~~~~~~~~~~~~~~~~~~~~~~~~~~~~~

ALMOST HUMAN

∽ THE SECOND TRILOGY ∽

VOLUME 2

DESCENDANT OF DARKNESS

BY

MELANIE NOWAK

~~~~~~~~~~~~~~~~~~~~~~~~~~~~~

Praise for Melanie Nowak's Venomous Vampire series
ALMOST HUMAN

"It's extremely rare to find an author who can write engaging plotlines, captivating settings, and powerful, life-like characters that live deep in a reader's heart long after the story is over. Melanie Nowak possesses this unique gift. This thrilling novel depicts intriguing external and internal conflicts, while the engaging plot flows smoothly through many unexpected turns and twists! Descendant of Darkness is another brilliant addition to the Almost Human world!"
- Gigi Lupo, www.ParanormalRomanceGuild.com

"This series has continued to be consistently excellent and I have to say I am seriously impressed that the level has remained so outstanding with each book. If you aren't reading this series, you should be!"
– Melanie Newton, www.NerdGirlOfficial.com

"This book is filled with emotions that run deep and brings the characters into new challenges. The ever-continuing series of vampires and "almost-humans" continues to expand and add more excitement on this journey that is certainly addictive! Nowak writes an intriguing tale of darkness, well written, deeply vampiric and paranormal, with twists of humanity and challenges."
- Amy C. Shannon, Amy's Bookshelf Reviews

"These characters are fascinating, their interaction flows easily. Reading about their conflicts, lost love, tragedy and quest for happiness made me feel pity, love and sadness. When an author can awake those feelings in a reader then the desired effect has been accomplished. Nowak's writing just flows, her stories are easy to read, and her writing style is fantastic!"
- www.ReadingDiva.com

*ALMOST HUMAN - The First Series was originally published as a trilogy of novels, now broken into novellas as an alternate format. The story is told in a serial succession - not stand-alone books. Each novella is meant to be read in order, as the story unfolds chronologically. Each series will be contained enough to be read on its own, with a certain amount of main storyline closure with the last novella, but there will also be some story-ties leading from one series into the next.

If you enjoy this book, please take a moment to leave a review online, on your favorite book review website! Questions and comments can be directed to: WoodWitchDame@aol.com

You can join author/reader discussions about the series, and get updates on upcoming book releases for this series on the author's web site at:

www.MelanieNowak.com

Copyright 2012, 2018
Melanie Nowak, WoodWitchDame Publications
Cover Artwork, Book formatting/Editing: Melanie Nowak

DESCENDANT OF DARKNESS
ISBN: 0-9824102-5-5
ISBN-13: 978-0-9824102-5-7

~~~~~~~~~~~~~~~~~~~~~~~~~~~~~~~

A Special Thanks to

~~~

My Mom & Step-Dad, Adele and David Weitzel
who have always given their love and support

~~~

My dearly departed brother, John,
who is loved, and missed each day

~~~

And to my wonderful and loving husband,
Scott,
and our sons, William & Eric,

who had patience when I was obsessed with writing,
gave me never-ending confidence and inspiration,
and for whom I am forever grateful
and blessed to have in my life.
I love you dearly.

~~~~~~~~~~~~~~~~~~~~~~~~~~~~~~~

ALMOST HUMAN was originally published as a series of novels, now also broken into novellas as an alternate format. These are not stand-alone books - they are meant to be read in order, as the story unfolds chronologically.

ALMOST HUMAN ~ The First Series
<u>FATAL INFATUATION</u>
Part 1: Captivating Vampires
Part 2: Tempting Transgressions
Part 3: Venomous Revelations

<u>LOST REFLECTIONS</u>
Part 1: Persistent Persuasion
Part 2: Telling Tales
Part 3: Battles and Bliss

<u>EVOLVING ECSTASY</u>
Part 1: Ecstasy Unleashed
Part 2: Stakes and Sunshine
Part 3: Evolution of Love

ALMOST HUMAN ~ The Second Series
<u>BORN TO BLOOD</u>
Part 1: Vampiress Rising
Part 2: Exceeding Expectations
Part 3: Coping with Chaos
Part 4: Vampire Vertigo

<u>DESCENDENT OF DARKNESS</u>
Part 1: Determining Desires
Part 2: Undying Devotion
Part 3: Emotional Maelstrom
Part 4: Crossing the Line

<u>DESTINED FOR DIVINITY</u>
Part 1: Home of the Bloodthirsty
Part 2: Enemies and Allies
Part 3: Vicious Survival
Part 4: Divining Destiny

ALMOST HUMAN ~ The Third Series
<u>VAMPIRESS REIGNING</u>
Part 1: Uniting Vampires

ALMOST HUMAN ∽ THE SECOND TRILOGY
VOLUME 2 ∽ DESCENDANT OF DARKNESS

Contents

Part 1

Determining Desires

Dearest Felicity,

    I dreamt of you again yesterday, as I so often do. It was nothing that another would find very heartwarming or even interesting. I simply lay with you in the bed, and we talked for hours. I could feel the warmth of your body near to mine, and I could smell your sweet, subtle perfume. I heard and treasured the soft tones of earnest understanding in your voice. It was not a dream I could well describe to others, having no action or particular focus. It was only me, being with you. I have this dream often. It's my favorite.

    I envy Alyson more than she'll ever know. Not for her position, or the amazing gifts she has uncovered over these passing years; I envy her, for her ability to share her visions and dreams with you. I know that she does still have contact with you now and then, although she never speaks of it to me. To have that telepathic link, with you, is the only psychic skill I have ever truly coveted or desired in the least. I so miss the conversations we used to share.

    I miss the nights, after passion was spent, that we just lay in bed together talking. You have the most beautiful mind I have ever known. I love the way you approach a concept with such open acceptance, and yet have the keen intelligence to discern the truth at its core. I adore the way you discuss ideas with such fervor, and have

1

newly introduced me, with fresh perspective, to books that I thought I knew. I miss your patient explanations of modern methods, and my sharing of experienced insight over movies we had each seen separately, and yet only truly dissected and discovered in conversation together. I miss... everything about you. I miss you.

If only I had Alyson's ability, that we might truly connect within our dreams and speak within our minds. Even if I were to never physically see or hold you again, to speak with you each day would comfort. But alas, my only talent is to help those around me fulfill their dreams; my only supernatural ability ever discovered, the means by which I should take the lives of others; a gift I would gladly return for a life with you.

And so, I write. I pour out my heart through the ink of a pen, although I know full well that the hundreds of pages I have filled are letters that will never be sent. I know that you will never read these words, but I must write them. It is as though, even if only ink on paper, this silent communication is a driving desperate need. For if I do not express the feelings that ravage my soul, they may fade away. I am afraid that the heart you awakened will wither and die, and then I will have truly lost you.

As long as I know that you live and breathe, as long as I can envision your hopeful smile and know that somewhere your eyes shine with love for life and the world around you, I will take comfort in knowing that I did the right thing in letting you go. It is likely that your heart is now consumed with love for another, but I accept that painful knowledge as the price for your happiness and pay it gladly for you. I will continue to write these letters, which are useless as my unbeating heart, and then lock them away, to be hidden from the world, and my longing for you with them. They do console me, simple romantic that I am, as though speaking to paper eases my yearning for a time.

I am needed by the others. They look to me for strength and guidance. Alyson and Mattie are strong and well meaning, but they are still so young, and have been thrust into more responsibility than they even yet know. Others wander in and out of my life as well, needing assistance and direction. I help them as I can, and send them back out into the world. I need to be capable and steady for them all. I cannot afford to spend my nights indulging in depression. So I fool myself into believing that these letters do assuage me. Perhaps someday you will actually read them, with softly blushing smiles; but to believe that once again paints me as a naive, romantic fool.

Until a night when the prayers of this simple fool are answered, and ever after, I am eternally yours,

Cain

Chapter 1 - Home of the bloodthirsty

Elric

Entering the private community *Kana Susamış İçin Ev*
Montauk, Long Island, New York
An evening in early spring

Love, true and undying, had always been regarded as unattainable in Elric's eyes, for who could love death incarnate? That was what a vampire was; an animated corpse designed to bring death to others...not exactly romance material. If that wasn't enough, who could love the first lieutenant of a man some considered Satan himself? Yet, love had found him, insidiously disruptive as it was. Over the passing decades, love had wound its way into his heart, softening tissue that had once seemed stone, changing his hardened, jaded view of the world.

Elric was a large and imposing black man. His size and muscular stature painted him as intimidating to others, but he was also trusted and respected in his position, as second in command to the coven master, Arif. In most things, he was free to do as he pleased, as he had always acted in the best interest of his coven and its master, as far as anyone else knew anyway. This was useful for him when he found himself forced to enter the political/social arena of the coven. He usually remained aloof from the convoluted relationships, deals and manipulations of the others, but when he felt the need to act, he could do so with near impunity.

This made the current building tension all the more frustrating for him. This time, it seemed his choices were few, and all unsavory; his power and respect useless. He was being pressured by the coven towards an act that he had been dreading these past years. This was nothing so grand as assisting in plans for the evolution of a master vampire race, the domination of humankind, the invasion and destruction of other covens, or even the lesser distasteful things he had somehow become a part of. This current pressure

4

was of a far more personal and simple sort, yet it was more painful than any other horrid act he had committed, because of love.

Life in the coven was about rules. There were rules and routines to be followed for just about everything. Live within the system, and you could have anything your heart desired: wealth, comfort, and even freedom to an extent. Elric very much enjoyed his existence in the coven because of the comforts it brought him; of those, the most dear to his surprisingly softening heart, was the most intelligent, experienced, lovely, and lively woman of his harem, Latisha. Yet according to the ever-important rules, his time with her would soon be drawing to an end; it was time for her to leave him.

Although the end of her service to him steadily drew nearer, he had still not found a way to subvert this seemingly inevitable outcome. One way or another, he was going to lose her. It would be the last straw in a very large collection of indignities he had been quietly enduring under the rule of Coven Master Arif.

"Slow," he told the driver in the seat in front of him, as they passed through the gates and entered the coven's home compound, known to its inhabitants as *Kana Susamiş Için Ev*. Its name loosely translated as *Home of the Bloodthirsty*. Elric had resided comfortably in this private community for decades. He had orders to drive slowly upon approach, giving Arif time to recognize his mark and prepare for their meeting.

At the very tip of Long Island in New York, on the beautiful beaches of Montauk, east of The Hamptons, they were comfortably surrounded by almost 4000 acres of state-protected pine barrens. Their only true neighbors were Montauk Point State Park, and the Deep Hollow Ranch. The coven's estate, *Kana Susamiş Icin Ev*, saw nothing but forest and beach. Little more than two hours from Manhattan, and merely fifteen minutes from the beach bars, upscale clubs and summertime parties and events of the Hamptons, the coven's estate was nestled in private luxury.

The land had been passed down to Arif as a gift from his sire, who had purchased the property back in the late 1600's. At that time, Long Island had been considered true wilderness, inhabited only by a few farmers and fisherman, and the new cattle ranch that had just begun operation nearby. Back then, it had seemed the perfect private retreat. The city was close enough to be visited nightly, but secret forays to the cattle ranch provided access to blood at home as well.

Little did the vampires suspect that their quiet retreat would eventually become known as *The Hamptons*, a summer destination coveted by celebrities and millionaires; playground of the rich and famous. Still, the location only proved itself to be more perfect with every passing year, as vampires learned to live and play safely and secretly among humans, rather than having to hide from them. Much of the forest wilderness on the eastern end of Long Island had been cleared and converted into upscale residential areas, mansion estates and vineyards, but the buffer of state protected land still left around them was privacy enough.

Elric rolled up the darkly tinted window of the Hummer, to muffle the noise as the secluded road took them out of the woods to drive by the kennels. The dogs out in their runs barked furiously at the car's slow passing, and soon their sounds were mingled with the far more chilling and sinister sounds of baying and whining from the inner kennels, and those animals not quite *dog* anymore.

"What is that? Coyotes?" The frightened voice of the abducted cleaning-woman in the backseat still had a tone of confidence through her thick Spanish accent. "They don't sound right. Where are we?" Elric recognized her strength of spirit struggling to overcome her fear.

Elric closed his eyes, refusing to flinch at the sound of the hard smack she was given behind him. "I thought I told you to shut up," Anthony reminded her threateningly. Elric slowly turned to see the other vampire smiling, reveling in his position of power. The woman watched him warily, peering from beneath the ebony curls of her mussed hair. She did not have nearly as much fright in her large, dark eyes as Anthony would have liked to see, despite the bright red mark that showed clearly on her cheek. Judging by the vigorous and unrelenting fight she had put up earlier, she was no stranger to loud and violent men, and she was not yet privy to the fact that her captors were not truly human.

Forbidden to show his true nature as of yet, the vampire still tried to elicit a stronger response. He paused, cocking an ear towards the shrill sounds of howling in the night. "Maybe we should pull over and feed you to them," Anthony mused tauntingly.

Rather than shrink back, the woman sat up straighter, insulted by his attempt to scare her. Before anyone could realize what she would do, she spit directly into Anthony's face. Elric smiled and spoke, even as the enraged vampire drew himself up before her with a fist poised to strike. "Don't touch her again."

Anthony spun to face him through the space in between the seats, his fury barely contained. "That bitch isn't gonna disrespect me like that and get away with it! I'll drain her first."

Elric remained calm and in command, staring the vampire down. Anthony was a member of the lesser guard. Elric had seniority, and no matter how Anthony might complain to the master later, right now, Elric was in charge. "You will not lay another hand upon her. If you had done your job properly, she would not even be here. You did not, and that was your disrespect to her."

Anthony grimaced. "She shouldn't have been there. The house was supposed to be empty."

"Well it wasn't," Elric answered shortly. Anthony would have seen that, if he'd done a proper check beforehand. She could have been ushered out with minimal disruption before their business partners had even arrived. Instead, she was there for the entire transaction and that was unacceptable. There was no telling what incriminating things she may have seen or heard. If Elric had found her, he probably would have drained her to unconsciousness and left her there, claiming she was dead; he didn't feel she was much of a threat to their security. However, Anthony had discovered her, and that meant Elric had to set an example as mission leader and play strictly by the rules; no living witness left behind.

If Anthony had killed her when she had been discovered, it would have been within his rights, but the idiot had liked her look, and had wanted to bring her back with them instead. Elric ran a hand over his smooth, bald, head in an attempt to keep his temper, and reminded Anthony of his place. "Coven rules state that she is now property of the master, until such time as he initiates her and puts her up for trade. I can't very well let you mar the master's property, now can I? Such a beautiful woman should not be brought before him with a bruise upon her face, it would be an insult."

"I'm no one's property. I need to go home. I wouldn't say anything, I swear. You don't want to deal with people searching for me. Please just let me go." She spoke with quiet insistence to Elric, recognizing his reason and authority. Her vicious kicks, piercing screams and struggle earlier were now traded for quiet pleading, as she tried not to give up hope. Elric suppressed a sigh. Why hadn't Anthony just done his damn job?

Elric stared at her imposingly for a moment before answering, and watched her shrink further back into the seat, as she had been unwilling to do when dealing with Anthony. She was used to fighting against men like Anthony, but Elric had a quiet strength that was disconcerting to her. "Do not think to tell me what I can deal with. It would be much easier for me to kill you, than to try to explain your presence here to my superior. I let you live. I will treat you with the amount of dignity that you show me in return, but do not ask for what I cannot give. Release is not an option at the moment."

If he had been alone, he probably would have released her, despite the rules. He could surely convince her never to utter a word of what she had seen. That was too strong a rebellion against protocol though. He could not afford to stray with the eyes of others upon him. He needed to save his rebellion for more important matters. "What's your name?" he asked quietly.

She eyed him thoughtfully before answering, "Marguerite."

The name issued from her lips like a dark exotic whisper. He nodded in approval with a smile, ignoring Anthony, who now sat glowering in the corner. A beautiful name, well suited to her heart shaped face, full pouting lips and dark eyes. "You may call me Elric. Make no mistake, your situation is dire, but I will do what I can to ease things for you. Fate has dealt you an unfortunate hand. You must leave your life behind, and learn to thrive within these new circumstances. I know you would not have it this way, but the alternative is death. This is your new home. It does not have to be permanent, but it is your current reality. Accept that quietly, and wait until you are given your choices."

She seemed to brighten slightly when she heard that she would be given choices. She clung to that hope and gave a small nod of acceptance for now. All of her frenzied kicking and screaming earlier had earned her nothing, perhaps silence would help her to fare better.

Elric glanced out the window. They had already passed through the small apartment complex, and were now making their way past the sports complex. On their right, two sets of women played on the lighted tennis courts, the popping regular bounce of their ball a sound sharp and echoing, catching Marguerite's surprised attention, even through the car window. On the left side of the road, the swimming pools were silent and empty, although wisps of steam rose from the heated water in the crisp night air of early spring.

Elric lowered his window again, the noise from the dogs drifting away behind them as the animals settled down, to be replaced by slight strains of music. They were approaching the performance studio. Latisha would be there, teaching her dance class. Yes, he could feel her. She was visible at the front of the room through the large wall of windows.

He leaned across the seat to see her better through the right passenger-side window, as she led a group of women through a stretching exercise before beginning their routine. Dark and lovely as a Nubian princess, she wore her finely braided hair twisted into a ballerina's bun at the back of her head. She looked long and lean in her turquoise leotard and leggings, which stretched tightly over her firm thighs and the curving swell of her breasts.

The widely scooped neckline revealed much of her smooth shoulders and her long elegant neck. She would be turning fifty next month, and still she was the most captivating woman he had ever seen.

Others had beauty that tried to approach hers, but she had a twinkle in her eye that told of intelligence and humor that he found entrancing. She handled those around her as though every event in her life was perfectly orchestrated to suit her needs, and yet she was unspoiled and kind of heart. She coordinated his harem as she choreographed dance, with swift easy precision that never missed a beat. What would he ever do without her?

Latisha paused in the dance movement she had been demonstrating, and slyly turned her head to the window, soon frozen in a tableau of poise. She felt him. She knew that he was home. A smile stole upon her face, and then she finished the movement, directing her class without comment. Soon my love, he thought. First, there was business to attend to.

Marguerite had also noticed the dancers through the window, and watched them with a furrowed brow. Surely, the compound was not what she had expected. Next on that side of the road, they passed the dining hall. This building also was filled with windows, so that all activity within might be viewed by those without. The large building was filled with tables, inhabited by many people laughing, talking, and enjoying their meals. A keen observer might notice a certain similarity to these people, although most wouldn't catch it upon first glance. The majority of the diners were female, although there were a few males scattered throughout the room as well. They were also, without fail, fairly young and attractive, every one of them.

Elric recognized the psychic marks of three of his charges within, taking a meal together. Three more marked as his own were across the road, in the recreation hall, most likely playing pool.

Lastly, they came to what was known as the common house. It stood centered directly before them, so that the road must split to continue around it. It was a small building comprised of a few conference rooms, arranged around the center of its activity, a large sitting area called the common room. It was used as a meeting place for various purposes.

Vampires only really came to the common house for one of three reasons, based on what color flag was flying on the pole out front. The solid green flag of trade was not raised tonight; there was no bidding to be done this evening. The black flag promoting the discipline of a fellow vampire was very rarely ever flown. Unfortunately, the more sinister red flag of human punishment was raised tonight, and fluttering in the slight

9

breeze. Anthony's expression visibly brightened as he observed the flag. Elric was not as pleased. "Byron, stop the car."

Byron did as he was asked, observing both the flag and Elric with a weary expression from the driver's seat. After the car was in park, he turned to watch Elric exit the vehicle. "Should I meet you around the other side, or just go ahead?"

Elric eyed Marguerite in the back seat for a moment before answering. "You can pull around and go ahead into the driveway to wait. Keep her in the car." Elric glanced at Anthony, who was obviously eager to accompany him into the building. Marguerite was better off left alone with Byron anyway. After stopping in the common room, Elric and Anthony could continue through, out the exit on the other side to walk across to the car at their final destination, *Susuzluktan Saray*.

Anthony paused to mutter some hostile threat to the girl about staying in the vehicle, but Elric knew it was unnecessary. Byron would keep the doors locked, and could certainly be trusted to handle the girl with firm but civil control.

The common house was fairly empty this evening. Humans that might normally lounge and chat in the armchairs and sofas had no desire to inhabit the building while the red flag was raised. Two cadet vampires sat at the bar in the corner, speaking softly about something private, although they both nodded a respectful greeting when Elric entered.

He and Anthony crossed immediately to the cadet stationed at the small table in the corner, near the door leading to the basement below. He was a fairly new vampire, turned within the decade; a young, non-descript man who looked to have been in his twenties when turned. He dropped his magazine and straightened to attention as Elric and Anthony approached. Elric glanced at the book on the table before him, although it was upside down to his view. "Who's in the cellar?"

The vampire turned the book so that Elric might read it. "One of Cat's guys sir. His name's Craig." The man shared a disappointed scowl with Anthony at the disclosure. Surely, they both would have rather seen a female below.

Elric read the short entry in the book, and the list of three names and times below it. "What for?" he asked with furrowed brow. Normally there was at least a short summary of explanation. Beneath the man's name in the book was only the hastily scrawled word *'disrespect'*.

The cadet shrugged and looked again at the book. "I guess he was disrespectful. The master approved it," he said, pointing to Arif's signature in the top corner of the page.

Elric tilted his head and fixed the man in his gaze. There was always a story behind a night in the reform cellar, and very rarely was it unknown amongst the coven. The humans were terrible gossips, knowing everything that went on, and their vampires would surely have any interesting information about other harems out of them, so that they could then gossip among the other vampires. Elric found the whole rumor chain childish and tiring. He usually had no desire to delve into the business of others, but knowing Cat, he wasn't above wanting to know the details here. The reform cellar was not a punishment to be used lightly.

The cadet glanced around and then lowered his voice with a smile. "Well, we all know Cat's a freak. No one's got the exact details, but word is she tried to force him to do something fucked up and kinky, and he refused."

Anthony scoffed with an incredulous laugh. "What could she possibly want him to do that would be worse than the cellar?"

Elric didn't laugh. He'd seen and endured more than these younglings. He'd been through the Nazi camps and seen prisoners forced into circumstances others couldn't dream of. He could understand a human man valuing his pride enough to choose a night of torture above whatever bizarre sexual request Cat may have made. He glanced at the book again. There had been three visitors so far; none that he knew to be terribly vindictive. Perhaps Craig had made the better choice for himself. "I assume you made a proper inspection after each visit."

The cadet dropped his smile and nodded quickly. He didn't want to be written up. Elric had his doubts about the sincerity of his answer. The boy saw this too. "Alright, I didn't, but Bill was the last one down there, and said the guy's fine, conscious even. Bill would've been easy on him, and I'm sure he would've told me when he got down there, if there was a problem."

Elric shook his head in disapproval. A human in the reform cellar was to be checked on after each visit, to be sure they were left in suitable condition. Noting which vampires had visited, Elric understood why the cadet in charge would have assumed that the prisoner was resilient enough for whatever those vampires would do within the rules; but the man really should have been checked on. Hopefully he was in decent condition. No vampire wanted to be held responsible for the unapproved death of someone else's charge.

Elric weighed the trouble of reporting the young vampire, against the time and effort it would take on his part. "Lorelei hasn't been in?" he asked.

The boy widened his eyes. "No! I would have gone down after, if she had. It's only been those in the book."

Elric nodded. "Alright, but you're in no position to ignore the rules, cadet. I expect things to be in order under your supervision. I'm going down. Don't make me check up on you again."

The cadet nodded quickly. "Should I..." he gestured towards the book.

Elric opened the door to the stairs, with Anthony close behind. He shook his head at the book. "I'm just checking on him. You don't need to log it, unless you want to explain why I was doing *your* inspection."

The cadet quickly closed the book. "No. Thank you sir."

Anthony put a hand on his shoulder to stop him, as Elric began his descent. "You're not putting us in the book? There's only two glasses left."

Elric looked up over his shoulder. "We're not here to drink. Come back and do it on your own time."

Anthony was obviously annoyed. "But they'll be gone."

"That's not my problem," Elric mumbled as he resumed going down the stairs. As he reached the bottom, he was in a small landing entryway. Contrary to the vision that the title 'reform cellar' evoked, the space was actually a nicely finished basement. It was not particularly elegant, but it was a decently warm and inviting area, despite its purpose.

In the entryway, before the door to the larger room, they encountered a table, which did indeed have only two empty wine glasses left on it, next to a small but wickedly sharp knife.

Those who were brought to the reform cellar for punishment already belonged to a vampire within the coven. This meant that they bore the mark of that vampire, and could not be bitten by another. Visiting vampires could say or do just about anything to a human here, as long as it was not life threatening or permanently disfiguring. However, if they wanted to drink, they would need to cut the victim, rather than bite them.

Five glasses were placed upon the table at the start of confinement. A visiting vampire was only allowed one glass during the course of the evening, and to refill the glass was forbidden. This prevented the victim from losing more blood than they could withstand. Once the glasses were all taken, the victim's blood was off limits for the remainder of the night.

Vampires who did not care to bother with another's human for entertainment, still coveted those glasses of blood. Each had their own stable of humans to drink from, but there was never enough blood to satisfy. It must be rationed carefully to maintain human health, and animal blood made up the difference. How much animal blood you needed depended on your rank. Higher rank gave you more humans. New cadets especially were eager for an extra glass of fresh human blood when they could get it. Elric was happy to leave it to them.

Elric only paused for a moment before entering the prisoner's quarters, with Anthony close behind. The man lay naked on a mattress on the floor at the far end of the room. The manacles and chains that were fastened to his wrists and ankles looked strangely out of place in the comfortable room, secured with large bolted plates to the oak paneled wall behind him. The room looked as though it could be a cheerful game room or den, if not for its occupant and his restraints. The other strap tables and implements of torture remained concealed in their various closets. Craig was having a lucky night.

The man looked up wearily at their approach. He looked understandably apprehensive when seeing Elric's large and imposing form, followed by Anthony who was a smaller man, but surely wore a gleefully insidious expression.

Craig sat up, trying unsuccessfully to appear to have a shred of dignity left to him. The scent of fear joined the smell of sweat that hung in the windowless room. Elric stopped before him, and just stood there, surveying his injuries.

It was now apparent why the man didn't bother to try to stand. He had horrible bruises on his left ankle under the manacle. The skin there was dark with the purples and greens consistent with an older injury though, by a night or two at least, not from his confinement this evening. Most likely Cat had done it to hobble him, as punishment for going somewhere without permission. It wasn't broken, but it would slow him down.

The ankle was the least of Craig's current worries. He was trying to look at his visitors to gauge their intent, but could barely see them. His right eye was completely swollen shut, and his left was bloodshot beyond allowing clear vision. He had various cuts and bruises over his body, but a few good punches to the face seemed to have been the worst of it. His wrists were criss crossed with fresh slices from the knife, but they weren't too deep. The cuts were already crusting over, and weren't bleeding any longer.

The three vampires who had visited earlier had apparently knocked him around a bit as retaliation for disobedience, and they had certainly taken their full glass of blood each, but they didn't seem to have done anything more reprehensible than that. He had a few bruises on the front of his upper thighs that were probably from nastily placed kicks, but women usually fared far worse.

In over a century with the coven, Elric had never had occasion to confine one of his charges to the cellar for an evening, but then, he treated his humans better than most. Some vampires thought him too lenient, but Elric was really quite firm at home. The difference was that he understood the give and take of a long term, functioning household, and saw his relationship with the humans in his care as a symbiotic one, rather than that of master and slave. He cared for them and allowed them to live as they pleased, within the larger rules of the community, and they were happy to supply him with not only blood, but also to maintain personal relationships with him, of varying degrees. He had realistic but strict expectations of his charges, and if those expectations were not met, they knew the consequences. When disagreements occurred, he dealt with them swiftly at home. To him, the reform cellar was a last resort for a human completely out of control.

Elric turned to Anthony, who was standing with arms crossed, looking very annoyed over wasting his time down here without being allowed to drink. "Go up and get me a bottle of water from the bar," Elric told him.

Anthony gave him a look of disturbed questioning, but then turned to obey the request. As soon as he was on the stairs, Elric crouched by the injured man. Craig watched him warily, but did not speak.

"You'll be alright. There's only a few hours left," Elric whispered. He then shifted to expose his fangs. Craig flinched back from the vampire, startled, but Elric ignored him and punctured his own finger instead. Once bloodied, he brought his finger up before Craig's face. "Lean back," he ordered, with a quick glance over his shoulder. They were still alone. Craig did so, and Elric let a few drops of blood drip into the man's eyes. He stroked his finger over the worst of Craig's wounded brow, and then stood and backed away. Elric put the punctured finger to his own lips, cleaning the rest of the blood away as Anthony stomped back down the stairs.

Anthony tried to shove the water bottle at him, but Elric gestured to the man on the mattress in front of them instead. "It's not for me. Give it to him." Elric turned away without meeting the man's eyes again. The swelling should go down within the next half hour or so, but the redness had immediately cleared from Craig's un-swollen eye, so that he could see clearly again. The vampire blood would accelerate his healing, but not enough for Anthony to notice the difference. As Elric went through the doorway to the stairs, he heard Anthony begin to question the man about his reason for punishment, in a harsh and taunting tone. Elric paused without turning back. "Let's go, the master is waiting."

After assuring the cadet in charge that Craig was in decent shape, Elric left the building out the back double doors. He saw that the Hummer was waiting for them in the circular driveway of *Susuzluktan Saray* across the road. Anthony began to cross to the car, but Elric instead focused his attention off to the left, towards that side of the development of prestigious homes belonging to the senior guard. As head of the guard, Elric's home was the finest, and was situated right next to Arif's mansion here at the head of the community.

The community of *Kana Susamiş İçin Ev* was arranged in a long rectangular shape, the far end of which was the sandy beach coast. At the end of the community, in the center of the beachfront, stood the mansion of the Coven Master. Arif called it *Susuzluktan Saray, "The Palace of Thirst"*. The large and impressive homes of the Senior Guard were ranged around the mansion on either side, with Elric's to the left. Elric observed the marks within his own home. The last two charges of his harem were there, making all of his humans accounted for. The mark of the young vampire cadet assigned to him was clearly visible in the front room of the house. Everything was as it should be.

Anthony reached the Hummer before him, but leaned against it rather than opening a door. He was waiting for Elric's consent. He nodded once he was near enough, and Anthony rapped a knuckle on the window for Byron to open the locks. Anthony opened the back door, and reached a hand in to help Marguerite from the car. The vampire was commendably civil with her as she climbed down. Once on the driveway, Anthony kept a firm hold on her arm as he slammed the door closed behind her, making her jump.

Although she had surely been observing the house while waiting for them, her eyes were still wide as she took in the full glory of *Susuzluktan Saray*. The mansion was crafted to show as much splendor as could be accomplished upon a still fairly modern looking house. Its many turrets and towers topped by decorative finials gave the sprawling mansion the look of a castle, with the beautiful fountain centered behind the circular driveway, completing the effect.

Elric felt the mental acknowledgement of their master, and spoke to Byron, who was retrieving a large briefcase from the front seat as he exited the car. "We can go right up. He's waiting for us."

Anthony gave a rough pull on Marguerite's arm as they began walking towards the entrance. Elric gave him a commanding look to stop when they reached the porch, and then turned to address their guest. Marguerite lowered her eyes under his scrutiny as he spoke. "I will only say this once.

You are to behave yourself in a completely submissive and obedient manner. You will not speak unless spoken to, and you will obey directives without question at all times.

You are far from home, and far from help. Should you attempt to leave us, the dogs will find you, and I can assure you that the other creatures you heard are quite capable of making a meal of you, as Anthony suggested earlier. I'm sorry to have to voice such threats, but I speak only the truth. This does not have to be a terrible situation for you, as it seems, but you must act within the rules here. Marguerite…"

She met his eyes timidly at his pause after her name. He allowed her to glimpse a brief flash of his vampiric eyes. It made her breath catch sharply in her throat. Good. He had her full attention. He continued with a lowered voice. "There are creatures of the night far worse than you have imagined, and there are fates far worse than death. I like you, but I would sooner kill you in mercy than leave you to punishment at their hands. Be a good girl and do as you're told. Are we clear?"

Her eyes were wide as she nodded silently. Elric smiled at her indulgently and gently took her free arm to lead her inside, ignoring the fact that Anthony insisted on keeping hold of her other arm, almost tight enough to leave a bruise.

Marguerite observed with silent awe as they checked in with the door attendant and entered the house. They followed Byron, leading her through the opulent entryway, down hallways adorned with alcove shelves containing sculptures and displaying pieces of artwork to the point of garish excess, and up the grand staircase to the master's office. One of the lesser guardsmen stood outside the room, and watched them with interest as he noticed their prisoner. "The master awaits you," he said.

Elric guided Marguerite to a plush chair in the hall outside of the room. Anthony pushed her down into the chair as Elric released her and turned to the guard. "I will call for you to bring her shortly."

As they entered the office, Elric gave a nod of respectful greeting to the master, Arif, who sat at the far end of the room behind his large mahogany desk, the handsome Turk looking polished and composed as always.

Elric was surprised to see that Kieran sat in a chair to the master's right, looking through a stack of papers on the edge of the desk. Kieran gave him a warm smile before returning to his work.

Arif gestured for the men to take their seats before the desk. As senior guardsmen, Elric and Byron took the large leather seats directly before them, forcing Anthony to pull over a smaller chair from against the wall. "I trust all went as planned," Arif said, once they were settled.

In answer, Byron lifted the briefcase to the desk and opened it, revealing a very large amount of cash, their payment from the transaction. Arif barely glanced at the money. He was looking at Anthony, who squirmed uncomfortably. Byron gave the master the figures and prospective earnings for the future, ticking off numbers, and territories for their venture. Arif turned to him and cut him off. "So it went well and they want more," he said, cutting to the chase.

"Yes sir. They sold it all much quicker than they thought. You should see the amount of marks in the neighborhood. Ritzy restaurants full of businessmen and socialites, and they all wear the mark of our coven like common charges. The place looks like *Kana Susamiş İçin Ev* for God's sake. They want it undiluted though. These customers aren't like the druggies we sell to in the city. They think injection is distasteful. They like to slip it into their drinks."

Arif smiled. "That's fine. We'll simply charge them more."

Byron nodded. "They don't care, they can move it. They said they'd already sold out last week. They're calling it 'U', short for 'Euphoria'."

"Fine. That's just fine. We've plenty of venom to go around. I'll come spit in their drinks personally if they'd like!" he said, laughing at his fine joke. Elric and the others smiled obligingly as Kieran re-counted the money in the case. "I'll be interested to take a trip out next weekend and try out the control. It will be less without direct injection, but it should still be sufficient." Arif nodded to himself as he thought things over, and then suddenly turned his attention to Anthony once more. "So Anthony, tell me why this highly successful mission did not go as smoothly as planned."

Anthony squirmed like a student who'd brought a frog to school in his backpack. "I think the mission was a great success sir. Besides the business we went for, we've also brought home a new donor to feed the coven."

Arif's face did not betray his feelings on the matter with expression. "We are not in need of donors at the moment."

Elric could have sworn that he'd actually heard a *gulp,* as Anthony swallowed and searched for words. "I thought of you as soon as I saw her, sir. She is absolutely beautiful."

Now Arif gave a small smile of acknowledgment for the respect. "My harem is full." He contemplated, and then shifted his gaze to Elric. "However, that does remind me that a new donor will be called for shortly. I do believe that Elric is anticipating an opening in the near future."

Elric froze for a moment before lightly shaking his head as though unsure of the reference. Anthony jumped to his defense, knowing full well that Elric would be furious at him for this turn of the master's thinking. "Actually Master, I was hoping that I could keep her for myself once you had your fill of her."

Arif grinned. "So your motives were for yourself then, and not for her to join my own harem?"

Anthony lowered his eyes. "Any donor recruited enriches the population for us all, and you are entitled to first choice of those presented, without question, sir. Those of us below are honored to have opportunity to bid on those displaced whenever charges are shifted. I simply meant that at such a time as you grow weary of her, I hoped to have a chance to bid for her in trade." Elric knew his formal words were fragments of the guidelines he'd memorized long ago. He continued with a brief glance at Elric. "Elric would have first pick, as my superior. If he likes her, I'd be happy to then bid for whichever of his charges he puts up in trade."

Arif locked his eyes to Elric. "There will be no need for trade. By the time I have initiated her, and am ready to pass her down, Elric will be short one human. Doesn't one of your charges reach retirement age next month?"

Elric answered shortly. "Yes sir, Latisha. We have spoken of this."

Arif had the nerve to pretend he could not place the discussion, before finally feigning remembrance. "Have we? Ah yes, Latisha, the dance teacher."

"Yes sir. Perhaps we could discuss this later, in private."

Arif looked around the room, from Anthony, to Byron, to Kieran, as though to profess that he couldn't imagine what should not be discussed in their company. "I see no need. You will retire Latisha as planned, and then you may have this new girl in her place. What is there to discuss?"

Elric fixed him with a stony gaze. "If you remember, I had asked that she might have an extension. She is in perfect health."

Arif shook his head with a chuckle. "An extension? That sets a very bad precedent Elric. You know the rules."

Elric stole a glance at Byron and Anthony, who were both pretending to have no opinion on the matter. Kieran evinced to be very absorbed in marking entries on the papers before him. Elric lowered himself to plead with Arif for his cause. "She is invaluable to me sir. She is the coordinator for my guard and harem, and for the dance studio as well. Her current service does not end for three more years, and then I'd like to have her serve one more term. That's thirteen years sir."

"I know how to count," Arif replied in condescension.

"I ask that she have a stay of thirteen more years. She has shown unflinching loyalty."

Arif laughed in disbelief. "Another term of service? She is not even permitted to complete the term she is in at her age. Thirteen years? She'll be sixty-three! Now how would that look? Shall we keep a stable of senior citizens to feed from?" He nudged Kieran, who was obliged to give a sympathetic chuckle.

Elric continued. "Allow her to finish out her term at least. I understand she is reaching the age limit imposed by coven law, but three years is not much to ask. As master, it is your right to subvert the rules when a situation warrants."

"Of course it is my right! But I made those rules for a reason. Let her exit with graceful dignity. Those kept to drink from must be young and fit; kept in good health if they are going to produce the amount of blood needed without requiring constant replacement. Humans over the age of fifty become more of a burden than they are worth. Our medical expenses are more than I feel necessary as it is. I don't need to start shelling out money for heart medications and such."

Elric took a deep breath for calm. Arif knew that neither Latisha's health nor money was an issue. "As I said, she is in perfect health, sir. I would be willing to pay any medical expenses she might incur from my own earnings. She is more physically fit than any other her age. She teaches the exercise classes at the studio as well. Hers are the most attended classes there. She is well liked as a teacher."

Arif raised his eyebrows and questioned Anthony and Byron. "Is that so?" They nodded in Elric's defense. "Well, we can't have a bunch of fat harem girls, now can we? It is good that she inspires. Very well, seeing as she has been of such service to the coven, I will grant her retirement with double compensation. Very generous of me, don't you think?"

Elric sighed. How long was Arif planning to drag out this charade? "Very. But sir, she does not wish to retire."

"She would rather sacrifice? That decision is between the two of you. It would certainly save money, but my offer stands."

How dare he make such a suggestion! He was just trying to elicit an emotional response from Elric, so that he could accuse him of having weakness for his wards. He had hoped to plead his case without an audience, but Arif was giving him no choice; forcing him to do it now, and be more easily dismissed. Well Elric wasn't giving up without a fight. "No sir, not sacrifice. If the extension of her service cannot be granted, then I would like to propose another option; promotion."

Kieran had been about to close the briefcase before him, when he dropped the lid unconsciously in shock. It made a loudly audible click. Elric went on as though uninterrupted. "I want to turn her. She has been here longer than some of our vampires, sir. She understands our needs better than almost anyone. I believe she would be a very valuable member of the coven."

Arif leaned back in his chair and crossed his arms. "Promote her? It would seem that you have inappropriate attachment to your charge, Elric. She has served you well, but this alone does not make her suitable for my coven. You know how I feel about accepting women into the ranks. They lead with their hearts rather than their minds. They tend to instigate upset among the men and provide unnecessary drama. Look at the trouble Lorelei has caused. It was poor judgment to let her rise to Senior Guard, and she is on very unstable ground. I vowed not to make such a poor decision again. I only keep Cat because she has a wicked disposition easily controlled by greed. She'll never rise in our institution."

Elric suppressed the huff of disbelief that threatened to escape his lips. Cat was only kept around because she was a vampire with pink eyes, the only one in the coven, and she couldn't manage to pass pure enough blood to recreate the color in another. Elric knew if she were easily replaced by another of her breed, Arif would never tolerate her. Other members of the coven did not recognize the significance of various breed types to Arif's private project plans, but Elric knew the truth.

He refocused himself on the bargaining at hand. He could feel his hold on Latisha slipping away with every word Arif spoke. If Arif wanted to pretend control and rank was the issue, then let him. "Latisha can permanently remain cadet. We would accept that." Elric hated the sound of desperation he could hear creeping into his voice, and the fact that he let slip the word 'we', as though he made decisions based on the wishes of a mere human. He composed himself to retake control of the conversation. "She could be of great use sir. Not only is she loyal, she is clever; smarter than any vampire I've had charge over. She would serve you well."

Arif laughed, noting the subtle insult to those in their company. "Now what would I want with a clever woman? Has it ever occurred to you that a wise ruler keeps dull subjects? I don't need another cadet, especially one that will sway the thinking of my most senior guardsmen. You need to focus, man. You have been distracted of late, and now I see why. She clouds you. My decision is made."

Elric refused to let that be the end of it. "If not promotion, then grant the extension sir. The worry would be lifted from me, were you to grant her a few more years." Arif was unmoved. Elric straightened in his chair and looked at those around him. He had more service here than any of them, and damn it, he deserved to be granted this favor. He shouldn't have to beg for it. "She has served three ten-year service periods. Her fourth does not expire until three years from now. At least let her finish her service. As your most senior guardsmen, with a century of loyal service of my own, *I ask this of you.*"

Arif met his gaze and noted that Elric was unwilling to back down. Elric could tell that he was considering any benefit he might gain by granting this wish. "I will take it under consideration, but do not expect that I will change my mind. Rules run this coven and keep it strong. You must understand that I cannot make exceptions that I would not want to see become the rule. The others look to you for example, Elric. Order is of utmost importance here." Elric refused to answer, and only gave a slight nod of acknowledgement.

"Moving on," Arif said with a glance at Kieran. "Anthony, you are dismissed. I thank you for the recruitment." Anthony stood with a slight bow to the master, and left them. Elric knew that although he was likely annoyed to be left out of the remainder of the meeting, he was probably eager to return to the common house, and claim a glass from the reform cellar.

After he left, Arif resumed speaking. "As you can see, Kieran has returned. He has given me a full report of his surveillance these past months. Nothing seems to have changed. The vampire Alyson still resides as a ward of Cain at his estate, along with the other one, Mattie. She doesn't seem to have made many visible developments in her training. As you know, she has been discovered to possess exponential strength and speed, but none of her larger skills have been uncovered. She is a poor student and has a tendency to wander."

"Where does she go?" Elric asked with furrowed brow.

"No need for concern," Arif assured him.

"She's a kid," Kieran said with a shrug. "She hits concerts and clubs. They travel to party spots for spring break and stuff."

"She doesn't hunt," Arif continued, "and that keeps her weaker than she might be. However, she also seems unconcerned with her strong thirst. She feeds on animal blood and has remarkable control. That is not good. It means that she still feels that she does not need our help."

Byron shifted in his seat. "Why don't we just take her out now, while she's weak?" he asked.

Arif looked annoyed. "I don't want her dusted; I want her blood, a nice supply of it. That takes a bit more finesse. We cannot hope to infiltrate Cain's estate to abduct her. The Crimson Coven protects it, and they are too well organized and perceptive for anything less than an all out attack. We cannot afford that now. Only Kieran's unique skills have allowed him to observe unseen."

"So our best chance is to get her when she is outside his protection, on one of her pleasure trips?" Byron speculated.

Arif shook his head. "One would think. I have had Elric dispatch a few teams, to see if they might manage abduction, but so far, none have proved capable. It is a delicate matter when deadly force is out of the question. In any case, force may not be our best method. They are still acting as a coven. She wears Cain's mark, and likely has telepathic contact with him, as well as Mattie. It would be better if we could convince someone close to her that it is in her best interest to work with us. My business on the west coast these past years has kept me away over-long, but that may work in our favor. If we do not seem eager, perhaps they will not distrust our motives. We will make one more formal visit to their little coven. I am coordinating our schedules, and will soon give you the date of assignment. Elric, as Head of the Senior Guard, I would like you to accompany me. I believe our unique talents will be most persuasive in this instance, and as a pair rather than a group, we will seem less intimidating. Kieran will return to Cain's estate prior to our arrival, to watch unseen. Byron, you will have charge of the coven in our absence, with Tomas and Richard to advise you."

Byron and Kieran both nodded, but Elric was not happy. He was starting to wish he could step down as senior guardsmen and give the others the *honor* of being part of all the important missions. He'd rather stay home. Still, he had fought hard for his position, and hoped that rewards for his effort might still be forthcoming. He shielded his thoughts and nodded with a smile. "Thank you sir. As always, I'm honored to serve. I am sure your considerable powers of persuasion, combined with this cleverly chosen team will finally bring about the result you have desired."

Arif nodded in approval and then looked at each of them in turn. "You are dismissed." They stood to leave with quiet 'thank you's'.

"And send in the girl," Arif added as an afterthought. "I'll take a look at her and then have my coordinator ready her for initiation." He became thoughtful. "Elric," he called, causing him to pause before leaving the room. "We'll see how pretty she is; and whether she pleases me. If I decide

22

to keep her for a while, perhaps you can make do with your harem as it is; until she bores me."

Elric stared at him for a moment. Arif was providing that Latisha could stay until he decided to pass down Marguerite. Only a slight concession, but it was a start. "Thank you, sir." As he left the room, Elric said a silent prayer, that Arif would find Marguerite to be an incredibly intriguing woman.

Marguerite was still seated in the chair outside the door. The guardsman stationed there assured him that she had not misbehaved during her wait. Elric put his hand out to help her rise. He met her eyes as she stood, her lip slightly trembling as she tried to anticipate what lay ahead. "The master will see you now. Do not be afraid. He will treat you well if you relent to his wishes. Many lead full and happy lives here. It does not have to be a curse. No matter what is in your heart, believe me when I tell you that to fight him is useless. It will be better for you to gain his favor." She looked insulted that he would expect her to allow liberties to the man who would hold her prisoner, but then something in Elric's eyes must have shown his true concern for her. She softened and seemed to re-assess her situation.

The master was psychically calling for her to be brought in. There was no more time for talk. Elric took her hand firmly in his, to show the seriousness of his next words. "Marguerite," he whispered, "if you have any respect for the kindness I have shown, you will do your best to please him."

Her reaction was unsure, and then she was being ushered past him into the office by the guardsman at her side, who had also surely received the mental command for her to be brought into the room.

Kindness? In her eyes, he had kidnapped her and condemned her to a life of slavery against her will. Of course, he could have killed her, and the life she would lead here was easy and luxurious compared to any normal life out in the world; but would she see it that way?

He left *Susuzluktan Saray* to go and find Latisha, hoping against all hope that Marguerite would not spit in Arif's face.

Chapter 2 - The plan

Ben

Upstate New York
A Saturday in late May

Ben loosened his tie just a little more, fidgeted on the uncomfortable folding chair, and wished the sun would finally dip down behind the trees to give them all some relief. He'd been sitting out here in a field, in the direct sun for over an hour now, him and about 500 other people. He looked over the crowd in the rows ahead of him again, trying to pick out Felicity, but couldn't find her amidst the sea of yellow graduation caps.

The keynote speaker was still going on and on about the importance of having direction in life. Yes, we know. Have a plan, be prepared. The man made it sound like such a difficult endeavor. These students are all getting their degrees today. They must already *have* a plan, right? You choose your goal, and you follow the steps. Do other people really find that so difficult?

Ben never had those kinds of problems. He'd always felt that as long as you were unafraid to put in some hard work, it wasn't all that difficult to reach a realistic goal. He couldn't understand why the things that were supposed to be hard, came so easily to him; school, work, even fencing, he was a natural. But the things that other people seemed to handle effortlessly, those were the parts of Ben's life that he never felt able to figure out.

Take family for instance. How hard should it be, to have a somewhat decent relationship with one's only remaining parent? It's not as though either of them had any other close family to turn to. This was it! Yet Ben and his father were barely able to speak to one another about anything other than small talk and passing pleasantries. Why didn't his father feel he was worth the time for a real conversation? Was he such a disappointment? Ben felt he was more responsible than any other son his age could ever be expected to be, and yet his father couldn't trust him to have one important, honest conversation.

Ben ran his fingers through his thick, dark hair that tended to curl as soon as it grew out to any length, and glanced over at Felicity's oldest brother, sitting next to him on his left. Edmund was Ben's age. He was a nice guy. Ben had always gotten along with him well, but let's be honest; he'd made a few mistakes along the way. He had barely graduated from college, he'd needed to be bailed out of several unsavory situations by his parents over the last few years, and he had recently lost his girlfriend, because he'd been found in bed with someone else's. Not exactly a sterling reputation, but none of that seemed to matter. Edmund was a professional football player. Once he'd been picked up in the draft, you'd think the guy could do no wrong in his father's eyes. Of course, it was only by the Detroit Lions...who admittedly needed a lot of improvement to be taken seriously once again, but it was still professional football, and Ed's father couldn't be more proud.

Ben wasn't even sure that *his* father knew what he was doing at Columbia University. A scholarship to law school would make most parents very proud. Once Ben had told his father Bernard that he wasn't interested in public interest and rights, but in corporate law, Bernard had obviously dismissed *him* from interest.

Bernard did come to fencing meets, but his intent there seemed to be for criticism more than support. Whether Ben had won or lost the match, he had the annoying habit of rehashing every move Ben had made, and ended almost every diatribe with the phrase 'If this were real life, you would have been dead.' Ben's usual response, 'Thanks, dad.'

Ben sighed and dismissed thoughts of his father to concentrate on more pleasant things. Felicity was finally graduating! He wished he was the one finished with school, but this was almost as good. Felicity graduating meant that they could be together again. How he had been waiting for this day; the past year had been torture! Felicity had been finishing her schooling, while Ben had been living three hours away in the dorms at Columbia.

They had even agreed to see other people. It had been a tough decision to make. They'd been exclusively committed to each other for two and a half years before the separation, but they both recognized that they were young, and still discovering what they wanted from life. Their forced separation was the perfect opportunity to be sure of their feelings.

They'd set up all kinds of rules to try to keep each other from feeling guilty or jealous. They were only allowed one phone call a week, on

Wednesday nights, and neither was allowed to fish for information about dating; they could only talk about school, family and platonic friends. No talk about definite life plans for the future; no pressure. This had been a school year dedicated to freedom. They were no longer a couple. They spent one weekend a month together, leaving the rest of their time to do whatever they wanted, without being tied down.

In some ways, it almost felt as though they were setting themselves up for failure. What relationship could survive that? Ben had allowed himself to see other women, but not one of them was more than a party date, really. None of them could possibly compare to Felicity. There were plenty of pretty girls at school, but although they did have some classes and interests in common with him, most of them weren't very interesting to talk to. They just didn't seem to 'get him' like Liss did. After a few brief trysts, he'd found he didn't even really desire anyone else sexually. What was the point? It was Felicity he wanted. He didn't bother to bring dates to parties anymore; he'd rather be alone and wait for the next time he could see Liss. He lived for their weekends and Wednesday night phone calls.

He tried not to torture himself by wondering whom she might have been with, or what they'd been doing. When she was with Ben, she treated him as though he was the only man in the world, and that had been enough to sustain the hope that when their year of waiting was over, she would want to be with him always. He had a special suite booked for them at the Waldorf Astoria, and he couldn't wait until they were done with the graduation ceremony and family stuff, so he could whisk her away for time alone.

A baby's cry broke him from the daydream he had just begun, of how he would hopefully be undressing Liss later this evening. He felt a nudge on his right shoulder, and turned to find that Deidre was shoving her son into his lap. "Ben, hold him for me while I fix his bottle."

Baby Jerry Jr. winced, whined, and wriggled as Ben tried to figure out how to hold him without dropping him, or having him spit anything onto Ben's suit. Deidre was digging through a diaper bag big enough to live out of for a week.

Deidre, Felicity's best friend since childhood, had been having a rough time as of late. She'd dropped out of school after meeting Jerry, the 'love of her life'. They'd gotten a trailer together over in Walton, so that Jerry could be close enough to work in his dad's garage. The baby had come along while the wedding was still being planned. Apparently, the stress and responsibility of parenthood had convinced Jerry that he wasn't quite ready to let go of his freedom yet. He'd started staying out late drinking and partying with friends until Deidre had said that she wouldn't stand for it. At that point, Jerry declared that the wedding was off, and now she and the baby were living with her parents, while she tried to figure out a new plan for her life.

The baby stopped crying as Ben got him into a more comfortable hold. He gurgled and cooed, as he seemed to find something fascinating and comforting in Ben's eyes. Ben couldn't help but smile at the baby's pudgy little face. Deidre had found what she needed, and was mixing formula in a bottle, but had strewn various baby items all over her lap and on the grass at their feet in the process. The man sitting next to her did not look pleased.

In Ben's estimation, Deidre was a sweet kid, but she had a lot of growing up to do, and maybe a few lessons in priorities and decision making, before she should have even thought about being a mom. Why did it seem like everyone else his age was in such a rush? He looked forward to having a family, but it would be that much more rewarding when he knew he could do it right. However, it certainly wasn't for him to judge Deidre. She was trying to be responsible and make the best of it. He hoped things worked out for her. He leaned down closer to the baby, who had now taken hold of Ben's finger and was squeezing for all he was worth. "Good luck, kid," Ben whispered.

Deidre produced the bottle, and handed it over to Ben. "Would you mind? I have to clean all this up." The man next to her was inching her stuff away from him with his foot, annoyed at having his space invaded.

Ben tried to give the baby back. "That's okay; I'll clean it up for you. You can feed him."

Deidre was already draping a burp rag over his shoulder. "Don't be silly, you'll do fine." It was pretty obvious that Ben couldn't help her clean up anyway, from within the tight confines of the rows of folding chairs. "Just keep it tilted up so there's no air in the nipple."

Ben sighed and began to feed him. The baby was happy to take the bottle right away, without giving him any trouble. He even reached his chubby fingers up to try and grasp the bottle. Maybe this wasn't so bad, Ben thought with a smile.

"You're a natural," Deidre told him with an appraising grin. "Once you and Felicity get a place together, maybe you can baby-sit for me once in a while."

Ben looked over at her, first with a mocking little smile, but then in curiosity. "What makes you think we're getting a place together? We've been dating other people. I haven't even seen her in weeks."

Deidre laughed. "Give me a break, lover-boy. You are so totally committed to her. It's obvious! You think any other guy would come sit through hours of bullshit speeches just to see her graduate?"

Ben grinned and looked around. "How do you know there isn't some other guy in the crowd waiting for her?"

"Well, if there is, he doesn't get the brownie points you score for sitting with the family. Anyway, don't tell her I said so, but there's nobody else."

"Really?" Ben tried not to sound too desperately hopeful.

"Nobody important. A new name comes up now and then, but never more than once. Mostly, all she talks about is you." Ben shifted the bottle for the baby and tried not to seem too obviously relieved. "How about you?" Deidre continued. "Since you're sitting *here*, I'm thinking there isn't really anybody else, is there?"

Ben decided to tip his hand with a smile. "My oats are sown. There hasn't been anyone but her for a while now, and never anybody important. There's nobody like Liss. I'm going to marry that girl someday."

Ben accidentally jerked the bottle from the baby when Deidre squealed in delighted surprise. "Oh my God!"

After giving Deidre a fierce warning glare to keep her voice down, Ben glanced around in the hopes that the people sitting around them would think it was the baby causing the disturbance. Deidre tried to subdue her glee, leaning closer to speak to Ben in a whisper that still seemed too loud for his taste. "Did you say marriage? You're going to marry her! It's about freakin' time!"

Baby Jerry began to fidget, annoyed that his meal had been interrupted. Ben shoved the bottle at Deidre and then carefully but quickly handed the baby over. "Someday. Not today. Would you be quiet!" he whispered harshly.

Ben was given a firm nudge from Felicity's brother Ed, sitting on his left. "You'd better keep it quiet, because if mom hears, she'll have the whole thing planned before you even go out and get a ring," Ed informed him with a chuckle. Ben responded with a sheepish smile as Ed continued. "She's the only girl out of the four of us, so you know you're not going to get away with anything less than a huge formal affair, but don't let that scare you. I'd be happy to have you for a brother."

Ben grinned. "Thanks. I still have some school left though. Changing my major early on kind of threw me off track. One more year. I can't go making big wedding plans until I'm settled at a law firm."

Deidre scoffed at him as she lifted the baby to her shoulder for burping. "This is the perfect time to make plans! You *do* realize that a wedding of that magnitude has to be booked at least a year ahead of time anyway, right? Then there's the florist, the caterer, a band…"

Ed laughed. "You're really trying to scare the shit out of him, aren't you?"

Ben laughed, shaking his head. "Look, I have a plan, a timeline. I like to know that things are going according to plan. I know it's not romantically spontaneous, but it's reassuring, and I think Felicity's cool with it. I have one more year of school, and then, provided I find a good position somewhere, maybe we can start thinking marriage."

"Maybe in a year? How exciting," Deidre whispered sarcastically.

Ben gave her a resentful stare. The speaker at the podium had stepped down, and they were going to begin calling up the graduates. Felicity's last name was 'Snow', so they still had some time to kill. Ben turned thoughtful for a moment, and then grinned. "Fine, you want romantic? This is supposed to be a big secret, so you can't say anything…"

Dee scooted closer in anticipation. "A secret! Oh my gosh, what is it? Do you have a ring?"

Ben sighed while Ed laughed. "I'm not talking about the ring."

"That doesn't come until further in the plan. Weren't you listening?" Ed answered her with a snicker.

"I notice he didn't say that he didn't have one though," Dee answered grumpily. "Do you?" Ben just smiled, refusing to answer. "You do, don't you?" She asked in excitement. "I bet he's got one for her. He could give her the ring early."

Ben slumped his shoulders and waited for attention. "That's not the surprise I was talking about. I do have another year, but I also have connections. It turns out one of my professors has a wife who's a teacher at an primary school near Columbia, and she is retiring this year."

Deidre stared at him, trying to figure out how this was a surprise. "So?"

Ed smiled. "So, Felicity just got her teaching degree, and maybe she can snag that job!"

Ben nodded. "If all goes well. My professor said his wife has already agreed to put in a good word for her. I also scoped out some really nice apartments near the University."

Dee shook her head. "That close to Central Park West, I'll bet they cost a fortune!"

"You'd be surprised. There are some reasonable places out there. Don't forget, if Felicity gets the job, she'll be making a nice salary," Ben assured her.

"So let me get this straight," Ed interjected. "Your surprise is that my sister can get a job to support an apartment for you guys close to your school, so you can move out of the dorms and live in sin? Mom and dad will be so proud!"

Ben sighed and shook his head. After a moment, he turned to Ed with a serious demeanor. "Look, I am in love with your sister, totally. I know we haven't been close lately, what with being at different schools, and maybe she doesn't feel the same about me as she used to…"

"She does," Deidre interjected, shifting the baby to her other shoulder for another burp.

"I hope so," he replied with a smile. "I can't wait to see her tonight, and see what she's been thinking about for the future, but even if it turns out that she's not really on the same page I am, it's still a good job. I'm still giving her an opportunity for a good teaching job, and I hope she gets it. She'll need an apartment, but I can stay in the dorms and we can take things slow…or not at all, but I hope she'd like me to be with her. And, if things do sort of pick up where we left off, and seem to be progressing the way I'd like them to…I do have a ring."

Deidre squealed again, causing Felicity's younger brother Richie, sitting next to Ed, to lean forward and shush them on a cue from his mother. Ben glanced in their direction and Felicity's mom gave him a curious but reprimanding look. "Sorry," he whispered.

Deidre smacked him on the shoulder, although it made the baby tilt precariously. He jerked his hands up towards the baby but she shooed him away with a loud whisper. "He's fine. I knew you had a ring! See Ed, when he didn't deny it, I just knew!"

"It was my mom's," Ben admitted quietly. "I'd love to give it to her when the time comes, but for now, I'd just like to know that she's willing to leave with me after the family dinner."

Ed laughed. "Are you kidding? Dude, why wouldn't she? You've got the total package, man. Good looking guy, a couple of years older than her, with a cool car, ready to finish law school? It might not quite be professional ball player status," he said with a smirk, "but it's still pretty much the definition of 'desirable' in a girl's book. Am I right?" he asked Deidre.

She'd been gazing at Ben a little too longingly, and now gave a self-conscious nod and began adjusting her hold on her son, who had fallen asleep in her lap. "I'll say," she muttered. "You're like the perfect guy."

He laughed. "Thanks," Ben told them with a smile. "We'll see."

Perfect might be an exaggeration, but he'd certainly always tried to do the right thing. So why did he feel as though he always fell short when it counted most? He studied and got good grades, worked hard and paid his bills on time; no matter how unimpressed his father might be, he was a model son!

Girls always seemed easily impressed by him. Getting dates had never been a problem. When his relationship with Felicity had transitioned into more, he'd even handled that very well, for almost three years! He hadn't felt trapped, or gotten bored and developed an itch to wander from her, as he had secretly been afraid he might. His time together with Felicity was the most happy and secure he had ever felt in his life.

When she had suggested they see other people for the first year he would be away at Columbia, he had been somewhat shocked. Honestly, he couldn't tell if it was because she wanted it for herself, or because she thought he might have the urge to cheat on her and was simply sparing herself the grief. He had offered that he would like to stay committed, but she was the one who had said she thought it would be better this way, so he'd followed her wishes. Whatever the incentive, the final outcome had been to make him want her even more. He could only hope that it had done the same for her feelings for him. Absence makes the heart grow fonder, and all of that.

He was a good boyfriend, wasn't he? They'd had a few rocky moments in the beginning, before they'd let the events of the past fade behind them, and they'd found their footing as a couple, but together they made a great team. She understood him and always knew how to make him happy, and he had tried very hard to do the same for her. For once, he would have a long lasting, healthy, and positive relationship in his life.

Others may see him as perfect, but looking back, he knew he was far from it. His important personal relationships were all marked by large failings on his part. Whether others thought it was his fault or not, he always felt as though he'd missed the signs and failed to do what was needed before it was too late.

His brief relationship with Sindy had been the start of it. Only after she had run away, disappearing from the neighborhood and his life, had he realized that she had been sexually abused at home. Rumors and gossip had put together for him the awful truth that he had not even noticed right under his nose. She had never said a word to him of it, but surely she had looked to him to make her feel protected and safe, and he had been blindly wrapped up in his own concerns. He must have seemed so selfish and uncaring!

When she had returned, he'd been stricken to find that she'd become a vampire and was temporarily obsessed with turning him into one as well. At that point, all he could do was avoid her as best he could. An apology just wasn't going to cut it. She wasn't even really the girl he had known anymore, was she? He had failed her; the first in a long list of family and friends he had disappointed and been forced to let go of. His Dad, his Mom, Davy, Mattie, …Allie. He always seemed to miss the signs or mess things up.

When he had begun to recognize how much he cared for Felicity, he'd sworn to himself that it would be different. He would protect her and keep her safe. He wouldn't miss a thing. It was bad enough that he had almost lost her when she'd given her heart to the vampire Cain. When Cain had left, it was as though she'd practically been handed to him. He didn't completely understand the circumstances, but he wasn't going to mess up his chance. He would keep her safe, love her truly, and be everything she would ever need; vampires be damned.

Over time, he had learned to stop trying to constantly shield her, or worry that her judgment might have been clouded by her time with Cain. Vampires were no longer a nightly concern, or even a topic of conversation, for a very long time now. Ben and Felicity had become a loving, caring couple, sharing their lives with mutual respect and understanding. Over the past year he had given her the freedom she had requested, but had also always tried to be sure she knew that his feelings for her never wavered. He loved her. If she still loved him too, they had a bright and hopeful future ahead of them.

Ben was startled from his thoughts as he heard the announcer say the name he had been waiting for. "Felicity Snow." Ben searched the stage, and then saw her as she climbed the steps to receive her degree.

Her hair shown with a radiant auburn glow in the bright sunlight, as it cascaded over her shoulders from underneath the golden yellow graduation cap. She turned and looked out over the crowd as she took her diploma, her cheeks flushed from the heat and excitement, her smile beaming. Her sweeping gaze finally found her parents, and she froze for them to take a picture. Just before moving on across the stage, her eyes swept along, taking in her brothers. Then, she saw him.

Her eyes seemed to sparkle as they met Ben's and he could practically see her heart swell in her chest beneath the graduation gown. He hadn't told her he was coming, but had she really thought he wouldn't be there? Her sincere appreciation was clearly apparent. They hadn't seen each other in a month, yet he could almost feel the love she had for him pouring forth across the distance. The crowd didn't matter; they were sharing a private understanding in that one fleeting moment.

The announcer had taken her elbow and was ushering her off the stage so that the next name could be called. She had to break their gaze and make her way down the steps to her seat.

It didn't matter. Ben's anxious anticipation had gelled into a more sedate sort of expectance. He was eager to see her, but now he knew. She still loved him, and he was going to be sure that he would always be everything that she would ever need. For once in his life, everything would go according to plan.

Chapter 3
Old friends and new discoveries

Allie

Upper West Side, New York City
A Saturday evening in early December

Allie drifted swiftly earthward, and then lightly touched down on the ground in the alley behind Lion's Head Tavern, almost surprised by the feeling of weight coming back to her as she let herself rely once again on the pavement for support. Once she was settled firmly on the ground, she couldn't help but giggle a bit to herself at the discovery of this new skill.

She had started out the journey thinking she'd rely on her supernatural vampire speed to travel from Buffalo down into Manhattan. She had tirelessly run about half the distance, and judging by the traffic on the highway she'd been paralleling, she was doing better than 90 mph. She had easily outdistanced every car she'd passed with giddy glee. She didn't even worry who might see her. Her coven-mates Cain and Mattie might not approve, but she knew she was little more than a blur before she was gone from the sight of mortal eyes; hardly something she was going to waste time worrying about. Besides, she'd thought with a humorously wicked grin, Cain and Mattie weren't here to tell her not to, were they?

At times, it was faster to stray from the road, finding her way nimbly over the mountaintops, rather than winding around and through the valleys between them with the roadways. This was the longest and fastest she had ever pushed herself. Traveling by her own power, unfettered, was so freeing, and fun!

At one point, she had crested the peak of a hill, and had been about to begin her descent down the other side, when she'd decided to make a grand leap, rather than run. As her feet had left the ground, she'd felt an odd sense of release and a dizzy sort of weightlessness. She'd felt as though she could walk on the air, with no need to obey the laws of gravity, or to touch down again at the end of her sailing jump. She'd automatically shifted her body weight and had actually felt it alter and adjust to keep her levitating in the air, mid-leap. She floated and teetered precariously for a moment and then stabilized; she was flying!

The wind resistance took on new importance, making the crisp cold air feel like a living thing around her. She found that she could anticipate its shifts and gusts, to counter against them and keep afloat. After a few anxious seconds of frightened wonder, still expecting to fall at any moment, she'd given a cautious laugh and willed herself to rise a little higher. To her amazement, her body had obeyed.

Allie had risen higher in the air until she had hung about ten feet above the ground, in the disconcerting way that a 5' 2" girl of about a hundred pounds shouldn't; no matter how petite she may seem. It was exactly like the dreams she'd had now and again, where she could defy gravity at will to soar among the treetops. But those dreams always had a surreal quality to them that let her know they weren't real. They always began mid-flight, and they never considered practical things like wind, or the need to get back down. This was real! She was flying! Oh my God, should she try to land?

Part of her felt that she should, just to be sure that she could reach the ground again at will, but her daring, stubborn streak quickly took over. What if she landed, and could never get back up into the air again? This was an experience not to be wasted! When the time came to touch ground again, she would figure it out. For now, she was an unfettered kite, broken free of string and earthly restraint, and floating up ever higher on the wind.

She'd begun to experiment with increasing abandon until she was rising and falling with ease. She became more daring still, moving forwards and back, and finally executing a very wobbly and uncertain tumble-salt, nearly losing her tinted glasses in the process. Dizzy and off balance for a moment, she righted herself and then stood straight and tall on nothing. She was still standing on air, and it didn't seem that she was going to plummet to the earth any time soon.

Then, she had made up her mind to rise as high as she could go, to test the limit. She'd passed the treetops, and risen up to be surrounded by stars. A fog had formed on the lenses of her rose tinted glasses, and she'd taken them off to fold them and put them into her pocket. She didn't suffer for lack of oxygen, because her body didn't need to breathe, but she could feel the air turning ever colder. Finally, she'd stopped to look down and see the tiny sparse lights of civilization far down below. She was high enough, she'd decided.

Alyson had hung there for a moment, just taking in the awesome wonder of weightlessness and height. Lyrics from the song *Learning to Fly* by Pink Floyd were running through her head. *'There's no sensation to compare with this; suspended animation, in a state of bliss,'* So true. She'd inhaled a deep lungful of frigid night air and then gotten her bearings to assess her direction. She'd resumed travel, to find that just a slight shift in the desired direction would take her sailing smoothly forward. From her new height, she'd been able to cover the distance in no time!

Over bridges and past landmarks she'd flown, gazing in amazement as she'd recognized the Empire State Building, among the bright lights of the skyline up ahead. She'd closed her eyes and consulted her memory of the map she had studied for this secret plan, trying to remember just where it was she needed to go. Once she had found Central Park, the large, darkened area of green foliage easy to pick out amongst the multitude of city lights, it had been simple to figure out how to reach her final destination. She'd managed to find the Upper West Side, and done a roundabout circuit of the area, before deciding to land in the alley behind Lion's Head Tavern, to be close to her goal without attracting notice upon landing. Felicity's apartment should be only a few blocks away.

Landing had been simple, just another shift in body weight, consciously making herself gradually heavy enough to touch the ground again. Just as a quick test, she rose up a foot into the air again, and then came back down. Now that she had the hang of it, she could levitate herself at will! Wait until the guys found out; this had to be the best power yet! Cain had mentioned having something new that he wanted to work on with her when he returned from his trip. She wondered if he had known she could be capable of flight all along, or if there was something else.

He was away, investigating some brutal murders that had made the news from down in Maryland, which had all the signs of being caused by a vampire. He had told them that he expected to return within the month. It had been a nice break from training, but now she was excited for him to return, so she could share her new discovery.

Allie's clothes were damp from flying through the precipitation of low clouds in the cold night air, but nothing could dampen her spirits after that flight. She brushed the hair back out of her eyes and put her tinted glasses back on. Her hair was wet too. Hopefully it wasn't too much of a mess. She wove her fingers through it a few times to help it lay straight.

During the first year or so after her change, she'd kept up buzzing her hair short, because she wasn't sure how else she could keep it easily neat, without being able to see her reflection in a mirror, but it'd just seemed so boring after a while. She couldn't really apply make-up without a reflection, and having a platinum blonde buzz-cut just seemed so masculine and uninteresting. Even Mattie had remarked that he missed her often varied and surprising styles of the past. In response, she had dyed her very short blonde hair bright neon pink; a signature color for streaking in the past. Mattie had laughed that the color change wasn't quite what he'd had in mind, but she wasn't going to bother to try to change it. At least she felt a little more like herself, knowing that she looked so unique.

Eventually she'd stopped cutting it. She hadn't let her hair grow out to any real length in years; she'd always shaved the back, and just let the top grow a few extra inches for styling. Now she had let it all grow out to a chin length bob. Fairly straight, and parted in the middle, she imagined that it would look very ordinary, except for the fact that she'd never cut off that bright pink color. She had about an inch and a half of bright pink ends that satisfied her creative side. It was cool to have hair long enough that she could actually see it for a change. Maybe she would just keep letting it grow. It took some getting used to, having hair in her face now and then, but she'd just pull it back into a ponytail once it was long enough.

Satisfied that she looked as inconspicuous as a tiny girl with pink hair, wearing wet clothes and knee high leather boots, coming out of a city alley at midnight was going to look, she prepared to step out onto the street. Before she had quite reached the end of the dark alleyway, she felt a sudden, forceful surge of thirst come over her like a wave. She needed blood, badly. She stood stunned in dazed confusion for a moment as the thirst strongly ripped through her again. She'd drunk so much before she'd left, that Mattie had asked if she was planning to run clear around the world. How could she possibly need more?

Someone was coming. She took a step back into the shadows as a man walked by on the street. He didn't notice her at all. He was stumbling slowly by, hugging his coat closed and mumbling something to himself as he walked. She could feel him…she could smell him. It didn't matter that he stunk of sweat and grime; he was *warm*, large, and full of what she needed. His blood called to her like a siren's song. He took on shades of red as her vision shifted, urging her towards easy prey. She could grab him and pull him into the alley before he even knew she was there.

She swallowed back the thirst and cleared the heat gauge from her vision. He was gone, past the opening and continuing on into the night. Why was her body so damned desperate to be fed? It must have been the flight. She was always thirsty after she ran for any length of time at super speed, flying must use up that much more of her body's resources. It wanted her to replenish herself. Still, she had never drunk from a human, and she wasn't about to start now. There must be something else.

The metal of the flask she had brought was freezing cold against her leg, between her snug jeans and the inside of her tall leather boot. She had no body heat to keep it warm, and although the blood had been fresh and warm when she'd filled the flask, the altitude of her recent flight in the cool night air had now thoroughly chilled it. Cold blood...yuck. She'd save that for later. Maybe she could warm it up at Felicity's. She had better find something else to assuage her thirst now though. It would not be a very good idea to show up to visit her human friend for the first time in years, while bloodthirsty and on the verge of losing control.

Alyson paused to assess her surroundings. The hulking skyscrapers around her felt so enclosing. She much preferred to feel the living essence of the tall pines of the forest. The clean fresh smell of open air in the woods was better too. To her sensitive nose, the heavy stench of the city seemed almost unbearable. How did other vampires live here? Must be something you got used to. With her vampire sight, she could see the life energy of not only people, but animals and plants as well. She was oppressively surrounded by people at the moment, hidden and living out their lives packed into the buildings all around her, but the alley itself felt dead and empty. Well...not entirely empty.

She turned and slowly walked towards a dumpster, now hearing a rustle of paper from behind it. Amidst the general scents of filth, rotting food, vermin and disgustingly enough, human feces, she could also smell cat piss. Sure enough, as she neared the container, a frightened cat shot out from behind it with a screech. It stopped to hiss at her from a few feet away.

Her fangs unsheathed themselves, and she found herself practically hissing back at it, even as a part of her mind was thinking, *No, don't eat the kitty!* She watched while it stood frozen, staring at her with its head dipped low and its back arched high. It was a mangy thing, grey and black striped, and certainly underfed. She knew she could catch it easily, but she didn't move. It would be warm and filling, and it wouldn't be the first time she'd snatched up a small mammal out of desperation, but despite being more of a dog person, she wasn't quite desperate enough to kill a cat, no matter how evil it might be acting towards her. A sharp pang of hunger clamped her stomach. Okay, maybe she *was* beginning to feel rather desperate, but there had to be another option.

She deliberately turned away from the cat to scan the rest of the alley. Her heat seeking vision swept by the dumpsters and found what she was looking for. Rats, at least three. Not exactly a gourmet meal, but they would contain nice warm blood and that was all that mattered. Most likely, the cat had been hunting them. *Sorry kitty, they're mine now.*

She caught the first one almost without thought. It was pathetically slow, compared to her swift movements, and the papers and soda cans on the street were poor cover for its radiantly warm blood that practically glowed in her vampire vision. She was sure not to breathe in its scent as she sunk in her fangs, puncturing through the greasy fur and skin. Rather than actually suck the blood out of it, she tore it with her fangs and then held it up to squeeze and pour the blood into her mouth, so she wouldn't have to touch hair to her lips again. It seemed a disgustingly uncivilized meal, but it was so good to feel warm blood on her tongue, that all she could think of was the fact that she wanted more. The small amount she could gain from the tiny animal seemed a tease.

She threw it aside and instantly found another, catching and treating it just the same. The last rat was actually inside the dumpster. She thought about jumping in after it, but she didn't really want to show up at Felicity's smelling of garbage. Having rat blood breath was bad enough.

She made her way to the back corner of the dumpster, where a rusted hole near the bottom had given the rodent entrance. She squatted down on her heels, unwilling to rest her knees on the dirty pavement, and sent out waves of curious enticement to the creature. She could feel its little rat mind, wondering what was so interesting out there, as it twitched its nose and tried to pick up the scent of food. *Yes, there's food out here. Come and get it.* She gave the rat a mental nudge and it finally came wandering out of the hole. Although cautious and skittery, it never even noticed her through the mental blinders she'd thrown up at it. Rats were pretty single-minded when hungry, making them easy for her to fool. It ventured further and further from safety.

She let it get about a foot from the dumpster, and then she just reached out and grabbed it. The poor thing never stood a chance. Blood, so warm, so good…so little. She actually did find herself sucking at this one, trying to get every last drop. Once it was nothing but a limp and hollow carcass, she dropped it to the ground, wiping her mouth on her sleeve.

Alyson paused and spit once or twice onto the cement at her feet, finding to her disgust that she had a rat hair in her mouth. She closed her eyes and chased the revolting realization from her mind. *You are a powerful vampire; an immortal super-being who can fly,* she told herself. *Having a rat hair or two in your mouth is a small price to pay.* Her thirst had calmed a bit, barely quelled for now. She would need more soon, but the alley seemed empty of all energy but hers. The cat was long gone. Lucky for the cat, because now that she'd begun drinking, she was starting to think that feline blood wouldn't be so unwelcome after all. In fact, just the thought of it made her thirst intensify. A cat must have at least the same amount of blood as three rats, right? She shouldn't have let it escape.

It probably hadn't gone far; she'd have to wait though. She had some place else to be. She shifted back to human form, and concentrated on resuming her journey. She sincerely hoped that Felicity didn't own a cat.

Once out on the street, it wasn't long before she found the building that she was looking for. She made her way up to the right floor, and began to mentally attune herself to thoughts of Felicity, as she searched out the right apartment.

She hadn't psychically connected with Felicity in a while. In her first months as a vampire, she'd found that it would happen randomly, through dreams or just during moments when Felicity might be thinking of her, allowing Allie to 'pick up' the thoughts. However, since Alyson had better learned to control her powers, she tended to shut out any outside transmittance automatically.

Occasionally, she thought of her old friend. She wondered what she was doing, and whether she was still seeing Ben, Allie's close friend since childhood, now estranged. It still hurt that she couldn't share her new vampire experiences with Ben, not that he would ever properly appreciate them anyway. She knew in her heart that someday she was going to go back and talk to him, to make him understand and be her dear friend again. She was just waiting for the right time. She wanted to be sure that she fully understood things herself; that she was in complete control.

The last time she had seen Ben, she'd made the stupid blunder of unconsciously speaking to him telepathically and totally freaking him out. She wanted to be confident and able to present things to him in the most acceptable way. Or…maybe she was just procrastinating, scared that no matter what preparations she might try to make, things wouldn't work out as she hoped.

There had been times that she had checked in on Felicity throughout the past few years. She knew that Ben and Felicity still kept in touch, although their relationship seemed to wax and wane. She knew that Felicity loved him, but was worried that she might have rushed into their relationship. It seemed to Allie that Ben was pretty devoted, by the thoughts and memories she saw through Felicity. It was Felicity who was holding back. Allie couldn't help but wonder if the girl still harbored feelings for Cain. Felicity didn't actively think of him anymore, as far as

Allie could tell, but she didn't really dig to try to seek out the girl's inner feelings. It felt wrong to so invasively read another's thoughts and emotions without their knowledge.

It was nice for Allie to feel she had a connection with another woman once in a while though. Normally she spent all of her time with Mattie and Cain. Truthfully, she had always been more comfortable with men than women anyway, but it was nice to have a break from them sometimes. She was really looking forward to this visit. She'd been remiss in not coming back to see Felicity sooner. With Cain being away, she had the perfect opportunity. It was time.

Now that she was allowing it, she could feel Felicity clearly. In fact, it was the girl's thoughts that led her to the right door, rather than the apartment number. She could feel her inside, working hard on some kind of paperwork, even though it was rather late. After a few moments of enjoying the familiar feel of her friend, Alyson knocked on the door.

She felt Felicity's surprise at having such a late night visitor. Allie put on a smile as she felt her friend approach the door to look through the peephole. Felicity didn't recognize her at first, and even once she did, she didn't believe her eyes. Allie gave her a quick mental nudge. *Yeah, it's me.*

The sound of metal locks being worked came from within, and after a moment the door was swung open wide. "Allie?" Felicity asked in surprised disbelief. "Oh, my God; Allie is that you?"

Alyson spread her arms wide with a smile. "In the flesh."

"Allie!" Felicity repeated with squeaky delight. "I can't believe you're here! How did you find me? Look at your hair; I love it! And you're…" she faltered slightly as she gathered Allie into her arms, "…you're wet." She let Allie go and backed away a little, to better observe her. "Is it raining?"

Allie laughed dismissively. "It was a little," she lied, "but it stopped now. Can I come in?"

"Of course, come in!" she exclaimed without the slightest hesitation as she backed into the apartment.

Alyson stepped through the doorway and took a quick look around before settling her attention back on Felicity. It was a pleasant little apartment, nicely decorated, but there was a good-sized pile of boxes taking up most of the living room floor. Knowing that Felicity had moved in some time ago, Alyson was going to ask about them, but got distracted when she took a good look at Felicity. "Look at you. You look great," she said with a grin.

Felicity had cut her hair almost as short as Alyson's, to just barely above her shoulders, and had it very straight, in choppy, modern layers

41

framing her face. The color was still that naturally gorgeous dark red, which stood out strikingly next to her fair skin. It was a nice look for her, but the next thing Allie immediately noticed was how thin her friend's face looked. She took a step back to survey Felicity's newly thinned frame. "Holy cow girl, you got skinny! Does your boyfriend have you on some kind of super-model water diet? You'd better start eating again!"

Felicity laughed and smoothed her hands down over her thighs, turning a bit to model her jeans. "Do I look good though? Would you believe these are a size 8? An 8 Allie! I know to someone who has spent life as a size 0 that probably doesn't sound very impressive, but I haven't been able to fit into jeans this size since tenth grade!" Allie was just giving her a tolerant little smile, so Felicity continued. "No, it has nothing to do with Ben. I wanted to lose some weight for me. I started going to a gym. Then I moved in here, I started a new job, and things have been so crazy and stressful, that I don't even have time to eat. The last two months, I feel like the pounds just keep falling off. That doesn't happen for me, *ever*, so I wasn't going to fight it."

Alyson found that her eyes kept trying to shift into the heat spectrum again as she studied Felicity. Another hunger cramp of blood thirst rumbled through her. The rats had hardly been enough to keep her thinking clearly, and her body knew that however much weight Felicity might have lost, she still had a hell of a lot more blood in her than a rat. Allie slowly blinked her eyes, fought back the thirst, and re-assessed Felicity's figure. "You look good, but I think you should start eating again." Allie shook her head with a sigh. "It'd be a damn shame not to properly appreciate good tasting food."

Felicity looked at her oddly. "Can't you taste stuff?"

She shrugged. "I can, but it's not the same as it used to be. Nothing tastes as good," *as blood,* she added mentally, editing herself at the last second. "It's more the texture of food that's interesting now."

Felicity just stared at her mutely for a moment. "My God Allie, I still can't believe it. I can't believe you're really…really…"

"Yep. Really, really. You processed it all way back when, and I know you've thought about it since." She hadn't expected Felicity to be very shocked. She'd been close to vampires before. "The new me is old news by now."

"I know but, it's not like I had much time to take it in before you left, and it's been years. You haven't been back for *years,* Allie. Look at you. You look mostly the same, except for your hair, which I truly love by the way, but gosh Allie, you're so pale."

"Am I?" She asked, slightly self-consciously. It was her need for blood; she was spent.

Felicity came forward, taking Allie's hands into her own. "And you're cold as ice! Can I make you some hot tea?" Felicity asked in concern.

Allie chuckled. "No thanks, I brought my own." She bent to slide her hand down her leg and retrieve the flask from within her boot.

Felicity stared at it for a second and then stepped into the kitchen. She found Allie a mug, and handed it to her, trying to seem unfazed. It had been a few years since she'd watched anyone prepare to drink blood, and she probably hadn't been very comfortable with it then either. Allie apologized. "Sorry to barge in and put bodily fluids in your microwave." Felicity blanched as Allie poured the contents of the flask into the mug. "I'd wait, but I'm pretty parched, so it's probably better if I just go ahead and…"

Felicity was looking at the contents of the mug with thinly veiled disgust. "Yeah. Go ahead," she said, waving a hand towards the microwave.

Alyson studied Felicity as the microwave hummed and warmed the mug of blood. She was obviously uncomfortable. "Don't make me feel all weird about coming. I've been really looking forward to seeing you."

"Oh no, Allie, I'm glad you came, really. It's just been a while since I've thought about the practical side of this sort of thing," she said, waving towards the microwave. She took Allie by the shoulders, pulling her in for a quick hug. "I am so happy to see you! You shouldn't have stayed away so long!" She leaned back to meet her friend's eyes. "How is everything? Is it all you hoped it would be?"

"And more," Allie answered with a chuckle.

Felicity flicked her eyes downward for a moment. Oddly, she wasn't jealous, as Allie thought she'd be. Instead, she was worried that Allie wasn't being truthful; putting on a brave face to cover any misgivings she might have over her decisions. Alyson gave her a small mental wave of reassurance. Felicity didn't seem to be conscious of the deliberateness of it, but she looked up at Allie with a smile. "I'm glad you're okay. I worried about you."

Allie laughed as the microwave beeped. "Me? I was worried about you."

"Why?"

"I left you with some pretty intense stuff to deal with. You held him together." For some reason she couldn't quite bring herself to say Ben's name yet. It didn't matter. Felicity knew whom she meant. "I'm glad you were there for him, and that you decided to stick around for a while after."

Felicity gave her a thoughtful grin. "He needed me. I love him." She said it matter of factly, without hesitation. However their relationship had waxed and waned, she obviously had no doubt of her feelings.

Allie took her mug from the microwave and gave it a swirl before taking a sip. "Real love, huh?" Allie asked with a chuckle. "Has he finally realized that he loves you too?"

Felicity nodded. "I think so." Her gaze only grazed the blood within Allie's mug for a moment, and then she turned around and busied herself with making a cup of tea. "You know what else I figured out?" she asked as she put her own mug in for heating. "I love me when I'm with him. I love the way he makes me feel…he empowers me. He tries to come on all strong and protective, but he needs me to be strong too, and I love that. He makes me feel so special and confident. He believes in me."

"Wow. That's a good thing to have, someone who believes in you. I'm pretty lucky that way too, with Mattie. I have to remind myself of that sometimes, so I don't screw it up."

Felicity grinned. "Well, I'm glad Mattie believes in you, but I can't imagine you ever being any less headstrong and confident than you've always been. Before *I* met you guys, I was such a wishy-washy milksop. When I liked a guy, I would be trying so hard to be everything I thought he wanted me to be, that I would forget who I am. I was the incredible disappearing girl. I'm not like that with Ben. What a loser I was."

"You know you weren't, 'cause I'm not friends with losers. Don't be so hard on yourself. You're not the only one that happens to. I've seen it before, lots of times. Never understood it myself, but I'm glad he gives you strength that way."

Allie could feel Felicity become withdrawn in contemplation for a moment before adding comment. "Actually, I have to give credit where credit is due. It was *Cain* who brought that out in me." Her voice slightly faltered as she said the name, but she continued. "It was Cain who first believed in me as I was, and refused to let me lose myself in him. He always encouraged me to be strong and to have my own opinions; to allow myself to be happy on my own terms. Even when he left, it was because he knew what I wanted for my life, in my heart, and he wouldn't let me give it up for him."

Even without the betraying tremble in her voice, Alyson could feel the heartbreak still within her. The scars had healed and she had some emotional distance from it now, but her love for Cain and the sorrow over the loss of their relationship was still there. Alyson put a hand on her arm, unsure what to say. Felicity continued. "If it weren't for Cain, I never would have been strong enough to make it work with Ben. Kind of ironic, huh?"

Allie shrugged. "They say everyone comes into our lives for a reason. Maybe that was his."

"Maybe." She grew quiet and doubtful as she said it. "Somehow I always thought there'd be more."

"More what?"

"More to us."

Allie met her eyes for a moment, feeling the disappointment within her. It was softer now though. An old familiar ache that had simply become a part of who Felicity was, a testament to the injustices in life, and proof of strength to move beyond them.

Alyson broke the gaze and swept her eyes around the apartment for a change in subject. "So what's with the boxes? You're not moving out are you?"

Felicity was pulled from her reminiscence back to reality. She finished fixing her tea and moved with Allie into the living room. "No. Actually, Ben's moving in."

Allie's eyes widened in surprise. "Really? How did I miss that? I have to start paying closer attention."

"Allie, it has been a few years."

"Yeah, but even though I knew you guys were together, it seemed kind of on-again off-again. By the way you were talking, obviously it was *on* at the moment, but I didn't know you two had gotten so serious."

Felicity seemed confused by Allie's reaction. "We did stop seeing each other for a while, but we've been pretty serious since the summer. How would you even know that?"

"We need to talk. I've got to catch you up to speed," Allie said, putting a hand on her shoulder and glancing at the door, "but isn't he coming home soon? It's pretty late."

Felicity plopped herself down on the couch, unconcerned, and then patted the seat for Allie to join her. "No, not tonight. He's over at student housing. He has his room there until the end of term actually, but he stays here most nights. He just finished getting the last of his stuff out of the dorm and his roommate's giving him a goodbye party."

Allie raised an eyebrow as she took the proffered seat. "A goodbye party? It's only right down the road."

"Pretty much, but those guys will use any excuse to throw a party."

"So how come you're not there? It's Friday night!"

"Loud drunken law students aren't really my thing. Besides, I have a bunch of papers I have to correct over the weekend and give back on Monday." She gave Allie a glowing smile as she realized her new profession was news to share. "I'm a teacher now."

"I know, congratulations! Do you love it?" Allie was suitably happy for her, but Felicity still seemed off-put.

"Yes, I do, but how do you know this stuff?"

Allie sighed and shook her head. Obviously, Felicity hadn't caught on to their psychic connection. "Do you ever think about me?"

"Sure I think about you. I mean, things have been pretty busy lately," she admitted apologetically, "but I used to think about you all the time; I'd have vivid dreams even. They were so intense I even started writing them down."

"Really?"

"I have a journal full of them somewhere. What does that have to do with anything? Of course, I missed you, Allie. So badly, I used to wish we could talk. Who else could understand the things Ben and I have been through?" She gave Allie a sheepish grin. "I even used to talk to you sometimes, when I was alone. I know it's dumb, but it made me feel better."

"It's not dumb. I heard you. Not always, but sometimes. And those dreams, I had them too. I think most of them were probably real."

"Real? I don't understand. How could you hear me?"

Allie sat back, crossing her legs and resting them up on the coffee table. "Turns out, I'm not your ordinary average vampire."

Felicity remained sitting rigidly serious in her confusion. "Allie, I don't consider *any* vampire ordinary or average in any way. What are you talking about?"

"Let me fill you in from the beginning. We never knew it, but vampires actually come in different breeds, and you can tell the breeds apart by the color of their eyes."

"Okay," Felicity answered dubiously.

"Well, each breed also has certain powers, special things they can do."

"Like what? Leaving different marks? Is it like a venom thing? Because other than that, I've only ever seen them drink blood and make more vampires."

"No, some things all vampires can do. We all have venom. It's more specialized than that." Allie shifted impatiently, wishing she could just dump all of the information directly into Felicity's head. That was a little too drastically assuming though. She didn't want Felicity to freak out on her as Ben had. She sat up and folded her legs under herself, pretzel-style on the couch, and tried again to explain. "There are vampires with pink eyes, that can run super fast and they're strong and agile too. They could run by you, climb up the side of a building, and leap across to the next, before you barely even knew they were there."

Felicity didn't look very pleased by the example. "That's not very comforting. I hope there aren't too many of them."

"No, hardly any. The really special breeds are pretty rare," Allie assured her. She attempted again to engage Felicity in the excitement of the discovery. "There's another kind that can actually fly! And vampires with purple eyes are telepathic. They can speak to people without saying anything. They can read minds, and they can even put someone in thrall just by staring at them."

"Wow. Is that what you are?" Felicity was thinking about Allie's knowledge of her relationship with Ben, trying to put things together.

"Sort of."

You can really read my mind? Felicity asked within her thoughts.

Yes. That's how I knew about you and Ben, and about your new job. I don't usually go poking around in people's heads and stuff without permission. I was just checking in once in a while, to make sure you were okay. I should've come to visit sooner.

That's okay. "What can vampires with yellow eyes do?" Obviously, she was thinking of Cain.

Allie hesitated, unprepared for that shift in questioning, but then answered truthfully. "I don't know. We don't come with instruction manuals. Most of this stuff is hard-core old school vampire lore. It's the kind of information that a maker is supposed to pass down, but things aren't so formal these days. Half the vampires around don't even know who made them. They don't know what *they* can do, let alone other breeds. Even old vamps don't know much about it. You just have to kind of learn by trial and error."

"What about vampires with red eyes? What's their talent, being supreme bitch sluts?"

Allie laughed softly. She was clearly referring to Sindy. "I don't know, maybe. Mattie has orange eyes, and we haven't figured out anything special that he can do either."

"Yellow, red and orange, that's all I've ever seen. So what about you? Your eyes are purple? Can I see them?" She had eager anticipation in her voice.

It reminded Allie of when she'd first asked Mattie what color her own eyes were, and her disappointment at the answer. "Sure. They're not purple though."

"I thought you said it was the purple kind who could read minds and stuff."

"Yeah, but I also said that I'm a special case. My eyes are white."

"White?"

"M-hmm. See?" Alyson shifted to reveal the bright white eyes that had caused such concern since her change. Felicity was just staring at them transfixed, until Allie smiled, revealing the tips of her fangs.

It made Felicity lean back a little. "Whoa."

"I know, right?"

"They're really pretty." Felicity gazed at her in speculation until Alyson changed back, worried that she might be putting her friend into some sort of trance. Felicity blinked a few times, as though there were spots before her eyes, and then asked uncertainly, "So what does white mean?"

"Everything. If you took every color and mixed them all together, you get white."

"Wouldn't that make brown?"

"No. It's not like mixing paint! It's like when you shine white light through a raindrop and it gives you a rainbow. I'm a mix of everything."

"Everything? How did that happen? I thought Mattie made you?"

"He did. It's a long story. No one was more surprised than we were."

"You can do *everything?*" Felicity asked uncertainly as she tried to put it all together. "You can read minds, and run fast, and be strong and…fly?"

"Sweet deal, huh? Check it out." Allie put down her empty mug on the coffee table. She kept her position of sitting cross-legged Indian style next to Felicity on the couch, but now she concentrated on the air around her and caused herself to slowly float up into it. The motion was a little jerky at first as she figured out the control, but in a moment, she was levitating about four feet above the couch. Felicity almost choked on the last of her tea.

"I know! I just learned this one. I am so psyched! I think it's my favorite power so far."

Felicity couldn't stop staring at the empty space underneath Alyson. "Oh my God Allie, that's amazing!"

Allie let herself settle back down onto the couch again, vindicated by Felicity's positive reaction. "See, that's why I wanted to come see you! You're so cool about this stuff. I knew I could talk to you and you wouldn't get all freaked out and emotionally scarred or anything."

Felicity sighed. "Like Ben?"

"The king of denial. I miss him. I have Mattie, and he's wonderful, but I still miss you guys. I can't even reach Ben telepathically. It's like he is totally closed to me. It sucks. I can't usually read humans from too far away, but you and I seem to have a strong connection; I guess because we understand each other about most stuff. I seem to be able to reach you no matter where you are. I can always reach Mattie too, but Ben... I couldn't even tell you if he was in the building. It almost feels like he's doing it on purpose. I guess he's just so mad at me, that he's unconsciously throwing up walls. Does he still hate me?"

"He doesn't hate you. He just doesn't agree with your choice, and he worries that it changed you. He would rather think of you as being dead, than think of you as a monster," she admitted apologetically. "He misses you though."

"I'm not a monster," Allie assured her.

"I know."

"I don't drink from humans, at all; not ever." Even as she said it, greens and blues washed over her vision, trying to make the blood within Felicity stand out in a tempting glow of red. Her body kept trying to let the predator within her out to hunt. She was using her powers too much, using up the blood within her faster than she was replacing it. She was going to have to do some heavy feeding if she was going to manage to get home again before sunrise. She briefly wondered how many rats could live between here and the Hudson River.

Felicity was obviously relieved to learn that Alyson wasn't drinking from people. If she had seen another flash of Alyson's vampire eyes, she pretended not to notice. "That's good. Is it hard?"

"Sometimes. Sometimes it's *really* hard, and I wonder what the hell I've gotten myself into." Felicity was sitting very still. She was completely trusting, but Alyson's internal struggle felt so strong, that she wondered if Felicity could feel it somehow. "It's good too though," Allie quickly added. "The powers are definitely a bonus, but it can get pretty intense.

Would you believe that there are legends about me? Well, they're not about *me*, but they're about a vampire with white eyes. As far as I know, I'm the only one around. They even have a title for me. I'm called *The United One*, since I bring together all the breeds. There are stories that say I'm supposed to be a sign or something. Like I'm supposed to usher in a whole new age for vampires."

"A new age? What does that mean?"

"Beats me. It's really strange. It's supposed to be a secret, so you can't tell anyone, not even Ben. I'm not even really supposed to be here, but it's been so long and I really wanted to see you. I have to be careful not to let other vampires see my eyes, or they act all weird. Strong ones, ones that act almost like regular people, if they see that my eyes are different, it makes them kind of uneasy. They start asking all kinds of questions and they expect me to know what it means; like they want me to do something important with it.

Weaker ones just seem to follow me around. It's kind of creepy. From the way some of them act, you'd think they were waiting for me to take over the world or something." Felicity seemed to find that mildly alarming. "Relax, it's not on my to-do list. I'm just hanging out with Mattie, having a good time. I think it's important for me to figure out everything I can do though. I don't like not knowing, so we've been kind of working on that."

"It must be scary, not even knowing what you're capable of."

"It can be, but Mattie's there for me, and…there are some other vampires we've met that have helped me out. Older vampires, that know some stuff."

"Really?" The mention of other vampires seemed to bring Felicity to attention. "Are there a lot of them?"

"Well, no. We don't like to keep in touch with too many, because of the whole secrecy thing. There's only one…or two that we see on a regular basis." It felt ridiculously obvious that she was referring to Cain, but Alyson tried to keep her face neutral and hoped that Felicity wouldn't dwell on it.

"Oh." She answered simply, but was consumed with contemplation. "I'm glad you're not alone," she finally added sincerely.

Allie smiled. "Me too."

Alyson dared to stay and visit for another hour before finally admitting that she would need to leave in order to allow for travel time before dawn. She had to laugh when Felicity offered to drive her to the train station. "Thanks, but I didn't come by train."

Felicity nodded. "Still have the old orange Charger huh?"

"Yeah I do, but the damn thing is in the shop again. Shit!" she exclaimed as she remembered something. "Can I use your phone? I was supposed to call them."

Felicity glanced at the clock on the wall. "Sure, but I think they're closed," she said with a chuckle. "It's after one in the morning."

Allie went and picked up the receiver as she dug the business card out of her pocket. "I know. I have to leave a message. It's a damn pain in the ass that I can't leave the house during business hours. Everything is always closed! I can't wait for daylight savings!" She turned her attention to the phone after hearing the beep from the machine on the other end. "Hi, this is Allie with the '69 Charger. Got your message. You can go ahead and do the work, just charge it to my card. You'll have to let me know when you're open late, so I can pick it up after work one night once it's done. Thanks."

She turned to Felicity as she hung up the phone and shoved the card back into her pocket. "Thanks. I meant to call before I left the house. I dropped my cell phone service. What do I need a cell for? Being telepathic does have its advantages."

Allie spotted a photo laying next to the phone on the table. It was a picture of Felicity and Ben, each on horseback and wearing cowboy hats. She picked it up for closer examination. It was a candid shot and they were both obviously having a good time. They seemed to be riding on a trail. Felicity was in front, but Ben was edging his horse up alongside of her and they were laughing. Ben looked good, tan, happy, and healthy; a sight for sore eyes. "This is a great shot of you guys."

Felicity glanced at the picture and smiled. "Yeah, I want to get a frame for it. Ben took me to a ranch for my birthday weekend. We lucked out that the weather was still warm. We had a great time."

"Happy birthday miss twenty-two year old."

"Thanks," Felicity said as she came to give Allie a hug goodbye. "I'm so glad you came to visit Allie. Try not to forget about me. I know my life isn't exciting like yours, but now that I know we can talk anytime…"

"Of course. Yeah, I know I haven't been checking in like I should have. You'd be surprised how easy it is to let time slip by when you don't have to keep to schedules or anything. The more I'm starting to realize what it means to live outside of humans and mortality, the more I seem to take time for granted, even though I shouldn't. Weeks seem to fly by like days, since I don't particularly have to keep track. I'll try to remember to check in though, even if it's only telepathically."

"Okay. Take care, and be safe," Felicity said, giving her a last squeeze.

"You too." She wanted to add take care of Ben for me, but stopped herself. She didn't want to bring him up again. If she'd been meant to confront him, he would have been here. It was better that she hadn't come face to face with him unexpectedly anyway. That reunion was going to have to wait.

~~~~~~~~~~~~~~~~~~~~~~~~~~~~~~

Allie touched down to the ground to walk the rest of the distance, almost home. She was behind schedule, but dawn was still at least an hour off. As she got closer, she could feel Mattie's comforting mark reaching for her. He was on the road nearby, returning home from somewhere. She could feel him slow as he noticed her approach. She finally saw him parked up ahead on the side of the road, waiting for her. He was on Cain's Harley Davidson.

He turned to face her with a smile as she came to give him a hug and kiss. He held her tightly close before letting her go. "You're late. I was starting to worry."

"You would know if anything had gone wrong."

"How'd it go?" he asked. She could feel the tension begin leave him. Now that she was back safely in his arms, he could relax.

"Fine and dandy. No trouble."

"Was Ben there?" he asked shortly.

"No." That had been his main concern. He worried about another confrontation with Ben, that and about what could happen to her while traveling. He wasn't very interested in details about her visit with Felicity. Alyson also opted not to mention that there was now considerably less of a rodent problem in Riverside Park.

"Felicity's doing well. She and Ben are moving in together." That drew little more response than a raised eyebrow and a slight shrug. He refused to care. She fished around a little to see if she could read any more from him, but he was closed to the subject. He was done with Ben. It didn't concern him anymore.

The news of her newly discovered power of flight was bubbling within her, waiting to burst out. She stood for a moment, wondering just how Mattie would react if she suddenly lifted into the air. He was looking at her as though a great weight had lifted from him with her return. "Got it all out of your system now?" he asked. "No more back and forth over wondering if you should visit? I'm so glad you're home and things can get back to normal," he told her.

Allie smiled. Normal…right. Maybe she'd better wait until Cain was around as a buffer before she unveiled yet another paranormal aberration. Who ever heard of a flying vampire? She gave him another kiss and then got onto the bike behind him. "Yeah, I'm done with that for a while. I missed you too. Everything here alright?"

He nodded as he revved the engine. She could hear him better in her mind than with her ears as he quietly answered. "Cain's back early." She couldn't help but flinch like a kid playing hooky who'd just found out dad was home. She should have realized that Cain was back. How else could Mattie have used his motorcycle? Mattie could surely feel her alarm at that news, but he reassured her quickly. "Don't worry, it's fine. I told him you wanted to go check out some band over in Buffalo, and I was going to meet you there...*and* that I made you promise to be careful. You *were* careful right?"

She grinned as she leaned into his back, urging him to get moving. "Of course I was. Aren't I always?" She could feel the vibration of a chuckle as he pulled back out onto the road to drive them home.

Allie punched in the security code when they paused at the gate, and before long, the house came into view. Surely, Cain heard them approach on the loud motorcycle as they rode up the drive, but although they could feel his presence, they couldn't see him anywhere. It felt as though he was beyond the house, around behind it, rather than in it. "I think Cain is around back. Should we go say hi?" she asked as they slowed at the top of the driveway.

Mattie stopped the bike and glanced uncomfortably in the direction from which they could feel Cain's mark. "It's almost daylight." She shrugged off the comment. They still had plenty of time; he just didn't want to go. He glanced in Cain's direction again. "No thanks."

It only took Allie a moment to discern what Cain might be doing that Mattie would be uncomfortable with. She hopped off the motorcycle, letting Mattie pull it into the garage alone. "Well, I'm going to say hi," she told him with an unconcerned wave. She began walking around the house to where she could feel Cain. He was staying still, giving off a very calm and soothing presence. She was silent in her approach.

Cain knew she was there now, and she could feel the telepathic greeting he gave as she gently let herself be known in his mind. He was glad she was home with time to spare. Of the three of them, Alyson was the least tolerant to sunlight, and usually found herself falling practically comatose as the sun rose. She really should plan to be indoors well before dawn, but she was known to cut it close sometimes. As she came around the side of the house, she could see Cain in the far corner of the manicured lawn, at the edge of the woods. He was not alone.

A very large doe stood at Cain's side, wearing his mark. He knelt by her, gently stroking the deer and whispering calming things to her as he glanced up at Alyson. Allie paused as the deer flicked an ear in her direction. *She won't bolt, will she?* Allie asked Cain silently. He gave a slight shake of his head.

Alyson knew how to use her power of empathy to project calming vibes, giving animals a sense of reassurance in her presence. This deer was Cain's though. It was familiar with vampires and their practices, but was still a wild animal, and it didn't know her. It was already a little edgy, and probably not entirely comfortable with the thin hollow straw of bamboo that was currently sticking out of its neck.

It was a technique Cain had shown her long ago. A thin hollow stick of bamboo, sharpened at one end, was used to puncture the animal's throat. A thin stream of blood flowed out of the straw into a waiting container. Once enough blood was collected, the straw would be removed and a tiny amount of vampire blood rubbed over the spot, to help it heal quickly. Collecting blood this way was much more aesthetically pleasing than drinking from the deer directly, and allowed some to be saved for future evenings. Cain only needed to actually bite the animal to renew his mark and venom to help control it.

Alyson slowly approached the pair as she projected waves of tranquility towards the deer. After a few moments, the animal took its eyes off her and let itself be at ease. She untensed as well, and knelt on the grass beside Cain. He was monitoring the flow of blood into the bucket, which was only a quarter full.

Allie lowered herself to sit, and slowly reached up to stroke the deer, which twitched its skin under her touch, but didn't seem to mind. "She's a beauty."

Cain smiled. "Isn't she? She's the largest doe on the property by far."

The distinct phrase *Big Mama* came through from Cain's thoughts. Allie snickered. "I thought you said you didn't name them."

Cain lowered his eyes with a sheepish smile. "I don't really, nothing to actually call them by, but I do know them each individually. I have to think of them by some sort of designation. I just didn't want you to think I went walking through the woods calling them in for supper." He cupped a hand to his mouth and pretended to call out with a whisper, "Come here Big Mama." They shared a laugh. "She's had three sets of twins over the past three seasons, and as I said, she is the largest I've seen."

"Big Mama. Wow, that's a lot of babies. Do they all have that many?"

"There are single births, but twins are fairly normal. It's good. Keeps the population strong. I like to spread things out, keep a nice rotation of who is collected from. I wouldn't want us to be too large a burden on any of them."

"Don't you worry about them getting overcrowded? They don't have many natural predators here, right? Except for us I mean," she added, as she watched Cain press his finger to the deer's fur at the point where the dart-straw entered its flesh. He put some pressure to it, and then used his other hand to pull the straw out. The deer flinched and tensed to run, but he soothed it with strokes and whispers.

Cain put his finger to his mouth and quickly punctured it with his newly unsheathed fangs. Alyson looked up at his eyes in fascination as he quickly changed them back from golden vampire yellow to a deep human blue. No matter how many times she saw it, it always sent a small thrill through her, to see this calm and friendly man suddenly reveal the predator within. Mattie always hesitated when changing, and behaved as though it was something shameful and disgusting. Cain did it smoothly, naturally, the way that she did.

Cain held his finger horizontally to let some blood bead at the puncture, before parting the deer's fur and rubbing it at the site of her wound. Once he was satisfied that her cut would heal well, he leaned close to the doe's ear. "Thank you," he whispered. He then gave her a strong pat on the rump, which sent her trotting off towards the woods.

He turned back to Alyson to continue their conversation. "The property is well planted for them all. Apple trees, berries, and there's an alfalfa field at the other end as well. There's plenty to sustain them. As for predators, we do get coy dogs and coyotes now and then, if they can squeeze through the fence. We've even had true wolves wander through." He seemed to watch her carefully for expression, although she couldn't imagine why her reaction on the subject should be of interest. "The Crimson Coven runs them off."

She grinned as Cain wiped his hands on the knees of his jeans and stood. He lent down a hand to help her up, as though she needed any; ever the gentleman. She gave him a playful push once she was upright. "The Crimson Coven. Finally throwing me a scrap of information about them, huh? I will have you know that I am very proud of myself."

Cain chuckled. "Are you?"

"Yes, I am. You told me not to snoop, and that if I did what you asked, you would tell me everything at the right time. Well it has been three years Cain, three! I have not been asking questions, I haven't gone sneaking off to where I'm not supposed to, and I have waited pretty patiently. Do you have any idea how hard it's been for me? I have been ridiculously well behaved, and you still haven't told me a damn thing about them! They haven't been to the Christmas party since the first year, and I haven't seen one single naked person in your garage since then either. They're obviously avoiding me now. Why won't you tell me about them? Am I that unworthy of sharing a secret with?"

Cain was too busy laughing at her to respond immediately. "Ridiculously well behaved? Do you honestly think I don't know what goes on around here? I may not read minds, but I'm not so preoccupied as to not notice what's right under my nose. I'll admit that you have been respectful of the coven's privacy, and I deeply appreciate that, I do, but I'd say *ridiculously well behaved* is going a bit far."

She rolled her eyes at him and put her hands to her hips, unwilling to agree. He smiled and continued. "As far as doing what I have asked, well, that would be true if you were ever actually here. It's no wonder I can barely teach you anything, I can't even find you most nights, and that's *with* the mark!"

Alyson dropped her eyes and shrugged with a pout. "I get bored easy. We're supposed to be working on discovering all my powers, which sounds like fun, but you're so damn slow and methodical with everything, it's taking forever! I get so frustrated that I need a break now and then, or I'll go out of my mind." She gave him a sly look as a new thought occurred. "Besides, you're just as bad."

"What?" he asked in disbelief.

"Always running off to help someone, or investigate some suspicious activity that could be a rogue vampire…always right after the first of the month. Don't think I haven't noticed a pattern here."

Cain looked away and wouldn't meet her eyes as he spoke. "I don't know what you're talking about."

Allie laughed. "You can't lie to me, Cain. I can read your mind!" He looked up in sharp affront. "I'm not," she added quickly, "but I could." She waited until he would look at her again to speak. "Look, I know what this is about and you're making a big deal out of nothing. The three of us agreed that it was important to continue drinking each other's blood to keep up the mark of the coven. It makes a strong united front, and keeps a close connection between us in case there's ever a problem. We all agreed."

"Yes, you know I support that," he agreed quietly.

"Okay. So, it's not your fault if your body happens to find my blood incredibly orgasmic." As soon as the word was out of her mouth, she knew it was too much. Cain made a huff of embarrassed disbelief at her words and turned as though to walk to the house. She reached out to take his arm and turn him back around to face her. "Well, it's true, and avoiding me for nights afterward is so stupid. You don't have to worry about it, Cain. I get it. It's okay."

"I know that *you* don't see it as a problem, but it feels disrespectful to Mattie. I will not be 'the other man'. Never again."

Allie stared at him for a moment, wondering when Cain had ever been in that position in the past. She held back the question. "Well you're not fuckin' me, so we don't have a problem."

He gave her a fierce glare for her bluntness. She gave him a little smile and mental apology to keep him from going off to brood alone. Cain told her quietly, "I will not threaten the dynamics of your relationship with Mattie."

"You're not. Cain, you are always completely appropriate, to the point of overkill prudeness even. Sharing blood feels good, and my blood happens to affect you kind of sexually. It's not on purpose and Mattie knows it. If we're gonna last for eternity, we'd better be able to stand more than that!" Allie pointed out. "I'm the only one who can be inside both of your heads, so you're just going to have to trust me. I know how you feel about it, and I know how Mattie feels too. He's not jealous of you like that, not much anyway. We can handle it. Trust me."

"It's only a few nights a month that I make myself scarce. The heightened sensitivity to each other afterwards is awkward for me, and that lessens after a week or so. I like to get the first few nights behind us, that's all."

Allie took his hand and gave it a little squeeze, noting the electric shiver of marked connection between them. "You told us that the shared mark of a coven is a family tie. It's a bond of brotherhood, and that's how we see it, Mattie and I both. You're not a third wheel, you're a part of our family. Yes, there's a bit of attraction between you and I, but it's purely a physical thing driven by the blood, and we both know that it will never be anything more, so it's not worth thinking about."

Cain gave her an annoyed look of disapproval, as though unwilling to admit any mutual attraction, regardless of Allie's empathetic awareness. "The attraction... I don't see you that way, *at all*."

"I know," she assured him.

"It's just the blood."

"I know."

He stared at her for a few moments, sensing that she wasn't quite as resolute about it as he was. It just wasn't a big deal to her. So she found Cain attractive, so what? It wasn't like she would ever do anything about it. He was a good-looking guy, and being able to see into a persons' true feelings was an even bigger turn on than appearance. He was a truly good person and she appreciated that. It also made sharing blood with him something that she thoroughly enjoyed. But that was it. She didn't see anything wrong with that and neither should he. He was always a little skittish about it though. He insisted on trying to give it firm parameters. "You should be looking at me as a father figure if anything," he informed her.

Allie laughed, giving him a look of physical appraisal. "A father? I don't think so, no matter how old you actually are. A brother maybe."

Cain sighed. "A brother then."

"I treated Ben like my brother, and even he knew how to take a little harmless flirting once in a while. Cain, after all this time I can't believe you are still uneasy about this. We're fine...all three of us. I don't have to pretend you're my brother to justify things. You are the only one worrying about it, so just chill out. When I get close to the house and I feel that shiver that tells me you're there, it's comforting to me. It's not awkward or indecent. It makes me feel happy and safe. I know it makes you feel that way too."

"Yes, I worry about you. Part of sharing the mark of the coven, is that one feels incomplete when the coven is divided. You know that I care for you in a completely platonic way, regardless of how my body views your blood. I will do my best to deal more appropriately with the situation."

He shook his head with an exasperated sigh. "There is so much more for us to be focusing on. No matter my own feelings, it will still be difficult for me to work with you if *you aren't here*. I will not let you change the subject by turning the table. My short outings are nothing compared to the jaunts you disappear on. You need to commit to this, Alyson."

"I'm committed! I just need to get my fun on once in a while."

Cain crossed his arms and she could feel the disapproval within him. "I understand that you and Mattie need private time now and then, and I give you space for that, but you need to stop wandering off. As far as being slow and methodical with explorations of your power, I think that is how it should be. Anything less could be dangerous."

She knew that he was probably right, but it was just so frustrating to have this new power and freedom, and not be allowed to use it. This probably wasn't the time to mention her newfound flying ability. Instead, she stood her ground and waited for him to wrap up the lecture. "Alyson, you have known from the beginning that this would be a gradual and controlled process, for good reason. Your cache of skills is something akin to Pandora's Box. Opened without care it can wreak all sorts of havoc.

Think of the box as containing many compartments. If we were to open them all at once, it could be disaster. We must carefully open but one at a time. Only when you can have complete control of a skill without even needing thought for it, should you move on to learn the next. Like with your telepathy, you have mastered that now, as well as your powers of suggestive manipulation, and even your physical skills of supernatural speed and strength. You've come so far! Your thirst is now more easily controlled, and I'm very proud of how you have adjusted."

She opted not to mention that the only reason they thought her thirst was under better control, was because she had stopped complaining about it, and taken to going out and finding herself forest animals to drink from. "See, I'm doing good."

"You are, *when you're here*. I understand your desire for freedom, I really do. However, there is a big difference between a vacation, and disappearing for months!"

"It hasn't been months," she said with a derisive snort.

"Not this time. What about when you two left for New Orleans, back in March?"

"It was Mardi Gras!"

"When you said you were going for Mardi Gras, I expected you to be gone for a week or so, not for two months."

"It wasn't that long."

"All right, well, six weeks at least. My mark was off you both by the time you returned, remember? That's why we adopted the 'first of the month' policy for marking, to eliminate discontinuity."

Alyson looked at the ground as she kicked at the grass with her foot. "We were having a good time," she said with quiet apology.

Cain took her by the shoulders. His touch was light, but the force of their strong connection through shared marks startled her. She looked up to see his eyes soften. "I know. I just worry is all. You were having such a good time that you were careless and let other vampires see your eyes. Remember the three that followed you home? They were mooning over you like zealots and constantly trying to lead you away with them. It took me almost two weeks to convince them that you had nothing to offer them and to send them on their way; and it wasn't even the first time you've let it happen. We can't have mistakes like that, and we need to stop wasting time. Things have been very quiet for us and it feels like the calm before the storm. I worry that the storm will come, and we'll have squandered all the time we should have been using to prepare. I want you to be strong and ready, in case a problem should arise."

"I am strong. But I would be stronger if you'd hurry up and let me figure out what else I can do. It's gonna happen anyway. I discover new things about myself all the time, Cain. You can't stop it."

"What new things?"

She gave him an impish smile. "I'll show you...if you promise to lighten up a little."

"I will, if you promise to stop gallivanting off around the world for extended periods, and take your training here a little more seriously."

"It's a deal. I'll stick around for a while if you will. You're the one who keeps changing the subject though. You were finally going to tell me more about the Crimson Coven, weren't you?"

He gave her a secret sort of smile. "The subjects are connected actually. The fact is, I have been planning to tell you everything about them, I was just waiting for something...someone. There was someone that I very much expected to have joined us by now. But they haven't, and perhaps I was very wrong in my judgment to believe that they would."

She stared at him for a moment impatiently. He seemed lost in thought and wasn't elaborating. "Who?"

He looked up at her and shook his head. "Never mind. And don't you go fishing for it either," he warned. "Things will happen as they are meant to. I'm not even certain you're ready for the knowledge the Crimson Coven holds. We've got some work to do first. I want to review some things and then, if you are ready as you say, we'll move forward, alright?"

Allie gave him a sullen nod. She briefly considered trying to read it from his mind, even after his warning, but then decided against it. She could surely pull the information, but he could always tell when she'd been reading him. It would really piss him off. She'd just have to wait.

"Have you discovered something new?" Cain prodded again.

"You'll see," she answered with a coy smile, "when I think you're ready." He gave her an exasperated sigh. She turned her attention to the mostly full bucket of blood on the ground at their feet. "Think I could have some of that before it gets cold?"

"As long as you promise to leave some," he said teasingly. She had been learning better control, but her thirst was still at least double that of the guys'.

She lifted the heavy bucket easily in one hand, starting towards the house. "I've promised you enough already. You want some, you'll have to keep up."

Cain was running unhindered, while she needed to temper her supernatural speed with smooth and agile balance, so as not to spill the bucket, but she still managed to beat him to the door.

~~~~~~~~~~~~~~~~~~~~~~~~~~~~~~

Mattie walked into the kitchen, camera in hand, and began rifling through a drawer for something. "You two still at it?" he asked with an air of boredom.

It drew Cain's attention for a moment and allowed Allie to progress in the slight hold she was gaining over him. "Yup," she answered with a grin.

Cain sat across from her, with his arm outstretched, facing upwards with a closed fist on the kitchen table. Mattie took a seat and began using a butter-knife to tinker with something on the camera. After a moment, Allie was pleased to see Cain slowly opening his hand to reveal the quarter in his grasp. As his palm became exposed, she reached over and snatched her prize. "Thank you!" she said gleefully.

Cain let out a weary sigh and gave Mattie an annoyed glance for the distraction. Mattie looked up with only vague interest. "All that for a quarter?"

Allie smiled. "It's not the money, it's the method."

Cain shook his head. "I just spent the better part of an hour keeping that from her. You walk in and in a moments distraction she manages to take full control of my body and forces me to open my hand. God help any vampire who isn't ready for you," he told Allie with a smirk.

Allie balanced the quarter on its edge and gave it a good spin. "Yeah, but I have to have some venom in them or it won't work at all. I can only control *humans* I haven't bitten. Vampires are too tough."

Mattie tossed the knife behind him into the sink and put down the camera. "This ring is shot. I don't know how I managed to bend the damn thing."

Allie barely even glanced at it. "You aren't gonna go buy *another* camera are you? You must have dozens, and we don't even show up on film!"

Cain looked up in amusement. "They didn't even have cameras when I was human. Don't listen to her, Mattie. You're a wonderful nature photographer. I love your prints." He gestured towards the wall behind them, at one of the many matted and framed photographs Mattie had taken. Cain then reached out and poked a finger at Allie's quarter to stop it from spinning. "As much as I'd like to blame Mattie, I wasn't going to be able to hold out against you for much longer anyway."

She took the coin and put it into her pocket. "Are you finally ready to admit that I know what I'm doing? You've spent weeks testing me at just about everything I can do, and I am awesome at all of it. Can we move on?"

Mattie shook his head with sympathy for Cain. "Awesome she is, humble she's not."

"I'm just telling the truth and Cain knows it," Allie insisted.

"I couldn't very well let you start developing a new talent while we were busy preparing for the holidays now could I?" Cain asked. The large annual vampire gathering had come and gone as usual this year. The novelty had mostly worn off for Allie and she had begun to see how Cain could view it as a perfunctory chore more than anything else. It had been nice to visit with Fiona and a few of the others she had made acquaintance with, but there were so many other things she would rather be focusing on. Cain got up from the table and glanced at the clock. It was still early. "Alright. I can tell you're eager to show off some new parlor trick."

Mattie turned to Allie in concerned surprise. "Trick? What trick? You found something new?" She gave a little nod. He glanced at Cain, and then back to Allie, a little hurt by her exclusion. "Why didn't you tell me?"

She stood up from the table and pushed in her chair, waving her hand dismissively at Cain. "He doesn't know what it is either. Cain was all busy testing me with stuff before I was allowed to work on anything new. Besides, it's kind of a big one. I thought we should all be alone together."

Mattie slumped his shoulders. "Oh great. I hate this."

Alyson came around behind him to hug his shoulders. "Why? It's fun!"

"Sure it is, for you. For me it's just something else I have to worry you're going to get yourself into trouble with."

She just laughed and nudged him to get up. "This is a good one though. You'll see. Come on. I think it's better if I show you outside."

Once she had them standing out on the lawn, and back from her a pace, she asked, "Are you ready?" They nodded and then she stopped for thought. "Do you want to guess what it is first?"

Mattie hung his head in exasperation. "No, just do it." Then he held up a hand to stop her. "Wait. It's not like, some kind of weapon type thing, is it?"

Allie looked at Cain with a raised eyebrow. "What kind of weapon-type things are there?"

Cain laughed. "None that I know of. Relax," he told Mattie.

Alyson turned to him with a mental wave of reassurance. "Take it easy, hon. It's definitely more *def*ensive than offensive. This is a cool one. Watch."

She took a deep breath, held her arms out from her sides a bit, and slowly let herself rise straight up into the air about five feet from the ground. She'd been practicing a little in secret, and had learned to rise and fall smoothly now. She'd wanted to be sure that she looked in complete control before showing it to them.

Mattie sat down on the ground in shock. Cain laughed to himself quietly. "Nicely done. I was wondering when you were going to stumble onto that one."

Mattie looked at Cain in disbelief. "She can fly. You knew she could fly?"

Alyson looked down at him in mock reprimand. "Cain, I can't believe you knew! You don't just *not* tell someone they can fly!"

He laughed. "If you knew about that skill first, I'd never be able to get you down onto the ground long enough to practice the others. Flight is a trademark skill of the blue-eyed vampire. I believe that Elric of Arif's coven shares the gift. It's rather rare."

Mattie stood up and walked over to Allie, circling her feet, which were now at about eye level for him. "How are you doing this?"

She shrugged, bobbing a bit in the air. "I don't know. I just think about being light and going up. Want a ride?"

He gave her a startled look as she lowered herself down to meet his gaze, keeping herself half a foot off the ground to even their heights. "What?"

"A ride." She lowered herself to put her arm around his waist before he could protest. "Come on, I'll take you up."

He tried to shrug himself out of her grasp. "Bad idea."

"Why not? I can hold you. I'm super strong, remember?"

"Yes, but that's just physical. You don't know if your power's strong enough to carry another person up in the air. What if we get fifty feet up into the sky and your flight gives out?"

Allie tilted her head and shrugged. "Then I guess we'll plummet to the ground. It won't kill you."

He laughed at her nonchalance. "No thanks."

"Come on, don't be a baby. We can test it before we go high. You guys are all into me testing stuff, right? I should know what I can do. What if I have to fly you to safety one night?"

Mattie crossed his arms. "I'm going to go out on a limb and say that I'll manage to avoid putting myself in that situation." He turned to Cain for his assessment. "Do you think her flight is strong enough to hold another person?"

"I have no idea, but I'd guess she could do it."

Alyson was letting herself float about now, moving in lazy figure eights with her arms out like Superman. She could feel that Mattie wasn't afraid to try it; he just really didn't think she would be able to lift more than herself. In fact, he was hesitant because he didn't want her to be disappointed if she failed. It was touching, but she just couldn't believe that she wouldn't be able to do it. She came closer to him, urging him to let her try. Mattie watched her use her new skill with interested envy. "It does seem really cool. Have you gone high before? Is it amazing? It must feel amazing."

She came back to him. "Yeah, it's pretty wild. I like this one. I really like this one," she admitted with glee. Most times she tried not to make too much of her powers in front of Mattie, because she felt bad that he didn't have them, but this was flying. How could she hold in excitement over something like flying?

"Okay. Take me up," he relented with a smile, holding out his arms for her to embrace him. She happily came and wrapped her arms around him, making sure he felt secure. It only took a moment for her to feel Mattie's anxiousness melt into excited wonder as they lifted from the ground.

She made them rise slowly and then paused at about ten feet, even though Mattie showed no signs of wanting them to stop. He turned to meet her eyes with a loving smile. "You can really do it. We're flying! Oh my God, this is crazy!"

She was relieved and vindicated to find that it wasn't even difficult. It felt no harder than it would be to lift him physically while on the ground, which may have not been easy while she was human, but was certainly simple for her now. "Don't you love it? Should we go higher?"

Mattie gave her a quick nod and a squeeze as she took them higher still. The crisp winter air was blowing past them as they sped faster and higher into the night sky until they came out above the treetops to see the moon and stars unhindered. She could feel Mattie's amazement. "You didn't think I could do it," she accused him teasingly.

"It's *your* power," he responded quietly, "why should you be able to carry someone else?"

"I knew that I could do it," she said confidently.

"How did you know?"

"Because I *couldn't* have this, and not share it with you."

Mattie gazed at her lovingly for a moment, realizing that she would push herself to the very limits for him if she had to. "Is it hard? Are you straining?"

She shook her head. "I'm okay, but I'm gonna need one hell of a drink when we get back down."

Mattie laughed. "Don't worry, I'll make sure we get you plenty." He looked around again in wonder. "Look at this view. It's beautiful."

"I'm sorry that you can't do this for yourself," she said regretfully.

"That's okay. I have you. Besides, you're the kite, I'm just the string, remember?" He was referring to the tattoo on her hip; the kite with a large 'A' on it to represent her, and the string that wound intimately down the inside of her thigh to spell his name. She smiled fondly at the thought of it, as Mattie continued. "You've always had something special in you Allie. You're meant to fly. Even then, we knew it. I've never felt special that way. Are you sure I'm not holding you back?"

Allie wrapped her arms around him tighter. "Ever seen a kite after someone's let go of the string?" she asked.

"Sure. They fly really high."

"Yeah, until they come crashing down, out of control. I'd rather be grounded. Besides, in case you haven't noticed, you're not holding me down, I'm lifting you up."

She could feel the grateful acceptance of her statement in his heart as he said, "I love you."

"I love you too Mattie, really." She felt the need to make him understand the sincerity of it. "I know I do stupid things sometimes, but I love you so much. I never want you to doubt it. See this?" She brought her hand around to show him the ring he had given her on the night of her change. She never took it off. "This means forever to me. It means you never have to question; you don't even have to think about it. I will always love you."

He brought his ring from her into view as well. "You know I feel the same. I know there will be times that we disagree and it won't always be easy, but I will always love you Allie, always."

He met her lips for a kiss heated with desire, driven by their shared emotional commitment. The warm and intimate current of sensation from their shared mark embraced and bonded them both. High above the earth in their own private heaven, Alyson showed him the powerful love that she felt through the depths of their kiss. As Allie focused on loving him, she felt them lose a bit of altitude. She regretfully reined back her passion to concentrate on their flight and to begin their gentle descent to the ground.

Even as their feet touched the earth, they continued the kiss, now able to give it full attention, until Cain interrupted them by clearing his throat. "I was beginning to wonder if you were ever planning to come back down. Obviously carrying someone wasn't a problem."

No, but thirst might be. Alyson didn't even realize that in her emotional state she had shifted into her vampire aspect, until she turned to Cain and saw that he was painted in shades of blue and green through her vampire sight. Her desire for blood was almost overwhelming, begging her to drink more than passion from her lover's lips. She tried to swallow back her thirst for the moment, unwilling to let it concern the others, and quickly resumed her human visage. "Nope, it was easy," she said with confidence. She unwound herself from Mattie as he stepped back from her, and then she turned to Cain with a grin, opening her arms to him. "Wanna go for a spin?"

Cain laughed softly from where he was relaxing on the grass. "No thanks."

She tilted her head in disbelief. "Come on, it's your turn. What's the matter, are you scared of heights?"

Cain never even moved to get up. "No. Just knowing that you can fly me to safety should I need it, is comfort enough," he teased. He then continued comment not in voice, but in thought. *This is something special. Let this be for you two.*

~~~~~~~~~~~~~~~~~~~~~~~~~~~~~~~

"Time?" Cain asked after completing his trek across the lawn from the house.

"Forty two minutes," Mattie answered after a glance at his watch.

It had snowed during the day as they'd slept, coating the forest pines in white, and making the coven's peaceful surroundings seem almost something from a fairytale. Alyson focused intently on the images and strains of music from *Peter and the Wolf* that drifted through Cain's mind as he surveyed the glistening white woods. He recognized her presence in his thoughts and smiled up at her, although she was really too high up in the sky for eye contact. *How are you doing?* he asked her silently.

I'm thirsty. Does it count if I lower myself just enough to scoop up something to drink?

That would rather defeat the purpose, don't you think? Cain thought back to her in amusement.

They had set out to determine just how long Alyson could remain aloft of her own power before being forced to land. So far, they had not uncovered any limit other than her thirst, but it seemed that would be her undoing. Just to share her misery, she unleashed a powerful wave of thirst on the guys below, through their empathetic connection. Cain was taken aback by the forcefulness of it. *Dear Lord Alyson, it hasn't even been an hour yet. Didn't you drink anything before you went up?*

You told me that I shouldn't drink any more than usual, or it wouldn't be a fair test, she reminded him.

Yes, but you usually drink a lot!

Apparently, Alyson was relaying the conversation to Mattie as well. He turned to Cain with a shake of his head. "No vampire should have to drink as much as she does, Cain. If she were drinking people, she'd have wiped out a small city by now! It's getting really hard to keep up with."

"Which is why I keep telling her that she is not to use her powers more than necessary," Cain said aloud, although the statement was more for Alyson to hear. "It takes blood to fuel those abilities."

I know, I know. I do have to learn my limits though, and pushing to the limit works up an appetite. Are you stocked back at the house? Because if not, I might have to go thin out your herd a little.

Don't you dare touch my deer. He warned her. He was still bitter over the last one she'd accidentally killed. He had allowed her a few to practice controlled feeding and exercise venom use on. Unfortunately, she still needed a lot more practice. She'd needed to ask him for more than one replacement.

Alyson gave them the equivalent of a mental sigh. *Alright, relax. I'll wait a few more minutes just to round out the hour, and then I'm coming down. But I want it going on record that I didn't run out of power, I'm just damn thirsty.*

Duly noted. Cain answered with a grin. He had begun his return to the house, when he caught a wave of interested excitement from Allie.

You have got to be shitting me! she exclaimed in thought.

Cain turned to share a look of confusion with Mattie. Mattie spoke aloud for Cain to hear, knowing that Alyson could still pick up the thought. "Something going on that you want to share, hon?"

I can't even believe it! Look, North East, at the edge of the property.

"What are we looking for?" Mattie asked.

"Marks," Cain answered with quiet concentration. "Well what do you know?" he asked rhetorically in astonishment.

Mattie kicked at the snow in annoyance. "Hello? I hate when you guys do this. I can't see it yet. Who are we looking at?"

Allie answered. *Sorry babe, I just can't believe it.* Sindy's back, *with friends.*

Mattie suppressed a sigh of annoyance as he shifted his weight and anxiously waited for Sindy's mark to come into view. "How many friends?"

Cain answered as he focused on them. "Three I think, although they may not all be in range yet. They're moving rather quickly though. Yes, it's three, but I don't think they're friends. They aren't *with* her, they're chasing her."

It wasn't long before Sindy entered Mattie's range and he could see her mark for himself. Alyson read the question from him before he asked it. *You're right; those are Crimson Coven aren't they? I've seen their marks before, but they don't usually come this close to the house. Why would they be chasing her?*

"I can't imagine," Cain replied in concern. "They've never met, but I've told them of her, and I think they should recognize her. I wonder what they're doing."

Alyson didn't need more of an invitation than that. *I'll go find out.* Before the men even finished their protests, she was off like a shot, flying on route to intercept the four marks, which were quickly approaching from the opposite direction. *Don't worry, they'll never even notice me up here,* she assured Mattie and Cain, as she slowed and drifted slightly downward.

Alyson chose a small clearing that would be in Sindy's path, and then descended to perch among the treetops to watch unobserved. Alyson tensed as Sindy's mark sped closer. She could hear slight crunching sounds of approach in the snow, but was very surprised at the figure that burst through into the clearing. She'd been expecting to see a tall, dark haired, seductive beauty of a young woman, but the figure attached to Sindy's mark did not even have human shape.

A large, dark wolf loped into view, so deeply grey that it was almost black. It was running at full speed, and even in her surprise Alyson had to note what a gorgeous creature it was. Alyson waited to see if Sindy was following behind it, but the wolf was alone for the moment. The marks that had been closing in from behind seemed to have inexplicably scattered and then disappeared as though cloaked. She stared at the wolf as it sped by, thinking there must be some mistake, but the animal was not marked *by* Sindy, it carried the mark of Sindy herself.

Allie barely had time to wonder at the sight of the animal, when another wolf burst through the brush unexpectedly from the other side of the glade. It had circled around to surprise her. This wolf had shades of brown in its coat, but was also a beautiful example of the species. Unfortunately, it allowed no time to be admired as it bared it's incredibly large fangs and raised its hackles, ready to attack.

The dark wolf skidded to a stop, but two lighter grey wolves now caught up from behind, growling and worrying their dark foe until it was practically forced into the jaws of its opponent. The brown wolf jumped, forcing the darker wolf to also rear in order to meet it head on.

They stood on their hind legs, gripping, pawing, straining, and twisting to bite each other amidst vicious growls. Each tried in vain to get a strangle hold on the other, but were rewarded only with mouthfuls of fur, and no real purchase. The other two lighter grey wolves kept their distance, barking and circling the fray.

The black threw the brown off, but it was unfazed and attacked again almost immediately. The black essentially lost the fight in that moment, as the brown jumped at it again, twisting its body to strike at an angle, bowling the black over onto its back to expose its stomach. Its brown foe dipped its head down between flailing forepaws and got a grip on the black's throat. Holding the dark wolf pinned with its powerful jaws, the brown brought up a rear foot to score on the black's underbelly.

With one mighty raking of its claws, it flayed open the soft flesh, as the black let out a piercing cry followed by a pitiful whine. As though vindicated by the act, the brown released its victim and backed off. It surveyed the damage done, and then simply turned and left it there, to join the other wolves at the edge of the clearing. Alyson was confused and surprised. From what she knew of wolves, she had expected the others to rush in for the kill, but they all seemed abruptly unconcerned. They melted into the suddenly silent forest and disappeared.

The wounded dark wolf had curled into a ball on its side, but there was a quickly spreading stain of bright red leaking out onto the snow from beneath it. Alyson had sat in stunned silence upon her branch while observing the melee, and now left her perch, allowing herself to drift gently down to the forest floor. Once landed, she looked back to the wolf, who had not yet noticed her. It seemed on the verge of losing consciousness, and did not even lick its wounds. As she watched, it un-tensed its muscles and then let its head loll to the side.

Alyson took a hesitant step towards it, still mired in confusion. She shifted to her vampire state and observed the wolf with that spectrum of vision. It must be greatly wounded, for it almost seemed something already dead. Its body was colored in cold tones, and what little warmth it had was quickly becoming lost to the snow with its blood.

Alyson took another crunching step closer in the dried leaves and light snow. The wolf came back to awareness, flinching and then tracking Allie's approach with its eyes. They were eyes of red, deeply beautiful glittering red, with a strangely upright black pupil. Even as Alyson sought to connect that observation with the mark that permeated the creature, something incredible happened.

The wolf seemed to melt into itself like a poorly built sand castle disintegrating under an ocean wave. Allie stepped back in unsettled astonishment and returned to human vision to try to process what she was seeing. Was it Sindy? Was she dead? But the creature hadn't truly turned to dust as she had seen when other vampires had ceased to exist. The wolf had disappeared but there was still an odd hazy mist hovering in its place.

Alyson observed, dumbfounded, as the dark mist pulled together and reshaped itself to resemble a human form. It lightened in color as it solidified into the body Alyson had always known as Sindy.

She was completely nude, lying in the snow with her long black hair fanned out darkly beneath her. Alyson's gaze drifted from Sindy's face to see her body horribly marred by four raking claw marks from just under her breastbone all the way down the length of her abdomen to below her belly.

The skin was shredded, but oddly, the site was unbloodied; at least for the first few seconds that Alyson saw it, then blood began to pool and leak from the area to stain the fair skin. Apparently, when changing form, the body had attempted to put itself back together properly, but had been unsuccessful. Alyson met Sindy's eyes, but they appeared almost unseeing, glazed, and staring at the sky.

Even without a blood bond, Sindy's agony was forceful enough to be felt empathetically. Allie crouched next to her in shock, unsure what to do. She fumbled to grip Sindy's hand. She felt a light tension there, although it wasn't strong enough to be considered a squeeze. Sindy blinked and tried to lift her head, seeming now to realize Alyson's presence.

Allie could feel the woman struggling to overcome her injuries. When Allie looked back to the wound, she found that she could actually see the skin trying to come together over the dark and glistening insides that threatened to spill. But then Sindy lost her slight grip on consciousness. She had spent the last reserves of her energy. Her body shuddered and rolled slightly to the side, her hand falling out of Allie's grasp as she went limp.

At the same moment, the awful wound opened further, as though completely giving up on trying to heal itself. Intestines spilled from her body through the ragged strips of flesh straining to hold her together.

Alyson backed away in horror, not knowing what to do. After a second of shock, she let out a desperate mental call. *CAIN!*

Now that she had opened herself to communication again, it was Mattie that she heard answer from first. *Allie, are you okay? Don't ever leave us hanging like that! What's going on?*

I'm fine but I'm gonna need help, she answered shakily.

She felt Cain address her, calm and reassuring amidst Mattie's worry. *Calm down and tell us what's wrong, Alyson. Did you find Sindy?*

I found her alright. She's hurt. You have to come, now! Allie ordered.

Cain remained composed, trying to help ease her anxiousness. *What's happened? Hurt how?*

Alyson stood staring at Sindy's mangled stomach, at a loss for words. *She's…it's bad.*

How bad? Cain asked forcefully.

Like disemboweled bad! Hurry up and get here!

Chapter 4 - Part 1: The bitch is back

Cain

Cain's estate, near Buffalo New York
An evening in January

Cain felt Alyson's panic over the severely injured state Sindy must be in. As awful as it may be, she needed to calm down and assess the situation as a vampire rather than a human. Cain worried about Sindy himself, but in all likelihood, she would be fine, no matter how desperate her circumstances of the moment.

Mattie began to run towards the trees to find them, but Cain turned to run the other way, to the house. "I'll be right behind you, I need to get something," he called over his shoulder.

Cain burst through the door of the house and sprinted to one of the guest bedrooms in the back. He grabbed the coverlet off the bed and wound it up in his arms. He navigated through the hallways and back to the door in a flash. Through Alyson, Cain could feel Mattie's reaction as he came upon the scene. He was horrified. *Holy shit, what happened? Did she get attacked by Wolverine?*

Alyson simply blasted out another telepathic message. *Cain, hurry up!*

I'm coming. Don't worry, she'll be alright. Cain assured her as he left the house.

He could feel Alyson's doubt. She kept fading in and out of his mind as her attention was drawn to Mattie and Sindy. *I don't know, Cain, you haven't seen her. It's pretty bad.*

Cain practically flew across the lawn and entered the glistening winter forest, weaving through the trees using the marks of his friends as a guide. *Trust me, I have cared for more than my share of injured vampires. If she hasn't turned to dust, she'll be alright. Just keep her calm.*

She isn't even conscious, so calm isn't a problem, but she's…oozing… like, her intestines and stuff. This is awful Cain, what should I do? Should we try to put them back in? Alyson was trying her best to be helpful and practical, but he could feel her thinly veiled panic.

That would be helpful, but if you don't feel you're up to it, just stay put, he insisted. *I should be there in a moment.*

Cain could see their marks, and thankfully, Sindy's as well. He finally came out into a clearing where Alyson and Mattie huddled on the ground over Sindy's still form. He noted Sindy's long bare legs, and allowed himself only a brief glance at her pale body distorted by a large swath of dark red where her torso should be. The snow was drenched with the crimson stain of her blood. Her state of undress told him that she must have been changing forms. Without risking the distraction of getting a better look, Cain flung the blanket out to straighten it, and spread it on the ground. Before it had even settled, he was crouching by Sindy's side.

Alyson made way for him and seemed rather surprised when he let out a sigh of relief. Mattie remained kneeling next to Sindy with his hands cupped over the side of the lower part of her stomach, covered in blood. Ragged slashes tore down her body leaving a mess of blood, skin, and viscera where her abdomen should be.

Although her injury was far worse than his hands could cover, Mattie was trying to keep the worst of it contained. He lightly tipped a hand to the side to show Cain the extent of the trauma. Stopping the blood from escaping was impossible, and there didn't seem much left at this point, it was her actual intestines Mattie was trying to keep in place. Cain gave a nod to show that he understood, and Mattie lowered his hand again.

Sindy was in a horrific state, but to Cain's eyes, it could have been much worse. A quick assessment assured him that her basic figure was intact, with all of her limbs still attached. It looked as though her intestines had been sliced through, which would take a long time to heal, and could be problematic, but he could handle it. Internal injuries were terribly painful, taking much rest and recovery, but it was a far easier project than trying to re-attach something severed. This would be a simple matter of making sure everything stayed inside and then wrapping her up to heal.

He spared a moment to lean over her face. Her eyes were closed and she was completely unconscious, as Alyson had said. Good, better that she not see herself this way. Her face had the pale deathly pallor of a corpse, her eyelids seeming dark and sunken. She had lost a massive amount of blood. If she were left in this state, exposed and unable to feed, it could take her weeks to recover. The tree cover was slight here in the clearing, and if she were to lie out in the sun, she very well might truly die. Luckily, she was not alone.

Cain let his fingers lightly caress her cheek, although she did not acknowledge his presence in the least. Mattie was already doing what he could to keep everything in place where it should be, but once he removed his hands, it would be for naught. Cain turned to Mattie, once again taking on the practical urgency necessary. "I want to lift her onto the blanket, but that's not going to do well enough. I think we'll have to wrap her injury first or she'll be all undone by the time we get to the house."

After a brief pause for thought, Cain reached up and pulled off his shirt. It was a thin, long sleeved tee. Once he got it off, Mattie helped him to place the shirt over the worst of her injury and wrap it around underneath, using the sleeves to bind it securely. "That will have to do. It's just until we get her inside. Help me lift her to the blanket."

Cain moved behind her head so that he could grip Sindy under her arms while Mattie moved to grasp her legs. Alyson hovered near, trying to clear most of the leaves, twigs, and snow from her hair and body as they got her settled. Cain wrapped her with the blanket, lifted her, and started towards the house.

"I can get her there faster if you want," Allie offered.

Cain hugged Sindy's light, lifeless body closely as he walked as quickly as possible without jarring her too badly. "No, I've got her. Speed isn't an issue, she'll be alright." Cain was studying Sindy's still face as he made his way out of the forest and across the lawn. She had finally returned. He'd been waiting and hoping that she would. It had been frustrating to know that he had connections to help her, and yet she chose to make things difficult for herself. His refusal to accept her intimately had wounded her pride, but at least she hadn't been so stubborn as to never return.

Now that she had, look what had become of it. Why had the Crimson Coven attacked her? It had to have been one of them. Sindy's flesh had been shredded by claws, deeper than any natural animal could have done, unless there was a grizzly bear nearby, which he very much doubted. It was the work of a Crimson wolf, but why?

Mattie and Alyson helped him get her into the house and settled into a bedroom upstairs; the same one he had given her to stay in for the holidays the last time she'd been here. It was right next to his room so he could easily keep an eye on her, even during the day.

Once Sindy was on the bed and unwrapped from the blanket, Cain removed his makeshift bandage as well. It was bloodied from the jostling of him carrying her, but the wound wasn't really bleeding anymore. She had lost a lot, and what little vampire blood she had left was actively trying to stay inside, clotting and retreating to other uninjured places of refuge within her body.

Cain positioned the blanket over her legs, to just below the injury, and then drew a bed sheet across her chest for modesty as he studied her wound. Allie came in from the bathroom to hand him a washcloth soaked in warm water.

"What can we do?" Mattie asked. "Do you want me to get some blood?"

"Not from the kitchen," he replied, as he took the cloth and gingerly cleaned up the edges of Sindy's skin, making sure all was where it should be for proper healing. He spared a glance up at Mattie. "She'll heal faster with stronger fare. Can you get me a knife, and a cup?"

Mattie left to do as he asked, while Alyson sat on the edge of the bed next to Sindy. Cain looked up at her with a grateful smile. "This will be the one and only time that I shall thank you for taking off and poking your nose into the business of others. She's lucky you were there to help, or it may have been a much longer and more painful recovery."

Allie wrinkled her nose while looking over Sindy's wound. "She's really gonna recover from that?"

Cain nodded with a smile. "Isn't being dead grand?" Impatient for Mattie's return, Cain shifted into his vampire state to bite and tear his finger. One look at Sindy with his vampire sight told him she would be unconscious for some time. She had very little blood left within her. What blood she had was too busy trying to heal her gaping wound, to expend unnecessary energy on things like waking thought.

He left the larger part of her injury to be dealt with upon Mattie's return. For now, he used his bloodied finger to caress smaller cuts, coaxing them to close. She had several gashes and bites less serious than the main wound, and he smeared his blood on the edges of them. He watched them slowly regain a healthy skin color, pull closed and seal again right before their eyes while Alyson gasped in amazement.

Then he focused on her internal injuries, making sure all was in place as it should be. Mattie returned with a knife and empty mug as requested. Cain took the knife and gestured for him to leave the cup on the bedside table for now. "Ah, thank you. Now I can really get to work." He promptly slit his wrist with a deep vertical gash from his hand almost to his elbow.

Even Mattie winced at the act, as Alyson let out a small cry of disbelief. "Oh My God. Careful, you don't bleed to death!"

Cain bared his teeth at the stinging pain, but it felt good, sharply focused to what needed to be done. He'd felt so dulled to the world over the last few years that he actually appreciated the strong sensation. He dismissed Alyson's anxiousness. "You needn't worry on that account. I just want to make sure I get as much as I can in there before it starts to close; heal the inside as well as out." As blood quickly seeped from his wound, he moved his arm over Sindy, letting it flow into her cuts to heal from within. He reopened his cut once more as his arm tried to heal. Mattie and Alyson watched in fascination until his blood stopped flowing freely and began to clot again. "That's probably enough for the inside. Help me close the wound."

He had Mattie gently hold the edges of Sindy's largest gaping wound closed, as he made a smaller cut on his arm to let a little more blood drip onto the surface of her skin. "Alyson, would you be a dear and see if you can tear a strip of material from one of the sheets? I'm afraid we don't have bandages in the house."

Alyson used the knife to cut a long swath of material from the bottom edge of a sheet from the bed, and then helped Cain and Mattie wrap the worst of Sindy's wound to keep it closed until it held on its own. Cain used the washcloth to clean up his arm. "That's a good start," he remarked as he assessed their handiwork. The wound had begun to close even as they were wrapping it. She would be alright with another night or two of rest.

As he was looking over Sindy, Alyson was assessing him. "Cain, I'm going to bring you a drink from the kitchen. I'm getting thirsty just watching you lose all that blood. You need a refill," Alyson informed him.

Mattie questioned Cain as he sat quietly watching over Sindy, lost in thought. "What do you think happened? What could do that to her?"

"Alyson didn't say?" Cain asked, sparing a glance at him before giving his attention back to Sindy.

Mattie shook his head. "Allie said she found her that way."

"I guess we'll find out when she wakes up. I've got my suspicions. You needn't worry about it though. I'm sure we're as safe here as we've always been."

Mattie didn't seem so sure. "I'd like to hear what *she* thinks about that," he said with a nod towards Sindy. "How long do you think it will take her to revive?"

"It might be a while. She's suffered a lot of blood loss, and severe internal injuries really knock you out."

Alyson returned with a warm mug for him to drink from, which he accepted gratefully. "Anything else we can do?" she asked as she took a sip from a mug of her own.

"Would you mind bringing her up some clothing from the garage? I'd like to have it here for her when she wakes. Then you two can head back downstairs. Thanks for the help, but it's probably better if she doesn't wake up to everyone hovering over her."

~~~~~~~~~~~~~~~~~~~~~~~~~~~~~~

The sun would be rising soon. Sindy hadn't even flinched over the past few hours that Cain had sat with her. He'd decided to unwrap Sindy's bandage to give her wound a final influx of blood from his wrist before turning in for the day. Her largest wound wasn't yet closed, but it was definitely looking better. As the first drop of Cain's blood fell upon her skin, he saw Sindy's eyelids flutter open.

"Cain?" Her voice was husky and struggling to overcome the grogginess of deep healing sleep.

"Welcome back."

She was looking at his face with confused recognition, as though she distrusted her eyes. Then she seemed to notice the blood dripping onto her from his arm. "What are you doing?"

"Fixing you." She leaned up to see better, as her hand lifted almost involuntarily to her stomach. "Don't touch," he cautioned her quietly.

She stared at the stripes that marred her body. They were beginning to hold closed on their own, but remained stubbornly puckered and raw in some spots, and surely there remained unhealed damage beneath. Still, bad as they were, they looked like injuries from some ordeal a week past, rather than something as recent as a few hours ago. He could see her remembering whatever incident had brought her here. "You rescued me." It was more a statement than a question. She looked at him with quiet disbelief as he could see her trying to recall the details of the prior event.

"Question is, from what?"

She shook her head lightly. "My own stupidity, pretty much."

He raised a questioning eyebrow. "Want to tell me what happened?"

She met his eyes with a plea for discretion. "I really don't, if that's okay." She watched him carefully as he concentrated on letting the blood of his slit wrist drip onto her skin. He could tell that she was wondering how much he had seen.

It didn't matter that he hadn't seen anything really. He could guess what had happened well enough. "You know I don't allow such hostilities on my property, and I enforce that rule when necessary. I can't do that if you don't tell me who I'm after."

"No, you don't have to enforce anything." She paused in thought and then shook her head, apparently ashamed of the actions that caused her injury. "It was my fault, I deserved it. You should have just left me there."

Cain gave a slight chuckle as he worked. "Right. As though I would leave you lying on the ground in agony in my backyard for a week or so while you waited for it to heal on its own."

She looked down at her wound, which thanks to Cain's care was now beginning to look more like pink scar tissue rather than the awful shredded appearance it had earlier. "A week?"

"At least. Maybe even a month without assistance. If you were human, you certainly would have died. You'll be alright now though. Mattie and Alyson helped me get you settled here, and I've put you well along your way to recovery. You'll probably only be out of commission for a few nights with proper care." She tried to sit up and examine her wound better, but he reprimanded her. "Don't sit up, you'll make it tear open again."

She lay back as ordered. After a moment, he found she was staring curiously at his bare chest. However used to walking around half-naked she might be, she knew it wasn't very like him. "Where's your shirt?"

He nodded to it, bloodied and crumpled on the floor. "Makeshift bandage."

She gave him a sly smirk. "See, even when I'm unconscious I can get you to take your clothes off." He grinned as he used the washcloth to clean up his arm again, now that he'd stopped bleeding. "How did you even find me?" she asked.

"Actually, Alyson found you. I'm just the one putting you back together."

"Oh…right. Alyson." He could see the statement jog her memory, and she sat silently trying to recall things more clearly. "What did she say?"

"Just that you'd probably be in need of assistance…considering the fact that some of your insides were on the outside."

She blanched at his description. After a moment, she collected herself and seemed almost annoyed. "Oh. And naturally she called you, because rescuing damsels in distress is your thing." She stared at him pointedly for a moment. "I should have remembered. Of course, I'm not used to being on *this* side of it."

Cain met her eyes. The last 'damsel' he'd saved in Sindy's memory was most likely Felicity, whom he'd rescued by pulling Sindy off her and throwing the vampiress into the street. Surely not a fond memory for Sindy. He gave her an endearing smile. "Oh, I'm not nearly so exclusive these days. I'll rescue just about anyone; damsels in distress, insolent wayward vampires, matter of fact, I'm so needy for the gratitude I'm about *this* close to rescuing little old ladies' cats out of trees."

She lost the bitter stare she'd been holding, and couldn't help but chuckle, which made her immediately wince with pain. "Don't make me laugh, it hurts."

"Don't make me explain why I'd want to help you." She met his eyes again and gave him a surprisingly tender smile. He sighed and lightly ran his fingers over her wounds, testing them. It still made her flinch, but the cuts had mostly all closed now and left only lines of pink scar tissue across her torso. Only the largest wasn't quite entirely sealed over yet. "I think that'll do it. You just need time now. Lets bandage you up again though, until the muscle inside has had a good chance to bond well, so you don't have to worry about impeding your movement."

He took out another of the sheet strips Alyson had left for him, and slid a hand underneath the small of her back to help lift her from the bed a little. "Just let me pass this under," he said as she grimaced. Once he had the material wrapped around her middle and secured, he helped her to adjust the sheet so that it spread out over the bed again and could properly cover her completely. "There, now you can stop looking at it. You must be thirsty. You lost a lot of blood." He used his head to gesture towards the nightstand on the other side of the bed. "There's a full mug there for you. It's about as fresh as you can get, and hopefully not too cold."

The cup was in easy reach. He helped her to lean up a bit, as he moved the pillow to support her. She looked very grateful for the blood. "Thank you." She took a small sip and then looked up at Cain in curious surprise.

He watched her for a moment and then asked, "Is it not to your liking?"

She hesitated, but then slowly ran her tongue across her top lip to confirm her suspicions. "It's...*yours*, isn't it?"

"It'll help you to heal faster."

"But you never let anyone drink your blood."

Cain smiled. "That's not true. I'm just a bit more discriminating than some. You need it." She resumed drinking, but was obviously sipping it slowly, to savor it. "Don't be afraid to drink up. You can have as much as you require."

She let out a small breath of bewildered amusement. "Thank you. I have to admit, your blood is probably the last thing I ever thought I'd taste. You really do care about me, don't you?"

Cain grinned, lightly shaking his head at how much she underestimated his regard for her. As though sexuality defined the capacity at which someone could feel any degree of devotion. "Would this be an inappropriate time to say I told you so?"

She let a smile play on her lips as she met his gaze and searched his eyes for further evidence of emotion. He sat quietly and let her look, unsure what her observations told her. He did care about her, but when a person had swum in the ocean, no other body of water ever seemed as deep. His ocean was contained within a young human woman who was out of reach now, a world away it seemed, and no one else compared.

Sindy's eyes seemed to hold an honest depth of feeling he was unused to seeing there. She spoke quietly, sincerely. "Sorry I took off like that."

She was thinking of the night he'd meant to introduce her to the Crimson Coven; the night he'd tried to explain how he could help her to better understand herself, and all she would hear from him was rejection. "I'm glad you came back. It took you long enough. I was beginning to wonder if you ever would."

She shrugged it off. "Yeah well, can't blame a girl for playing hard to get. Sorry I let myself be sidetracked along the way though. This wasn't quite the entrance I'd had in mind." She lowered her eyes sheepishly and finished her drink.

It would be nice to start over, putting the past behind them. "Don't give it another thought. Need more?" he asked, reaching to retrieve the empty cup from her hand. She nodded, passing it to him as he changed, letting his fangs descend.

Sindy's eyes slightly widened at the unexpected action. He was preparing to bite his wrist, when he noticed her puzzled expression. If he was going to share his blood, and she was obviously well enough to drink at this point, why was he not just letting her take it directly? "You can't bite me," he explained. She sat up a bit, looking confused, as though he didn't want to let her infect him with her venom. That might complicate things, but that really wasn't the problem. "I'm marked," he clarified, "by Mattie and Alyson." Sindy would not be able to cross that mark to bite him. His aura was cloaked; she hadn't known.

She sat back again with a bit of a lost look in her eyes. "Went and made yourself a little coven, did you?"

"We might include you, if you'd like," he offered quietly.

She let out a small breath of shock. "No way. I mean, thanks but I doubt that'll happen. You might be able to talk Mattie into it, but there's no way that Allie would ever share blood with me."

Cain closed his eyes to reflect on how alike both girls could be in their stubborn and sometimes misguided demeanors. "Don't be so sure. I don't think either of you girls gives the other enough credit. Besides, from what I've heard, it wouldn't be the first time."

"What do you mean?"

"You've drunk from her before," he reminded her.

She seemed to find the comment ridiculous in this context. "She was human then, and it wasn't exactly voluntary!"

True as that may be, it didn't change the fact that the girls were linked through an odd twist of fate. "She's got some of your blood within her as well."

Sindy was genuinely confused. "No she doesn't. What are you talking about?"

Cain leaned forward and spoke quietly. "Do you remember an incident during which she licked a stake?"

As soon as he said it, Sindy made a face of disgust. "Oh. That was the most conceitedly childish gesture, I mean, *really*."

Cain had to agree with a grin. "Well, be that as it may, that act of childish conceit just may have changed the course of history for our entire species."

Sindy looked incredulous. "Huh?" He sympathized with her reaction to the statement. It was just so bizarre how things worked out sometimes. He was about to explain, when she suddenly closed her eyes and put her hand to her head as though dizzy. Sindy lay back again, trying to regain her composure, which only seemed to remind her that her stomach hurt worse than her head.

"Forgive me," Cain implored her. "I'm sitting here chatting when you are in serious need of blood and rest. We've plenty of time to talk later. Right now, you should drink." Cain bit his wrist. Rather than reach for the mug, he looked to see how he might angle his arm to feed her directly. She couldn't bite him, but she could still drink what he offered, and it would be more effective to let her take what she needed directly, than to awkwardly ask for more and wait for him to keep refilling the mug. He sat next to her on bed. "Do you mind?"

She opened her eyes to give him a weak snort of derision. "Yeah, you know how shy I am," she answered sarcastically.

Cain smiled. "Can you roll to your side at all, or is that painful? The wound is almost fully closed, and the bandage is providing secure pressure for it, so it should be fine." Cain used a hand to help roll her away, so she could lay with her back towards him. He lay behind her on top of the covers, and brought his arm up around her in a tender hug, giving her his wrist to feed from. She seemed pleasantly surprised to be offered his blood this way, but answered only with a grateful smile. Without further comment, she took hold of his bleeding wrist and then suckled it gently.

The pull of her thirst drew his blood strongly, her venomous saliva having just enough presence to keep the wound from closing. If she was feeling any resistance from the marks he wore, she overcame it. Once begun, her thirst overwhelmed her, although she was obviously trying to moderate it. After such a severe injury, her body wanted to take full advantage of the resource at hand.

It felt good to him, to lie next to her on the bed in the comfort of an embrace and give freely. No guilt, no awkward associations, or venomous indecencies. She needed him and he could be there to give her what she needed. He ignored the aching warnings that his body tried to provide, to inform him of its depletion. Let her take what she could. He was old and strong. He could survive it. He simply laid his head on the pillow next to her, closed his eyes, and let himself revel in the fulfillment of beneficence.

~~~~~~~~~~~~~~~~~~~~~~~~~~~~~

Cain felt Sindy awaken with a stir. Vampire sleep was so deep and still, that consciousness was easily betrayed as it brought life back into a body that had the semblance of death. He had woken up a short time before, but had needed that time to realize where he was and whom he was with. To awaken and find that he was not alone was such an odd occurrence. It was his thirst that had woken him, terrible in its intensity.

Cain had originally meant to retreat to his own bedroom once Sindy had drunk her fill from him, but he had fallen asleep. Upon awakening this evening, he'd made no move to leave, loathe to disturb her. Just to lay there with her and feel needed was a simple pleasure. His arm was still draped over Sindy as she unconsciously held it to her lips in a loose but loving grasp, the way she'd fallen asleep while drinking. Cain felt horribly starved and desperate for blood, his body trying to force him to find the back of Sindy's neck beyond the dark hair next to him on the pillow, or drive him from the bed to fulfill his need.

He'd fought to keep still and subdue his thirst, annoyed that the vampire essence within him should seek to control his actions and try to force him to bite her or retreat. With his eyes closed, the comfort and peaceful satisfaction of caring for Sindy the night before had come back to him quickly enough once he'd focused on it. He'd used his thoughts to try to tame his urgent desire for blood.

She woke now, and seemed surprised to find that she still held his arm against her lips, although the skin was now smooth and unbroken. She glanced at him over her shoulder and saw that he was awake. "You stayed here with me all day?" she asked in quiet wonder.

Cain gave her a little nod, and then lightly tugged his arm from her. "You umm, wouldn't let go."

She answered with sheepish embarrassment. "Oh, sorry."

"That's alright. I'm not complaining." As he moved to rise, he had to slow himself, feeling weak and lightheaded. He'd lost a severe amount of blood.

Sindy turned and then let out a gasp once she fully faced him. "Oh Cain! I'm sorry," she said in stumbled apology, "I think I…took too much from you."

"No, it's fine," he rushed to assure her. He brought his hand to the side of his face to find that his cheek felt sunken and hollow beneath its light stubble. "I knew. I was *pouring* my blood out onto you for heaven's sake. I knew I'd be depleted. It's alright. Are you okay?"

She was still staring at him in glazed shock over his pale, gaunt appearance. Finally, she tore her eyes away to peek under the covers. "I think so." After a few moments struggle, she managed to produce the unwound bandage from under the sheets. "It's all closed. I'm fine," she told him as she dropped the bandage to the floor next to the bed. "Thank you," She said as she looked back up to meet his eyes. It seemed she could not stop thinking about how drained he appeared. "You must be starving. Does it hurt?"

He gave a small smile. "No. I'm a bit weak and terribly ravenous, but it's nothing a few pints won't fix. I'm old enough to stand it."

"Did I look like that?" she asked.

"No, although you might have if we'd waited any longer. We got to you pretty quickly."

She was thoughtful for a moment, playing with the edge of the sheet in distraction. "What about the other time, a few years ago? Remember when you drained me, to keep me from Ben?"

There was an act he had tried to forget, such a vampiristic act of dominance over her. He should have found a more human way to deal with the situation. He dropped his gaze in embarrassment. "I didn't take *that* much. It was only enough to knock you out."

She grinned. "Good, 'cause I never want to look like that," she said teasingly, as she raised a hand to lightly touch his face. "Go get something to drink, will you?" He chuckled and ignored the cold heaviness that came over him as he rose from the bed. He could imagine that he probably looked a fright. She grasped his hand before he moved out of reach and gave it a squeeze. "Thank you," she told him again, sincerely.

He nodded, and then let go of her hand to head for the door. "I'm going downstairs for that drink, because I sorely need it. If you feel you're up to joining me, there's some clothing for you on the chair," he told her over his shoulder. "Otherwise, stay here and rest, and I'll bring you something up in a bit, alright?"

She answered hesitantly, "I think I'll stay in bed for a while."

He nodded and left the room, needing to slow his pace due to light-headed dizziness. He thought of stopping to put on a shirt first, but sharp and almost crippling stabs of blood thirst were clenching his insides in spasms at the thought of getting nourishment, so he made straight for the stairs.

Mattie and Alyson were hanging about in the kitchen. He could feel them before he even got there. Just his luck. When he wanted to find them to work on something or have an important conversation, they were always sequestered away in their trailer for privacy, or mysteriously difficult to find, and now that he wanted to slip into the kitchen alone for a drink, there would be no avoiding them.

Alyson surely felt the strength of his thirst before he entered the room. When he stepped through the doorway, she was already staring at him with her mouth open in shock. Whether it was the severity of his thirst pangs or the sight of his blood-starved face that had shocked her more, he was unsure. The two had been working together on a large jigsaw puzzle at the table. Mattie was still intent on fitting his piece, and hadn't noticed anything amiss. Cain walked past without really looking at them and made straight for the refrigerator. "Good evening."

He should have known he wouldn't get away with that. "What the hell did she do to you?" Alyson demanded as he opened the fridge.

He took out the half-full gallon container of blood and swirled it around a little. "She needed blood," he answered simply.

"So do you," Alyson pointed out irately. He should have stopped to put a shirt on, if not for modesty, at least for the fact that without one he looked all the more emaciated. Too late now. His attention was purely commanded by the container of blood in his hand. After a moment's indecision, he decided to take the top off and just swig it down cold. It tasted awful that way, but at this point, he didn't really care.

As Alyson watched him in disgust, Mattie looked up, noticing his condition. "Holy cow Cain, you look even worse than I feel after a session with Allie."

"Hey," Allie interjected defensively. "I don't take that much...at least I have the decency to put it back. I certainly wouldn't send you out looking like that! Seriously Cain, you look like the living dead."

Cain lowered the container and wiped the corner of his mouth with the back of his hand. "I am the living dead," he replied drolly.

They all turned their attention to the doorway as Sindy's voice came from out on the stairs. "Cain?"

"Come back to bed honey, I'm still thirsty," Alyson whispered mockingly.

Mattie gave her a look of reprimand. "You're one to talk."

Cain answered Sindy, ignoring them. "I'm in the kitchen. Are you alright?"

Sindy's quiet footsteps padded across the wood floor, and she began to speak even before reaching the doorway. "I feel great, thanks to you. Just thirsty. Oh...I didn't know you weren't alone."

She wore only the black unisex hospital-scrub type shirt that Alyson had brought up for her from the garage. Cain kept a supply of clothing there for the Crimson Coven if needed. The shirt was a bit large and apparently, Sindy had opted not to bother with the pants, even though her height made the shirt indecently short on her. Her complexion was still a little pale, especially next to the dark fabric and her long black hair, but she seemed healthy and strong.

There was an awkward pause as she eyed Mattie and Alyson, until Mattie smiled and spoke. "You're looking much better than the last time I saw you."

Sindy gazed at him leisurely and then returned the smile. "Really? Then I must have been worse off than I thought, because I'm pretty sure that the last time you saw me, I was naked."

Cain sighed as Alyson let out a huff of annoyance. "I think he was too busy staring at the gaping holes in your stomach to notice," Allie said pointedly.

Sindy's eyes slowly left Mattie's flushed face to meet Alyson' irate stare. "Right. Keep telling yourself that."

Alyson spoke to the guys telepathically while still staring Sindy down. *Why did I help her?*

Cain replied with a mental chuckle. *Because you're a good person. Selflessness is a wonderful leadership quality.*

I never asked to be a leader, she reminded him.

You may not be given a choice.

Sindy finally unlocked her eyes from Allie's, and longingly played them over the container of blood in Cain's hand, before trying to gauge their reaction to her. Based on the silence in the room during their telepathic exchange, it seemed a cold reception. "Well, thanks for the help and hospitality, but maybe I should get going."

Cain knew she had no intention of leaving. She was only looking for him to jump in and tell her how much he wanted her to stay, to diffuse any hostility Allie might have brewing. After Sindy's inciting comment, he was tempted to say 'Okay, bye now', if only just to see how she'd react. Instead, he settled for a long and uncomfortable pause before he spoke. "Nonsense. If you've come down out of bed, you must be thirsty. Let me get something for you."

He'd planned to finish the container himself, but now took out a mug with the intention of heating some for her. He should probably go and get her a new container from the garage refrigerator, considering the fact that he'd been drinking directly from this one, but he didn't think she'd really care. He wasn't up to leaving the room for the other, and she was in no position to complain after her behavior.

Alyson stood and snatched the container from his hand. "Sit down, you've served her enough." He obeyed silently. Truthfully, he was feeling rather weak, as Allie surely knew, and he was grateful for the rest.

Allie poured the blood into the mug and then put it into the microwave. Mattie spoke to fill the tense silence as they waited for it to beep. "Just for the record," he said to Sindy, "I'm sure you *were* worse off than you thought. And, shredded flesh and guts...not very sexy, even to a vampire."

Sindy's hand moved unconsciously to guard her stomach as she took in the severity of Mattie's gaze. "Well, I guess that depends on the vampire."

The microwave sounded, and Allie took the mug from it. Sindy held her hand out for it, expectantly, but Alyson walked right past her and handed the mug to Cain. "Don't ever drink it cold like that in front of me again, it's disgusting." She turned to Sindy who was staring open mouthed at her audacity. "It's on the counter," Allie told her with a nod of her head. "Get your own."

Sindy's eyes became hard slits, but Cain ignored the exchange as he drank the blood he'd been offered. Sindy was going to have to temper her attitude if she planned to stay for any length of time. She'd known what she was walking into when she came downstairs, and it was her own demeanor that had set the tone.

Sindy finally went to retrieve a mug of her own from the cabinet. She opened the wrong one. Cain was going to tell her where to look, but she found it on the next try. She poured the last of the blood into her cup and put it into the microwave without comment. When she turned to face the table while waiting, she found that they were all watching her.

Mattie seemed most mesmerized by her movements, but not for any indecent reason. "Are you really all healed?" he asked in disbelief. "Doesn't it hurt even a little?"

She smiled. "Nope. I'm good as new. Want to see?" she asked, reaching down to the top of her thighs and grasping the hem of her shirt, as though willing to raise it.

"I'll take your word for it," he responded dryly. "What happened to you?"

Sindy shrugged as the microwave sounded. "Momentary lapse in judgment," she said as she tended her beverage.

"During what, a swordfight?" Mattie asked incredulously.

"You were attacked by the Crimson Coven," Cain provided, "Am I right?"

Sindy nodded as she sipped from her mug. Mattie still pried. "Are they carrying machetes now?" he asked facetiously.

"They were claw marks," Alyson told him quietly.

"I don't understand. What kind of claws? Aren't they all vampires? And I thought the Crimson Coven wasn't dangerous," he said, turning to Cain warily.

"They are vampires, and all vampires are dangerous," Cain replied quietly. "But we do have a mutual understanding." Cain changed the subject, unwilling to delve into things further in front of Mattie and Alyson. He wanted to learn the specifics for himself first, before getting into things he wasn't sure the others were ready for. "Pity we haven't any food in the house."

Mattie looked at him oddly, partly annoyed for the change in topic, but also curious over the statement. "What do you need food for?"

"I don't, she does," he explained with a nod towards Sindy. "I'm afraid there was some damage to your intestines," he told her. "They may seal off while healing. You'll lose the ability to pass food. Not a devastating development, but the ability to eat in front of others can be useful, and you might miss it after a few years. It's better to keep things working properly. If you get some food in there during healing, it will be forced to remain open and functioning. I guess we'll have to go to the market and get you something."

"I have food," Alyson offered hesitantly.

Cain and Mattie both turned to her in surprise. "You do?" Cain asked.

"M-hmm." She stood and reached towards a cabinet over the refrigerator. Cain could tell she had been about to levitate herself to reach it, when she thought better of doing so in front of Sindy. After quickly catching herself, she instead pointed towards it and Mattie swiftly stepped forward to open it for her.

"I've got cookies, potato chips…chocolate," she added the last after a slight pause, as though hesitant to share. "I have a stash back at the trailer too, and there might be some ice cream in the freezer."

Mattie looked at her oddly. "I never knew that."

"That's because I eat it when you're not around."

Mattie still seemed to think it was odd. "What do you need food for?"

Allie slumped her shoulders in exasperation over his lack of understanding. "It's comforting."

Surprisingly, it was Sindy who interjected on Allie's behalf. "You can't just expect a girl to give up chocolate!" Sindy rolled her eyes at the idea. "Men," she muttered, giving Alyson an empathetic smile. After a moment, Allie returned the smile, grateful for the shared understanding.

Cain was glad to see some small connection between the two girls. Maybe this wouldn't be a disaster after all. "I think a cookie would be best for a start. You'll have to eat it very slowly though. Small nibbles," he instructed as Allie handed Sindy one from the package. "Give your body time to get things working again. It might be a bit painful, I'm afraid."

Sindy didn't look thrilled at the prospect, but took a dainty bite as directed. Mattie resumed questioning her. "So, what exactly happened to you?" She ignored him, focusing on her snack. Mattie would not relent. "As the guy who was in charge of putting your guts back in, I'd kind of like to know."

Cain was going to say something to deter them, when Alyson joined in the questioning. "Yeah Sindy, what exactly happened? I'd like to hear it myself."

Sindy finished the last sip from her cup and then put her hand to her stomach, rather dramatically. "Actually, I'm not feeling very well. Maybe I'd better go and lie down." She looked to Cain for sympathy. "I'll finish this up in my room. Would that be alright? We can talk later."

Cain smiled in accommodation. "Of course. Can you manage?"

Sindy nodded as she slowly made for the doorway. "I'll be okay. I just need some rest."

As she left the room, Allie was shaking her head. "Can you believe her?" she asked sarcastically.

Mattie was looking to Cain for answers. "Do you know what happened?"

"No, but after I get a bit more blood into me, I plan to visit the Crimson Coven and find out."

~~~~~~~~~~~~~~~~~~~~~~~~~~~~

"She's a slut." The woman said the words as though spitting them onto the ground, making Cain wonder if she was truly as volatile as her name.

Tempest was a lovely young woman of color, with full lips, and a nose that was slightly broad and nicely complimented the round plumpness of her cheeks. But it was her eyes that demanded full attention to her face. Her eyes were large, dark, and enticingly seductive. She wore her hair completely natural, so that it was a dark, thick halo around her head and flowing down over her shoulders in a cloud of tight curls. It appeared to have a life of its own, as it was tugged and shifted with the breeze. Her body seemed the perfect balance of lean muscle and full, voluptuous curves. This could be seen very clearly, because despite the cold, she stood before him unabashedly nude.

The Crimson Coven was comprised solely of the rare breed of red-eyed, shape-shifting vampires, and they were not in the habit of wearing clothing, as it would restrict them from changing form. Cain stood in the area that the coven called the 'speaking circle'. It was a clearing within the deep woods, which held a bonfire surrounded by three large concentric rings of log seats. There was no official gathering this evening, and there were only a few small groups of vampires scattered about the circle. All kept a respectful distance from their leader, Khalon, as he spoke privately with Tempest and Cain, their guest.

Cain knew this was a gathering place where human form was expected, as it was the only form in which they could all speak to one another. The woods around them were surely populated with many vampires of the coven, but they were difficult to see among the trees, as they seemed to keep mostly to their wolf or bat forms. Every once in a while Cain was startled when a bat or wolf would silently and unobtrusively approach the edge of the circle and then suddenly shift into a swirling cloud of smoke to re-shape into human form and walk through.

"Sindy got what she deserved," Tempest continued, as she stood before Cain and Khalon, picking the dirt from under her long fingernails with a small splinter of wood. "She's been sniffing around our coven for almost a year."

Cain interrupted her in surprise. "A year?" He looked to Khalon as Tempest nodded in confirmation. "Did you know about this?" Khalon dipped his head to show that he did, although he didn't seem to think it was important. "Why didn't I know about this?" Cain asked him.

"It's not my place to tell you," Khalon answered simply. "She would let herself be known in her own time. She comes and goes. She has been watching us long enough to know that I am the leader here, and she has not spoken to me yet. If she wants my help she can ask for it," he replied with a shrug.

"Perhaps she didn't need help…before now," Cain added, with a sharp look at Tempest.

Tempest discarded the wood, putting her hands on her hips with an attitude of severity. "She's also been watching long enough to know that I'm the dominant female of this coven. I am the oldest and the most skilled," she informed him, holding her head a bit higher. "I'm the strongest, fastest, deadliest, and most beautiful woman of the coven. I will not stand to be betrayed and humiliated."

Cain gave her a nod of acknowledgement, to show that he was appropriately impressed. He had a feeling of impending unease with the direction of the conversation, though. Sindy had many impressive qualities as well, when she let them show through. Unfortunately, respect for others was not usually one of them. "Fair enough. So what is your problem with Sindy?"

Tempest folded her arms in uncompromising negativity. "My problem with Sindy is that she was fucking my man."

Cain took a deep breath, and sighed. He kept expecting Sindy to conduct herself with the dignity he saw within her when they were alone, and yet every time she went off on her own she resorted back to her same old disappointing ways. It wasn't for him to say how she should conduct her private life, but why did she only seem to value something if she could take it away from someone else? "I see. Well, I understand your frustration, believe me, I do. The fact is you have a perfect right to defend your relationship and position within your coven. However, Sindy is *not* a member of your coven. While she has been tolerated on this land, she has never been formally accepted or included in any way. Therefore she is still under my jurisdiction, and my rules clearly state that I will not tolerate such hostility."

Tempest snorted in contempt. "It was only a warning. I didn't kill her. I just wanted to make her suffer…a lot…for a very long time."

Cain lightly shook his head. He did sympathize with the woman, but he had never been comfortable with the way vampires sometimes conducted themselves among their own kind. It was so…inhuman. "With all due respect, while I do acknowledge Sindy's fault here, she is not alone in it. I assume the man in question *is* a member of your coven. Considering his actions and the fact that you consider him to be *your* man, perhaps you should have taken this up with him."

Tempest gave him a mirthless smirk. "Oh, I have. And he is very lucky that as a vampire, things can be re-attached."

Khalon interjected before Cain could even decide how to reply. "This girl Sindy, she was greatly injured?"

"I've taken care of it," Cain assured him. "She's healed now."

Khalon assessed his disposition with concern. Cain knew that although the color had returned to his face, he had not yet fully recovered from giving Sindy so much blood, and still looked a bit haggard. "No wonder you are looking so drained. You will be compensated."

Tempest was staring at him in shock. "She can't be healed."

Cain did not want Khalon to make more of the problem than it was. He knew that punishment could be severe within the coven. After learning the circumstances, he had to admit that Sindy had probably brought it on herself, and there was no permanent damage. "I can assure you, she is fine. You needn't be overly concerned. She was already up and about when I left."

Tempest was still staring at him as though he was being less than truthful. She'd obviously hoped to have had a greater effect on Sindy. "No. That can't be. It was only last night! I sliced her belly. It was long and deep." She turned to Khalon with intensity, although Cain would have thought she would be happy to minimize the damage for her own sake. Apparently, pride in her performance was more important to her. She would rather defend her dangerous reputation than escape reprimand. "I severed intestine. That kind of injury will take at least a week to heal."

Cain remained quietly calm and sincere. "Not in my care."

Khalon held up a hand to show Tempest that he wanted no more from her. "I have heard enough. Tempest, you will be informed of how you will repay Cain for the healing, and for your indiscretion. You are dismissed."

Tempest did not say more. She simply nodded in acknowledgement to them both, and then turned and walked away. Once she was gone, Khalon turned his attention back to Cain. "This wound, was it as she said?" he asked thoughtfully.

"Yes. Four deep slashes from breastbone to pelvis. The center cut did slice through muscle to reach the organs beneath, but she'll be alright."

"No doubt she will, but how is she right now?"

Cain shrugged. What further description was required? "As I said, she is walking and drinking. She only has mild discomfort now. I took care of her."

Khalon chuckled softly to himself. "Friend, I have suspected something for a long while that I think does not even occur to you. Your breed, with golden-yellow eyes, they are rare, aren't they?"

"Yes," Cain agreed, although confused by the shift in discussion. "I've never met another of my kind."

"And yet even before your own well deserved reputation, those of the breed were known as caregivers who helped others."

"That is true," Cain admitted. "I've heard it before."

Khalon nodded thoughtfully, and then motioned for Cain to wait as he stepped towards the fire ring. On the ground near enough to the bonfire to be warm and dry, rather than covered in snow, was an ornamental wooden box. Khalon lifted the lid and brought out a sharp knife. He returned to Cain. "Watch," he said as he used the knife to make a slice on the inside of his own arm. Once there was a good cut there, they watched as his blood pooled, but did not spill. The cut seemed to pull together just a bit and was no longer bleeding, but it did not heal completely. The skin was still puckered, red, and raw.

Cain looked at Khalon curiously. "How did you heal Sindy?" Khalon asked.

"As you'd expect, with my blood."

"Would you be so kind as to repeat it?" Khalon asked, offering his sliced arm. Cain began to feel déjà vu creep over him. He used the knife to slice in his wrist and then let a few drops of blood fall onto Khalon's wound. He was careful not to use too much. He'd been sharing blood with Alyson for the mark of the coven these past years, and surely had her special blood within him. He'd discussed with Mattie and Alyson the possible repercussions of letting her blood mix with others, something they tried to prevent for the most part, but they really did not know if it mattered. Hopefully this wasn't enough to make a difference. With Sindy, he hadn't much of a choice.

He watched Khalon's wound as his blood dripped onto it. The change was noticeable in seconds. The edges of the skin around the cut pulled tighter together, and before long it was fully closed, looking mostly smooth and of normal skin tone. Khalon remarked on the obvious. "You are a healer, my friend. What could take me an hour or more to heal, your blood can do in minutes."

Cain was staring at Khalon's arm in confusion. "All vampires have accelerated healing. That would take you almost an hour?"

"Of a certainty. We heal quicker than humans do, but none among us heals as quickly as you. Have you ever been greatly injured?"

"I've endured my share, but I've never compared my healing to that of others," he admitted. Or had he? An elusive memory danced out of reach.

"It seems your skill is uncovered."

"You think it is the talent of my breed?" he asked dubiously.

"Of course. Healers, teachers, guardians, these are all names that those of yellow eyes have been known by, but none of us have known why. Now at least some of that is clear. What else would it be?" Khalon asked with a smile.

What else indeed. The feeling of déjà vu that had been haunting him was suddenly placed; Arif. A similar conversation had taken place between him and Arif years before, but his rapid healing had not been discussed in terms of breed skill. In fact, Arif had turned the entire conversation in a much different direction. Arif had wanted to discuss Cain's practice of subsisting on animal blood rather than drinking from humans, and his 'crusade' to teach other vampires to exist among humans with moral dignity.

In fact, although he had not truly spoken it, Arif had manipulated the conversation to suggest that it was Cain's ethical practices alone that set him apart from other vampires. He had tried to lead Cain to believe that his rapid healing from injury caused by holy water and cross were evidence of holy forgiveness, rather than a skill shared by his entire breed. The audacity of the man, to withhold breed skill information that he surely knew, and let Cain believe that it was divine intervention! He had played Cain for a fool, holding out the thin promise of heavenly forgiveness. Although cautious and humble over the matter, in his deepest heart of hearts, Cain had dared to believe it.

Cain was lost in thought as he watched the cut on his own arm heal. Khalon seemed to notice the change in Cain's demeanor. "Are you disappointed by such a discovery?"

Cain shook his head and forced a smile. "No. Thank you for sharing these thoughts and helping me to see what I should have known all along. *You* have always been truthful with me."

"Of course I have. What purpose is there in lying? It is society that covets such skills of deceit and manipulation of truth. That is why I prefer the forest. My coven holds close the values that drove us to live apart from the world. We don't need all of that," he said with a gesture meant to encompass outside civilization. "We know what holds true merit.

Now let us discuss the debt that my coven owes you. There must be some way that Tempest can repay you for your troubles. Although she should not have been so boastful, her claims were all true. She is certainly the most beautifully skilled woman of the coven."

Cain gave his friend a thoughtful smile. "Actually, I did have something specific in mind."

Chapter 4 - Part 2: Love... eternal

Cain was lounging in the parlor before the fireplace, thinking about the arrangement he had put into place with Khalon, to have Tempest repay him for her trespass. Hopefully it would work out as perfectly as it fit together in his mind.

Cain had refused to divulge any information about it to Alyson and Mattie yet, so they had left the estate on some errand of their own this evening, leaving Cain to ponder recent developments alone in quiet.

Sindy had declined to get up this evening. She was suffering some discomfort as her insides worked out the kinks from her injury. Cain was also under the impression that she might be pouting because he had refrained from fussing over her once he had finished giving her blood.

He was happy that she had returned, and did not begrudge healing her, but he didn't approve of her behavior. He certainly didn't intend to spend his time coaxing her out of her room, or trying to get Alyson and Mattie to accept her. He'd done his part the first time around in trying to hold her hand and offer assistance, and she had misconstrued it and then taken off on him. This time, she could build her own relationships and ask for help if needed, or deal with the consequences.

He felt so weary this evening. It was more than his recent draining of blood could account for. He was almost fully recovered from the blood loss. Mattie and Alyson had assured him it no longer showed in his appearance; this was a weariness of the soul. He was tired of having to carefully coordinate things. Worrying about special powers, Alyson and Mattie, the Crimson Coven, Arif... Worrying about what Sindy might expect from him: how he was going to keep her at a distance without pushing her away; relationships that intertwined everyone and needed a careful balance of interaction... He was tired of deciding which information some should know and others should not. It all made his head hurt.

He had gone to his desk to write, as he often did to comfort himself, but even words had deserted him. He didn't care to write about recent developments, and the ache within was not something he could express through a pen tonight. It had all been written dozens of times before. There was nothing left to say. He stared at the fire in the grate, hoping it could somehow warm his heart as it did his skin.

Cain was startled from his thoughts by the sound of the buzzer for the front gate. It took him a moment to even place the noise. He very rarely had visitors, and everyone in residence knew the code. No one ever rang the buzzer.

Cain made his way to the console and turned on the intercom. He'd never gotten around to putting in security cameras, but in his defense, most of his visitors wouldn't show up on film anyway. The speaker system served the purpose well enough. "Hello?" he asked, once the crackle of static that let him know it was in operation subsided. There was no answer. "Is someone there?" He turned up the volume a bit, although his enhanced hearing should easily pick up any response. He almost thought he could hear someone breathing near the microphone.

"Cain?" It was a simple inquiry. Only his chosen name, spoken to him millions of times, and yet it froze him instantly with the shock of recognition. That voice: that soft, feminine, hopeful and yet uncertain voice, rang through him with a cognizance he dared not trust himself to acknowledge. "Is that you?" she asked timidly. It was she. There was no doubt in his mind that this was not hopeful fantasy. It was Felicity. Felicity was at his gate.

He could not even speak to answer. Felicity was here? How was that possible? Dare he see her? Denying her wasn't even a serious consideration. He could not seem to work his voice, but wasted not a second to ponder it more. He pushed the button that would unlock the gate, and then ran for the door. Surely, the large iron gates were still swinging slowly inward, while he was already outside of the house and beginning his descent down the drive at breakneck speed.

The winter night was crisp and cool, the moon nearly full, and his surroundings seemed almost surreal as he ran beyond the snow-covered lawn and down the long wood-lined driveway. He almost expected to find that he was the butt of a cruel joke, his imagination run away with him; that he would reach the gate and find no one there at all. He could not see the end of the driveway, being too far from the top of the small hill, but he now saw the glow of headlights on the surrounding trees. A car had come through.

He topped the rise that would bring him down to the entrance, finally able to see the source. Headlights loomed as a car he did not recognize made its way slowly towards him. He slowed his pace and moved to the side of the road. The car also slowed, as its driver spied him. It did not pull to the side, but eventually it stopped dead still in the center of the road. It was still some distance away from him. Maddeningly, the headlights kept Cain from being able to see the person behind the wheel, the lone occupant of the vehicle.

When the driver's door opened, it seemed that time froze. Would it be her? Would his desperately lonely heart be given this amazing gift? He watched as she climbed from the car and stood, taking only a moment, although it seemed an eternity. The glare from the headlights still hindered his vision, as he tried to begin the assessment of identity. The open car door was making a steady soft bell tone alarm sound from within. She'd left the keys in the ignition.

She walked around the car door, stopped to gaze at him for a moment, and then swung the door shut, to stop the ringing alarm. She seemed a little tall, but he realized that she was wearing high, stylish boots with her jeans. He squinted a little in the headlights, trying to see her better. Her hair was different, still long, but only just to her shoulders now, smooth and straightly styled. In this lighting, he could only barely see a hint of the beautiful reddish color in it that he loved. He took a step closer. It was her, it had to be her. Her face was a bit thinner, her lips just the same and looking kissable as ever. He wanted to see her eyes. Damn those lights.

As though reading his mind, she slowly came around to stand a bit in front of the car, partially blocking the left headlight and giving his eyes a chance to adjust. His keen night vision began to return, and he was able to finally meet her gaze. Felicity, his lovely Felicity had come to him like an answered prayer! Just as their eyes met, he found himself moving forward, almost without thought. He was drawn to her with a force that could not be stopped. The very moment he began to move, she was running to him as well.

He opened his arms and gathered her in like a deep breath of air after the stillness of death, and she held him in a crushing embrace just as desperate and grateful as his own. He drank in her scent as though it was blood, his lips closed and pressed against the side of her throat reveling in even just the feel of her skin against them. Eyes closed, tangled in her hair and holding her as though the world was trying to rip her from his arms, he lifted her lightly from the ground.

"Felicity." He mumbled her name against her throat, and then gently loosened his hold so that she could regain her feet, and he could truly speak. His lips brushed her cheek as he set her down and leaned slightly away, and words were forgotten. Instead he found her mouth with his own, his lips eager to meet hers after years of only dreams.

She seemed almost startled for a moment, but kissed him in return after only the barest hesitation, with a sweet surrender. Time meant nothing. It was as though he had kissed her thusly only yesterday, and yet there was also the overwhelming resurgence of passion too long unsatisfied, to lend an urgent delight to the endearment. He found her tongue with his own and abandoned restraint as his heart sang with the long-awaited reunion. Engaged in gloriously sensual bliss, he savored her attentions with intense pleasure. He kept the kiss far longer than he should have, but distressingly suspected that he may not get another. Finally, he forced himself to end it.

As her lips left his, she drew a sorely needed, ragged breath of air, but then came back to taste him once or twice more before pulling away. He closed his eyes and relished the sweet pull of her final kiss as it ended. His sweet Felicity. He could feel the blood pulsing through her with each rapid heartbeat, and his body longed to taste what flowed just beneath her smooth warm skin.

He had not been so close to a living person since the night he had left her, and all the little signs of life within her were terribly enticing to the predator within him. His heart was full of longing to keep her crushed to him, to steal more kisses, but he needed to keep himself in check, more so now than ever. He filed his thirst away, along with the lustful urges that surged within him upon seeing her again. When he looked down at her, she had tears in her eyes, but was gazing up at him with a curious little smile. "I guess you aren't mad that I came," she said playfully.

He gave a little laugh and shook his head, although he should probably be reprimanding her. "How did you even find me?" he asked in quiet wonder.

"Through Allie. But don't be angry with her," she quickly added. "She doesn't even realize that I know." Felicity became thoughtful for a moment, and then corrected herself. "Well, she *didn't*. She probably knows now. She tends to pick up very strong emotions."

"Yes, I know," he informed her with an embarrassed smirk, thinking of all the times Alyson had seemed to draw the raw feelings straight from his heart and bare them unapologetically before him. "We're working on dampening that. But I still don't understand how you found your way here."

Felicity shrugged. "I'll explain later. It took a little Nancy Drew work on my part, and I know I shouldn't have, but I didn't think you'd mind." Her gaze dropped to the ground for a moment. "After the way you left me standing in that parking lot, I kind of figured you owe me."

Without warning, his eyes filled with remorseful tears at her words, and he hopefully searched her beautiful green eyes for a glimpse of forgiveness. "I didn't want it to be like that," he quietly explained. "I didn't want to leave that way…but you *did* know that I was leaving, and you wouldn't let me go. I didn't have much of a choice. There was no easy way to do it."

"I know." Her voice was stiff with old resentment, but he could see in her eyes that she understood.

"I never stopped loving you," he assured her sincerely. "I did what I felt was right for you, though it broke my heart, but I will *always* love you." The words caused her to meet his eyes again and she couldn't help but smile. It seemed he had confirmed a secret hope that she had dared to hold onto. She should never have doubted it, but separation could easily breed such insecurities. After a quiet moment of confirmation, he asked, "Has it taken you this long to forgive me?"

Her smile grew, but then faded as she pulled up the memory of her feelings after he'd left. "I was hurt. Sad and angry, but mostly I was just frustrated." She took a deep breath and sighed. "I understood, and I forgave you a long time ago." A weight lifted from him with that knowledge. "It's been hard though, and I missed you." He nodded, sharing her pain. "I still loved you too. I don't think I've ever stopped loving you." She paused for a moment with a slight grimace, "and it makes things really complicated. I needed to see you." She said the last with an almost accusing, distraught intensity that surprised him.

He took her shoulders with a quiet but almost desperate worry. "Have I ruined things for you?" he asked.

Her distress fled at his touch, and he could feel her comfort in his concern. She smiled and shook her head, re-assessing things and obviously forcing herself not to stir up turmoil. She looked into his eyes with sweet sincerity. "No. No regrets." The simple statement threatened to undo him, as he remembered the first time she had uttered it to him, long ago, on the night that she had decided to give herself to him and consummate their love.

"I've been okay," she insisted. "Life is good, as they say," she continued, forcing herself to smile. "I have a good life, but it's changed so much. Everything is changing, and I really needed to see you before..." She trailed off, and he made himself imagine what changes she might be speaking of. "Before it changes *too* much," she made herself conclude.

It was another man. It had to be. That was why she had first hesitated at his kiss, sweet though it had been when she'd given over to it. It had been over three years since he had seen her last. The count ticked off in his head, another date to remember always. Of course, there had been other men in her life since he'd left. She was twenty-two years old now. She was still very young, but at the age when true-life plans were beginning to take shape.

He could guess what sorts of upcoming changes might require such closure; what she might consider important and irreversible. "I see," he said with quiet acceptance. Had she come to ascertain her options for the future? He was resigned that she should have the life she'd always truly wanted.

He watched her take another deep breath to calm the trembling of nerves she seemed to be fighting. He took her warm, soft hands into his own and glanced at their surroundings; the first time they had taken their eyes off each other since her arrival. "Well, let's get out of the middle of the road," he suggested. "We can go up to the house and talk. You can tell me about your life," he added with a smile.

"I'd like that." She let go of one hand and used the other to lead him back towards her car. As they reached it, they parted to go around to their sides, and he was now able to see it better without the lights in his face. It was a smart little four-door maroon colored car. A Toyota, he could see by the little plastic logo design on the front grill. It wasn't brand new, but nicely kept.

"You got a new car," he said as he stood before the front passenger door.

She opened her door and began to get into the driver's seat. "Oh yeah, a couple of years ago. The old one was a piece of junk," she said with a chuckle.

He opened his door, but remained standing outside. Finally, he leaned down to see her within, and felt the oppressive thickness of repellent force urging him out, for his lack of invitation. "You'll need to invite me in," he gently reminded.

"Sorry, come in." She shook her head at her own misstep, and was staring at him thoughtfully. "I can't believe I forgot that."

He felt the air seem to thin, the oppression dissipating through the magic of her spoken acceptance, and he slid easily into the seat. She was gazing at him in wonder. He just gave a little shrug and watched her as she finally put the car into gear and began to resume the journey up the driveway to the house. He found himself staring at her most of the way. Her familiar beauty was mesmerizing to him. She kept turning to see him as well. In fact, at one point, their eyes locked, and she nearly drove off into the woods. "You might need to watch the road," he told her gently, as they felt the car begin to bump over uneven ground.

She jerked the wheel back with a start, over-compensating a bit. "Oh, sorry." She flushed prettily with embarrassment. "I just can't stop looking at you. You look *exactly* the same."

He always would, a cruel reminder of their differences. "You're more beautiful than memory." He could see the thrill that ran through her at his words. She looked away and busied herself driving the car up the hill.

As they crested the peak, she saw the lights of the house come into view. "Wow," she exclaimed with quiet disbelief. "Is that your *house?*"

He glanced down, feeling awkward over the grand image it presented. "I hardly ever stayed here until recently. I prefer to be on the road. It's just convenient to have someplace big enough for large gatherings when needed."

She smiled at him with reassuring approval that he shouldn't feel the need to explain. "It's gorgeous."

"Thanks. You can just pull up the side there by the garage." As she did, he took in the little differences time had made in her. The way she did her hair, her make-up and style of clothing, all came together to give her a look of confident maturity. She'd lost a bit of weight he noticed, not that he felt she'd needed to. She now presented a tall, thin, statuesque impression. He could see by the way she moved, her self-image had been positively affected by it, although truthfully, he'd preferred her fuller curves. It didn't matter though. Nothing in her outward looks would ever matter. Just being close to her, it was as though he could feel the warm and comforting presence of her caring heart. It was his Felicity. Whether she belonged to another man in her true life or not, even if he could not truly claim her as he'd so like to; for this private moment in his mind, she was his.

She put the car into park and turned to him. He didn't want to remain in the confines of the car, although he did enjoy its privacy. He worried for who else might wander upon them. He wanted no interruption. This was *their* time. "Come, let me show you inside." He got out, going around and opening her door as well, and trying to decide where he should take her. He preferred the back parlor with the fireplace, but everyone knew that was where to find him. Still, it was where he'd like to take her. Perhaps it would serve if he locked the doors.

As they approached the entrance and he opened the front door for her, he could see that she was very impressed and almost intimidated by her surroundings. Vast high ceilings, rich dark wood, and wrought iron fixtures gave the entry a prepossessing air that did not feel right to him for this reunion. He ushered her past the grand curving staircase and the threshold to the ballroom, as she gazed about in wonder. He brought her through to the parlor, feeling its comfortable warmth of character and fire glow close about them. Lighting that fireplace was usually the first thing he did upon waking, and by this time, it was burning steadily. There was no comfort like sitting before a warm fire. Once she was within, he closed the room's double door and turned the lock.

He always considered the room his parlor, although it was rather large, and he remembered the real estate agent referring to it as a 'Great Room'; a very pompous sounding description he'd never cared for. He spoke to Felicity casually as he walked over and locked both pairs of double doors that led through to the ballroom. They'd already been closed, so hopefully it didn't seem too obvious that he was sequestering them away in secret. "Please, make yourself comfortable. Shall I take your coat?" The words sounded almost ridiculously formal, as though he was the butler. He was just trying to fill the silence as he prepared the room so that they could then ignore all else.

She didn't comment, and seemed at ease as she removed her short, stylish jacket. She laid it on a chair, waving her hand that he needn't bother to come and take it. She observed the paintings and furnishings of the room with a smile of approval. "This is lovely."

He glanced across the room, to the doors on either side of the fireplace, which led to a small suite of guest rooms. They were already closed, and he knew that no one should be within. He relaxed and smiled, allowing himself to concentrate on her again. He picked up the poker for the fire, a final detail, and gave it a rustle to stir the wood and enliven the flames.

"Would you like a drink?" he asked. He could practically see her thought process as she considered, and then seemed to decide that she wanted to keep her head clear. She smiled and shook her head no. The thought of inebriation made him realize that she might have felt effect from the venom in his kiss earlier. She must have, the first renewal of it in years. He couldn't help but wonder if she minded that. In a practical sense, it probably wasn't fair of him to introduce it to her again. But he hadn't been thinking of that at all, and he couldn't say he would have done it any differently. He wouldn't have given up that kiss for anything.

He approached her as she stood, just watching him as though in a trance. As he came and took her hands, she demurely lowered her eyes. He smiled and gave her a slight nudge to look at him. "It's alright; I can't take my eyes off of you either. There's no shame in it. I still can't believe that you're here. I keep thinking it must be a dream."

She gave his hands a squeeze and then let them go, moving to sit on the loveseat. He joined her there. She seemed to withdraw a little, and he could see that she was beginning to worry that she shouldn't have come. He was being too affectionate, and she was unsure how to react. He needed to remember that her daily life did not include him, although thoughts of her pervaded his existence nightly. He spoke of less intimate things. "So, where are you living now?"

She gave a little laugh while glancing around, "Someplace a far cry from this." He looked away, uncomfortable with the comparison. He'd the means to support her in every luxury she could dream of. She must know that. Still, wealth was a poor reason to give up humanity, and not a way in which he ever hoped to win her. She noticed his discomfort and smiled. "It's nice though. It's not a house, it's an apartment, in the city."

"Manhattan," he replied brightly. "That must be exciting for you."

"It's definitely a lot different from what I'm used to. I'm sort of between the Hudson River and Central Park West, not that I can see either of them from my apartment. I'm near Columbia University."

"Oh, do you attend there?"

She paused, and then answered quietly. "No, I don't. I've already graduated. I'm a teacher."

He smiled with widened eyes. "A professor?"

She chuckled. "No, not at the college. I'm an elementary school teacher. P.S. 165. I teach second grade."

"That is absolutely brilliant," he exclaimed happily. He took her hands back. He couldn't help it, he needed to feel her warm skin and communicate his delight at being near her, through the grasping of her fingers, if he was not to hold her. She didn't seem to mind, and he imagined that she was secretly pleased with his touch. "A teacher. It's perfect for you. How old are they?"

"Seven and eight-year-olds. They're great kids." Her broad smile conveyed how enamored she was of them.

"I'm sure you're wonderful with them."

"Well, I don't know about that, but I try." He gave her a reprimanding look for being unsure. She suddenly seemed more like her old self than ever. Although her confidence had grown, she was still humble and unpresuming. She graciously accepted the rebuke and corrected herself. "Actually, I do think I'm pretty good at it, but this is only my first year. Sometimes they look at me like they have no idea what I'm trying to show them, and I feel like an idiot that I can't make them understand," she admitted with a laugh. "But then we go at it another way, and their eyes light up and you can see them get it. It's just the best feeling in the world."

He nodded with admiration, almost envious of her. He hadn't spent time with a child in ages. He knew it was a special feeling, to be part of a child's life. He missed that. She went on. "I don't know what I'm going to do all summer. I'll miss them terribly."

With a tolerant smile, he changed the subject, happy for her, but needing to soothe his own heart from its bitter loss. "I still don't understand how you've made your way here. You can't gain information from Alyson's mind without her knowledge, can you? I hadn't thought that possible. The telepathic ability is *hers*, not to be bent to the will of the subject."

"Oh, it wasn't anything supernatural. Just good, old-fashioned snooping on my part. She came to visit me a few months ago."

"Did she?" he interjected with surprised disapproval.

Felicity continued cautiously. "Yes. I don't know how she got there, because she said her car was in the shop. She used my phone to see if it was done. After she left, I hit redial. It was West Herr Dodge in Orchard Park."

She watched him raise his eyebrows at her findings, before going on. "The other piece of the puzzle was *sort of* telepathic, I guess. I had a weird dream a couple of years back; quite a few of them actually. I even started keeping a dream journal so I could try to figure them out. That's how bizarre it was. They were dreams that I was with Allie…well, it was more like I *was* Allie; like I felt that she was there, but I couldn't see her. I didn't understand at the time, but we've talked about it since and I guess I kind of get it now. It doesn't really happen anymore though.

Anyway, in one dream, and it was just a little snippet of a dream, nothing much, we were riding in a car, and I could see the same things that she did. I just remember a green street sign with white letters that said 'Webster Road'. I never thought anything of it. You know how many 'Webster roads' there must be? In fact, I'd completely forgotten it. But then during her visit, Allie explained to me about her visions and how we could sometimes share dreams, especially early on, before she knew how to control it.

After she left, I started thinking about maybe trying to see you. I looked up that car dealer on the computer. Right there, just a few blocks away was Webster Rd., staring right at me from the 'Google Maps' screen. The dream just popped back into my head, and I realized that it might have been something that was real, and could be near where she lived. I figured all along that she and Mattie might be staying with you. I just couldn't decide if I should come...until now."

Cain was sure that she could read the blank steadiness of his expression to be growing ire that Alyson had been so careless. Felicity quickly tried to reassure him. "That visit was the first time I'd actually seen Alyson in all these years. She never mentioned you, not once. We've spoken since, but even the few times that I asked her if she still saw you, she wouldn't give me a straight answer. She told me once that you were fine, and I shouldn't worry, and then she wouldn't talk about you anymore. I knew you'd probably told her not to. I guess you thought that would make it easier for me to let you go." She looked directly into his eyes with a steadfast sincerity. "I never will though, not completely."

He felt his eyes fill with unshed tears, and he tried not to betray how happy that made him. It wasn't fair of him. She was better off being able to move on. He tried to detach himself from his feelings, but she refused to let him become distant and seal himself off from her. "I know I shouldn't be here, and I hope you aren't mad that I invaded your privacy," she said with a teasing smile, "but I had to see you," she insisted. "I drove over six hours to get here, and then up and down Webster road for the better part of an hour before I found the private path to your house. Even then, it was just a long dirt road that ended with a gate and a speaker. I had no idea if it was really your house, or who would answer. I took a chance, and pushed the button. I can't even tell you the shock I felt when I heard your voice. Even after all this time, I knew right away it was you."

He looked into her eyes, feeling their connection stronger than ever, a loving bond that seemed to surpass all else and make him believe that things had to work out somehow. She did still love him, just as he loved her. He forced himself to re-examine his reasons for departure from her. Were they insurmountable?

"That night," he began quietly, "the night that I left, it wasn't only because I thought *I* knew what was best for you. It's not for me to decide the course of another's life. I did believe I was doing the right thing in leaving, but when you asked me to change you, I turned you down for reasons other than my own." She just watched him quietly, without prompt or comment.

He swallowed and tried to explain. "I believed that you had made your decision, not because you wanted to change what you were, but only because you wanted to be with me." He furrowed his brow and lightly shook his head. "It may have seemed an acceptable compromise to you, but I didn't think so. I could not take away your humanity, knowing that it wasn't truly what you wanted. You are a woman full of light, and to condemn you to darkness based on your wish to accompany me was simply unthinkable.

Life has so much to offer you, more than I ever could. You enjoy the company of your family, and your peers; you're accomplishing something good with your career. I wouldn't ask you to give that up for me. Not then, and not now. You've come all this way to see me, and I do know that your love for me is strong, but you never really wanted to give up being human. I don't blame you. You shouldn't have to sacrifice so much for love. I know that you *would*, but you shouldn't. So nothing has really changed, has it?" She opened her mouth to speak, to protest it seemed. He cut her off with a question. "What of your children?"

She seemed perplexed, and then shook her head and shrugged. "There are plenty of other teachers."

"Not those children...*your* children."

She gazed at him in confusion for a moment before answering. "I don't have any children."

He gave her a small smile and reached up to let his fingers graze her cheek and chin. "Precisely my point."

She closed her eyes and then tipped her head downward as his hand left her face. "I didn't come here to ask you to turn me," she admitted hesitantly. "You're right. It wasn't really what I wanted." She sat up straighter, meeting his gaze, severely serious that he grasp her sincerity. "I would have gone through with it though, and I would have loved being with you, and that might have made it alright." Her eyes left his, and stared unfocused over his shoulder for a moment. There was a little indignation there, uncertainty. She was happy with her life, but she could still see the enticement of what might have been.

They could have had at least a decade he was sure, a decade of happiness, maybe even two; but then the weight of the life she could never get back probably would have begun to settle upon her. That was something that would slowly destroy them with resentment and regret. He had needed to be strong and see things past the short-term future that she had been acting upon. Her gaze came back to him and she gave him a resigned sort of nod. "But I've accepted things as they are."

He watched her carefully, interpreting what he saw in her eyes. "You're committed to another man, aren't you?" He probably shouldn't have just blurted it out like that, but he didn't want her to feel as though she had to hide anything. "It's alright, you can say it," he assured her. He could see in her eyes that she worried to hurt him.

"Yes. We're not married..."

He gave her a tender smile. "But it won't be long." He coaxed a small smile from her as well.

"Probably not," she admitted over the lump in her throat. She reached to the neckline of her blouse, fumbling with something there. She drew out a chain that was about her neck. Strung on the necklace was a ring, a large diamond engagement ring.

He stared at it for a moment, knowing fully what it meant, and not wanting to let disappointment show on his face. He shouldn't be disappointed, he should be happy for her. "That is a big, beautiful ring."

She gave him a bittersweet smile. "I haven't worn it. I told him it was too big and I was afraid to lose it. We're supposed to get it sized. But really, I think I was waiting."

"For what?" he prompted quietly.

She blinked back the tears in her eyes. "For you," she admitted softly.

There were tears in his eyes as well, but he smiled through them. "Come now, all this time and you're still thinking of me?" he admonished her teasingly.

She looked shyly at the ring and then dropped it to hang from the chain again. "Do you ever think of me?" she asked falteringly.

"Every night," he answered without hesitation. "And every day too," he added in admission. She was obviously thrilled at the answer, although he felt it was unfair of him to reveal. "I shouldn't have told you, but it is the truth."

"It's nice to know," she assured him. He was glad it didn't seem to bring out more regret in her. During difficult times, it would be good that she could always hold those words dear, knowing that he loved and thought of her always.

Still, he needed to allow her to move forward. "That doesn't mean that you can't be with another. It does not mean that you shouldn't live your human life. That's why I left, so you could have that."

She swallowed back her tears and gave a small nod of acceptance. "Are you lonely?" she asked.

Why did she have to delve into his feelings? She shouldn't worry about him. It would only make things more difficult for her. "I'm not," he comforted her. "I do miss you, but I've spent most of my life alone. Besides, I have Mattie and Alyson here with me now. They're young, they need guidance. Alyson especially should have someone watching over her, and it's quite a task. Mattie needs all the help he can get," he confided with a chuckle. "It's good that I am here for them. It's nice to be needed. Don't worry about me."

Her eyes wouldn't leave his face and she was obviously trying to determine if he was just putting up a front for her. He spoke again, shaking her a bit from her thoughts. "Should I be worrying about you?" She seemed unsure how to answer. "Does he love you?" he forced himself to ask. "Is he loyal and good to you?" She nodded mutely. "More importantly, *do you love him?* I've told you before that I know you've got a big heart. There's room in there for you to love another." He lightly touched his fingers to her breastbone with a wink. "As much as I don't want to say the words, I hope you love him more than you do me, because he'll be able to truly share your life and make you happy."

Tears threatened to spill from her eyes, as he asked, "Does he…make you happy? Does he listen to you?" He shook his head a little, giving her warning. "I know you sometimes tend to follow the lead of others, but you are *so* smart. Make sure he listens to you." She gave him a little nod. "Do you have fun together?" he asked. She gazed at him, words still failing her. "Say something. Tell me that he is all of those things for you, and that you are happy. I want to know that. It doesn't wound me," he lied. "I *want* to know that you are happy." That was true, he did. He just wished with all of his soul that he could be human, to take her hand and share the future with her. No use asking for the impossible though; better to let her be happy with the attainable.

She took his hands and squeezed them tightly. "He's a good man, and he's good to me." She waited to see the affect of the statement. He gave her a relieved smile. He did want to know that she had someone worthy and loving to be with, even if it couldn't be him.

Reassured by his acceptance, she continued. "We do have fun, and I love him dearly, I really do." Cain tried to keep his face neutral and confirm his approval for her, without giving in to selfish jealousy. She held his gaze for a moment, before adding, "But he's not you."

The façade was lost and tears spilled from his eyes. He looked down and tried not let it completely overwhelm him. Her lips trembled a bit as she tried not to grimace as she continued. "I shouldn't have come. I don't know what I'm doing here. I don't know what I thought would happen."

"I do," he told her quietly. "You needed to give your heart permission to submit entirely to someone else. And you should. It won't change how I feel about you, and you can always know that; no matter what happens, or how difficult life can be. Even when you feel as though everything has gone wrong and everyone is against you, and I'm sorry to say that there will be times like that in life, there just will; you can always know that *I* love you. I believe in you, and I'm proud of you, and you will always be in my heart."

She was truly crying now. There was no keeping the tears from freely spilling down her cheeks. "I came here to prove something to myself," she explained. "I thought I knew what I wanted. I was happy, and thought I was going to show myself that I was doing the right thing. As much as I've missed you, these past years have still been good, and I thought I loved him enough that it wouldn't matter if I saw you again. But here you are, and I didn't account for how you could still touch my heart and make me feel. I thought maybe it had faded, but what I feel for you is just as strong as when you left. It isn't gone, it's just been waiting. So now, instead of confirming what I want for my life, I'm more confused than ever!"

She was so distraught, that it forced him to be strong for her. He gathered his will and took her shoulders firmly, taking her attention with them. He did not tell her the words that were trying to pound their way out of his heart in lieu of a beat. He did not tell her that he wanted to take her into his arms and steal her away from life to be with him. He did not tell her that he would like to shower her with luxuries and affections, making her forget the love of a human man who could not possibly adore and appreciate her as he did. He told her...what she needed to hear. He told her the truth that seemed pale compared to the passion in his heart. It was the truth though, and it would serve her well. If she did not live her life, then all he had gone through to try to give it to her was for naught.

"Felicity, look at me. It's not wrong that you're here. It's commendable that you want to be sure of yourself. A man who wants to spend his life with you, deserves for you to have that certainty. If you've lost sight of it within yourself, than I shall help give it back to you. If you loved him before seeing me tonight, then you love him still. What you feel for me doesn't have to ruin that. You know that I love you just as powerfully in return, but I cannot be with you in your life, and he can. That doesn't mean that you're settling for anything less special; it means that between two men who love you, you are making the decision to be with the one who can give you a human life and family.

I hope that man *is* everything that you deserve, and I am so glad that you do have that choice. There is no shame in making it. Love him. Love him truly and strongly with all of your heart, so that your life can include all of the wonders that you deserve. Having someone to go through life with, to share and realize your dreams with, is something I would never want for you to forgo because of me. If the man in your life now is not all that you need, then give yourself time to find another; but do not keep yourself from human love because of me, because that is the one thing that I cannot give you."

She had stopped crying and was silently mulling over all that he had said. "I do love him," she told him with quiet confidence. "I don't want you to think that I'm only with him because he'll be a good husband and father. He will," she admitted with a smile; a smile not for him but for the other man; the man in her real life. Cain tried not to let it hurt as she continued, "he will, but that's not why I'm with him. I do love him."

Cain forced himself to smile in reassurance, and wiped a tear from her eye. "There, see? Now stop doubting yourself." She would have a good life and be happy. He hadn't ruined things for her. The other man was a lucky one, and hopefully he would take good care of her tender heart; he'd better. "Tell me, what do you want in life?"

She smiled and laughed a little through her tears, shaking her head. "I don't know. That's such a broad question."

"Where do you see yourself in a few years? Where do you want to be?" Her cheeks had become flushed pink as she shrugged and tried not to answer. He grinned and gave her a small nudge. "Come on, there must be something you think about for the time to come."

"I feel silly. I mean, look at your life. Granted you have an awful lot of time on me, but still. Your life has been amazing. You find other vampires and you help them; you convince them to stop killing people. That is so grand scale. I mean, you're saving people's lives. Not just a few people, but every single victim that each vampire would have killed for years to come. That is huge! You have a purpose, and it's so noble and selfless. The kind of stuff I want isn't anything special, not compared to that." He gave her a look of reprimand for belittling her own expectations. She continued with a smile. "You want to save the world. I just want to be a PTA mom," she admitted with a giggle.

It brought warmth to his heart that surely showed in his eyes and his smile. He took back her hands into his own, holding them tightly. "Being a mom is a *very* special thing. It's something I would want for you as well. I've always known it was important to you, although I have no idea what a PTA is."

She laughed, "It stands for Parent Teacher Association. We have meetings once a month at school to talk about changes for the curriculum and to set up fun things for the kids. I go as a teacher, but when I'm there, I see all these parents that seem such good friends. They get involved and work together, and do nice things for their children. They have fun. I'm there, but I'm not a part of it the way that they are. I want to be a part of something like that. I want to have children, and be there for them as a good mom, taking care of my family with a good husband by my side. It seems so simple, but that's really all I want."

Now he was the one getting teary eyed. "Sounds wonderful to me." The words seemed almost to wound her as she realized that he wanted the very same thing, but could not have it. He quickly admonished her. "Now don't give me that look. I had my life. I screwed it up terribly, but I did have it. I got to be the husband and the daddy, at least for a little while. That's behind me now. Now it's your turn. If that is what you want, then have it, and enjoy it, and don't you dare try to tell me that it isn't important and special."

She stared at him thoughtfully for a few moments, lost in his eyes or her own ponderings he couldn't tell. Finally, she patted the back of his hands that held hers, and then let them go. "Time does strange things. You are just as I remembered. But somehow, as time went by, I started to wonder if maybe you didn't love me as I'd thought you did, or whether I was embellishing things about you in my memory.

At first, I was afraid to come, because I might find that you weren't really as I remembered at all. Time tricked me into thinking that in your amazing life, the few months you spent with me were long forgotten, and that you would think I was stupid to believe you'd want to see me again." Surely, she could see how the words hurt him, to know that she would think such things, but she continued. "I think that's why I finally decided to come after all. Because faced with letting you go," she took hold of the ring that hung about her neck, "faced with really letting you go, I thought it would be better if I showed myself that you didn't want me anyway.

I was so stupid. Forgive me, for being stupid enough to ever doubt you, and to think that I was going to come here and prove to myself that you didn't love me, and I was hanging on to nothing. I thought I would be so strong and unshakable in my relationship at home, and you would be cold and distant, wondering why I was even here; just some human girl you had a fling with."

It was entirely the wrong thing to do, but as she sat there looking lost and unsure of herself, admitting she had been unsure of him, he broke his horrified stare and found himself taking her into his arms. He pulled her close and kissed her once again. He kissed her lips with the same passion and desperation of their earlier reunion, but this time with the force of wanting to prove her wrong, to show her just how powerful his feelings truly were.

As before, she held back at first, but couldn't help but give into him after only a token resistance. She still loved him too much to turn away. The renewed warmth and familiarity of being with her, talking to her, knowing her again, made the kiss all the more sweet. He savored it for as long as he dared, being sure to convey all of the love he had for her through it. Finally, he drew back and held her face softly in his hands. "Don't ever doubt me. My love for you is eternal, no matter what the future holds."

She peered into his eyes and gave a small nod. Eventually she broke the gaze and then smiled at him coyly. "If you expect me to commit to another man, you're going to have to stop kissing me like that."

He gave her an apologetic grin. "Consider it a kiss goodbye. That'd be allowable, wouldn't it?"

"I guess, but…can I stay for the night? Just to talk," she added quickly. "There is so much more I want to say; things I didn't think to tell you until it was too late. So many times I'll be reading a book and think, 'Cain would love this', or something would happen and I'd think, 'Cain would understand', but you're not there to tell. I just want to talk some more. I've missed you. I can stay until dawn. Would that be alright?"

Alright? It was more than he had hoped for. "I would love that."

She took him back into her arms for a last hug and whispered to him, "Thank you." He knew that she meant not just for allowing her to stay, but more for confirming her feelings and giving her what she needed from him, the affirmation of affection, and the closure.

He held her longer than he probably should have and as he did, once again he was enveloped in her warm and pulsating liveliness. The smell of her hair, the warmth of her skin, the beat of her heart...the flow of her blood. A surge of thirst rushed through him and he firmly pushed her away as he held it back. When his eyes met hers, she was seen through shades of blue and he was abashed to realize that his thirst was showing; his eyes had changed.

He blinked and turned them human again in an instant, but she must have seen it. For a second he was nervous that it would frighten her, but she was unafraid. She did look at him oddly for a moment though, as if only just remembering the other aspects of his nature. "I'm sorry. I never even thought about the position I was putting you in. How difficult it must be," she conjectured, remorsefully.

He stared into her eyes, forcing his thirst to subside even as he took a breath to draw in her scent, unwilling to remove the temptation entirely. He wanted to take in every aspect of her that he could, knowing that she would soon be gone from him. Difficult? It was torture, but it was also passion more intense than anything he'd felt since he had left her, and he wouldn't give it up.

"Is it hard for you?" she asked in innocent concern.

"Like you wouldn't believe," he admitted with a whisper, "and I wouldn't trade it for the world." She watched him, assessing his control, he imagined, and then she gave him a tender smile. He shook his head, flustered that she should even have to think about such things. "I'm fine. Let me get myself a drink, and I'll bring you a cup of tea. Then we can sit by the fire and talk, all night; just as we have in my thoughts a thousand times."

She nodded in pleased agreement. "Yes, I'd like that." He stood and made for the door, when her voice stopped him. "Cain..." Her tone suddenly became faltering and solemn, "After tonight, I think I probably shouldn't see you again," she told him in regretful resignation.

He nodded in quiet understanding. She was right that they shouldn't see each other again. But for tonight...even if quiet conversation must be accepted in lieu of loving kisses, for tonight he would have her all to himself.

Chapter 5 - Anything you can do, I can do better

Sindy

Cain's Estate, Upstate, New York
An evening in March

Sindy tossed her magazine onto the chair in the corner of the room. She'd like to become engrossed in something to give herself an excuse to stay in her bedroom, but she'd read the magazine cover to cover twice and there was nothing left in it that could keep her attention. She glanced at the folded clothes stacked on the chair and debated getting up and dressed, actually come out of her room for a change tonight.

She scooched herself up further on the bed and reached over to move the curtain aside from the window. It was a beautiful night, clear, crisp and cold with a nearly full moon. She wasn't ready to head out into the woods and risk running into the Crimson Coven again just yet, but she couldn't spend another night cooped up in the house. Maybe she could go take a walk around the immediate grounds, following the pathways through the landscaped bushes that were prettily covered with snow.

Her gaze wandered to the top of the driveway and she lost all ambition to leave the bed. The driveway was empty now, but she could clearly envision the car she had seen there the other night. It had been a sleek little dark red car, driven by a lovely, sophisticated woman with dark red hair; a woman who'd turned out to be someone Sindy had hoped never to see again.

Felicity had come to visit. Cain had gotten out of the passenger side of the car and rushed around to open the door for her as though practically tripping over himself to treat her with the utmost chivalry. From her view out the bedroom window, Sindy could see just by the way Cain looked at Felicity, that he adored her just as much as he had in the past, if not more.

Felicity had definitely changed. Not only was she better dressed than usual, wearing high-end boots and a chic, tailored jacket, her posture was straight and tall, filled with confidence, probably at least partially fueled by the fact that she'd dropped a few pounds. It also couldn't hurt that Cain was obviously mesmerized by her presence; the woman was in complete control. Sindy had to admit that before, the girl had been pretty, with an innocence that guys could find appealing, but over just the past few years, she had grown into a beautiful woman, in command of herself and entering the prime of her life. Even in a pair of snug and shapely jeans, Felicity had managed to look polished and mature.

Sindy let the curtain fall back over the window with a snort of disgust, blocking out the imaginary replay. Personally, Sindy had always felt confident and in command. She'd been forced into adulthood far earlier than she might have liked, and had been carrying herself with the poise and confidence of a woman since well before the age of sixteen. Once she had rid herself of her maker and her father, in that order, very few people could make her feel like any less than the powerful woman she envisioned herself to be. But looking out that window and seeing how the passing years had worked changes in Felicity, made her feel a sliver of doubt that was now eating her up inside.

Just a few short years. What differences might there have been in Sindy, if she had just been given three or four more years to be human? If she had been turned into a vampire at the age of twenty, rather than sixteen, would there have been any noticeable difference? She'd always been mature for her age, and with the right clothes and make-up, she'd begun passing for twenty-one to enter bars long before she'd become a vamp. By this time, chronologically, Sindy was 24, but her body was that of a lithe 16 year old. She'd always felt that she fully looked like the adult she was, but how did she really look to others? It was horrifying to think that others might perceive her as a teenager playing dress-up, to think that *Cain* might see her that way.

It didn't matter. She didn't have any clothing with her now, only the boring black pajamas Cain had left for her. He'd barely even spoken to her since healing her injuries. To be given his blood, in such a loving and intimate way, had been so much more than she had ever expected or hoped for from him. She had thought that he'd definitely changed his way of thinking about her. Then she'd come downstairs and everything had been awkward and put her on the defensive. After that first night, she'd taken to bed to avoid Mattie and Alyson.

Then she'd seen Cain out on the driveway with Felicity a few nights ago. When they'd entered the house, Sindy had not dared to do more than open her bedroom door a crack and try to listen, but Cain had closed them away in the parlor, out of earshot. She'd heard him getting drinks from the kitchen, but other than that, she could not even guess the direction their visit had taken.

Sindy had given up and gone back to bed. She'd toyed with the idea of coming downstairs partially dressed, but never actually left her room. She knew that the look on Felicity's face would be priceless, but Cain would surely be furious with her. It wasn't worth getting kicked out, especially in front of *her*.

Felicity's car had remained in the driveway until Sindy had heard it pull away well after sunrise. After an interminable amount of time, Sindy had heard Cain ascend the stairs and come down the hallway. She'd laid still in bed, hoping that he would stop to check in on her, since she'd left the door open a crack, but the next thing she'd heard was the closing of his bedroom door. She had not seen him since. During the nights after, she could guess from the near silence, he had spent a good amount of time alone, locked away in his room.

Mattie and Alyson were easy enough to avoid. Apparently, Cain had requested privacy, because Sindy heard nothing from them for a few nights after Felicity left. She couldn't see their trailer from her window, but even once she heard them begin to come around again, they never entered the house until at least an hour after sunset. It had become her habit to sneak downstairs as early as possible, before it was even full dark. That way she could prepare herself a huge helping of blood from the refrigerator, drink it down quickly and bring another up to her room before anyone else was up and about. Cain seemed to begin his nights alone at the desk in his room. She could hear the chair being moved on the hardwood floor. So far, she had always managed to get back into her room before he came out of his. She desperately wanted to see him, but she wanted him to come to her.

He *hadn't* come to her, though. Eventually she'd begun to hear regular activity in the house again, but no one ever came to her door to bother with her. She wasn't sure if she should be relieved, or insulted. Maybe she should just get dressed and go talk to him. Suck it up, so to speak. She couldn't spend forever haunting his house like a ghost. Thoughts of the day he'd spent in her bed feeding her, gave her warm shivers. She wanted so badly to see him.

Sindy was startled to hear her doorknob turn. She barely had time to sit up better in the bed, throwing the covers back to expose her shapely legs in the hope that Cain was entering the room. When the door opened however, she was severely disappointed. Alyson stood there, unapologetically, and appraised Sindy's appearance.

Sindy tugged the sheet back over herself and gave Allie an irate glare. "Don't you knock?"

Allie just cocked an eyebrow. "How long you plannin' on hiding out up here?"

Sindy turned away from Allie in disdain to look out the window. "I'm not hiding. I just haven't felt like seeing anyone."

"Except for Cain," Alyson conjectured.

Sindy looked back at her with a falsely self-assured smirk. "Cain is exceptional."

Allie was quick to correct her. "I think you mean Cain is *an exception.*"

"No, he's exceptional," she repeated with a thoughtfully wicked grin.

Allie rolled her eyes. "You never give up do you?"

"Why should I?" Cain had originally invited her here. She had no reason to believe he didn't want her to stay, did she? Was it so irrational to think he might want more? Alyson must know more about Cain's visit with Felicity than Sindy did. She would never give Allie the satisfaction of being asked about Felicity, but she couldn't help wondering what Allie knew about Cain's true feelings. Alyson was a pain in the ass, but she could usually be counted on for a straight answer. Finally, Sindy just came out and asked. "What does he think of me?"

Allie smiled with bemused surprise that Sindy would ask her. She paused in thought before answering. "Jury's still out on that."

Sindy dismissed the uninformative answer. "He wouldn't tell you anyway."

"He wouldn't have to. I'm really good at reading people. He just doesn't know what he thinks of you yet. He does have a soft spot for you, God knows why, but you keep doing things to piss him off."

Sindy chuckled. "He'll get over it. Gives him a reason to try to tame me. Guys like a challenge."

Alyson shifted her weight, her arms crossed over her slight chest. "There's a big difference between playing hard to get, and acting like a low class whore."

Sindy squinted at her for a second in disbelief. "Get out of my room."

Allie ignored the request. "Nice try, but technically you don't live here. Cain brought you in, but I guess he hasn't formally invited you to stay, so this isn't *your* room, and you can't un-invite me." She watched Sindy with an annoying, self-assured smirk before going on. "I know what you did, and that it's why you got your ass whipped by that girl from the Crimson Coven. I don't know how things work over there, but intentionally screwing someone else's boyfriend is frowned upon pretty much anywhere. Cain went and talked to them. He knows about the whole thing." She shook her head mockingly. "He's very disappointed in you."

"Shut up."

Allie laughed and sat perched on the corner of the dresser. "Relax. He will get over it. He's kind of sweet on you, in a distanced sort of way. Be patient and give him space or you'll push him away."

Sindy watched warily as Allie made herself at home, hopping up to sit better on the dresser. "Why are you giving me advice?"

Alyson looked at her long and hard. It almost felt as though she were looking inside of Sindy to what others couldn't see. It was very uncomfortable. Finally, she answered, "Because he needs someone, and maybe it could be you, if you aren't stupid enough to screw it up."

Sindy thought about that and then leaned back with a sigh. "I don't get you. You're the one who found me out there in the woods, right?" Alyson gave a small nod while watching Sindy discerningly. "So you called Cain to come help me, because you thought he might be lonely? I'm sure there was a part of you that wouldn't have minded just leaving me there."

Allie chuckled. "Can't deny that. But if I didn't get you put back together, I wouldn't have a chance to ask you all of the interesting questions I've got." Sindy looked at her inquiringly. "I saw you...before you got gutted like a fish. I saw the whole fight." Sindy tried not to give her the satisfaction of flinching at her harsh description. Allie continued with a smirk. "So…what, now you're a werewolf too?"

"I'm not a werewolf!" Sindy spat back in disgust. "I'm a vampire, same as you. Well," she added with a smug smile, "not *just* the same as you. I'm a special breed."

"Let me guess, red eyes, right?"

"That's right. And with those eyes come talents most vampires never even knew existed."

"Like turning into a wolf." Allie shook her head in disbelief over the amazement of it. "What is with that? If anything, you'd think vampires turned into bats," she said jokingly.

Sindy gave her a sly grin. "I can do that too."

Allie hopped down off the dresser in amazement. "You lie!"

"No it's true. I can fly," Sindy said with a smile, enjoying the effect of the statement more than the actual act. The truth was, she hated trying to fly. It was terrifying. Still, the look on Allie's face was worth the boast.

Hopefully she wouldn't have to back it up any time soon. "Girl, I've got skills you've never even dreamed of."

After a moment of soaking in the information, Allie gave her a strangely cunning grin. "Is that right? I hope you're having fun up on that high horse, because you aren't going to be there for long."

"What are you talking about?" It was very disconcerting, looking up at Allie from where Sindy lay on the bed. The girl was wearing tall leather boots that gave her normally tiny frame a nice bit of height. Sindy wished she would sit down again, rather than hover over her.

Sindy sat up taller, folding her legs underneath her. Alyson sensed her discomfort and sat next to her on the bed to speak more confidentially, still sporting that annoying, crafty smile. "I'm a special breed too," she announced. "As a matter of fact, I'm about as special as they come. Maybe even one of a kind."

"Yeah right," Sindy replied sarcastically. "What color are your eyes?"

"White."

"*White?* What's so special about that? What can you do?"

Allie laughed. "What can't I? Ever seen a prism?" She was met with a blank stare. "Like when white sunlight shines through a raindrop and refracts into every color to make a rainbow." She paused, but Sindy didn't grasp the implication. "That's me."

"So now you're Rainbo-Brite? What the hell does that mean?"

Allie broke into a broad grin and sang in a soft and lilting voice "Anything you can do, I can do better. I can do anything better than you."

"No you can't," Sindy answered, unintentionally giving the next lyric to the song.

"Yes I can." Allie finished the verse. "Don't you get it? I'm all breeds in one. Every color, every power, all within me, just waitin' to be discovered. The wolf thing kind of threw me, though. Never expected that one. Thanks for introducing me to such a nifty addition to my bag of tricks."

Sindy just sat there staring at the girl. Could it possibly be true? She had noticed a few oddities about Alyson since she'd been changed, but she hadn't yet seen her in her vampire state. Her mark was damn bright though, brighter than any normal mark should be.

Alyson gave her a little clap on the shoulder. "Actually, I guess I kind of owe *you* a thanks anyway. It's all your fault, you know. I could have been a regular vampire with no notable powers and nothing particular to do, hanging out with my boyfriend and loving death. Thanks to you, I get to be a *Descendant of Darkness*. Training and responsibility, looking over my shoulder for all of eternity in case among the groupies trying to worship me, there's some creep trying to kill me to keep me from spreading my special blood. Great gig, huh? Got to admit though, it's got its perks."

This was all going a bit fast to follow. "I don't get it. What's a *Descendant of Darkness?*"

"Never mind. Actually, my official title is *The United One.* I have the blood of all breeds in me, united, and it's all thanks to you."

"You keep saying that. What does your blood have to do with me?"

Allie eyed her in mock sympathy. "It's about your breed. See, Mattie had most of 'em when he turned me, most but not all. In fact, he's got all but one. Guess which one he's missing."

"Red."

"That's right, and lucky me, I already had the missing piece, just waiting for the puzzle. See where this is going? 'Member when I staked you?"

Sindy thought back over the occurrence. "You missed…and you licked it." Outraged realization came over her as she remembered Cain mentioning the incident as well, and put together what had happened. "You licked the stake, you fuckin' freak, and now *my* blood is in there turning you into some kind of super vamp?"

"Yup. Remember at the dance, when you said that you were a *lioness* and we humans were all just a bunch of little jumpin' gazelles?" Alyson stood up over the bed, spreading her arms. "Meet the lion tamer," Allie announced with glee.

Sindy shook her head in disdain. "Is there no justice?"

"Seems pretty *just* to me, after all the shit you put me through."

"I never cared about you. It was Ben I was after. You should've stayed out of the way."

"I figure I'm collecting on Ben's behalf too, since he was too soft to dust you when he should have."

Sindy smiled. "Ben was never *soft* around me, trust me." Allie was obviously getting ready to lose her cool. Sindy decided to back off a bit. Well, maybe after just one more dig. "I'm guessing you don't see him much these days," she asked in a softer tone, although she couldn't quite hide her smirk.

Alyson eyed her stonily. "No. And I never want to hear *you* mention his name again."

"Touchy, aren't we?" Sindy considered taking it further, but after a moment, the fleeting urge to needle her passed. Still, she wasn't planning to spend the rest of her time here worrying about offending this biotch. "If you didn't want to hear from me, you should've just left me in the woods after the fight," Sindy informed her.

Allie just stared at her for a minute before sitting back down on the bed. "I know. Guess I'm a better person than I would have thought. Lucky you."

Sindy shrugged. "Wouldn't have killed me anyway."

"Maybe not, but it sure would have been a slow and painful recovery, assuming the Crimson Coven didn't decide to come back and finish the job."

Sindy let out a small breath of a laugh. "If they'd wanted me dead, they would have just killed me. Long and painful was what she'd had in mind. It was a warning."

"That girl Tempest, everyone in the Crimson Coven, they're like you?"

"Honey, nobody is like me."

"They can turn into wolves," Allie clarified. Sindy nodded in confirmation. "And you can't change with your clothes on, can you? That's why I found you naked," Allie concluded. "That's why the Crimson Coven is always walking around naked too. It'd be a pain in the ass to keep changing clothes every time you wanted to change forms." Allie pondered that for a moment. "Cain keeps clothes for them in the garage, in case they need to be out in public. He knows."

Sindy gave Allie a reprimanding look for her slow wit. "Of course he knows. They've been living on his land for over a century. He knows about me too."

Allie knew she was right, but seemed very bothered by it for some reason. "But if he knows, why didn't he tell *me?*"

Sindy smiled. "Maybe you're not as special as you thought; not in his eyes."

Allie shook her head. "You've got a lot to learn about how things work around here these days. He didn't tell me because he's trying to slow me down, make me be careful."

"Yeah? How's that working out?"

She and Allie shared a grin at the thought of Alyson meekly following careful direction. Finally, Alyson stood from the bed. "This could work. We're not finished here. You and I are going to have some pretty interesting chats ahead of us. You are going to show me the rest of those impressive skills you were bragging about, and I'll see if I can get Cain to come around for you. But you'd better stop acting like such a bitch, because not only does it try my patience, it's totally turning Cain off. I'm not a miracle worker."

Alyson walked over to the door, to leave Sindy to ponder this interesting new development. She opened the door and then turned to Sindy before leaving. "And by the way, stay the fuck away from *my* boyfriend or I'll make you wish Tempest had finished the job. I don't do warnings."

~~~~~~~~~~~~~~~~~~~~~~~~~~~~~~

The United One. It sounded so official and important. Was Allie really as big a deal as she seemed to think she was? Whether she was or not, she seemed to have Cain's attention at the moment, judging by the way he allowed her to act as though she owned the place, and…by the fact that he had shared blood with her.

Cain had forged a blood bond with Mattie and Alyson. Why would he go and do that? He'd spent plenty of time with other vampires, including Sindy and her little coven…before things had gotten out of hand. He'd certainly never offered to share blood with them. If he went so far as to not only mark Mattie and Alyson, but to let them mark him back, there must be something important going on. That was a serious display of loyalty. It seemed as though the three had been here together since she'd left a few years back. For Cain to keep them together as a coven, and practice blood sharing for that long on a regular basis, meant it was probably a safety issue. Knowing Cain, that was the only thing that made sense. He thought they were in danger. He wanted Mattie and Alyson kept close.

Now the question was what he wanted to do with Sindy: keep her around, send her back over to the Crimson Coven, or send her packing in earnest. He'd offered to include her in their coven, but he'd been healing her at the time, and felt badly over her surprise to learn the three of them were marked. She couldn't treat it as a serious offer…yet.

She'd decided to spend one more night alone in her room. She was interested to see if Alyson truly planned to talk to Cain on her behalf. She wasn't sure she liked the idea of gaining help from Alyson, or that she needed it, but it wouldn't hurt to spend another night in her room until she decided just how she should play things.

Sure enough, the next night there was a knock at her door as soon as the moon rose. "Sindy?"

It was Cain. Sindy hadn't gone downstairs early as usual. She'd been lying in bed, awake and thirsty, lost in thought over her conversation with Alyson. Cain rapped lightly on the door once more. "You're still in there aren't you? Can I come in?"

She rolled over in bed towards the door, smoothed her hair to lay prettily on the pillow, and then did her best to sound sleepy to account for her hesitation. "Yeah, sure. Come on in."

Cain opened the door and entered, carefully balancing two mugs in one hand. "I hope I didn't wake you. It's full dark." She sat up and shook her head, making space for him to sit next to her as he entered the room and handed her one of the mugs. "I was waiting for you downstairs," he explained. "I know your habit has been to go down early. When you didn't come down, I decided to bring something up to you."

"Thanks." She was looking at him curiously. He was taking a sip from his own mug, when he glanced up and noticed her observation. "Why were you waiting for me?" she asked.

"Because I have been a terrible host this past week."

"I know how to help myself."

"Yes, but it was unfair of me to leave you alone for so long without even checking in. I'm afraid I had some things of my own to deal with. Forgive me."

She certainly wasn't planning to ask about it, and have him bring up Felicity. She shrugged as though it made no difference. After a moment of indecision she asked, "Did Allie tell you to come talk to me?"

He looked surprised by her question. "Why would you think that? No, she hasn't said a word." Sindy just stared at him for a moment until he had to confess. "Well, she didn't *say* anything, but she did give me a mental nudge."

"A what?"

"Alyson has got telepathic abilities. She can speak within one's mind. She planted a seed of thought for me to seek you out. It was little more than your name, but she knew it would force me to stop selfishly focusing on myself, and come to see you. She thought she was being subtle I'm sure, but I can always tell when she's been poking around," he said with a slight tap to his temple.

"Can she read minds?" Sindy asked in mild alarm.

Cain nodded, "Usually. She has a harder time with vampires that haven't shared blood, but she's an empath too, so she picks up the general implications if not the details."

"What's an empath? Is that like a lie detector?"

Cain laughed. "It can be. Empathy is the ability to share another's feelings or emotions. I should think that would make Alyson a very difficult person to lie to."

File that away under annoying information to remember. "Good to know."

Cain shook his head with a smile. "I suppose I should tell you that Alyson is a very gifted vampire. Telepathy is not her only skill. She does in fact have the rare advantage of accessing every talent available to vampire kind." Sindy raised her eyebrows as though surprised, while listening attentively. It seemed that what Allie had told her was true. Lucky bitch.

Cain continued. "She was made with a mixture of blood from every species. An accident of incredible odds, but...there you have it. There are old stories that tell of such vampires, legends that say all were such until somehow split into the breeds we see today. The coming together of blood to re-create this ancient united breed is an event of prophecy. The vampire of all breeds is called The United One, and is supposed to be a leader for the species, destined to take a position of divine royalty."

"Royalty?"

Cain gave her a small sympathetic smile for her disbelief. "That's how the story goes. That doesn't make it true. Few are left who've even heard the legends, let alone believe them. You and I know that Alyson is still...Alyson. However, don't discount the legends entirely. Her eyes do shine with the light of power, and there is no doubt that she has been gifted with a special sense of command over other vampires. I've seen those lesser made become mesmerized at the sight of her vampire eyes."

"Arif can control others like that."

"This is even more so. She controls them almost unconsciously. She may not have plans to become a leader, but she has been given the opportunity, accidental or not."

"What does she think of that?" Sindy asked.

"Not much, yet. She enjoys her abilities, but she hasn't got designs beyond her own personal existence with Mattie. I'm glad for that, but she needs to be prepared for whatever position she may find herself forced into in the future. That is why I've requested for them to stay here for the time being, and why we share a coven mark. She may find herself in need of guidance and protection, at least until she becomes more experienced."

Sindy nodded thoughtfully. "I was wondering why the three of you seemed so close. I mean, you always kept yourself pretty distanced from the other vampires you helped." He lowered his eyes, regretfully. He had never allowed himself to be so close with Sindy in the past, when he'd been trying to guide *her*. She felt a little better knowing that Allie had special circumstances. It wasn't personal. She met his eyes with another question. "So if she has every ability, does that mean she can shift shape too?"

"I believe so, although I don't think she's encountered it yet. I've been encouraging her to focus on only one ability at a time, so as not to be overwhelmed. I'd rather you didn't mention it to her just yet. Why did you think she sent me to see you tonight? Have you two been talking?"

Sindy didn't even hesitate. "Not really. I figured she'd send you up here to find out when I'm leaving. I've been here for a while now and I'm sure she can't wait to get rid of me."

Cain shook his head. "No. I think she just felt I was being neglectful and should come see you. How've you been feeling?"

The gentle concern in his eyes could just make her melt; and he probably wasn't even trying to be anything but platonically nice. She tried not to show how his attention affected her. "Better."

"Does everything seem to have healed properly? I trust you didn't have any trouble with the cookies."

"I'm fine. Everything works." She chose not to provide details about how incredibly painful it had been though. Digesting those cookies had felt as though she'd swallowed a gut full of glass. Whatever scuffles she might find herself getting into in the future, she would never again forget to guard her intestines.

Judging by the pitiful look he gave her, Cain was familiar with the painful process. "I'm glad you're alright."

How embarrassing. Here she was hoping that Cain might see her as a romantic prospect, and so far, their conversation had consisted of how he'd been neglecting her to sulk over Felicity, Alyson's talents, and whether or not Sindy could take a shit. This visit definitely needed a change in direction.

Sindy took another sip of the blood in her mug and summoned the courage for a real apology. That would be the mature thing to do, wouldn't it? Better to get it out of the way now and put it behind them. "I'm sorry about all the trouble I caused. I shouldn't have come hanging around your property without even letting you know I was back. It was disrespectful."

Cain dipped his head in a slow nod. He agreed, but accepted her apology. She continued. "I was just curious about the Crimson Coven. I've never met anyone else who can do the things that I can do. I wanted to see what it looked like, from the outside, and how they handled things."

"I understand that completely. That's why I wanted to introduce you to them. However, I can't say how you'll be received by them now. Tempest is a highly respected member of their community, and I doubt she's willing to accept you at this point."

"I never meant to make anyone mad at me. I was skirting the top north corner of the property, where the woods meet that field. Nick was patrolling the perimeter and he saw me. He was in his wolf form, but I knew who he was; I'd been hanging around for a while by then, and I'd seen him before. I recognized his mark. I haven't really shown myself to anyone in my other form, and he was very appreciative of it. He's seen plenty of wolves besides me, so it was pretty flattering. He makes such a large, strong wolf, and I was curious…"

Cain cut her off with his hand held up flatly before her. "Spare me the details. Did you know that he was attached to Tempest?"

She gave a slight nod of admission and a shrug. "It didn't seem to bother *him* any. He came back to meet me there more than once." Not to sound as though she were bragging, but she didn't want Cain to think that she was here at the house begging for attention, as though she didn't have any other prospects. He put on an impressive display of not caring one way or another. Couldn't his feelings for her elicit just a little sliver of jealousy to satisfy her ego?

"I'm not here to judge either of you. Tempest has already dealt with each of you as she saw fit. You're consenting adults and your activities are none of my business or interest," he informed her impartially, but then he took on an annoying expression of disappointment, as though he felt she'd been naïve somehow. "It just seems a bit short-sighted on your part. Do you realize that you've hindered your opportunity to gain knowledge and experience in shifting from the only true coven of shifting vampires known to be on this continent?"

Really? …Damn. Being with Nick was a pretty memorable experience though. Maybe it was worth it. Cain was still staring at her in disapproval, waiting for comment. "No, I didn't know that. Tempest isn't coven master though, Khalon is. Can't he just tell her to get over it?"

"Khalon may be leader, but his loyalty to his coven demands that he support a respected member over an outsider, especially when most would sympathize with her position. Why should he throw his community into social upheaval for you?"

She didn't have an answer for that. What did he want her to say? "So, do you want me to leave?"

He gave her a tender smile. "No, I don't. I just wish you would think about the implications of your actions…before they get you into trouble. As far as actions already taken, you'll just have to deal with the results."

"Results as in, the Crimson Coven hates me now."

"They don't hate you. Most wouldn't even know who you were without Tempest spreading ill reputation for you. And Tempest is a proud sort, so I've a feeling she isn't going to be speaking to many of the incident. I understand that Nick has left the coven to travel back down south for the time being. I'm sure it will blow over. The coven will eventually accept you, if Tempest allows it."

"If Tempest allows it? Why would she want me hanging out with her coven? Even if *they* don't all hate me, I'm sure *she* does."

"You could be right, although I believe the wound she gave you should be considered sufficient payback for the ordeal. I'm sure she'll need some time to cool her temper, but I think I've found a way to settle things between you. I've taken the liberty of making use of a loophole in coven law, to be used to our advantage for the situation."

Sindy furrowed her brow at the use of the word *our*. Was Cain just including himself as being on her side? It sounded like something more. "What loophole?"

"Well, if you were a part of the coven, it would be within Tempest's rights to deal with you as she saw fit, in light of your…disagreement. If you wanted to argue that, you could take it up with Khalon."

"But I'm not a part of their coven."

"Precisely. That means that you are covered under my house rules as a guest of my property. She tried to argue that you were trespassing, but I had already told them to expect you, and you had been given a standing invitation. My rules clearly state that there is to be no hostility on my property. That applies to anyone not covered by Crimson Coven law, and Tempest broke that rule."

"What does that mean?" Sindy asked. "Do I get to gut her?"

"No. It means she is in debt to me for her indiscretion. I have found a way for her to pay that debt, which will accomplish something I'd already been planning, in a more controlled environment than I had hoped for.

I'm going to require that Tempest report here at the house on a regular basis for a time, to be a trainer for Alyson in the art of shifting. I had planned all along for Alyson to eventually learn from the coven. I think learning from a private tutor will be more advantageous than being thrown into a group, and according to Khalon, there is no better teacher than Tempest."

Sindy just stared at him for a moment, slightly insulted. Why wasn't he asking Sindy to teach Allie how to shift? Didn't he think she was capable? *Alyson* had been happy to ask for her help. Admittedly, Tempest was over half a century older than her, and very good with her skills, but once you figured out how to take the form, what else was there to know? Besides, Sindy was the one who was supposed to be getting special attention and help from the coven, not Allie! "So what does that have to do with me?"

"Well, I thought we could kill two birds with one stone. My original intention was to have you learn from the coven as well. You can join Alyson in her lessons and have opportunity to ask any questions you've been harboring." Sindy looked at him in disbelief. "That way it can be done here at the house, and you can spare yourself acclimation into the coven until all has blown over. Tempest is under obligation to me to be on her best behavior as a fair and honest teacher, and it will give you two a chance to clear the air and start anew. I don't plan to have her start until the fall though. She has a trip planned to visit a coven out west for a few months, and collect a red-eyed vampire from them to join the others here. I thought it better to wait until her return, than to rush her here now. Give her a chance to settle her ire. I think it will work out fine."

"Fall…as in next year?" They were still buried in snow at the moment.

"About six months from now. I hope you'll remain as my guest until then, unless you have obligations elsewhere."

She pretended to think about it for a minute. "I guess I could stay. I don't know if it was worth all the trouble though. I don't know about Allie, but I don't need *lessons*. I've figured everything out just fine by myself. I was just hanging around for a little observation, that's all."

Cain smiled, looking as though he was humoring her. She tried not to let it piss her off. "From what I saw, you do have very impressive control. But I would never venture to say that there was nothing left to learn. If there is no new knowledge or experience left to be gained, then what is the point of existence? Always be open to new perceptions. You'll find it invaluable as your mind ages, something to keep you from growing weary of the world. There should always be a hope for something new." He looked very tired as he said it, as though his mind had wandered to his own expectations and disappointments.

He wanted the possibility for something new? She'd bet she could teach him a thing or two if he gave her the chance. "Fair enough." She took the last sip from her mug and placed it on the nightstand, laying back a bit on the bed. "So," she began with a hint of a grin, "what do you want to do from now until fall?"

He returned her smile in earnest, finished what was left in his own mug and collected hers as he stood from the bed. "Well, for a start, I was hoping you might accompany me on a walk outside."

She held his gaze for a moment. She'd rather have him here on the bed, but that was obviously not on his mind. She slipped out from under the covers and slowly crossed to retrieve the pants that were folded on the chair.

She took her time, giving him a nice view of her long legs before covering them. Were all of her artful displays of her body just a waste of time? She wished she knew for sure if he even noticed. Much of the time he seemed to act as though he was above even bothering to look, but she knew men. She liked to think of this as laying the groundwork. He may pretend not to notice, or to be unaffected, and maybe he really wasn't thinking of her that way at the moment, but the image was there for him. He would find himself catching a glimpse now and then, in spite of his best intentions. At some point, when he was feeling more receptive and thinking about her, those carefully placed poses she had shown him would come to mind to fan his fire.

A short time later found them lazily following the paths around the house, wandering between snow-covered evergreens and small holly bushes. Cain asked if she'd like him to find her something to cover her feet, but she knew he wouldn't have anything to offer other than a pair of his own boots. She was perfectly happy walking barefoot in the snow and feeling the soft, cold crystals between her toes. It was oddly like walking barefoot at the beach on a cool night, only squishier. The cold didn't sting and hurt the way she remembered it feeling when she had been human. It was just...cold.

Cain filled her in on some of the things he and Mattie had been working on with Allie, and told her more about his relationship with the Crimson Coven. He asked what she had been doing these past years, before she had come back to his estate, but she broad-stroked over the details.

She had basically just wandered North-Western New York, practicing her shape changing, hunting small animals, and loving the freedom of it. Whenever she'd grown tired of being a lone wolf in the woods, she visited a few colleges for company. Colleges could always be relied on when she needed a place to stay and a few good meals. The parties were fun and she could fit right in with the age group without raising suspicion. The guys were always accommodating, more than happy to let her crash for the day in their dorm rooms. She could drink her fill of drunken frat boy blood without even being noticed, as long as she was careful not to take too much from any one guy.

When she'd become bored with wandering, she'd visited Arif's coven. She'd come across them by accident, but it had been an interesting diversion. But Arif wouldn't allow her a true place there yet, and she'd found herself curious about the Crimson Coven once again. Re-visiting Cain, now that her pride had healed, was a welcome idea. She'd made her way to his estate to observe the shifters and think about whether or not she might give things with Cain another try. It hadn't gone quite as she'd hoped, but now that she was here, out walking through the snow with him in the moonlight, she was glad she'd come.

Finally, she and Cain wound up lying on the ground in the snow, out in the middle of the front lawn where they could best look at the stars. Cain turned to her, resting his head on his elbow and playfully tossed a small snowball at her.

It was good that she was keeping things casual, and not being too forward. She could just tell that he felt incredibly relieved to be able to relax and enjoy himself with her, without having to worry that it meant anything in particular. She got the impression that although he was close with Mattie and Alyson, and enjoyed their company, they were often wrapped up in each other. She could understand how he might sometimes feel like a third wheel. He enjoyed the fact that Sindy truly wanted to spend time with him.

He was watching her with a smile as she shook the snow from her hair. "Do you think you might be persuaded to change for me?" he asked.

What kind of change, she wondered defensively. She'd given up her coven of followers, and stopped killing people. Wasn't that enough of a change? What the hell more did he want from her? "What do you want me to change?"

"Into your wolf form," he clarified.

Oh…that. She tried not to show how stupid she felt for misreading the question. She shook her head lightly. "You don't have to act all interested, like it's some kind of novelty. You see the Crimson Coven do it all the time."

"I told you that I'm not very close with them. I've seen them shift, but I don't spend time with them really. I approve of their wish to be independent from society, and not hunt humans, but we don't have much else in common.

Besides, it's not a matter of wanting to see the act of shifting itself. I wanted to see you…in your other form. From the glimpse I was given that New Year's Eve, it was beautiful. I wanted to see you that way again, if you were so inclined."

After a request like that, how could she say no? Without a word, she stood from the ground and brushed the snow from herself. Her clothing was only mildly damp, since she had no true body heat to melt the snow.

She stripped herself of her clothing, laying it aside on the ground. Cain didn't turn away for modesty or seem uncomfortable with it. Neither did he seem very affected by her nudity, but he watched her attentively with a gentle smile.

Now she was a little nervous. She hadn't often shifted in front of anyone before. She'd done it recently a few quick times with Nick, but that had been done in a haze of passion and haste. It was much different to have someone sitting there watching you with full attention.

She met Cain's eyes and held his gaze as long as she could, as she let herself slowly disintegrate into a thick cloud of dark smoke. Tiny particles of Sindy, floating in the air, only barely able to retain awareness of her surroundings. Sometimes she felt inclined to stay this way, just let herself float on the breeze without a care, but it was impossible. She didn't have the strength to keep herself in this state for more than a moment or two. She could already feel the inexorable pulling together, a demand to take form. If she didn't choose one, she would revert back to her default human shape.

She pictured the wolf in her mind, large, strong, dark, and sleek. The blueprint for the form was already inherent within her. Somehow, the blood knew how to form the wolf that she pictured in her mind. Good thing, because she had only a vague idea of all the organs and functioning parts needed to actually build such an animal. Not that she actually needed any of those organs, but the blood seemed to insist that she form an exact replica.

She felt herself lowering towards the ground and settling at about half her normal height. As with most of the Crimson Coven, she was fairly large for a wolf, but not unnaturally so. Now that her blood had been given the command on how to reform her body, it was a swift and automatic reformation. Without further thought, Sindy felt herself settle into the solid, muscular shape of a large dark wolf. The slight breeze ruffled through her fur. She closed her eyes and lifted her snout slightly to catch the scents around her on the wind.

Cain took back her attention. She could smell the subtle scent of his aftershave. He'd made some small sound of amazement, just a hushed intake of breath. Her ears swiveled to catch the sound and she opened her eyes to see him smiling back at her.

He sat up in his place in the snow, and observed her with undisguised appreciation. His form looked very pale to her, because she was seeing him mostly through shades of gray, though each edge was in sharp relief.

She shifted into her vampire state, preferring her more colorful heat seeking vision. As her eyes shifted spectrum, she felt her vampire fangs distend beside her canines. Now she was wolf and vampire. If she were to hunt, she could inject her venom with a single bite and take her prey down easily.

She took a few steps towards Cain, who now stood, and was smiling broadly, as he gazed into her red vampire eyes. "You are absolutely beautiful." He said it with complete sincerity. "I never know how to react around a vampire wolf," he admitted with a self-conscious laugh. "My natural inclination is to reach forward and run my hand over your fur. It looks so thick and soft, inviting to touch. Is that rude, to pet you like a dog?" he asked tentatively. "I'm not close with any of the Crimson Coven as I am with you. I wouldn't dare to touch them unbidden, but you I feel comfortable to ask."

She wished she could laugh. He was smiling with the delight of a child, but also looked cautious, and almost shy. It was very unlike him. She moved closer and nudged his hand gently with her nose. She could understand how odd it might be, to feel as though he were with an animal, but to know full well that the mind of a full grown, independent woman was within. He wanted to fondle her freely as he would a pet, but as he would not dare allow himself to when she was a woman.

It felt so good to feel his strong hands on her. Hesitant at first but soon more fully, he stroked the fur down the length of her back. It wasn't long before he became comfortable enough to more intimately brush his fingers from the tip of her snout down to the soft fur of her cheek, beneath her eye, and then ruffle the scruff under her throat.

After a few moments of this, she teased him by quickly turning and gently catching his hand in her jaws. It startled him to jump, and then laugh at himself. She released him and lay down in the soft snow, her mouth open, tongue lolling, and her tail thumping lightly to clearly show her playful humor.

He sat down next to her, still appreciatively running his hand down her side in repeated strokes from her ribcage down to her soft belly. It felt wonderful, even accounting for the scar tissue that was still present from her injury. How strange it seemed that only in this form he felt unashamed to admire and fondle her this way, as never before. She wondered how he would react if she suddenly shifted back into the form of a woman. He would immediately withdraw, she decided. She didn't do it.

He spoke to her quietly, admiring different aspects of her shape and occasionally asking a question, although she couldn't properly answer. She absolutely loved her wolf form. It made her feel powerful, independent, and unafraid, in the way that becoming a vampire had made her feel in comparison to being human. As a vampire, she had the tools to seduce men with her body, drug them with her venom to gain whatever she needed, and was unafraid for them to truly harm her. As a wolf, she had the tools to be even more independent than that. She was stronger, faster and could hunt animals for her food without fear of harm or discovery. She didn't need anything from anyone, except maybe attention. To have Cain fawning over her like this made the form even more rewarding. Its only downfall...its lack of speech. It would be nice to be able to speak to him as a wolf, but then again, that would probably ruin the illusion and bring back his sense of polite personal space.

Sindy knew from observation that the Crimson Coven had perfected communication in their alternate forms of wolf and bat. Not only had they learned the signals of body language, combined with a few simple sounds to give meaning, as true animals did, but they had their own patterns of language as well. For one thing, she knew they used their marks to communicate. She had seen them take down deer while in small hunting parties. They had mastered complete control of their marks and would dim, flash and show them in patterns to mean different things as they split up and surrounded their prey. The deer could not see the marks, and there was no audible evidence of the vampire wolves trailing and silently closing in on them.

Some of the coven seemed to be slightly telepathic as well. She'd be willing to bet that none of them could use telepathy on the level that Alyson was probably using it, from what Cain had told her, but they could get their meaning across. Simple commands sometimes came through to her, as she lay hidden, a mental eavesdropper watching the coven coordinate an attack.

Try as she might, she couldn't accomplish a single mental word that was acknowledged by another. She just didn't have the gift. It was very disappointing, but she could tell that many others in the coven didn't have it either, so she was not alone. It was just one of those random vampiric talents sometimes carried through from mixed blood, not a true trait of the breed.

Sindy tried now to express herself to Cain telepathically, but it was no use. His conversation was forced to be one-sided. Finally, she grew impatient at being unable to speak to him, however comfortable his gentle caresses were. As his hand rested lightly on her side, she allowed herself to disassemble into a smoke cloud once more. She tried to shift into her womanly body as quickly as possible, but he removed his hand as soon as she began to change.

Sindy once again appeared as her human self, lounging in the snow beside him, nude. He sat awestruck for a moment, and then handed her the shirt she had worn out here. She took it, but laid it aside without putting it on. Honestly, he didn't even seem to notice. He was still tickled over her shape change.

"That is absolutely amazing," he told her quietly. "I don't think you understand just how much I admire not only your abilities, but the strength of character and poise with which you *own* them. I could never handle the things you've discovered with the grace and determination that you have. To find such unexpected gifts, and then have the courage to practice and hone them until you have mastered them to this degree, without any support or even prior knowledge of their existence, is very impressive indeed. It speaks volumes of the woman you truly are, Sindy."

She gazed at him in assessment and then gave him a smirk of a smile. "I've finally impressed you, huh?" She rolled onto her stomach in the snow and made swirling patterns on the ground layer with her finger. She shivered as the cold snow pressed against her breasts and caused her nipples to harden. "I think it's more than that." Cain looked at her curiously, as he lay down similarly, opposite to face her. She propped herself up on her elbows, hoping to give him a better view of her pert breasts beneath her.

She looked up to watch him thoughtfully before explaining herself. "I think it excites you. I think that you like the idea of having a little *wild* in your woman. You just don't want to admit it." There was a bit of sheepish guilt in his expression, although he shook his head in dissent, playing with the snow distractedly. "It doesn't make you a bad guy you know. It's not like you're under some kind of moral obligation to only be attracted to a woman who's pure as the driven snow." She tossed a light handful of the stuff at him for emphasis.

He put his hands up to guard his face, catching most of it, but rather than smile as she'd expected, he became sullen and quiet. He played with it in his hands while deep in thought, and then finally spoke what was on his mind. "Snow... I don't even know if she exists any longer. Felicity *Snow* is soon to be no more. She'll be taking some other man's name now; become some other man's wife."

It took a few minutes to register. That's right, Felicity's last name was Snow. If she'd remembered, Sindy would have done anything to keep from reminding him of her, even though they were out here laying in the stuff.

"Felicity's getting married?" she finally asked in surprise. "I didn't think you'd allow that. Isn't she supposed to be inconsolably pining away for you, until you finally give in and decide to go back for her?"

He took the acid comment better than expected, and answered her seriously. "No. Where's the point in that? I told her to go and live her life. What kind of life would it be, spent brooding alone?"

Sindy couldn't help but raise an eyebrow, and chuckle at his answer. "Maybe you ought to ask yourself that."

"I'm not alone," he responded, sitting up defensively. "I have Mattie and Alyson," he reminded her.

"Right. Tell me, do they comfort you during the long days when you can't sleep because thoughts of *what could have been* keep swirling around in your head, making you question every decision you've ever made?" He eyed her accusingly for speaking the truth aloud, and making him acknowledge it, but he didn't answer. "I didn't think so."

She sat up and scooped more snow into her hands, turning it over and firmly pressing it to no avail. "Look at this. I can't even pack a damn snowball," she said with a laugh. "I'm too cold. It won't melt enough to stick. Must be time to go hunt, and get some warm new blood in these veins." He looked up from his private introspection with slight alarm over her statement. "Don't worry, nothing big. Just something to take the edge off."

He didn't acknowledge her. He was lost in thought again. She stood, dusted herself off, and took a step towards the woods. She would change as she reached the tree line.

Now Cain sat up more fully, realizing that she was leaving. "Stay."

She stopped and turned towards him with some disdain. "I'm a wolf, not a dog. I don't *do* commands." She put her hands on her hips and took a step back towards him. He had such a pitifully forlorn expression. "You need me to stay and take your mind off things," she asked, "so you don't have to think about the future Mrs. Whatever-her-name-will-be?" He didn't say anything. She couldn't imagine what he could say. "Well, I think I deserve to be more than a distraction. I'm going on my hunt now, and then I'll be retiring to my room, if that's okay with you," she told him sarcastically. "When *I'm* the one on your mind…then you can give me a whistle and see if I come." With that, she changed back into the wolf and took off into the woods.

Part 2

Undying Devotion

Chapter 6 - 'Til death do us part

Felicity

Upstate, New York
An early Saturday morning in late June

The flowers were late. The flowers were late, her dress was too tight, because somehow she had suddenly gained five pounds, and she was never going to make it on time because although the limo had arrived as scheduled, her hair still wasn't done. What else could go wrong on her wedding day?

Felicity was ushered into the limousine in a daze. She wasn't listening to Deidre chatting away beside her from beneath a mound of teal taffeta, but she came back to awareness as she saw the church pass by outside her window. "Where are we going?" she asked in a panic as the church disappeared from view.

"Oh…there was a slight snag. I'm afraid the church wouldn't accept you," Deidre informed her.

"What? Why wouldn't they accept us?"

"Don't worry. It's all been worked out. You'll just go with plan B."

Felicity regarded her friend's optimism with confusion. "I had a plan B?"

Deidre leaned in confidentially. "Of course. Don't you think everyone knows? You've always had a plan B!" Before Felicity could voice the flushed guilt and embarrassment that she could feel creeping over her, Deidre continued in a manner far too cheerful, "And good news, the florist finally showed up!"

Felicity found her door being opened, and she was led out of the car and through a gate by someone she couldn't quite see. She began to recognize the indistinct swimming feeling of haziness and confusion that told her this might not be what it seemed. Was she dreaming? She tried to see the faces of those around her, but although she'd stepped out into a crowd, there was no one familiar in sight. This must be a dream.

She entered a small courtyard where all was quiet and serene. No, it wasn't a courtyard, it was a cemetery. The graves were all covered with mounds of white roses, and ribbons were strung from headstone to headstone, to line the aisle that had been laid out with a white runner over the grass. It actually looked rather pretty in an odd way.

Someone thrust a bouquet of flowers into her hands, but she was suddenly alone in the silent space. Friends and relatives were nowhere to be found. Who would attend a wedding in a cemetery?

The sun shone brightly over the graves, and she slowly made her way down the aisle, looking down at the flowers she held. She found that a cluster of black roses was clasped in her hands. That wasn't right. "I'm supposed to have Ben's roses, with all the colors and their special meanings. They shouldn't be black. What do black roses even mean?"

As though summoned by his name, Ben suddenly stood before her. "I think they symbolize death."

Felicity looked up at him with a smile, grateful for his presence. He was radiantly handsome in the sunshine, as his honey brown eyes gazed upon her lovingly. "Ben!" She said his name with relief, as though she'd been lost and he was there to rescue her.

"Hey there, beautiful," he replied with a smile.

"Wait, you're not supposed to see me. It's bad luck!"

He shrugged. "I don't believe in luck. Besides, I'm actually kind of busy right now. I didn't think you'd notice. You're not really thinking of me anyway."

Felicity backed away a pace in disgruntlement, as Ben drew his rapier from his hip, and she realized that he was dressed in his fencing garb. She wanted to ask what he was talking about, but he continued. "That's alright. I've been waiting. When you're ready, I'll be there for you."

Felicity tried to tell him that she *was* ready, but he'd already taken up his position in en-garde stance, to cross blades with his father, Bernard. As they moved into a sparring match, she turned away and continued up the aisle, the zinging sounds of sword fighting filling the silence of the cemetery.

It suddenly became ominously dark, which worried her, but then the moon came out, bathing the surroundings in beautiful silver-blue moonlight. She left the cemetery behind, and approached the archway of flowers at the end of the aisle, its white roses practically glowing. A man stood beneath them. It wasn't Ben. Could it be…?

Cain turned to face her. He was a heart-meltingly handsome vision of a gentleman in his tuxedo. His face was cleanly shaven, his lips turned slightly in a humble smile, and his blue eyes glistened with joy upon seeing her.

"Cain." She spoke his name quietly, like a secret treasured.

He held out a single red rose to her as she met him. "You forgot this."

She saw that the tines of the lovely emerald hair comb he had given her, were once again woven through its stem, as when he'd returned it to her the last time she'd left it behind. "Oh yes, I almost forgot!" She took it eagerly and placed the comb into her hair.

He clasped her hand as she finished, and she expected to feel the warm and magical current of his mark on her skin...but it wasn't there. She wasn't his. She met his eyes and the surge of love she felt course through her was quickly replaced with trepidation. "But how are you even here? I thought you said we couldn't be together. You wanted me to live. Has that changed? Is that why my roses are black?"

Cain looked at her black bouquet in distaste. "No. No black roses for you. I won't allow it." He took them from her, casting them aside. "You're right though. I shouldn't be here. I just wanted you to know that I love you. Perhaps I love you too much, but I always will, regardless of rings; 'til death do us part."

"I can arrange that." Bernard's words cut through their private moment as his sword came flashing down in a swinging arc determined to separate Cain's head from his body.

"**NO!**" The screamed rebuke erupted from Felicity's lips even as she heard the sword strike unexpectedly against metal with an ear-splitting clang.

It was Ben's rapier that had clashed against his father's sword; both blades were held crossed before Cain in a surreal tableau.

Ben moved his rapier to push against the inside of his father's blade, as if to parry it away. Instead he took a small step closer to Bernard, brought his weapon to point almost vertically, and with a quick flick of his wrist suddenly pointed his blade down again on the other side of his father's, causing it to wrap around and jerk Bernard's sword from his grip, disarming him.

Hikari, Bernard's beloved katana, lay on the grass a few feet away. Bernard nodded to his son, as if to say 'well done'. He then retrieved the sword and disappeared, as Felicity turned in shock to face Cain and Ben once again.

Ben's blade was still raised up before Cain's face, but Cain stood passive and silent. Felicity, severely shaken, spoke to Ben in grateful surprise. Cain was not only a vampire, but a vampire that Ben knew vied for her heart. The last thing she would ever expect was for Ben to protect him. "I don't understand. Why didn't you let Bernard kill him?"

Ben sheathed his sword, stating simply, "It would've made you unhappy."

Felicity glanced at Cain in quiet sorrow as he silently backed away into the darkness. She turned back to Ben with a discerning stare. "You know I love him," she admitted apologetically.

"I know. And I love you. Have you noticed? I can make you happy, if you let me."

She was gazing into his eyes, her heart torn over the shock of recent events, but feeling overwhelming appreciation that he would do anything to make her happy, even if it meant protecting a vampire. "I love you too, I do."

Ben smiled. "Are you ready?"

"Ready for what?"

"To wake up."

Felicity's eyes opened with a start as she heard something bang down next to her head. It was someone slamming down the snooze button on her alarm clock.

"Wake up," Deidre repeated demandingly. "You have to get ready to say *I do!*" Felicity tried to focus her eyes. Seeing she was awake, Deidre began bustling around her, giving the bed a shake as she went to open the curtains. "Felicity, your alarm has been going off forever. Couldn't you hear it?"

Deidre sat down on the bed with a thump and then leaned closer with a smile as Felicity rubbed the sleep from her eyes. "Are you even awake yet? You have three hours to prepare to become Mrs. Benjamin Everheart!" Deidre informed her with barely contained glee.

Felicity was still trying to catch the last fleeting memories of her dream before they fled from reach. She met Deidre's eyes in a daze of serious thought. "He does love me, doesn't he?"

Deidre raised an eyebrow with a smirk. "Are you kidding? He's crazy about you! But if you're having second thoughts, I'd be happy to take him off your hands, not that I could fit into your dress. Ben adores you, and that makes you pretty much the luckiest girl alive! Now get a move on. It's your wedding day!"

~~~~~~~~~~~~~~~~~~~~~~~~~~~~~~~~~~~

The flowers were already laid out in her mom's living room. Felicity's dress fit perfectly, and her hair was beautifully coiffed before the limousine had even arrived. "Oh gosh, I almost forgot again!" Felicity stood while Deidre was still fussing with her headpiece.

"Felicity, sit down! Where are you going? You could've given me some warning. I almost ripped it off your head when you jumped up like that!"

Felicity was digging through a drawer in the dresser behind them. They were in her old bedroom in her mom's house. There were boxes of photo albums and things her parents didn't have storage for elsewhere, but it was still her room, and her belongings left behind had remained untouched.

Finally, she found what she was looking for, under layers of scarves in the drawer. She pulled out her prize and unwrapped it lovingly from its protective scarf. "Sorry. I can't believe I almost forgot this again."

It was the emerald hair comb Cain had given her long ago. She'd hidden it here on one of her trips back home a few years ago. The antique hair comb was as gorgeous as she'd remembered, perhaps even more so. Its swirling design of tiny little diamonds, emeralds, and sapphires across the top was so extravagantly elegant.

She never really had occasion to wear it, and had never shown it to anyone. That was probably for the best, as it was surely a very expensive antique, and she didn't want to explain where she'd gotten it. It was a private treasure. She handed the comb to Deidre. "You have to help me work this in. You can put it in the back, under my veil."

Deidre wasn't even listening to her; she was just staring at the comb and running her fingers over its jewels. "Are these real? My God Felicity, this is gorgeous! Where did you get it?"

"It was a gift, from a dear friend. I want to wear it." Part of her felt a bit blasphemous for wanting to wear something for Cain on the day of her wedding to Ben, but she couldn't *not* wear it. Cain could not share this day with her. She was moving on, and her love for Ben was true, but she couldn't help but feel that Cain deserved this acknowledgement. He'd stepped back for her to have this life with Ben, and she loved his dear heart for it.

Deidre was turning it over in her hands and holding it to different places near Felicity's hair. "It doesn't match. It can't even be your *something blue*. It's mostly green. I don't know where to put it."

Felicity took the comb from her. "It's got some blue. It's something old. Like, 400 years old at least. I told you, put it under my veil, in the back." She held it up, trying to position it as she wanted according to her limited view in the mirror.

Deidre did as instructed, but still seemed dubious about the placement. "You can't even see it."

"Good. That's fine. *I* know it's there."

Her mother entered the room in a swish of midnight blue satin. "Oh sweetie, stand up so I can look at you again. That gown is so perfect on you. You look like a princess!" she exclaimed, dabbing her eyes with a tissue to prevent make-up smearing tears.

It was a beautiful wedding dress. Felicity turned to see herself in the mirror again. She had chosen a traditional ball gown of silk with a full skirt and train, and a fitted bodice delicately embellished with a petite design of pearls and crystal swirled across the neckline. It gave her a prideful rush of happiness to think of how Ben would see her walking down the aisle in it.

Preparations continued, pictures were taken, and although Felicity was caught up and drawn into the excitement of it all, she still found herself recalling bits and pieces of her dream now and then.

She remembered hearing from somewhere that the dream a woman had on the morning of her wedding day was supposed to be prophetic, or have some sort of symbolic importance. Was that true? In her dream, Ben had stopped Bernard from killing Cain. She didn't truly expect that to happen, but what bothered her most was that in those circumstances, she really wasn't sure *what* Ben would actually do. She couldn't imagine him protecting a vampire. What did that mean?

The more she tried to recall and interpret details, the further from reach they seemed to slip. The fact that she wasn't given a quiet moment to think was frustrating as well. She considered giving up her efforts at contemplation and just trying to enjoy her wedding preparations, but it kept nagging at her.

As they entered the church, and were escorted into their respective waiting areas, they were informed that they had actually made it there a little early, and had a few minutes to spare before the minister was ready for them. Felicity approached the small group of cousins and friends acting as her bridesmaids, and pulled Deidre aside. "Dee, I have to go find Ben."

"What? He's probably up at the altar, Felicity. You'll see him soon enough!"

"No. We're early. Only the ushers are out there. He's got to be in a back room somewhere getting ready. I have to go talk to him."

Deidre grabbed her arm to keep her from leaving the room. "Why? Oh my God, you're not gonna go turn him down are you? Are you taking off like one of those runaway brides?"

"No! I'm not running away from him, I need to see him. It's important. You have to find my dad and stall. Cover for me Dee, please."

"Alright but you owe me; and if you don't come back, I have no reservations about being a very available shoulder for him to cry on, even if you are my best friend."

"Fine. Thank you. No comforting necessary. I'll be back!" she whispered over her shoulder as she slipped through the door. She navigated hallways, making her way unobserved around to the back of the sanctuary where she hoped to find Ben waiting in a back room. She had seen that her brothers were all busy ushering people to their seats in the pews, so hopefully Ben would be alone. She peeked through windows and cracked open doors until she finally found him standing alone before a full-length mirror. "Ben!" She caught his attention with a whisper as she entered the room and quickly closed the door behind her.

"Liss...you look gorgeous." He stood in awe upon seeing her, with a look in his eyes that was priceless. She wished she had more time to savor it.

He was looking dapper as ever. His thick, dark hair was slicked back, but still had a bit of unruly wave and curl to it. His face seemed made of such clean lines, with a strong, straight jaw and square chin, but full kissable lips to soften it. His large honey-brown eyes sparkled with his smile. He could've stepped right off a page from one of her bridal magazines. "Thanks. You too, you always are."

"I thought I wasn't supposed to see you until the ceremony," he said in confusion, as he moved forward to place his hands on her hips and lean in for a kiss. "Isn't it bad luck or something?"

She returned the kiss quickly and backed out of his grasp. "I know you don't believe in luck. I really needed to talk to you."

"Why? Is everything alright?"

"Yes, it's just...you love me, don't you?"

He furrowed his brow in understandable confusion and spread his hands to indicate their surroundings, as if to say, 'why do you think we're doing all this?'. "Of course I do, Liss! You know I do."

"You want me to be happy, right?" she asked with quiet uncertainty.

"Yes, always. I... I thought we were happy." He moved forward to try to hold her again, suddenly unsure of her. "Don't I make you happy?"

She gave him a reassuring smile. "Yes, you do. I just needed to know, hypothetically..." She turned her attention away from him, trying to find a way to ask what she wanted, without giving specifics, "Would you do something *just* to make me happy, even if it wasn't something that you really wanted?"

"Felicity, what is this about? Because we're getting married in like ten minutes, and you're really freaking me out here."

"I'm sorry. I just wanted to be fair to you, and ask *before* you said 'I do', because it's important to me." She moved closer to him again, feeling guilty for upsetting him, but still needing to ease her mind. "I would do anything for you, Ben. Would you do anything for me?"

"Well…yes. What kind of anything? Like, pay to add a few days onto our honeymoon, anything; or hiding bodies, anything? Give me some scale here, Liss. What are we talking about?"

She took a deep breath and laid it out. "Vampires. We're talking about the general acceptance and not killing of vampires. Except in self-defense, of course."

Ben became very still, his gaze hard with disgruntled disappointment over the topic. "Of course." He watched her for a moment before asking with a stern attempt to restrain his emotion, "What brought this on? Were you out visiting vampires last night?"

"No," she refuted vigorously, annoyed at his accusation. "I had a dream," she added lamely. "It just made me think about some things, and it's important to me to know where you stand about this. I love you. You make me happy and the life we are building together does *not* include vampires. I'm good with that, really." His mind seemed a bit eased with her statement, and he relented in his severity with a small smile. Hesitantly, she continued. "But, like it or not, we both know some vampires personally, and I would just feel better to know that if you happen to come across one, you aren't going to dust them."

"Except in self-defense."

"Except in clear self-defense, right," she repeated.

"And you would do anything for me?" She nodded in agreement. "Even if I asked you to never have voluntary contact with another vampire again, ever?"

She hoped her eyes didn't become too wide with reaction. How could he ask that of her? That brought up a whole new slew of problems and explanations she didn't want to have to get into. She was telepathically connected to Alyson, even if she hadn't heard from her vampire friend in weeks. He didn't know that, but how could she try to make a promise against it? "If that's what you want from me," she began falteringly, "and it's that important to you, I guess I would have to find a way to make and keep that promise." Hopefully that was not too ambiguous an answer. She truly wanted to respect his wishes, even if they were impossible.

He was still staring at her stonily. "Liss, I trust you, so I'm not going to ask that of you, because I shouldn't have to tell you what would make me happy. You can do whatever you want, but if what you want, is a life with me, then I hope you would act accordingly. I also hope that you trust me, like I trust you."

"I do," she said with loving relief. "I just need to know that you wouldn't do something, *or stand by and watch someone else do something*, which would make me so unhappy. I'm just looking for a general 'live and let live' sort of deal."

"As applied to the undead," he added mockingly. He sighed. "I'm not even going to ask which particular vampire you're thinking of, because I doubt I'd like the answer. It doesn't even matter. Why should vampires have anything to do with our happiness? They aren't a part of our lives."

She took his shoulders and moved closer still, wishing she could just kiss him and not give him upsetting thoughts to ponder. "No, they truly aren't, but I need you to promise me this, so that I don't have to think about it anymore."

"It's not like I would kill somebody unless it was self-defense anyway. What kind of person do you think I am? I thought you knew me better than that."

Unlike your father...she thought to herself. She held her tongue and took a deep breath. "I do. Ben, please, just make me feel better and promise anyway."

"Fine, I promise." He sounded defeated.

She felt bad to have brought this to him now, but terribly relieved to have the promise out of him. "Thank you."

"Are you expecting me to come across one?" he asked warily.

"No. I just wanted to put my mind at ease, that's all. I had this stupid dream that kind of spooked me. I know and love the man that you are, but I just had to be sure. I would never want to see you that way, as a killer." He was looking at her oddly, most likely wondering where she would suddenly come up with such thoughts. "I know how hurt you've been in the past."

She looked down at her engagement ring, which had once belonged to his mother. As a teenager, Ben had found his mom, who had been blessed with recent remission from cancer, in their driveway, drained of blood, as a message to his father, the Vampire Hunter. Ben knew, despite public claims of defeat by cancer, a vampire had killed his mom, although he'd never admitted it to her. He had to know that she had guessed the truth. Did he know why his mother was killed?

He also looked down at the ring while she spoke. "That kind of thing can drive a person to store all kinds of pent up anger and resentment," she told him with tender understanding. "I'm glad you can put it behind you. We can move on with our lives, without having to think about that kind of hostility ever again." There were tears in his eyes and she felt terrible for making him think of the loss of his mom on this day that should be full of joy. She watched him blink back tears and rally his emotions.

"How does the saying go?" he asked. "Today is the first day of the rest of our lives. I will promise you anything Liss. Just say you'll be my wife."

She threw her arms up around him in a hug of relief and happiness that they could focus only on their wedding day now. "Oh Ben, I will. I love you so much. I will make you so happy, you'll see."

He found her lips for a kiss of passionate excitement for the future. They savored it until they could both feel the impending sense that their stolen private time together should come to a close. Someone was bound to come looking for one of them soon. Ben ended the kiss, tipping his forehead against hers with a sigh. "Can we just skip all this hoopla and go to Tahiti now?" he asked her jokingly.

She laughed. "I'm not letting you out on that beach without a ring on your finger." She paused for a moment, actually thinking about the prospect of Ben noticing other girls as they walked by in their skimpy swimwear. "Are you sure you want to spend the rest of your life with *me?*"

He answered with immediate assurance. "Absolutely positive, and I'm the one getting the better part of the deal." He took her by the shoulders and turned her to face the mirror behind them. "Look at you. Not only are you my sweet lovable Liss, but you are breathtakingly gorgeous too. Who wouldn't want to spend their life with you?"

She rolled her eyes, looking away with a smile. He gave her a nudge to look up at the mirror again. "Hey, take a good look, because when I see you tomorrow, the next day, and every day after that, this is what I'll see. This is the woman who is going to be my wife, and she is *always* the most beautiful woman in the room, not just for today. I love everything about her and I always will.

Baggy sweats, messy hair, that stuff can't touch what I see in you. And as beautiful as you look today, it's still only a small glimpse of the beautiful person I see inside. I want to spend my life with you, Liss. Now let's find our minister and get this show on the road."

~~~~~~~~~~~~~~~~~~~~~~~~~~~~~~~~~

Felicity made her way down the aisle of the church and was relieved to find that it was nothing like her dream at all. There was no sense of wrongness, and rather than lost, she felt as though she'd been found. Her friends and family were all gathered about her with teary-eyed smiles as she passed by, and for once she truly felt that all eyes were on her for good reason, instead of worrying and speculating about some self-depreciating flaw from the collection she kept in the back of her mind. She was proud and confident, and it felt good, really good. This was her day; it was for her and Ben, and it was right.

She couldn't meet Ben's eyes until she was only a few feet away, because she was afraid she would have to fight back tears if she looked at him sooner. When it finally came time, her father lifted back her veil, gave her a kiss, and offered her hand to Ben. She met her future husband's gaze, and the pride, love, and loyalty she saw reflected there instantly calmed her racing heart. As long as she had Ben beside her, she would always feel comforted, safe, and loved.

The bouquet she held was composed only of gorgeous full roses, tied with a white silk ribbon. Five roses, each of a different shade. Yellow for the friendship they had always shared. Lavender to represent the enchantment of love at first sight; for even though it had not been acted upon, they'd both felt that the other was special and important to them, from the first time they'd laid eyes on one another. Orange stood for the passion of fervent desire, felt when they finally had recognized their respective feelings. Pink was for the gratitude and appreciation they each felt for the dedication and loyalty they'd shared, from even before their romance had begun. The last rose in her bouquet was white, the color of pure new beginnings. All five of the flowers were beautiful, full, and fragrant.

Ben held the final rose, a rich deep red, the color of love. He held it out to her as she met him at the foot of the altar. "Felicity, this red rose represents love, deep, strong, and everlasting. This is what I feel for you, and what I offer you in our new life together. Will you accept it from me?"

She looked up at him with a smile of loving confidence. No matter the disagreements they sometimes had, or whatever dramatic difficulties may try to surround them out in the world, she knew his heart. Ben loved her, and he would spend his life wanting to make her happy; keeping her safe and helping her to fulfill the dreams for the future that they had together.

He offered her his red rose, and she voiced her acceptance with a smile "I will," and allowed him to slide the flower into the center of her bouquet.

She was grateful her mom had been sure to loosen the ribbon around the flowers so that this addition could slide right in, because she and Ben couldn't seem to take their eyes off each other in order to ensure the flower was fitted properly. Finally, she broke their gaze as the minister spoke to usher them closer before him. The red rose was gorgeous, poking up a bit taller than the rest. After a quick glance to ensure her bouquet was as it should be, she passed it to Deidre and stepped up to join Ben before the altar.

She tried to listen to all of the opening remarks that the minister gave, but she kept finding herself lost in thought, looking at Ben and smiling over the fact that he would soon be her husband.

Six months ago, she had gone on her little adventure, traveling based on speculation and guesswork to visit Cain. At the time, she had already accepted Ben's proposal, and wedding plans had tentatively begun, but as much as she loved Ben, she had felt slightly unsure in her heart. There'd always been that grain of uncertainty in her that was trying to hold on to Cain. It was one thing to spend all of her time with Ben, loving him and having fun, but when it came to making a decision in front of friends, family and God, that she would permanently give her heart to him, forsaking all others, it had been serious enough to make her falter.

Seeing Cain had been a wonderful experience and a heart-wrenching devastation all rolled into one. He had been more handsome than memory (something she hadn't thought possible) and more loving and accepting of her than she had ever allowed herself to believe he would be. He truly was the man that she remembered him to be, and he still loved her, four years later; it wasn't just a passing thing for him, he loved her even still.

The kisses they had shared...it took a lot to try to dislodge those from her thoughts. She did love Ben, and if asked, she would have said that her love life with him left her perfectly satisfied, but those secret kisses Cain had stolen were a private memory to be treasured.

Afterwards, they had talked for hours about everything she could think of, including the course of her life. He'd kept impressing upon her how lucky she was to be born in this century. Women had so many choices open to them now. She had the same opportunities and education available to her as a man. Whether she chose a demanding career, or to be a housewife, or both, it was her choice. Of course, these were things she had always known, growing up as a young lady in 21st century America, but the way Cain regarded it all as such a privilege caused her to truly realize that women of the past had not always had such advantages. She was not forced to marry for money or title. She could marry strictly for love.

If she had been the type of woman who desired to become successful in the business world, seeking power, wealth, and professional respect, she could have pursued that. She also had the sneaking suspicion that if she had, as she'd turned older, after she had conquered what she'd sought, Cain would have come back to her. Cain would have been happy to step in and bring her to a new phase of life after she'd lived her life in the human world.

But what now? What she wanted was not temporary. What she wanted involved a commitment to last a lifetime. She wasn't looking for power or wealth. She had no head for business, and no interest in that type of career. What she loved was family. She loved kids. She loved to teach them, and she wanted to have children of her own. However old-fashioned it might seem, all she really wanted was that ideal image of a happy family, sharing life together. She wanted to be with a man she could depend on, that she could have fun with and share her feelings with; someone who respected and loved her, and who would be a good husband and father. Cain was not that man.

Were he human, he certainly could have been, but in this stage of his life, as a vampire, Cain had other goals and obligations that did not fit with her dreams. He could not have children, nor was being a father to young children something he could handle in a practical way, even if he wanted to adopt some. His children were the lost vampires that he sought out to mentor and help. He was needed elsewhere, and were it not for meeting and falling in love with Felicity, he would be perfectly happy with that. He dearly missed having a partner to love, but his larger purpose was fulfilling to him. She would never take him away from that, to try to live a human life with her.

She still loved him. It wasn't even a secret really; if asked, she couldn't even try to deny it. She loved Cain, but she was accepting of the fact that they needed to go their separate ways. Their time together was precious to her, and the conversation they had shared on that last visit was more valuable than she ever would have guessed it could be. He understood, had known all along really, and he wanted her to move on to pursue her life and be happy. He had helped her to realize that her love for her human fiancé was just as real. She would be forever grateful to Cain for that selfless act.

Ben was everything that she had ever dreamed of when she lay in bed at night as a little girl and tried to picture who her future husband would be. Not only was he sexy and charming enough to continually make her heart flutter, being with him was such a comfortable camaraderie, fun and special, without worry or reservation. They'd had their rocky times, as any couple would, but the one thing she never questioned was his undying devotion to her. She had given him ample opportunity to look elsewhere, as she'd given herself the freedom to explore her own options. But she had found only that she missed him terribly even when she was with someone else, and he was always there waiting for her with open arms.

She loved Ben, in a very real and human way. She would never stop loving Cain, but she was truly ready to stop looking back and move on. Ben was not made of the gentle mysterious magic that Cain evoked, but in some ways, he was so much more. Ben was such a large part of her real life. Not only was he handsome and devoted, wanting the same things that she desired, for him to be her husband and the father of her children, he was thoughtful, passionate, inspiring, and fun; and she loved every headstrong bit of him. She could not imagine leaving him to go off and have some other kind of life elsewhere. She needed him. She loved him, and now, she would be his wife.

Finally, the time had come, and the minister asked, "Felicity Snow, do you take this man, Benjamin Everheart, to be your wedded husband, to share your life in sickness and in health, in joy and in sorrow, in hardship and in ease, to cherish and to love, so long as you both shall live?"

"I do."

"And Benjamin Everheart, do you take this woman, Felicity Snow, to be your wedded wife, to share your life in sickness and in health, in joy and in sorrow, in hardship and in ease, to cherish and to love, so long as you both shall live?"

"I do."

"Then you may turn to one another, and recite the vows you have written."

Ben turned to her and took a deep breath to calm his nervousness. She expected him to take out the small piece of note paper that she had seen him writing out his vows on, although he'd never let her read them. To her surprise, he didn't. He must have memorized them, even though he'd told her many times that he'd never be able to remember what to say without assistance. He had kept telling her that he'd be too busy gazing into her eyes to recall the words, no matter how many remarks and arguments he could memorize for the courtroom. He must have decided that she didn't find it romantic for him to recite from paper, even though she'd told him it was fine. It made her smile to know he'd memorized it.

"Liss, from the time that I first met you, my heart knew that you were different. With you beside me, I felt secure in a way that I had never known. You spoke to something inside of me that demanded my attention, and caused me to focus on you like no one else in my life before or after.

As our friendship grew, not only did that focus allow me to overcome emotional obstacles in my life, but it began to rise above everything. When life is frustrating, frightening, and difficult, I think of you, and I know that I can be strong for us both. Together we can transcend anything life puts in our way.

I finally understand what it means to love someone more than life itself. I want to always take care of you and protect you, just as you have taken care of me in times when I needed you. You taught me how to love, and my heart belongs to you, Felicity Snow, now and for always."

The flutter of her heart and the joyful tears she needed to blink back from her eyes commanded her attention, to the point that she forgot it was her turn to speak. She just stood there smiling and looking into his eyes until Ben prompted her with a nudge. She began breathing again with a start, but forced herself to take a moment of calm composure before meeting his gaze again to speak her own vows.

"Ben, when I first met you, I hoped that you would be my friend. Now, not only am I lucky enough to know that you always will be, that friendship has grown into so much more, and now I get to spend the rest of my life with you; a life you saved more than once.

At times when I thought my life was over, when there was so much sorrow, fear and pain that I couldn't believe that I could survive, you rescued me; you pulled me out of the darkness. You have always been there for me, unconditionally. Even when we disagree, you show me that you will still be there for me, to support me, to make me feel special, and to love me, no matter what. I love you Benjamin Everheart, and I look forward to sharing our lives together."

Ben took her hand into his own, and they exchanged rings as they had practiced in rehearsal. Once finished, the minister spoke the words that made it all official. "Then by the power vested in me, I now pronounce you husband and wife. You may kiss the bride."

Ben pulled her close and took her lips with a passionate hunger that far surpassed the modest church kiss they had talked about in rehearsal. Felicity was too engaged to care. Her heart sang with the warmth of his love and the knowledge that from this day forward, they would always be together, as husband and wife. A joyous cheer from those around them suddenly brought them back to the present, and they ended the kiss. They shared a sheepish smile over the display, but then Ben raised her hand up in his own, triumphantly, and they made their way down the aisle, ready to face the world, together.

~~~~~~~~~~~~~~~~~~~~~~~~~~~~~~~

The reception hall was every bit as beautiful as she had pictured in her teenage dreams and fantasies of what her wedding would be like. They took pictures in the gardens, and as guests enjoyed the cocktail hour inside, she and Ben were able to sneak some private time alone in the gazebo, watching the sunset, and settling into being Mr. and Mrs. Everheart.

They entered the hall after the D.J.'s formal introduction of the bridal party, and they danced their way into the ballroom through a makeshift tunnel of bouquets held by their bridesmaids and groomsmen. It all seemed to go by in a whirlwind of music, dancing and visiting tables of well wishing friends and family.

"I've been wondering dear, what did you mean in your vows, when you said that he had saved your life? Were you in some sort of accident?"

Felicity smiled at the older woman before her, and shrugged. "It was figurative. You know, teenage girls always feel like their life is about to end unless prince charming comes along." The woman smiled and took another sip of her drink with a polite little laugh. Felicity finally disengaged herself from speaking to this great aunt that she barely knew, so that she could join Ben at their reception table at the head of the room. She approached to find Ben's friend Pete sitting in her high backed wicker chair sharing an animated conversation with Ben that seemed to involve positioning water glasses and drawing diagrams on the tablecloth with a wet finger.

Both guys looked up as she approached, and Pete guiltily stood from her chair. She grinned. "It's alright, you can stay," she told him. "I just thought I'd check in."

She leaned over the table for a kiss from Ben. "Hey babe," he said. "My dad was just looking for you."

"He was?" she asked in hesitant surprise. "What for?"

Ben prefaced his answer with a look of apology. "I think he had some kind of 'Welcome to the family' speech prepared for you."

Felicity rolled her eyes with a sigh. "I can hardly wait."

"He just went out into the courtyard. Do you want me to come?"

The offer was sincere, but she knew he was hoping she'd turn him down. "No, that's okay. You can stay here and hang out with Pete. I'll go talk to him."

Pete grinned and gave Ben a friendly nudge. "Dude, your wife is awesome."

Ben met her gaze with a look of loving thanks. "Isn't she? Liss, I'll come if you want. I know how he can be."

"It's okay," she insisted. "But if I'm not back in twenty minutes I fully expect you to come and rescue me."

He stood to lean across the table and give her another kiss. "Will do."

Felicity navigated her way through the guests to the door that would let her out into the courtyard. She could see that Bernard was out there alone, leaning against the gazebo and lighting a cigarette. He wore a tuxedo similar to Ben's, but his was a much longer coat with a looser cut that set him apart from the wedding party. He took a drag from his cigarette, making the end glow brightly in the newly darkened sky, and then looked up at her approach.

"Hello, dear; just stepped out for a smoke. Pesky rules don't allow it inside."

She stepped closer to allow him a kiss on the cheek. "Probably my fault," she admitted. "I thought the guests might like to breathe." He grinned at her unapologetic sarcasm. She spread her hands to indicate their surroundings as fair compensation. "It's beautiful out here though, isn't it?"

"Yes, it is a beautiful night, but not half as lovely as you my dear. Have I told you what a vision you are?"

Felicity made a conscious effort not to lower her eyes. While getting dressed this morning, her mother had impressed upon her that she should accept all compliments gracefully. She fully deserved them and she should break her habit of shyly trying to dismiss them out of hand. She was forced to realize that her mother was right, and some graceful confidence was long overdue. "Thank you."

Bernard seemed to notice and approve of her steady posture and graciousness. He took her hands into his own and she could tell it was time for whatever speech he had planned for her. "I also want you to know how very pleased I am to have you join our little family. Benjamin is a lucky man, and I believe that your marriage will be a strong and joyful one for many years to come. Your devotion to each others' happiness is very inspiring."

For some reason, his words were more heartfelt and touching than she had expected from him. She gave him a genuine smile. "Thank you. That's very kind of you to say."

"It's true. And of course it goes without saying that as an Everheart, you are under my devout protection." Felicity tried to keep the smile plastered onto her face rather than show the deflated annoyance she felt, that he had to ruin it for her by bringing up the hero bit again. "You and your future family needn't worry for supernatural interference. I will be keeping a very watchful eye to ensure your well being."

"That is kind of you," she said with forced sweetness, "but I don't expect we'll need protecting." She patted the hand that held hers with reassurance that was perhaps a bit too condescending, but she wanted her feelings to be clear. She dropped his hands and stepped back to walk away, not wanting the conversation to go further, but he stood between her and the door. It would probably be a little too rude for her to just walk away from him anyway.

"Bold words from a brave girl," he said with a hint of disapproval. "I understand that your brief experience with paranormal peril is years behind you now. You've let the memory lessen and have felt the danger fade, but believe me when I tell you, the dangers of the night are still very active. You would be foolish to discount them and forgo the protection I can provide."

She took a deep breath and sighed. Why did everything have to be about vampires with him? Couldn't he let just one evening in their life go by, focused on something else? It was probably best just to thank him and go back inside to Ben. If Bernard wanted to say anything further on the subject, let him say it in front of his son. "Bernard…"

He wasn't even looking at her as she began to speak, but raised a hand to pause her. "Shh."

Felicity furrowed her brow in confused outrage. "Did you just shush me?" she asked in disbelief.

He did it again, while concentrating on something outside of the courtyard to their left. Felicity shook her head in dismissal and was about to simply move around him to the door, when she heard noise coming from the bushes. After a moment, a man stepped through.

He was a young Latino man, with dark hair and eyes. He wore black pants and a white shirt, making him resemble a member of the wait staff. The man ran a hand back through his hair as he stepped through the shrubbery, and barely spared them a glance as he walked towards the door to the reception hall.

Bernard stood at attention before the door and spoke before the man got there. "Excuse me, but this is a private party; invitation only."

The man let out a little laugh, as though Bernard was ridiculous to try to bar his entrance. "I'm not here for the party; I just need to see someone inside."

Bernard kept his ground. "You're not invited."

The man smiled. "It's a public building though, isn't it? Don't worry *Papi,* I'm not here for the food."

Felicity looked at the man oddly. "Excuse me, do you work here?"

Now he spared her a quick glance. "Yeah, I do. You're lookin' really hot tonight, mama. Congratulations to you and your lucky man. I'm just here to pick up my paycheck. I'll be in and out in ten minutes."

Bernard did not move to admit him. "I'm afraid that I can't allow that."

The guy was obviously annoyed, and did not plan to be delayed any further by them. "Step aside, old man." He reached out a hand to push Bernard aside, but Bernard shoved him back hard for it. As the man stumbled backwards from the unexpected resistance, Bernard reached up behind his head, and to Felicity's great surprise and dread, he drew his sword from an unseen holder under his jacket, fastened down his back between his shoulder blades.

The man only had time to look up at Bernard when the sword came swinging down in an arc through the man's throat to separate his head from his body in one swift motion.

Felicity let out a choked scream, as she'd barely even had time to draw a breath before seeing this warped echo of the dreaded action begun in her dream, followed through and realized.

The man fell to his knees before his head tilted oddly to fall forward into his lap. Thankfully, as Felicity drew another breath to scream again in earnest, she was halted by the fascinating realization that the man's entire form was now turning into ash. It held for a moment as a solidified replica of the man composed of dust, and then crumpled and fell in on itself to be nothing more than a pile of dirt on the ground.

Felicity took a ragged, hiccupping breath as Bernard quickly re-sheathed his sword. It disappeared under his coat, down his back as Felicity glanced up in shaken horror. The reception went on, behind closed doors of glass, not fifteen feet from where this disturbing occurrence had just taken place. Not a single person seemed to have noticed. She stood there in stunned silence, with her mouth open, and watched everyone standing around talking, laughing, and dancing, completely oblivious to the act. The music of the DJ even seemed to have disguised her scream.

She stood frozen, watching her wedding guests enjoy themselves for a moment, and then turned to Bernard in baffled outrage. "Oh my God! Are you kidding me?" He just stood there looking concerned for her well being, while she felt herself trying to hold back an internal volcano of emotion over the fact that she shouldn't have to deal with this sort of thing on her wedding day.

Perhaps she should have felt frightened, or even grateful, but the emotion that seemed to override all others to boil out was sheer anger. She kept a thin façade of civility in her voice but actually stalked up to her new father-in-law and shoved him, much as the vampire had done moments before. Hopefully he wouldn't behead her for it.

"What did you do, stage this? Did you arrange for me to be out here, so I could watch you kill some random vampire? Am I supposed to be all grateful and beholden to you or something?" He just stood there, having the nerve to look surprised at her reaction. She gestured almost hysterically towards the pile of ash that now dirtied the white patio stones. "Who was that?"

Bernard obediently looked at the ash and then shrugged. "I have no idea. I didn't plan this." He placed his hands on Felicity's shoulders to calm her. It took all of her will not to shove him off and break away. Bernard spoke again, sounding infuriatingly reasonable. "Perhaps he was following me. Please accept my sincere apology for subjecting you to this display."

Felicity covered her face with her hands, subsequently making Bernard let go of her in the process. She rubbed her face trying to wipe away her distress and resume some semblance of reasonable normalcy without terribly ruining her make-up. She looked up again, her hands joined before her face as though in prayer, and spoke to him in a much softer tone, trying to make sense of things. "If he was following you, wouldn't he have known who you were? Do you always behead people for trespassing?" She spread her hands in askance, as she wondered why her nice normal life had this annoying habit of becoming so bizarre at such inconvenient times.

"He was not a person," Bernard reminded her calmly, "he was a vampire. And you must admit that he was unlikely to have been here with good intentions. You didn't actually believe that he was here to pick up his pay, did you? He may have been getting paid, but it wasn't by *this* establishment, I can assure you."

"Who would pay a vampire to sneak into my wedding? And I can't believe that you brought that *thing* to my reception." She gestured almost violently towards Bernard's shoulder, trying to indicate his sword.

"What thing? Hikari is not a thing, she is practically an extension of my arm, and she never leaves my person once the sun goes down. Considering the circumstances, I would say that it is a very good thing that she was here."

Felicity rolled her eyes at his childish determination to continue speaking of the sword as though it was a person. "Look, I know you're feeling all smug and proud of yourself right now." He raised his eyebrows at her and she realized she was being overly harsh as a result of being so disturbingly shaken.

She took another deep breath and nodded her head to accede that what he had done should probably not be considered an entirely bad thing. "I suppose I *am* glad to know that all of my guests will survive the reception, so I appreciate your diligence, I really do, but…"

He folded his arms waiting for her to continue and his self-righteous seeming appearance flared her anger again. "But this thing you do…in the future I would like for you to do it far the hell away from me. I don't want to know about it, and I certainly don't want to see it. I can take care of myself; me and my *future family*, no matter what you may think. I don't want your protection, and unless you plan to have a very revealing talk with Ben, you can be damn sure that he doesn't want your protection either. If you aren't willing to be open about it, I certainly don't need to feel like you're spending your time sneaking around for our benefit. Play hero somewhere else, but when you're with me, I want you to keep that sword put away. I never want to see it again!"

Felicity stormed her way past him and flung open the door to the reception hall, to be suddenly engulfed in the cool air conditioning, the warm glow of light, and the noise of the party. She began to stalk across the floor, navigating by watching people's legs so she wouldn't need to make eye contact with anyone, when she suddenly felt herself crash into someone who had stepped directly into her path.

She looked up in aggravation, to find her new husband standing before her. He put his arms around her with a smile. "Liss, I was just coming to rescue you, I swear."

She tried to take a few calming breaths to keep the crowded dance floor from making her feel suddenly claustrophobic. Ben must have seen how red in the face she was, and that she looked ready to either burst into tears or start yelling at someone, although she couldn't have said which would be more likely. "What's wrong? Did something happen? He couldn't have had anything *that* bad to say," he added with an attempt at levity.

She forced herself to let the emotion drain from her face, to be replaced with a smile for Ben. It wasn't that Bernard was so difficult to deal with, although he did rub her the wrong way at times. It was just awfully jarring to see him so closely mimic his actions from her dream, and it had really freaked her out. "No, it's fine. I can handle your dad. Could have done without the talk, but he was trying to be sweet. I just really have to get to the ladies room."

He gave her a quick kiss and let her go. "Are you sure you're okay? Because you looked kind of upset."

"Nope, I'm fine, really," she said with another forced smile. "Just a little anxious over the prospect of holding eleven yards of silk and crinoline over my head in order to pee." She moved towards the bridal suite, hoping for a little time alone to compose herself.

"Do you need me to get Deidre?" Ben asked as she hurried away.

"No thanks, I can do it," she called over her shoulder. She made her way out into the empty lobby and then quickly into the bridal suite bathroom. Once there, she closed the door behind her with a sigh of relief. She just needed some quiet to think straight and process things. A glance across the way at the wall full of mirrors told her that the room was empty; no feet showed from under the stalls. After a pause, she turned and slipped the bolt to lock the door, and then made her way over to the mirror.

Felicity leaned over the counter, resting her head in her hands. She should not have blown up at Bernard the way she had. The truth was, he trying to be helpful. What would she have done if he hadn't been there? There was no way to know if that vampire would have attacked her, or why he was there at all, but things could have gone very badly if he hadn't been stopped. It was just so unexpected and violent.

She took a deep breath and let it out slow, looking up to examine her face in the mirror. Somehow, her eye make-up was still perfectly in place, a testament to the miracle of smudge-proof mascara. She did look a bit weary though.

"Relax, you look gorgeous."

Felicity stifled a yelp of surprise, spinning at the sound of the voice behind her. As soon as she caught her breath, a large grin spread across her face. "Allie!"

Sure enough, Alyson stood behind her, leaning against the wall in the corner of the room. She was wearing a sexy black jumpsuit that had a halter-top fastened behind her neck and split to the waist, and wide legs that almost appeared to be a skirt when she stood still. It was formal enough to fit in with the wedding guests, but still very *Allie*. Her hair was slicked back and twisted up with just a bit of the pink ends showing from behind. She came forward and gave Felicity a big hug. "Congratulations."

Felicity was grinning from ear to ear. A visit with Allie seemed just what she needed right now. "You came!"

"Of course I did. You think I'd miss it? Well, technically I did miss it. Sorry I didn't get to see you walk down the aisle."

"My fault. Daytime ceremony, Ben insisted. He didn't want to wait around all day being nervous."

Alyson grinned. "How'd he do?"

Felicity felt herself fill with joy at the thought of the day. "He did great. Oh Allie, you should have heard the vows he wrote for me, they were so sweet! And he memorized them, too; it was very romantic. When he gave me the rose...did I tell you about the roses?"

Allie gave a quick nod. "Yeah, I bet it was beautiful. I wish I could have come. Would you mind if I..." she lifted her hand to lightly touch her temple.

It took Felicity a second to understand what she might mean, and then she was taken aback, but agreeable. "Sure, go ahead." She stood still, trying to be aware of anything that might indicate that Allie was maneuvering through her thoughts, but there was no hint to her of what Allie might be seeing. Nothing inward anyway, but one look at Allie's teary-eyed smile let her know that her friend had found whatever images she'd sought.

Allie gave a nod and a smile. "He looks good. I'm so happy for you guys. I wish I could just go see him. We really need to talk."

Felicity hoped the wave of trepidation that washed over her didn't seem too apparent to Allie, or too selfish. "I'm sorry Allie, but I really don't think it's a good idea. Not tonight."

Allie nodded with a shrug. "I know. It's okay. I don't blame you for not wanting him traumatized on your wedding night."

Felicity put a hand on her shoulder, sharing the disappointment. She wanted to see them reunite as friends, but regardless of the time gone by, Ben still didn't seem ready, especially not tonight. "I am sorry. Truthfully you shouldn't even be here." The words came out automatically, but as she heard them, she realized how significant they really were. "Really Allie, it's dangerous!"

Allie shrugged it off. "Don't worry, I was careful."

Felicity's voice was infused with a new sense of urgency. "No, you don't understand. It's not just about being seen by one of Ben's friends or something, *it's his dad...*"

Before she could explain further, she was stopped by the serious look in Allie's eyes. "I know. Dangerous guy with a penchant for vamp hunting. I've been given the scoop, but if I didn't believe it before, I sure as hell do now. I can't believe he beheaded that guy right in front of you!"

Felicity felt the shock come rushing back, thrilled that she could let out her pent up outrage over it. "I know! Wasn't that insane?" After a moment's thought she added, tentatively, "He wasn't…with *you*, was he?"

"No," Allie quickly shook her head. "Mattie and I are exclusive now," she added with a little smile, flashing Felicity her own ring. "I don't know who that guy was. I'm here alone. I travel better by myself. I had just gotten here and was trying to figure out where you were. I wasn't really snooping, but I felt you getting all agitated, so I tuned in."

"That's okay, but how did you know about Bernard? Did you get that from me?" Felicity asked.

"Uh-uh. Before tonight, I didn't even know that you knew about him. I try not to go rummaging around in people's heads, and I never really noticed it in your surface thoughts before."

"I've been trying to block it out," Felicity admitted.

"So how do you know? He told you? Oh my God, does Ben know?"

"No, Bernard won't tell him. He thinks that Ben doesn't even know vampires exist."

"So why did he tell you?"

"Believe me, I wish I didn't know. When Ben first introduced me to him, I was still marked…by Cain. He saw it. I tried to pretend that I didn't understand what it was, but Bernard wasn't buying it. He sort of cornered me, and I had to tell him something, so I pretended like it was a random attack. I think he loves the fact that I'm 'in the know', because now he's got someone he can protect and brag to, that actually knows what's out there to be protected from. Still, the whole thing gives me the willies. I know he'd like me to think of him as a hero, but the idea that he's some kind of vindictive killer keeps creeping into my mind."

"Wait a minute. What do you mean he saw it? You mean he saw the bite on your neck?"

"No, my *mark*. He could tell it was from a really strong elder vampire too. I couldn't deny it."

"How is that even possible? People can't see marks."

"It's a long story that I also wish I didn't know, but the bottom line is that he ingested a lot of vampire blood and now he can see marks. That's how he tracks and kills vampires so easily. They can't sneak up on him in the dark, and they can't hide from him in the daytime." She eyed Allie nervously. "You're cloaked, right?"

"Always. I still can't believe he can see marks though, just from drinking some vampire blood. I didn't know people could gain abilities that way, without being turned. Can he do anything else?"

Felicity shook her head. "That's all he can do as far as I know."

Allie's eyes suddenly widened a bit. "You knew that it was possible to get powers that way, though," Allie insisted falteringly. "You knew all about it, considered it even! Oh my God, you and Cain have talked about it before. Did you ever drink any?"

"No." Felicity answered shortly, flustered by Allie pulling the information from her. "Why even ask me? You can just read it straight out of my head."

Alyson was immediately repentant. "Sorry. That was really rude. I try not to do that, I just get ahead of myself sometimes, before I realize."

Felicity couldn't imagine what it would be like to have everyone's thoughts open to her for the reading. The temptation to pull any information needed would be difficult to reign in for anyone. She gave Allie a smile and nod. "It's alright."

It was just unsettling to Felicity, because memories and thoughts of Cain seemed very private, yet Allie had read them as though they were an open book.

She elaborated on the information Allie had been referring to. "Cain and I did discuss it once. He's had a little experience with a human gaining abilities by drinking vampire blood, but he said it's very dangerous. It's unpredictable and hard to control. I admit it sounded kind of interesting, but he wouldn't give me any. The last person he'd given it to died, and even when he tried to turn her, it didn't work out well."

Allie nodded soberly. "Well, Bernard isn't having any problems with it."

"You said you'd been given the scoop," Felicity said thoughtfully. "You knew before you got here? Who told you? I didn't think anyone else knew."

Allie chuckled. "A hobby like vampire killing doesn't exactly go unnoticed in my circle. Vampires talk. But don't worry, I am safely invisible to the psychic eye. He'll never even know I was here. So let's not waste anymore time talking about it."

Just then, someone startled them by rapping on the door. After a slight pause, Felicity rushed to the door, looking back at Allie in trepidation. "Sorry, I'm in here. You can use the ladies room behind the bar," she called out. There was silence, and then the person moved off down the hall. Felicity came back to Allie with a giggle. "Well, I am the bride. I can hang out in the bathroom if I want, right?"

Allie nodded. "Until Ben comes looking for you." She grabbed Felicity's hand to give it a squeeze, but became distracted by her wedding and engagement rings. "Nice rock," she said with a wink.

"It was his mom's," Felicity said quietly.

Allie gave a little nod, understanding how special it was to Ben. "I know. He really loves you. So tell me how it feels to be Mrs. Benjamin Everheart."

Felicity answered with a sincere smile. "It feels great."

"Good, then it's official. Now he's your problem."

They shared a laugh, and then Felicity put a reassuring hand on Allie's shoulder. "He will eventually come around about you. I've been working on him. It's just that for now, it's been good for us to be able to concentrate on getting our lives in order and just be regular people, you know?"

Allie nodded, although it seemed her bottom lip was slightly trembling. Felicity squeezed her shoulder and Allie looked back up at her with a smile. "I always thought I'd be a part of it, the day that Ben got married. You know, stand by his side as some sort of unconventional best man or something."

"He had my brothers."

"Oh."

"I'm so glad you're here though, Allie. It really means a lot to me. I've missed you."

"Who was your maid of honor?" Allie asked in an impartial monotone. She seemed to have reigned in her emotions. She was trying to appear strong and unaffected by the fact that she was so removed from the event.

"My friend Deidre," Felicity answered. After a moment's thought, she added. "She used to be my best friend."

"Used to be?"

"We used to talk on the phone almost every night, for hours, even after seeing each other in school all day. I can't even say what we talked about. We would just go over everything from the day, and we could each relate to what the other was going through. We've grown apart though. It's not her fault. I guess I'm the one who's changed. I have a different perspective on things now, one she can't really understand. She's still my friend, she's just not my best friend."

Allie was watching her closely. "So who's your best friend now?"

Felicity shrugged. "I guess I'm in the market for a new one. Tough job, though. It has to be someone who's willing to be available for a couple of hours a week, not physically, but at least to talk to. They'd have to be a good listener, understand my feelings, and try not to judge, but be willing to give advice. They'd also have to promise not to disappear for months without checking in, and they'd have to be there for me in times of emotional crisis, even if it's inconvenient. It's kind of a rough gig. I'd do all that in return though. So it's an even trade."

Allie was trying not to grin. "That's a tall order. I have a lot of demands on me right now, which is kind of new for me, and I can't say I'm good at not letting people down. But I am loyal and understanding, so if you think it would work out, I wouldn't mind trying the position."

Felicity raised her eyebrows, feigning surprise. "Sure you're up for it? I *was* thinking it was kind of a waste to be telepathically in tune with someone who barely makes any time for me, but I still hoped you'd be up for the challenge."

"Well you've been all preoccupied with wedding stuff," Allie began, defensively. "Maybe that's part of a best friend's job, but every time I tuned in, you were picking out napkin colors or tasting wedding cake; which by the way is very frustrating to someone who can't even hardly taste stuff anymore. You can't blame me for tuning back out for a while. It's not like I was gonna be much help on whether the place cards should have had little ribbons glued to them or not."

Felicity kept Allie in a steady stare, refusing to let her off the hook. Finally, Allie relented. "Okay, you're right, I should have checked in more often. I'm sorry. But I have a lot of stuff going on too. Stuff you wouldn't believe."

"I'm sure you do. You know, you're welcome to talk about it any time. I'm a good listener. Just because I'm not a vampire, doesn't mean I couldn't still be a good best friend."

Allie lowered her gaze guiltily. "It's not because you're human, there's just some stuff that I don't think I should share. Please don't be mad at me."

"It's Cain, isn't it? You see him…like all the time, and it makes it awkward for you to talk to me, having to edit him out of everything. Am I right?"

Allie acceded with a tilt of her head. "It does put me in an odd position. I don't want to bring up old stuff and maybe mess up what you have now. You and Ben are so good together and you guys are gonna have a wonderful life."

Felicity cocked her head inquisitively. "How do you know? Do you have some special vampire power that lets you see into the future?"

Allie chuckled. "No dummy, I just know it. Don't you? I *saw* the way he was looking at you as you came down that aisle, and judging by the amount of love for him I feel in you, I'd say it's a sure thing. You guys are gonna do great."

Felicity welled up and grabbed Allie for another hug. "Thank you Allie. Thank you for coming. It's the best present I could have asked for."

Allie looked away as she let go. "Yeah about that, I didn't actually *buy* you a present. Mattie called me cheap, but honestly, I know you too well to think you want another china gravy boat or some nonsense. So I'm giving you something you can really use. In fact, it fits in well with the whole 'best friend' deal."

Felicity gave her a look of surprise and leaned back against the counter with arms crossed, waiting to hear about this interesting gift. "Okay."

"Like you said, it seems kind of waste to be telepathically in tune with someone, and not get anything out of it, right?"

"That's not exactly what I said," Felicity told her with a laugh.

"Close enough. The thing is, as a vampire prodigy, I'm in a position to do some interesting favors." She held up a hand to stop Felicity's protest before it could be made. "And being such a good person and all, I know you would never take advantage of that, or ask me for anything of dramatic proportion. But what good is being able to do stuff, if you can't figure out how to help your friends with it, right?

I haven't really figured out anything clever or unexpected to do for you, in fact, I don't even *know* everything that I can do. So here's your present."

Allie reached into her pocket and pulled out a little slip of paper. "Remember when you were a kid, and you couldn't afford to buy real presents for your parents, so you'd give them silly coupons for hugs or chores and stuff? It looks kind of dumb, but hear me out." She handed the paper to Felicity. It was a note of the size you would find inside a fortune cookie. It read:

Felicity – I.O.U. a Favor – A

"I am giving you a monumental favor, to be called in at any time, no questions asked. You screw things up, your life is overwhelming, and you don't know what to do, call me. No judging or reprimand for whatever mess you need cleaned up, I will just come and do whatever you need me to, to put things right again. Pretty awesome gift, huh?"

Felicity laughed, "Awesome and unique. Thank you Allie."

"So you don't have to feel guilty about asking, it's a gift. I know you wouldn't normally ask me, but I'll tell you straight out, brainwashing and subtle memory alteration, are quickly becoming some of my specialties. Probably not something I should be proud of, or use often, but I'm sure they could come in very handy somewhere along the way. I am at your service for a secret favor of questionable ethics when you need it. I know most people give money at weddings, but I thought this could be more useful. Congratulations."

"I will try to use it wisely."

"Oh, I almost forgot! I have a real present for you too." Allie reached down into the other pocket in her flowy pants and pulled out a sealed envelope.

"You didn't have to," Felicity insisted.

"This one's not from me," Allie told her as she handed over the card.

Felicity froze as an anxious chill ran through her. "Who's it from?" Allie just stared at her, knowing no answer was needed. Felicity couldn't help the wave of indecent guilt that flowed over her at the thought of Cain. She shouldn't be thinking of or speaking about Cain here on her wedding night.

"Oh relax, it's just a card," Allie said impatiently. "Take it."

It was a plain, large ivory envelope, unmarked. Felicity turned it over in her hands without opening it. "He knows?"

"Well, yeah. I had to tell him. He seemed to expect it though. You guys must have talked about it, right?" Felicity nodded mutely. "But when I mentioned it, the only vision in his mind was you. He didn't seem to have a face for the groom, so I didn't name names. He doesn't know that it's Ben?"

Felicity shook her head, trying to decide how to voice her feeling over it. "I don't know why, I just couldn't tell him. I thought it would be easier for him if he didn't have to picture anyone. It's enough that he knows I've moved on."

"You still love *him* too, don't you? I don't have to *read* that," she added in quick defense, "it's pretty clear."

Felicity looked up with an almost frightened expression of guilt. "Does that make me a terrible person?"

Allie quickly shook her head. "No, you're not a bad person at all. You truly love Ben, and you're starting a new life together. You don't have to stop loving Cain. He's in the past. You love Ben more than him now, and you'll love Ben a little more every day. It's okay." She gestured towards the card. "He's happy for you. It's hard on him, but he's really trying to be happy. Open it."

With slight trepidation, Felicity slid her fingernail under the edge of the flap and ripped the seal. It was a large, beautiful wedding card, covered with lovely embossed designs of flowers and doves. She held her breath as she silently read his hand written inscription.

Dear Felicity,

Congratulations on this momentous occasion in your life. Please accept my blessing, and know that I wish you and your husband nothing but the best experiences that life has to offer.

May you always believe in yourself as I believe in you, and may the light of joy always shine upon you and your family.

While money definitely does not ensure happiness, life is always a bit easier when you have something in the bank, so please accept this gift. I hope that it gives you the freedom to make choices for your family from the heart, and that it makes the future just a bit brighter.

With deepest regards,

Cain

Felicity stood staring at his perfectly neat and flowing penmanship, with its old-fashioned swirls. She could picture him sitting alone at a desk, in a dimly lit room late into the night, trying to decide what he could write, that would be considered appropriate and still show the depth of his caring for her.

Tears came to her eyes and she had the inconsequential thought that although it had put in a good showing, there was no way that her waterproof mascara was going to survive this. She raised her hand to her face and tried to keep the large teardrops from ruining the ink on the card or falling onto her silk gown. Allie quickly handed her a tissue without comment.

Cain wanted so much for her to be happy; she knew that he did. He wanted to see her have a family and a human life. Only she knew how badly he must wish that he could be the one to share it with her.

Alyson stood silent, seeming to understand that Felicity didn't really want words of reassurance. There was nothing to say. She seemed to feel a warm current of comfort from her friend though, and it helped her to take a deep breath and pull herself together.

Felicity read the last paragraph of the note again. A gift? She turned the page of the card and realized that there was a folded paper there, between the pretty tissue paper backing, and the actual back of the card. As she took out the paper and unfolded it, she found her legs becoming weak and she immediately backed up to sit in the parlor chair behind her.

As it turned out, the chair wasn't actually *behind* her, but off to the side. Allie caught her and quickly guided her to the seat. "What is it?"

Felicity stared at the paper, trying to be sure that it was what she thought. "It's a cashier's check."

"That's nice, that he sent you a present. I thought he might."

Felicity met Allie's eyes. "It's…it's a half a million dollars."

Allie's eyes widened. She truly hadn't known. "Wow. *Really* nice."

"It's crazy!"

"No it isn't. A million might have been a little much, but $500,000 is just enough to buy a house."

"An amazing house," Felicity insisted, trying to impress her shock on Allie, who seemed far too easily tolerant of the whole thing. "I can't accept this."

Allie crossed her arms with a huff. "Sure you can. He wants you to have it. It's a gift. It's not like you don't need it."

Felicity sat back indignantly. "We'd do okay without it."

"Of course you would, but wouldn't it be nice not to have a mortgage? Are you gonna tell me you couldn't use that money? He's got it to spare, and he wants to see you off to a good start. I think it's really sweet."

Felicity shook her head, trying to make peace with the idea that she couldn't keep the money. "Ben would never accept it."

"Why not? He knew Cain too. They were friends…kinda." Felicity almost laughed at the stretch. "Okay, maybe not really, but it's not like they're still rivals or something. Ben is your husband now. He won. Why shouldn't he accept the money? It's not awkward, like you still see Cain all the time or anything. You had one visit in four years…" Allie stopped speaking in sudden shock. *"You kissed him?"* she suddenly asked in surprised accusation.

Felicity covered her mouth as though she'd spoken the secret rather than Allie having pulled it from her thoughts. "I wish you wouldn't do that," she mumbled in reprimand. "It was a kiss goodbye."

"Twice?" Allie asked, without making apology for reading her mind.

"And a hello kiss," Felicity admitted. "I hadn't seen him in years, and we had a lot of unresolved stuff to work through. It is over though. I told him I can never see him again."

"Good. Then it's okay for you to accept the money."

"I know he is trying to show me that he's okay with things, and it is very generous and thoughtful of him to want me to have this security, but Ben would never accept it! What is this, my dowry? This is the twenty-first century and I am married to Mr. Prideful, remember?"

"Well you have to take the money because it will break Cain's heart if you don't. He is trying so hard to be gracious about everything, and I don't need him thinking you're insulted or mad at him. Just take the money and tell Ben it's from a rich uncle."

Should she? Felicity knew that it wasn't nearly as consequential to Cain as she was making it out to be. For him it was probably just a kind gesture, giving him peace of mind that he could make things a little easier for her. He was so worried that after leaving her to a human life, it might not turn out to be all that she'd hoped it would. This was his way of trying to watch over her, seeing as he couldn't be there himself. Truthfully, she thought it was sweet and had no real problem accepting it from him. But what about Ben? Would the rich uncle idea work? She looked back up at Allie. "There is no way Ben is going to accept a gift like that from someone he's never met or couldn't thank in person."

Allie raised an eyebrow. "Well you'd better figure something out, because I'm not letting you use up your favor from me on something silly like this," she suddenly looked toward the door with an odd expression on her face, "and I think he's coming."

Felicity desperately looked for some place that she could put the card and check. Finally, she tucked the check into her corset, but the card was too big. She wasn't willing to leave it. After a moment's indecision, she carefully ripped out the tissue page with Cain's writing on it, folded it up, and stuffed that down into her corset as well. She probably should have just thrown it away, but that felt unappreciative somehow.

Meanwhile, Allie was standing pressed up against the door. She wasn't listening with her ear to it, as you would expect a person to do. Instead, she had one hand pressed to it as though she could feel right through the wood. Her head was tilted a bit to the side and she had a bittersweet smile on her face.

They both jumped a bit when he knocked. "Liss, are you in there?"

Allie was just standing there, in the way. Finally, Felicity came up behind her to answer. "Yes, I'm here. I'll be out in a second. Just freshening up."

"Are you okay?" he asked. "I've been worried about you."

A big grin spread on Allie's face as she nodded in affirmation of his words. Felicity gave her a lop-sided smile in return. "Don't worry, I'm fine. Just takes a while to get everything back into place. I'll be right out."

"Okay, well we don't have a lot of time left. I want a few more dances with my beautiful bride before we have to leave. Hurry up. I miss you."

Felicity wanted to unlock the door, to give him a quick kiss and ask him to wait, but Allie shook her head, anticipating the action. If she did, Ben would surely push his way in for time alone with her, and then he'd see Allie. Felicity sighed. "Just another minute, I promise."

They listened to Ben walk away, and then Allie turned to her in happy excitement. "I could feel him. I could hear him! In his head, I mean. Last time he was all angry and dark inside and he pushed me out. I thought maybe he would always be closed to me and I couldn't read him ever, but he was just too far away. He's so happy, Felicity. Oh God, he loves you so much and he is so happy. He really deserves it too. He hasn't had things all that easy."

Allie paused for a second's thought and then began speaking almost too quickly for Felicity to keep up with. "I could probably still read him, even from here, now that I know what he feels like. I could pick him out of the crowd. I wonder what he thinks of me. He couldn't still be mad, right? He's had so much time to think about things. He couldn't possibly still feel the same way. If I take a peek into how he really feels, I'll know better how to handle it, and then I could come out for a real visit, and maybe I could make things good again between us."

Felicity took her by the shoulders. "Slow down. Allie, don't. It's a bad idea. Listen to me. I know it's got to be tempting to search his thoughts, and I know you mean well, but you can't do that. Not only is it unfair to Ben, but if you go digging around where you don't belong, you're apt to find something you'll wish you hadn't. It'll just hurt that much more. You have to give him the opportunity to put his thoughts into the right words. If you just go snooping for yourself, you might not interpret things the way he really means them. Give him a chance. You know he is slow to change, but he will come around eventually. I truly believe that. This is a big deal to him. *You* are a big deal to him. I know it seems like it's been forever, but he needs some more time. Trust me."

Allie sighed, defeated. After a few moments of thought, she gave Felicity a tight hug. "Alright. Thanks. You'd better get out there. Don't keep your handsome hubby waiting."

"Okay. And don't forget to check on me now and then, when you're not out flying around the world being superwoman."

Allie laughed. "I promise. I'll be thinking of you."

Felicity slipped out the door into the empty lobby. As she made her way towards the reception, someone came to meet her, but it wasn't Ben. Bernard came to her with a look of apologetic concern. "Felicity, I'm so glad I've found you. I feel terrible that you were so upset by the confrontation in the courtyard."

She quickly looked around for Ben, and then pulled his father off to the side, as what she hoped was a brilliant idea popped into her head. "Forget it," she told him quickly, "Look, I need you to do something for me, and then we'll be good, okay?"

He seemed taken aback, but interested. Felicity reached down into her corset and pulled out the check from Cain. She had to stifle a giggle at the expression of indecent surprise on Bernard's face when she reached into her cleavage for it. He looked around to be sure they weren't observed. She glanced down to be sure it was the check and not the note, but she had the right paper. She handed it to Bernard. "This was a wedding gift, sent to me by my ex. I haven't seen him in years," she fudged a little. "He's a sweet guy, and he's got some money and was just trying to be nice."

Bernard looked at the check and then back up at Felicity in stern seriousness. "That's quite a gift."

She shrugged as though it was not nearly as staggering to her as it really was. "He's very generous. He knows he'll never see me again. It was just a nice gesture. The thing is, I know Ben wouldn't want to accept it."

Bernard glanced down at the check again. "Probably not."

"But we could do a lot with that money. It was a gift to *me*, and *I* want us to have it. I want you to tell him it's from you."

"What?" he asked in confused astonishment.

"I know things have been a little strained between you, but Ben really cares about what you think. You're always so busy, that it would mean a lot to him for you to be truly *interested* in our lives. **Not** in a stalkery, hanging around outside to protect us from evil kind of way, just *interested*. He doesn't need you to be his hero. He just wants you to be his dad. He's used to you giving money as gifts and he would accept it from you. Tell him that you really want to see us off to a good start, because I know that's true."

Bernard gave her a warm smile, seeming heartened that she wanted to see him strengthen his relationship with Ben. Before he had a chance to answer, the groom himself came to find them.

"There you are. I thought you were coming to dance with me," Ben said, giving Felicity a kiss and putting his arm around her waist. She had to smile. He thought he was rescuing her, as he had been meant to earlier.

She beamed a smile at him. "I was, but I got snagged by your dad here. He wants to give us another gift." She gestured towards the check in Bernard's hand, which he then obediently held out to them at her prompt.

Ben took it with a grin. "Dad, you already gave us your gift."

"I know, but it wasn't nearly enough. I wanted you to have something that showed you just how interested I am in seeing you and your new bride off to a good start in life. I'm very proud of you, son. Your accomplishments in school, passing the bar, and having the good sense to marry a beautiful young lady of such uncommon intelligence... I wish I could do more to show you how I feel."

Ben seemed truly bewildered by his father's words, but not nearly as surprised as he was when he saw the amount on the check. "Holy cow. Dad, can you afford this?" Ben asked, showing it to Felicity, and then holding the check out to his father.

Bernard just pushed the check back at him. "It's yours, for both of you. See, I've even put it in Felicity's name, because she'll have the good sense to put it in the bank, rather than try to give it back. Put it in right away, before you get bogged down in paperwork over name changes."

Ben shared a glance with her, during which she did her best to seem suitably shocked and grateful. She hugged Bernard. "Thank you so much!"

Ben finally folded the check and put it into his pocket. "Dad, I don't even know what to say. Thank you. Thank you for everything."

Felicity knew that the words from his father were bringing Ben to tears, rather than the money. He gave his dad a hug and she felt vindicated that she'd done the right thing. She felt bad not to give Cain credit for his generosity, but hopefully he would understand if he had known.

Bernard let go of his son and gave him a friendly shove towards Felicity. "Now you two go and dance. Enjoy this memorable evening, being together and loving each other."

Ben took her into his arms. "Thank you. We definitely will."

~~~~~~~~~~~~~~~~~~~~~~~~~~~~

Ben hoisted Felicity up into his arms without warning. She laughed and clung to him, although she felt very secure in his strong arms. "I thought you were going to open the door first," she exclaimed with a giggle, explaining her surprise.

Ben stood there in the hotel hallway, with his arms full of Felicity and voluminous mounds of wedding gown silk and crinoline. "I guess that would have been the smarter way to go, huh?"

She laughed. "Is the key in your pocket?" He nodded and she dug past her skirts to fish the plastic card from the pocket of his tux. Ben angled her to reach the lock and swipe the card through. It took a few tries for her to be able to swipe it and turn the doorknob before the little light turned back from green to red. She imagined that by the time they actually got into the room, poor Ben was going to drop her from exhaustion.

The door opened to reveal a gorgeous suite of gigantic proportion. Felicity stared at it in appreciative awe. Their bags had been brought upstairs earlier, when they'd first arrived for the reception, so neither of them had seen the room yet. Even Ben stood and took in the sight of the beautiful room for a moment, rather than rush in to set her feet down on the floor. She glanced up at him. "Don't you need to put me down?" she asked.

He smiled. "I will…when I find the bed."

She laughed. "I think it's probably through there," she said with a nod of her head towards an archway off to the right. Ben kicked the door closed with his foot, made his way past the entryway table that was covered in a cascade of beautiful flowers, and through to the archway. He took his time entering the bedroom, seeming unfazed to continue carrying her. "You must be working out more than I thought," Felicity teased.

He hefted her up a bit higher with a grin. "Never underestimate me, I'm full of surprises."

He carried her into the bedroom and then laid her down on the king sized bed, giving her an extra little toss as she landed, making her bounce. She felt practically buried in skirts as she sunk into the soft, plush down coverlet.

Felicity unwound the wrist strap from her satin bag of wedding cards, and pulled open the drawstring to reveal the many gifts within. "Look at all these cards! Did we invite this many people?"

Ben smiled and gently took the bag from her. "They probably all have money in them too, so let's not lose them. I'll put them on the dresser for now."

"Don't you want to open them first? Maybe dump them on the bed...roll around and bury ourselves in them or something?" she asked with a giggle.

Ben closed the bag and tossed it onto the dresser top. "The only thing I want to bury myself in right now...is you," he told her with a throaty voice that sent a shiver down her spine, abruptly cutting off her giggling. His light honey brown eyes were looking unusually dark, seductive and quite serious.

He stood next to the bed and gave her a moment to recognize his desire, then held out his hand. She slipped her fingers into his grasp with a quiet smile and he helped her to sit up. He leaned over to meet her lips with a kiss. "If that's alright with you, *Mrs. Benjamin Everheart*," he added with a whisper.

His kiss was soft, but thorough and full of promises for a pleasurable evening ahead. As it ended, he leaned back, allowing her to raise herself up and better arrange her gown on the bed. She'd taken her hair down earlier, and been sure to put the hair clip from Cain, along with his note, fished out of her corset, away in a safe place with the things going back to her mom's house. She would treasure them both always, but they had no place here. Tonight was about Ben, and only Ben, as would be every night hereafter.

He brushed a curl of hair from her face and let his fingers brush her cheek. "Beautiful," he told her sincerely, sounding almost reverent as he paused, seeming entranced by her. Then he glanced down at her wedding dress with a grin. "I've been eyeing your body in this elegant gown all evening." He lightly traced his finger along the neckline of the dress, causing little chills of excitement to race across her skin wherever his finger dipped down off the fabric.

He continued to speak in that enticing, throaty voice that was deliciously full of anticipation. "While you are gorgeous in it, I know you're even more beautiful without it," he told her, as his fingers travelled over her shoulder and down, meticulously sliding slowly over every single button that fastened the sheer material inset bordered by lace that ran down her back. "Unfortunately, I think it might take me a good part of the night just to get it off." He finished the sentence with a chuckle as he let his fingers rest on the last button, daringly low, but still demure enough to be lady-like...just barely. "So I'd better start right on it, all twenty seven buttons worth."

Now she couldn't help but laugh. "You counted them?"

"More than once," he admitted with a sly wink.

She reached behind to take his hand and bring it around so that she could bestow a kiss on his fingertips. "Well, then you'll be very happy to hear that you don't have to actually unfasten any of them." He looked at her curiously. She guided his arm around her again, and brought his hand up to feel the start of the buttons at the top edge of the dress. "Feel that little piece of satin that runs down alongside the buttons?" He nodded, with knitted brows. "Hidden zipper," she told him with impish glee.

He blindly moved the material aside, found the zipper behind her back, and pulled it down, his smile growing as he listened to the very rewarding hissing sound of her being freed from the gown with a sigh of metal and plastic. "Now I *really* like this dress."

He let go of the zipper to wrap his arms around her, and pull her in for another kiss, after which she made him let her go, so that she could help him to take off his clothes. It had been a while since they'd shared intimate time together…too long. She noticed that her hands were lightly shaking as she tried to fumble with all of the buttons, cufflinks, and clasps for his shirt and cummerbund. Her eyes danced over each strong, masculine line of his body as it was revealed in bits and pieces, causing a dull, warm ache between her legs.

She ran her hands lovingly over his sculpted torso, admiring the toned muscles of his abdomen. Then her gaze dropped lower to observe the impressive bulge in his pants, straining the material tightly; it looked very uncomfortable for him. She unclasped the waistband, slid down the zipper, and stood, deftly sliding her hand down between the material of the pants and the warmth of his stomach. As her fingers gently found and repositioned his sex, it grew even larger in her hand. "Better?" she whispered.

He smiled and leaned down to repay her with a kiss. "It would be better if you took them off."

She obliged with a smile, grasping the waistband of his pants and shorts together. She tugged them down, to unveil the flushed tip and eventually the hard length of his penis, her hands running the material smoothly down the outside of his thighs against his warm skin. As she did, she couldn't help herself but to pause and place one soft kiss upon his still-growing erection as it jerked further upwards and stiffened before her. She heard Ben's sharp intake of breath caused by her actions, but she willed herself to back away and finish helping him to remove his trousers. By the time they had managed to get him entirely out of his tuxedo, they were both feeling terribly impatient, burning with tightly coiled anticipation.

Finally, Felicity stood and let her gown drop down to the floor, needing a hand from Ben to step out of it over the sizeable heap of material at her feet. She unclipped her stockings from the lace garter belt she wore. He lovingly took each leg into his hands and helped her to roll her stockings down and take them off, along with the belt.

As they approached the bed, she noticed Ben observing her body as though it was a living sculpture of fascinating beauty. He drank in every curve and swell of her with his eyes, and she imagined she could actually feel his gaze on her skin like a soft caress. She trembled, wishing he would touch her. Her loving husband, the only man who would ever have the right to touch her again…and as she met his eyes and saw the sweet love and desire there, she knew that would be just fine with her. What more could she want? This wonderful man knew her, loved her, and wanted nothing more than to make her happy, always. Knowing the good man that he was, she was very happy to let him.

He came and knelt on the bed next to her, and then slowly slid her panties down to remove them. Once she was completely bared, he held himself over her where she lay, making her feel small and safely guarded from the world. "You are mesmerizing," he told her, sounding genuinely fascinated by the effect she had on him. He dipped his head down to bequeath small kisses down the length of her throat to her breastbone, his strong arms holding his weight firmly above her.

Her breath caught as he moved his head to the side of her body and playfully nudged the heavy weight of her breast with his face, before moving to take her swiftly hardening nipple into his mouth. Her heart was pounding as he suckled her gently, and then slowly swirled his tongue in designs that dizzyingly heightened her arousal.

She turned her head aside and let her eyes take in the subtly toned curves of muscle that flexed and bulged in his biceps as he kept himself lifted over her. His knee nudged between her thighs, resting on the bed, keeping his full, thick erection from touching her. She arched and caused her hips to brush against it, and then reached down to encircle the shaft delicately with her fingers. Once she had her hand wrapped around him, she stroked more purposefully, and he rewarded her with a throaty moan of approval. So familiar, so natural; having her hands on his body felt like reuniting with an integral part of herself.

There had been a time when she had felt slightly unsure, and had purposely kept herself from Ben to discover the world without him. But what she had discovered was that although she could stand on her own, in her heart she needed Ben, not just anyone, Ben. He understood her like no one else seemed to. She needed the comfort, love, and unspoken understanding that always permeated their time together. Whether they were arguing over something inconsequential with headstrong stubbornness, or confiding in each other over deep-seated fears with emotional vulnerability, together she and Ben had learned to rely upon on each other always. It didn't matter if they were sometimes at odds, they knew that their love was unfaltering. Their underlying sentiment: I'll always be there for you.

Making love with Ben was unconditional ecstasy. Focused only on pleasing her, Ben knew how to seduce her body with an intimate tenderness that connected directly to her heart. His feelings for her never wavered, he wanted nothing more than to delight her.

Ben lifted his hand from the bed to caress her leg. He trailed his finger along the sensitive skin of one of her thighs, until he found and explored the depth between them with lavish attention. It was amazing how he knew just what could make her squirm and what would drive her to passionate frenzy. He took his time, always knowing when to slow the pace and make her want more. His intuitive touch had a way of wooing her and making her feel the recipient of extravagant luxuries of sensation.

Felicity rubbed her thumb over the tip of his erection, spreading the small bead of moisture that had formed there. The anticipation of the day was still tightly wound within her, and she could barely contain herself with each stroke of his skilled touch. She couldn't help but think that there'd be plenty of time for foreplay and erotic antics during their honeymoon. Right now, she wanted fulfillment. There was no waiting; teasing torment was something she would not be able to endure. "I need you," she whispered to him pleadingly. "I need you now, Ben."

Needing no further invitation, Ben gave her a final stroke for readiness with his hand, and then guided himself to enter her. Ready as she was, her body still gave small resistance as he gently pushed his way inside her. He felt so huge, but she shifted and drew up her knees to ease things for him.

His mouth met hers for a kiss, his tongue lightly exploring the seam of her lips until she allowed it entry to twirl and dance with her own. As it entered, his hips thrust him deeper inside of her, filling her aching need. She wrapped her legs around him, moaning with delicious abandon as her body stretched to accommodate him.

Together, in body, in spirit, in life...this was her destiny, wasn't it? To be together with Ben in this magical union would fulfill everything she wanted from life. The snug and soothing feel of his body intertwined with hers became comfortable and easy, as the delicious push and pull of their actions became intensely heated and slick.

Instinctively she moved with him, wanting ever more. The thick length of him filled her even as love for him filled her heart. Hot flares of desire seemed to tremble through her, as she came temptingly close to climax, which always seemed to be maddeningly just beyond the next stroke.

Ben's fierce need drove him harder, faster, and she loved the carnal roughness of it, his unrestrained vigor. He knew her. He knew that it would peak her desires just as it did his. No longer was she the hesitant young woman he'd once been afraid to intimidate. She urged him on with little more than a rumbling in her throat and a squeeze of her tightly gripped hands. Pleasure built within her, pulsing with radiant jolts of rapture that suddenly exploded.

Ben's orgasm surged through him in reaction to her own clenched muscles and sweet moans. He held her tightly, spasms shuddering through him, until all strength left them both, and they collapsed with exhausted gasps for breath.

She fell against him as he rolled to his back, and she rested her head on his heaving chest. Sweet satisfaction and beaming joy permeated her. She and Ben were now truly husband and wife.

Once they had regained their breath, Ben brought his hand to stroke her hair as he whispered, "I'll love you always, Liss. 'Till death do us part."

Chapter 7 - Meet the maker

Elric

Cain's Estate, Upstate, New York
A warm Summer evening

Elric put the car into drive as the large iron gate swung slowly inward. Only Arif sat in the car beside him. The coven master had insisted that they make the unannounced trip by themselves, so as not to seem threatening. Cain had not answered the intercom himself; another young man had admitted them. It was probably Mattie, although he had surely had a quick conference with Cain before letting them enter the grounds. From what the coven's surveillance had observed, there were very few vampires in residence at the house, and no humans. Cain did not keep human guards. Then again, he didn't need them, not with the Crimson Coven patrolling the area.

It should not have come back to this. Arif's mental voice reverberated through Elric's mind. Although they were alone in the car, he would not risk speaking aloud in uncertain territory. *I have planned for it, of course, but this should have been taken care of by now. Are your forces so incompetent as to be unable to apprehend one small girl?*

Elric sighed. Perhaps he hadn't truly been trying as hard as he should have, but in the strictest sense, he had followed his orders. He answered in thought. *Perhaps if I'd been given seasoned fighters, they would have been more successful. Forgive me for saying, but sending half of our forces off with Lorelei on whatever covert mission you felt was more important than this, has left me with little to rely on. You've only permitted me to send Cadets, and obviously stronger measures were needed.*

Elric could feel the annoyance in Arif's response. *She cannot even use her powers yet. You've heard Kieran's reports. She revels in her flight skill like a child with a new toy. She still spends her time wrestling with her boyfriend, and testing her speed by racing the deer through the forest. She knows nothing of true defense. Cadets should have been more than sufficient. They are not trying to kill her, only to bring her to me.*

A directive that requires skill and finesse, as compared to a simple execution, sir. Elric answered defensively. *Obviously, she's mastered projecting influence over lesser vampires. The group sent to recruit her from her trip to Louisiana stayed with her for weeks, and could not sway her to our ends. They accompanied her back to this very estate, and yet they returned to me empty-handed, completely bewildered with stories of her glory. She listens only to her trusted coven, and cannot be persuaded by outsiders.*

Arif shook his head, annoyed at their repeated failures using subtle means. *That is why you were then given permission to use force. Still no report from the last pair?*

Elric hesitated, but knew he would have to give up the most recently acquired information. The two he'd sent to follow and abduct her on her last outing, a wedding reception it seemed, had also failed in their mission. *Their last report was that they had isolated her in a public building and had split up to approach from both entrances, trapping her. She could not have escaped without risking exposure through a blatant display in front of many humans, something that would surely make her hesitate, but it seems the pair somehow failed. My follow up team discovered ash in the courtyard they believe to have been Enrique. There has been no sign of Luis. Either he was also killed, or perhaps upon learning he was alone in the mission, he fled.*

Arif turned to him in disbelief. *You believe he would abandon his directive? Those two were acquired together. They were prominent members of a greatly feared gang in life.* After a pause, he accepted that the new vampire might very well have decided to flee with his newfound immortality, rather than fight for a cause not his own after the loss of his friend. His loyalty to the coven had not yet been tested. *Give him one week to return. After that, if he is seen by a coven member, he is to be killed on sight.*

They pulled into the parking area at the top of the long driveway. The house was impressive, yet welcoming. Elric wished he had a friendly social reason to be here. Cain himself was standing outside on the front porch to greet them.

The man had a very interesting presence about him. In appearance, Cain did not seem very threatening. He wasn't a small man by any means, but he had a very soft spoken and calming demeanor, gentle and friendly. He always looked thoughtful and understanding. However, he had a wariness about him as well. Something in his eyes told you he was wise beyond the age of his physical appearance, and that he was not one to tolerate deceit.

Cain's mark flared into mental view to complete his image. The mark would make you think twice about confronting the man, if his kind appearance hadn't. He was old, almost three times Elric's age. He was well made, meaning that his intelligence and memories were fully intact, and he had decent vampiric power as well, even if it was mostly untapped. A vampire could feel the cautionary urge for respect at the sight of that mark. It was inherent to want to obey ones elders, or treat them considerately, at the very least.

Cain's mark still bore the signature of his small coven upon it, linking him with Mattie and Alyson. It was a blatant display that those two were under his protection. By its brightness, they had shared blood very recently. So even if the girl was not here, Cain could not claim to have lost track of her entirely. Elric respected their solidarity, but it would have been easier for all if Cain would just let her go off on her own. Young Mattie exited the house to stand behind Cain as they drew near. Alyson was nowhere in sight.

Arif spoke upon their approach. "Cain, my friend, so good to see you. Forgive me for staying so long out of touch. I hope all has been well. But of course, you would have contacted me if there was cause for concern."

"Of course," Cain answered shortly. He was staring at Arif levelly, without a trace of his usual friendliness. Something seemed to have lowered his esteem for the master.

Arif noted his coldness. "I hope you don't mind our dropping by without notice, but we were nearby, and I simply could not in good conscience return home without asking after our dear Alyson."

Cain stood with arms crossed, unwelcoming. "Put your mind at ease. She's quite well."

"As I see by your shared mark," Arif said with a slight nod meant to indicate the Mark of the Coven that shone around Cain's psychic aura. "Glad to know she is still able to share blood with you, without losing control."

Mattie was immediately visibly offended. "Of course she can. She's fine."

Arif simply gave him a benign smile. "That is good news. Is she here?"

Cain answered promptly, without a glance at Mattie. "Not at the moment."

Arif just stared at him for a few seconds in challenge before asking, "I expect she will return shortly, no? May we come in and wait for her? I would very much like to reassure myself of her well being, and perhaps have a chat."

Cain appeared insulted. "My assurance should be more than sufficient. There has been no change to cause alarm. I'm happy to say that your predictions were erroneous. However, you are welcome to stay for a drink if you'd like. I've already prepared refreshments for us out here on the veranda."

Arif shared a glance with Elric, noting the slight against them, that they should take drinks outside rather than be invited in. Rather than remarking on it, Arif simply nodded and followed Cain and Mattie up onto the wrap-around deck and around to the side of the house where a carafe and glasses stood awaiting them on a patio table. They each took seats. As Mattie poured them drinks, Arif asked, "Have you been training her in controlled discovery and restraint of her powers as suggested? She must learn to contain herself. Power of her sort can be over-whelming. She must learn to lock it away, for her own good and ours."

Elric took a sip of the blood provided, and was pleased to find that it was far better than he'd expected. He could feel Arif broadcast his distaste for it as he took a small polite sip. Arif never drank blood from anything other than a human. He deigned it to be beneath him. However, men in the ranks of the coven regularly supplemented with animal blood out of sheer necessity. They each had a stable of humans assigned to them, its size based on their rank, but it would take numbers greater than they could easily support, to feed every vampire in the coven indefinitely. To Elric's palette, this blood was better than any animal blood purchased or raised at *Kana Susamış Icin Ev*. The blood was that of a creature wild, healthy, and free, and was flavored with a slight hint of the delicious tang that pheromones of fear could bring.

"I'm very pleased with Alyson's progress," Cain said guardedly. "I don't believe she'll have any of the problems you described. She is quite confident in her control."

"Are you sure? As you must know, a vampire's thirst is an insidious thing. It creeps upon one with furtive stealth, and can very suddenly take control of even the most diligent of humanitarians. She will crave more than you currently provide here, with your neat little preserve. Power of her magnitude will not remain sated by animals forever."

Cain only glared at him while Mattie refuted the statement. "Yes it will. Other than Alyson's, *I've* never tasted human blood in my entire existence."

Arif looked amused by the admittance. "Young man, you hold a pale fraction of the darkness possessed by your protégé. *She* is a true, pure vampire; a magnificent example of evil magicks beyond your comprehension, while you are little more than a human boy playing at being a vampire by comparison."

Cain sat up angrily in his chair. "I've heard quite enough."

"No, Cain, you do not know the depth of the darkness within her. She may contain it now, but it will emerge, and you will be unready for it. What will become of her, when that desire for human blood overtakes her reason? She is not one of these weak younglings that you pride yourself in mentoring." Arif gestured towards Mattie, who sat scowling at him. "She is *The United One,* a descendant of darkness the likes of which you cannot even imagine. When she wants to taste more than what your civil pitchers can provide, what then? Without careful and controlled outlet for her needs, she will turn savage, and completely beyond your control."

Mattie practically spat out his reply. "Don't be ridiculous. Cain, we don't have to listen to this."

Arif eyed Mattie thoughtfully. "You are angry not because you believe it untrue, but because you fear I am right. You've always feared it. You feel the strength of her thirst. You know her better than any, and you know she is struggling. I have a compound on Long Island, only a few hours from here. Nestled safely within it, a stable of dozens of humans, who can help her to slake her thirst, in a controlled atmosphere. How long before she begins to test the limits you've set for her here, and seeks the human blood she truly longs for? How long before she begins to kill?"

"She wouldn't do that," Mattie told them quietly. He seemed slightly unsure, but desperate to believe it.

Cain took back Arif's attention. "Why do you care? Don't tell me that you're concerned over the lives of humans."

Arif smiled. No matter the other's positions on killing humans, it was true that *he* felt their lives and deaths were nothing more than an inconvenience to him. "I am concerned that stronger fuel brings stronger power, and if she unleashes it unsupervised, she will be given a true taste of the horror she is destined to become. She has the ability to control all of our kind, you must see that within her. She could be a queen among servants if that was her wish. Her eyes shine with the light of sovereign control, bestowed upon her by dark forces that our kind are better off not remembering. A small taste in a controlled setting may satisfy her, and teach her restraint, but if she unleashes it on her own, there will be no boundaries.

Once she truly discovers what she is capable of, she will not renounce that power! She will rise up and usurp not only the two of you, her sire and her rightful coven master, but elders and leaders everywhere among our kind. She will upset the proper order, and give vampires the world over a taste for anarchy and chaos. It will throw our kind back into the depths of the dark ages from which we have ever so slowly begun to crawl. Do you want to live only in darkness again? Do you want humans to once again know and fear us, while our kind follow her in an attempt to conquer the world?

I know that you frown upon my practices. I have taken a role as master of my domain, and I enforce coven law upon all of those within my territories, whether they choose to swear fealty to me or not. I know you disapprove, but you cannot deny that I keep order and civility among vampires, as often you cannot. Do you really want to see that dissolved?

Giving the girl freedom is a recipe for disaster. She must be carefully monitored and guided for the safety of us all. You attempt that here, alone... with the help only of this youngling. Do you really believe that will be enough?"

"I do," Cain insisted. "My guidance has been sufficient thus far. I see no reason why it should not remain so. Alyson has no designs for power. She is not the uncontrollable force that you paint her to be. As you can see by our mark, we have a close relationship. I am confident in that, and I will not let her go astray."

Arif gently shook his head. "Complete confidence is often the mark of a misled fool."

Mattie stood from his chair in quiet outrage. "My wife is not a power hungry tyrant. We'll leave that to you. *The United One* is just a fancy title for the condition of her blood, it's not *who* she is. Just leave her alone and we won't have any problems."

Arif gave him a condescending smile. "Dear boy, I am not your enemy, nor am I a tyrant. I am simply a realist. I want only what is best for Alyson, as do we all. It worries me that you so underestimate the demon within her. It lies dormant, overshadowed by the girl, but it must be bound before it is awakened. You cannot care for her needs as I can. You've wasted so much time."

Mattie became too distracted for reply. Elric shared a glance with Arif. *The United One approaches.* The master told him silently. He must have picked up on the hum of telepathic communication between she and Mattie.

Cain replied to Arif as though there were no interruption. "Our time is not wasted. She has learned much, and there is nothing you can do for her, that we three cannot accomplish together."

Arif gave a small shrug. "I disagree."

There was no sound or mark to betray the approach of Alyson, only a subtle, obscure change felt in their company. It seemed that she almost magically appeared before them. She had been moving too fast for their eyes to truly track, and had now joined them. She was standing silent, pale, and still as an apparition. Arif stood, in acknowledgement of her presence, and the others followed suit. "Perhaps the lady herself would like to make that judgment."

Alyson was remarkably quiet and motionless, very unlike her. It gave her a presence of confident command that Elric had never observed in her before. Perhaps her abilities were maturing her disposition. She took her time inspecting those in attendance. Finally, she gave them a smile that was almost eerie in its impish nature. "I didn't know we were expecting company."

Arif gave her a small but formal bow, which she seemed to take delight in. "Forgive me, but we were unexpected. I wanted very much to visit with you though, and see that you were well."

"Well, isn't that sweet? I'm fine and dandy," Alyson still wore her smile, but it seemed a bit patronizing now.

Arif accepted her answer with a nod. "That is good, but I am still concerned for you. I was just explaining to your coven-mates, that your thirst differs from that of a typical vampire. *You,* are of course, anything *but* typical." He said it as though they were dear friends sharing a private joke. She just watched him calculatingly. "My dear, you are made from stronger forces than they know, and your thirst is equally strong. You try valiantly to slake it in ways of which they approve, but animal blood does not satisfy, does it?"

Elric could see in her eyes that Arif was right. He wondered if the others knew, or if they blinded themselves to it. Alyson never even glanced at them. "I make do alright."

Arif seemed full of sympathetic concern. "It's getting harder. You don't have to voice it, I know it is true." She didn't correct him, or look at the others. "It seems unfair that your coven master forces you to struggle, existing by standards even lesser vampires find difficult to uphold. You are *The United One*, and your needs are greater than ours."

Arif spared a glance at Cain in disapproval, before returning his focus to Alyson. "Containment of your thirst is like building a dam. If you do not give it controlled release, the pressure builds until it bursts, causing destruction. The animal blood you drink is barely a slight hole in the dam, hardly enough to ease its pressure. You must learn to allow a spillway; the carefully moderated drinking of human blood, the only kind that will satisfy enough to ease your struggle."

For the first time since Arif had begun, Alyson looked doubtful and ready to dismiss him. He took back her gaze, and spoke in earnest confidence. "I know you don't want to speak of this in front of your coven.

They do not understand, and take offense to such things. But please do not dismiss what I tell you, because you may need to rely upon it when the thirst overwhelms you, regardless of your master's edicts."

"He's not my master," Alyson replied in a quiet voice, with a slight apologetic glance for Cain's benefit.

Arif responded with bemused surprise. "No? Then you have accepted to be true, what you must know in your heart. *The United One* has no master, for *The United One* is meant to *be* the master of us all. Yet you exist like any youngling, looking for guidance and shelter here. You are part of a coven bound by blood, and Cain is the eldest among you. If you do not recognize your own status, then this gives him inherent control; the right to lead." He sounded deceivingly rational and on Cain's side, although Elric knew he was happy to see Alyson explore the opposite direction.

Mattie looked wounded by Alyson's small defiance, but Cain spoke steadily, without betrayal of emotion. "We are allied by blood, but I do not seek leadership here."

Mattie nodded. "That's right. We don't need a *master* here. We came together as a coven of equals."

Arif laughed at his words and turned to Cain. "That is very gracious of you Cain, gracious of both of you," he said, looking to Alyson as well, "for an elder of such impressive age, and a creature as powerful as *The United One,* to allow this nondescript youngling to consider himself your equal." Before any could protest, he addressed Mattie. "You must be held in high regard."

Alyson sent out what could only be described as a wave of command for attention. "He is," she told them with authority. "We're all independent here. I'm not looking for status, or special treatment, and I don't need a master trying to tell me what to do." She looked pointedly at Arif, as he was the only vampire in her slight experience to have ever had the arrogance to call himself *master.*

She continued, with a gracious smile at Cain. "Cain's not my master, but he is an elder with more experience than me. More importantly, he's also a wise man with a kind heart. He's my friend, and I trust him. He doesn't give orders, but I appreciate his advice.

Mattie is my lover and my maker. I would *never* act against him. So get this straight. I'm only a part of a coven by choice, and it's not a power-thing. I make my own decisions, but I'm not stupid enough not to listen to anybody else," *Most of the time...* The last was a mental admission broadcast to all with a lilt of humor that made Elric smile. "And so far, you haven't told me anything that would make me think for a second that I should be listening to you."

Arif weighed her statement and then gave her a reasonable smile. "Then perhaps you should listen to this offer I have for you. I would very much like for you to come and visit my coven for a short while. I have a luxury estate not terribly far from here, called *Kana Susamış Icin Ev*. Living there, on my coven's private compound, are nearly two hundred willing humans, happy to give all the blood you require, in thanks for the carefree life that they live by my provision.

Each member of my coven receives a group of private donors. You are welcome to come and stay as an honorary coven member, you and your maker, of course. You could have private living quarters, access to our private beach and all of our amenities. I could offer you as many donors as you need to give you the strong human blood you require, in order to keep your thirst from being such a distraction. It is as though you are currently trying to control hunger with breadcrumbs."

Mattie crossed his arms and replied with disdain, "And it's like you want her to control alcoholism with alcohol."

Alyson seemed troubled over making a decision about the offer, but finally shook her head. "I don't need that. I don't need human blood."

Arif nodded, although it was obvious he didn't accept what she'd said. "Do you need knowledge? For *that* is the larger treasure that I have to offer you. You are trying to define and control your powers, yes? Shall we use another analogy? How do you learn to drive from a man without a car?" he asked with a sly glance at Cain. "My coven is comprised of every breed of vampire. You can be taught restraint from those who truly know what it is you are trying to harness."

Elric was surprised to find that master included him in the next exchange, a private telepathic conference with Alyson that the others were not a part of. *Has Cain been teaching you how to be selective in your thought reading? Can he show you how to be sure your telepathic communications are private? Can he sympathize, when it seems that all the voices in the world are closing in about you, or teach you how to shut them out for your own sanity? He may give you advice, but only I can truly understand.* "Elric."

Elric was startled to attention by the spoken command of his name. It was time for his demonstration. He moved to stand before Alyson, and offered his hand. The others seemed brought to alert, as though he were coming close to hurt her, how stupid. He looked into her eyes and could feel her reading his intent and telling the others to stand down.

He dwarfed her with his height and the breadth of his shoulders. You could fit this delicate seeming, finely featured little girl into the frame of his muscular body twice over and still have room to spare. They seemed opposite in every way. His skin was dark as black coffee, while she was pale, with platinum hair and light blue eyes, but her spirit, her spirit was strong and stubborn as his own. In spirit, they were not all that different really. He had no doubt that she loved to fly.

She looked to her coven-mates. That irked him. Was she so uncertain of herself that she could not make a simple decision without their approval? Then he realized that she wasn't really looking for permission. She had consulted with them mentally out of respect. After all, as benign a master as Cain might be, he was still the oldest vampire any of them had ever known.

She tentatively reached for his hand, still slightly unsure of what he meant to do. He spoke three simple words to her in the barest of whispers. "Fly with me." As her fingers barely brushed the tips of his, he took off like a shot. Straight up into the air, with the freedom of the wind rushing over him, he left the others far below. Although startled, she followed after him immediately, even managing to keep contact with his hand and catch up enough to slip her own small fingers further into his grasp. They penetrated the slight cloud cover and came out above to see the stars. Now Elric slowed and finally stopped to admire the night sky.

She came to a halt next to him, letting her hand slide away from his. He could tell that she was experiencing the miracle for the first time; the miracle that it was to be up here untouched by another, and yet not alone. To have company that could fly of their own power was interesting and oddly exhilarating to her. He noticed that she kept herself floating with her feet a bit higher than his, in order to equalize their heights. It made him smile.

They were high enough for privacy, and they didn't have much time. "Don't go with him."

She lost the gleeful grin flight had brought, and looked at him curiously. He continued. "Tell him you will consider his offer, but don't go."

He could not risk more than that. The master was going to find it odd already that Elric had taken her so high out of his psychic range, rather than the mild demonstration they had planned. He reached out for her hand once again and began to descend. She came willingly. Before long, they were setting feet to the ground. Alyson was still smiling like a schoolgirl. Elric could see that although annoyed by the departure from plan, the master was pleased that Elric had impressed her so. Her husband seemed less pleased.

She turned to Elric as though they had never spoken. "How long have you been flying?" she asked.

He knitted his brows to think. His skill had been uncovered so long ago, that he stopped his mental count. "Over a hundred years."

Alyson's eyes widened appreciatively and she gave him a sly smile. "You must know all the tricks by now."

Elric spared a glance for the master, pleased that this was visibly unfolding just as he'd hoped. "Every nuance."

Arif interrupted with an annoying tone of smugness. "Flying is but one of the talents at my disposal." As though Elric's skill *belonged* to the master. "I have access to all talents."

"Such as healing?" Cain interrupted. "I'm told greatly accelerated healing is a rare talent, and surely a valuable one to a coven responsible for the care of so many. Is there a breed of *that* talent at your disposal?"

Even Elric, not having been taken into confidence, and relying only on his small gatherings of knowledge gained while in the master's employ, understood Cain's ire. Elric had been present for a demonstration Arif had held years back, in which he'd showed that Cain could heal himself more quickly than any other among them. He'd made it appear that Cain was protected from holy water and cross, receiving divine healing from such items that greatly injured other vampires. It was insinuated that Cain was somehow special, perhaps under God's protective wing, as a vampire living by religious restraint as opposed to being a killer.

It struck fear in the coven, that Cain was seemingly immune to that which could destroy them. It gave them respect for Cain, but more importantly, it showed them that they needed the protection of their master, Arif. If they believed that Arif had a good relationship with Cain, it would then protect the coven from him. Although Cain was known as a teacher to many, he was also known for frowning upon the practice of feeding from humans, a practice most coven members were unwilling to forfeit. They did not want Cain coming after them, to force them to change their ways, especially if they had few effective weapons against him. If he was immune to holy water and cross, who knew if anything else could destroy him?

What Elric now realized, was what Cain must have recently learned as well. Healing at such an accelerated rate was not mysterious divine protection bestowed upon him by his God. Cain was not immune to injury, it was simply the talent of his breed to heal so quickly that most small damages done were of almost no consequence. Perhaps with Arif's goading, Cain himself had even been led to believe that Godly forgiveness was at the root of his repaired body. If Arif knew the powers of *all* breeds, as he now claimed, then he had known Cain's talent. Yet he had not given Cain explanation for his gift, and instead deliberately led his suppositions astray. Cain knew that now, and was very annoyed.

Elric knew that they did not currently have a vampire of yellow eyes in the coven, but when they had, her talent had been kept secret. She was a crazy old woman, and Elric was unsure what secrets of her talents she might have shared with Arif, but it seemed likely to Elric that the master knew more of Cain's abilities than Cain did. That bothered Elric almost as much as it did Cain.

Arif did not give the question direct answer. "While it is true all vampires heal more quickly than humans, and from injuries a human cannot sustain and live, a breed of incredibly rapid healing is good to have access to. I do have such an acquaintance. But that is not a talent Alyson needs to concern herself with."

Arif approached Alyson with a smarmy smile and open arms to show his concern for her. "There is so much for you to learn. So you see, I felt that I needed to come and reiterate my invitation to you. When we last met in Atlantic City, I don't think you were yet fully aware of what I had to offer, just as you were not yet aware of the powers and struggles you would have to deal with, within yourself. To have the care of a vampire such as yourself in my hands would be a great responsibility, but I am happy to provide for you, if you will come. It puts my mind at ease, to know that your great power will be mentored properly, with utmost safety for all."

Alyson did not meet the eyes of the master, *or* those of her coven, which Elric could see worried them all to no end. Apparently, she was not mentally conferring with them. She was staring off into the distance, at the stars over their heads. After an interminable amount of time, she turned her attention to the master with direct focus. "That is a very generous offer. I don't drink human blood, but even if you had animals to draw from, I could easily drink you out of house and home, I'm sure," she told him with a smile.

Arif returned her grin. "Have no concern. I am happy to provide."

"I've never met anyone who can do the things that I can do." She was obviously still impressed by Elric's flight, as well as Arif's ability to use telepathy. She was also doubtless aware of the master's ability to mentally manipulate others, if she had found it in herself. It was a power that stemmed from the telepathy and something that probably took much practice and control. She could learn that from Arif better than any other. To practice these gifts with others who could truly share them, this was something she had to have thought about before. Her lover, Mattie, looked ill. She kept her attention on the master. "I'm sure there is a lot that your coven could teach me."

"Without a doubt," Arif agreed.

"You don't need an answer now, do you?" For the first time since her return to the earth, she gave Mattie and Cain the look of reassurance they obviously needed. "I'd like to think about it; have time to talk to my friends."

Arif was more than amicable, certain that he was finally beginning to sway her. "Of course, my offer stands. However, I do hope you will not wait too long before exploring what I can provide. You may find that you need the support of other breed kin sooner than you think. Harnessing power such as yours is not to be taken lightly. I think there is much we can do to help you."

Alyson nodded thoughtfully. "Thanks. I'll keep it in mind."

~~~~~~~~~~~~~~~~~~~~~~~~~~~~~~~

Elric punched the code into the alarm keypad, and opened his front door. He'd just begun to swing it open, when he heard someone rush into the entryway behind it. When he opened the door further, he saw the cadet assigned to his house, standing at attention to receive him. Obviously, the cadet had been surprised by his arrival, and rushed to the door. Elric wasn't expected to return until the next evening.

"Yes, I'm early. I couldn't stomach another day on the road." He'd managed to persuade Arif to let them travel home, rather than spend yet another day closeted away in a hotel room with only hired women for company.

He glanced into the living room, where the cadet had been relaxing before turning in for the day. The television was on, connected to a bundle of wires and black plastic on the coffee table. He must have been playing some sort of video game. "I'll be staying. You can retire to your own quarters for the remainder of the evening," he told the cadet, "and take that with you."

"Thank you, sir."

"Anything to report?" Elric asked as the cadet gathered his things.

"No, sir. Your house runs like clockwork," he admitted with a chuckle. Surely not all of his assignments were as simple. "The log is there with everyone accounted for. They're all in for the night."

Elric nodded and dismissed the man as he walked over to the entry table to glance at the logbook. Every member of his household was logged into and out of the book for each occasion that they left the house. There were dozens of entries for even just the short time he was away.

On his orders, during the past three days and nights, his nine charges had been allowed to maintain their normal schedules. They had permission to come and go for classes, meals, and community duties as usual. When Elric was home, he never bothered with the logbook, but the cadet was required to strictly follow coven protocol. If a human left the house, it was logged into the book with the time of departure. If they were being sent without escort, it was the cadet's responsibility to radio their destination and be sure they arrived there, also to be logged into the book. Everyone was accounted for, at every moment.

As the front door closed behind him, Elric barely flipped through the book and then stashed it into a drawer, hoping it would not be needed again anytime soon. He was glad to be home. He could feel that all of his charges were within at the moment, as the cadet had said. It was well after midnight. Most likely, most of them were sleeping. However, one of his marks did feel as though they were nearby, rather than upstairs.

Elric put down his things and made his way down the hall, into the back of the house. He could see a warm glow of light coming from the kitchen. He smiled as he slowly walked into the room. Just the woman he'd come home to see.

Latisha sat at the kitchen table, alone. She was having a late meal, quietly eating what looked like grilled chicken and vegetables while reading a book. As usual, she was dressed in her dance clothing. She wore a full leotard of dark, royal purple, with a very loose white tee shirt draped over it, the sleeves and neckline cut so as not to inhibit movement. Her hair was not in its usual ballet bun though. She had unwound her dozens of fine braids to spread over her shoulders and down her back. She looked up with a quiet smile at his approach. She was very glad to have him back. "Welcome home."

He came to give her a soft kiss hello. "It's good to be back." She smelled divine. A hundred years could go by and he would be able to close his eyes, picture his Latisha, and remember that scent. He'd drunk his fill of blood elsewhere earlier, but being close to her always made him want a taste. He fought the urge and forced himself to back away a step. He watched her for a moment, sitting sedately at the table with only her book for company, until now. He shook his head mildly. "Why are you having your meal all alone?"

"I had a late dance class. With you away, everyone else has gone up to bed." He nodded. No reason to keep nocturnal hours, without their vampire in residence. The smile faded from Latisha's lips and she lowered her eyes as she used her fork to move the pieces of chicken around on her plate. "Besides, I should probably get used to being alone, shouldn't I?"

Elric sighed. It wasn't a jab at him, but a plea that he either confirm the fact or change it. Latisha knew she was on borrowed time, and spending each day wondering when the master would decide to send her away was wearing on them both. She had lived here for nearly her entire life, embraced by Elric, and her adopted siblings of the harem. The idea of having to be sent out into the world alone, was very depressing to her, no matter how financially compensated she would be. "No."

She looked up at him, daring to hope that he had good news. Unfortunately, he had nothing concrete to reassure her with. Their situation was just the same. He had nothing new to tell her, only his passion that refused to lose her. "I won't let it happen."

She looked back to her food, unwilling to express a lack of confidence in him, but worried all the same. He sat at the table across from her and gestured towards her plate. It was one of the cafeteria take-out trays. "Is that any good?"

She shrugged. "Not bad. No chef on duty right now, so it's just the community service staff. Not exactly a gourmet meal, but it's okay."

"Why didn't you eat in the dining hall? It wasn't empty. You could have had some company."

She shrugged again. "I felt like being alone."

He eyed her speculatively for a moment. "You knew I'd returned early."

She cracked a small smile, which she quickly hid. "I knew." She said it off-handedly, as though it made no difference, because she hadn't been waiting for him.

"I came home early because I missed you."

She stood from the table, clearing her place and effecting indifference. "It's not my night," she said as she threw the tray in the garbage.

He laughed. "Does that matter? This is *my* house, isn't it?" he asked, his deep voice sounding intimidating without effort. He was the vampire here, and unquestionably the superior of all within his home. Who was to say whom he could spend his time with? "Whose night is it?"

Now she was the one to laugh, a beautifully rich, deep and throaty chuckle. "You don't know?"

He sighed. "I don't really care." He was surprised to see that she hadn't expected that from him. She knew he felt strongly for all the humans in his home. He enjoyed their company and had close relationships with each of them in various ways. Latisha was not only the head of his harem, it was also well known that she was his favorite. However, his harem did not have a clear pecking order beyond that, as most did. He did not rank his charges, beyond Latisha, but treated them equally. Latisha knew that, but seemed to secretly suspect that he still had a private ranking order for them in his heart, desiring the company of some over others.

The truth was, he was happy to spend time with any of them, but it was Latisha that he had missed while away. She didn't bother to tell him who was assigned to await him in his bedroom and feed him, should he require more blood this evening. She finished clearing her place and then reached for her bookmark across the table. He handed it to her, letting his fingers brush over the soft, supple skin of her hand. "The night's half over anyway," he observed. His assigned companion's shift would end at dawn. "Switch with someone for tomorrow."

She just grinned at him, unswayed. "Yes it is your house, but you gave *me* authority over the schedules here. You'll mess everything up." She took her hand back, placing the bookmark in her book and then moving to the sink. She washed and dried her hands, and then stood with them resting on her hips.

The schedule for a vampire's household was carefully coordinated. Each member of the house was on call to their vampire for one 24-hour rotation period. Their shift began at dawn, and it was that charge's sole responsibility not only to be a consort during the day and following night, running errands for him when needed, but also to feed him during that time. He still needed to supplement with animal blood, so as not to take enough to harm any of them, but during their assigned shift, he would drink as much blood from each charge as they were safely able to give. Changing the order of the schedule could require one of his charges to give him blood before they'd had sufficient time to rebuild their strength.

"I've been away for three nights," he reminded her. "You've all had time to recuperate. It won't matter." He could see her fighting the desire to give in to his request. She always enjoyed their time together. She'd missed him just as he had missed her while he'd been away. Why was she being resistant? She should know better than to believe that he wanted only a warm body in his bed. "Latisha, I don't thirst, I don't ask you to my bed if you're not inclined, I just have a lot on my mind. I want to talk with you. Let me run you a bath. You can soak and ease your muscles, and I'll run the sponge over you and unburden my thoughts."

"Beverly is waiting for you upstairs. I'm sure she'd love a bath." The suggestion was delivered quietly, with less bite than another might have used to voice it, but it served to help him understand her reluctance. He knew she wasn't jealous of her harem sisters. Something else was bothering her.

Latisha knew that he was intimate with the other women of his harem, as was his right. How unhappy would they be, to believe that they were undesirable to him? Only Jordan, the sole male human in his home, did not regularly share his bed, despite the fact that the man was gay. Elric preferred women. Jordan was a blood donor, a friend, and a guard and escort to Elric's harem when needed. He was free to share his body with other humans of the community if he wished, and Elric did not worry for his self-esteem. Jordan knew his value to Elric. But the women…he would not insult them by shunning them in the bedroom.

Unlike some vampires, Elric had no rules of fidelity for his charges, nor did he ever require them to do anything that made them uncomfortable. His harem was free to have sexual relationships with other humans in the community if they so desired. But as their provider, it was also Elric's privilege to be intimate with each of them. Technically, their bodies belonged to him along with their blood. Were he to display desire for some of them more than others, it would create hostility and discontent between them. The last thing he needed in his house was drama.

He was only as intimate with them as they each preferred, sometimes spending the day simply holding them in sleep, other times having an entire day of active and fulfilling escapades. They were each given attention as fairly as possible in his home and in his bed; they expected it and were satisfied to be treated fairly, with the exception of Latisha. She had been with him far longer than any of the others, was the designated head of his harem, and was acknowledged by all as having earned his special favor. Latisha was often known to accompany him in bed for an extra day during Jordan's feeding shift. As his favorite, the extra time was hers to claim if she wanted it.

Latisha was satisfied with the system, and was not being jealous. She was frightened that she would soon be asked to leave him. "No one understands me like you," he admitted to her. "And I understand you just as well. I know what you're doing, trying to push me off on spending time with the others, so you can distance yourself from me. What do you think that will accomplish? You've been my charge since you were thirteen! You think a few weeks of distance will erase the past thirty-seven years so simply?"

"I have to do something. Don't I have a right to prepare myself?"

He watched her silently for a moment. "Do you *want* to leave? You still have many years of life left, and your compensation would let you live comfortably without ever wanting for anything. You could open your own dance studio. You are such a beautiful and talented woman, surely you could be happy out there. Perhaps you could find a man to keep all to yourself."

He knew that it wasn't what she wanted, but he had to offer it now and again. He didn't want her to think that she didn't have a choice. She looked at him as though the mere suggestion was ludicrous. "I don't want a *man,* I want you. Besides, what would I do with a man all to myself? What a pain in the ass!

Hunger for me, pamper me, love me, and show me respect. Give me your full attention when I am with you, and then leave me to do my own things. They can have you the other nights of the week; give me some peace." She said with a coy smirk, and then turned her back on him to attend something at the sink.

He knew that she just didn't want to meet his eyes and seem foolishly sentimental. Life at the compound taught one not to openly express too much emotional attachment. A charge should be enamored of their vampire and seek to please them, but tears were just considered an annoying display.

Of course, she knew better than to believe Elric felt that way in private, but old habits died hard. He came up behind her, wrapping her in his strong arms, engulfing her thin frame. She brought up her arms to hold his; she had such long and graceful limbs. "You're sure you want to stay then?" he whispered.

She cocked her head to meet his eyes. "You know I do. I would never leave you. This is my life. I *need* to stay."

He couldn't help but smile as a memory came to mind. "You *need* to stay, the way you *needed* me to bring you here?" She looked at him curiously. "Remember the night I met you?"

She grinned sheepishly. "Don't go getting all nostalgic on me now," she told him, slipping out of his embrace.

It had been just another night for him. Just another job with his men; another group of humans to be killed for some thing or another that the master didn't like. It was automatic for him, monotonous. Obeying orders in return for safe haven and fresh blood. Back then, his small stable of charges were just convenient company and regular warm meals. He wasn't cruel to them, but they didn't matter. His body was dead, and his spirit with it.

"You were thirteen years old," he reiterated from memory. "A scrawny, gangly thing, all arms and legs." She gave him a playful swat for the description, however accurate. "And you stormed up to me with courage I'd never seen, and demanded that you needed me to take you with me. It completely blew my mind." She shrugged. It had been a very long time since they'd talked about that night, but it was a vivid memory for them both. "You knew what we were," he insisted incredulously. "You'd seen us all drink and brutally kill those men."

"If you knew what they did to me on nights you weren't there, you wouldn't be so surprised by my reaction."

He shook his head. "I'll still never understand why you didn't run screaming from the room."

"Run to where? To whom? Back home was worse than where you found me. You were different. Dangerous murderers maybe, but you showed me that there were things out there I didn't understand. All I could think, was that you lived differently from me, and anything different couldn't be any worse than what I had. Even if you'd killed me, at least it was an escape from the trap that was my life."

He lowered his eyes. He knew her early years were a blur of nightmares, but it was something he never pushed her to talk about. It didn't matter now. "Why me? Of all the vampires in the room, why did you come to me?"

She grinned, tracing a finger over the bulging muscles of his folded arms. "Isn't it obvious?"

"My charming good looks?" he asked teasingly. He knew that he was a man of chiseled, handsome features, but at 6' 7" and close to three hundred pounds of muscle, most found his stature intimidating to the point of being unapproachable. Thirteen-year-old Latisha, swallowing her fear and standing up to him that night had made quite an impression.

She stretched up to give him a quick kiss. "You were the biggest, baddest thing in that room! I figured if you didn't kill me, you would be able to protect me from all the others." He chuckled at her logic. "And I was right."

"They thought I was insane to bring you back, but spirit like that had to be rewarded. Besides, I knew all you really needed were a few good meals and a respite from the beatings you'd obviously been getting, and you'd have the opportunity to grow into the graceful, gorgeous woman you are today. You certainly proved yourself useful from the moment you got here."

"I had to make sure that you couldn't give me up. I was always good at organizing things. It wasn't hard to pick up on the way things work around here."

"Ever regret it?"

She gave him a look of reprimand. "You know I don't. You've given me a better life than I ever would have had. You treated me with more love and decency than anyone I had ever known…and it was here that I learned to dance," she added, in fond recollection. "The fact that I wasn't more seriously injured or on crack before you found me is a miracle. The only reason I wasn't pregnant was because I hadn't truly hit puberty yet. I've always been happy here. I've never wanted to leave."

He smiled. "Liar." She knitted her brows at the accusation. "Your sixteenth birthday," he clarified. She blushed beautifully at the reminder. He couldn't resist recounting it for her. "Stowed away in my bed, insisting that you were grown, and it was time for me to initiate you into the harem."

"The others treated me like a child," she told him defensively. "Besides, I was ready."

He laughed. "No you weren't." She'd been so insulted and humiliated by his refusal to bed her, that she had run away. He hadn't sounded an alarm or gone after her. She'd never even left the grounds, and had come back to him the very next night, at which time he had informed her that she would become a fully initiated member of his harem at the age of twenty-one, and no sooner. When she'd insisted that the edict was preposterous, he'd asked her if she'd like to be traded to another vampire who would be happy to take full advantage of her body. She'd declined, but held a bit of a grudge against him for a good long while for it.

"You were being ridiculous. You never even gave me a proper kiss until I was eighteen," she recounted with a bitter edge.

He smiled. "And a sweet kiss it was." Let her try to pretend that he'd been unfair to make her wait. He wouldn't have changed a thing. Her twenty-first birthday had been worth the wait, for both of them, he was sure. "By the time you were twenty-one, you would truly understand this life, and could make a real decision about staying or leaving. Your ten-year service would end soon after that, and it seemed a good compromise. I gave you two full years of being a full-fledged harem member, and then you were given the offer to leave with compensation."

"I never really considered leaving. Sure, I've briefly thought about what it would be like to have a nice full bank account and start a new life somewhere, but it's not a fantasy of mine. The thoughts make me *unhappy* more than anything else. How could the grass be any greener? Jordan and my sisters respect me and we all get along well. I live in this beautiful house, spend my time doing things that I love…dine on fairly decent food," she added with a laugh. "And to top it off, I have the love and attention of a man who makes me swoon, and still pauses to watch me walk by, his eyes blazing with desire."

He smiled and dipped his head in acceptance, pleased that she was still truly happy here. "I won't let him make you leave."

She met his gaze in serious contemplation. "Elric, you've worked very hard to rise in the ranks to where you are. You can't give that up. The rules are the rules."

"The rules need to change."

"Perhaps, but I won't let you give up all you've worked for by acting against him. Even if you were to just abandon it all, you know he would never let you leave in peace. He's held that out to you as a lure for years, but he'll never truly let you go. He depends on you too strongly. Your reward will be only to be bound tighter to him. Were you to leave, he would have you hunted for the insult. You know that."

He stood in silent contemplation. She was right; they both knew it. She moved closer to him and traced her long elegant fingers along the curves of his arms once again. "We may still have some time. I think Marguerite is adjusting well."

He let out a small sigh of relief. He'd been wondering, but that was information vampires did not share among themselves. Arif could have been keeping the woman chained in his basement for all Elric knew. The humans, on the other hand, usually knew everything that went on in each household. The women especially loved to talk. Latisha smiled and nodded, reassuringly. "She's begun a belly dancing class. She's quite graceful with the scarves."

"That's good. He'll like that. Does she speak of the outside?" That was always a dead giveaway. Humans new to the compound either let go of their past and embraced their new existence, or they tried to hold on to outside connections, talking endlessly about people they missed and aspects of their old daily routine. Those who could not let go, were the ones who would eventually try to escape before their ten-year service was up, and usually needed much discipline before they settled in. There were always the rare few who could not be converted to harem life. He sincerely hoped it would be easier than that with Marguerite.

"She's only mentioned her past once or twice during class. She was a good prospect. She has no children, no lover, and yet she is old enough to know that life isn't easy. I think she was pleasantly surprised by what she has been offered here. She doesn't complain about her duties, and she seems to enjoy her training."

Elric took Latisha into his arms and held her tightly. Perhaps the master would not try to rip her away from him after all. "That's good. That's very good."

"She tolerates him well." Elric nodded, his face resting lightly on the top of her head, losing himself in the pleasantly mild scent of the oils in her hair used to smooth her braids. He knew what Latisha meant. Marguerite showed no bruises or signs that she tried to resist Arif. Of course, if she made the mistake of meeting his gaze, he could control her flawlessly. Resistance would be impossible. "I think she actually doesn't mind him," Latisha clarified. "Perhaps she's intrigued by his power, and he's not unattractive."

Elric didn't bother to comment. Every single human in the compound spent a time of initiation with the master before being assigned to another vampire, even Latisha. It was a private matter whether he took sexual liberties with them, but he always drank from them, to secure their submission to the coven. If the master liked them, he kept them for a while. When he was ready to release them to the coven, he would let their mark wear off, and then send them to the common house for auction.

Any interested vampire with the highest rank could claim them, putting up a human of their own in return, so as to keep only their allotted stable size. In this manner, the humans were traded down the ranks until all vampires were satisfied. It had been very lucky for Elric that he had been able to claim Latisha for himself. He had not held a very high rank back then, but luckily, not many of the others had been patient or foresighted enough to want a gangly young upstart of a girl. He'd been able to pull a favor or two to keep others from bidding, and gained Latisha for himself. He did not know what had passed between her and Arif for the six weeks she had spent at *Susuzluktan Saray,* but he knew that she had been happy to move in with Elric afterwards, and that was all he needed to know.

"You have three years left in your service, if not cut off by age. Perhaps he'll let you serve them out. Unless Marguerite seriously offends him, I believe that will be his ruling."

Latisha hugged him tighter. "Then we'll make those years count."

"Come upstairs with me. I won't have you spend the day alone. You need me to ease your worries," he told her, as he gently pulled her by the hand to follow him from the room. *These years will count, and when they are over, things will change,* Elric vowed to himself. No more wasted time. Now was the time to plan for the future; a future without Arif's rules.

~~~~~~~~~~~~~~~~~~~~~~~~~~~~

Elric sat in Arif's private conference room with five other vampires, the full Senior Guard, trying in vain not to be annoyed by Kieran's incessant tapping on the table. He was about to reprimand Kieran for the irritating behavior, when his attention was drawn by a moan from across the room.

Lorelei sat brandishing her wickedly serrated little curved knife, admiring the glistening blood on the tip of the blade. A human man, stripped naked to the waist, lay draped over a chair next to where she crouched on the floor. He was a handsome man with dark skin and a tousle of black curls. She reluctantly put down the knife and turned her attention to meet the man's eyes, putting him back into thrall. Gingerly, she grasped his wrist once again, and held it so that the fresh slice she had just made could drip blood into a glass. Lorelei had been put in charge of refreshments for the meeting.

When the glass she held was sufficiently full, she placed the man's wrist on the arm of his chair, facing upwards to keep the wound from dripping. The man was completely under her spell, oblivious to his surroundings and the company of vampires that shared the room. Lorelei stared into the man's large brown eyes, giving him some last mental command to maintain his motionless obedience, before she retrieved her knife and stood to face the room.

Tall, blonde, and beautiful in a sharp, intimidating sort of way, she reminded him of Uma Thurman, the actress in the *Kill Bill* movie franchise. Of course, Lorelei was a bit more subtle and demure than *The Bride* of the movies, but certainly no less violent or lethal. Her evil manipulations made her just as dangerous as the fictional cinematic assassin, and Elric knew she was every bit as good with a sword as she was with her wiles.

She squinted at Kieran, and Elric knew that his tapping had been every bit as annoying to her as it had to him. She tossed back her waist-long, blonde hair, and sauntered over to Kieran with the glass of blood. He looked up at her, called back from his own distracted thoughts.

"Here," she said bluntly, offering him the glass and then adopting a falsely polite smile. "Have a drink and find something else to occupy yourself with, before I claim those fingers for my own." She lifted her nasty little knife for emphasis, carefully licking the blood from it with her long tongue. Kieran took the glass without comment.

Lorelei folded the cleaned switchblade while meeting Elric's gaze with a smirk. She knew Kieran's impatient nature annoyed him. She was always trying to paint herself as Elric's ally, no matter how he despised her. He held her coveted former role as head of the senior guard, and confidant of the master; a role she would do anything to regain. She hated the fact that the power she once held so dear was now not only his, but was not even properly appreciated by him in her eyes. She'd lost the position through her own greedy, selfish weakness, and he refused to pity her, as she tried to claw her way back into the master's good graces.

Elric gave a nod towards the human from whom she had gathered blood. He was one of three human men who sat motionless, scattered about the room. "He isn't one of yours?" She had used her *dragon's claw* to collect the blood, and the man did not wear a mark.

She glanced over at the man and shook her head. "Not yet," she replied with a grin. "Master asked me to pick up a few extras off the street. Apparently, we're having guests."

"Doesn't he usually prefer you to take women? They're easier to control."

She gave a huff of a laugh, indifferent to what troubles another vampire might have with these humans when she was done with them. Her psychic power of manipulation made the size and strength of victims irrelevant to her. "Makes no difference to me. Besides, human women are so weak and pathetic. I need to feed a roomful here. What am I going to do with some tiny little pretty girl that goes comatose after a pint? You male vampires are ridiculous with your harems full of petite beauties. They're so inefficient."

Elric chuckled. "It's not just about survival. A man needs to retain some aesthetic pleasures."

She looked down her nose at him haughtily. "Are you saying a large woman isn't aesthetically pleasing?" Like most vampires, Lorelei was gracefully proportioned. A vampire's body shed its stored fat over time, rather than carry the extra dead weight. She was lean and not overly muscular, but at six feet tall, she was more Amazon than fragile femme petite. Her six-inch spiked stilettos made her height almost equal to Elric's, something he didn't encounter often, especially in a female. The thought of tangling with a woman who might actually attempt to match him in size, if not strength, was interesting, but Lorelei wasn't someone he'd ever find appealing. She was too brash and crude to seem attractively feminine in his eyes.

Elric didn't bother to stand. Let her feel she was looking down on him. He knew who held the upper hand. "I have women of many shapes and sizes in my harem, though none of your considerable stature. But you see, I've chosen my stable for more than quantity of blood, or quality of bed partners. It is their individual natures and characteristics of companionship that I find aesthetically pleasing. I'm very discerning about who I choose to spend my time with." Now he stood, equaling her height and letting his eyes boldly meet hers. "If you'll excuse me."

Elric left her standing there, leaving without waiting for response, to accentuate the fact that she was not among those whom he valued for companionship. He'd rather pace the room.

Tomas, Richard, and Kieran remained sitting at the large mahogany conference table. Lorelei took his vacated seat there, as Elric made his way towards Byron, who stood at the window. The master was approaching. Byron met his gaze and nodded to show that he felt it, just as Elric did. As Arif's presence grew stronger, Elric crossed the room and opened the door for him.

Arif met him at the doorway with a smile and slight nod of his head, pleased that his most senior guardsman had anticipated him and risen to open the door as a sign of respect. It would look good in the eyes of his guests. Elric backed up behind the widely opened door to allow them entry.

An immediate hush fell over the room as the senior guard all stood at attention to receive their master. Arif entered, and then moved aside with an outstretched arm to admit his two guests. The first was a tall and strikingly handsome, pale man, with dark hair and a very arrogant, commanding expression. He wore an expensive black suit and entered the room as though he owned it. His manner piqued Elric's interest, that and the fact that Master Arif seemed to defer to the man. A very odd and not entirely unwelcome sight.

Behind him, entered a woman of rich beauty, her countenance bringing to mind the glamour of classic royalty, although she wore a modern black cocktail dress. Her copper hair was worn twisted up, accentuating her high cheekbones and delicate features. She entered the room and stood beside her companion, surveying the vampires within with mild interest and a slight smile. She clearly enjoyed having the full attention of the room.

Arif entered, taking a place beside them. Elric closed the door and then stood aside with his hands clasped behind him, awaiting introductions.

Arif swept his hand before him, indicating the vampires in the room as he dipped his head and spoke to his guests. "My Senior Guard." As the couple looked them over, Arif lifted his head and addressed his coven. "It is my honor and esteemed pleasure to present…my sire." It seemed all the vampires could do to keep a hush upon the room. Even Elric swallowed back a gasp. Other than Cain, the coven had never met a vampire older than the master. He had certainly never given any indication that his sire still survived.

After letting the title sink in, Arif continued. "The vampire Drake, and his vampiress consort, the lady Maribeth." Drake barely dipped his head in a nod of acceptance for the introduction. He wore a guarded expression and did not reveal his mark, as was common practice among most vampires upon introduction. The lady however, lowered her lovely blue eyes, turned her head to the side, and executed a gracefully simple curtsy, letting her mark blaze brightly into psychic view, before giving the room a shrewd smile.

Her mark was amazing. Elric took it in with fascinated awe. It was not that she was terribly strong in power, but she was centuries old. Reading the aging of a mark was a complex and inexact skill, but the only mark that Elric had ever seen that approached the apparent age of this graceful woman, was the vampire Cain.

In addition to her age, her aura was compelling because it was intertwined with the mark of another vampire. She had been bitten and drunk from recently. If the mark was from Arif's sire, which was likely by the way he now held his arm wrapped around her covetously, Drake was a very powerful vampire indeed. Elric could not tell his true age by this second-hand imprint, but he must be close in age to Maribeth, and twice as strong in magical skill.

After giving the vampires a moment to acknowledge the two, Arif continued. "I wanted to be absolutely sure that my full senior guard makes your acquaintance, because they are to acknowledge that you have complete, unrestricted access to the entire community during your stay." Arif explained to his guests.

Drake nodded and then addressed the coven. "This is my first visit to *Kana Susamiş Icin Ev*, although I have heard about it endlessly over the past century." His accent was European, but difficult to place. He sounded smug, and a bit bothered to have been brought here. "It is interesting to see what Arif has done with this parcel of property that was nothing more than woodlands when I bequeathed it to him; another pet project for his collection of interests.

I returned from abroad a few years ago, and Arif has finally convinced me to come and pay a visit. You keep your own humans here, is that right?"

Maribeth's smile lit up in refined but mischievous glee. "I don't think I've ever seen so many marks in one place. The local aura's lit like Christmas!" Her accent was different from his, thick and more traditionally British upper class.

Arif's lips curved into a smug smile. "Yes, we endeavor to be as self-sufficient for blood as possible here. Of course, you are welcome to sample from any within our community walls. We house nearly two hundred humans here."

"Two hundred?" Maribeth repeated in shock.

"One hundred and eighty three at the moment, to be exact. They are kept in careful count I can assure you," Arif told them proudly. Actually, Elric knew that number to be a bit off, even accounting for an extra pet Elric knew the master had been keeping. Strange for the master to over-estimate like that. He was usually very aware of such things. He must be giving less attention to the compound with other things on his mind. Elric did not see fit to correct him, and let him continue. "There is no killing here. We keep only the finest and healthiest of donors."

Maribeth responded with a polite, maidenly chuckle as Drake rolled his eyes and commented, "A lot of unnecessary work if you ask me."

Maribeth nodded, "It does sound quite the burden. Surely you don't need so many."

"To be honest, if caring for them weren't a burden, I would say we needed more. As it is, we supplement to those lower in the ranks with animal blood harvested from the nearby ranch," Arif confided.

Maribeth made a small mew of disgust. "With so many humans I would think it would be better to ration lightly and make do, rather than drink from animals. They're never nearly as good."

"Our humans give all they are safely able, on a regular basis. If a vampire is away on business for more than a few nights, their stable is brought to our medical center regularly for blood collection. Vampires who wish to have more blood than their own stable provides, can earn credits for collected human blood from our bar, rather than be limited to the animal blood we keep in strong supply there.

Vampires of my coven also have opportunity to earn leave for hunting expeditions, or possibly earn a higher rank through loyalty and devotion, giving them a larger stable of humans to feed from. Those of high rank are eager to keep their places, and the rewards rank brings," Arif explained, gesturing around the room at his senior guard, "and those below are very motivated to show me their worth. It is a good system. I have vampires who are connected to me throughout the nation, who wish to earn my favor for a spot here in our little community.

But you needn't trouble yourselves with our blood rationing. You are welcome to have all that you desire. We have thirty-seven vampires in residence here at *Kana Susamiş Icin Ev,* and each of them will be instructed to allow you access to their stables upon request."

Drake's interest was regained by that information. "Thirty-seven?" he asked incredulously. "That's rather ambitious. Most covens tend to fall apart much beyond twenty members."

Arif stood a little straighter, answering proudly, "As you know, my extended coven is actually quite a bit more grand in comparison, but yes, my immediate coven in residence is impressive on its own. Things run smoothly here. Discipline is the key. I have a strict system of checks and balances. Each of my senior guardsmen..." Elric could tell by the look Lorelei shot the master, and his slight pause, that she was bold enough to give him mental reprimand. "And guardswoman," he added, "has command over two lesser guards, and four cadets; with the exception of Kieran, who is my personal scout. All have duties that keep the community running smoothly and under strict supervision."

"How very militant," Maribeth remarked with a slight edge of contempt.

Arif chose to continue as though uninterrupted. "And of course all are at my disposal for whatever special assignments I might need them to take care of. Those loyal vampires who follow the rules are well rewarded for it, and are very content in their residence here."

Drake crossed his arms as he surveyed Kieran and the five senior guard vampires of the coven once again. "And I should hope that of those in residence here, not all are privy to the details of your many endeavors, no matter how loyal."

"Discretion is an art I know well," Arif assured him. "I am truly shined upon by good fortune to have such a competent senior guard. They each have certain projects that they oversee for me, to keep our interests moving forward."

Drake fixed Arif with a steady gaze. "There is only one interest I have here. Your hobbies and dabblings do not concern me. I want an update on the girl."

Elric noticed that the other vampires of the room were listening keenly. As far as he knew, Tomas and Richard had not been trusted with knowledge of the vampiress Alyson, and her significant powers. Byron and Lorelei knew of her, but were not directly connected to the situation. Aware that the conversation should not go any further in present company, Arif nodded sedately. "Of course. Let me dismiss those uninvolved, and I can tell you all that you wish to know."

Arif gave Elric a mental command that he and Kieran should stay, and then addressed the guard aloud. "You are all dismissed. Make your underlings aware of our guests and their elite status here. They are permitted entry wherever they would like, and may have carte blanche at our blood bar. They are to be given full access to all humans upon request as well."

As Arif nodded their dismissal, and all readied themselves to leave, Lorelei boldly raised her hand to be given leave to speak. "May I ask how long we have the honor of expecting their presence here?" she asked, after giving Arif only a brief moment to acknowledge her.

Arif looked to his guests. Drake gave him a look of boredom that Elric interpreted as his aloof version of a shrug. "We'll see."

Lorelei was not satisfied to be dismissed. "Is there anything else I can do for you, sire?" She was not only offering her services, she wanted to be sure that the visitors knew that she was Arif's offspring, hopefully to be treated with extra favor.

Arif stared at her levelly. There was no way for Elric to know if Lorelei ever received mental rebuke for her forwardness, but Arif rarely reprimanded her vocally. She'd always been a favorite. "Lorelei, why don't you stay and see if our guests would like some refreshment?" She dipped her head with a smile and retrieved some crystal glasses from the table, to fill from one of her captives.

Arif turned back to his guests and gestured that they should make themselves at home. "Please, sit. Lorelei will bring you each a drink, and we can discuss some exciting recent developments."

Drake pulled out a chair for Maribeth at the conference table, before taking a seat himself. Kieran, Elric, and Arif joined them, while Lorelei served drinks.

Drake rested his elbows on the table and folded his hands, leaning his chin upon them. "May I speak plainly here?"

Arif glanced at the vampires present. "Yes, these have all been trusted with my cause."

"Arif, you have been chasing after this dream of creating The United One for the better part of a century. Researching myths, collecting vampires of all breeds, performing your blood experiments...and every time that you have told me you were on the verge of producing this powerful creature, I have known better than to think it could be true."

Arif was obviously a bit annoyed to be spoken to this way in front of his coven, but after a moment, he replied with a sly smile. "But this time we are beyond speculation, it is undeniable. My plan has finally come to fruition and I have produced The United One, without a doubt."

Lorelei had obviously been unaware of this information, and joined them at the table with great interest. She seemed nervous. Elric guessed that she might wonder and worry that it was her original target in her failed mission, the son of the vampire hunter, who had now been turned into this vampire prodigy.

Drake spoke quietly with his chin still resting on his folded hands. "I believe you."

Arif smiled broadly. "You have faith that my foresight was justified?"

"I've seen her," Drake answered simply.

Elric wondered if any other noted the relief on Lorelei's face, that The United One was female, and therefore not the child of her former lover.

Arif was astonished, but given no time to speak as Drake went on. "I have seen her, spoken to her and danced with her. I caused her to ingest my blood and shared her visions. The United One walks among us, just as you say. But she is not your creation, nor is she under your control."

The room was silent. Arif was frankly flabbergasted to think that Drake had such intimate knowledge of The Untied One, before Arif had even gotten the chance to tell him. And then to have the credit taken away as though her creation was a mere accident? Perhaps it was, but an accident born from years of preparation on his part.

Maribeth broke the silence by lightly running her finger along the lip of her crystal glass, making a lovely chiming sound. "I didn't think she was all that impressive."

Drake corrected her. "She was young and uneducated, but the power within her was quite impressive indeed. It struck me as a very pleasant and unexpected surprise. I knew what she was the moment I saw her vampire eyes. It was but a glimpse across a crowded room, but they shone with radiance unlike any other. After that, I observed her closely and learned what I could, my original intentions for attending the gathering all but forgotten."

"I still don't understand why you wanted to go in the first place," Maribeth said sulkily. "You barely even gave me time to visit. Taking me there, and then dragging me away before I'd had my fill. You're such a tease. Haven't I a right to spend time with my eldest protégé?"

Drake dismissed her with a wave of his hand. "You haven't been close to Cain in decades."

Could this woman truly be Cain's sire? Before Elric had the chance to speculate further, Arif spoke up to take their attention. Something telepathic must have passed between Arif and his sire, because Drake was not at all unhappy over the interruption. "Maribeth, I know Drake has not fully embraced the slice of paradise I've created here, but surely you can appreciate its finer luxuries. Why don't I have Lorelei give you a private tour of the compound? You ladies can visit the salon, or perhaps Lorelei can have some of her handsome humans escort you for a stroll on our private beach. It's beautiful in the full moonlight."

Maribeth looked perfectly happy to be left out of the remainder of the conversation, in exchange for the promised tour and companionship. Lorelei however was very annoyed and insulted. Arif pretended not to notice. "Lorelei, escort the lady Maribeth to endeavors more of her interest. Perhaps rouse two of these humans you've brought us. They're unmarked as of yet, and I'm sure you and the lady would enjoy an unrestricted drink from such strong and virile sources. Take them with you to a secluded setting more to your liking."

Lorelei fixed him with an icy glare. "As you wish, Master."

Maribeth glanced around the room until her gaze settled on a handsome, fair-skinned blonde man near the window. "I like that one. May I?" Lorelei gave a slight shrug and looked away in a manner that seemed almost rude, to show it made no difference to her. Maribeth didn't bother to acknowledge the woman's ire at having to leave the room. She rose and approached the man.

He was draped over a chair, his head slumped to one side, and looked to be in his early twenties. He wore only a pair of jeans, his strong and well-muscled arms and chest bare, to provide better access for blood letting. There were only a few crusted over wounds from Lorelei's knife, but any vampire in the room could smell the enticing aroma of his blood.

Maribeth knelt to see his face, and ran her hand over his body in bold familiarity. She let her finger trace down the chiseled lines that separated the muscles of his abdomen until she skimmed over his navel, reaching the denim of his jeans. "He'll do nicely." She looked up at the man's unresponsive face. "Is he drugged?"

Lorelei gave a small snort of a laugh. "Of course not, you'd taste it. How unappealing. I'll rouse him," she said, as she came to stand before the man. She took his chin in her hand so that he might face her, although his eyes were still closed. "Wake up, sunshine."

Elric was surprised to see the man begin to come around immediately. He could see Kieran was surprised as well, but Arif and Drake didn't seem to find the transaction at all interesting.

The man's eyes fluttered open and he focused on the two women before him. "Sorry...did I fall asleep?" he asked Lorelei groggily. "Hey, is your friend joining us? I'm down for that," he said with a grin.

Maribeth smiled and clapped her hands like a schoolgirl. "Marvelous," she remarked to Lorelei. "How do you do it?"

Lorelei was visibly pleased by the appreciation of her talents. "When you can get into their heads, it's easy. He wasn't in a normal state of sleep, he was only sleeping because I told him to. I put him in thrall; hypnotized him. Sunshine was a code word."

The man knitted his brows and tried to make sense of the ladies' conversation as he sat up a bit straighter in the chair. He glanced down at himself to see that he was shirtless, and noticed the scabbed-over wounds on his arms. "What the hell?" For the first time he seemed to realize that there might be cause for alarm.

Lorelei shifted to reveal her entrancing violet vampire eyes, as she cupped his face in her hands to make him meet her gaze. "It's alright," she told him. "See that pretty red-head there?" Lorelei let him break their gaze to glance at Maribeth for a moment before taking back his attention. "That's my friend Maribeth. She'd like to spend some time with you. You be very nice to her, and do whatever she tells you to, okay?"

As Lorelei released him, the man nodded and stood to approach Maribeth, who was watching him with interest. "Hey baby, let's get out of here."

Maribeth raised an eyebrow at the way he addressed her, but then laughed and took his arm. Lorelei chose the dark skinned man she'd drawn blood from just before the guests had arrived. She woke him in the same manner she had the other, and then brought him to join Maribeth at the door.

Maribeth glanced back at Drake as her prize opened the door for her. "See you later, darling," she told her vampire lover.

He gave her a tolerant smile. "Have fun."

As they left, Lorelei took a moment to look back at the master. She gestured towards the last human man that was left on a couch at the back of the room. "He's all yours."

Arif nodded his head, dismissing her. "Thank you, Lorelei."

As the ladies left with their escorts, Drake spoke to Arif, Kieran, and Elric. "Maribeth is a lovely creature, isn't she? So graceful and charming, and of an admirable age. I love ladies of refinement, especially when they harbor an appreciation for viciousness beneath their civil exteriors of powder and lace."

Arif gave him an agreeable smile. "Why do you think I was drawn to turn Lorelei?" Elric and Kieran shared a glance of amusement. Vicious might describe Lorelei well, but lady-like lace and refinement were a bit beyond her reach.

Drake continued. "I came across her in England, and we've been traveling about together for the past few decades. It's much more suitable for me over there now. The vampire population has thinned considerably, and the hunting is excellent. Bit of a werewolf problem though…mangy things.

You can imagine my annoyance when we returned to the states, to find that the place is practically over-run with the undead. They're proliferating like vermin over here. Have you no control at all? We used to clear out the younglings from our territories. Now I find they are being sheperded like lost sheep!"

Arif lowered his eyes. "I've been focused on other things."

"Obviously. Don't you find it irritating to have such competition for your hunting area?" Drake asked, including Kieran and Elric in the question. They both knew better than to answer.

"Ah, but we have little need to hunt. Our harem stables provide all the blood and entertainment we could want from humans," Arif told him smugly.

"How nice for you," Drake replied drolly. "There are still those of us who prefer to hunt nightly prey, and would like to spend an evening without tripping over younglings to do it. Even without actively eradicating the young and unprotected, most used to perish after a few years on their own. However, the vampires here seem well educated in the arts of survival, and on the whole, less violent than most.

I'd heard that there was a single vampire responsible for this. A man named Cain. I had sought him out to see if he might be eliminated, in order to stop encouraging such growth in our numbers, but then I was presented with proof of The United One, and all further concerns fled my mind. You can imagine my surprise, not only to find the very creature you have dedicated so much time to producing, but to find her unfettered, free and completely beyond your reach."

Arif took the discussion back in hand, insulted by Drake's statement. "It is true that The Untied One was created outside of my supervision, but it was only due to my careful coordination that she was produced at all, and we have had her under strict observation from nearly the night she was awakened. Kieran is a shade, and has been reporting her doings to me since she was discovered."

"Then why did you not collect her upon discovery, and bring her here?" Drake asked shrewdly.

Arif was annoyed that he made it sound so simple. "There are many factors at play. She has connections that protect her, an entire coven of shifters, and an elder that is best not made an enemy. Cain, the very vampire that you described, has made it his personal duty to mentor her."

"I don't find him all that formidable." Drake's stare bore into Arif like a laser, steady and unflinching. "You could have taken The United One swiftly, before they even understood her significance. They would not have known to trace it to you. Your hesitation lost her for you. You will not take her now. You'll have to try and create another."

Arif shook his head, refusing to admit that Drake was right. Elric knew that partly due to his own actions, Alyson was not brought to the master's attention until she was well established at Cain's estate. It sounded simple to abandon her to make another of her breed, but all of Arif's attempts had failed. That was also due to Elric's meddling. Making a new United One probably could be accomplished under controlled circumstances, if Elric wasn't involved to sabotage it. Elric hoped that Arif never figured that out.

"Oh no," Arif said with a shake of his head. "It won't come to that. I've left her an open doorway, that she will surely be persuaded to make use of. She will come to me, you'll see. Already the seeds of doubt I've planted are beginning to grow within her."

Elric put very little stock in the effect their last visit might have had on Alyson. It had seemed as though she might be swayed at first, but in the weeks that had gone by since then, they had not heard from her. Kieran reported that she still seemed satisfied to stay where she was. Maybe she was heeding Elric's secret warning. Drake did not seem to put much faith in Arif's plan either. "That is very little to place your hopes on."

"Never fear, it will be enough when combined with the fact that I have Kieran to watch over her, telling me of her every move. And Kieran is not the only agent I have guiding her towards my interests."

Drake shrugged and leaned back in his chair. "Do as you please. This is your pet project, not mine. I find her an interesting curiosity, nothing more. But I admit that I would like to learn more of your plans, should you manage to obtain access to the powerful blood you seek."

Arif stood, seeming almost unable to contain his excitement. "Yes! This is why I have wanted you to come," he said, gesturing for Drake to leave the room with him. "Elric, Kieran, you are dismissed. Elric, you're to take Lorelei's last captive to a holding cell, and meet me back here one hour before dawn for further instruction. Kieran, visit your stable and drink your fill, for you'll be returning to your post watching over The United One at nightfall tomorrow evening."

Elric and Kieran stood, nodding acceptance of their orders as Arif and Drake moved to leave the room. "I think you will be quite impressed," Arif was telling his sire. "Let me show you the vessels I have prepared."

Chapter 8 - Time to Shift the Scales

Allie

Cain's Estate, Upstate, New York
An evening in early Autumn

Sorrow. Like drowning in the dark depths of a silent sea, misery pulled at her senses, threatening to drag her further in, like a merciless undertow. Every now and then, hard truths of failure and sharp jagged edges of self-doubt would come upon her, as though she were being pummeled by them; rocks at the bottom of this unforgiving ocean.

It had started as a vague discomfort. Alyson was out shopping, just randomly flipping through the CDs in the music store at the mall, looking for a way to kill the night without having to be at home taking direction from anyone. It was much more fun to spend her time practicing her powers. Tonight she was reading minds and seeing just how much control she could have over others without their realization of it; something she was better off doing alone, so as not to be reprimanded for disregard of privacy.

At first, she had thought it was someone at the mall. She kept getting these waves of unhappiness. But it was not long before she felt the intimate personality within the emotion. It was Cain, she just knew that it was. But he was at home, wasn't he? That was pretty far away. She shouldn't be feeling him from here. Another flowing wave of despair washed over her. It didn't matter where he was physically, he was most definitely in her heart.

She left the store and made her way out of the mall, walking sedately at first, her head cocked to the side as she listened for thoughts and tried to figure out what was going on. Soon she found herself pushing past teenagers and desperately trying to get out of sight so she could take to the air and get home.

She tried to communicate with him, but got no response. Either he couldn't hear her from so far away, or he was shutting her out. Where was Mattie? A quick check told her that he was still at the swap meet, rifling through old camera parts and looking for something interesting to bring home and tinker with. He was still feeling a bit sullen over the fact that she hadn't wanted to go.

It wasn't so much that she didn't want to shop, as the fact that she greatly valued the chance to be alone for a change. He'd been acting so smothering lately, wanting to be with her every moment, and focusing on things that seemed so mundane and…human. If she had joined him and then he'd caught her focusing on playing with her powers rather than giving him her attention, it would probably have been worse than not going.

Mattie had no idea she was checking on him, or what was up with Cain. She left him be for now. She'd be home in a moment to assess the situation. As she rose into the night sky, the chill from the height better matched the misery that was growing stronger within her. It took all of her focus just to get home. She almost found herself wishing she could just plummet to the ground, to curl up and cry.

As she neared the house, the strength of feeling almost doubled; something she would not have thought possible. She was close enough to actually feel him now, not only through her empathy, but through their shared mark as well. She practically dove for the ground and then hit the lawn running. "Cain?" She burst through the front entrance and took a quick survey of the house with her senses. Nothing but emotional pain. "Cain?"

She strode purposefully for the back parlor where Cain was known to sit by the fire. It was empty, and the fire grate was cold and black. She stopped to judge his direction through her feel for him. Upstairs. She didn't even bother with the grand staircase. She simply ran out to the entryway and rose straight up to the upper hallway loft that overlooked the front door. He was in his room.

She walked to the door, wondering if she dared to disturb him while he was closed within. "Cain," she called again meekly. She felt so drained. Her strength was becoming quickly sapped, between her flight and the emotional distress of his sadness. My God, but he felt so desperately hopeless that she half cringed to think that he might even be planning to dust himself. He didn't answer and she still couldn't make any telepathic sense of his thoughts, it was just too heavy a wall of depression to slosh through. In a sudden panic, she thrust open the door and entered, ready to find him in a terrifying state, and to stop him from whatever drastic measures he might be taking due to his emotional defeat. "Cain!"

She quickly assessed the room. Impeccably neat, and other than the bookshelves, almost too empty to look lived in. The only thing out of place was the wooden chair, pulled away from its home at the desk. Her eyes darted from the desk, past the plush, but empty, reading chair and ottoman by the window, and over to the bed. There he was.

Cain lay on the bed. Dressed, silent, and staring at the ceiling, he didn't even acknowledge her entrance into the room. She stalked over to the bed, still worried, but now that she had found him whole, also just a bit pissed off. "Cain!"

His eyes slowly focused on her standing over him. He was still unmoving, but rather than seeming too exhausted to move, he looked to be straining with great effort to keep himself still. "What?" he asked through gritted teeth.

She slumped herself down to sit next to him on the bed, glad to find him responsive. Jeez, you would have thought he was under some sort of evil spell or something. But no, now that he acknowledged her, his mind opened for her as well. There was no frightening paranormal reason for his state. It was just Cain, tensely upset and feeling absolutely miserable.

The force of it was daunting. If the man could have easily killed himself, he might have. *No*, she could hear him respond wearily in her mind to her worried concerns of suicide. *I wouldn't so irresponsibly abandon God's work for me here on earth. Apparently, I am meant to forever exist in pain.*

"Stop it," she demanded in exasperation. She'd been feeling his bouts of depression since she and Mattie had taken up residence here, although never like this. She was thoroughly tired of it, unsympathetic as that may seem. How much could she take? The feelings weren't even hers! This had to be the worst, though. She'd never felt him so desperately hopeless and unresponsive. "Cain," she tried again, in a softer tone.

He looked at her stonily. He still felt stiff and tense. He was pissed that she'd burst into his room. "What do you want?"

She was speechless for a moment. "I... I don't want anything, I just..."

"Then please leave." He turned his eyes back to the ceiling without even giving her a chance to meet his gaze.

"No," she insisted indignantly. "You don't get to do this to me."

Now he looked at her with true awareness and emotion. "To *you*? I'm terribly sorry if my heartbroken depression and misery are an inconvenience to you. I certainly never meant to spoil your evening with my own personal sorrow." She'd never really heard him use sarcasm before, and with such a biting edge that she'd be happy if she never heard it again. "Feel free to shut me out," he added.

"I can't," she said in forceful annoyance.

"Well, I guess that's something else you need to practice control of then."

She put a hand on his shoulder and gave him a light shove. "That's not the point. I can't just leave you like this. You're my friend, Cain, and you should let me help you deal with stuff. I want to help."

He sighed, loosening up a little. He was still giving off every bit the same amount of sadness, but now sounded sorry for inflicting it on her. "Well, you can't, so I suggest you work on shutting me out so I don't drag you down with me."

"I tried," she admitted. "I can't. I don't know if it's because we've shared blood recently, or just because you're scaring me with all this, but I can't just make it go away and ignore you. It's like you're strangling me with it."

"Well, I'm sorry. That certainly wasn't my intention."

Allie lay down next to him, although he refused to move over and give her room. She fit anyway; it was a large bed. She lay on her side facing him as he stubbornly stared at the ceiling. "What's all this about?"

He spared her a glance as though to ask if she were truly *that* insensitive and stupid. Alright, she knew it was Felicity, but *still?* When she'd talked to him about the wedding, he had shown impressive restraint and control. He'd said he wanted it for Felicity, a human husband and family. Alyson had known it was difficult for him, but he did truly seem to want Felicity to be happy with her new life. He'd found Allie the very next evening and given her the card, desperate to know that she'd deliver it for him; that it wasn't too late. The wedding had been two months ago now, but she hadn't really spoken to him about it afterwards. She hadn't wanted to bring it up again because she'd thought he was handling it well. Guess not.

"Don't you understand?" Cain pleaded quietly. "She's truly gone now. She's beyond my reach. No matter my undying devotion and love for her, I can never touch her again, not after this. She's gone."

Another wave of heartbreak rushed over her from him, as Alyson tried to console him with her own soothing emotion. "But you knew that was how it would be," she told him with quiet reason. "You hadn't seen her in so long, and even after she came, you sent her back. What did you think would happen?"

"I know. I want it for her, I really do. I don't mean to try to change it. It just hurts." He seemed to rally his emotions and wiped his face. "I never meant for anyone to see me this way. I gave Sindy some money and sent her out clothes shopping. I wanted to be alone. I'm sorry my feelings were broadcast to you. I must seem so damn weak."

Allie was afraid to ask just how much money Cain had given Sindy in order to buy some time alone, but at least maybe she would come home with some clothes to discourage her penchant for walking around half-naked all the time. Allie gently wiped his face with her hand as well. "You aren't weak. Weakness would be taking Felicity's happiness away because you couldn't stand it. It takes strength to choose someone else's happiness over your own. This..." she said, gesturing towards his tear streaked face, "this just makes you human."

He arched his brow and wore a bit of a smile. "Almost," he added. "If I were human I wouldn't have the tenacious endurance to torture myself for so long. I would have moved on by now." He looked over at her with new worry. "Did I do the right thing, sending the card? It wasn't over-stepping, was it?"

"No, not at all," she assured him. "It was thoughtful."

"Did you read it?"

She looked at him with mild indignation. "No. I wouldn't open your personal correspondence."

He smiled. "I didn't ask if you opened it, I asked if you read it."

After a second, she dropped her eyes with a sheepish grin. "Okay, you caught me. I read it from Felicity." Felicity might have shown her the card if she'd asked, but it was easier, although questionably ethical, just to pull it from her thoughts while she was reading.

Cain didn't seem to mind. "Was it alright? I tried to write it in such a way that she wouldn't have to worry over showing it to another."

"It was fine."

"It wasn't too impersonal though, was it? I was trying so hard not to be overly emotional, but I hope she could still sense the depth of feeling; how much I care for her."

"She loved it, Cain. It made her cry."

"Oh great. I made her cry on her wedding day. Aren't I a sporting chap?"

"It was a beautiful gesture. So was the generous gift."

"It's only money. How was the wedding? Was it everything she could have hoped for?"

Alyson nodded to reassure him. "It was really nice, a childhood dream come true."

Cain smiled as he tried to picture it. "What sort of gown did she wear? I'll bet it was a classic ball gown. I know she loves that sort of thing."

"Yes, she looked like a princess."

"Did she wear her hair up?"

Alyson had to laugh at his desire for such detail. "Mostly up, but there were some pieces left down too."

"Ringlets," Cain supplied for her, picturing it. "I'm sure she was gorgeous. I wish I could have seen her." Cain lay there thoughtfully staring at the ceiling, his sorrow replaced by fond imagination for the moment. Suddenly he sat up, startling Allie. He stared at her with direct intensity. "Show me."

She gave him an odd look, as though unsure of his meaning, as she considered the implications. He pressed on. "Don't pretend that you don't know what I mean. I know you can do it. If you can pull memories out of my mind to experience them as full sensory visions, as you have in the past, there is no reason why you couldn't project your memories to me. I want to see her."

"I don't think that's a good idea, Cain."

He narrowed his eyes. "I ask for so little. How can you deny me that? You have your love with you always. I have almost nothing."

She sat up and tried to soothe him with emotional current, but he rejected it with intense force. She tried to reason with him. "Cain, I'm afraid it will just make things worse. Why torture yourself? You have to let her go."

He calmed, and used a new tactic. "I will. I'll let her go, but I need closure."

"Isn't that what her visit was all about? You were supposed to have closure then, when you kissed her goodbye."

He chose to ignore the tone of reprimand for kissing her. "Alyson, please. I want to see her, in her wedding gown, happy to begin her new life. It will make it real for me. Then I can move on."

She stared at him for a second and then lay back down on the bed with a huff of indecisive aggravation. This was a bad idea. She knew it was a bad idea. But how was she supposed to refuse? The poor guy was heartbroken. "I wish you were human," she told him accusingly.

He gave a bitter chuckle as he lay back down next to her on his back. "You and me both."

"If you were human," she explained, "I would know what to do. I've helped guy friends get over heartbreak before."

He turned to look at her. "How's that?"

"It usually involves large amounts of alcohol."

"Ahhh."

"Someone should invent liquor that works better on vampires."

"Yes, I think I could use that."

She turned to face him in thoughtful contemplation. "Actually, there is something that works." He just looked at her without anticipating her thought. "Venom," she supplied.

He considered it briefly, and then gave her an appreciative but dismissive smile. "Thanks, but I can make do without. I just need time." They lay in silence until he finally turned back to her pleadingly. "Just show her to me. Please? I can handle it. I'll never ask you again."

Allie sighed. He sat watching her with his large and hopeful blue eyes. She knew she was going to give in. Why prolong it and make him suffer? She nodded and felt the tension in him immediately ease. "Do you need anything from me?" he asked eagerly.

"No, just lay still so I can focus." She gently put a hand on his shoulder to help her settle her attention. "I'm not going through the whole wedding," she warned him. "I'm only going to show you Felicity alone."

"Fine, anything. Thank you," he told her agreeably.

Alyson sorted through her memories, trying to decide what would be suitable. She decided that showing Cain her visit with Felicity at the wedding probably wasn't the best choice. They had spent most of the time talking about Ben and Bernard. She could show him the vision without letting him hear the conversation, but Felicity had seemed a bit drained by events at the time. It had not been the happiest moment of the day. There must be a better alternative.

Finally, Alyson decided to show him Felicity's morning spent getting ready. This was a memory of a time that Alyson had not been present for, but she had pulled it from Felicity during her visit. Being a second-hand vision as it was, Allie wasn't sure if it would be as clear, but it still seemed the most joyous choice that did not involve Ben directly. She would relay it without sound, because she'd only been able to retrieve snippets of the conversation, but she didn't think Cain would mind.

Alyson closed her eyes and replayed the memory in her thoughts, doing her best to broadcast it to Cain. She'd never done anything quite this ambitious before, but she had sent Mattie a small flash of a vision now and then, to show him a picture of something he hadn't seen, so it wasn't an entirely new endeavor.

Felicity stood before a full-length mirror in a bedroom somewhere. She wore her wedding dress of creamy, rich white silk, and was swishing and smoothing it, admiring the full bell shape of the skirt, and turning to try to see the train stretching out behind her. Her hair had been curled by rollers, and was pulled back in a temporary clip, but her make-up was already done. She looked absolutely beautiful. She reached up to remove the clip, and let the waves of her deep red hair tumble down about her shoulders.

Alyson could feel Cain gasp beside her, as his heart swelled at the vision. The depth of his emotion for Felicity, restrained for a time during his talk with Alyson, suddenly came rushing back, overwhelming her, and causing her to lose the vision for a second. Multi-tasking was still beyond her. She needed to concentrate on one thing at a time. Although Cain's thoughts might slip through now and then, she needed to try to stop reading things from him, to concentrate on sending the memory.

Alyson found the memory again, showing Cain the vision of his love. Felicity sat down in a chair before a vanity table, and began speaking to a friend who was fussing with her hair. They couldn't hear what was said, but it didn't matter. Felicity was smiling and laughing, stopping every now and then to stare dreamy-eyed into the mirror, and imagine hopes and visions of her own. Cain and Alyson were silent voyeurs, watching Felicity have her hair pinned into just the right arrangement, transforming her into what came through as a Victorian-era beauty to Cain's mind.

Felicity's friend was placing the headpiece and veil into Felicity's hair, when her subject startled all by jumping up and rushing across the room. Felicity retrieved something from a drawer and came back to give it to her friend. It was a stunning antique hair-comb, covered in jewels. Alyson shared the same awe as Felicity's friend as they admired the piece, but then the vision fell apart.

Cain had unwittingly interrupted her. His reaction to the scene was beyond anything Alyson could account for. The hair-comb was lovely, but why did it affect him so? Alyson barely had time to interpret his emotion, before he was impatiently urging her to bring back the memory for him. Allie was hesitating, wanting to understand. "It was a gift," Cain explained to her through his tears, "from me. I gave it to her years ago, before I left. Did she wear it?" he asked in quiet and gratified disbelief.

Alyson had no choice but to continue showing him the memory. They watched together as Felicity seemed to express the deep attachment she had to the piece, and to insist that her friend place it properly in her hair. When they were done, the lovely comb barely showed, its jewels of green peeking out from its place in the back above her curls. It didn't matter. Felicity was well satisfied just to have it with her, and apparently so was Cain.

He couldn't hold back his emotions any more. They swept over Alyson, making her lose her thoughts. As the vision dissipated, she was forced to turn her attention to Cain, gently weeping beside her. She couldn't say she was sorry she had shown him. Although overcome with emotion, it was not the same as the misery she had felt from him before. He was happy for Felicity, and thrilled to know that he had been in her thoughts on her special day.

Alyson did her best to disengage herself from him and assess his state. As grateful as he was for the vision, and although it had helped in a way, she still could not leave him like this. "Now would be the time for the alcohol," she said decisively.

Cain still lay on his back with his eyes closed, quietly trying to contain himself. He didn't even flinch when she firmly took his arm into her hands. Without further thought, Alyson extended her fangs and bit down into his forearm. She felt the rush of adrenaline race through her as her venom was injected through her fangs to infect her victim with its hypnotizing narcotic.

Alyson could feel Cain start as she punctured his skin, but he didn't pull away, and the venom began its work on him quickly. She did her best to keep her fangs sunken into his arm, although the vampire within her desperately wanted to remove them to taste his blood. A few more seconds, she kept telling herself. Just give him a few more second's worth.

Cain noticeably calmed and then sunk into a hazy bliss of the remembered visions soothed by Alyson's powerful drug. Alyson herself could not even spare another thought for whatever Cain was feeling, because her own bodily demands were boldly urging her to meet their needs. She needed blood. The flight, fighting off Cain's despair, the visions, using of all those powers had drained her. She had nothing left to draw on for restraint. Self-control disintegrated and she withdrew her fangs to take a much-needed drink of blood from Cain's arm.

She sucked and pulled on his skin to draw the blood as quickly as she could. It filled her mouth as a rich reward. More, she needed more. Impatient and craving, she took his blood as quickly as she could. Oh God, the thirst within her was so strong that she could barely think, but the predator within her was still alert to the fact that someone had entered the room.

Alyson swallowed what was in her mouth and forced herself not to take any more until she had analyzed her surroundings. The vampire within her wanted to turn and hiss at the intrusion, chasing off whoever dared to keep her from her feast. She'd only barely begun! She needed the blood before her, and nothing else could possibly be as important.

Alyson fought for control and forced herself to recognize that it was the mark of her lover nearby. It was Mattie who had entered the room, and now stood staring from the doorway. Alyson looked up, battling her urges, keeping her movements steady and smooth, rather than turning on him like a wild thing.

A small trickle of blood escaped her lips and her tongue retrieved it before she could bring her arm to her mouth to wipe it away. Neither gesture would present a very civilized picture, but she still wished she'd been quick enough to wipe it with her sleeve rather than betray that she couldn't bear to waste a single drop.

Her eyes fought to keep Mattie in shades of blue and green, while her mind struggled to make her body shift, and present herself as human. She couldn't do it. She needed blood far too badly to give up her predatory form. Mattie just stood there staring at her, painted in the cold tones of her heat vision, waiting for an explanation. "Cain was having a bad night," she told him.

Mattie stood there observing Cain, lying on the bed unconscious, with a bloodied bite on his arm. "I'd say he still is," was Mattie's quiet reply. "Then again, maybe not," he reconsidered. "He always did enjoy having you drink from him. Is this your idea of helping him out?"

Alyson sat up more fully, trying to contain her ire over the accusing tone of Mattie's voice. Jeez...it's not as though he'd found them in bed together! Well, technically, they *were* on the bed, but still...

Mattie dropped his eyes from her. He knew better than to meet her line of sight when she wielded her vampire gaze. She forced her annoyance to recede and instead sought his understanding. "I had to do something. He was overwhelming me with his emotions. It was because of the wedding. He's taking it really hard."

"I thought you were at the mall," Mattie's voice still had a slight lilt of accusation...and an undercurrent of hurt.

"I was," she told him. "He was here alone, drowning in misery. It was so strong I couldn't hold it off...even from the mall," she insisted pleadingly. "I had to come home and do something. The venom always calms him. I thought it would be better if he could sleep. I didn't know what else to do. It was really bad."

He believed her. She could feel it. He was slowly coming around, letting the indignation of finding them like this slip away. As upsetting as it had seemed, Mattie knew Cain well enough not to expect anything indecent from him. It was a bit distressing to Alyson, that Cain's loyalty came to Mattie's mind before her own, but she was just glad he wasn't too mad at her.

She stood from the bed. As she dropped Cain's arm, the small beads of blood that had formed over the puncture of her bite, shifted and began to flow a little down his skin. It took every bit of will within her, to keep from going back to lick it clean. "I barely took anything," she told Mattie, desperate to make him understand and admire her restraint. "I wasn't planning to drink from him. It's the venom that knocked him out. I'd only just started when you got here, I swear. I didn't take much at all." She could hear the desperation in her own voice as she tried to explain her need without unleashing the strength of her thirst on him through empathy. "But I'm so thirsty, Mattie. I can barely stand it."

He came towards her, accepting her plea with open arms. "It's okay. We can fix that." He wanted to take her in for a re-assuring hug. He wanted to bring her downstairs and get her a drink of something dead and preserved from the refrigerator. She understood that, but it was never going to fly. Her body wanted blood live, warm, and straight from the source. To think that she was going to calmly walk downstairs and wait as he prepared something cold and clotted, needing to be stirred and reheated in the microwave was a joke.

She came into his arms and immediately sank her fangs into his throat. He couldn't even put up a token resistance. Her needle-like eyeteeth had punctured his skin and begun to drug him with venom before he even understood that she was biting him. Mattie's blood wasn't exactly alive, but the vampiric qualities in it more than made up for that, and it was a far cry from what was in the fridge.

Mmm... Mattie's blood was always the best. Cain's blood was wonderful in its own right, tasting of his age and the concentrated purity that came from years of mostly keeping it to himself, but Mattie's blood was the source of her existence; it was the force of her creation and the first blood she had ever drunk. There was just nothing else like it.

She drank from him steadily and briefly wondered what human blood might taste like. Vampire blood was slightly warmer than room temperature, but not nearly as hot as the living blood she had drunk from live animals. Vampire blood's appeal was not so much the warmth, but that it was such a powerful and complex solution, while animal blood was simple, thick, and heavy with life. Would human blood have a complexity reminiscent of a vampire's, mixed with true heat and those heavy, life-burdened cells found in animals? Why was she even questioning it? She would never know. Back to the source at hand.

She lowered Mattie to the floor as she drank, until she rested on her knees and held him over her lap. He'd passed out now. She hadn't taken care to give him a large dose of venom, but she had taken enough blood that he'd lost consciousness. He hated when she did that, and she usually tried to show more restraint. However, since Arif's visit he'd been extra-understanding of her struggles, so maybe he wouldn't give her a hard time.

Allie took a final pull from his throat, and then lowered him to lie in her lap. Not that her thirst was completely sated…it was never completely sated, but she shouldn't take any more from him. It was bad enough that she'd knocked him out from blood loss, she didn't want to take so much that it showed in his appearance. She was going to have enough to explain without Mattie waking up gaunt from depletion.

She should probably carry him out to the trailer. Luckily, with her strength it wouldn't be a problem. She glanced up at Cain, over on the bed. He was just as she'd left him when Mattie had interrupted her. She gently moved Mattie from her lap onto the floor and stood to approach the bed.

The bite she had given Cain had healed, and there was only the slightest discoloration to show where blood had dripped down his arm. His eyes were closed. It was always odd to watch a vampire sleep; all of the little signs of life that one might be used to, were not present. There was no rise and fall of his chest, no sound of breath, none of the little twitches or movements that one would expect to observe in a person asleep. He was still as death. His mind was at rest also. She was very glad to have been able to do him that favor, at least.

She was still seeing him with her heat vision. She hadn't shifted back since drinking from Mattie, although at this point, she had enough control to change. Cain's form had a general hue of blues and greens at his extremities, but there was still a core of yellow within him, and at the center of his body, there were even some slight tones of orange and red. Spreading in thin lines throughout, she could see that there was still some warm blood within him.

She sat down on the bed next to him and took his arm back into her hands. She was just lifting it to her lips when he pulled it away. His eyelids were still heavy, but she could feel that his mind was no longer as groggy as it had seemed. She immediately blinked her eyes, allowing herself to appear human again, re-sheathing her fangs repentantly. "You're back early," she said with a lilt of sheepish humor.

He gave her a weak smile. "I'm a healer. Nothing works on me for long." He glanced towards the doorway. "Unlike Mattie, whom it seems will be turning in early this morning."

"He'll be okay."

"Will you?"

"Yeah, sure."

His eyes watched her carefully now. "Is this a problem?"

She shook her head. "No. I talked to him. He understands why I bit you. It's no big deal."

Cain was glad to hear that, but she knew that it was only partially what he was talking about. He didn't want to cause problems between her and Mattie, but his main concern was her control. He said as much. "And your thirst?"

"I think I've been doing really well. You have no idea how hard it is, Cain." He arched an eyebrow at her with a smirk. He was a vampire, too. But her thirst was greater than others, even Arif had said so. "Don't you think I've been handling it okay?" she asked with a sudden flash of self-doubt.

"I did," he agreed, "until you came back for seconds." He lifted his arm for emphasis.

"Sorry."

She could feel him gathering his thoughts through the venomed haze to try to voice his concerns. She didn't really want to hear it. Mostly because she wasn't even sure she knew the answers to the questions he would ask. He asked anyway. "The things that Arif said about your thirst, were they true?"

She shrugged. "It's been getting harder," she admitted, "but I'm okay. I don't drink from humans. I never have," she insisted.

"I know. You've managed to mark almost every large animal outside of my estate for a ten mile radius," he pointed out with a grin, "but that's alright, as long as it's enough."

She didn't realize that he'd noticed. She'd never said anything to the guys about her outside hunting trips. She knew Mattie suspected, but she really didn't think that Cain knew. "I'm always careful," she assured him.

He nodded. He knew she was, because if she were killing the animals, there wouldn't be so many that were marked. She'd made a few mistakes, but she was a pretty good judge of things now. Leaving so many marks in plain sight may not be the wisest strategy for someone theoretically trying to maintain a low profile, but what choice did she have? The stuff from the fridge didn't always cut it for her. Luckily, most vampires couldn't see marks from very far away.

"What did you think of Arif's offer?" Cain asked. He was worried. He could see where she might find the invitation appealing.

"Don't worry. I'm not going anywhere." Cain just nodded. "Except to bed," she added. "I think things will go a lot more smoothly if Mattie wakes up next to me in bed instead of on the floor."

Cain smiled as she stood and went over to lift Mattie, who still showed no signs of waking. She was about to leave, when Cain called to her. "Alyson," she turned back to see him sitting up and watching her with a tear in his eye. He was thinking of Felicity again. He gave her a warm smile. "Thank you."

~~~~~~~~~~~~~~~~~~~~~~~~~~~~~~

Alyson approached Cain's house, relieved to feel that Mattie was definitely inside. Comforting, but strange. He rarely left their trailer before she awoke, even though he often rose much earlier. Mattie usually spent the early evening having a drink while watching the last colors of sunset fade from the sky and waiting for Allie to wake and join him. Maybe he was still annoyed with her.

On top of everything else last night, she'd somehow managed to smash one of the mirrored closet doors in their bedroom while getting undressed. She'd only meant to close it, but it had slid closed a bit more easily than she had accounted for…or maybe she just hadn't really been paying attention. Being super strong was something that still took some getting used to. Add it to the list of things they would have to fix because of her carelessness. It had been very close to dawn and she had been too groggy to clean it up properly. The stunt with Cain last night was enough reason for Mattie to be mad at her, she hoped he hadn't also stepped in the pile of broken glass she'd swept aside to clean up later.

Alyson found that she couldn't manage to wake before full dark these days. It had been a gradual shift, but a steady one. Try as anyone might to wake her, she was groggy and mostly unresponsive until no trace of light was left in the sky. Only upon full darkness did she begin to feel the surge of strength and alertness through her that made her feel invincible and ready to experience all the world had to offer.

She entered the house, but although she could feel Mattie's proximity, he didn't feel as though he were in the kitchen or parlor, where she would expect to find him. She followed the feeling of his mark, and sought the entrance to the basement stairs. Now his presence became stronger as she grew closer. As she descended, she began to hear evidence of him as well. She followed the odd noise combination of death metal music, simulated machine gun fire, and furniture being roughly abused. She entered the media room just as he slammed the controller in his hand down upon the arm of his chair with a curse. He picked it back up almost instantly and resumed his activity without sparing her a glance.

Alyson's senses were assaulted by the seven-foot-wide television screen mounted on the back wall of the room. It was showing the fast-moving images of soldiers racing through a previously-bombed city, while images of weapons, statistics, and messages flashed up on various parts of the screen. Mattie was practically jumping up and down on an oversized leather armchair, while playing the video game, and apparently losing.

Alyson stood there for a minute, taking it all in, and then crossed her arms and sent a mental nudge to Mattie for attention. He ignored her until the music signaling the end of the match was over, and the final kill was replayed for dissective criticism. Finally, he put down the controller and swiveled his chair to face her.

Alyson glanced over at the table in front of him. "You brought the Playstation over here?"

Mattie chuckled at the obviousness of the answer. "Are you also going to ask me why? Look at the size of this screen!"

"Call of Duty?" she asked, gesturing towards his game.

"The new one. Picked it up tonight."

Alyson was about to turn from it to speak to him, when something caught her eye. The game was over, and the pre-game lobby screen was on as Mattie waited for new players to join up for the next match. One of the names listed on the right side of the screen was familiar. "Is that *Ben?*"

Mattie answered in tense monotone. "Yup."

"Does he know it's you?" she asked incredulously.

"Nope. I changed my screen name."

Allie chewed on her lip to keep from smiling. "Still can't beat him huh?"

"I will. I definitely owe Everheart a few ass-whoopin's. I can play all night every night if I have to. I'll beat him."

Alyson shook her head. "All night, every night? Would it be really mean to tell you how pathetic that sounds?"

"I'm pathetic? He's the one playing Modern Warfare on his honeymoon."

Allie laughed. "They've been home for weeks now."

"Still, the guy is supposed to have a real life now, right, a job and a wife? There is no way he has more time to practice this shit than I do. I'll beat him."

Alyson thought better of pointing out the fact that Mattie considered himself to have a wife too. He was usually all about togetherness, which was nice, but it might be nicer to have a few un-smothered moments alone. Besides, if he was still pissed at her, let him play and take out his aggressions on the game. "Go get him, tiger."

Alyson left Mattie to his game and wandered back upstairs, only to be intercepted by Cain. He called to her from the parlor as she passed through the kitchen. "Alyson, is that you?"

She'd almost like to sneak back out, but she was too thirsty to leave the kitchen without a drink. He could feel her presence anyway, through their shared mark. He was just letting her know he'd like to see her. "Yeah, it's me."

She fixed herself a large helping from the refrigerator and then went to join him. He was sitting before the fireplace, in his favorite chair. The flat screen television above the fire was on, showing some sort of musical stage play; it looked like an opera. "Wouldn't you rather watch that in the media room? Why'd you put Mattie downstairs?"

"Mattie is down there because the media room is sound-proofed, and he is making a great deal of noise," Cain informed her with a chuckle. "I'm not really watching this anyway. I was just waiting for you. It's good that he's busy."

Allie's shoulders slumped. "Why do I have the feeling that I'm about to be busy too?"

"Because I have a task for you." He smiled at her sour expression. "Don't worry, this time you'll enjoy getting busy."

"Really?" Now she cracked a smile and let alternate meanings for the phrase *getting busy* telepathically flash through his mind.

He rolled his eyes and tried to hide the flush of embarrassment that momentarily rushed over him. "Very funny. Not what I've got in mind. You are going to enjoy this, though."

"More than I would enjoy going back to the mall?"

"Most definitely."

She took the last swig from her mug, trying not to grimace at the fact that it was nowhere near as good as blood from a living source would be. The last thing she wanted to do was go out hunting and give the guys reason to reprimand her for her insatiable thirst. She assessed Cain's calm demeanor. He was gentle, composed, and friendly as always. You would never know that the man was an emotional wreck inside most nights. "Are you okay?"

He gave a small, bitter little smile and nodded soberly. "I'm fine."

Good to know he had things under control again. Unfortunately, that also meant that he had probably been thinking over her behavior with a level head. "Are we going to have to talk about last night?"

He eyed her quietly. "No, not if you don't want to."

"Then count me in. What are we doing?"

"I recognize that using your powers has been draining for you, and that is most likely the source of your increased thirst."

"I thought we weren't going to talk about it."

"We're not really, but I am going to give you a better outlet for it."

"Now I'm intrigued," she told him with a smile.

Cain switched off the television and signaled for Allie to follow him outside. It was a beautiful, autumn night, the air just beginning to cool as winter winds tried to come chase summer warmth away. Cain led them to the back patio and gestured for her to take a seat. Rather than sit at the patio table, she chose to recline in one of the lounge chairs. He sat up straightly sideways on the one next to her, with his elbows on his knees. "Are you certain you aren't entertaining Arif's offer? I'm very glad that you want to stay, but I can see where access to other vampires of varied powers could be appealing."

She smiled. "Na. Your dedication can be really annoying sometimes, but I'd still rather hang here and figure stuff out with you, than let *him* teach me stuff."

"Thanks," he said with a laugh.

"Besides, I get the feeling he's got ulterior motives. I can't read him. We haven't shared blood, and anyway, I think he knows how to shield his thoughts from me. Bad vibes, though."

Cain nodded in agreement. "Do you understand why I'm so dedicated to helping you learn control? It is for your well-being, but that's not the only reason. Everyone has motives."

That threw her for a second. She'd grown used to reading Cain fairly well, and knew that he'd always had her best interest in mind. It took her a little thought, before she realized what he meant. "You believe Arif, that I'm not just a freak of nature. You think I'm *meant* to be special and turn into some kind of vampire leader. I know you've said it before, that because I can control others with my eyes, they might think of me that way, but I never thought you really believed it *like that*. I'm not that special Cain, trust me."

"I believe that everything happens for a reason. I can't find it in myself to think that you would be given such power, and such domination over others, if it weren't meant to be used for a purpose."

"Arif thinks that too, doesn't he?"

"Perhaps, but I hope you don't think that makes me like him. Because I believe that the purpose I have in mind is surely far different from his."

Alyson smiled in reassurance. "I know what you want. It's the same thing you've always wanted. You want vampires to stop hurting people.

You want vampires to evolve; think of themselves as a new responsible, moral race, separate from the old way of thinking. No more Draculas and Lestats. Gonna change your name to Cullen now? If we're good little vampires, do you think we'll get all sparkly in the sunlight, too?" she asked him with a smirk.

She was surprised to see him place the references, shaking his head with a laugh. Then again, you couldn't be completely unaware of pop-culture vamps these days, could you? "Please don't think I am so naïve as to believe life is a fairy tale. I am just as much of a realist as Arif. The difference is that within my reality, I also have faith.

I have faith that you were given your gifts for a reason, and while they are your gifts to wield, I hope you see the potential for good in them. Do you realize that you could quickly accomplish through your divine influence, the shift in mentality of vampires as a species that I have spent over a century trying to bring about? To that way of thinking, how can I not believe that you were put into my path for a reason? If you were led into my care through higher powers, isn't it my sacred duty to guide you to be a morally responsible and ethical leader? I don't know what the future holds, or how far off change will be. However, you do have power to make change. If you were thrust into taking control unready, I would consider it my own personal failing."

Alyson pondered what he'd said, but couldn't bring herself to offer an opinion on it. "I'm still not sure what you mean by me being thrust into power. By who? Why would anything change? I'm just doing my own thing."

"You've seen how other vampires sometimes react to you. They see your eyes and become almost mesmerized, those not very strong-minded anyway. Any young one who was not well made, and did not have a mentor, would naturally turn to you if they knew of your existence, just as they often turn to me for my age. You've brought home followers in the past, whom I've had to help as I could and then shoo off. Without caution, you could find yourself saddled with a flock of young vampires just waiting for you to give them direction. Do you see?"

She shrugged. "We've talked about that before. Most of the time, I can just lose them. That doesn't bother me so much. What creeps me out, is the idea that someone might think about my blood as something bad, the way Arif talked about it in Atlantic City. I don't need somebody thinking I'm too strong for my own good, and that I should be killed before I can make more vamps just like me. I'm not planning to use my blood like that, but I would like to hang on to what I've got."

Cain smiled. "Protection is important, and one of the most valuable skills you can learn for protection is that of camouflage."

Alyson sat up and pulled her thinly folded tinted glasses from her pocket to slide on. "These aren't enough?"

"You can do much better. What I have in mind will give you a more satisfying outlet for your thirst as well, in giving you the ability to hunt animal prey outside my property unseen. That's why I've called you out here. We're expecting some company."

Alyson tilted her head to gaze at him curiously. "Who?"

"A member of the Crimson Coven."

Allie broke into a broad smile. "Oh…this is gonna be the big night huh? Finally plan to unveil the mystery?"

Cain grinned, taking a quick glance around. "Yes. We're a bit early. We're to be met out here at ten, but that's alright. It will give me an opportunity to explain a few things first."

Alyson swung her legs over the other side of the lounge and hopped up out of her chair. "I hate to take the wind out of your sails, but before you start explaining stuff, there's something you might want to see."

Cain looked up at her with a wary sense of premonition. "What?"

Alyson began to unbuckle her jeans, which drew a raised eyebrow from Cain. She laughed, reflecting on how her actions would look if he didn't already know what she was planning. She decided not to bother with taking off her clothing. She could find her way out of it while shifting, and she could barely contain herself. She'd been looking forward to this for a while. Without another word, she took a step back and changed, just as Sindy had taught her to. Alyson closed her eyes and let her body loosen and separate as though it was only a temporary form, holding shape for everything that she truly was inside.

Alyson became transparent, as every molecule in her body slightly moved apart from its neighbor. The tiny pieces shifted and moved until her shape became distorted and lost, a nebulous cloud of dark fog. Her clothing fell to the ground in a heap, and it took her a few moments to completely navigate her way out of it, but she managed. It felt wonderfully free and without care or restraint, as she hovered there before Cain as nothing more than mist.

He almost fell off the chair. She paused to enjoy his surprise, and then focused on the wolf form she wanted to take. With just that hint of direction, the particles that would construct her new body knew what to do. The vampire blood remembered this shape, as though it was pre-programmed, and knew how to instruct her molecules to make it just right.

In the blink of an eye, the mist that was Alyson pulled itself together into the shape of an almost purely white wolf. Alyson shook herself, feeling the ruffling of fur, and enjoying shaking out her tail. Cain was just sitting there, staring at her. She sat down on her haunches, and stared right back.

Finally he spoke. "Oh my... You're... ...Alyson, I think I am speechless," he admitted with a laugh. He stood and approached her. "Gorgeous, and flawlessly executed, I might add. I never will be able to keep you steady at my pace, will I? Always rushing ahead. Look at you." He bent slightly to cup the side of her face, his fingers resting lightly under her chin. She looked up at him proudly. "Still with those beautiful blue eyes, they look lovely."

At his words, she shifted to her vampire sight, revealing her white eyes and bringing forth a startled huff of breath from him. "Brilliant," he whispered. "How did you discover this? I can't imagine you came upon it on your own. Have you been sneaking about the Crimson Coven too, or did Sindy tell you?"

I told you I've been staying away from them. It was Sindy, but not on purpose.

Cain was again startled for a moment, and took a step back, dropping his hand from her. "Your telepathy... Of course, you can answer. I'd forgotten. Sindy can't communicate in this form."

Oh yeah, I guess she can't. Wow, that must be frustrating as all hell.

"It surely is. But I'll tell you a secret. I think she'd get on much better with those around her *without* speaking."

Alyson replied with a mental chuckle. *She knew you wanted it to be a secret, but I saw her change, and she couldn't deny it. I made her show me how.*

"And why didn't you tell me?"

Alyson did her best to simulate a shrug, although it was just a slight flinch of her canine shoulders, and the meaning came across better mentally. *I just liked having it to myself for a little while first.*

Cain stood before her, reaching out again to feel her soft fur. He couldn't seem to help himself. "Does Mattie know?"

She shook her head. *Aw heck no. I felt bad not to tell him, but he is the original open book. He can't keep a secret, and I wasn't ready for it to turn into a whole big thing yet. Besides, I have a feeling he might need your support on this one.*

"You're probably right. It is a very altering talent. It will take some getting used to for him, since he can't share it, and it's far beyond his current realm of experience. The other talents are amazing, but when you use them, you're still *you.*"

Alyson stood, lightly flaring her nostrils to take in the scents of the surrounding forest in the newly crisp autumn air. She lightly raked a claw across the wooden plank of the deck. *I'm still me,* she reminded him indignantly.

"I know that, but I'm used to dealing with people in different forms. Mattie's not, and you'll have to give him a chance to soak it all in." Cain glanced up in the direction of the forest, although nothing could be seen amongst the trees.

Someone was near. Allie could sense it, although there was no definitive mark to be seen. She wasn't alarmed, though. Cain had said they'd be expecting company. Cain brought back her attention with a question. "Has Sindy shown you her third form as well?"

She can become a bat, right? No, I've never seen it. She says she doesn't like it, that bats are just disgusting rodents with wings, but I know that's not all there is to it. She's frightened of that form for some reason. It spooks her.

"She's never shown it to me either, although I haven't asked." Cain just shook his head with a shrug. "Well, you needn't worry about it. A member of the Crimson Coven owes me a favor, and she's going to repay me by assisting you and Sindy in learning the art of shifting. Whatever there is to it that you haven't already mastered, that is. She and Sindy should both be here shortly. Her name is Tempest."

Tempest? The woman that ripped up Sindy in the woods?

"Told you about that, did she?"

This should be an interesting night.

"Tempest is an elder vampire, and although her temper may have gotten the better of her, I trust she has put that behind her now, and will act accordingly."

There was a slight rustling in the brush that could either be a small animal moving carelessly, or a larger one, stepping lightly. It was hard to tell. Allie tried to peer through the dark cover of brush, wondering if it was Tempest. *Just how old is she?*

"I'm not sure, but elder is a term commonly applied to anyone who's lived past a century, and she is certainly older and more experienced than either of you. I think she'll have a lot to teach you."

If Sindy doesn't try to rip her throat out first.

"Leave Sindy to me. I've asked her for tolerance out of respect for me, and I believe she'll comply." Alyson couldn't argue with that. Sindy would probably do just about anything if Cain directly asked it of her.

A wolf stepped out from the cover of the forest, and after a moment of surveillance, began to lope across the lawn to join them. It wasn't Tempest. It was Sindy. Her mark was hidden, but Allie recognized the long black wolf as it strode towards them. Sindy slowed as she reached the house, and then daintily climbed the steps onto the deck to stand next to Alyson, facing Cain.

Sindy made a bit larger of a wolf than Alyson. Her eyes were a dark soft brown, while Allie had let hers shift back to her normal blue. Cain took in the image of the black and white wolves standing side by side. "Well, don't you two make quite the pair? Yin and Yang… although I couldn't tell you who should be which," he said with a light shake of his head. He looked at Sindy directly. "So much for keeping a secret."

Sindy shifted into her human form and stood there before him, proudly naked, with one hand on her hip, and a smirk of a smile. She glanced over at Alyson before answering to Cain. "I managed to keep it from you," she pointed out smugly.

Cain just smiled at her in acknowledgment, and averted his eyes from her body. It seemed to Alyson that although he pretended to be disappointed, he was secretly pleased to see the two girls getting along.

Sindy was still posing for him. It was amazing to Allie, the amount of calculation and thought that went into Sindy's every move almost automatically. She had never noticed it before being able to pick up snippets of it telepathically. The woman was constantly slightly altering her stance to meet with subtle deductions going on almost unconsciously in the back of her mind, to show her body at its most attractive angles. She was always vaguely aware of the best way to flex her calves, raise her chest, keep her shoulders back, turn her head just so for the light… It was second nature to Sindy, from years of trying to impress and manipulate men. To Alyson it seemed exhausting.

Although Cain didn't pay her any undue attention for it, Alyson had to admit that the woman looked good. Whether he was conscious of it or not, on some level, Cain did notice. Sindy smiled at him. "I told you we didn't need any lessons."

Alyson would have rolled her eyes if she hadn't already let her form slip into mist, so she could also regain her human body. As she re-formed, Cain politely looked away. She gave him a slight mental nudge. *Relax Cain.*

Now that I can do this shifting thing out in the open, it's gonna be a pain in the ass to try and have a conversation, if you're always afraid to look at me.

Cain sighed and finally met her eyes, being carefully aware not to let his gaze dip any lower. *You're going to have to tell Mattie about this new talent tonight. I don't want any secrets from him.*

Allie nodded. *Soon as school's out,* she replied, gesturing to the lawn.

Tempest was charging towards them in wolf form. As she reached the deck, she let herself disperse into smoke mid-stride. She joined them as a beautiful dark skinned young woman, perhaps in her mid-twenties at death. The feature that most caught Allie's attention was her long, natural, nappy hair that seemed made of millions of tiny, soft ringlet curls in a cloud about her. However, once Allie took in the view of the whole woman, she had to admit that Tempest had to have one of the most voluptuous and yet toned, and subtly muscular bodies that she had ever seen. Alyson remembered having met her briefly once before, but seeing her *shift* into her form was somehow much more impressive.

Her transition had been smooth and swift. Alyson smiled in appreciation of her talent, and glanced over at Sindy, who was still maintaining her attitude that this was a waste of time. "I don't know," Allie told her. "I'm kind of interested to hear what she's got to say."

Sindy shot Alyson a quick look of betrayal, that Allie chose to ignore. Tempest nodded a greeting to Cain, and then eyed her new pupils, noticing Sindy's unyielding attitude. "I saw your wolves from the woods. Not bad, but I could still easily gut either of you with one swipe. If you want to learn how to make that *not* happen, I suggest you stick around for the instruction."

Cain met Sindy's gaze for a long moment, as though asking her for graciousness. "Are we all set here then? You'll stay for a bit, won't you, to give Alyson some support?" he asked quietly. Sindy gave him a small and almost imperceptible nod. She liked the fact that he was waiting for her to accept. He gave her a warm smile and then observed their little group. "Well…being surrounded by three such lovely nude and lethal ladies is a bit more than I'm up to handling at the moment, so I think I'll be on my way and leave you to it."

As Cain went back into the house, Tempest and Sindy stood eying each other haughtily. Once they heard the house door slide shut, Tempest spoke with a bit of a sneer. "You've got a lot of guts coming back here. I guess I left some in there after all."

Sindy stopped herself from automatically moving her arm to guard her stomach. Allie could feel Sindy's phantom shivers of remembered pain from where Tempest had sliced her open. She adopted a conceited look of unconcern. "It's not my fault that you couldn't keep your man's attention."

Alyson was focused on Tempest. She couldn't exactly read the woman, but she could feel her age and confidence. Although slightly hostile, she didn't seem unreasonable, or quick to petty anger as Sindy often was, but Tempest was definitely a force to be reckoned with. Allie kind of liked her.

Allie could feel Tempest assessing Sindy, and then consciously deciding to let go of her hostility with a shrug. "If a man doesn't know how to appreciate what he's got, then he doesn't deserve to have it."

Sindy tilted her head slightly in acceptance. "True enough. Does that mean Nick is back on the market?"

Her question pushed Tempest back to the edge of irritation again. Cain was right, Sindy should learn when to shut her mouth. "That's right," Tempest answered. "He went crawling back to West Virginia with his tail between his legs. Feel free to follow him."

Sindy smiled. Secretly she was glad Nick had left, because when actually faced with Tempest's composed, natural beauty, Sindy was thinking it might not be much of a competition. She'd turned Nick's head a few times and caused him to be unfaithful, but if he had to choose between the two women, Sindy was afraid that Tempest was the obvious choice. It made Allie pause, to realize that there was actually a lot more self-doubt under Sindy's harshness than she ever let show. "I don't need your rejects," Sindy informed Tempest. "I was just curious."

Suddenly, Allie placed whom they were talking about. Nick was the first Crimson Coven member she had ever seen, 'naked man' from the garage. She said as much privately to Sindy. *Nick from West Virginia? You were doin' it with 'naked man'? Nice...* For reference, she sent Sindy her mental image of Nick from when she and Mattie had unexpectedly walked in on him a few years back, standing tall, built, and naked in Cain's garage.

Sindy grinned broadly at the image. *Yes, he certainly was.*

Allie quickly composed herself a bit for Sindy's sake. *I still think you were acting like a slut, but for that guy, I can almost sympathize.*

Alyson wondered if Tempest suspected her telepathy. Tempest was just standing there staring at them. "Look, I'm here to help Cain out by showing Alyson a few things. Whether or not you want to stay and join us, is your call, but I don't have all night, so stop wasting my time."

Sindy weighed her possible responses and finally folded her arms and said, "Fine. Why don't you try and show me something worth staying for, and then we'll see whose time is wasted."

Alyson couldn't help but give her a warning glance. *Don't be stupid Sindy. Maybe you should shut up and learn something.*

Tempest found the goad so ridiculous, she didn't even bother to let it ruffle her. "You want to be impressed? I can put you in a world of hurt without even thinking about it. You put up a decent fight out in those woods, but the fact is, you couldn't kill me if I let you try. You shouldn't talk shit until you can back it up."

Allie interrupted them, hoping to turn the evening into something productive. "Why? Why couldn't she kill you?"

Tempest smiled and inhaled deeply, letting it out slowly and resuming her teaching role. "How are you going to kill a vampire?"

Allie smiled and shrugged. "Stake you, I guess."

"Good old fashioned stake through the heart? Not mine, and you'll never guess why." Allie couldn't even begin to follow where she might be going, and let her continue. "You wouldn't know it, but I'm about three inches shorter than I was when I was human. Any guess why?"

Sindy answered with an air of boredom. "Your spinal cartilage rotted away before you were turned?"

Tempest didn't even glance in her direction. "Because when I take form, I make conscious choices about my construction. I don't need to be 5' 8". I'd rather use the material somewhere else; like to encase my heart in solid bone, for example."

Alyson widened her eyes as a glimmer of an entire new world of possibilities suddenly began to shine before her. Even Sindy couldn't pretend not to be interested or impressed.

Tempest nodded at their amazement and continued. "We have an amazing array of abilities that far outweigh even the magic of taking animal shape. We are vampires that are truly gifted to last for eternity. The trick is learning how to use and manipulate what you've got, because no matter what you learn to construct, you only have a finite amount of time and resources to construct it with."

Allie could feel the wheels in her mind spinning faster than they had in years. She wished she was a better problem solver. She felt as though she could just grasp the tip of the implications Tempest was giving her, but couldn't quite figure things out for herself. She tried to voice everything to make sure she was clear. "So you're saying that the body we died with is all we have, but because we have the talent of red-eyed vampires, our blood can take that body apart and make it into whatever we want?"

"I knew it!" Sindy interjected. "No woman has a body that damn perfect. You *made* it look that way!"

Tempest laughed. "Not so fast honey. You think it's that easy? I may shift a few things here and there, but you'd still recognize me from a photo, believe me."

Alyson ignored Sindy's accusation. "So we just can't become anything larger than our human bodies…or much smaller."

Sindy seemed very annoyed. "I can't become anything else at all. Just the wolf and that stupid bat, which *is* pretty damn small by the way."

Tempest knitted her brows at Sindy's insult. "A bat is an elegant creature, especially the flying foxes that we take the shape of. You'll notice that the wingspan of your bat is always just a shade shorter than your height as a human. We're smaller, true, but as humans, we're used to carrying a lot of extra water and organ weight that we don't need to carry as vampires. Our vampire bodies are much lighter, and can be condensed into the smaller form of the bat without changing very much of our mass. There may be a bit of magic involved, but the rules only stretch so far."

"What else?" Allie asked eagerly.

"We only have those three pre-designated forms; human, wolf and bat. And of course, each of those forms has its vampire counter-part. For whatever reason, those are the forms that our vampire blood is familiar with, and are the only choices on the menu. A very talented vampire can change those preset forms to make alterations of their own construction, but it is a skill that takes years to develop, and most give up trying before they get very far." She turned her gaze to Sindy. "It takes great discipline, a rare trait to find these days."

Alyson moved forward to take Tempest by the arm and urge her to sit on the lounge chair next to her. Sindy remained standing, leaning against the rail. "Tempest, what other modifications have you made for protection?" Allie asked.

"Yeah," Sindy chimed in. "What's to stop me from chopping your head off?"

Tempest smiled. "Like I'd ever let you get that close to me with a weapon. But even if you did, my throat is encased in bone from collarbone to skull. Good luck." She stretched up her long and graceful neck, although there was nothing amiss there from what the girls could see. "And my skin is about an inch thick all around, so you'd have trouble getting through that as well. Soft, but strong."

"No wonder Nick left," Sindy couldn't help but comment. "You can't be much fun in bed, all bony and un-bite-able."

Even Tempest couldn't help but laugh at that remark. "I can leave vulnerable spots where I want them. I've spent a lot of time studying human anatomy and physiology. You might want to do the same. We're getting way ahead of ourselves though. I'm just letting you in on the possibilities. The truth is, you two still need to work on the basics. Then you can pick a trait to alter, and work on it until it becomes an automatic part of your blueprint. You only have a small window of time to change in, so if you don't have the form already set in your mind the way you want it, you'll never have time to materialize it."

"Why don't we have time?" Allie asked in confusion.

Both women looked at her as though they didn't understand the question. Sindy answered first. "You just don't. You can't just hang around as smoke forever. Your body wants to pull back together and be something. You have a few seconds to pick a form, or go back to what you were before you shifted. You don't have a choice."

Alyson just sat there thinking about that, as Tempest nodded in agreement with Sindy. Finally, Allie stood from the chair. "I've never felt that. I just shift into the wolf because I want to, but I don't feel rushed about it."

Tempest nodded towards her. "Do it again, you'll see."

As instructed, Allie let herself shift into smoke. She became a misty cloud of tiny particles that would make up a form that she chose...*if* she chose one. This time she didn't pick a form to change into, but instead only concentrated on her surroundings.

It was difficult to focus on Tempest and Sindy, as she was seeing with her vampiric sense of the life forces around her, rather than true sight. She could see Tempest's mark, which revealed her to have significant age and power, as Cain had claimed, but Sindy's mark was cloaked. Allie could not hear them either, but when they spoke, her telepathy helped to relay what was said. She couldn't read Tempest well, but Sindy had always been open enough to her psychically for surface thoughts to come through.

"Why isn't she changing?" Sindy asked.

Alyson just hung there before them, very aware of the autumn breeze trying to disrupt her and pull her apart. She managed to keep herself gathered into one area, but allowed her nebulous cloud shape to spread out a little thinner, to be less noticeable to the human eye; just a darker pocket of air, lazily floating a few feet above the ground.

Curious, she let herself rise, as she was used to doing during flight. It was the same! She could control her movements, even in this misty state. This could be fun! She moved around a little, practicing thinning and stretching into different configurations, until she realized that the women before her were trying to get her attention. Reluctantly, she let herself shift back into her human body.

Sindy looked annoyed that Alyson had discovered yet another thing that she could excel in. Tempest was staring at her with open amazement. "I've never seen anything like that," she admitted. "It's like a whole separate talent in itself."

Allie shrugged. "It must be something that another breed can do. I assumed it went along with what you guys did. I didn't realize that red-eyed vampires were limited to forms like that."

Tempest looked almost flabbergasted that someone would describe her vast array of abilities as *limited*. Still, she could not deny what she had seen. "Cain told me that you were a special creature, but I wasn't expecting… I don't know what I was expecting. Are you truly The United One?"

Sindy let out a snort of disgust that sounded like it should have come from the wolf rather than the woman, although she still stood nude and human looking, leaning against the rail. Alyson let out a deep sigh. "That's what they tell me." Tempest was still staring at her, so she decided that she might as well show them and get it over with, so they could move on. Cain had already trusted her with the information, so revealing her eyes shouldn't make a difference. She shifted into her vampire state.

Tempest was immediately affected. She gazed at Alyson's eyes as though they were mesmerizing. After a moment or two of silence, Sindy moved closer to see what had taken Tempest's attention. Allie had only shown Sindy her eyes once before, and although Sindy would not like to admit it, she found Allie's eyes fascinating as well.

These women were strong, independent vampires though, with whom she had never shared blood. They were able to break her gaze and resume normal conversation. Alyson had come upon others in her travels that were not as strong.

Some vampires could find themselves almost in thrall, even through the shield of Allie's human eye covering. Her white eyes shone through and caught their attention, drawing them under her spell like a moth to a flame. It was very annoying.

She would be standing in a crowd, on the street, or at the movies, and suddenly find someone staring at her, as though unable to look away. She would break eye contact and move on, but would often have some vampire following after her, going on about how 'bright and beautiful she was', and asking, 'was she some kind of vampire goddess? Could she help them?' *No*, she would invariably answer, *I'm nobody. Go away.* After a few of those episodes, she was careful never to leave the house without her tinted glasses, and she tried not to look strangers in the eye.

Tempest was suitably impressed. "Cain was right, you have great power."

Sindy just sat in stunned silence, irritated and mildly jealous, cursing fate for letting things turn out as they had. Alyson shifted her eyes back to blue and used the stairs off the deck, down onto the lawn. "Power isn't much good if I don't know how to use it." She wanted to practice more shifting. Tempest and Sindy shared a glance and then followed her out onto the grass.

"Let's get to work."

~~~~~~~~~~~~~~~~~~~~~~~~~~~~~

Allie sat on the edge of the bed as Mattie questioned her, yet again. "Seriously? You're not messing with me?"

"I swear, Mattie."

"Wow...you always hear about vampires turning into bats in the movies and stuff, but it just seemed too far-fetched to ever be true."

"I know, right? And whoever heard of a vampire changing into a wolf?"

Mattie sat down next her, thoughtfully. "Dracula could become a wolf. He used to do the mist thing, too. That's how he would get in, through the keyhole."

"Really? I bet I could do that, with a little practice."

Mattie laughed. "So am I going to get to see this, or what?"

"Sure, I just wanted to make sure you were okay about it first."

"Why wouldn't I be?"

"I don't know. I didn't want to just turn into a wolf without fair warning and freak you out."

"I appreciate the warning, but as long as you aren't going to go all *'American Werewolf in London'* on me, I think I can handle it. It's just straight to smoke, and then wolf, right? No disgusting, scary, in-between stages?"

She laughed. "There is no stretching, skin ripping, or anything of the kind, I promise. Believe me, I'm just as relieved to know that as you are."

"Is it scary, though? For you, I mean. I can't imagine suddenly exploding into a million microscopic pieces. You must have been terrified!"

She took his hand and shook her head. He was a little miffed that he didn't get to sit in on her first lesson, to comfort and support her. She appreciated the sentiment, but she didn't need half as much support as he always seemed to think she should. "It wasn't bad at all. I got to see Sindy do it first, so I wasn't scared. It's kind of cool, actually. It feels like…letting go. I like being the wolf, too. We went running through the woods, and I even caught a rabbit!"

Mattie's eyes widened. "To drink?"

She nodded yes, remembering the thrill of the chase and the catch. She'd actually been hunting in wolf form with Sindy for a couple of months now, to supplement her drinking at home, not that she'd ever let Mattie know. Sindy had told her it would be far more fulfilling then drinking stuff from the fridge, and boy was she right. There was something about drinking *live* blood…

"Did you kill it?" Mattie asked, with trepidation.

"Rabbits aren't very big, Mattie. Even taking all of its blood was hardly worth the effort."

"I guess. Poor bunny."

She tried not to roll her eyes. "There's millions of them out there."

Mattie looked at her oddly. "There are millions of people out there, too. I hope *that's* not your line of reasoning." She just made a face of exasperation at him. "So what do I get to see first?" he asked, changing the subject back to the matter at hand.

"Well, it'll have to be the wolf. I haven't learned the bat yet. Sindy already knew the wolf, so we started there. I was a little nervous to play around with the bat by myself."

"You're going to be having these lessons for a while right, a couple of nights a week? Think I could come watch next time?"

Allie shrugged. "I guess that's up to Sindy and Tempest. I don't mind, but I don't know how they feel about you observing a class that's taught in the nude."

Mattie raised an eyebrow at her, as if to accuse her of jealousy. She didn't bother to point out that it was totally unwarranted. He could look at whomever he wanted, as long as he was always honest with her about it. But truthfully, she also knew that no one would care if he wanted to watch. He'd already seen Tempest nude when they'd first met her, and she hadn't minded then, and Sindy would probably love the idea of having him watch.

Allie was the one who wasn't in a rush for him to come. Not because of jealousy, but more because she liked having something to do that didn't involve him. Was that mean? She'd spent all night, almost every night with him since she'd been turned. She loved it, but she liked having a reason to go do her own thing sometimes too. In fact, she'd found herself looking for excuses to get out on her own lately. Mostly it had been to sneak out and hunt, but sometimes she just wanted some quiet time alone, to do nothing in particular. Like last night, when she'd gone to the mall…and look how that had turned out, with Mattie coming home and finding her drinking from Cain. Guilt washed over her and she looked up at him with an apologetic smile. "Sure you can come. No one will mind. It'll be cool to have you there."

He looked very happy that she'd reconsidered. She didn't want him to feel too left out…but she also kind of hoped he would only come once or twice, and then get bored and go back to playing video games. It was cool to have an *all girls* activity. She'd never been a part of anything like that before.

"What's Tempest like?" Mattie asked. "Isn't it weird having her teach Sindy stuff, after she went all *Freddy Krueger* on her in the woods?"

"They've called a truce. They traded a few gibes, but it was okay, and Tempest certainly knows what she's doing. I've learned so much already." She stood from their bed, quickly stripped off her clothing and moved across to stand before the closet doors. "Show time."

Alyson shifted into mist, trying to make it happen slowly this time, rather than enact her usual race to see if she could beat Sindy to form. She wanted to let Mattie observe it as closely as he might want to, so that he could feel like he understood it better. He was the kind of guy that liked to take things apart and see how they worked. If he couldn't share this with her, she could at least give him a thorough showing of it.

He gasped and moved back on the bed to give her room. She could read all of his amazed reaction through his thoughts, and it spurred her to want to show him more. She let herself remain in smoke form, and moved closer, drifting over the bed. Mattie was enrapt. She did something she'd never really had the opportunity to do before. She saw herself in this state, through Mattie's eyes.

She and Mattie were so close, sharing vision was almost as easy as sharing thoughts. *Sending* visions to him was something they hadn't practiced as often, but after that session with Cain, she knew she could do that just as well. But at this point, when she spoke to Mattie telepathically, she was often able to read what he was seeing through his eyes, pulling the visions from his mind with the thoughts.

Seeing herself now, through Mattie's eyes, was an amazing experience. She willed herself to drift upwards, and she could see the result. It made her bold and daring, to try experimenting more with movement. Without actual eyes, she'd been frightened to move about too much in mist form. She could only see through her psychic mark sense of the life energies around her. Here in the trailer, there was barely any life at all. She could just barely sense the hard cold lines of the edges of the furniture, and it would take a lot of practice to learn maneuvering successfully through that type of environment. She sent Mattie thoughts to explain as much.

He was happy to let her play with her new state through use of his vision. She had an idea for something she wanted to try. First, she settled herself over him as he lay back on the bed, engulfing him within her in an odd sort of hug. Then, with the aid of Mattie's feedback, she lifted herself and stretched out her shape until she had made a long, thin column of smoke. She chose a side, and decided to spin herself circularly in that direction. It worked! After a moment, she had a spinning column, whipping around and around. Mattie laughed in appreciative awe. "You're a mini tornado!"

She suddenly let her particles disperse in a silent explosion, startling Mattie, and spreading herself out into a large cloud that rose up to practically cover the ceiling. It was as thin as she dared stretch herself. She was worried that if she lost too much cohesion, spreading too thinly, she might have trouble pulling herself back together. She was alright for now though, and remained a dark shadow of fog, hovering near the ceiling.

"Allie, do you realize how incredible this is? You might as well be invisible! You could hide from anyone, and never be found."

She hadn't thought of it like that. Definitely a talent that could be useful someday. But now, it was time for the second half of her display. She pulled herself together and floated to the floor, where she then reformed into the wolf.

Mattie was leaning towards the edge of the bed intently, watching her reform. She tried to do it as slowly as she could, but once the instruction to take shape was given to her blood, it took over the process and created the body for her at its own swift pace. It was still cool to watch though, seeing it from Mattie's perspective. It looked like a million pieces of sand, suddenly sucking together out of the cloudy air to build a wolf. The bones and tissues of her insides were created first, and then layer upon layer of flesh, skin, hair and everything else that went into making her, but it all happened almost too fast to follow.

Once she was finished, she gathered her haunches and made the small jump up onto the bed next to Mattie. He jerked back, but then immediately reached out to touch her, running his fingers through her thick white fur. "You look like a Husky!"

She sent him a mental chuckle and gave him a sloppy wet lick on the face that startled him into laughter. They rolled on the bed in roughhouse play. It felt so good to hook her paws around him and mock bite his arms. It conjured up fond memories from Mattie, of playing with his family dog; a normal human memory that seemed so far removed from his life now. She was happy to bring that back for him, and it gave them both a nice, unburdened stress release. It was great fun.

She spent a good long time letting him appreciate her wolf form. Being able to see herself through him was a very cool experience. She looked just like a real wolf! The light coloring did render her a little more dog-like than Sindy and Tempest, but she could still look very fierce and wild when she wanted to. No one would ever suspect that this wasn't the form she was born to.

Finally, she shifted back into Allie-shape, and stretched out on the bed next to Mattie. Perhaps she hadn't given him enough credit. He may like to play things on the safe side, but he was handling this whole shape-shifting thing just fine. She felt bad for not sharing it with him sooner. "That stuff didn't freak you out?"

Mattie chuckled and caressed her bare thigh, still a bit awed by the whole experience. "No. I mean, it's weird, but I think it's cool too."

"I owe you an apology. I guess I underestimated you."

"Allie, we have known each other practically forever. I've seen you do some freaky things, but I love you. Stuff like this isn't going to scare me away."

"Glad to hear it." As she lifted herself enough to give him a kiss, she noticed the familiar heaviness of the coming dawn beginning to creep over her. "Sun's coming soon. I have to turn in now." She slid herself down under the covers. "Are you going to stay up for a bit?"

"Na, I'll come to bed."

The sun always affected her much more strongly than it did Mattie. It seemed like such a gyp. She would find herself getting exhausted long before there was any real sunlight in the sky, and she never woke up before it was full dark anymore. He had at least two hours more to his nights than she did. "Are you sure? I mean, you don't have to. I know you've probably got another hour."

"Let's see, stay up and watch lame morning shows on T.V., or snuggle in bed with you... I think I'll come to bed." He stripped down to his boxers and climbed under the covers next to her, giving her a teasing squeeze. "Boy, for a telepathic chic with empathy, you don't read me very well these days."

She laughed. "I guess that's because everybody keeps telling me not to pry into their thoughts."

"Don't try to pretend you don't. I know you try to be respectful, but you must take a quick peak, now and then. Who wouldn't? So, what am I thinking right now?" he asked mischievously.

"Things that we don't have time for," she told him regrettably. She could barely keep her eyes open.

"We must have a little time. Enough for a quickie at least?"

"That depends. How insulted will you be if I end up comatose before we're done?" After a second, she shrugged. "What the hell, if I don't make it, it's my loss. I knock you out all the time, so I guess turn about's fair play."

Mattie took her into his arms, although his demeanor was more serious than romantic. "Being *drunk* to unconsciousness isn't quite the same, but I know you're trying to work on that. We're both learning how to handle all of this. As long as I can recover, I don't mind." He squeezed her tightly for a moment and then began to let his hands wander over her body. "What I mind, is being denied my Allie lovin' because you're too busy playing with your new powers and schoolin' with Cain, Tempest and Sindy. All I get is the last fifteen minutes before you pass out? You're going to have to start planning your timing better, babe."

She felt drugged. Damn morning sun. "I'll try. Now, shut up and give this night a happy ending."

~~~~~~~~~~~~~~~~~~~~~~~~~~~~~~~

"What about the bat?" Alyson asked impatiently.

Tempest had been walking through the crunching leaves on the ground to head for the wood-line, but paused, turning back and glancing first at Alyson, and then Sindy. "What about it?"

"That's it? We're not getting into that tonight? I've been waiting forever." Allie asked in disappointment.

Once all the basics of the wolf form had been gone over, Tempest had begun teaching them about modification. They'd been working on editing their wolf forms in order to make alterations. First, they were practicing simple color changes, but once they mastered that, Tempest promised they would move on to something useful, like extra sharp claws. Internal modifications, like Tempest's bone encased heart, were too difficult for beginners. They needed to learn how to alter things from the set imprint first, and it was much easier when you could see the results.

There was actually a bit of artistry to it, and although it wasn't easy, Allie found it very engrossing and enjoyable to work on. Sindy had been having a difficult time of it, but Allie had been making wonderful progress these past weeks. Allie's short attention span couldn't help but want to switch it up now and work on something new. She was itching to learn how to become a bat.

"We're done for the night. That's too long a lesson to start this close to dawn. Besides, you're not ready."

Alyson threw Sindy an incriminating glare. Although the lessons hadn't been easy for Sindy, Allie got the feeling she didn't even want to learn the bat form. She seemed to be stalling. "*I'm* ready."

Tempest followed Allie's gaze to Sindy, who stood silently, with arms folded. "Well she's not, and I'm not going through everything twice. Relax, we'll get there. Anyway, flying's hard as hell. Smash face first into a few trees, and you'll wish you'd never tried it."

Alyson levitated herself a few feet off the ground with a smirk. "It's not all that hard." She flashed a grin at Sindy who looked away in a disgusted sulk.

Tempest laughed. "Nothing's hard for you is it? But you're not infallible. Remember that, or one of these night's you're going to get your ass handed to you. We'll pick it up again next week. You want to fly with wings? Talk to your friend."

As soon as Tempest entered the woods, Sindy turned to Allie with a discriminating gaze. "Don't ask. I'm not doing it," she insisted in a throaty growl.

Alyson floated closer to Sindy, her flight making her a bit taller than the dark haired vampiress for a change. "What's the big deal? You're so good at the wolf. Wouldn't it be cool to have another form too? It's the only way you'll ever get to fly, and let me tell you, it's pretty sweet up here."

Sindy reached out and grabbed Allie's arm, pulling her back down to the ground with a hard yank. "I didn't say I couldn't do it, I said I won't. First of all, what she said is totally true. Flying is ridiculously impossible…the crash landings are painful, and frankly, the whole thing's scary like you wouldn't believe."

Alyson didn't quite suppress her chuckle, but did manage to evoke a look of sympathy afterward. "We can help you. I'm sure it just takes lots of practice."

Sindy knitted her brows, unappreciative of the offer. "And secondly, have you got any idea what it's like to be so damn small?"

Alyson looked down at herself and then back up to Sindy, who was at least a good six inches taller, and spread her hands. "Seriously? Do *I* know what it's like to be small?"

Sindy put her hands on her hips, and dismissed the response. "Not five foot two, tiny. We're talking really tiny."

"Actually, we'll be pretty big for bats. I think their bodies are just a little under a foot long. That's not too bad."

"When's the last time you were that small? Small as in vulnerable, floundering on the ground, unable to walk properly with these wings flopping and in the way, that seem freakin' giant in proportion to your little body. You're helpless, easily stepped on, and very probably eaten by something before you can even figure out what the hell you are."

Alyson stared at her for a moment. "We already know what we are." She delved deeper, quickly diving into and sorting through Sindy's thoughts. Sindy wasn't expecting it. A guarded vampire was almost impossible for Allie to probe unless they'd shared blood, but she managed to sift through before Sindy even thought to block her out. "Oh-ho. Fox, was it?"

Sindy blinked, startled. "What? Shut up. Let's go."

She started to walk out into the field, but Allie came around in front to stop her. "So that's what happened to you, why you're so freaked out to be the bat. The first time you changed, it took you by surprise, and you didn't even know what you were, huh?"

Sindy sighed, giving in to the fact that Allie wasn't going to drop it or let her walk away. "Yes," she answered shortly.

"A fox came after you?"

"It was a fucking nightmare. The thing played with me like I was a toy, and I couldn't even figure out how to run. It was nothing but yelping whines and snapping teeth."

"Why didn't you just change back?"

"Gee, why didn't I think of that?" Sindy spat out with a snarl. "Don't you think I tried? I was all flustered, and the thing was tearing me up. Every time I began to change, it would grab me and shake me, and I'd lose my concentration. It felt like it took forever before I got a grip and was able to shift."

Alyson looked at the ground, reading the experience from Sindy as she told it. It had really traumatized her. She'd gotten pretty badly injured from it too. "At least you knew it couldn't kill you."

Sindy wasn't exactly comforted. "Thanks. I wonder how much of me it would have eaten, before it gave up and wandered away. Think I'd regenerate and recover on my own, or would someone have to go sorting through fox shit for the pieces?" She shook her head. "Tempest is right, your cocky stupidity is gonna get you killed."

"I don't quite remember her saying that."

"Not dying of old age doesn't make you immortal. Just because you can survive a lot of stuff, doesn't mean nothing can kill you. And just because you don't *think* something can kill you, doesn't mean you should give it a chance to try.

I don't know about you, but I really like my new vampire body, and the things that it can do. I'm not going to put myself into a situation where it can be taken away from me, not now, after all I've been through. You want to turn into a little flying rodent because you think it might be neat, go ahead. I'm going to stick with the wolf; strong, fast and deadly. It suits me."

"You said you'd tried to fly. That couldn't have been the first time, with the fox. You tried it again?"

"Yeah, I tried it again. It's not like I just dismissed the form out of hand. I'm not an idiot. After I healed and got over the initial fear of it, I realized what the form was, and that it could have some advantages, so I tried again. It was a disaster. I spent one very long and difficult night bashing my brains against trees, plummeting in wild spirals to the ground, and suffering some serious vertigo. Then, I decided it wasn't worth it. You think you'll do better, be my guest. Maybe I'll stay and watch for a good laugh."

Sindy began to slowly walk into the clearing that stretched out before the house, and Allie followed. "Fine. I'll tell Tempest I'm doing it solo."

A gust of crisp autumn wind began to blow, and a cascade of leaves fluttered out into the clearing on their way to the ground. Sindy plucked a falling leaf from the swirl, and began picking it apart as they walked. "Hey, I heard you had a visit from Arif the other night."

Allie stopped walking. After a moment, Sindy turned to face her. "Yeah, I did. Where were you?" Allie asked.

"Out on the grounds. I saw him on his way out."

"That must have been a nice little reunion," Allie said with a bitter smile. "Isn't he a bosom buddy of yours?"

Sindy let out a little huff of a laugh. "I wouldn't exactly say that. He killed my maker. Then he helped me out for a little while afterward, but he doesn't really give a shit about me."

Alyson stared at her steadily. "Really? 'Cause as I recall, one of the things he helped you out with, was abducting me and Ben."

A slow smile crept over Sindy's face. "Oh yeah. That was a pretty good favor he did me, wasn't it?"

"Not from where I'm standing."

Sindy blew off her annoyance. "We barely even did anything to you. That night was all about Ben. I just needed to make sure you were going to stay out of the way."

Alyson refused to let it be dismissed so easily. "You gave me a concussion!"

Sindy shrugged. "You lived. It was totally worth being in debt for," she reminisced. "Best drink I ever had."

Allie shook her head in disgust. "All you did was make Ben hate you even more."

"Are you kidding?" Sindy asked with a chuckle. "I did him a favor. He got to experience something that he'd been fantasizing about, without any of the guilt, because it was out of his control."

Alyson was staring at her as though she was insane. "How can you possibly be so delusional about his feelings for you?"

"How can you?" Sindy asked in reply. "Can't you just go peeking into his head and see all those deep hidden desires he never wants anyone else to know? 'Cause if you did, I'll bet you'd find out that I know him even better than you do. I'd also bet that he secretly wishes I'd come back and do it again."

Alyson refused to be shaken. Ben may have been into Sindy when she'd been human, but that interest was long gone since she'd changed. There was no way Ben would want anything to do with her now. "Not only does he hate you, he hasn't even thought about you in years. Ben is now a happily married man."

Allie could tell that Sindy was actually a bit wounded by her words. Being hated wasn't disturbing to her. Hate was a strong emotion, worthy of her. It was the idea that she was dismissed and not thought of that hurt. She threw up a mental wall, blocking Allie out of her thoughts. She was learning. Sindy ignored the insult and commented on the information. "No kidding? Everheart tied the knot? Anyone I know? Who's the lucky girl?"

She could almost feel how badly Sindy wished she could delve into Alyson's thoughts the way that Allie could read hers. Allie grinned in response. "Not you." She stared into Sindy's eyes, wishing the woman would lose her concentration and give her another peek into her head. "So, did you ever pay Arif back for that favor?" Sindy showed no visible response to the question, and her mental concentration kept Allie blocked from her mind. Allie could always try shifting, letting her alluring vampire eyes distract Sindy into letting her in, but that would tip her off that Allie really wanted to know some more. Better to play it casually.

After a moment, Sindy just shrugged and began walking towards the house. "Yeah, it wasn't a big deal. Why was he here?"

Allie saw no reason not to be truthful about it. Cain had already told Sindy that Allie was The United One, and she probably knew that Arif knew it too. "He made me an offer to come stay with his coven at some compound where they have humans who give blood."

Sindy stopped her, turning and grabbing her arms, so that Allie had to face her. "*Kana Susamis Icin Ev?*" she asked in disbelief.

"I guess."

Sindy shook Allie by the hold she had on her wrists for emphasis. "On Long Island, in the Hamptons?" Allie just nodded. "You lucky bitch!"

Allie shrugged out of Sindy's hold. "Why, what is it?"

"Only amazing. The place is like a luxury resort for vampires." Sindy looked very put out by Allie's lack of appreciation for the offer.

"You've been there?"

"I wish. No, it's totally elite. Only Arif's top favorites get to stay there. I used to hear his guys talking about it. It's like a whole private neighborhood of McMansions, and they have a huge heated pool, an exclusive beach, and a private cinema, a salon... I can't believe you scored an invite!"

Alyson refused to be impressed. "What do I need a luxury resort for? Look at where I live now." She turned and swept her hands to encompass the house before them. Mattie stood at the rail of the deck waiting for her. He gave her a wave in response to her gesture. He looked so small in comparison to the house. They were just far enough away to truly take in the whole building. It really was beautiful, and surely to be considered a true mansion in its own right. Cain may not have bothered with amenities like a pool, but it was certainly nicer than anyplace Allie had ever stayed for any amount of time. Technically, she and Mattie stayed in their trailer, but they had always had open invitation to the house too.

Sindy lowered her voice in seriousness. "All the human blood you can drink. No strings attached." She leaned back and smiled with raised eyebrows, as though that should be an undeniably compelling argument.

Allie shook her head. "I'm sure there are some strings. There always are."

"Maybe, but guilt isn't one of them. All you have to do is let Arif be in charge, and he takes care of everything. Just like every vampire there, you'd probably get a group of blood donors willing to feed you, and do anything else you want! There's no killing. He feeds and supports them, gives them medical care to keep 'em all rosy healthy, and you've got your own private group of venom addicts just falling over themselves to please you, so that you'll bite them again."

For Allie, Sindy's description brought back the disturbing image of the coven Sindy had kept years ago, bound to her by blood, and striving to please her. They had been vampires though, not venom addicted humans. Sindy may have been hoping to model things after Arif's coven, but apparently she wasn't able to keep her humans alive long enough to achieve it, and had turned them all instead. "Sounds pretty twisted to me," Allie remarked.

Sindy licked her lips and met Allie's eyes. "Don't knock it until you've tried it. Have you ever even drunk from a human?"

"You know I haven't."

"Why not? I don't know what your hang up is. It's not like I'm saying it would be good to go out and hurt people, but a drink? I mean, do you know how easy it is, to go dance with a guy in a club, and then just lean in for a little nip? A wet kiss on the neck makes the spot a little numb, and then you just slide those long sharp fangs right in. If they've had a few beers, they barely even feel it, and even if they do, the venom spaces them out before they can complain. You take a few good pulls, the song ends, and you go on your way. No fuss, no muss."

Was it really so easy? Allie thought back to when she'd stolen a pair of sunglasses from a convenience store, with the cashier's thrall induced approval. It probably *would* be easy for her, everything was. She wouldn't admit it though. "What if someone sees you? Or what if they do feel it, or someone sees the blood? Oh sorry, I accidentally bit you on the neck while we were dancing... It seems like an awful lot of trouble to go through, when you can drink all you want right here."

Sindy rolled her eyes. "Let me ask you something. Which do you prefer, deer blood out of the fridge, or rabbit blood out in the field?"

That was a no-brainer. "The rabbit, definitely. But the deer blood is better when you drink it straight from the deer."

Sindy's eyes widened. She and Sindy had only ever brought down rabbits in their little hunting forays together as wolves. Sindy didn't know that Allie had been out hunting on her own, and Alyson could bring down larger game than Sindy was easily capable of. Sindy quickly realized that with Allie's extra speed and strength, she could probably take down anything she wanted to. "You know the difference," Sindy agreed. "When the blood is still live, you get more out of it. The stronger the prey, the better the drink, and to have their heart actually pumping it to you with every sucking pull...and those are just animals. What's it like when you drink from Mattie? He doesn't even have a living, pumping heart. All he's giving you is used blood, combined with whatever vampire stuff is in there keeping us going. It's not the same as drinking from a human; nothing is."

Allie just stared at her, unwilling to admit that it was a very intriguing notion. "It doesn't matter. I'm not going to run out to the Hamptons for a vampcation with Arif, just so I can drink human blood."

Sindy gave her a hopeful smile. "Well, the Hamptons are better in the summer anyway but…you sure? 'Cause if you just didn't want to go alone, I'd be happy to tag along. Could be fun."

Allie gave her a withering glance. "You and me hangin' with Arif and a bunch of venom groupies? Not my idea of fun. No thanks. Anyway, he said I could bring Mattie with me if I wanted to."

Sindy was incredulous of Allie's offhandedness over the generous offer. "And you still turned him down?"

Allie locked eyes with her for a moment. Sometimes she wished she could decipher her own feelings as easily as she managed to read others. "I didn't turn him down. I said I'd think about it." Stupid thing to say. She wasn't actually considering the offer…was she?

"Good thinking. Make him wait and take you in come July when the clubs open and the music starts pumpin'. I'm telling you the place gets *hot*. It's where all the best celebrities go to party."

Rather than reply, Alyson shifted into her wolf form and loped towards the house, although she was probably running from her own urges, more than the other woman. Sindy may have discovered the ability to shift into a wolf first, but Allie was just as acclimated to it now, and there was no match for her strength and speed, in any form. She left Sindy far behind.

As she neared the house, she saw Mattie leave his place of observation at the deck railing, to go inside in anticipation of her arrival. He would be preparing blood for her. He knew that she was always ravenous after practice.

Alyson leapt into the air and dispersed into mist, to reform and land in her human body as she reached the deck. Changing was so exhilarating! She had never felt so excitingly strong and in command of her powers. Tempest was a wonderful teacher, and even Sindy could be decent company and support during their sessions. After having a hunt out behind the house, and then practicing various aspects of her shifting powers with the girls, she got to come back and spend the remainder of her evening with Mattie. How could things be any better? She would have to remember to thank Cain once again for arranging this for her. She was very grateful for her comfortable situation.

Allie chose pants and a top from the folded clothing left out for her and Sindy, put them on, and went into the house. Mattie met her at the doorway with a warm mug of blood, which she eagerly chugged down. Mattie laughed as she finished and put the mug on the counter. "You savage. You don't even have time for a 'hello' and a 'thank you' first? Even bloodthirsty monsters can have manners."

She delicately used her middle finger to wipe a drop of blood from the corner of her mouth, and then licked it clean, before moving into his arms for a hug. "Hello," she whispered as she met his lips with a kiss, "and thank you."

Allie moved from his embrace to turn and face the glass patio door as it slid open behind them. Sindy stepped through wearing nothing but a look of annoyance. She hadn't bothered to dress before entering. "You could have waited for me."

Mattie looked at Allie with a smile. "See, you have no manners at all."

Alyson didn't even acknowledge the comment. She was too busy irately glaring at Sindy, who stood with her hands on her hips, posing nude before Mattie...again. She wasn't truly jealous of how Mattie might view Sindy's body, but just how much was she supposed to ignore? "Sindy, you know Cain has a rule about wearing clothing in the house."

Sindy had the nerve to let her eyes focus on Mattie, rather than answer Alyson directly. "Does he?" she asked with an annoyingly false lilt of innocent questioning. Mattie briefly met Sindy's eyes and then looked away, trying to appear indifferent and unaffected.

"You know damn well he does," Alyson growled, drawing back attention.

Sindy turned to her with a smile. "Sorry, but Mattie here spent so much time squinting across the field trying to get a glimpse from the deck, that I thought he deserved a nice close-up view before turning in for the day. Sweet dreams," she told Mattie, as she passed him to go up to her room.

Mattie was suitably flustered, and did his best not to glance at her as she went by him. Instead, he approached Allie, who was trying valiantly to keep her temper. "I was only out there waiting for you, I swear. I mean, I watch sometimes, but not for that."

"I know." Things between she and Sindy had been better lately, but every once in a while Sindy just couldn't resist a little dig. It seemed she knew just how to get Allie riled, walking the line without quite taking it far enough for Alyson to truly justify retaliation. It didn't seem Sindy would be leaving any time soon, so unless she and Mattie were planning to pull up stakes, they were just going to have to deal with her. *Think of Cain,* Allie told herself. *It's been good for Cain that she's here.*

Just then, Cain entered the kitchen with a greeting. Mattie practically pounced upon him, feeling the need to show Allie that he didn't favor Sindy at all. "Cain, does Sindy really need to stay here? She healed up months ago and she obviously doesn't need any help shifting. Isn't it time you sent her on her way?"

Cain was understandably taken aback by the plea. Alyson could feel his exasperation at having to wonder, *what has she done now?*

Alyson swallowed back her aggravation, and tried to consider things from Cain's point of view. "And you say I've got no manners. Mattie, we're guests here too, remember. That was really rude."

"Well she was just really rude to Allie," Mattie explained to Cain defensively. "I only said what you were thinking," he told Alyson quietly.

"No, actually I wasn't thinking that at all. Sorry, Cain. I don't really mind Sindy, honest. She just purposely says things to get under my skin sometimes, but there's no real harm done. I can take it. It's a good exercise in restraint."

Cain gave her a sympathetic smile. "I'm sorry if she's been goading you. I'll talk to her."

Mattie put his arms around Allie from behind, trying to comfort her, as a sort of apology for having to take the abuse. She glanced up at him in reassurance, as she continued. "Cain's been going through a rough time, and it's hard to be alone. He's got as much right to get some as anybody else."

Cain stared at her for a moment, as though trying to make sure he was properly interpreting what she'd said. "Excuse me?" Cain finally interjected indignantly. "That's not why she's here. I am not looking to *get some*, as you so quaintly put it."

Mattie gave her a little shove from behind. "I told you they weren't together like that."

Allie dropped her gaze to the floor with a smirk. "Not yet, but all guys need some now and then. Maybe it's just taking a while." Cain was gazing at her in insulted annoyance. No, he didn't consciously think that way, but he was still a guy wasn't he? She gave him an apologetic little smile, looking for him to admit that she wasn't completely off base. "Come on, it's not like you couldn't use the distraction."

Cain rolled his eyes. "That's enough. I'm not trying to sleep with her, and forgive the disparagement to Sindy, but if that were what I was looking for, it wouldn't be taking this long. I did not invite her here to seduce her, or to distract myself by using her in any way," he insisted. "I wanted to help her, and... I just... I'm hurting and I'm lonely, and it's nice to have someone to talk to when you two are off on your own. I'm not using her," he declared again. It sounded as though he was trying to convince himself more than the others.

"Cain, I didn't mean it like that," Allie said quietly.

He was very upset by the idea that he might be taking advantage of Sindy somehow. Jeez, the guy hadn't even touched her. Besides, he had to know that Sindy was here because it was exactly what *she* wanted, regardless of how Cain felt. "You're not using her," Allie assured him.

"Then why does it feel that way? Maybe you two are right, maybe I am. That was not my intention, honestly. I've never needed anyone to lean on before. Being alone was my specialty. I didn't think it would be this hard. I just want it to be over already."

Mattie's voice was infused with sympathy, but he didn't understand. "What to be over?"

"The pain!" Cain answered desperately. "I know you're sick of hearing about it, and I'm just supposed to 'get over it', but it's not like flipping a switch! I don't think either of you can truly understand how I feel. I have never felt love for someone the way that I feel love for Felicity, and I have lived a damn long time looking for it, believe me. I've had ill-fated affairs and short-lived, badly ended romances, but not true love. No one has ever permeated my soul the way that she has. I know that we weren't together for very long, but that doesn't matter. Felicity is a part of me, forever entwined. I *love* her, as a bird loves to fly.

Finally, I've found true love. And yet, I knew I would ruin it if I took her life. Even if I didn't turn her, to keep her with me, holding her back from experiencing life would be just as harmful. She didn't deserve that from me, so I trusted that in doing the right thing, we would somehow be rewarded."

Alyson could clearly feel Cain's shift from pleading desperation to cheated anger. He felt an idiot to have let her go, but that it was the only fair choice he could have made in her best interest. As he continued, his voice was a low growl of resentment. "My reward thus far? Pain. Can't I have a single bloody emotion without it ending in pain? Three and a half centuries I have been waiting for the pain to end, and it never does. I just keep getting pelted with new incarnations of it, each more emotionally damaging that the last. Does it never end?"

Allie took his attention, giving him a telepathic slap of sorts for clarity, meeting his eyes and speaking firmly. He knew that she was sympathetic, but what's done is done. He was going to have to suck it up, pull himself together, and move on. "No, Cain, it doesn't. It never ends until we're dust." She gave him a teasing lilt of a smile. "It took you over three hundred years to figure out that life sucks?"

She felt the tension break, as he laughed a little at himself. "Call me an optimist," he told them with a hint of a lopsided grin.

Mattie shook his head as he clapped Cain lightly on the shoulder. "No offense, Cain, but if *you're* the optimist in this group, then heaven help us all!"

Even Cain had to smile at that remark. "I do spend a good amount of my time looking at the empty half of my glass these days, don't I?"

Allie grabbed his hands for a squeeze. "I know it's been hard, but you should start allowing yourself to be happy again. There are good things going on here. Look at how much you've helped me! I can't even tell you how grateful I am for all you've done for Mattie and me." Mattie was nodding behind her in emphatic agreement. "And you've been a big help to Sindy too, despite the fact that she can be an ungrateful bitch."

Cain winced at the description. "She's not *that* bad, is she? Tell me she's getting better."

Allie smiled. "She is. I know she's had her own stuff to work through, and it hasn't been easy for her, but she is getting better, thanks to you. It's not wrong for you to enjoy having her here. Especially when with you, is exactly where she wants to be. You don't have to analyze it. Just let yourself be happy for a change. And for my part, I will try my very best not to rip her open, Tempest style."

Cain laughed. "Thank you. I appreciate the restraint."

Mattie met his eyes in all seriousness. "You should, because I don't think she's kidding."

~~~~~~~~~~~~~~~~~~~~~~~~~~~~~~~~

Khalon and Cain stood quietly consulting with each other, as Tempest instructed Sindy on details to perfect the modifications she was trying to make to her wolf claws. Tempest was showing her how to make them a bit longer, thinner, and sharp enough to slice open others, the way that Tempest had sliced her.

Alyson wasn't paying them much attention. She'd been playing around with the alteration exercise all evening, and had gotten fairly good at it. Instead, she was focusing on Cain and Khalon, who had stopped by to evaluate the girl's progress.

Khalon was speaking, as he watched Tempest demonstrate the finer features of the technique for Sindy. "I think it's gone remarkably well. Tempest is happiest when she has a project to work on. And when Tempest is happy, it is better for everyone."

"She's been a marvelous teacher," Cain agreed. "I'm sure I haven't provided the most malleable of students," he said, glancing over to Alyson with a teasing grin, "yet they all seem well satisfied."

Khalon nodded with a smile. "Three headstrong women…this could have been a catastrophe. Instead, I am happy to see that it is harmony born of hard work." He leaned closer, speaking to Cain confidentially. "I had told her that about two months should be sufficient, but it's been more than three, and Tempest has not even asked for a release date. She takes pride in her work. She will continue until no longer needed."

"Well, I hope she knows how much I appreciate that. As much as I asked her here for Alyson, Sindy has benefited greatly as well, and it's affected a change in her for the better."

As Cain finished speaking, Sindy shifted into her wolf form to see if she could create the deadly, razor-sharp claws Tempest had shown her. It struck Alyson as almost comical to see the large, dark wolf sit down docile on her haunches and give Tempest her paw for inspection, like a pet performing tricks for a treat.

Tempest gave Sindy's paw pad a little squeeze, to better extract her claws, and then gave her a grin. "Wonderful! I think you've got it this time." Tempest ran her finger under the claw and it drew a shallow line of blood from her finger. "With a little power behind it, I bet that'd slice clean through to the bone."

Alyson felt Sindy mentally nudging her for attention. She wanted Allie to translate, since Sindy couldn't speak for herself in this form. "You think?" she asked Tempest.

"One way to find out," Tempest replied with a smile.

Allie laughed at Sindy's telepathic response. "I don't suppose you're volunteering?" she asked for Sindy.

Tempest grinned. "You wish. Let's go catch something and try them out." Tempest swiftly shifted into her wolf form, which Sindy promptly gave a playful swat with her paw.

Allie also shifted into her wolf, as she broadcast, *I'm all for that.*

Cain stopped them before they took off into the woods. He looked a bit put off. "Are you three seriously going to go and torture small animals?" he asked them in distaste.

Allie just blinked at him for a moment. The man was a vampire. Was there no predator in him at all? *Don't worry, we'll drug them first,* she told him. *Better squirrels than people, right?*

"Remind me to never buy you a puppy," he said with slight grimace. "I'm going to go back to the coven circle with Khalon for a bit. We need to discuss security preparations for the holiday gathering. I wish we could forgo it this year, but I suppose that isn't really an option. I just want to focus on keeping things as low key and smooth as possible. I'll see you ladies back at the house."

Alyson acknowledged him, and then realized that Mattie had made his way towards them from the house while she had been distracted. He was practically upon them. She was glad that she was in wolf form, so she didn't have to try to suppress the weary sigh she probably would have let out, hurting Mattie's feelings.

Cain gave them all a wave, and followed Khalon into the forest. Tempest and Sindy were also eager to leave, both pacing in their wolf forms, waiting for her. *Sorry, I'll just be a sec.* Allie shifted back to her human form as Mattie reached them.

"Here you all are."

"Hi hon," she said, as she met him with a quick kiss. "I thought you were going to wait back at the house tonight?"

Mattie glanced at the two wolves impatiently pacing the wood line. "I was, but you said you'd be done at 3 o'clock…which was like an hour ago. We were going to watch that DVD, remember?"

"Oh right, sorry. We've been working on something, and I think we may have finally gotten it. We were just about to go and test it out."

Mattie didn't seem to understand that she was getting at needing him to give her a little more time. "Okay," he said agreeably. "I'll come with."

Allie put her arms around his waist and gave a little squeeze as she looked up and gently told him, "Well… you can't really. It's wolf stuff."

Mattie paused for a moment of disappointed reflection, and then replied. "Uh-huh. And when is it time for Mattie stuff?"

Allie slumped her shoulders, giving his waist another squeeze. "I don't know hon. I don't want you to be left out, it's just that this is important right now."

"You mean exciting. That stuff is more exciting."

Sindy let out a small whine of impatience. She wanted to go off into the woods and hunt, but liked having Alyson there as a buffer between she and Tempest. On one hand, Allie was annoyed, because Sindy could easily have spoken to her telepathically without making it seem such a display in front of Mattie, but at the same time, she realized that Sindy was trying to give Mattie incentive to just drop it and let them all leave. However unfair that might seem for Mattie, Allie was almost grateful for it.

She batted her eyes at him soulfully for understanding. "There will be time babe, really, just not right now." She could feel him wanting to reply, but he just stood there, looking out into the darkened woods. It wasn't the movie. It wasn't the fact that she liked going off and doing this stuff sometimes. That was okay with him. It was the big picture.

When and how would there be time for him in her life? He knew she loved him, but he couldn't see how to fit this new vampire stuff into the quiet existence he wanted to live. He couldn't put it into words without sounding like he was demeaning the important things she was trying to figure out. He knew he didn't have to say it, she could read it from him.

She could not deal with this right now. Allie gave him an emotional wave of reassurance. *Don't worry, babe. We'll figure it all out. One night at a time. I'll be back in an hour, okay?* She was itching to shift. Tempest and Sindy had already slunk off into the brush. Mattie gave her a small nod of acknowledgement, and it was all she needed. She stretched up to give him a kiss, and then disintegrated into mist in his arms. She briefly swirled around him, giving him a quick mental nudge of thanks, and then drifted to the ground, to become the wolf and disappear into the thicket.

~~~~~~~~~~~~~~~~~~~~~~~~~~~~~~~

Sindy flinched and jerked her head away from Allie's hand. "Ow! Damn it Allie! Forget it already, just take them out." She reached up to feel one of the offending earrings gingerly.

The holidays had passed quickly, as such anticipated days usually do, with as little drama and difficulty as one could hope for from such a large event. In fact, it had seemed rather quiet this year. The usual group of younglings had descended upon the estate to check in with Cain on how they were progressing out on their own, and a few elders that he'd met over the decades came to pay their respects, but no one that Allie found particularly interesting. Allie, Mattie, and Sindy had constantly speculated about whether Cain's maker, Maribeth, and her consort Drake would attend, but the pair never showed.

Cain seemed very relieved over that fact, and Allie had noticed that he'd tended to lean quite heavily on Sindy throughout the holiday week for emotional support and private company, although the two were still not intimately involved.

As a token of appreciation, Cain had given Sindy a nicely sized pair of diamond stud earrings as a gift; earrings that were now causing both she and Allie a great deal of grief.

Sindy wanted to have a second piercing done in her ears for them, so she could wear them above the large hoop earrings she already wore, but she worried that Cain would be angry if she went to have it done by the lady at the mall. What would happen when the woman tried to show Sindy her work in the mirror? Or what if a sample of Sindy's blood, or skin had been left behind? Probably not a real concern, but the last thing she wanted, was to have Cain frown upon her actions.

Without aid of a mirror, that meant her only real choice had been to ask Allie to do it. Allie didn't really mind, and was certainly capable, but every time Sindy changed into a wolf, they fell out, along with all of her other jewelry, onto the ground with her clothing. Then if she wanted to put them back in, new holes needed to be pierced. How annoying! Alyson kept her *Claddagh* ring from Mattie, in a keepsake box back at the trailer, and didn't even bother to wear jewelry anymore, unless she was planning to stay with Mattie all evening, in human shape. But Sindy was determined to wear these earrings, and she wanted a second set of holes for them. Allie had pierced them again for her last night after their hunt, and Sindy hadn't shifted form since. She had assumed that after having some time to heal, the holes would be established, but now she was complaining about how much they hurt. What a wuss.

Sindy tried to sit still on the chair at the dressing table in her bedroom, as Allie inspected Sindy's ears, which looked perfectly normal. "Sorry. I don't know what the problem is. I did all mine myself. It's not like they can get infected or anything, right?" Allie worked the backing off the topmost earring, only to have the diamond leave Sindy's ear and fall to the floor, quickly to be lost in a groove between the hardwood floorboards. "Shit."

"What? What'd you do to me now?" Sindy asked accusingly, her hand reaching up to feel for damage in her ear.

"Nothing," Allie assured her. "I dropped it."

Sindy turned to glare at her. "You lost it?" Her eyes quickly scanned the floor to no avail. She turned the angry glare upon Alyson once again. "Those were real you know."

"I know. I'm sorry. I don't know what happened. It just kind of popped out of your ear."

Sindy shooed Allie's hand away, as she reached to take out the other one. "Yeah, nice work. Just forget it. I'll get the other one out myself."

As Sindy began to remove the other earring, Allie looked up to see Cain observing them from the hall. He'd paused by the doorway upon leaving his own room, after hearing their disgruntlement. "What's going on?"

Wanting to rectify things before Sindy could place too much blame on her, Allie squatted on the hard wood floor, next to the crack that had swallowed the earring, and tried to find it. Sindy answered sarcastically, "Oh nothing. I was just stupid enough to let Allie pierce my ears, and now they hurt like hell."

Cain looked at her oddly. "Your ears are already pierced."

"I know, but I wanted a second set."

Allie looked up from where she had been trying, unsuccessfully to use her long pinky fingernail to fish for the diamond. "I thought dumb stuff like that wasn't supposed to hurt us anymore?"

Cain stood with arms crossed over his chest and grinned. "Everything hurts. It just won't kill you."

Sindy sneered at Alyson, while speaking to Cain and taking the other earring out of her ear. "Yeah, well she put in those beautiful new diamond studs you gave me, but it feels like she cleaned them with holy water first."

Allie looked up with a grin. "That'd be a pretty funny trick."

"Hilarious," Sindy answered drolly.

Sindy gave Allie a withering look while Cain moved closer into the room to ask, "So she made a new hole in your ear?"

"Yeah, with the diamonds you bought me." Sindy held up the second earring to show him, while batting her eyes coyly. "I love them. You're so good to me."

"I am, aren't I?" Cain replied with a playful smile.

Alyson rolled her eyes. *You gave me a set of books,* she pointed out to him, with mental reprimand. Cain looked hurt, but she immediately reassured him that she was teasing. *They're good books though. Probably too many big words for her anyway.*

Cain tried to hide his smile as Sindy eyed him suspiciously. "Would you guys please not have private conversations right in front of me? It's really rude. If anything you should be pissed at her," Sindy told Cain, holding up her lone earring for emphasis. "She lost one," she added with an accusing glance at Alyson.

Cain took the earring from her without even sparing Allie a glance. "What keeps it in your ear?" Sindy held up the little gold backing for him to see, and then showed him how it fit onto the earring. "Well no wonder it hurts."

"What do you mean?"

"You poked a *foreign object* through your flesh, and *forced* it to stay there."

Both Alyson and Sindy gave him blank stares for a moment. Sindy spoke while rubbing her ear. "It's just an earring Cain. My others don't hurt."

Allie stood, giving up looking for the lost diamond, and moving her hair to expose the many holes in her left ear. "Yeah, what's the big deal? I've got seven."

Cain smiled and handed Sindy back her earring. "Yes, but you had those *before*, didn't you?" Allie shrugged and nodded. "They're already established. Your body assumes that they're supposed to be like that. But a *new* hole in your ear will heal, just like any other injury." He turned his gaze back to Sindy. "You should know that."

"Yeah, but…I just figured the earring would be there, so the hole couldn't close. Why does it hurt so much?"

"Because your body keeps trying to expel it. It's constantly pushing against the earring to try to get it out. It'll never heal."

Sindy rubbed at her ear some more. "*Now* he tells me."

Cain shook his head with a laugh. "You'll just have to settle for wearing one pair at a time."

Sindy slumped her shoulders as she admired to lone earring she had left. "I guess that won't be a problem."

Cain touched the side of her face, to have her look up and give him attention. "If you can't find it, I'll buy you another," he told her. He turned to leave, but then stopped suddenly. Something seemed to have caught his eye at Sindy's window. He froze for a moment, and then quickly crossed the room.

Allie was watching him in mild alarm. "What's the matter?" She could feel his sudden tense worry.

Cain answered her telepathically rather than with speech, which Allie also found odd and alarming. *I saw something, at the window. I think we're being watched.* Cain slowly approached the window and slid the glass pane upwards, until it was fully open and he could lean out.

Allie quickly broadcast the news to Sindy, telling her to keep quiet and stay put as Allie approached the window beside Cain. *Want me to go check it out?*

No, I definitely do not want you outside right now. Stay here while I take a look. Cain climbed carefully out the window onto the roof. It was slick with frost, but he knew how to choose his footing cautiously, keeping his balance.

Allie protested as he crouched there. *You're gonna fall. Just let me do it, I can fly out there and take a quick peek, no problem.*

Cain turned to give her a glance of disapproval. He may not be able to fly, but he resented being considered incapable. *I was climbing in and out of windows, and across London rooftops, for two centuries before you were even born. I think I can handle it.*

He turned and scanned the night sky, before making his way further out, and ducking down next to the peaked rooftop of the window. He was watching something, and had ducked down and frozen. He was certain that he had not yet been seen, and wanted to keep it that way.

Sindy moved behind Alyson at the window, and began to speak, before realizing she'd been told to keep quiet. "What's out there?"

Allie answered aloud, hoping to sound natural and unaware of observation, just in case. "Nothing. It was probably just a Crimson bat. I'm sure plenty of them would be thrilled to get a peek in your window." She abruptly pulled closed the curtain, in the hopes that anyone watching would believe they'd escaped unnoticed. She gave Sindy a stern look, and went to sit down on the bed, and check in telepathically with Cain.

The fierce protectiveness she felt from him was a bit startling. He was worried for Alyson's safety, and furious that someone would seek to infiltrate his estate and invade their privacy. He sat unmoving, waiting for the unknown party to give themselves away.

Maybe it was *a crimson bat.* Allie suggested.

No, not unless they were in the process of shifting, while twenty feet above the ground. It didn't have clear form. I think it was a shade.

Allie put a hand out to stop Sindy, who had been about to go look out the window. "Sit," she mumbled. *What's a shade?*

Not a true shade, but another vampire, Cain explained. *Those with the ability to remain in-between forms, as you do. They're known as shades.*

What color breed is that?

I wish I knew. I've never actually met one. I've heard of them, but I wasn't sure they truly existed until I saw you do it. If it's a talent in your arsenal, then there must be a breed that specializes in it as well. I think I can just see it, a dark patch hovering out over the snow on the lawn. I wish it would shift into a form I could recognize.

Allie was surprised to feel that not only did Cain want to recognize it, he was tensed, ready to jump to the ground and stake the thing. His hand kept hovering near his leg, where a stake was tucked into the top of his boot beneath his pant leg. *You keep a stake on you, even in the house?* she asked him incredulously.

I don't take my role as your mentor lightly. I'm not just the pain in the ass trying to keep you focused and get you trained, I consider myself your personal protector as well.

He was dead serious. Allie was a little taken aback, as she picked him up empathetically. He felt very menacing at the moment, coiled and ready to attack if necessary. It was touching…and kind of hot. *You'd put yourself in danger for me?*

Of course I would. You're my coven sister, not to mention being the United One. Damn. It's moving around to the front of the house where I can't see it. He began to slowly creep across the roof until he could cross the center peak and find a place to perch out of sight on the other side.

Sindy gave Alyson a nudge for attention. "Is he coming back in, or what?" she asked in a whisper.

Allie just held up her finger for Sindy to wait a minute. *Can you get to it?* she asked Cain.

Pointless. If it remains in mist form, I can't do anything to it. It'd be like fighting a shadow. You know that. I don't know if it saw me, but it doesn't seem to be in a rush to leave.

Allie shook her head, before remembering that Cain couldn't see her. *I doubt it saw you. We can't really see much when we're all dispersed like that. We mostly have to rely on psychic sight, life forces, and marks. It had to take form if it was going to do any real spying. It probably didn't change into smoke until you came to the window, and then it would have been too busy trying to navigate leaving, to see you come out. It's hard to move around when you can barely see where you're going. You're cloaked, so if it's still a shade, I doubt it knows where you are.*

Good to know. Cain answered. *I'm sure whoever it is, has more practice traveling in that form than you do, but I think if it saw me, it'd be moving with more purpose.* Allie waited tensely for another report, but Cain was silent. Earlier he'd been purposely allowing the relay of his actions to her, but now he wasn't paying her much attention, focused only on his subject. Finally, she tried to connect with him more fully, to see what he was seeing. It took a minute, because Cain was in the habit of keeping his thoughts fairly guarded when not purposely communicating, but after a few mental nudges, she was able to get him to loosen up and let her see through his eyes.

Alyson focused on the dark shadow Cain was watching just in time to see it swirl into tighter formation and purposefully shoot across the lawn, to disappear into the woods. Cain untensed his muscles with a grunt of annoyed defeat. Allie was too curious to give up yet. *Maybe I can follow it,* she suggested.

Absolutely not. You could be charging right into a trap.

Allie scoffed at the idea. *Whoever it was, they didn't know we were watching. I'll bet they're here alone.*

Probably, but even so, what would you do if you found them? Whoever it is, you can be sure they are likely to have more experience using their skills combatively than you do. Cain finished the thought as he began climbing back in the window. Once in, he turned and shut it behind him, locking it with a loud click.

"Well?" Sindy prompted impatiently.

"We were definitely under surveillance, although I don't know by whom. It was a shade: a vampire who can disperse into mist for indefinite periods. They're gone now, but there is no telling if they will be back, or even if this was their first time here.

I'm afraid we're going to have to operate more alertly around here from now on. Both the house and the trailer are guarded by the need for invitation, so they should be secure places to retire. You'll have to be wary out on the property, though.

Alyson, you should get in touch with Mattie and have him come straight home. I'll alert the Crimson Coven that we will need them to be on guard, and then it should be relatively safe, as long as you are careful and observant of your surroundings. No more hunting."

"What?" both Allie and Sindy asked in affronted unison.

"You'll be too distracted to stay safe, and I'm afraid all wandering expeditions off premises will have to come to an end for a while as well."

"What do you mean, like we can't go anywhere?" Sindy asked in outrage.

"That is exactly what I mean."

"But that blows!" Sindy exclaimed. Alyson shared the sentiment, but let Cain fight it out with Sindy first. If he wasn't going to let Sindy go anywhere, he certainly wouldn't be keen on letting the United One go jaunting off without protection.

"We have no idea who that was, or what they were doing," Cain explained reasonably.

"Right, so maybe it was nothing. You're being paranoid," she informed him.

"I am being careful. If someone wants to cause Alyson harm, we don't need to make it easy for them."

"Like who?" Sindy turned to Allie accusingly. "Did you piss someone off at the party? I know you're usually good at that."

Cain answered before Allie could. "Unfortunately, Alyson is at risk just for being who she is. We have tried to keep things fairly secret, and I know she was extra careful during the holiday, but I'm afraid she's been followed home by interested parties on more than one occasion in the past," he pointed out with a reprimanding glance at Allie. "So far her admirers have seemed harmless enough, but that could easily change. We have to be careful until we know what we're dealing with."

"So? That's her problem, not mine," Sindy insisted.

Cain crossed his arms over his chest, giving her a look of disapproval for her lack of solidarity. Alyson didn't expect much more from Sindy, though. In all the time she had been here, Sindy and Cain were still on little more than friendly terms, with nothing more than some mild flirting going on. Alyson knew that since Sindy's initial healing, Cain had not shared his blood with her again, so while Cain might call Allie his coven sister, what was Sindy to any of them?

She was a guest in Cain's home, and a companion for Allie to practice shifting skills with, but Sindy had never been offered more. Mattie, Alyson, and Cain still regularly continued their monthly marking, but they had never invited Sindy to join them in it. Alyson and Mattie kept waiting with trepidation for Cain to ask, but he never did, and oddly enough, although Sindy surely noticed the shared mark of the coven on them, she never mentioned it, or requested inclusion.

Cain continued to explain to Sindy why Alyson's worries should affect her. "If Alyson is kept well protected, and you go blundering out into the hands of someone seeking to harm her, what is to stop them from using you as a hostage? If it is Alyson that they want, they might easily decide that torturing you is a good way to make me give her to them."

Sindy eyed him with discerning interest. "What's the difference? You wouldn't give her up for me anyway, would you?"

There was no way that Cain was stupid enough to answer that question. He simply sighed and said, "Stay on the grounds."

Sindy wasn't exactly pleased with his reply, or the sudden house arrest. She turned to Allie with a stare like a stab of ice. "Thanks a lot."

Allie stood silent, glaring back at Sindy and trying to decide if all this caution was truly necessary. Cain came up behind Sindy to take her by the shoulders with his strong hands, instantly disarming her, making her practically melt into him. Allie knew that Cain hadn't given Sindy much hope that they might move further into any sort of relationship. Allie could see the potential there, but it was taking much longer than Sindy had expected, and the vixen had begun to give up. Instead of spending her time uselessly trying to flirt with Cain, she'd begun hunting men in town for trysts and little drinks.

Neither she nor Allie had thought Cain realized that, but Alyson now saw that this was foolish. Just because Cain did not voice his disapproval, did not mean that he was oblivious. He knew. She could now clearly read from him that he had been tolerating Sindy's excursions because he wasn't prepared to offer her anything more at home. He still wasn't, but he knew that it would ease her disgruntlement over the limitation, if he were planning to pay her more attention.

"Is it really so distasteful to think that you might be trapped here with me, rather than continuing your nightly excursions into town?" he asked Sindy quietly.

Sindy lowered her eyes, considering her answer while enjoying the feel of Cain up against her back. He let his arms wrap further around her shoulders in a more familiar hold. Allie could tell Sindy was clearly aware that she was being played into submission, but she was happy to play. "I guess I can stick around, if you're willing to help keep me occupied," she said seductively.

It was clearly evident to Allie, that Cain was not at all willing to take things as far as Sindy would like them to go, but he would try to appease her with his undiluted platonic attention if nothing more. "I make no promises," he cautioned, "but I have missed your company lately."

Sindy met Alyson's eyes, from within Cain's light embrace from behind. A long time ago, Alyson had promised to put in a good word for Sindy with Cain when she could. Every time Sindy mentioned it to her in private, she would tell the woman to stop being impatient. Cain's attention was worth waiting for. She hadn't pushed the man, because she didn't want to urge him into anything that wasn't right for him. However, annoying as Sindy could be, the understanding and attraction the two seemed to share was undeniable, and this did seem a small step in the right direction. Sindy gave Allie a sly smile at the small victory.

When Alyson looked up to meet Cain's eyes however, all she saw there was worry. "I'm very protective of those I care for," he told the girls. Sindy seemed to feel the statement was for her, but Allie knew Cain meant to include she and Mattie as well. "I want to know that you're safe."

Allie gave him a warm smile. "Don't worry, we'll be fine."

Chapter 9 - Surprise!

Ben

Restaurant, New York City
An evening in June

Ben watched Felicity pick at her dinner, and wondered how he should begin the important conversation that he wanted to have. She seemed *off* tonight.

They'd been planning this evening for weeks. After all, it was their one-year anniversary celebration! Earlier, they'd gone to a wonderful new show on Broadway that she'd been dying to see. He'd gotten them a very extravagant hotel suite for the evening, but first, a late dinner at their favorite restaurant. It may not be the most luxurious place for dinner, but he knew she always loved the food. He just wished she seemed to be enjoying it more.

She absently swiped a curl of glossy auburn hair back behind her ear as she pushed the food around on her plate with her fork. She looked absolutely gorgeous this evening, with her hair mostly pulled back into a loose French-twist, and wearing a new emerald green dress that brought out the deep hue of her eyes and hugged her in all the right places. He'd noticed that she'd been letting those curves fill out a little again, and it definitely suited her.

"You were right babe, the show was great, wasn't it?" he asked.

She looked up, offering him a weak smile. She'd claimed to be having a good time, but seemed preoccupied. "Hmmm? Oh, yes. Definitely worth seeing."

"Is your dinner alright? You're barely eating."

She gave him a more heartfelt smile, wanting to re-assure him that his well-planned evening wasn't going to waste. "It's delicious. I'm just not all that hungry."

"You sure you wouldn't like a glass of wine? You're making me drink alone here. I told you that you don't have to worry about driving. This is my one and only drink," he reminded her, tipping up his 7 & 7 to her before taking a swig.

She chuckled and took a sip from her water glass. "No thanks. Go ahead and enjoy it."

"I guess I can toast you with water, but I'm not sure it'll take as well."

He held up his glass and she obediently clinked hers against it. "I'm sure that will work just fine. What's the toast?" she asked.

"To my beautiful wife, who has made our first year of marriage even better than I could have dreamed. Thank you for putting up with my crazy schedule, my study cramming for the bar, my complaints about civil service commitments and generally being a workaholic. I wish I could have been spending more time appreciating what a lucky man I am to have you. I hope you know that even on hectic days when I barely get to kiss you goodbye, and you're already sleeping when I get home, I still thank God that you're in my life. I love you Liss."

He could see her eyes fill with unshed tears, as she drank to his toast, and then leaned across the table to kiss him. "That is so sweet." She dabbed at the corner of her eye with her napkin, trying not to smear her make-up. "I love you too, so very much. I just can't believe how quickly the year has gone by. It's been such a whirlwind, but I wouldn't change a thing. I know you've had to put in a lot of time for work, but I'm so proud of you. Passing the bar, and getting such firm footing under your career. It'll pay off, you'll see."

He grinned. "Speaking of rewards from hard work... What would you say if I told you that we have a beach house in Sagaponack?"

Felicity froze for a moment, mid-sip, and then put down her glass, with a look of understandable confusion on her face. "I'd say, no we don't, and where the heck is Sagaponack?"

"We could... It's on Long Island, near the Hamptons," he told her enticingly.

She was too stunned to be impressed. "You bought a house?"

Ben reached over to hold her hand and reassure her. "I wouldn't do that without you! Relax, I haven't signed anything, but it's ours if we want it. Our own beach house. Could you imagine it?"

"A beach house...in the Hamptons? That must cost a fortune! We'll have nothing left."

She should know better than to be so concerned. He was always the frugal one, worrying about their finances. If he wasn't anxious over it, she certainly didn't need to be. "No, we can actually get it for just a little more than half of what we have in savings, and property is a great investment, especially in such a desirable area. Remember that lawyer I introduced you to, Connor Fitzgerald?"

She sat back a little, trying to place the name. "The older man, the one that was mentoring you?"

"That's the one. He's retiring. He and his wife are moving to the Bahamas."

She raised an eyebrow in disbelief. "The Bahamas?"

"I know. They're loaded. Anyway, they have this summer home that he used to use to schmooze clients, and he said I could buy it from him for this ridiculous price. The place is gorgeous. I mean, wait until you see it, it's like a million dollar house. I was in shock."

"You've seen it?"

Ben shook his head, reassuring her that he wouldn't take such steps without her. "Only pictures, but we can go check it out next weekend. He only gave me a few shots of it, but look at this place Liss."

He dug the photos out of his jacket pocket, excited to show her this amazing opportunity. She gasped as he put them down, suitably impressed. "What a cute place," she said, upon seeing the initial front shot of the house. Then he pointed to the next photo, with the back deck and stairs to the beach. "Is that the back? Oh my God, it's breathtaking! Look at all those windows!"

Ben smiled. "I know. They do that on the beach. It's all about the view. There are skylights too. It looks very open and airy; cathedral ceilings, and look at this kitchen."

Felicity had picked up a photo and was holding onto it, as though afraid it was unreal. "This looks like something out of a magazine. We could *live* there?"

"I know it's not what we talked about, but trading up to a bigger place here in the city would be half the size for the same money. Honestly, Liss, I'm over Manhattan. Aren't you? It's been exciting, but I think we're ready to move on. He told me about this place and I couldn't help thinking…if we are seriously going to start trying for a baby in a few months, maybe we should start thinking about getting out of the city, at least part time. It can be a summer home."

He could see the gleam of acceptance in her eyes. She loved the idea. "Or…" he continued, "if you want to look for a teaching position out there, there's a company office close by in Riverhead that they said I could work out of. We could live there full time, if you like it. It's not just a vacation area. It's a real community, with a good school district. It looks like a nice place to raise a family."

A beautiful smile spread over her face. "A nice place to raise a family, huh?"

"I thought so. That is the plan, right?"

Felicity looked positively gleeful. "Yes. We are definitely on the same page."

Ben took her hands as she put down the photo, worried that she might have second thoughts when considering things long term. "Unless you would rather live closer to your parents. I know this puts us even further away from them. It's supposed to be a really nice area though. And if you'd rather, we could still just use it for a summer place. I think it's worth looking at. It's too good an offer to pass up. Don't you think?"

"I think it sounds perfect."

Ben gave her hands a joyful squeeze. "Really? I'll tell him in the morning and we can set up a visit. Liss this is so amazing. Are you excited?"

"Oh, I'm excited alright. I actually had something I wanted to talk about with you too," she told him with a strangely coy smile.

"I knew you had something on your mind. Something going on at school?"

"No, it's not a school thing. My thing is…something big for both of us, actually. We're, um, going to have to move up the schedule a little." She hesitated, running her finger around the rim of her glass. "I'm pregnant," she finally announced quietly.

He could not have heard that correctly. "What?"

"We're having a baby." She was serious.

"Now?" he asked incredulously.

"Well, I think it'll probably take about nine months," she said with a chuckle, "but yes, I'm pregnant now."

Before he could truly take in what that meant, Ben felt he needed to clear up the confusion. "How? I mean, I thought we said September?"

Felicity gave him an apologetic smile. "It's not an exact science, Ben."

"I know but, you're on birth control. I thought we were going to start trying in August or September, so you could have the baby in spring. That way you could take your maternity leave, and have the summer off," he reminded her.

"I know the plan Ben." Her smile began to crumple as her lip slightly trembled. "It's my fault, I screwed up."

Ben quickly leaned forward to try to hold and reassure her. "No! Liss, don't say that. This isn't a screw up, this is…this is wonderful!"

"It's okay?" she asked hesitantly.

"Of course it's okay! It's just…unexpected, and I'm in shock, and… it's incredible! We're having a baby!" My God, it was really happening, already. They were going to be parents! "Are you sure?" he asked, sitting back again in shock.

"Pretty sure. I haven't seen the doctor yet, but I spent a good portion of my morning peeing on sticks with little blue lines on them, and they all seemed to be in cahoots. I made an appointment for Monday morning." She seemed very pleased that he couldn't wipe the grin from his face. It may be ahead of schedule, but could she really have been worried to tell him? He was thrilled!

She tried to explain the circumstances. "I'm sorry for the timing. I'm such a dope. See, the last time I was at the Ob/Gyn, she told me that it could take three to four months for birth control pills to leave your system, so it could take a while to get pregnant, even after I stopped taking them. I started to worry that I wouldn't even be fertile until Christmas, end up being nine months pregnant in September and mess up the whole school year, and I panicked. I stopped taking them last month, so that there would be plenty of time for me to get fertile again before we really started trying."

"A month ago?"

"Not even. I can't believe it could have happened so quickly! I know we've had a few romantic evenings since then, but I've been on birth control *forever*. I just didn't think it could work out this way. Guess I'm pretty fertile after all."

Ben was shaking his head with a huge grin, and trying to mentally count months. "When are we due?"

"It's kind of soon to tell, but if I really am pregnant, I guess it would be at the end of February."

"Boy, you really missed that April mark, didn't you?" he teased. "Don't worry, it's fine. We'll make it work." He tried to reach over to her again but couldn't stand the table between them. He got up and went to stand her up out of her chair for a real hug. "We're having a baby!"

With all of their news and plans laid out before them, the rest of dinner was a very enjoyable flurry of conjectures and excitement. By the end of their meal, neither of them could stop smiling.

Felicity was making a last visit to the ladies room as Ben went to bring the car around. Candidates for baby names and possibilities for future events kept playing out in his head as he walked. The summer night was warm and humid, the city air still and heavy around him after the air-conditioning of the restaurant. There was no valet parking, but luckily, there was a garage right next door.

A father, he was going to be a father! It was an idea that had always been an abstract plan for the future, but to put a timetable on it and start the countdown…now it was real. Exciting, scary, anxious, joyous, and *real*.

Ben entered the parking garage, and noticed that the attendant was not at his post. He would be collecting the car on his own anyway, so it didn't really matter. He made his way into the large parking facility, dimly lit by flickering fluorescents. Hopefully the garage being unattended didn't mean his car hadn't been kept safe and secure.

His car…he was probably going to have to trade that in, wasn't he? His prized yellow Mustang was a beloved possession. An eighteenth birthday present from his dad, it was probably the only true gift the man had ever bought him, other than the sword he'd received upon turning twenty-one, which was still wrapped up in the bottom of a closet somewhere. But the car…now there was a practical gift that really meant something to him. Bernard had even taken him to the lot and let Ben pick it out himself. Ben had always treated the car like gold, and done many of the improvements to it on his own. It was a two-door though, not exactly a practical, family-friendly vehicle. Maybe he could still keep it, and they could trade in Felicity's car for a minivan. If not, well, he would do whatever he had to. Beginning their family was the important focus.

He would have a family to take care of now. Not just he and Felicity, each fairly self-sufficient and able to get through anything that should be thrown at them, now there would be an infant depending entirely on them. Of course, they would be a team, Ben taking on as much of the parenting as Felicity when he could, but in the beginning especially, she was going to have her own bodily changes and concerns to deal with. The birth, recovery, breastfeeding and whatnot…it was on him to be the strong provider and take care of the family.

When he rounded the bend that would take him to his car, he noticed a couple making out up against the wall. So *that* was where the lot attendant had gone. Ben politely averted his eyes with an annoyed shake of his head. He was giving them wide clearance as he began to pass them, when something made him suddenly stop and do a double take.

At first glance, they were just two figures sharing an amorous moment, but as he looked away, he realized that something seemed strange. As he processed what he had seen, he recognized that both of the figures were men. One, Ben recognized as the lot attendant, the other figure was wearing a dark coat, but looked like another man. Not entirely unheard of, but also not what he had expected to see. It caused him to turn back and better assess the tableau.

Yes, although the figures weren't of a large build, even in the dim lighting, he could tell that they were both definitely men, and they weren't kissing… Even as a tremor of alarm went through him, one of the men looked up at him. His eyes were an inhuman, reflective orange.

Vampire. Even after almost five years of relative peace and normalcy, the feeling of slightly sick and angry recognition came immediately, followed by the uneasy realization that he was not prepared for this in the least. Ben reached to his collar and fumbled at the chain on his neck until he was able to pull out the gold cross, although a mumbled curse left his lips rather than a prayer.

He and Felicity had not seen nor spoken of vampires in ages. He'd begun to let his guard down. He always wore a cross, but he had stopped being so diligent about carrying a stake with him. He kept one stowed under the seat of his car…a lot of good it was going to do there. It had felt good to live a normal life, unconcerned with what others would consider paranoid fantasy. The tiny gold cross he wore seemed flimsy protection, when actually faced with those gleaming eyes, knowing they were attached to some very sharp fangs.

Obviously, he was more prepared than the parking attendant had been, at least he knew what he was up against, but if the thing turned on him, he didn't even have a decent weapon. Ben wasn't given time to react further. The moment the vampire met his eyes, it released the parking attendant, who slid to the floor in an unconscious slump, and began to advance on Ben. Whether the vampire saw him as another victim, or simply a witness to be eliminated, Ben was in trouble.

The thing looked to have been a man in his thirties, but haggard and worn by its previous life. Wrinkles and a general weariness had stamped its features in a way that even the false health of immortality could not erase. The man had dark, stringy hair, thinning and unkempt, paired with the thin and patchy beginnings of a beard. His eyes were almost too large for his face, and although he looked to be of slim build under his dark over-coat, the mere expression on his face sent a stab of intimidation through Ben at his swift approach.

Ben took another quick appraisal of his surroundings. Back here in the bowels of the dimly lit parking garage, there was nothing much he could use to help his situation, and killing a vampire with one's bare hands was nearly impossible, no matter how often he went to the gym. A sea of parked cars, a fire extinguisher on the wall, a rubber traffic cone and a metal sign stand in the middle of the lane, proclaiming which way driver's should exit, were the only objects that offered. Wasn't anything made of fucking wood anymore? Ben took a quick mental inventory of his pockets, but he didn't even have a damn pencil. *Never leaving the house again without a stake...ever.*

As the vampire reached him, it bared its fangs with a hiss. Alright, so this was how it would be. Not even a thin charade of civil humanity, no trickery or manipulation. Just an inhuman demon bent on killing him. Fine. At least he knew where he stood.

Ben wasted no time, but moved in to punch the thing in the face before it could try to grab him. Knowing it would be his best chance at a good clean shot, Ben was sure to put as much power as he could possibly muster into the strike, adrenaline helping to fuel its force so that Ben felt the slight crunch of shattered bone as his fist indented the man's cheekbone, nose and eye socket.

The look of shock on its face just before Ben's fist connected, was almost comical. Apparently, although Ben was a large man in good physical shape, the vampire had expected him to be frightened, or at least surprised by its demonic countenance. "Save the theatrics, I've seen it," Ben told the thing as it rocked back from the blow.

It hadn't the advantageous element of surprise it had expected, but it wasn't about to be bested by a mere human without a hell of a fight. Ben knew that vampire's felt pain just the same as human's did, but this thing just regained its balance and came right back at him. If anything, now it was really pissed.

"Then you should have run," the thing advised him in a harsh growl.

Run, and leave this thing here to kill the next poor soul who wouldn't even have a chance? It had never really seemed an option. Besides, he didn't know how fast the thing was, but Ben would probably just get turned around in the garage and disoriented. A good straight fight was preferable to a game of cat and mouse amongst the cars. At least in a straight fight, Ben felt he had a chance to inflict some real damage on the thing.

The vampire didn't seem to think so. It didn't seem intimidated in the least, despite Ben's well-thrown punch. It lunged back at Ben, grabbing his shoulders and trying to get itself into a position to bite. There was a smear of blood down its chin, and Ben found himself wondering if it was a result of his punch, or if the vampire was just a sloppy feeder. He held the vampire off as best he could, but was momentarily overwhelmed by being engulfed in the stench of his attacker.

It probably wasn't the vampire that smelled, but the over-coat it wore. Ben's knees buckled as he was smothered in the thick smell of wool soaked with sweat, piss, and a fetid rotting food odor reminiscent of a dumpster. Why was this thing wearing an over-coat in June? Ben wondered who was stupider, the vampire for wearing the thing out of season, after most likely stealing it off a bum in an alley somewhere, or himself for not immediately noticing how out of place it looked.

As Ben involuntarily gagged at the stench, the vampire bent to find his throat, but then backed off with a grunt of annoyance. It must have touched Ben's cross, and been distracted by the pain it caused. After a second of disorientation, it found the chain of the necklace, grabbed it, and pulled. The digging burn of the chain cut into Ben's skin before it finally snapped. The vampire threw it to the ground in disgust, and then while holding Ben's collar with one hand, gave him a solid blow with the other.

Ben was knocked back, blinded by pain, but still managed to kick the vampire away. It came back at him immediately, grabbing him by the shoulders and keeping him pressed towards the ground. The vampire dove down with exposed fangs, trying to puncture his skin. Ben struggled, and only narrowly avoided being bitten. He couldn't quite gather the strength and leverage to throw the vampire off...until the sharp tips of its fangs actually touched his flesh.

As needle-like teeth pricked his throat, the sensation called up memories of every vampire attack he had ever warded off...and the *one* to which he'd been forced to submit. When Sindy had bitten him, the venom she had injected was like nothing he'd ever felt before, and nothing he would ever be able to forget. It had brought about many reactions from him, some of which he worked very hard to block from memory, but one thing was certain, once she had infected him with her poison, his will and ability to fight had fled. That *could* not happen here.

Ben found new vigor and shoved against the vampire for all he was worth. His sudden renewed aggression was more than the vampire had expected. It still had the advantage of standing above him, but was shoved back, losing its purchase on Ben's throat, a fact it complained of with a disappointed hiss.

The instant's reprieve was all Ben needed to effectively continue his offensive retaliation. He brought his head up sharply to butt against the man's face. The vampire's chin and teeth crunched under Ben's forehead. The blinding knock of pain hurt Ben as much as the vampire, but he was ready for it, while the demon was not. Ben hoped he'd somehow managed to snap a fang off the thing.

The creature let go of him and Ben was able to stand, ignoring the pounding ache in his head. He advanced on the vampire, noting that while its fangs still gleamed, long and sharp as ever, the vampire had lost a few of its lesser teeth. Fangs must be made of harder stuff. Ben punched it again, bruising his knuckles against the creature's temple, but knocking the vampire to the concrete.

Ben gave it a good kick in the side, as anger and resentment rushed through him with a frightening force. This inhuman, unholy abomination dared to think it was going to make a meal of him? Here he was, a hard working, upstanding man, just minding his own business, and this thing thought it could just step out of the shadows and take him away from his life?

His wife, carrying their unborn child, would receive news from some policeman or E.M.T saying, *I'm sorry Mrs. Everheart, we aren't sure what happened. I'm afraid your husband has been found dead.* Fuck that. He bent down to punch the thing again, harder than ever. He struck it again, and again, feeling the creature's flesh surrender under his barrage of blows. That was *not* how his life was going to end. That was not how he would leave his family, God damn it.

It wasn't moving. Ben straightened and took a deep breath, allowing the dusty scent of concrete and lingering exhaust fumes to carry away the stench of the thing's coat. He gave the vampire a final kick. Although it wasn't fighting back, the thing was still conscious. The vampire seemed very confused and debilitated by Ben's assault. It lay on the ground, dazed and trying to protect its head. Maybe it thought that Ben would just leave it there, satisfied that it was out of commission. So it could regain its strength, and attack the next passer-by? Not a chance.

Ben kicked it again and then looked around at his surroundings, hoping to be inspired with a way to kill the thing. The fire extinguisher was surely nice and heavy, but even crushing a vampire's skull would not ensure its death, not definitively. Ben would be satisfied with nothing less than dust.

He stalked over to the freestanding metal parking sign, yanked the legs of it out of their weighted feet, and brought it over to the vampire. It was thin sheet metal, but thick enough to be sturdy, and it had a nice edge to it. Ben flipped the sign upside down, holding it out before him, and then rolled the vampire onto its back with his foot. Its eyes were closed, but they flicked open to look at him with their ill-orange orbs and thin upright black pupils.

Those eyes…they looked just like the eyes of the first vampire that had ever attacked him, late at night behind a gas station with his friends Allie, Mattie, and David. He'd been humoring Alyson and they had all treated the stakeout like some kind of joke…until he'd been attacked. Alyson had saved him, almost staking him along with the vampire, as her small body, coiled with energy, drove a makeshift spear right through the thing's back, and made a shallow puncture in Ben's chest as well. After that, he'd had no choice but to believe her wild tales of demons in the night. His life had never been the same.

Thoughts of Alyson brought an unexpected tear to his eye and he quickly turned to rub his face against his shoulder to wipe it away. She was gone now, all because of horrid creatures like this one. Allie, Mattie, David…all gone. The vampire on the cement beneath his foot finally realized that playing possum wasn't going to help, so it bared its fangs at him once more. It didn't seem to understand Ben's intention though. Ben stepped down harder on the vampire's chest, gripped both legs of the sign and brought its top edge down with the angry force of over ten years of resentment, right onto the vampire's throat.

Its head separated from its body with a very sickening but satisfying pop, as the sign thunked down to the cement beneath. After an odd second of feeling his foot slightly sink into the thing's chest as it began to disintegrate, it completely turned to ash, and Ben was left standing in little more than a pile of dirt.

It was strange, to be so pumped with defensive violence, and then to suddenly find yourself standing all alone, your adversary nothing but dust on the concrete. Ben let out a ragged breath, tossing the sign aside. It hit the cement with a loud, echoing clang. After finally being able to take in a true inhalation, he exhaled in relief. It was gone. Done. He, and therefore his family, were safe for another night. Is this what his father felt? Maybe they weren't so different after all.

Bernard Everheart, the feared and revered vampire hunter. Yes, he knew his father's secret identity all too well. The man might be good at killing the undead, but he was also an alcoholic and a braggart. His machinations to hide his nightly activities from his son were not nearly as successful as he thought they were. Ben liked to think of himself as fairly intelligent and observant, even as a teenager. Once given the information that there was truth to fear in the paranormal, it hadn't taken long for him to piece together things he knew about his father.

Weapons, secrecy, snippets of phone conversations between his father and heaven knows who…and remembered visions of a woman; a woman that Ben had seen many times out his window at night as a young child. She had very long, flowing blonde hair, and eerily beautiful violet eyes that almost seemed to glow in the dim light. She wore a sword in a belt at her hip, and she was just as tall as his dad. Back then, Ben had thought that she looked like a warrior princess. He had seen his father speaking with her in hushed tones out on the driveway, sometimes with intimate familiarity, other times just a shade away from drawing blades. He never knew who she was, but he knew that his father dealt with people who were not a part of the normal world.

He'd always resented the fact that his father did not see fit to tell him the truth. After all, he wasn't a child anymore. He hadn't felt the pampered security and safety of being a 'child' since his mother's death when he was sixteen. His mother had been killed by a vampire. He wished he could remain in stubborn denial, and believe that her cancer had dealt the final blow, but he knew the truth. It had turned the exciting, privileged knowledge of the paranormal, into a harsh and bitter reality.

His father was involved with those things somehow. How could he have let that happen? He blamed his father, but it was difficult to truly hate the man, because it seemed Ben's father blamed himself as well. That was when the heavy drinking had started. So they lived their lives, separate but together. Bernard had apparently decided that his family needed his utmost protection. Considering that Ben *was* the only family now, it was like closing the barn door after the horses had gone, wasn't it? Too late dad. I don't want your protection. You should have protected mom.

Their silence over the paranormal had become a sort of contest of wills. Ben refused to reveal his understanding and confront his father with the topic, because he resented that Bernard wouldn't come to him with it on his own. Bernard was happier living in denial, believing that he was doing the ultimate justice to his son by protecting him from that which he had been unable to save his wife from, fostering the false appearance of a normal, happy life.

There was a time, just before his mother had died, when Ben had been preparing to approach his father, to reveal what he knew. After the incident with Allie, Ben had put it all together and begun to idealize his father, as some sort of superhero. I know the battle you fight dad, and I want to fight by your side.

Then he had found his mother, lying in the driveway, moments from death. It was just another normal weeknight. His dad was working late, and Ben had stayed home alone to study for finals rather than accompany his mom to the store. She'd honked the horn after pulling into the driveway, and he'd gone to put on his shoes before coming out. He'd come to help carry groceries, and she was just lying there, behind the car, with a trickle of blood running down the side of her throat. He'd looked up in a desperate panic, seeking help...or cause.

It wasn't late, but it was dark and no one was around, except...the woman with the long blonde hair stood nearby, watching with gleaming purple eyes, before disappearing from view behind the trees. Ben had recognized her from somewhere in the depths of his childhood memories. The warrior princess he had seen with his dad. Only she wasn't some beautiful fantasy figure he imagined his dad was helping to save the world. She was a vampire, and she had killed his mom.

No. He was not like his dad at all.

~~~~~~~~~~~~~~~~~~~~~~~~~~~~~~

Felicity noticed Ben cautiously observing the alley next to the restaurant, as he pulled up to the curb. She glanced around nervously before getting in. "What took so long? I was beginning to wonder if you'd freaked and skipped out on me."

Ben let out a shaky laugh and shook his head. "Never," he told her quietly, as she got in and closed the door. She turned to him as she buckled her seat belt, but he was too busy observing the city streets around them. It was late, but there were people everywhere. That's Manhattan for you, the city that never sleeps; wonderful place to be a vampire. Were the people in the streets all around him just harmless humans? Ben would never know, unless one of them turned on him.

The sound of sirens could be heard in the distance. Good, paramedics were on their way then. The parking lot attendant had still been breathing when Ben had made the 911 call on his cell. Perhaps he should have stayed, but he just couldn't leave Felicity alone any longer, and he wasn't sure he could face questions.

She could tell that he was shaken, even though he had done his best to straighten himself up and erase all signs of the scuffle before picking her up. She observed the way he was watching the people around them with a thinly veiled expression of distrustful paranoia, as he pulled the car away from the curb. He couldn't find words for Felicity yet. He just wanted to get the hell out of here.

"Still creeps you out too, huh?" she asked gently. Ben glanced at her with a guilty start. "The dark," she clarified. "It's still scary sometimes," she admitted, looking out the window.

Ben shook his head. "This is not being scared, it's being aware. I'm done being scared." He surprised her with a laugh. "Honestly, you should pity the thing that attacks me in the dark." She looked at him curiously, but he wouldn't meet her eyes. "You can never let your guard down Liss. It's when life seems to be just perfect, that everything gets pulled out from under you. Vampires screwed with my life enough in the past. It may have been a long time ago, but you don't forget lessons like that...or at least we shouldn't let ourselves forget."

She was staring at him intently as they pulled up to a red light. She was beginning to realize that something was wrong. She was staring at his temple. He was probably going to have a nice bump and bruise there from head-butting the vampire. It may have even left teeth marks. It still hurt like hell, and it had given him a pounding headache.

"Ben?" She was really concerned now. She'd definitely noticed, even in the dark. "Are you okay? Did something happen?"

"We're just a block from the hotel. I'll tell you when we get there. Don't worry. We're going to be just fine."

Part 3

Emotional Maelstrom

Chapter 10 - Let go

Cain

Cain's Estate, Upstate, New York
A summer evening

Mattie was sitting on the steps to the front porch, watching Tempest try to instruct Alyson on the finer points of transforming herself into a large bat out on the front lawn. Cain joined him, also marveling at the sight of the two women intermittently fogging their human bodies into clouds of dark mist, and then re-appearing as small winged mammals.

Tempest was able to reform in mid-air, to almost instantly take off into the sky, gracefully swooping in circles before reforming as human again. Unfortunately, Alyson was much less graceful, floundering awkwardly on the ground as she tried to perfect moving around in the form, before she could even consider flight.

The summer air was warm and thick, even in the darkness. Although the sky was deeply black and colorless at the moment, it wouldn't be long before the sun rose again to make the temperature climb even further. Noting the time and the frustration level of her student, Tempest ended the lesson and sent Alyson back to the house with instructions to practice more on her own over the next few evenings.

Alyson dematerialized to travel towards them as a shadowy cloud. Cain politely rose and walked to the end of the porch, to enjoy the view elsewhere so that she could don the clothing Mattie had for her. After giving her a few moments to dress, Cain rejoined the couple. Allie offered a quick apology. "Sorry, I've figured out how to dematerialize into mist without having to undress first, but I still have to form a body before I can put my clothes back on."

Cain chuckled. "Perfectly understandable. I see you've graduated from wolf to bat. Congratulations."

Cain winced as Allie gave the corner post of the railing a half hearted punch with a thump. Luckily she remembered to keep her strength reigned in. "It's way harder than I thought it'd be."

"Well, you've only just started."

Mattie chuckled, as he sat with his elbows resting on his knees. "She's gotten too used to everything being easy. What's the matter, forget what it's like to put in a little hard work?"

She made a face at him and gave him a nudge with her foot. "I'll get it."

Mattie sighed. "I'm sure you will. At least you've had beautiful weather."

Cain leaned against the post next to them. "I hope Tempest doesn't mind having to practice so close to the house under our watchful eyes."

Allie shrugged. "We'll need an open area like the lawn once we start getting into flying anyway. I can't wait to fly! I mean, levitating is one thing, but won't it be cool when I can fly like a real bat? I could be out there swooping around, flying free, right in the open, and nobody would suspect a thing! I could do it in public even!"

Cain smiled at her enthusiasm, although Mattie didn't seem quite so ecstatic over the prospect. Alyson observed his somber countenance, and moved closer to sit and join him in looking up at the stars. "It is beautiful out tonight, isn't it? I don't know when I've seen so many stars. It'd be a good night for fireworks. I feel bad that we missed them this year. Remember when we used to go and watch them at the lake for the Fourth?"

Mattie nodded with a sigh. "You know what I miss? Summer barbecues! Remember family cookouts on a Saturday afternoon? You'd spend the day playing touch football...except you'd be all dirty and sore from being tackled, because nobody really respects the 'touch' rule. Then there'd be burgers and hot dogs, and baked beans with a little maple syrup in the sauce...and brown sugar! My mom always used to put in a little brown sugar."

Allie put a sympathetic arm around him. "Your mom always was an awesome cook."

Mattie continued in his nostalgia. "Everyone sitting around on a hot summer day just before twilight, laughing, and talking, and eating; trying to stay out of the barbecue smoke, but knowing that's the only real way to keep the mosquitoes away."

"That's one thing I don't miss," Allie said with a smile and another playful nudge, "mosquitoes! Who'd have thought having no scent or body heat would be so convenient?"

Mattie just shook his head. "I loved days like that. I always watched my dad, sitting around with his buddies after they let the grill go out, playing cards, and drinking a few beers; talking about how damn big the kids were getting, and how it made him feel old. It was so…human."

Cain knew all too well how it felt, to remember what is was to be human, and to wonder what could have been. It was very hard to let go of every expectation you had for your life, and feel so alienated from all you knew. "You'll make new memories now," he told Mattie comfortingly. "You'll start new traditions, and do things others never dreamed of."

"I know, but I always thought that would be me one day. I thought for sure I'd have a mess of kids, and a wife that knew how to make homemade potato salad better than you get at the deli. I thought I'd be having a beer and swapping stories with friends while the kids ran around catching fireflies. I thought one day it would be my turn at the grill. But that'll never happen now…not for me."

Alyson seemed at a loss for what to say. "I can make you potato salad," she finally told him, trying to make him smile.

It did manage to make him laugh a little. "Nice try, but you were a rotten cook even before you stopped eating." His humor was short lived. "Besides, that's hardly the point. You don't even really get it, do you? How can you not get it?"

"Yes I do. I'm sorry, I guess that's just not the kind of thing that I ever fantasized about or wanted."

Their attention was drawn to the sky as silent heat lightning flashed overhead, lighting the lawn for a brief moment. There was a pregnant pause as they waited to see if there would be thunder, but it never came. Finally, Mattie sighed. He didn't seem very comforted by Alyson's answer. "Right. Well it might be nice if maybe, just for once, things could be about what *I* want for a change." He stood and walked into the house before anything else could be said.

The sky flashed yellow once more, but it wasn't nearly as startling as the first time, even though there was a bit of rumbling thunder to go with it. Allie gave Cain a look as though to apologize for Mattie. "I don't know what his problem is. Sometimes he just gets all moody. What does he want me to do, make him human again? He's got to let it go. It's not my fault he's a vampire."

"No, but you must admit, that you get far more pleasure from it than he ever has. I suppose that's just difficult for him to stomach sometimes."

"I guess. Still, if he knew how hard it is to concentrate on much of anything when you feel completely ravaged by thirst all the time, he might not be so jealous. It's a very good thing I have these talents to focus on, or I'd be going nuts."

"Is your thirst that bad?" Cain asked, trying to discern if she was being dramatic, but worrying that was not the case.

Allie gave him a level look and then shook her head. "It's just been extra distracting lately. I can manage. I'd better go cheer him up."

~~~~~~~~~~~~~~~~~~~~~~~~~~~~~~

The next evening, Cain found himself trying to analyze his own thirst for blood as he woke and made his way down to the kitchen. It was always strong enough to wake him, and was a nagging uneasiness within him until he fed his body the blood it desired, but he wasn't really troubled by it normally.

With access to a constant supply of animal blood and limited involvement with humans, he didn't pay his thirst much mind at all. In fact, many evenings he would intentionally ignore his needs, letting the thirst build and brew within him before drinking a few hours after the night was underway. The rumbling need for blood stirring inside him felt almost oddly comforting in an irritating way, like something pressing and focused to break up the sometimes flat and unchanging state of his existence. The uncomfortable intensity of his thirst helped to remind him why he'd left Felicity to live her human life without him.

Alyson didn't seem to have that luxury though. She claimed it was impossible to ignore her thirst for any amount of time, and normally drank before even leaving the trailer she and Mattie shared. Then, when they came to visit him at the house, she could still rarely be found without a glass in her hand. The exception was when she was out in the woods shape shifting with Tempest. After her lessons and a good run through the forest as a wolf, she seemed satisfied for a time.

Cain knew that the girls drank from animals while out in the forest. Drinking from a living source was always more effective than drinking anything collected and stored for a time. Cain knew from his own experiences, that fresh blood was most satisfying, and after drinking from a human, his thirst would subside for a good long while, not that he took advantage of that fact. Perhaps the hunting restrictions the girls were currently trying to abide by were making Alyson's thirsty needs seem almost too difficult to fulfill.

Cain could feel she and Mattie approaching the house as he waited for his coffee to finish brewing. He was interested to assess her control, and see if perhaps she was having a harder time than she let on.

He heard the couple enter through the glass door in the back parlor, and make their way through into the kitchen to him. As they entered, he gave them a nod of good evening, and poured himself a mug of coffee. He was feeling a bit somber tonight. Alyson however, seemed to be in a mood that was practically jovial.

Mattie didn't share her glee as he quietly came inside. His mood did not seem to have improved much from last night. Alyson's smile however, was positively beaming as she entered the room. Maybe Cain's worry over her thirst was misplaced. In fact, her joyous mood in itself almost seemed cause for concern.

She hopped up to sit on the counter, something Cain was normally apt to reprimand her for, but he only gave her a disapproving glance. "What are you so happy about?"

She immediately tried to lessen her smile, but still seemed too exuberant to account for. "Can't I just be in a good mood?"

Cain shared a glance with Mattie, who merely shrugged. Cain turned back to her discerningly. "You and Sindy have been moping around here for weeks due to the hunting restriction, and now you are suddenly happy as can be. You can understand my concern."

Alyson immediately sought to reassure him. "It's nothing. I was just thinking about something really happy, and it stuck with me. I'm just in a good mood, honest. Relax."

Mattie rolled his eyes. "She's been high as a kite all evening. Sometimes she just wakes up that way. Go figure." Alyson just chuckled at his response.

After a moment of reflection, Cain sighed. If Mattie didn't know what she was happy about, Cain could imagine who else she might have been communicating with this evening to put her in such good spirits...Felicity. Cain took his coffee and sat at the table, resolute not to inquire further. Allie continued to reassure him. "I haven't been sneaking out or anything, I swear."

She was telling the truth. He knew that between Mattie, Tempest and himself, Alyson was never given a moment alone to transgress anyway. Sindy however, was not so innocent of such things. Alyson knew it too, although she wasn't going to be the one to bring it up.

Sindy had not yet come downstairs. She had snuck out into the woods last night for a quick hunt. She thought Cain didn't know, but he'd seen her through his bedroom window, as she'd shifted out on the lawn and run off into the brush. She couldn't have gone far, because she'd come back in only about twenty minutes. She'd surely found herself a rabbit or something to drink from, and then come straight back. It wasn't the first time she'd done that in these past few months. His restrictions were wearing on her. Perhaps he was being overly cautious, but he was too worried not to be.

The Crimson Coven had only reported a few scattered incidents of seeing the spying shade on the grounds since his encounter, nothing terribly troubling, but their privacy *was* compromised, and that was reason enough to worry. Honestly, Cain didn't particularly care for the girls' hunting practices anyway, and was in no rush to give them leave to take them up again, if they could manage just as well on the blood carefully and humanely collected for them from his deer herd. But perhaps they needed fresh blood more than he had realized. Their shifting skills would certainly use up much of their energy, and if drinking from a living source helped to replace that more efficiently, maybe he should allow them to continue it. Hunting small game gave them an emotional outlet as well. The girls were chafing under their current restraints, and all of them were beginning to find their patience with each other wearing thin.

Allie watched thoughtfully as Cain mixed the contents of his coffee mug. "Why do you like coffee so much?" she asked, looking to change the subject. "I mean, I never see you really eat or drink anything else, except maybe the occasional glass of rum and coke. Why coffee?"

Cain shrugged. Mattie gave a dismissive smile as he joined Cain at the kitchen table. "The man likes his coffee."

Cain stared into his cup, and then startled them by responding quietly, "I don't actually. Not all that much, anyway."

Mattie looked at him oddly. "Sure you do."

Cain laughed. "It's alright, but mostly, I like *making* coffee, the routine of it. I like mixing the coffee with the cream and sugar; watching the colors swirl 'round, and I really like having something hot and steaming to hold in my hands."

Alyson and Mattie were watching him in wonder as he continued. "I do drink it. I like that it's hot. The idea that this body of mine has gone cold...and dead..." He paused for a slight shudder with a distant look in his eyes. "I can't actually feel the difference, but I like the idea of drinking something warm to lessen the cold inside."

He looked up to find the others staring at him. What did they expect? Centuries of mostly solitary evenings had caused him to become partial to somber introspection. He should probably keep it to himself, and try to lighten up a bit, but surely Mattie at least could relate.

Cain smiled. "You know what else I like? I like that it is so blessedly normal; such a mundane combination of actions. The methods of it have changed a bit since my human days, but it's still something that I do upon waking. It's something I can share with more than half the people in the world; just the same as anyone. I wake up and I make coffee. Place the filter, measure out grounds that smell strong and fresh, to fill it. Pour the water through and listen to it perk. Sit and think about my plans for the next few hours, as the rich aroma fills the room. It's something I can have in common with any man on the street. Yet another thing to help me feel almost human. You aren't the only one who misses that sometimes," he added giving Mattie a warm smile of camaraderie.

Mattie looked appreciative and understanding of the explanation. "Wow, that's some deep coffee."

Allie remained sitting on the counter and shrugged it off, giving Cain a smile. "We don't need to be human. What's so great about being human anyway? I'm damn glad I'm a vampire."

Sindy entered the room, giving Allie a high five as she walked by. "Amen to that, sister." She opened the refrigerator and just stood there, staring into it with a dissatisfied look on her face. "Cain, when are we allowed to hunt again? Even squirrel would be better than something cold and reheated."

As though she hadn't drunk live blood in weeks… Cain stared at her for a moment, without a trace of sympathy, and then gestured towards the blood in the refrigerator. "I live on that every night of my life."

"Me, too," Mattie added. "You girls are so spoiled."

Sindy let out a derogatory laugh as she pulled out a container of blood and began pouring it into a mug. "Spoiled? You think having to drink through a mouthful of fur is being spoiled?"

Allie made a face and shook her head. "You're better off making a bigger opening, holding it up and just pouring it," she told her, lifting her arms into the air as though holding up an unlucky animal.

Cain blanched at her description. Mattie looked positively ill. "Never tell me about that again," Mattie instructed her.

Allie chuckled. "I don't do it that way often. I usually hunt in wolf form. A wolf's snout isn't really made for sucking," she explained to the guys. "So we usually just chunk down the whole thing. That's the benefit of hunting small game. You can't do that with a deer. You either have to lap it up with your tongue, which would take forever, or change and suck through fur."

Mattie got up from the table to fix some blood from the fridge, and get away from the immediate conversation. "And she just keeps talking." Cain watched the girls levelly, as Mattie added. "You wouldn't have to drink through fur, if you just drank what's been collected into a container."

Sindy crossed her arms, and arched an eyebrow in amusement. "You know what doesn't have fur? Humans. If I could take a nice controlled drink from a hot blooded hunk once in a while, I wouldn't have to figure out how to keep rabbit hair from getting stuck between my teeth."

Cain saw that Alyson could feel the impending debate, and decided to head it off with a change of topic. "You know," Allie said, giving Sindy a nudge, "I still think you're missing a golden opportunity by not practicing the bat form."

Sindy gave a growl of annoyance. "Enough with that already."

"Well, you are. I haven't gotten very good at it yet, but the form's still gonna be a big advantage when it comes to feeding."

Cain looked up at her with interest. "How is that?"

"You're small," she told him, as though that were the answer to his question. Everyone continued to watch her, waiting for elaboration. "When you're in a smaller form, it doesn't take as much blood to keep you going. It's way easier to drink, because you're stealthy. You can fly down and land on the back of a sleeping cow, and they don't even notice.

At least that's what Tempest says. Obviously, I'm not up to that yet. But she says it doesn't take nearly as much blood to satisfy you, and once you drink your fill, as long as you stay in bat form for an hour or so afterwards, you aren't even thirsty for the rest of the night! I can't wait to get this form down." She turned her attention back to Sindy. "You should really reconsider trying it with me. It may take a lot of practice, but at least it'd take your mind off not being able to head out into the woods every night."

Cain sighed. "Perhaps it wouldn't be a problem to let you two spend time out in the woods again. I know Tempest dislikes trying to teach her lessons so close to the house, and it's obvious that I'm going to have to give you girls something to keep you busy and out of trouble."

Both girls let wide grins spread across their faces, but surprisingly, it was Mattie who came to pat his shoulder appreciatively, as he rejoined Cain at the table. "Thank you. Don't get me wrong, I love having her to myself for most of the night, but I've had to spend half my time fighting her off from drinking me dry!"

Allie answered with a derisive snort, but there was little doubt in Cain's mind that it was true. "I hope you don't think I've been too over-protective," he continued quietly. "I just worry. Let me talk to Khalon. I still don't like the idea of you two going out on your own if there may be danger lurking, but perhaps you could join one of the Crimson hunting parties now and then."

Allie gave him a big smile as Sindy placed a grateful kiss on his cheek. "Thank you," Sindy purred. "If there's anything I can do to show my appreciation, please let me know," she whispered seductively.

Cain laughed off her offer, not in the mood for her flirting. "Just keep your fangs out of hot-blooded hunks please. I think we should be keeping a low profile for a while, and we don't need your marks lighting up the neighborhood."

Sindy mouthed him a little kiss. "If you want to jealously keep me all to yourself, you can just say so."

Cain sighed. He really didn't feel like playing this game tonight. He answered with a tone of serious authority. "And don't go out hunting in the woods again until I've spoken to Khalon, alright? I find lack of respect rather unattractive."

That changed her manner quickly enough. She didn't act repentant though. "Fine. Sorry," she answered with a sarcastic edge.

Mattie took his drink and stood up from the table. "I think I'm going to head downstairs. I've got a video game grudge match to settle."

Sindy glanced his way as she stirred the contents of her mug, happy for a distraction. "What are you playing?"

Allie chuckled. "He's anonymously fighting Ben Everheart in Modern Warfare."

"Are you kidding?" Sindy asked incredulously. "This I've got to see."

Allie moved to join them, as Sindy followed Mattie from the room, but Cain reached out to touch her arm and stop her as she passed. "Actually, I thought it was time that we got back to working on a few things." She did not look pleased. "You've been so busy with Tempest that we've completely neglected your basic training," he explained.

Allie's joyous mood quickly fled. "I'm not neglecting it, I've moved on."

Why did she always insist on refuting him? "Alyson, I know that you have learned to use your skills, but you need more than ability, you need to master them. You need to practice control."

"Control?" she asked in disbelief. "I have control. Don't I spend enough time working? They get to go play, and I'm stuck here doing pointless demonstrations?" she asked with a wave of her arm towards the basement stairs where Sindy and Mattie had disappeared. "It's a waste of time! I know what I'm doing."

Cain furrowed his brow in indignation. "Pointless? You want to talk about control?" He stood and stalked over to a kitchen drawer, opened it and pulled something out for Alyson to see. "Why don't we talk about this impressive display of control? What's this?"

Alyson lowered her eyes in a sulk. "Half a butter knife."

"Right. Half of a butter knife. A knife I had asked you to bend at a right angle for me. Remember that?"

"Oh, big deal," she replied, rolling her eyes at him. "I was in a bad mood. I was all tense and I went a little overboard."

Cain held the piece a little higher for emphasis. "Alyson, you snapped it in half!"

She sat down in a chair with a thump. They both flinched for a moment as she did it. It wasn't all that long ago that she'd broken a leg off one that way. Alyson froze for a moment, realizing that her carelessness would not prove her point well, but then relaxed when the chair held. "It was a cheap knife," she said sulkily.

Cain let out a small bark of a laugh as he tossed it onto the table. "That is my good, thick solid silver thank you."

She looked up in amusement, that he might be insulted that she had disparaged his cutlery. "What do you need tableware for anyway? You don't even eat!"

"That's not the point! You call that control? You've had increased strength for a couple of years now. It's nothing new. Being tense is no excuse! You may be under great pressure one night, and be called to do something requiring precise control. Say you came across a child, lying injured in a ravine or something? I'm sure you'd rather lift them out to safety, than snap them in half!"

Alyson squinted at him in disbelief. "Well if I'm ever out rescuing helpless children, I promise to be more careful."

He smiled. "It was an unlikely example, but you know what I mean. You need to be able to navigate through situations, not just plow over them, no matter what kind of mood you're in. Control should be your mantra. Control your thirst, control your temper and your powers, no excuses."

Alyson met his eyes across the table as he sat back down. She knew he was right, he could just tell. She gave him a grudging smile that still seemed a bit facetious. "Okay teach. What do you want me to work on?"

He grinned and reached across the table to grasp her hands for a moment. "Alyson, I know that to you, the responsibility these powers bring can be a great annoyance. I just want you to know how much I appreciate you letting me work with you to harness all of it."

She shrugged. "I know it's important to you."

"I'd like for it to be important to you, too. Have you thought any more about our talk over the influence you might have on others? About using your position to help guide vampires into leading a less violent existence?"

She gazed at him thoughtfully. "I'll tell you what, I don't particularly have any plans to guide vampire-kind, but if I find myself in that kind of position, yeah, I guess it wouldn't be a bad way to shift things. Don't think I'm going to make it my life's work or anything, though. I don't plan to go out looking for other vampires, just so I can convince them to stop killing people."

"I understand."

She chewed her lip for a moment. "Actually saying that out loud sounds really selfish and callous, doesn't it?"

He gave her hands a squeeze and let them go. "The task I've set for myself isn't yours. You need to make your own decisions for how you will spend your time. I had more selfish and callous years of existence than I would ever care to admit. I would hope that my time of indulgence was far worse than anything you have in mind. I'm not asking you to give up your life for my cause. I'd just like to know that you're in my corner."

"Of course I am. I don't have any sympathy for vicious killers, believe me. If I can stop them, then I guess I should, and I'll certainly try. I just need some more time to sink into all of this."

Cain gave her a broad smile. "Fair enough. You know how happy it makes me, to know that I'll have your assistance in such things, don't you? I've had quite an uphill battle on my own."

"I know you have, and you know what? As wonderful as it is that you've spent so much time helping people, I think it's been good for you to take a break and be here with us these past few years. You've had the occasional trip out to investigate a serial killer in the papers, and spent a week here or there dealing with new vamps, but for the most part, you've been here with us. It's changed you."

"It has?" he asked in quiet surprise.

"Sure it has. I can see it. I think you needed some time for you."

"I'm not sure that's what you're seeing at all. I think the change that you see in me, is the joy I've had over having a new sense of purpose. To think that perhaps divine intervention has brought you to me for guidance…"

Alyson sighed, but she must feel that from him. With all of her powers of empathy and telepathy, she couldn't read it incorrectly. Yes, having a sense of family and comfortable existence for a change had been restful and healing for him, but it was his role as mentor to The United One that had truly made a change in his demeanor; this new avenue to continue what he considered to be God's work.

"You're wrong," Alyson said, reading his thoughts from him. "Well, not *wrong*, but I don't think you give social interaction enough credit. I know you think helping me is a big deal and all, but your happiness is a big deal too, you know. What do you think has been missing all these years? It's not like you've been unhappy your whole life because you were waiting for me. Being with Felicity made you realize how much you needed to feel loved again." She sent him a soothing current of apology for the mention of Felicity, but continued. "I know that didn't work out well, but it did bring you to a place where you could accept and appreciate the friendship and company of a family. I know we aren't the love of your life, but I think it's been good for you to have us around. Allowing yourself to invest in others is important."

"I invest in others," he muttered.

"You are the epitome of selfless and helpful to others, but that's not really investing in them is it? I mean, you do everything you can for others, but you aren't expecting or needing anything in return. I'm talking about carrying on long term relationships with people that go both ways. Not those you help, who leave to go back into the world without you, people who want to stay and care about you in return. Me, Mattie, Sindy…yeah, even Sindy. We've been good for you. *She's* been good for you. I know she isn't the woman you wanted, but she isn't as bad as she comes off sometimes."

Surely, Allie could read his surprise that she was arguing Sindy's case. She smiled and continued. "We never used to get along, and I know she's done some rotten things, but people look a little different when you can see them from the inside. She hasn't handled it all that well, but I guess she's just a little lost and misguided…like everybody is. She's not all that bad. She has potential. But you already knew that, didn't you?"

He allowed a small grin to steal upon his face. "Why do you think I never gave up on her? I come across many young vampires with violent pasts. There are those who not only don't care to change, but seem to have lost all sense of moral conscience; such vampires are beyond anything my advice might do for them. But sometimes, young vampires are just scared, lost, and alone, acting out against all of the injustice they've been through. There is no true excuse or vindication for their actions, but I feel their pain. I understand, and feel I can reach someone in that position; someone like Sindy. She has changed since I've met her, hasn't she; regained her sense of accountability for her actions? She is who she is, but I'd like to think that I've caused her to better consider her options, and travel a more productive path for herself."

"Definitely," Allie agreed.

Alyson continued to hold his gaze, wearing a slight grin and watching him as though she expected him to say something more. "What?" he finally asked.

Allie shook her head, as though he was missing something terribly obvious. "Could you see yourself with her? I mean you're practically *with* her now, except for leaving out all the fun stuff." He rolled his eyes with a laugh. "Really though. I know how much you love Felicity, but…maybe it's time to let go. Wouldn't it be nice to truly move on and let yourself have a good time, guilt free?"

"Life isn't all about having a good time."

"It's not all about torturing yourself either. Fine, forget the good time. Could you ever see yourself loving her?"

"Sindy?" He asked as though he'd never considered the idea, but Alyson knew he was just buying time because he didn't know what to say. The fact was, that although he might not like to admit it to himself, he had. He already did feel love for her to a certain degree, even though he hadn't allowed it to manifest romantically.

To him, Sindy was a very intriguing mixture of strength and vulnerability. She was a woman of harsh, hostile edges, who still held a delicate and fragile heart hidden inside. He was very glad to have met her before the world had caused that heart to turn entirely cold and cruel. He'd seen that before, vampires who could not find it within themselves to come back from the violent and vengeful persona they had constructed as armor to ward off the world.

Sindy had never truly known loving care, and had only vaguely, consciously recognized the void it had left within her, needing to be filled. He could not help but want to fill it for her. Even when his heart had been taken by another, he had wanted to reach out to show Sindy that not everyone in the world was uncaring.

There was nothing to hold him back now...nothing but his own hesitance and heartbreak. Not only could his love fill Sindy's needs, it would do so without taking anything away from her. Unlike his true love Felicity, Sindy could accept love from him that would heal rather than hurt, a soothing realization. *If* he could allow himself to love her, it would be a relationship untainted by guilt or regret. It seemed a wonderfully comforting prospect, happiness without a price. But could he?

He met Alyson's eyes with an uncomfortable little cough. "Don't you worry so much about my heart. You've got your own to look after."

She shrugged him off with a smirk. "Mattie and I are fine."

"Good. Enough stalling then. We've got work to do."

Chapter 11 - Live a little

Allie

Cain's Estate, Upstate, New York
An evening in Autumn

Alyson rounded the corner of the house quietly, and made her way down through the apple orchard to the clearing before the woods began on that side. Someone was there. It didn't sound like an animal, and she was having a hard time picking up a life-force aura from anything of a decent size over there, other than plants. That meant that it was either a machine of some sort, which was doubtful, or a cloaked vampire.

She'd originally thought it might be the vampire shade that had been hanging around the grounds, but if that was the case, they weren't being particularly stealthy this evening, and what were they doing? It sounded like someone digging with a shovel. In fact, now that she placed it, that was exactly what it sounded like. Who would be out here digging? Cain and Mattie were inside, and the Crimson Coven kept themselves far from the house normally.

She crept closer, and then allowed herself to relax as she came through the bushes and found the source of the mysterious sound. Just as she had suspected, it was someone digging with a shovel, but not *who* she would have expected. It was Sindy. Looking very out of place for doing yard work, wearing a tight, low cut red top with a large studded belt, leggings and tall leather boots, Sindy seemed to be well underway in her work, but Allie couldn't tell what she was trying to accomplish. It looked as though a good portion of the area had been turned over, but there was no hole. Maybe she had buried something and was filling the hole back in.

Sindy paused, with her back to Alyson, resting her foot on the top edge of the shovel scoop. With one hand on the shovel handle, she obviously wanted to use her other hand to brush the hair from her face, but her hands were filthy with dirt. She finally settled on trying to clear her face with the back of her arm, as Alyson approached behind her. "Oh my God. Who'd you kill?"

Sindy jumped and spun around, startled. When she realized it was just Allie, she let out an annoyed huff of breath. "What? I didn't kill anybody."

"Uh-huh." Allie nodded towards the plot of newly over turned dirt. "So who're you burying?"

Sindy rolled her eyes and leaned against her shovel standing upright in the dirt. "I'm not *burying* anybody." She averted her eyes self consciously before admitting her task. "I'm making a garden."

Allie raised her eyebrows with an incredulous smirk on her face. "*You?*" Sindy just nodded. "You're...*gardening?*"

"Yeah. What's the big deal?"

"Like, actually digging and planting stuff?"

"That's what a garden is, stupid. Did you want something?"

"No. I was just seeing what you were doing. Why are you doing this? I mean, sorry, but you just don't seem like the 'green thumb' type."

Sindy shifted her weight, using her elbow to prop up the shovel handle as she tried to brush the dirt from her hands. "I'm not. I'm making it for Cain."

Allie placed her hands on her hips and watched her with a little smirk. She was telling the truth, but Allie could sense that Sindy thought Allie still believed she was burying someone and trying to make up a lie to hide it. Who could blame her? It seemed kind of an unlikely activity. "You're making a garden for Cain? What's he gonna do with it? Doesn't he already have gardeners, landscapers or something?"

"They just mow the lawn. This is different. Something we can work on ourselves. Believe it or not, he's really into this stuff. He's been telling me about his life...before. Did you know he used to be a *farmer?*"

"No! *Cain?*"

"For real."

"When was that, back in England?"

"No. Back in England, he was the son of a *nobleman.* Says he lived in a big old mansion and spent his teenage years out drinkin' and whorin' every night. Can you believe it? Wish I'd known him *then.*"

Allie laughed. "Are you sure he's not puttin' you on?"

"No, really. Then his brother made him move here when he was like 18. They had a farm. You should have heard him talking about it. I'm telling you, he was a total farm boy. He misses it, I could just tell."

"So what are you gonna do, grow corn and stuff?"

"No. I'm not going to grow *food*. That'd be dumb; we don't even eat. I'll plant flowers, things that bloom at night and smell nice. I haven't gotten the plants yet; right now, I'm just turning the dirt over and planning it out. But when I'm done, he can help take care of them, and add to it once in a while, like a hobby. God knows we haven't been doing much else together.

I saw this beautiful bench we could put in the corner. I thought it'd be a cool place to come sit and talk. That old one he's got up by the deck is just stuck there with zero ambience. This would be all pretty and secluded, under the moonlight..." Sindy had been growing animatedly excited at the idea, but now became aware of Allie once again, and looked away in embarrassment. After a second, she looked up to gauge her reaction to the idea. "You think he'll like it?"

Allie surveyed Sindy's work and broke into a big smile. "He's gonna love it." She turned back to see pride on Sindy's face. "He'll love that you did it for him."

Sindy dropped her smile and looked away, trying not to let Allie see how pleased she was by the approval. "Cool. Well, just do me a favor? Don't say anything. I want it to be a surprise."

"Sure, no problem. It's kind of late in the season though, isn't it? I mean, how are you gonna be able to get it done before the first frost?"

"I know, I've got crappy timing. I wish I'd thought of it sooner. I guess I'll just get it laid out now, and I'll have to wait to do most of it in the spring."

"You need some help?"

"That's okay. *I* wanna do it."

~~~~~~~~~~~~~~~~~~~~~~~~~~~~

Felicity lay on the bed in her panties, with her maternity shirt hiked up to just under her breasts, and her pants kicked off onto the floor. She lay with her hands on her newly swelled belly, as she intently focused and waited to feel an elusive flutter of movement from within.

She'd felt the faint but definitely independent rolls and rumblings of her unborn child for the first time just a bit earlier, and had anxiously shared it with Ben the moment he'd gotten home from work. He'd placed his hand on her stomach and waited with bated breath until rewarded with a few kicks and bumps. The young couple had been absolutely tickled by the sensations, and Felicity was anxious to feel more response from this child, whom she could not wait to meet, but true to the contrary nature of most children, now the baby was quiet and still.

Ben walked into the bedroom while loosening his tie. "Well, all of the paperwork's been submitted and the house should be ours by next month. We will officially own a home in the Hamptons…well, close to the Hamptons anyway. I'm going to put in for a few days off in October so we can take a long weekend out there, and really figure out how we want to do this, okay?" he asked, as he began getting undressed across the room.

She wasn't truly listening for anything but signs of new life from inside her, at the moment. She had taken the year off from teaching for the pregnancy; since they were considering moving, it had seemed the best option. Luckily, losing her salary for the year wasn't too terrible a blow to their finances, thanks to their savings account and careful management, even after buying the house. Thank goodness for Ben, taking care of the business end of everything. These days Felicity found it hard to concentrate on anything but her changing body. Finally, she spoke without taking her eyes from her belly. "I wish the baby would move again," she said with a pout.

"I'm sure it won't be long before the little guy is wiggling around so much that we won't have a moment alone together," he said with a good-natured chuckle.

She sighed, longingly. "I just can't wait to feel it again. It was so amazing."

"Yes," he agreed, "It was incredible, and I'm looking forward to it too. In the meantime, I think your husband is in need of some assistance."

She moved her hand to a different spot on her stomach as she gestured with the other towards the corner of the room, replying without a glance. "There's clean pajamas in the laundry basket on the floor. I just haven't put them away yet."

Ben moved closer to the bed, to stand right next to her, forcing her to look at him. He was fully nude…and partially aroused. "That's not the kind of assistance I need," he told her with a smile.

Now that she let her eyes play over the sight of her husband's gloriously naked body…broad shoulders, muscular torso, the defined ridges of his abdomen and his very large manhood, now proudly pointing upwards towards her, she had to receive the sight with a smile.

He gestured towards her on the bed. "Look at you laying there all gorgeous and glowing. I miss those soft curves and smooth skin. The doctor said we could continue things as usual, as long as I'm gentle, right?" he asked her hopefully.

She nodded with a slightly guilty grin. It was true, but she hadn't been much in the mood over the past six weeks or so, barely evincing interest in this poor, patient man. It was only a very recent development that she'd begun to feel less nauseous and more like herself, and starting to think romantic thoughts again.

Ben smiled and sat down next to her. "I thought maybe now that you're in the second trimester, and the morning sickness period seems to have passed...well, shouldn't the increased libido be kicking in?"

She laughed. "You've been reading the book I gave you!"

"I told you I would." He placed his hand lightly on her belly. "How are you feeling?"

"A lot more receptive to my handsome, well-read husband, I have to admit."

He moved his hand and gave her a quick kiss and a smile. "Only if you feel like it. I'm sure it must feel strange to have all these changes going on. But seeing you laying there like that, I just had to give it a shot."

She patted his leg. "I know it's been a while."

He shook his head, eager to make sure she understood that he didn't mind. "It's okay. I just miss your sexy body," he said, giving her thigh a little squeeze for emphasis.

She laughed. "Well, you might be missing my *sexy* body for a long time, because it seems to have been replaced by this new one that I'm not all that familiar with, whose belly is growing by the day."

Ben began trailing his fingers lightly on her skin. It always gave her shivers of delight when he did that, his light touch knowingly seeking out her most sensitive places. He knew just how to build desire in her, just barely touching her, always just skirting the spots she would most like him to caress, making her anxiously anticipate his attention.

As his hand whispered over the new swell of her stomach, he paused to look at her lovingly with those soft, honey brown eyes. "Are you kidding? That's the best part." She raised her eyebrows, questioning him. "Okay, maybe it's not *the* best part, but it is definitely one of my favorite body parts of the moment. It's a pretty good part," he assured her.

She sighed. "Sure, right now it's all new and still kind of cute. It's going to get a lot bigger than that. You might not feel the same in another month or two. You sure it's not going to turn you off?"

Ben gave her a reprimanding look. "Alright, now you just sound crazy. It's almost embarrassing," he told her, shaking his head with mock disgust. "Don't you remember me telling you that my wife, mother of my unborn child, is *always* the most beautiful woman in the room?"

"I'm the only woman in the room," she pointed out with a smirk.

"Doesn't matter, the concept still holds, and I'd like to add that you will *always* turn me on, pregnant or otherwise. I'll still be saying this when you're eighty."

"Promise?"

"Oh yes, easy promise." He leaned down to touch his lips to hers, his soft kiss quickly turning into a more thorough display of his passion.

As his tongue gently requested entrance between her lips, she found herself igniting with desire in a way that she hadn't in weeks. All of her past feelings of unsexy discomfort were quickly left behind, to be replaced by the joyous tingle of attraction and anticipation. Her husband knew how to fan embers of arousal into flames of all-consuming ecstasy, and now she was looking forward to the prospect.

"See?" he whispered, his newly-enlivened erection pressing against her as proof of his enamored interest. "I find you incredibly sexy."

She felt herself transported to a plane of dreamy pleasure as she closed her eyes and allowed him to run his hands freely over her body. His touch seemed somehow new and almost unfamiliar. Had it been so long? It was as though she was experiencing his amorous attention for the first time, his soft caresses, and tender trailing fingers intimately new and exciting, as he stroked and massaged her in ways she was unused to.

She ran her hands over his firm, bare buttocks and then around his thigh to take hold of the hard length of his penis. Alyson gasped as she felt her fingers firmly close around the thickness of him. *Holy shit, he's huge!*

Alyson came to the abrupt awareness that this was not *her* experience, this was not *her* husband, and she was in fact somehow inadvertently eavesdropping in Felicity's head. Allie had been half-asleep, drifting slowly to consciousness after the sun had set, and had apparently been picking up Felicity's thoughts and observations, however private they may have been. Mentally she froze in awkward shock. *Whoa…sorry!*

Felicity still had her hands on Ben's body, her physical actions being beyond Allie's control, but she'd frozen upon picking up Alyson's exclamation of surprise, and the sudden realization that she and her husband were not exactly alone.

Alyson was still acclimating herself to the actual context of the situation, and preparing for a swift exit, but found herself making another mental comment before she could censor herself. *Are you sure that thing won't hurt the baby? Damn!*

Felicity's thoughts erupted into completely understandable outrage and confusion. "What?" *No… I mean yes! Get out of my head!*

Ben stopped kissing her neck and leaned up to see her face. "What's the matter?"

Felicity moved her hand to less intimate territory, while trying to reassure him that she was still feeling amicable. "Nothing. I'm good. Feels nice."

He gave her an odd look at her obvious change in mood. She gave him a reassuring smile and stood from the bed. "Sorry. This is all good, really. Just give me a second in the bathroom, okay? Seriously, don't move."

As Felicity entered the bathroom, Alyson was frantically trying to telepathically apologize. *I am so sorry, really. It was a complete accident. I wasn't trying to intrude, I swear. I was half-asleep and I guess I was picking stuff up and I didn't realize what was going on right away. It was like having a dream, but all of a sudden, it was Ben, and weird and... I'm leaving now, and don't worry, I won't be tuning back in anytime soon, believe me! Sorry!*

How humiliating! Alyson forced her mind to go blank as she lay there alone in her own bed. Why couldn't she just have kept her big mental mouth shut? She should have kept her thoughts to herself, and quickly extricated herself from the vision with some decorum, rather than interrupt and make Felicity feel uncomfortable about it. Felicity hadn't needed to know about the faux pas. Now they were both going to feel all self-conscious over it.

Wow, that was an odd experience. Made even weirder by the fact that she was still feeling totally turned on...by Ben. How weird was that? She had never looked at him that way before. She still didn't think of him that way, it almost seemed kind of incestuous, even though they weren't related. But she was undeniably still feeling revved and ready to go. Before she'd realized who he was, she had to admit, she was totally digging it. Her body still felt the phantom tingling trails from his touch.

She opened her eyes, reprimanding herself and trying to think of something else. It wasn't even really *her* skin that had been touched. It was amazing how strong empathy and telepathy could be!

She suddenly realized that the tingling she was feeling wasn't only a phantom remembrance, it was a mark. Mattie was approaching and she could feel the slight current of their shared mark getting stronger. Now *there* was a pleasant feeling she could go with. A visit from her own man was just what she needed.

Mattie entered the room fully dressed and seemed to have his mind on something else, because he didn't even look at her until he had retrieved the car keys from the dresser. He glanced over at the bed before leaving the room, and realized she wasn't sleeping. "Hey, you're up. You've been sleeping awfully late these days."

"Yeah, seems like I never wake up before it's pitch black out. Sorry."

Mattie shrugged. "You don't have to apologize, it's not like you can help it. I wake up early and you don't. All vampires are different, I guess. I don't mind."

He looked like he was planning to leave the room after speaking. She quickly stopped him. "Good. Come back to bed with me."

He gave her an odd look and spread his hands as though asking her to notice that he was fully dressed and obviously engaged in doing something else. She refused to let him leave though. She pushed back the covers and crawled to the end of the bed near him seductively. "Come on, Mattie, please?"

"Cain's waiting for me." He leaned down for a quick kiss before leaving.

He should have known better; if he had really wanted to leave, the kiss was a mistake. His coming that close to her made her not only want him in bed, but it also caused her to realize that she was thirsty as hell. She could not take no for an answer. She wrapped her arms around his neck, refusing to let him go. She began to nuzzle his throat with little kisses, valiantly fighting her urges to keep herself from piercing his skin with her newly unsheathed fangs. "Let him wait. I need you way more than he does."

Mattie tried to stand. She let him, but still wouldn't let go, instead getting up onto her knees to keep her hold. He shook his head, not meeting her eyes. "I'm not really in the mood."

"You're just going to run out on me? Where are you going?"

"I didn't think you'd care. You're always busy anyway. Cain wants to go into Buffalo for supplies, and he has an appointment with his accountant. They're staying open late for him. I said I'd drive. I thought it'd be good for us to have a little *guy* time for a change. I was going to leave you a note."

"You guys get to go out and I'm stuck here...all unprotected?" she added, hoping to guilt him into staying.

Mattie laughed. "Sindy's home too. We're running errands, it's not like we're planning to have great fun. And you're not unprotected, there are about fifty shape-shifting vampires in the backyard ready to come running at your telepathic call."

She sighed and then resumed her kisses about his neck. "Well the least you could do is give me a drink before you go." He didn't seem receptive to the idea at first, but she couldn't imagine that he was actually going to deny her. She let a telepathic empathy wave of thirst and naked desire wash over him, pleading for him to understand her needs.

His knees practically buckled under the onslaught. "My God, Allie."

"See," she whispered. She gave him a stronger pull with her hands, which were still wrapped behind his neck. She tugged him forward and made him join her on the bed. "Just let me take a little, hmmm?" She was already licking and numbing the side of his throat, when he nodded and gave her his unspoken permission.

The moment that her fangs penetrated his flesh, he moaned in appreciation of her venom, and she knew that he'd be staying for more than a drink. Her venom had a definite aphrodisial effect on him, and each sucking pull of blood she took would only heighten the effect. Who needed foreplay? She rolled him onto his back and took only a small amount of blood before stopping for a kiss. She needed to be sure not to push him over the brink of passion before she had a chance to ride…

~~~~~~~~~~~~~~~~~~~~~~~~~~~~~~~

Cain was sitting at the kitchen table, impatiently tapping his fingers, when Allie and Mattie finally made their way over to the house. Sindy was standing at the counter twirling a pen. "Oh yeah," Sindy said, apparently remembering something as they entered, and quickly writing it down on a scrap of paper.

Cain stood up at their arrival. "Finally. We were supposed to have left by now. I was getting ready to head out on my own."

Mattie looked down at the floor, sheepishly. "I know, sorry."

Allie smiled. "Sorry boss, entirely my fault." Rather than fully acknowledge Cain's stern look, she turned towards the cabinet to get herself a mug. "I'm starved," she explained as she opened the fridge.

"Are you kidding me?" Mattie asked. She just shrugged and poured herself some blood. She hadn't drunk all that much from Mattie. What did he expect? She was always starving! She popped her mug into the microwave.

Sindy had finished her list and handed it to Cain while pointing something out to him. "See this conditioner? Make sure it's the purple bottle. Don't get the mango one, the scent makes me gag."

Cain rolled his eyes. "Are you sure you wouldn't rather just come pick it out yourself?"

"Oh relax, it's only a few things. You can handle it. Besides, Allie's going to be teaching me how to shift into a bat tonight, aren't you Allie?"

Alyson shrugged while gulping down an enormous quantity of blood, non-stop. The others paused to stare at her, until she finally finished. "Sure," she answered. She looked around at their expressions of shocked amusement. "What? I'm thirsty."

Mattie asked Sindy curiously, "Why is Allie teaching you? I thought Tempest was doing the teaching."

Cain just lightly shook his head and made for the door. "Whatever. Let's go. We'll already be late as it is," he told Mattie. He paused for a moment at the door for last instructions. "Stay at the house, and call on Khalon if there's any cause for concern. We may be a while," he added, lifting Sindy's list for emphasis.

With that, he was out the door. Mattie was right behind him when Alyson put down her mug to call after him. "Don't I get a kiss goodbye?"

"I'll see you later," Mattie told her, barely pausing as he closed the door.

Sindy watched with raised eyebrows as Allie poured another mug and put it in the microwave. "No kiss?" Sindy observed. "Is the honeymoon over already?"

Allie gave her a sour look as the microwave beeped and she took out her mug. "I've known him more than half my life, Sindy. What we have, never needed a honeymoon. I get my share of kisses and more, believe me. Why do you think we were late?" She took a sip from her mug and then grimaced. She hadn't set it for long enough, and even thirsty as she was, cold blood was a quick turn-off.

Sindy eyed her expression with growing sympathy. "That stuff sucks. Let's go get something decent to drink."

"What, you mean go hunt?"

"Sure. They won't be back for hours. I don't know about you, but I am long overdue for a good hot meal. I once spent an entire summer on nothing but Slimfast, and it still wasn't as bad as living on this stuff."

"I thought you wanted to learn the bat form."

Sindy dismissed the comment with a wave of her hand. "Convenient alibi. They know I'm skittish about it, so they aren't going to ask me to show them until I'm ready. We can *work on it* for weeks. I'm going out. Are you coming?"

Allie took a last look at her mug full of luke-warm blood and then dumped it in the sink. "Definitely."

Sindy looked Allie over, with a hand on her hip. "Is that what you're wearing?"

Alyson rarely bothered with more than a simple tee shirt and jeans these days, unless she was playing sexy dress-up in the bedroom. What was the point? The only time she left the trailer was to come to the house, or shift into a wolf out in the woods. "Well, no. I was planning on wearing fur."

Sindy wore a sly grin. "Not for this hunt, honey."

Alyson grimaced as she realized Sindy's plan. "Where are you going?"

"I know a club out in Rochester that's pretty good. It's well out of Cain's mark range from here. I have a few regulars there."

Alyson felt her hopes deflate. The prospect of a good hunt was very appealing…when she'd been expecting to bag a deer. "You're hunting men?"

Sindy grinned. "We can hunt women if you want, but I'm kind of looking forward to a nice big catch. I won't have time for a double, so the first one's gotta have enough to spare. I'm pretty thirsty."

Allie shook her head. "You know I can't."

"Oh, that is *so* not the case. You can. You won't. Your loss."

"Why don't you just come out into the woods with me? I'll lure you a big buck. They're pretty satisfying."

"Satisfying? Am I supposed to believe that? Even *you* don't believe that. How can you even know what satisfied feels like, when you've never allowed yourself to be? I just don't get it, Allie. Why are you limiting yourself? To please them? They have no clue how you feel. I don't even truly know how you feel, but I know you're not satisfied, that's for damn sure." Alyson didn't answer. Sindy was right, so what could she say? Alyson sat down at the kitchen table, resting her chin on her hand.

Sindy joined her there. Turning her chair to better face Allie and leaning forward with her hands clasped in her lap, practically pleading with her. "Allie, I'll admit that seeing you have all these advantages is really frustrating for me sometimes. You have so many skills, and everybody just thinks you're little miss supervamp who can do no wrong. The way those guys dote on you is borderline revolting, seriously. Mattie is completely wrapped around your finger, and Cain… I've been here for a long time now, and he still doesn't look at me with even half the interest that he has when he looks at you."

Allie looked up at her curiously. "He doesn't think of me like that."

"Doesn't matter. He may not feel romantic about you, but he finds you fascinating, and you're still teacher's pet. I can see the three of you are still sharing marks. I'll bet he looks forward to that every month, even if he'll never admit it. That's got to be an interesting activity, having both of those burning hotties sucking on you on a regular basis. You've got to be the luckiest girl alive or dead."

Alyson allowed a guilty grin to steal over her face for a moment before answering. "It'd be a lot more interesting if the two of them would loosen up a little...but, yeah, I've got a pretty good gig, don't I?"

"And yet you're still not content," Sindy looked disgusted, as though she thought Alyson didn't have proper appreciation for her situation.

"Who says I'm not content?"

When she met Sindy's eyes again, the woman was dead serious, her brown eyes locked to Allie's blue ones. "Are you going to tell me that you're just naturally such a cranky bitch?"

"I guess you bring it out in me."

Sindy laughed. "Actually, I think it's just the opposite. Maybe the guys want to turn a blind eye to it, but I think you're tortured by thirst, making you irritable like a hungry diva on a diet. After you've gone out hunting with me, is probably the only time that you aren't consumed with wondering what you're going to drink next. It's because that shit just doesn't cut it," she added with a wave of her arm at the fridge. "Face it, Allie, you need live blood. Once it's a few hours old, it loses something; something that you need. You're constantly jonesing for it."

Alyson began tapping her fingers on the table, watching her purple lacquered nails strike the wood in a staccato rhythm, as she mulled over Sindy's theory. It was true that live animal blood held off her thirst much better than anything from the refrigerator.

Sindy took back her attention. "You know it's true. I'm right there with you. Sure, blood out of the fridge is good enough for them. They live like humans. They can get by on the bare minimum. But you and I need more. We've got real magic flowing through us, that we use all the time. You can't fuel that on cold dead blood, anymore than you could run your car on water instead of gasoline. You've got to be drinking jet fuel if you want to fly, honey!

Don't you deserve to live a little? You think drinking a big stag out in the woods is satisfying, when it only curbs your needs for a couple of hours? What do you think the live blood of a man would do?"

Alyson pondered the implication. She still could go hunt that stag. Leave Sindy to her own devices, and go hunt on her own. She didn't need Sindy to bring down large game. However, the idea of drinking something that would really last...something that would eradicate her thirst for any real length of time, was a proposition she couldn't allow herself to ignore.

Sindy leaned back and put her feet up on the table, crossing her legs. "I know it would be simpler if you could just look at me like I'm the evil voice of temptation. Then you could valiantly rise above it, and be all proud of yourself, but the fact is, you can't broad-stroke things that way. I'm not the bad guy. I don't really care what you do. I'll go get my fix with or without you. But I think you have a right to know the facts, because the guys sure as hell aren't going to tell you."

"You really think it would curb my thirst better than animal blood? 'Cause I need *a lot*, and I'm not going to kill anyone to get it."

"You only need that much because you're not drinking what you're made for. All the grape juice in the world still isn't the same as a glass of wine. Your body is made to run on the blood of a human. I drink a little from someone on the dance floor as an appetizer, then, I pick a lucky man to take me to a hotel for the main course. We have a good time, I'm full, and he's still breathing. Everybody wins. Sometimes it'll last me two nights before I'm thirsty again."

"Two? I've never had anything last me more than a few hours at most."

Sindy smiled. "It's true. I don't doubt you might need more than me, but I know you'll feel a difference. The powers you've got access to are mind boggling, and you're using them with nothing but dead blood to replenish your energy, with the occasional tease of live animal blood. Even when you drink from Mattie, he's not drinking anything better, so it can't help much. You're squashing your potential and putting yourself through hell, for what?

Because you're afraid you'll disappoint them, and feel like you're not worthy of what you've been given? The fact is, you deserve more. You're living on scraps like a beggar, when you have the potential to be a Queen."

Alyson was actually finding Sindy's argument to be surprisingly rational and compelling, but she was taking it a bit far. "Let's not get dramatic."

"Deny it? I think I'm right on the mark. Believe me, no one wants to admit it less than I do, but I look at your eyes and all you can do, and I can't pretend it's not true. You are vampire royalty, Allie, no doubt. If you wielded those eyes with a purpose, who could stop you? I think Queen is damn accurate, and they know it too. It scares the shit out of them. They don't know what to do with it, so they play it down and try to keep you harnessed and weak."

"That's not true. They aren't trying to hold me back."

Sindy shrugged. "Maybe not on purpose, but that's the result. How can you live like that? Who are they to tell you that you have to spend your nights thirsty and miserable, when you could easily live otherwise? What do you really think they would do if you drank human blood? Scold you? Order you to stop? You think they would leave you? They never would. Mattie would be lost without you. Anyone can see that. Cain didn't give up on *me* when I was on a psycho killing spree for revenge, and he doesn't even seem to care about me that much. You really think he's going to abandon *you?*

Only you know your needs, and no one has the right to try to force you to deny them. They gave you an alternative, but it's not enough. Now you have to be woman enough to stand up to them, and tell them what you need, with or without their consent. You don't have to be a killer, but at least give yourself a chance to be free of your overwhelming thirst."

Sindy stood, smoothing down her skirt. "I've got to go if I'm going to make it all the way to Rochester and back in time."

"It's not that far," Alyson told her thoughtfully, "as the crow flies."

"If by crow, you mean flying vampire," she said with a grin, "that would totally help me out. It'd be nice to have a little time to work the club, without having to take the first warm-blooded body who buys me a drink."

Allie hesitated. Was she really going to do this? It was only fair that she be allowed to make an informed decision, right? She should be allowed to know what she was missing. "Say I come with you, just to try a little, as an experiment, how do I know I'm not going to hurt anyone?"

"You won't. I've seen you hunt. You always leave the deer with enough to get by on."

"That's different! They're not people."

"It's not all that different really. You'd be surprised. Men and deer are both large mammals with a similar heartbeat. Just pay attention, and you'll know when to stop, just like you do in the woods."

"I'm not looking for a thrill or anything. I'm not taking anyone to a hotel or getting carried away, I just want a taste. I need to know if it will really quench my thirst. I think I should know."

"I agree."

"Then, I guess I'd better go get changed."

~~~~~~~~~~~~~~~~~~~~~~~~~~~~~~

Sindy let go of Allie, as soon as her heels touched the pavement. She began roughly combing her fingers through her long dark hair. "That was wild, but I must look like a fucking mess."

Allie stepped away from her, and assessed her appearance as she raked a few finger swipes through her own shoulder length locks. "You look fine, and I got us here nice and fast, didn't I?"

Sindy pulled a lipstick from the hip pocket of her skirt, and carefully applied a coat of blood wine burgundy, as Alyson tried to shake the inexplicable jitters that were creeping over her. "Jeez, I'm nervous as hell."

Sindy smacked her lips as she put the lipstick away. "Don't be. It's going to be easy," she said, as she made her way to the door of the club.

"That's what I'm afraid of."

They entered the darkened club to be engulfed in loud music, and the noise and warmth of a crowd of people. Sindy took on an image at once alluring and aloof, as she made her way through the throng to a place at the bar. She turned and leaned her back against it, as she surveyed her surroundings. "Now this is my world."

It was a decent sized dance club, with the bar along one wall, and a full dance floor ringed by small tables. Alyson felt at home as well, not realizing how she'd missed the familiar atmosphere from her barmaid days.

Before the girls had even gotten a chance to truly take in their surroundings, they were approached by two good-looking young men. The guys wanted to buy them drinks, and were scolding Sindy for staying away so long.

Both men were marked with her venom, although the marks were fading. They each gave Alyson a polite smile, and she could tell they were contemplating which of them should give up focusing on Sindy to include Allie instead.

Sindy gave Alyson a questioning glance. The marks were faint, Allie could probably overcome them, but the idea of drinking from someone who might know what they were in for, was daunting. What would the guy expect from her? She quickly shook her head. *Too intimidating,* she explained to Sindy mentally.

The girls had never shared blood, but their many hunting trips alone in the woods had acclimated Sindy to accepting Alyson's telepathy. Allie could usually share her thoughts, as long as Sindy wasn't purposely shutting her out. Sindy looked the guys over with a fresh eye. They were definitely worthy male specimens. *Really? They are top-shelf, but you're totally up for it.*

Allie just shook her head again. "No thanks."

Your call. Sindy declined the guys offer, giving them each a kiss on the cheek. "Sorry, but we're having a girl's night right now. Maybe I'll come get a drink from you later though," she told him with a wink.

As the guys reluctantly left for greener pastures, a popular new song came on, urging people to the dance floor and thinning out the crowd at the bar. Alyson noticed a very heavy man, sitting on a stool further down. He was alone, and looked a bit uncomfortable and out of place, but was nicely dressed. He seemed to be shyly trying to make eye contact with them, and get their attention. He also wore Sindy's mark, even brighter than the other two.

Allie turned to Sindy and subtly gestured towards the man with a raised eyebrow. "Really?"

"I was thirsty." She smiled and gave the guy a little wave. He awkwardly began making his way towards them through the crowd. "You know what?" she whispered to Allie. "He actually turned out to be a really good lay. Best I've had in a while. Sometimes charity pays off." The man approached. "Hi…"

Alyson could feel Sindy fumbling to produce the man's name. Alyson quickly delved into his mind to supply it for her. *George.*

"George," Sindy picked it up, barely missing a beat. "Nice to see you again."

He was visibly relieved to see that she remembered him, and was happy to acknowledge him, despite the fact that she was here with a friend. "Hi Sindy, how are you? I was really hoping I was going to see you tonight. You haven't been here in a while. I hope you enjoyed yourself when we went out the other night."

She smiled and put a familiar hand on his shoulder. "Oh George, you know I did. I'm afraid my schedule's been pretty full lately though."

He thrilled to her touch, remnants of her mark intensifying the excitement for him. It was amazing how these humans could feel so attracted to Sindy, and acknowledge their odd fascination with her, without truly questioning it. They kept themselves in denial that she could be anything more than a desirable, human woman. Alyson could feel George struggling not to seem too eager to spend time with Sindy and put her off. "Oh sure. I understand. Beautiful woman like you must have lots of dates."

She leaned forward to whisper to him. "None that know how to treat a lady like you do," she told him, placing a small kiss on his cheek. "But you need a nice girl, George. I'm no good for you."

"Don't be silly. You're plenty nice."

Sindy gave the man a smile, while cupping her hand to the side of his face. "You charmer," she teased. "I promised my friend it would just be us girls for now, but I'll see if maybe I've got a night free for you next week, okay? And don't waste all your time sitting in this dump looking for me, you're too good for this place. I know how to find you."

"Are you sure I can't buy you a drink? I'll buy one for your friend too."

She scrunched her nose at him, and gave him an apologetic little head shake. "Thanks George, but we've got to go."

The girls moved further down the bar, away from George, and became engulfed in the crowd. Allie spared a glance back at him as they left. *He's sweet. Don't hurt him,* she warned Sindy.

Sindy smiled. *I wouldn't dream of it. Relax, he's big enough to hold plenty of blood. It's not an issue. And I'm telling you, the guy's got skills. I think he must watch a lot of porn.*

Alyson was busy absorbing that, when Sindy grabbed her arm for attention and nudged her to look towards the door. A group of guys had just walked in, all young, handsome, joking, and loud. Booth-tanned despite the autumn cold outside, hair slicked and showing off their bulging biceps in sleeveless shirts as they stripped off their jackets, they looked like the cast of "Jersey-Shore". None of them wore marks. Sindy was obviously intrigued by them. *Ooh, fresh blood.*

Allie dismissed them. She wasn't looking to put on the type of show guys like that would require. She wasn't even sure what she was looking for. She probably shouldn't be looking at all. Why was she here? Like an answer to her internal question, a wave of thirst rumbled through her, sharp and demanding. It clenched her insides with cramps and drove her hesitation from her mind. She could not take this anymore. If human blood would make it stop, then it was time she try some.

Sindy was posing and non-chalantly beginning the back and forth flirting across the room that would get her noticed by the guys, but Allie found her attention drawn back to the bar instead. There were two young men sitting there having a friendly conversation, when one of them got up, clapped the other on the back and left.

The other was still finishing his drink before leaving. He was un-imposing, seeming casual and uninterested in trolling for women. He gave the lady bartender a very nice smile, but seemed ready to finish his drink and go. He had clean-cut dirty blonde hair, was wearing cargo pants, a fitted, white, long-sleeved tee shirt, and had a leather bomber jacket with a scarf tucked under the collar slung over the back of his chair. He gave the bartender a tip and flashed her that winning smile again. Wow, what a smile. He was really cute.

Sindy turned to Alyson, just as the guy was getting up to retrieve his jacket off the chair. "Come on, those guys are totally primed," she said, urging Allie to cross the room with her.

"No, I'm gonna stay here."

Sindy turned to see who she was looking at. The guy Allie was watching had been stopped by a man next to him to talk before leaving. A wide grin spread across Sindy's face. "Ah, blondie likes 'em wholesome. I should have known," she said, rolling her eyes. She was always commenting on Mattie's safe and simple ways, asking what Allie saw in him. Allie just flashed her a look of warning. "Well you'd better go after him before he leaves."

Wholesome...like Mattie. Who was she kidding? She couldn't go through with this. The guy was heading their way, having to pass them to get to the door. Allie turned her back to him. "Forget it," she whispered to Sindy. "Let's just go."

"Thank me later," Sindy whispered back. Allie was just looking up to ask what she meant, when Sindy shoved her backwards.

Allie stumbled into the man behind her in surprise. He reached out and caught her as she fell. Allie could have easily regained her balance, but she had been too busy forcing herself not to levitate to break her fall. She hadn't been out in a while, surrounded by humans like this, and had grown far too used to using her powers naturally around the house.

The guy caught and gently held her until she was standing again. "Whoa, you alright?" He was looking at her with a mixed expression of amusement and pity. He probably thought she was bombed.

Sindy spoke up with a laugh. "Sorry. She's not drunk, she's just a klutz." As she spoke, Sindy turned and perched herself onto a bar stool, to give Allie a little space with the guy.

Allie looked up at him in extreme embarrassment to apologize. "I am so sorry, really."

"That's okay." Now that great smile was aimed at her.

Allie quickly looked away. "I was just leaving."

"Can I walk you to your car?" he asked. He still had a gentle hold on her elbow, keeping her steady. "You're not driving, are you?"

On my God, she felt like such an ass. She looked back up at him, keeping a steady gaze so he could see that she was fine. "I'm not drunk, really."

He chuckled as he moved back to the bar. "Then maybe you should stay, so I can buy you a drink."

Was she blushing? How stupid, she was actually blushing. "No thanks."

Sindy was giving her a stern look. *Let him buy you a drink. Look at the way he is eyeing you. He totally wants you. It's all part of the hunt. You have to play the game.* Sindy insisted adamantly.

Allie wanted to protest, but the thirst was rising up in her again. She could smell him, a close, warm, masculine scent of aftershave, sweat, the wool of his scarf, and the leather of his coat. *I don't want to sleep with him, I just wanted a drink.*

Whatever floats your boat, but don't just stand there, he's going to get bored and leave.

"You sure?" he asked her gently.

Sindy kept urging her on in her head. It was really annoying. *Come on Allie, you're going to lose him.*

Alyson shot Sindy a look of reprimand. *Don't be an idiot. I don't need to play games. I can have anyone I want, any time.* She looked up at the guy. His eyes were a light, amber brown.

"I'm Josh," he introduced himself with a smile.

Allie smiled back, letting her own eyes flash into their vampiric magnificence as she replied. "Hi Josh. I'm Allie. Walk me outside?"

"Sure," he said, after a moment of gazing into her eyes.

As she let them lapse back into being blue again, he took her arm and began to guide her to the door. It was that simple, he was mesmerized. He'd do anything she asked. This was too easy. *Sindy come with me.*

What? Why?

Because I need you to make sure I don't go too far. I'm so thirsty I feel like I could drain the bar. What if I can't stop? I don't want to hurt him!

Sindy showed no signs of leaving her bar stool. *Relax, you won't. You'll be fine. You know how to handle yourself, I've seen you.*

You've seen me with animals, this is completely different. Get over here now!

Sindy stood, but seemed at a loss. *What am I supposed to do, just stand there and watch like a freak?*

Allie didn't answer, she just sent Sindy a wave of panic. If she didn't come, Allie would never forgive her. Sindy glanced around and spotted George still sitting a bit further down. She waved him over. "George, come walk me outside."

Alyson lost sight of her as Josh opened the door and led her through. *Now what?* He hesitated, waiting for her to indicate which car was hers.

She scanned the lot, looking for her car, which was not there, and then led them to a random vehicle in the back of the lot. She was very grateful to hear Sindy and George come through the door behind her.

As they walked across the lot, she could feel the vampire within her coiled and ready, anxious for the kill. No. No kill, this was just a simple drink. She just wanted a taste.

She gently leaned against the car, hoping against hope, that it didn't have an alarm. It remained quiet and she breathed a sigh of relief. What was she supposed to say to this guy? He was watching her with a quiet smile, little wisps of steam issuing from his lips in the cold night air. Actually, she didn't have to say anything, did she?

Alyson looked into his eyes with her own sparkling white ones once more. As he gazed into their depths, she could feel the wonder and compulsion she caused in his mind. So easy. He was hers. She mentally commanded him to let her do as she pleased, as he kept quiet and still. He would give her no trouble.

She leaned forward, stretching up on tiptoe to be near his face, and gave him a slight, soft kiss. He was willing and eager to kiss her back, but she turned her head from his lips in favor of his throat. His scent was overwhelming, and her thirst would no longer be denied.

She raised her arms around him and nestled her lips into the crook of his shoulder to find his skin beneath the scarf he wore. As soon as her lips felt warmth, her fangs further distended and she pierced his flesh in one smooth swift bite. *Ecstasy…*

She was careful not to tear his skin more than the small punctures her fangs had made, although normally she often opened a larger wound to allow her to drink more quickly. She knew that she would have to use whatever tricks she could, to force herself to drink slowly and not take too much. Her body was already trembling with satisfaction at being able to release venom into a human victim. The anticipation of drinking rose up in her, and she couldn't wait any longer. She removed her fangs and closed her lips over the bite.

As the first drop touched her tongue, she knew…this was meant to be. It was what her body had been longing for all along. Every pull was a luscious, extravagant swallow of thick, rich, warm bliss.

Josh moaned with a deliciously masculine rumble of pleasure, as she sucked more strongly. She could feel him, hard as lead as she pressed against his body to drink. Wow, she could definitely see where Sindy could enjoy mingling sex with her drinking, taking full advantage of her victims. It would be a nice enjoyable distraction, to break up the drink, giving her something else to focus on, reminding her not to take too much.

However, that was not the case here. The sexual urges she could feel emanating from the man in her grasp were tempting, but his blood was the irresistible pleasure. It was the most delectable nectar she could imagine, and she wanted nothing but more. Alyson tried to ignore the fierce urges within that wanted her to rip open his throat and bath her face in it. These small, simple holes in his neck were her only access, and she tried to suck gently, so as not to damage the skin around them. Cain thought she had imperfect control? Her actions here were an impressive display of restraint that even she wouldn't have believed she was capable of, but she was doing it.

She tried to curtail her immersion in tasting his blood, and focus instead on the man's heartbeat. Sindy was right. It wasn't all that different from the heartbeat of a deer really. She could try to transport her thoughts back to her past hunts in the woods, and her practice of stopping her drink before the deer's heartbeat would become too slow. The blood was so good though…better than anything she'd ever tasted from an animal by far. Just a little more, she didn't have to stop yet, did she?

Josh let out a small sigh in her ear, and let himself rest more strongly against her. It would not have even been noticeable, if she had let herself be carried away by the pleasure of her feast, but she was trying very hard to pay attention to such things, in tune with the intimate details of this stranger's body like none before him. His heart was slowing. Not alarming in itself, he was alright, but it was definitely time to end this rapturous experience.

She took a last savory mouthful, and then removed her lips from his skin. As she did, she was startled to feel someone place a hand upon her shoulder, making her jump. She'd allowed herself to be completely focused on her victim, and lost track of her surroundings, not a very wise move. Fortunately, it was only Sindy who had approached. Alyson took a shuddering breath, trying to clear her mind, and keep herself from going back for more blood. God but she could still taste it, smell it… She licked her lips and forced herself to stillness, loosely holding Josh's slumped form in her arms. He shifted, taking his full weight from her as he stood more fully on his own, regaining awareness, although still groggy.

"See," Sindy said gently, "I told you that you could handle it."

~~~~~~~~~~~~~~~~~~~~~~~~~~~~~~~~~~~

Alyson opened the sliding glass door that led into the parlor, and quietly eased it closed behind her. She'd come home last night before Mattie had even missed her. He and Cain didn't get home until well after the girls, and thought them to have been practicing shifting at the house all evening. Although Allie had been bursting with energy, and thrilled to find that her thirst was sated as never before, she'd managed to keep Mattie from noticing. It had been mostly by avoiding him until she turned in for the day, which had possibly annoyed him a bit, but at least he didn't suspect anything. He had gone to bed none the wiser.

She had woken up alone. When she'd first reached out psychically for him, he'd seemed far away and hard to find. She'd thought maybe he was over here at Cain's, in the media room playing video games again, but now that she was here, she still couldn't feel him. If he were on the immediate premises, she would feel it through their shared mark. Cain was there, she could feel him, but Mattie was nowhere to be found.

Now she was nervous. He usually waited for her to awaken before doing anything, and he never left without at least a note. She sat down on the edge of the armchair by the fire, and reached out for him again; full throttle, no fooling around this time. She had to find him. Where the heck could he be? What if he was in trouble? What if he needed her? What if he knew about last night...?

Auras of vampires and venom-marked animals began to fill her awareness in an ever-broadening circle around her. The lighted marks of the Crimson Coven were spread over the property like a glowing blanket, interwoven with deer they had drunk from. It was too much to sort through. He wouldn't be out in the woods with them anyway.

She turned her attention towards town. Now the marks thinned out to consist mostly of dimly marked animals she had drunk from in passing, weeks ago. Sindy had marked a few of her own...along with a couple of humans just beyond town. She ought to be more careful, they were a little close for comfort. Alyson wondered if Cain had noticed. They were probably out of his range, unless he was out wandering. She was very glad that she and Sindy had made damn sure to conduct their little expedition nowhere near here last night. Where was Sindy now? Allie couldn't see her. Not having shared blood, she couldn't feel her either. As long as she was cloaked, Sindy could be in the next room or the next county. Allie couldn't tell.

Where the hell was Mattie? She reached out for him psychically again. Why was he so hard to get through to? Usually she could read him as well as her own thoughts. Wait... There, she could sense him. Like wading through thick muddy waters, she finally found and felt his presence. *Mattie, where are you? Are you okay?*

His response felt as though a curtain was slowly lifting, as she eagerly tried to peer beneath and see what had been shielded from her. *I'm fine.* She could see him now, picking up bits of his surroundings through his eyes. He was sitting at a table, raising a warm cup to his lips. There was a window next to him, but it was too fogged and streaked with rain to see through. A coffee shop maybe?

Where are you? She asked in confusion. It wasn't raining here at the house.

Out.

No kidding. Why were you so hard to reach? You had me worried sick! You didn't even leave a note. He still felt distant. He knew nothing of her outing with Sindy. Mattie wore his heart too plainly on his sleeve to hide knowledge of that sort. If he knew, she'd know about it. So what was going on? He didn't seem to have much of a reaction to her desperation. What the hell?

She could feel a wave of weariness wash over him as he replied. *Honestly, I wasn't even sure you'd notice. I just thought I'd get out of your way for a while. It's no big deal. Go do your thing.*

She sat there dumbfounded, as she realized why she'd had such a difficult time finding him. He had completely shut her out! He was hanging out in some damn coffee shop, purposely far the hell out of her range. He knew damn well that she would have no idea where he was, and he had blocked her out! *What the fuck Mattie? Are you pissed at me because I hung out with Sindy last night instead of you? Are you serious? You're the one who went out without me, and when you got home, I was busy. What are you doing, acting out like a freakin' toddler?*

She could feel him, calm and almost fatigued, as though her ire couldn't even irk him. He was just fed up and defeated. He felt that it didn't really matter what he did. She would always do whatever she wanted anyway. She was who she was, and they would always be linked more intimately than any other couple could ever truly hope to be. He loved her, and she knew that no matter what she did, he always would. He would never truly leave her, but he was getting damn tired of feeling ignored.

It wasn't that bad, was it? Yes, last night was a transgression he wouldn't understand, but he didn't even know about last night! She was usually there for him. They did stuff together. Of course, the stuff they did was mostly him watching, while she showed him her stuff...

His reply was quiet and resigned. *Just go do your thing. You know I'll be back.* The curtain came down again with a psychic thud. He was gone.

Blocked. When had he learned how to do that? Jeez, he may have a legitimate reason to be mad at her, but did he have to be such a drama queen?

He wasn't, and she knew it. She knew he wasn't doing anything that wasn't perfectly justified. He wasn't even throwing a fit, arguing with her, or truly acting out. Those things she could deal with. He didn't like the way she had been treating him, so he had just walked away. He knew she had turned a blind eye to his gentle pleas for attention, putting him off, and refusing to recognize his needs. If he kept confronting her over it, it would just become an argument. But she couldn't fight with someone who wasn't there. Mature, responsible Mattie, forcing her to see herself through his eyes, rather than try to argue on her ground.

Allie let out a disgruntled huff of a sigh. Okay, maybe she needed to re-assess some things. But first, a drink. She didn't really need blood, (an amazing realization!) but she should probably keep up appearances for Cain. She'd get a glass for show…maybe with some rum in it.

Alyson rose and entered the kitchen with grim determination. It wasn't her fault she'd turned into The United One. She didn't ask for any of this. She couldn't help it if she had powers that Mattie didn't. She needed to learn how to use them, and that took up a lot of her time. It didn't help that using them made her ravenously thirsty, and then she usually had to spend the rest of the evening hunting to slake that thirst. He had to be a little understanding. What the hell did he want her to do? Stay at the trailer and play house all night? Right, like she would ever be Martha fucking Stewart! He knew damn well that wasn't her.

Alyson was startled to find Cain watching her quietly from the kitchen table, with various odd looking implements laid out before him. She'd been so distracted, that she hadn't even realized he was there. He smiled at her surprise. "Good evening. It's a rare occasion when someone startles you. A lot on your mind?"

She took a deep breath and let it out, enjoying the feeling of air whooshing in and out of her lungs. Breathing wasn't a necessity anymore except for speech, and taking such a full breath felt good, like stretching neglected muscles. She couldn't decide how to answer, so she just shrugged and headed for the fridge. It would look odd to Cain if she didn't immediately get herself a drink as usual.

"I'm glad you're here. I thought we could do some more exercises in manipulation control."

"Yeah. There's always something I'm supposed to be doing, isn't there?" she asked. It probably came out a bit more harshly than intended, but her exchange with Mattie was giving her an impatient edge. "Can we do it later?" she added more softly. He just nodded, watching her inquisitively. She gestured to the table and all the stuff laid out on it. "What's all that? Part of the exercise you wanted to do?" she asked as she prepared her drink.

"No, this is for me." Cain was preparing something as well. He was stirring something in a little cup that smelled of an odd mix of blood and paint. "Inking time," he told her, holding up his arm for emphasis. She turned to better assess what he was doing.

Now she recognized the equipment on the table. It was a tattoo machine and its various accessories. A simple, traditional hand held v-machine, attached to a power pack with a foot pedal. She shed her disgruntlement and came to the table with interest. "You do it yourself?"

"M-hmmm. I had it done professionally the first time, but I've found it easier to just re-ink it myself when needed. It's not nearly as difficult as trying to avoid mirrors in a tattoo parlor. Besides, I'm better off mixing my own ink. I hadn't gotten it done until long after I was a vampire, and tattoos don't really take well on our skin. Our bodies eventually reject the ink like a toxin."

The microwave beeped as Alyson was inspecting the very faded tattoo on the inside of his forearm thoughtfully. It read *Genesis 4:7* in fancy calligraphy-type script. "God's advice to Cain in the bible, right? What's the quote?" she asked, gesturing to the tattoo as she retrieved her mug. He didn't say anything as she added an unseemly amount of alcohol to her cup.

Cain gave her a bittersweet smile. He'd recited the verse to her before, but knew that she liked to hear it now and then. "If you do what is right, will you not be accepted? But if you do not do what is right, sin is crouching at your door; it desires to have you, but you must master it."

She nodded as she chewed her lip thoughtfully. "You always keep it the same?" she asked of the tattoo.

"It always fits," he answered simply, still stirring his cup.

She felt her eyes suddenly begin to cloud. She blinked and cleared her vision. "What's so great about being accepted anyway? Accepted by who?"

Cain gave her a small, sympathetic chuckle. "I used to think it meant society. I spent a long time mourning that I could never regain human acceptance. But does that matter?

Then I began to think it was God who would accept or deny me, based on my morality or sin. Did you know that I can hold a cross with only a fraction of the pain and damage that most vampires would sustain? Is that acceptance? No, I've come to find it's nothing more than accelerated healing due to my breed. I've found that I have been alternately accepted across the threshold of a church, or denied entrance like a lack of invitation, depending on the night I choose to visit. Who can tell why? Is it based on my intentions, a balance of good or evil within me? I've no idea. I know only that I have been welcomed with a feeling of grateful relief, just as many times as I've been barred like a blasphemous outcast. I've stopped trying to figure it out. I'll drive myself mad.

You know what I have figured out, though? If I sincerely seek to be a good person, doing what is right, by at least my own standards, I can accept myself. Seems a small, simple thing, but it feels like a step up the stair. I've done things in the past that I find hard to accept in myself. I don't want to feel that way over my actions anymore. I want to be able to accept who I am with pride. I may never reach heaven's gates, but I won't lay down in defeat.

Sin is crouching at my door, but I've promised myself to ever step up away from it as best I can. I will do my best to master it. It's not easy though. Sometimes I am so damn weary of the fight to do good, and to resist temptation, that I forget that promise. That promise is what I aim to remind myself of. Hence the tattoo."

Allie nodded towards the inked reminder on his arm. "Does it work?"

He chuckled. "Sometimes," he told her. "We are in difficult positions, as vampires. Humans can seem so vulnerable. I don't have your eyes, my power lies in venom and experience; the gathered observations of over three hundred years, and yet that is more than enough. When I hunted humans, I found it depressingly simple to charm and seduce my victims. No matter how far above those past actions I'd like to try and hold myself, I still think it is good to keep the reminders; to never allow myself to forget. You've got an arsenal of skills and techniques that I can barely even fathom the effects of, were you to use them thusly."

Alyson found herself sitting very still. Did he know about last night? He never talked about the time when he used to drink from humans. Why bring it up now? Somehow, did he know that she'd been out with Sindy last night...and that she'd drunk from a man? He couldn't know. Sindy would never tell him, and there was no way for him to read such things out of her mind, as she could read thoughts from his. He didn't know, but he knew of her struggles with thirst, and his intuition was uncanny. She nodded, looking wide-eyed and as innocent as she could manage.

He continued with his warning. "With greater powers, come greater temptations. Sin doesn't only crouch at your door, it opens it for you and bids you enter with wooing ease. Perhaps you could use a reminder as well.

No matter how powerful you are, no matter if not another soul in the world would be able to restrain you, you are responsible for your actions. Only you can accept the weight of the decisions you make. And just as no one else can take the blame for what you do, no one else can take the credit either. I know you're accustomed to reading people by their actions, and letting yours speak for you. Be sure that you can always be proud of them. I so want that for you."

Alyson swallowed over the lump in her throat and nodded. True, her conscience was clear on larger matters. She didn't have human deaths on her hands to atone for, but small scale? *If you do what is right, will you not be accepted?* She couldn't pretend she felt guilty for sating her thirst last night. It was the first time she could feel truly satisfied, filling a longing within herself that had been torturous. The guy was fine. She hadn't hurt anyone. But she did feel badly for knowing how it would disappoint Cain and Mattie, if they knew. Mattie already had enough reason to be unhappy with her, adding this might be enough to push things too far. Could she accept herself if she drove Mattie away? She had a tattoo reminder of her own, on her hip and thigh…a reminder of Mattie's love.

Cain stopped mixing and tapped his wooden stirrer on the edge of the cup, before placing it on a paper towel. He began readying his tattoo equipment, peeling open a needle package that was on the table before him, sliding out the long needle and gently bending it a bit, to make a mild arc before inserting it into the machine. He then slid the needle into the ink reservoir tube, fitting it through until only the barest tip was visible poking out of the end. His movements were methodical and calming. She could feel the tension ease in the room. Time to change the subject and lighten things.

Allie picked up and sniffed the cup of ink he'd been stirring as he finished his preparations. "So how do you get the tattoo to stay?"

"It's an imperfect process, but I mix my own blood in with the ink."

Allie nodded. "I knew I smelled your blood in there." She swirled it around a bit. It looked thoroughly black.

"I let some of my blood into a cup, then mix it with some of the ink. If I keep mixing it for a good long time, it seems to bond a bit, almost like dyeing the blood itself. Then I use that concoction for the tattoo. It's not exactly permanent, but it stays for a few months anyway. That's twice the time ink alone will last."

"Huh. I guess I'll have to do that when mine starts to fade. Ever seen it?" she asked, rising from the chair, and unbuttoning her pants to show off her artwork.

Cain laughed, and remained focused on his task, stepping on the power pedal for the machine a few times, as he dipped the needle into his cup to fill the reservoir with ink. "I think I see more of your body on a regular basis than is entirely proper already. I don't need Mattie walking in whilst you're in the process of stripping down your jeans."

Allie rolled her eyes, and continued to tug them down anyway. It's not like she wasn't wearing any underwear. Cain *had* seen her naked before anyway. Big deal. "Mattie's not even here," she told him.

He looked up at her with a level gaze for a moment before going back to his work. "I know."

Duh. Of course he knew. He and Mattie shared a mark too. He could feel that Mattie was nowhere near the house just as she could. He was just trying to make a point. She needed to show Mattie more respect. *Yeah, I know.* "It's not like it isn't relevant to the conversation. Besides, I hardly get to show it off to anyone."

She stood next to him with her pants around her knees, her tattooed hip level with the table, where his attention was focused on making adjustments to his ink gun. "Some things are private," he replied.

Cain knew that she wasn't trying to be flirty or indecent. Someone like *Sindy* would see it as an opportunity to show off her body, but Allie just wanted to use it as an opening to talk. "Not anymore," she said. "I know it's annoying sometimes, but we're a close coven, and nothing is very private when you can feel everything that's going on with one another." She wondered again if maybe somehow he *did* know. Well, she wasn't going to mention her thirst and open that debate, but maybe he could help her with her other concerns. "Maybe being so in tune with one another can be a good thing, because as it turns out, there's stuff that even The United One isn't very good at, like relationships. I could use some advice."

Cain sighed, but refused to spare her artwork a glance before beginning work on his own. Through her empathy, she could feel the needle sink into his skin with a burning sting that felt almost satisfying to him somehow. She could read from him that this was something he usually did alone, like meditation. He was willing to share the time with her, but this wasn't the advice he'd hoped she would be asking for. He vaguely nodded towards her hip without looking as he worked. "It's a kite, isn't it?" he asked over the hum of his tattooing.

She smiled. Obviously his eyes had strayed to it at some point or other. He'd probably noticed it during one of her shifting sessions. She pulled her jeans back up and fastened them so modesty wouldn't be an issue to make him uncomfortable. "Uh-huh, and there's an 'A' on it. The kite represents me."

Now Cain paused to look at her, his brow furrowed in interest. She continued. "The string for the kite winds down my thigh." And…she was losing him to impropriety again, painting such an intimate picture. He looked away but she took back his attention, getting to the point. "The string spells *Mattie*.

See back when we first got together, he used to marvel at how I never let anything bother me. He didn't understand how I could let things just roll off my back so easily. I told him that life wasn't fun when you let yourself get bogged down with stuff, so you're better off just rising above it. He seemed pretty impressed with that. Then he told me that if I could actually manage to keep that attitude all the time, without drugs or alcohol, I must be naturally high as a kite." She and Cain both laughed at the statement. "That just kind of stuck. Every time something would rile him up, I'd tell him to rise above it, and he would tell me to go fly a kite. It turned into a private joke."

"That's cute," Cain told her with a grin.

"After…" Allie tried not to falter, but it was always difficult to talk about this time in her life. "After he died, I was so devastated, Cain. I can't even try to describe it. I felt so helpless. I wasn't even there when it happened. I just came home to find Ben at my door telling me that Mattie was gone. I didn't know he'd been turned, I just thought he was dead. I was never going to see him again. To lose him like that, it was just awful."

"I know the feeling." Cain's eyes were glazed with tears of his own. He understood. In a life as long as his, he'd surely lost loved ones along the way.

"I went and got the tattoo. I wanted him to always be with me, no matter how high I flew, he could hang on and share the thrill. The tattoo artist kept trying to convince me that I had it backwards. Since Mattie had died, he should be the kite, flying up over the earth, and I should be the string on the ground, but that wasn't right. I was always the kite. Mattie, he was the grounded one.

When he came back, that tattoo made him so happy. You should have seen his face. Like, he'd thought I would just forget about him or something? He was so tickled with it. Not nearly as happy as I was to see him again, but…you know what I mean. I think he felt like he'd just lost everyone in his life, and to see his name on me like that, it meant he hadn't lost me, you know?"

She glanced up and found Cain's blue eyes gazing at her with quiet intensity. "Why are you getting into all of this? Are you two having problems?"

Why *was* she going into all of this with him? What could he possibly tell her that would help? Stop being selfish and thoughtless? She shook her head a little, lost in her uncertainty and shrugged. "It's not him, it's me."

"I know you've gotten a little more than you'd bargained for with all of this, but it's not a bad deal. You and Mattie are young lovers, united in immortality with a safe home and surrounded by friends. I should think that you've got everything you could want."

"I know. I don't mean to sound unappreciative. I thought this was what I wanted, it's just…I'm smothering, Cain. You guys are smothering me! Between you and Mattie I'm always getting tag-teamed…and not in a fun way."

Cain stopped the machine for a moment of silence. "That's not true. You asked me for space, and I've tried to give it to you. You may spend a lot of your time practicing your shifting skills lately, but you can't tell me that you don't enjoy it. As for Mattie, how much space do you expect him to give? He's your husband, not just some lover of convenience."

She let him feel how the statement wounded her. He didn't seem apologetic, though. Was that really how she'd been treating Mattie? Okay, maybe she deserved that. "I can't lose him though, Cain. I think back to that night when he died, and I just know that I never want to feel that again. I can't lose him."

Cain nodded in understanding. "Then you need to make sure he knows what he means to you."

"I know. I try. But he wants to be so involved in every damn thing. It's sweet, but these aren't his abilities, they're mine. Why can't he let me just be my own person? You know I love him to death, but you've got to admit that he's a little on the needy side. He loves me so much that he's making me want to run from him! Does that make any sense?"

Cain gave her a small smile. "You're a very independent person. There's nothing wrong with that. Mattie loves that about you too, so don't think that he wants you to change. You are very different people. He needs you, Alyson, and yet you don't need him in quite the same way. I know you say that you do, but he can't really see it. That frightens him sometimes. Not that he would have you change, he just doesn't want to be left behind."

"I wouldn't!" she assured him defensively. "I mean, I'm not planning to leave him, but I need to have *some* room to breathe, you know?"

"I know. You've been together for quite some time already. You've both changed a bit over the years; I'm surprised this type of situation hasn't arisen earlier," he said as he went back to work.

Allie shrugged. "It has, but we've always worked it out, and things just seem extra-intensified lately. Thing is, Mattie has always been the stable one, strong and secure, grounded in reality. I'll admit, I can be a little flighty. I know it. But it was okay because Mattie loved to see me fly. He didn't try to hold me down, he loved the idea that I wasn't afraid to do things that he wouldn't dare. And knowing that he was there, made things so easy. He would always be there to catch me, so I wasn't afraid to fall. It's like, I was a kite soaring high on the wind, and Mattie was happy to hold the string. He wasn't really trying to control me; he just wanted to hold on. I love him, I really do. But he's never going to fly, Cain! I want to fly!

I thought maybe he'd share that with me now. That without human concerns and responsibilities, he could let go of being so restrained, and we could truly share the adventure. Look at everything he's been given! He's young, free, and immortal! And what does he want? He wants to settle down and live a normal life. He wishes he could work a 9 to 5 and raise a family! I don't get that!"

Cain did not seem nearly as sympathetic as she'd hoped. In fact, he seemed a bit disappointed in her. "Alyson, Mattie is the same man he always was. Becoming a vampire doesn't always change who you are; and when it does, it's not usually for the better. Those of us who retain ourselves are just that – ourselves. You've known Mattie always, and you know that he hasn't been anyone but who he always was."

She tried to explain it without sounding ridiculous. Of course, she knew Mattie, but... "But I didn't! I mean, I know him, and I love him, and it's not like I want him to be anyone else, but...he seemed different when I was human; darker and sort of mysterious. He was so secretive."

Cain stopped the tattoo machine and put it down with a thud. "He was trying to protect you, not lure you on!"

"Maybe that's the problem, it made him more alluring than ever!"

"Allie, that's not fair."

She looked into his eyes and tried to force him to see things from her point of view. "I know, but it's true. Doesn't he know *me* at all? Doesn't he know that I don't want the things he wants? I'm not the docile, happy housewife type! He is absolutely devastated that he can't have children now. I never even wanted kids! I know he's traveled a little, but it was only because he was biding his time until he could come back home. He's not daring or adventurous! Why do you think he wants me with him? It's only with me, that he has any desire to explore what we are now at all!

If I didn't enjoy being a vampire so much, he'd hate it to the core! He only tentatively tries to accept being a vampire, because he knows that for me…it's integral! This is who I am now! Those don't even seem like the right words, it's more like this is who I was always meant to be! If he turns his back on the vampire and tries to be human, not only will he not succeed, but he'll also lose me in the process. So instead, he tries to control it. He tries to control it to death!

I have powers! Shouldn't I use them? I have thirst! Shouldn't I quench it? There are opportunities open to me beyond the wildest dreams of most people! Am I just supposed to ignore the possibilities, so I can comfort him into pretending that we can live a normal life? It's not fair! He gave me this incredible gift, and then makes me feel guilty every time I try to use it!" She could tell that Cain felt she was exaggerating a bit. Maybe she was, but she needed him to understand how she felt. "It's not my fault that he doesn't want to come to terms with what he can do, and who he can be!"

Cain let out a small, mirthless laugh that seemed almost laced with pity. "That's the problem. It's not a question of coming to terms with what he can be. It's the fact that he is already happy with who he is. You want him to want more…and he doesn't."

Her ire faded as she realized that as annoying as it was, he was absolutely right. She wanted him to side with her so badly, to sympathize, telling her that it wasn't her fault, but he was right. She was the one who needed to re-examine her view.

Cain reached out and took her hands into his own over the table. "Alyson, you and Mattie have your differences, and you may each want different things, but that doesn't mean your love can't last. Compromise is the key, for both of you. I know Mattie is trying, but it takes two. You have the gift of empathy, use it! Be willing to see things from his side, even if it isn't what you want to see. The past cannot be changed. All you can do is make things right between you now, no matter how difficult."

He gave her hands a little squeeze. "There is an old saying I've often turned to for comfort and strength: Each day, we must make every effort to do what is right, and pray that we have the strength to do it again tomorrow."

She squeezed his hands in return and let them go. "Maybe that's the tattoo *I* need."

He winked at her playfully. "I thought about it myself, but it's a bit long."

She shrugged. "I'm small, but I've still got plenty of space left." She lifted her leg to rest her foot on the edge of the table. "I've got a whole blank leg here. You can write it in that fancy calligraphy of yours, and dress it up with pretty colors."

He laughed and pushed her foot off the table, causing her leg to drop. "I've only got black. You're welcome to borrow the machine sometime, but leave me out of it. Tell you what, let's put off the manipulation exercises until another time. Somehow, I think that is your area of least concern," he added with a teasing smirk of disapproval. "Now why don't you go plan out how you might spend some quality time with your husband, and let me finish this."

She let her shoulders slump as she answered with a pout. "He went out somewhere and he's blocking me from finding him. I guess I brushed him off one too many times." She looked up, suddenly realizing that Mattie had broken Cain's ordinance that they remain on the grounds.

Cain didn't seem to care, although he recognized the sudden worry in her, that she'd ratted him out. He smiled. "I know where he is. He spoke to me before leaving…and no, I don't think it would be wise for you to go after him, no matter how it might help your marital troubles. It's too dangerous for you to be out wandering around on your own."

She shot him a look of betrayal to go with her pout, but he was unmoved. "He'll be back before dawn," Cain assured her. "If I were you, I'd go back to the trailer and plan him a proper welcome for his return."

She let out a resigned sigh, and stood from her chair, dumping her empty mug in the sink. After a moment of thought, she opened the cabinet behind her, took out the bottle of rum, and held it up for Cain's attention. "Mind if I take this?" she asked.

He chuckled. "Go ahead."

She lifted it to him in tribute. "Thanks…for everything," she told him sincerely, and then headed back to the trailer, making plans to show Mattie just how much she truly did need him.

~~~~~~~~~~~~~~~~~~~~~~~~~~~~~~~

Allie readjusted herself on the bed as she heard the trailer door open. She'd felt Mattie's return a little while ago, but he'd been taking his time before finally approaching the trailer. He must know she was in there. They could clearly feel each other physically through their marks at this close range.

Flower petals covered almost every surface of the bedroom where there wasn't a candle burning. Hopefully Cain wouldn't mind that she'd raided the rose bush by the back porch. They were past peak anyway this late in the season. She'd chosen to wear what she hoped was Mattie's favorite lingerie set, a sheer and frilly lavender number he'd given her a while back. She'd been into more leather than lace lately, but decided that feminine and docile was definitely more the way to go tonight, and traded her high-heeled, thigh-high leather boots for some dainty feathered slippers. Her shoulder length hair was down, and a bit mussed, in what she hoped was a playfully sexy fashion.

Mattie entered the trailer and took his time moving about the kitchen and front room before making his way back into the bedroom. By the time he got there, he seemed resigned and tired, as though he wasn't looking forward to seeing her. Even when he took in the state of the room and Allie's pose on the bed, he didn't give much of a smile. Apparently, this was going to take a bit more than good sex to smooth over.

"Hi," she said softly, with a hopeful lilt.

"Hey." He glanced around the room and then back at her. "You've been busy," he said, noting the flower petals.

"You like?"

He gave a half-hearted shrug. "It's nice."

She stared at him a moment, before sitting up and begging him with psychic current to give her his attention and forgiveness. "Talk to me. What's going on?"

He looked almost insulted that she felt the need to ask. Finally, he shrugged. "I feel like you're using me."

That wasn't quite what she'd expected to hear. "What?"

He furrowed his brow in disbelief that she'd dispute it. "Totally. Do you not get that? With your empathy, and telepathy, and everything…or do you only read what you want to read, just like you only hear what you want to hear?"

She opened her mouth with a bit of disdain at the accusation. Not knowing how to refute it, she finally insisted, "You know I love you."

"Yeah, I do, but I also feel like I'm just very convenient lately. You wake up in the evening and you drink from me. Then, if *you* feel like it, you jump my bones, and then you head out to do whatever it is you want to do. You come back to the trailer just before dawn, you drink from me again, and then you pass out. Sleep, wake, repeat."

"It's not *just* like that."

"Isn't it?"

She tried to give him a seductive smile. "Sometimes *you* jump *me*."

He squinted at her. "Really, when? Think about it. When is the last time *I* initiated? I doubt you can remember, because I sure as hell can't. 'Cause I'm not feelin' it, Allie. Not a whole lot of *romantic* going on here, with or without candles and flowers." Okay, she should probably admit if only to herself, that other than tonight, it had been a while since she truly worried about what would turn *him* on.

Mattie continued, reluctantly. "Even when we do make love, you're...bossy."

"You love when I'm bossy in bed," she reminded him, crossing her arms.

"I like when you play at being bossy," he corrected her. "Now you're just demanding, and impatient, and...I don't know, Allie, you're just not you lately."

"Really?" Despite the fact that she was supposed to be trying to make-up with him, she couldn't keep the harsh sarcasm out of her voice. "Then who the hell am I? Oh, I know. Maybe I'm a *descendant of darkness*. Am I evil? Is that it? Maybe Arif was right. You think this blood is changing me and making me *evil Allie?*"

Now his arms were crossed, and he looked annoyed more than alarmed. "Well, wouldn't that be convenient."

"Again with the *convenient*. What are you talking about?"

"Well, I'm sure it would be easy to blame everything on something beyond your control, but I don't buy it. You're stronger than that. The Allie I know, has a will stronger than any blood, United or not. Now if you've got a real problem, and you think you're getting out of control, then tell me, and we'll deal with it. Otherwise, own up and cut the shit."

After staring her down he finally un-tensed and sat next to her on the bed. Why did she have such a hard time admitting when she was wrong? She peeked up at him through her lashes. "I'm not evil," she told him quietly.

He smiled. "No kidding."

He'd tried to caution her gently so many times, and she'd just turned a blind eye and kept doing what she wanted, knowing he'd just take it. Why did she always have to push things to the limit? "I have been a selfish bitch though, huh?"

"Kind of, yeah."

"I'm sorry. I don't know why I get like that. I don't mean to be."

"I know. You have a lot going on, I get that. But I'm supposed to be a part of that…at least a little. I don't plan to spend eternity sitting on the sidelines."

"And I don't plan to leave you there. But I can't join you there either, if you can understand that." He understood what she meant, although he didn't like the fact that she thought his idea of a safe, happy, semi-normal existence was not something she could entirely embrace. There had to be a middle ground, though. They'd find it. "Forgive me?"

He sighed. "I want to."

"Look, no matter what else is going on, you and me, we have to be a top priority, because without us, nothing else matters. I'm sorry if I lost sight of that, but I won't again. I promise."

Now he was able to give her a small smile to go with his nod of agreement. He was wounded, but they'd be okay. He needed some cajoling to get things back to where they needed to be. That, she could handle. She snuggled closer to him and then undid the top string that held her nightie together. "Want to jump my bones? I'll be totally submissive, I swear. You can even tie me up."

He laughed. "Like anything could hold you." He shook his head gently. "I'm tired. Maybe tomorrow night."

He gave her a soft kiss on the forehead and stood to get undressed for bed. Vampires don't even get physically tired, just mentally weary. Wow, rejected. He never turned her down. Maybe that was the problem. He was so…comfortable, always there for her. He'd decided it was better to assert himself for a change and make her wait, make her work for it. Okay, she could handle that. "Not tomorrow," she said as he slid beneath the covers, his back to her. "Tomorrow I have something else planned for us."

Now he turned to look at her. "What?"

She smiled and turned out the light as possibilities flitted through her mind. "You'll see."

~~~~~~~~~~~~~~~~~~~~~~~~~~~~~~~

"Where?" Mattie asked.

"Out. Just you and me. I thought we'd hit a club or something. It's Saturday night, I'm sure there's something cool going on somewhere. I'd forgotten how much I miss going out to the bar. We used to have a good time dancing and drinking all night."

Now her outfit made sense to him. He eyed her boots and short leather skirt. She wasn't wearing any panties, and she silently let him know it. A slight flush rose in his cheeks, and then he allowed his gaze to travel up her legs and beyond, to her peaked nipples jutting proudly against the material of the flimsy top she wore. He was totally turned on by the look, but he still wasn't on board with the idea. "Allie, we can't. You know Cain wants us to stick to the grounds."

"He didn't care when you went out last night," she pointed out.

"It was a coffee shop, considerably more low key than anything you have in mind. Besides, I'm not the United One."

"Oh come on. It's not like I'm going out by myself, you'll be with me. We haven't been out alone together in forever! I know you like it when we go dancing."

He couldn't hide the little smirk that stole over his face. "Can't deny that I like to watch that body move," he admitted. "But we really shouldn't."

Her foray with Sindy had convinced her that there was no true harm in a secret outing. Why shouldn't Mattie benefit from her boldness? "Cain is totally over-reacting anyway. What have we got to worry about? So, there was one vampire shade hanging around for a little while. It could have been any lost vampire, who stumbled onto us, and stuck around to spy a little. It happens to Cain all the time. Young vamps come looking for *the teacher* they've heard about, and expect him to fix their lives. It probably had nothing to do with me. We haven't even seen the thing in ages. Come on," she urged with a little hip swivel, "I want to grind against you to the beat."

He laughed, trying without success to hide how her words affected him. "We do have a stereo here at home."

She held him with her human gaze, using her feminine wiles every bit as effectively as her vampire wiles would have worked. "I want to feel it pounding through me," she told him with a throaty purr. "I want to watch you watching me through flashing pulses of light, while the crowd all around just can't take their eyes off us. I want to see the other girls shyly watching and wishing they could touch you, while knowing that later I'll be letting you *take me* up against the building in the parking lot where they might even walk by... Take me out Mattie."

~~~~~~~~~~~~~~~~~~~~~~~~~~~~~~

Mattie was accompanying Alyson to the farthest back reaches of the property, to observe a hunt she would participate in with the Crimson Coven. A plausible lie. She and Sindy had been back there a few times already, and Sindy really was hunting with them this evening, with orders not to mention Alyson's absence. The grounds stretched far past Cain's psychic awareness, so he wouldn't expect to be able to feel or see their marks, and communication was not so fluent between Cain and the shape shifters for Allie to worry that she and Mattie would be missed for the few hours they'd be gone.

Downtown Syracuse had been the final destination. It was about a hundred and fifty miles away from home, twice as far as she'd gone with Sindy, but Allie had literally flown them down Interstate 90 in record time, and the distance gave Mattie the freedom to relax and focus on her, rather than worrying that Cain or anyone else might have seen or followed them. She was certain to assure him that he had her undivided attention, and it was something he obviously appreciated.

A club called *Fuel* was where Alyson had lured Mattie to let go of his inhibitions, and had fueled his fire to act out all that she'd described and more. It was about 4 a.m. when they found themselves leaning against the sidewall of an alcove on Clinton Street outside the club. Allie had her legs wrapped around his hips, and although his strong hands cupped her ass under her skirt, she levitated to keep her full weight from him. He leaned his head onto her shoulder, thoroughly spent and loving every minute of it.

The street was dark and quiet, the glow of the old-fashioned style street lamps making the red bricks along the sidewalks glisten, slick with frost. The club was closing now though, and sending its last patrons out the front door to disturb the cold and silent night. After not allowing herself to drink from Mattie during their escapade, Alyson could feel the predator within her practically screaming for her to hunt and bring it blood, but she ignored it as best as she could. The human blood she'd drunk the night before had lasted a long time, but the flight out here seemed to have wiped out the last of her reserves.

Mattie struggled to adjust his clothing properly as she lowered her legs to the ground and smoothed down her skirt. Loud and laughing college students stumbled past them down the street. Allie ignored their beckoning heartbeats, focusing instead on the rush of thrilling indecency than ran through her lover over their very close timing. He met her eyes, and they shared a laugh and a kiss. It had been a good night. Just what they'd needed.

Mattie glanced up at the sky. It was a clear and beautiful fall night with what looked to be a million stars in the sky. There was no sign of the approaching dawn. They still had a good three hours left until sunrise, and it wouldn't take them more than half of that time to get home. Still, she knew he liked to play it safe and she'd already pushed him pretty far out of his comfort zone this evening. It was time to head back. She tipped her face up towards his for another kiss first. He surprised her by making it a deep and fulfilling one; his last few moments of forgetting worries and the world to indulge in this little adventure with her.

He ended the kiss and then gave her a smile. "Beam me up, Allie."

She laughed and gave a quick glance around to assure they were alone again before lifting him into the air to begin their journey home. She generally liked to follow the roadways, because it was easier to keep her bearings without really paying attention, and at 4:30 a.m. no one was around to notice two people flying by fifty feet in the air above the street.

They were just outside of Rochester, about halfway home, flying over I-90 where it cut through Royal Coach Park, the normally lush, green space, now seeming barren and dead as the leafless trees prepared for the coming of winter. Allie and Mattie were making good time, with even a slight breeze helping them along, when Allie began to feel herself weakening. Her need for blood was borderline alarming, but that wasn't her only concern. She felt very oddly drained...or maybe dampened was a better word, as though a wet blanket had been thrown over the burning embers of her abilities. It was probably from lack of blood, but it felt different from times when she'd been depleted in the past. She was losing altitude and she couldn't account for why. Was she just running out of steam? She brought them down to ground-fall and told Mattie she needed a break.

There was a steep embankment on one side of the road. She made her way to it and sat leaning against the graveled side of the hill with her hands on her knees. They were in a stretch of state land that was quiet and deserted, and would probably stay that way without the usual weekday morning traffic, considering it was now a little after 5 a.m. on a Sunday.

Mattie followed her to the side of the road in concern. She looked up, feeling a bit uneasy, but not wanting to alarm him. "I don't know what's going on. I feel really drained, like I'm suddenly completely out of juice."

She scanned the area, hoping to see something warm-blooded, but nothing offered. She'd still felt so confidently satisfied from the human blood she'd drunk last night, that she hadn't even thought to bring a flask with her.

"Do you want to drink from me? Would that help?" Mattie asked.

"I don't know...maybe. You can't have anything with much oomph in it though. You haven't had anything to drink except what you drank from me before we left."

Mattie couldn't hide the smile that flashed across his face at the erotic memory. He'd refused to make love to her when they'd first awoken, but he'd done some very seductive drinking from various places on her body, without allowing her to take it back. She'd forced herself to obey his request, denying herself his blood. It had really fanned both of their desires and made the anticipation for the end of the evening that much more heightened. Realizing their current situation, Mattie quickly lost his smile to a flush of guilt, and came back to focusing on the matter at hand. "Yeah, but my blood has got to have more energy left in it than yours. I haven't been flying us across the city."

Allie took another look around. Across the interstate from them was mostly open flat land without much to see, but she knew that there were woods above and behind them. There had to be wildlife in there. She just wasn't able to sense it far enough in because of the embankment. "Maybe I should shift for a quick hunt."

Mattie immediately dismissed the idea. "No way. You aren't going off without me, and it's not a sure bet anyway. It'll be dawn in less than two hours, but we can still get home the old-fashioned way if we get moving. Let's start walking and get ready to stick your thumb out if a car comes by."

"I don't think I can fly, but maybe I can still run. I'll piggy-back you."

She knew he felt a little foolish, but when she presented her back to him, he allowed her to help him on. It was a struggle. In fact, it took only a second for Allie to realize it wasn't going to work. She couldn't really lift him, not for any length of time anyway. He seemed as heavy to her as…well, as a hundred and fifty-five pound guy should feel to a young woman of her petite stature. "What the hell is going on?"

"Your powers…all of your powers, not just the flight but the strength and probably your speed too, they're not working. Was it the long flight? I knew we shouldn't have gone so far."

She shook her head. "It's not that. Something weird is going on."

Mattie wasn't so sure. "You should drink from me, right now, before it gets worse, and then let's concentrate on getting home."

A scuffling noise startled Allie to turn and look up, just as some dirt and pebbles sifted down into her hair from the hilltop above. A young Asian man stood there above her, with an ominous grin on his face. "Drink all you want," he told her, "it won't help."

Mattie stood back a step to see the man better, as Allie fully turned and stood to be closer to Mattie and face the stranger. Before they could even really take in the fact that this man showed no psychic life-force aura, meaning that he must be a cloaked vampire, he was joined from behind by two others. Both were large, ill groomed Caucasian men. They looked as though they belonged in a biker gang, not a state park. One wore leather, the other denim, and neither looked very friendly.

What did the guy mean 'drinking won't help'? Her powers were gone? How was that possible? Before she could even decipher that, or what the three vampires might be doing there, all three men suddenly rushed at them, jumping down onto the road.

The two biker guys went straight for Mattie, who immediately yelled, "Allie, run!"

Run? No way was she leaving him there. She did turn, as though she was planning to take off down the road, but only to catch the Asian dude off guard as he came running after her. She suddenly stopped on a dime and spun with a well-placed kick at his head. She'd caught him off guard but didn't fully connect. His reflexes were quick, and he avoided most of the blow. Still, at least she'd rattled him a little. "My powers may be on the fritz, but I'm still a black belt in jui jitsu, creep. You don't know who you're dealing with."

She took a half-hearted swing at his face that was really a feint. As he reached out an arm to block her, she grabbed that arm, placed one foot on his knee and then jumped up to swing her other leg around over his head, to spin and flip him over her down to the ground. Considering her short skirt and lack of panties, she surely gave him quite a show in the process, but she wasn't in a state of mind to worry about it, and any distraction was an advantage.

Unfortunately, he was better trained than that. As soon as he hit the ground, he managed to roll and bend his arm before she could lock it into the arm-bar hold she wanted. He was far stronger than she was, and he knew how to counter what she'd done. In fact, he turned it on her, and she found herself suddenly pinned in a hold she was unfamiliar with. "Black belt, really?" he asked, taunting her. "'Cause, I don't see it."

A frightened chill ran through her as she realized this was someone who knew martial arts, far better than she did. She never did quite make it to black belt as she'd boasted, and she hadn't practiced anything at all in years. When she'd been a young human woman wanting to protect herself from vampires, her training had served her well. But since converting to the other side of that fight, she'd come to rely heavily on her vampiric abilities, and honestly never thought she'd need anything more. She was soft.

The guy wasn't beating the hell out of her though, he was holding her. If he was trying to kill her, wouldn't he have landed another blow immediately after pinning her?

"Allie!" Mattie had broken away from the other men and was rushing towards her. "Get off of her!" he yelled at her attacker. He didn't make it much farther. She couldn't see him from her angle, but she heard the others catch up to him, and his strangled yell as they resumed their fight. She hoped to God he'd be okay, as she concentrated on her own problem. Mattie hadn't truly been able to help her, but he'd been just the distraction she'd needed to get herself out of the situation she was in. As the man pinning her glanced up and made ready to ward off Mattie, Alyson was able to squirm out of his grasp.

She tried to roll him, but it didn't work, and her best avenue was to just back the hell away before he could grab hold of her again. She got to her feet and quickly swiped the hair from her face so she could see. The wind was picking up and not only her hair, but autumn leaves and twigs seemed to be flying everywhere.

Alyson involuntarily flinched as she felt a blast of pain wash over her and took a second to realize it wasn't hers. Her attention was drawn to find Mattie and the other vampires now fighting completely across the road and on the grass of the other side. The guy in leather was holding Mattie's arms behind his back as the other man punched him in the face. The guy had gotten in a really bad blow, but as he wound up for another, Mattie lifted his legs and managed to kick the man back away from him.

Alyson couldn't watch anymore, because the man she had been grappling with was coming towards her again. Oddly, he wasn't running at her or seeming to set up for a new fighting approach. He brushed himself off and smiled, seeming very self-assured about something. That worried her more than if he'd been running at her with a war cry.

She backed up a step as she smoothed down her skirt, and was startled to find she had backed into someone. She had been facing the road where Mattie and his attackers were, and the last time she'd checked, there had been nothing behind her but the steep hill. Someone else must have joined them while she was distracted.

She spun and was surprised to see that she'd backed into not a man, but a woman...a very tall and thin but shapely woman. She looked up to see a statuesque beauty, probably in her early thirties, with sharp features and incredibly long blonde hair blowing about her in the breeze. The woman wore a confident smirk on her face. "Thank you, Jin. I'll take it from here." She grabbed Allie by the bicep to pull her close, and before Allie could react, there was a wickedly sharp knife jabbing up against the side of her throat. Not something that could really kill her, but it was hard to fight instinct and allow yourself to be stabbed in the neck to try and escape. She probably wouldn't get far with Jin standing right there anyway.

The woman nudged her further with the point for emphasis. "That's enough rolling around. We're going to have a little girl talk. Act like a lady, and you and your boyfriend can go home when we're all done. Okay?"

She shoved Alyson towards Jin, who grabbed hold and twisted her hand into a wristlock to keep her controlled. The woman spoke to Jin, while she put the knife away. "You just hold her and keep your mojo focused no matter what. Clear?"

Jin twisted Allie's wrist a little to make her wince. "Crystal," he answered. Damn, where the hell was her strength? She had gotten so used to her extra vampiric powers, that she felt incredibly weak without them. At least they would be released unharmed, if the woman was to be trusted. What the hell was going on?

The woman stood before her, and crossed her arms as though deciding how to proceed. It gave Allie a chance to better assess her. She wore a tight black body suit that zipped up the front. It made her look vaguely like a comic super-villain or something, her long straight blonde hair swinging down behind her to replace the image of a cape, but honestly, the outfit was just the kind of thing Allie would wear, if she planned to do any fighting. She had a low-slung belt around her hips that held the sheath for what looked like a samurai sword. A sword…really? Who were these people?

The belt had a smaller sheath as well, where the knife had been housed. Also slung in with the weapons was something odd. It was a large, flat, clear plastic bag attached to a looped length of tubing, like they use for hospital I.V's. Alyson thought about teasing the woman with a quip about having a colostomy bag, but decided she'd better save it for when she was in a better position.

The woman smiled and Alyson was startled to see her eyes suddenly shift from their human brown color into a hypnotizing violet purple. Allie found herself fascinated, unable to look away from them, even though the whipping wind made her eyes water.

"Okay doll, item number one. You don't recognize me, and you never will. I might as well be invisible. Got that?" Alyson slowly blinked, trying to understand what the woman could mean. Of course she didn't recognize her. She'd never seen her before. The woman was staring at her intently.

After a moment, she spoke to Jin without breaking her gaze with Alyson. "She's got a lot of walls up in there. I hope I'm getting through. You sure she isn't more than you can handle?"

Alyson heard Jin answer from over her shoulder. "Shields down, Lorelei. Navigating her natural mental baggage is your problem."

"Damn it! Lorelei!" They were interrupted by a yell from across the road.

Lorelei grunted with supreme annoyance, before turning to see the two men chasing after Mattie, who was running towards them across the empty two-lane highway.

"Allie!" he yelled, as one of the guys took him down after only a short distance, tackling and rolling with him on the stretch of dirt in the median. The men dragged Mattie back across the road, to be further away from Lorelei, and not disturb her.

Lorelei looked livid. "Good grief, he is practically a boy. You'd think they could keep him occupied and shut him up for ten lousy minutes so I could concentrate. Must I do everything myself?"

Alyson blinked and focused her eyes on Mattie struggling in the street. "Mattie!" She tried to twist away from Jin's hold, but only managed to cause a severe stab of pain to shoot up her arm.

"Shut up," Lorelei barked at her, sweeping that violet gaze back to face her. As their eyes met, the heavens seemed to open up with a sudden fierce driving rain. Lorelei stared right through it, unfaltering, although large drops of water gathered and dripped from her lashes.

A screeching yell pierced the night, making Lorelei flinch, but she held her gaze steady. Jin looked across the road and apprised her of the situation. "Shit, John's been staked!"

Lorelei let out a huff of annoyance. "Where the hell did he get a stake?" Alyson smiled. She and Mattie always carried stakes, upon Cain's insistence. She had one in her boot too. She wished she'd pulled it out earlier, rather than trying to fight Jin in hand to hand combat. Her reflexes and habits were too attuned to her vampire powers. A lot of good that was doing now.

Lorelei raised a hand to touch Allie's chin, demanding full attention, although Alyson found herself unable to break eye contact anyway. "Don't move until I return." She let go and allowed her eyes to turn brown again as she turned to Jin. "Stay on her."

With that, Lorelei stalked across the street to where Mattie was lying face first in the dirt on the side of the road, with the large man in leather on top of him. The man had a knee pressing down onto the back of Mattie's neck while holding his arm twisted behind his back. Lorelei stopped a few feet away. "Ed, you're not having a problem here, are you? Because I really resent being interrupted." Alyson could just barely hear her through the wind and rain.

Ed looked up and gave Mattie's neck a little dig with his knee. "Don't worry, I've got him now. You want me to dust him? He took out John." The man nodded towards the place where his partner had been. The ash was becoming little more than a dark spot of sludge splattered across the concrete by the rain.

Lorelei barely spared it a glance. "I see that, but I want him *un*dead, if you can manage. She'll be much easier to manipulate if he's unharmed. Dust him, and she'll go psycho. I don't think even Jin could control her at that point."

Ed nodded. "It's okay, I've got him." He wound his hand into Mattie's hair and pulled, making Mattie crane his neck up to face he and Lorelei. "You'll calm down and be a good boy now, won't you, so we don't have to kill your girl?"

Even from across the road, Alyson could see Mattie's eyes go wide with recognition, and see a stab of fear and hatred go through him as he saw Lorelei before him.

"Hi there lover boy, remember me? We had such fun a few years back. You shouldn't have left my party so early. Things could have been much different." Alyson wondered what she could mean, but Mattie's mind was blank to her. She couldn't read where he might know the woman from.

Mattie scrunched his eyes closed tight, causing Lorelei to stomp the ground demandingly by his face. "Look at me when I'm talking to you." She gave a little kick that splashed muddy water from the fast forming puddles into Mattie's face, but he kept his eyes closed tightly. "Open your eyes, damn it."

Thunder rumbled and rolled overhead. It seemed to accentuate her frustration. Lorelei glanced at the sky and then backed away a step. She then crouched down close to Mattie's face and spoke in a softer tone. "Fine. Be that way. I took a lot of flak for losing you, and now…" she said with a sharply ironic laugh, "now you're practically worthless. Nothing but an annoying little shit." She stood and kicked a last bit of mud at him. "Maybe when we're done with her," she said with a nod towards Allie, "I'll come back and collect you for a pet."

"Hold him," she told Ed. "I'll just be a few minutes."

Large, stinging pellets of icy hail began to rain down around them as she turned to walk away. Ed kept his knee firmly against Mattie's neck, but let go of his hold on Mattie's hair to shield himself. "What the fuck? New York weather sucks."

Lorelei ignored him and rejoined the others. Jin was still holding Alyson by the wrist. They both involuntarily hunched over, ducking their heads to avoid the pelting balls of ice raining down around them that seemed to be increasing in size by the minute. Lorelei cast a quick eye towards the sky, sheltering her face with one hand. "At least we won't have to worry about an early sunrise through those clouds." She brought her now purple gaze back to meet Allie's eyes. "Let's finish this."

Jin shook his head. "I can't believe he took out John. I guess you underestimated the power of true love," he teased with a smirk.

Lorelei rolled her eyes as she took out something from a small pouch on her belt. "He's feisty," she told Allie with a smile. "I should have remembered. It's always the quiet ones you have to watch out for. Now where were we?" Allie began to struggle as she realized that what Lorelei had taken from her belt was a syringe, which was attached to the length of catheter tubing she'd noticed earlier.

"Stay still and you'll barely feel a thing," Lorelei ordered as she took Allie by her free wrist and exposed the inside of her arm. The hail stopped, and suddenly the wind died as well. All was strangely silent and calm. Lorelei looked up from where she'd been inspecting Allie's arm. "That's better," she said in thanks towards the sky. She touched the needle to Allie's skin, but as she applied pressure to puncture it, the sky lit up in a flash like daylight. The brightness was accompanied by an ear-splitting crack and blood-curdling scream, making Lorelei drop the syringe.

They were all drawn to look towards Mattie and Ed, just in time to see a very strange sight. Ed seemed to be glowing from within, and then he exploded into a cloud of dust.

After a second of shock, Lorelei asked in high-pitched alarm, "What the hell was that?"

Jin met her gaze in frightened awe. "I think he was struck by lightning."

Lorelei looked confused. "Can we be killed by lightning?"

Jin straightened from where he'd been hunched over them. "I'd add it to the list. It's like intense fire, right?"

Lorelei straightened as well. Alyson stood with them, one hand held in Lorelei's loose grasp, and the other still in Jin's grip, although no longer in a wristlock. They watched as Mattie rose from the ground and stood, slowly and shakily. He looked around and spotted them.

The wind unexpectedly returned with a vengeance, swirling around them for a moment like a private tornado. Mattie began walking towards them in the darkness with a look of eerie intensity. Lorelei let go of Alyson and shoved Jin's shoulder for attention. "It's him," she told Jin over the wind. "He's doing it. Stop him."

Jin glanced back at Alyson in worry. "I can't handle him and the girl too."

"If you don't, we're toast!" she insisted. Thunder sounded with a loud and ominous crash. The wind died out again to cause a scary stillness, and Lorelei's long blonde hair began to fan out oddly around her, charged and ionized. Lorelei grabbed Jin and pulled him from Allie to shove him out in front between she and Mattie, shielding herself. Her hair stood out around her like the needles of a sea urchin. She screamed at Jin in a desperate panic. "Dampen him or he'll fry me!"

Alyson was standing behind Jin next to Lorelei, staring at Mattie, forgotten by the others and trying to figure out what the hell was going on, when she suddenly felt strength flood back into her limbs. Her power was back, and it seemed that Lorelei's directive to stay still was no longer binding her either. With her powers unimpeded, she was psychically strong enough to over-ride such a confining order.

After a second of realization that she was free, she pulled the stake from her boot. Although she didn't understand Jin's control over her powers, he was certainly the most dangerous threat of the two vampires before her. She lunged at him with the stake, but he blocked her with his arm at the last second. He knew that in freeing her powers, he would have to try to protect himself from her.

The weather seemed to have calmed, and Lorelei's hair hung down damp and loose again. However, as soon as Jin took his eyes off Mattie to attend to Alyson, Lorelei screamed and ran to get behind them again. "Jin! Forget her, knock him out or something."

Lorelei pulled her sword and moved to separate Allie from Jin, putting the blade between them. Jin turned to meet Mattie before he reached the women, while Lorelei forced Allie's attention. "Call him off. You know I wasn't going to actually hurt you."

Alyson dropped the hand holding the stake back down to her side and almost laughed, despite the situation. "I don't control him. I've never even seen him do that before, but you really pissed him off. And you know what else?" she asked with a chuckle. "If he can do that," she said with a glance at the sky, "what do you think the odds are that I can too?"

Lorelei shifted into her vampire visage, betraying her panicky fear. Alyson could sense the woman's psychic command for obedience, but without a blood bond, her purple gaze couldn't have a strong effect on Alyson while she was on guard against it. Lorelei pointed her blade level with Alyson's throat, and Allie had no doubt that the woman knew how to use it. "I'll take your head clean off."

"Wouldn't that turn all my blood into ash?" she asked with a pointed glance at the empty bag at Lorelei's hip.

Lorelei suddenly turned and swung her blade around to threaten Mattie instead. "I don't need *his* blood though."

Jin had been holding Mattie at bay through a combination of power dampening and physical presence. Now he moved around behind Mattie to give Lorelei a clearer path with her sword. All three vampires stared at Alyson, wondering what her reaction to the threat would be. Lorelei's sword was held menacingly before Mattie. Surely, her skills were such that she could harm him with it before he could get safely out of the way.

Alyson's gaze bore into the woman. Allie could feel Jin flickering his dampening skills between her and Mattie alternately, ready to hold them wherever needed. Now that the weather had calmed, Alyson was fairly sure that Mattie would need to stoke it up to full force again before pulling off another lightning strike…if he even knew what the hell he was doing. She certainly had no idea how to do it.

Alyson let her eyes glaze over white, sending an icy stab of fear into the other vampires. "You wouldn't dare," she told Lorelei imposingly. "I'm pretty sure going home with an empty bag would be preferable to what you'd unleash if you harm even one more hair on his head."

Lorelei took in the sight of Alyson's white vampire eyes with her own glittering purple ones, and then dropped her gaze in surrender. She turned and gave Jin a meaningful look, and then re-sheathed her sword as though unconcerned. "Fine," she said looking back up at Allie.

Alyson felt Jin's attention focus on her again, her powers ebbing, but surely it was only so that he and Lorelei could safely retreat. "Forget me and the bag," Lorelei practically spat at her. She turned to look at Mattie in disdain. "Forget I was even here." She began backing away, letting her line of sight shift from Mattie to Alyson and then back again. "Let's go Jin." In an instant, the two were gone, over the embankment and out of sight.

"Should we go after him?" Allie asked shakily.

Mattie glanced in the direction the vampires had taken, but lightly shook his head. "He isn't worth it. We need to get home before the sun comes up. Let's get out of here."

~~~~~~~~~~~~~~~~~~~~~~~~~~~~~~~~~

Alyson lay in bed next to Mattie, trying to fight off the heavy veil of sleep that was trying to steal over her. Damn it, why couldn't she stay awake after sunrise like he could? They desperately needed to talk! The flight home had been a frantic race against the threatening daylight, and although she could read and vaguely respond to all of the confused and jumbled thoughts that were going through Mattie's head, what they needed now was a real talk. Unfortunately, the sun was rising. She was out of time.

Although she knew it was a question he couldn't truly answer, and she didn't have time to properly delve into, she couldn't help but ask him as she closed her eyes, "How did you do that?"

Mattie gently stroked the hair from her face, and gave her a kiss as she felt herself losing consciousness. "They were going to hurt you. I would never let anyone hurt you." She let the blanket of unconsciousness that always accompanied daylight steal upon her with a satisfied smile.

Hours later, Alyson slowly arose from the depths of deep sleep, sifting through befuddled dreams and waking thoughts. She'd been having an odd dream that someone else had been in her head, and had told her what to do. It was maddening because although she was aware of the act, she couldn't divine the directive. She wondered if the invasive intrusiveness of it, was what Mattie and Cain felt when she was in their heads.

Mattie never seemed to notice, but Cain could always seem to tell when she'd been reading his thoughts. Cain usually let her know that he'd recognized her trying to plant a subtle idea in his head or pull a piece of information. He'd called her on it often enough, that she'd stopped trying rather than upset him. Still, she had to experiment once in a while didn't she? But who could give *her* a psychic command? The only other vampire in the area that she'd been told had the power, was Arif, and she hadn't seen him in ages. It was just a strange dream.

As Alyson gradually woke, the first thing she noticed was the cold. She opened her eyes and half expected to see a cloud of fog exhale from her lips, until she remembered that not only wasn't she breathing, whatever air was inside her wouldn't be warm enough to cause fog anyway. She turned her head to see Mattie lying quietly next to her. "Why is it so cold in here?" she asked.

She looked to see what he was concentrating on. He was staring out the open window. The tinted glass had been slid aside to give a clear view of the darkened night sky. No wonder it was freezing in here. As she watched, delicate snowflakes began drifting down, a stray breeze causing a few of them to float inside and land on the exposed bed.

After a moment, she turned to Mattie with a smile. "Are you doing that?" He simply shrugged. "Oh my God, you're making it snow!"

He shrugged again. "It snows in November all the time."

"Not when the forecast said it was going to be over 40 degrees tonight." She gave him a playful nudge. "It's you. You're making it snow."

"Maybe."

A broad smile stole upon her face as she snuggled closer to him under the covers. "What you did last night was awesome."

"What I did last night, was kill two people. I've only killed once before."

She watched him as he quietly focused on the snow falling outside the window. "Are you feeling bad about it?"

The wind shifted, suddenly making the snow change direction, before settling back into a steady downward path again. "Not really." He looked at her and gave her a solemn little smile. "I'd do it again. It's just sobering."

She nodded respectfully, but after a second or too she couldn't help the excitement bubbling within her. "You found your power! I told you there was untapped magic in you. I could see it in your mark. There's a lot of power there for someone who thought he couldn't do anything."

He chuckled. "Yeah. And of all the amazing abilities there could be," he said, looking at her with a strange little smirk, "out of all the X-Men, I get to be *Storm?* Kind of lame."

Allie laughed. "Storm isn't lame, I think she's cool. Anyway, you're way better than her."

He arched an eyebrow. "At least she can fly. I make pretty snowflakes," he added facetiously.

Allie laughed again and tickled him under the covers. "You caused a freakin' maelstrom last night. Rain, wind, hail, and you totally fried that guy. That's pretty badass if you ask me. You're my hero."

"I guess." Mattie lay there quietly thoughtful while accepting a hug. "But you can do it too, now that we know."

"Maybe, but you'll be way better at it than me."

"How do you figure? You're great at everything."

"Yeah but this is your thing. You can focus all of your energy on just mastering this one thing. And it's really cool, 'cause there's lots of different aspects to it; fog, rain, snow, wind…lightning. I'm scattered all over the place trying to learn everything at once, while you can just focus on the weather. We can work on it together, which'll be fun, but I'll never be as good at it as you'll be. That's okay. It can be *your* thing."

He nodded. "Fair enough. But why couldn't I do it before?"

She shrugged. "You never had a reason to, I guess. You were pretty worked up last night."

He shook his head. "I've been mad before. Maybe not over anything that was life or death, but even you manage to piss me off mighty good sometimes. You'd think that would be worth a little thunder at least; a gust of wind, something."

"Maybe you just haven't noticed."

"I don't know. I've been a vampire for like eight years now, Allie. Don't you think I *would* have noticed? I've been thinking about it since I woke up. It does seem to rain a lot when I'm sad…"

"See."

"But I can't ever remember being angry in a thunder storm. Maybe it's a power that's always been there, but it seems strange that it's never gotten intense enough to be noticeable. What's changed?"

"Well, maybe I've had some kind of influence on you. I've been doing so much talking about tapping into powers, maybe it put you in the right mindset."

He gently shook his head. "I think it'd have to be more than that."

Allie teased him with an accusing smile. "Well, you drank so much from me last night before we left, maybe you sucked the skill right out of me."

She was only joking, but Mattie took her seriously. After thinking about it, he shook his head. "You can't gain powers that way. But if it was already within me to do, there is a chance that drinking stronger blood could awaken it. I've been drinking your blood all along though. I'm used to it. It never made a difference."

The idea sparked something in Allie's mind as well. She sat up in the bed. "You know, Sindy always says that our shifting powers come more easily when we've been drinking live blood. She says it makes our venom stronger, and gives us way better control than drinking butcher blood does."

Mattie sat up as well, catching interest to her train of thought. "Live blood…like straight from animals?"

"M-hmm. It loses something once it's been put in the fridge for a while."

Mattie was definitely interested in the idea. It made sense, but he suddenly became deflated. "Yeah, but you haven't even been hunting lately. Ever since Cain stopped letting you guys go off into the woods alone, you've been drinking nothing but refrigerated blood, same as me. When's the last time you hunted with the Crimson Coven? Over a week ago, right?

Damn, I thought we had it. It makes sense that I'd be stronger from drinking live blood through you, but you haven't hunted."

Not animals... Allie's thoughts were racing. "Oh my God."

"What?"

She shook her head. "Nothing."

"You don't say 'Oh my God' for nothing, Allie. What is it? Tell me." She couldn't think what to say. She couldn't tell him, now that he finally wasn't mad at her anymore. "You *have* been hunting haven't you?" he asked. She glanced up at him in guilt-ridden surprise. "I know Sindy has been sneaking out to hunt. You've been doing that too? When? We're always together."

She tried to figure out what she should say, as he pieced it together. "Just the other night," Mattie continued, "you and Sindy said you spent the whole night practicing bat form together in the basement, while Cain and I went for supplies. Were you actually out hunting? Why didn't you just tell me?"

"I knew you wouldn't like it."

"I don't really like it, but you could have told me. You always have before."

"This was different." She knew she shouldn't have said anything at all. She should have just said, 'I don't know why you got stronger' and shut her mouth, and left it at that. Would that have been so hard? But she felt guilty not to tell him, and part of her was so excited by the discovery, that she wanted Mattie to see the good that had come of it. It was human blood. She had drunk human blood, and it had brought out his powers and allowed him to use them to protect her. Was that such a bad thing?

"How was it different?" he asked warily.

He knew, didn't he? Even if he didn't, she couldn't really expect to keep it from him forever. The guilt and paranoia was eating at her over it. She didn't really feel guilty for doing it, but for hiding it. Time to come clean. She nodded her head, making peace with the idea that she had to tell him. "It was stronger. Your powers came out because you got stronger blood through me. The other night, I drank some human blood."

Mattie's mouth fell open in shock. "Like, from a person?"

She nodded. "I wanted to try it. I only took a little. It was hard to stop, but I did. I stayed in control, just like when you used to drink from me."

"It's nothing like when I drank from you. You knew the risks. You were my girlfriend. Who did you drink from?"

"Just some guy."

"Some guy?"

"I wanted a taste. That's all I did was take a little drink. I didn't hurt him. Mattie I can't believe you used to drink my blood and then go back to butcher bought crap! That stuff doesn't even satisfy me at all. I'm always thirsty, Mattie, always. The only thing that curbs it is live animal blood. That helps. When I hunt, I only have to drink like twice a night. Otherwise, I've always got a glass in my hand, always. You've seen me. It's overwhelming. But when I drank human blood, it was amazing, Mattie! Not only was it the most incredible thing I've ever tasted, other than yours of course, but it kept me full. It made me feel better. I wasn't even hardly thirsty the next night, not for hours!"

He was shaking his head, refusing to sympathize. She could feel that on some level, he did understand, and felt bad for her thirst, but in his conscious thoughts he refused to embrace the idea that drinking from a human was the solution. "Allie, I can't believe that you would do that! We don't hunt people! You've known that all along, it was a condition of my turning you!"

"Excuse me? A condition? You can't put conditions on my life! You can't tell me what to do Mattie."

"I made you."

As if that gave him authority? "So? That doesn't mean you get to control me! When your mother gave birth to you, I'm sure she had visions of you taking over the camera shop, getting married and giving her a few grandkids. Things didn't quite work out the way she'd hoped, did they? You can bring a child into the world, but you can't direct their destiny."

Mattie's mouth was set in a hard thin line. "You're not a child."

Alyson stood from the bed, insulted that he believed he had a right to control her. She could understand that he liked to discuss things, but if he didn't subscribe to her practice of drinking live blood, which she knew he would never completely condone, he certainly couldn't order her against it. "That's right, I'm not a child, I'm a Queen." She let her eyes flicker white for a moment of emphasis, although she didn't hold them that way to give him fuel to say she was arguing at unfair advantage. She didn't need mind control. She was speaking the truth. "I am Queen of a species that exists to drink the blood of humans. Are you going to try and tell me that I don't deserve a little taste?"

Mattie looked perfectly horrified. "Deserve? How can you even use that word, *your majesty?*" The words were dripping with condescension. Let him try to make fun of her. It didn't change the facts. "We're not talking about some kind of reward," he continued. "This isn't a cookie or a gold star. It's blood, Allie. Someone else's life-blood. You think anyone, not just you, but anyone, *deserves* the right to take that away from someone else?"

Allie slumped her shoulders, relaxing her stance. "Let's not get all dramatic. I didn't kill anyone. What kind of monster do you think I am? You're getting all bent out of shape because I took a little drink. Big deal. I didn't even hurt the guy. In fact, I think he kind of liked it."

"Are you really thinking *that's* going to make me okay with this?" He was probably right on that. Sucking on some other guy's neck was probably not the imagery she wanted to use for her argument. He shook his head and got out of bed, walking across the room away from her. "You promised! You promised me that you would live like I do."

"I do live like you, Mattie. It was one little drink, an experiment. Hell, I've been following the rules and doing everything I'm supposed to. I think I deserve a break now and then!"

"Again we're talking about what you deserve! What about me? What do I deserve? Did I deserve to die? Did I deserve to put my family through hell and watch from afar knowing that I can never speak to them again? Didn't I deserve my life? Fuck the stupid camera shop. Didn't I deserve to graduate high school, get into a good college, and earn myself a real career for all my hard work? I aced the SAT's, does anybody give a shit now? What about children? Didn't I deserve to be a husband and a father with a family of my own?"

"You are a husband, aren't you?"

"I don't know Allie, am I? A marriage is an equal partnership, not...whatever this is. And of all the things I've lost, *that's* what you pull out as my consolation? Fine. Everything else in my life has been taken away from me. It's gone and there's no way to change it. It's a bitter pill to swallow, but I've accepted all of it. It's done.

So what do I deserve now, Allie? I don't ask for much. I spent years trying to protect you from the dark side of this. I spent years testing the waters and poring over possibilities before I brought you into it. I would never let harm come to you, and I've always supported you no matter what. I waited patiently and my love for you has never wavered. All I ever wanted was to have you by my side.

I don't expect to control you, I never have, I never could, and I wouldn't want to, but I certainly don't plan to follow you around saying 'yes dear' while you turn into diva-bitch queen of the vampires!

I know you think that because I love you, I'll just accept everything you do, unconditionally. I loved you when you were experimenting with drugs even though it drove me mad with worry and made me sick to see you like that. I loved you even when I knew you were off in some other guy's bed. I'll always love you Allie, but someday you're going to do something that I just can't accept, and I can't promise I'll want to stick around to see it."

She sat watching him with wide eyes, feeling almost numb. "Is someday today?" she asked quietly.

He took a deep breath and let it out very slowly. She could hear his thoughts, sense him thinking over not only what she'd just told him, but their conversation last night, when they had made up and he'd thought things would be different. Finally, he sighed. "No."

She just nodded. She wasn't going to thank him, or plead with him that she would make things better. They both knew each other's hearts and understood their relationship. It wasn't perfect but it had always been solid. There was just too much to take in right now, so much to contemplate. He didn't agree with what she'd done, in drinking from a person, but in an odd way, part of him had believed it was inevitable.

"If you want to make a risky decision," he said quietly, "I guess I can't stop you. That's nothing new. But I expect you to at least have the decency to tell me about it. And I'll tell you what I *do* deserve, Alyson. I'm your friend, I'm your husband, and I'm your maker. At the very least, I think that I deserve your respect."

She walked over and took his hands, urging him to come back to the bed with her. "I'm sorry. You're right."

Once she had him sitting next to her, she turned to him very seriously. "I have to tell you, the truth is, Mattie, I need live blood. I *need* it. I can't even tell you how complicated and distracting it is to spend every waking moment wanting more. I think that's at least part of why I've been off doing my own thing without you.

Hunting is a huge release for me. It's really helping keep me sane through all this, but it's something we can't share. And after I drank that guy's blood...that was way better than anything I could get from an animal, Mattie. To find something that finally fills me... I can't see giving that up."

He was a bit hurt and resentful that she was openly admitting that she would do it again. She held his hands tighter, trying to show him that although she would make her own decisions, she cared what he thought. She just needed him to see it from her perspective. "I could finally stave off the thirst, and concentrate on other things. And my powers, I want them to be strong. I think if anything, last night should show you the benefit of that. We defended ourselves, both of us. That's an important ability to have. We *need* to be strong."

Mattie nodded his head thoughtfully, but wouldn't comment. Why couldn't he admit that it felt good to wield such power? "Tell me you don't feel the difference," she goaded him. "Don't you feel it, fueling you, and giving you strength? Wasn't it a rush, unleashing all of that? The wind, the hail… Could you control it? Were you directing it all?"

He thought about it for a moment, and then nodded with a little shrug. "Yeah, mostly. I mean, at first it just happened, but once I realized that it was coming from me, I made the conscious decision to do more. I was in control."

"It was amazing! And that's just the first glimpse of what you can do. What if it goes away? What if you can't fuel it on stuff from the fridge? You can't lose it now, you only just found it!"

He was a little off-put by the prospect, but tried not to let it show. "I don't need it. I never had it before."

She stood up and stared at him in disbelief. "Mattie?" It was a plea for a reality check. Was he really willing to let his power go? "It's your choice, but I think it's ridiculous. Mattie, you've given up so much, you said so yourself. Your body and your life were taken out of your control. So if you have a bright spot, if there is something that makes you feel powerful and in control, something you can enjoy to balance the scale, then damn it, Mattie, *that* is something you deserve."

He was giving her a level stare. "Sure, I like having my own magic ability. But at what price? What do you want me to do, start hunting? You know I won't."

"No… I don't know. That's not you, I get that." She looked up at him for understanding. "But it *is* something I can do. It's something I need to do, and I happen to be really good at it. Don't condemn me for it. And if you want to reap the benefits of it second hand, I'm okay with that too."

"We're talking about animals here, right?" he asked.

"I don't know, mostly." She looked away. Well…full honesty, right? "I don't want to make you a promise I might not be able to keep. I think the benefit outweighs the risk. I can be careful."

He thought about that for a minute. She waited for him to say it was unacceptable…but he didn't. He didn't say anything. He decided to put it aside for now. "We have to tell Cain."

That caught her off guard. "What? Why? He doesn't have to know."

"Are you kidding?" He gestured out the window. "Anyway, he's probably noticed the snow."

Allie glanced out the window and then smiled with some relief. "Oh, you can tell him about that. I thought you meant the other stuff."

"Your drinking, you mean."

"Well, yeah."

"Why do you care?" Mattie let out a mirthless chuckle. "What's the matter, afraid you might disappoint him? That he might think less of you? 'Cause that didn't seem to stop you from telling me. You hold his opinion in higher regard?"

She sat down on the bed in a slump. "Don't be stupid."

"So what are you afraid of? You're already grounded," he added with a smirk.

"I just don't think he'll understand."

"*I* don't fully understand," he reminded her.

"But you love me," she explained quietly.

"Cain loves you, too…in a different way, hopefully. What are you worried about? Are you afraid he'll send you away if he disapproves?" She shrugged. "Sindy drinks from people. He doesn't like it, but he accepts it."

"He expects more from me."

"He thinks you are a freakin' vampire prodigy dropped into his lap by God. He's not going to send you away, not for that. We need to talk to him, if not about that, then about everything else at least. We are a coven, and to me, that means there should be no secrets."

"You're right. Just give me some time on the drinking thing. He knows I hunt the grounds, that's enough for now. We have so much else to talk about. I can't wait for you to show him your powers!" Mattie wasn't as eager as she was. It almost seemed he felt nervous about it. "What's the matter, performance anxiety?" she asked with a little laugh. "Considering you just stumbled on it by accident, I think you're really good at it."

He just shook his head. "There are more important things to talk about. What about the attack?"

"Well, we can't tell him about that!" she protested.

"Why not?"

"He'll know we lied and snuck out."

"What are we, twelve? I'm not keeping another secret. He needs to know."

"What's the point? It all turned out okay. We got jumped by a couple of random vampire thugs. It doesn't have to be a big deal."

Mattie was staring at her intently. "I don't think it was random."

"No? Then what did they want?" It seemed a blur. She couldn't remember anything specific.

"To hurt you," Mattie told her steadily.

"You think?"

"They had to know who you were, Allie. They were prepared, making sure that guy could shut off your powers."

It came back to her with a jolt, as sharp and startling as Mattie's lightning bolt had been. "Jin." Mattie showed no recognition. "That was his name, the Asian guy who could keep me from using my powers."

"He told you?"

"No," she shuffled through vague memories, trying to remember. "Someone else called him that." She shook her head as she remembered how helpless she had felt. Jin was not a large man, but he was definitely a more experienced fighter. Then to be able to rob her of her powers as well...he had made her feel incredibly vulnerable. Thank goodness Mattie had rescued her. Although...she couldn't remember Jin actually trying to hurt her. After they had fought for a few moments, she had realized that he was trying to over-power her, not kill her. That had eased her panic a little, but she still didn't know what he wanted. "How could he make me lose my powers like that?"

Mattie was at a loss. "I don't know. I've never heard of that kind of ability, but to be fair, I didn't know vampires could do much of anything other than bite people, until I turned you. Most vampires don't even know about the powers *they've* got, or how to use them, let alone that of others. Did you see his eyes? What color were they?"

She shrugged and shook her head. "Dark brown. He never changed, not that I could see."

"Wouldn't he have to change to use his ability on you? You always change when you want to use your mind control."

She averted her eyes, guiltily. "That's different. I don't have to reveal my eyes to fly, or to shift. Mind control requires a more intense connection with someone."

"It seemed like an intense connection to me. Obviously, Jin could focus his skill, switching between you and me, but he couldn't shut us both down at the same time. He had to connect with one of us at a time."

"Maybe...or maybe that was only because I'm so strong, and you were having a conniption. Let's not jump to conclusions. We don't really know for sure. If he was only stopping something mild, like telepathy from more than one vampire, we don't know how far he could spread it. We shouldn't rule anything out."

Mattie sighed. "See, this is why we have to tell Cain. Maybe he knows more about it, and which breed has that skill."

"I doubt it. If he knew something like that existed, I think he would have warned us. I don't know what color Jin's eyes are, but I think we'd better go see Cain and try to figure it out."

Chapter 12 - Life

Felicity

A Hospital in New York City
A Saturday morning in February

Felicity lay swaddled in the cool, clean sheets of the hospital bed, sitting up and anxiously awaiting Ben's return. Hopefully he would be back with her ice chips before her contractions really started kicking in.

The last few months had been so jam-packed with life-changing decisions, that she still couldn't believe she was already here. She wasn't ready! They'd only just moved into the new house, and there was still so much left to do. Ben promised the nursery would be finished before she got home with the baby, but even her own clothes had not been completely unpacked!

Ben had been disappointed to learn that the law office in Riverhead only needed him during the spring, summer and early fall - peak season for the area. He was still the newest addition to the firm, and during the winter months, he would have to keep his position at the main office in the city to keep his superiors happy.

After weighing pros and cons, and swaying back and forth over the decision, she and Ben had purchased the house on Long Island anyway, because expensive as it was, it was still easily worth twice what they'd paid, and it had been far too good an offer to pass up. It was a beautiful house in a very nice neighborhood. Rather than relegate Ben to a ridiculous 2 ½ hour commute, they decided to keep their little apartment in the city to use during the winter months, at least for a few years, until school for the baby became an issue.

Closing on the house had taken longer than they'd hoped, especially with holiday chaos thrown into the mix, and it had only truly become theirs a few weeks ago. Furnishing and decorating on weekends while eight months pregnant was no easy task, but she hadn't wanted to wait. Ben's boss was transferring him to the new office in April, and they wanted the house to be move-in ready by then.

Ben and her brothers had done all of the actual lifting and moving for her, but it was frustrating not to be able to just do things herself. The house was mostly ready. Earlier this afternoon, Ben had been putting together the furniture for the nursery while Felicity had been unpacking boxes of spring and summer clothing, when her water had broken. Felicity had called for Ben in a state of panicked shock. How could her water break? She was supposed to have two more weeks!

She had to admit, Ben had been her calm and efficient hero through the last few hours, while she'd been a nervous wreck. The doctor had assured them over the phone that they had time to get back into the city, and use their hospital, as planned. She wasn't feeling any labor pains yet, but it was still the longest commute of her life, even with her mother on her cell phone trying to keep her mind off her worries.

Felicity had insisted that they stop at the apartment first. Once there, Ben had quickly helped her pack a hospital bag, since she had neglected to do it earlier, despite two weeks of keeping the empty bag in the bottom of the bedroom closet with good intentions of planning to choose what should go into it. He'd made the phone call to let her doctor know they were on the way, and then gotten her here and set up comfortably at the hospital, while she was desperately trying to remember something as simple as how she was supposed to breathe. Thank goodness he was there for her, so levelheaded and supportive, because if he hadn't been home when her water had broken, she didn't know what she would have done without him!

A young nurse in pink scrubs with her brown hair pulled back into a ponytail came in, all chipper smiles and efficiency as she handed Felicity a cup and checked her monitor. "Hi, I'm Vicki. How are we doing in here?"

Felicity smiled weakly, looking down at the cup of ice. "I'm okay I guess." She lifted the cup towards the nurse. "My husband just went to get me some."

"That's from him," Vicki explained. "His cell phone kept ringing, and he had to go outside to take the call. He said it was your mom. He'll be right back in."

Right back in…after finding the elevator and going down eight floors, navigating the lobby and heading out the front doors to where he could get a good signal… The nurse interpreted the worried look on her face. "Don't worry, I'm sure he won't be long. You want me to stay with you until he gets back?"

"Yes, please," Felicity answered in relief.

"How are the contractions? Anything strong yet?"

Felicity shook her head. "I had a few weak ones before, but they aren't regular or anything." The waiting was the worst part. Well, it was the worst part at the moment, but that opinion was sure to be revised shortly.

"The Pitocin should be kicking in soon." She checked her watch, took a look at the I.V. that was attached to Felicity's arm, and then looked at her chart. "If they haven't gotten stronger by the time your husband gets back, we'll increase the dose. Once they start, they do usually come on pretty quickly with the Pitocin though, so be prepared."

"Okay." Felicity's voice sounded shaky even in her own ears. She felt like such a wimp. She could handle this. She just needed to take a few deep breaths and be in control. A sharp spasm of pain ran through her lower abdomen and then settled in to grow stronger with a rumbling clench of muscles. Control? No, she was definitely not in control here!

The nurse noticed her discomfort, came to hold her hand and talked her through, even though this contraction was surely nothing, compared to what lay ahead. Once it passed, the nurse looked at her watch and made a mark on her chart. "That wasn't so bad, was it?" Before Felicity had the chance to disagree, the nurse was called for by someone out in the hall. She patted Felicity's hand and let it go. "I have to go take care of this. I'll try to send someone else in for you though, okay?"

She was practically out the door when Felicity stopped her with a question. "Vicki! Is it dark out yet?" The blinds were closed on her windows.

The nurse looked understandably puzzled. "I don't know. I came on at noon and I've been running ever since." She glanced at her watch again. "It's about a quarter after five so I'd expect the sun will be going down soon if it hasn't yet." She was clearly planning to ask Felicity why it mattered, but she was called from out in the hallway again, so she thought better of it and just gave Felicity a parting wave.

Felicity closed her eyes, trying to concentrate, but all the wishes in the world wouldn't help her communicate telepathically. It wasn't her gift. She needed someone telepathic to be checking in on her of their own accord. *Alyson where are you? Wake up! Alyson please, please check in on me! Don't make me go through this without you!*

Nothing. She popped a few ice chips into her mouth to crunch, just to keep herself occupied. Where the hell was her husband? Her parents lived two hours away, and had been called the moment she and Ben had left the house. They should be here by now! Her mother had probably spent a half an hour calling everyone she knew before they'd even gotten on the road though. Ben had better not be waiting for them out in the parking lot, knowing she was sitting up here by herself!

Another contraction began kicking in. *Already? Oh sure, now they'll be coming hard and fast, while I'm all alone,* Felicity thought to herself in annoyance, trying to distract herself from pain and panic. The pain began to get much stronger than anything she had felt thus far, and just as she was starting to worry that it was lasting way too long and she wouldn't get through it, a new distraction presented itself.

Felicity, are you okay? Are you hurt? What's going on? What the hell was that?

Alyson's telepathic voice of concern cut through the cramps, and made Felicity let go of the last receding pain with a sigh of relief. She laughed aloud before reminding herself not to actually answer Alyson in voice, but with her mind. *That was the beginning taste of what I get to enjoy for the next twelve hours or so during the wonder they call childbirth. Care to join me?*

You're having the baby? Alyson asked in shock. *I thought you had a week to go!*

*I was supposed to have two weeks left, but I guess the baby had other ideas. And by the way, that invitation for you to stay, was purely sarcasm, you know that, right? You **are** staying, and helping me through this, Allie. Please. You can't leave, okay? I'm such a wreck, I can't even remember my breathing techniques or anything. Stupid Lamaze…what a waste.*

At first Alyson seemed amused by her attitude, but before Felicity had time to get angry with her, Alyson headed her off with empathetic currents of soothing calm. *Relax, I'm not going anywhere. I wouldn't miss this for the world. I know you're a little freaked out, but look at what you get to do! How incredible is this? You're having a baby, Felicity! I'll never be able to do that, ever. I'm okay with that, but the fact that you want to share this with me, is pretty special. It's the closest to childbirth I'll ever get. I'm honored, and I won't let you down. We can handle it together.* Felicity couldn't even think of how to put her gratitude into words. Luckily, she didn't have to. Alyson continued to assess the situation. *Where's Ben, isn't he there? He'd damn well better be!*

Felicity laughed, but was cut short as she felt the beginnings of another contraction. *He just stepped out for a minute. He should be right back. Shit Allie, this hurts!*

Okay, take it easy. Maybe I can help. You said you don't remember the Lamaze, but I can help you with it.

You paid attention during the classes? Felicity asked hopefully.

No, Allie scoffed at the inquiry. *Totally boring, although it was cute watching Ben play coach. No, I don't know the techniques, but you do. I can probably fish them out of your memory, if I have a few minutes to poke around in your thoughts.*

The idea startled Felicity for a moment, but then the pain got worse and she couldn't even concentrate. *Deep, focused breaths... Why did I tell them I wanted a natural birth? Fuck this, I want drugs!*

Allie laughed, despite the pain of the moment, *Look, I've been known to sample more than my fair share of recreational pharmaceuticals, but I think you'll be able to get through without them in this case.*

Easy for you to say, you can tune it out! Felicity reprimanded her.

Just hang on and give me another second, Allie answered. Felicity was about to mentally yell at her for underestimating the intensity of the situation, when the pain suddenly dulled until it was all but gone. It was the strangest thing, because as she laid her hands on her stomach, she knew the contraction was not over. She could still feel it. It hurt a little, and she could feel her muscles contracting in spasms, but the pain had lessened considerably.

Better? Allie asked.

Is that from you? What did you do? Felicity asked in wonder.

Well, I was going to help you remember the Lamaze, when I realized all I really needed to do was dull the pain for you. As an empath, I can feel what you feel, but as a telepath, I can also project feelings to you. I can't take the pain away, but I can make you perceive it differently...at least that's the theory. It's working, right? I've never done anything like this before, but...

Yes! It's wonderful. Oh my God, Allie, thank you!

The nurse Vicki came rushing back in just as the contraction subsided. "Didn't Debbie come in to see you? I told her to get in here right away! I'm sorry hon, how are you doing? Was that another contraction just now?" Felicity nodded her head as the nurse checked the read-out from the monitor. "Wow, looks like it was a good one, too. We should be in business soon."

Just then, Ben entered the room, seeming very out of breath. "Hey babe, how are you? Sorry I took so long, I came back as soon as I could." He took her hand and gave her a kiss. "Your mom should be popping in right behind me. Your dad and your brothers are waiting downstairs, and Deidre's with them. I told them we'd call them back after the baby's here, but they want to wait. Are you okay?"

She gave him a broad smile. "I'm fine. Had a few contractions while you were gone though."

Ben squeezed her hand in concern. "Were they bad? Did it hurt? I'm so sorry you had to go through them alone."

Felicity smiled and reassured him. "I wasn't alone."

Ben spared a glance for the nurse, who was busy bringing a cart full of instruments closer to the bed and going through them. Ben lifted Felicity's hand to his lips for a kiss. "Well, I'm here for you now."

She smiled in appreciation and then squeezed his hand. "Good, 'cause here comes another one."

"Okay. Don't forget, You know, it's not too late to change your mind and take something. It's your call."

"It's okay. We've got this."

~~~~~~~~~~~~~~~~~~~~~~~~~~~~~

Several hours later, Felicity was trying to keep her eyes open as Ben stood next to her with their baby in his arms. Despite being exhausted, she didn't want to fall asleep yet and miss a second of this incredible night. A boy…they had a beautiful, healthy baby boy.

Ben sat down on the edge of her bed, their son in his arms, swaddled in a white, blue, and pink striped hospital blanket, and wearing a tiny blue knit hat on his head. "I can't stop looking at him. He is the most mesmerizing wonder I have ever seen…other than you," he added with a smile. "You were so amazing, Liss." Felicity shook her head but he wouldn't let her dismiss the compliment. "Yes, you were. No drugs and you were totally in control. It was astounding. I'm in awe."

She felt like such a fake. If not for Alyson, she probably would have been screaming her head off, or crying like a baby. How did other woman do it? Alyson chimed in telepathically. *You would have done it with or without me. I'm glad I could help make it easier, but don't sell yourself short. You did great.*

Felicity shrugged. "I had amazing help."

Ben smiled. "How were you able to focus like that? Did the Lamaze help? Were you thinking about anything in particular?"

She looked into his eyes and could practically feel Allie waiting for her answer with mentally baited breath. Was this the time to start this discussion? Probably not. It seemed like a good opening, but she was so emotionally depleted, she couldn't imagine bringing up Allie to Ben right now. "Ask me again sometime."

Ben gave her an inquisitive look, but it was Alyson who answered with a mental sigh. *Another time I guess. I've got to go. I am so totally drained, if I don't go find something to drink, I'm gonna drop.*

*That's some*thing *and not some*one, *right?* Felicity clarified.

Alyson had shared her drinking indiscretion, and while Felicity wasn't judgmental about it, she was convinced it was going to lead to trouble. *Yes Jiminy Cricket, I'll let my conscience be my guide, but if you start getting preachy on me, I'm going to have to stop telling you stuff.*

Don't you dare! As it was, Felicity already suspected that Alyson's first drink of blood from a human wouldn't be the last. She may have already repeated the act multiple times for all Felicity knew.

Relax and give me a last look at that gorgeous baby. So cute. Okay, I'm outta here. Later mama.

"Liss? You falling asleep?" Ben asked her gently, as he began to stand up with the baby. "You must be really tired."

"No, stay." She pulled him back to the bed as best she could. "I can't go to sleep until we give him a name. It just feels wrong. He needs a name." They still hadn't agreed on anything. Who'd have thought picking a name would be so hard?

"You're still not feeling William, huh?" Ben asked.

"It's a good solid name, but it just doesn't feel right to me. I still like Eric."

Ben shook his head. "Too trendy."

"Eric is the complete opposite of trendy! I looked it up. It means 'eternal'."

"I don't care what it means, it's just not my favorite name." Ben gave her a kiss and handed her the baby to hold. "Don't worry, we'll figure it out. Think about it and I'll be right back. I'm desperately in need of coffee. Do you want anything?"

She couldn't take her eyes off the baby, his tiny eyelids peacefully closed in sleep. "No," she answered. "I have everything I need right here."

She sat gazing at the baby as Ben left, and her eyes filled with tears. "You are so beautiful," she whispered to him. "I love your daddy so much, but right now, there is no one else in my world but you. You're everything."

She thought again about Allie's comment that as a vampire, this was the closest to having a child she would ever get…and honestly, it wasn't even close. The love that filled Felicity's heart for this baby was like nothing she'd ever experienced, it was the most fulfilling sense of peace and rightness in her world that she'd ever felt, and he was only an hour old! She wondered if Allie could pick up even a sliver of what this felt like…and whether it made her regret her decision.

To think, that Felicity herself had almost made Alyson's decision, to turn her back on human life. She lowered her face closer to the baby and gave him a soft kiss. "To think that I almost didn't have the opportunity to bring you into the world…thank God I got to have you." Thank God, Cain had known that deep in her heart she wanted this. It had been the furthest thing from her mind at the time, as she'd stood crying in the dark over his rejection, but he had known. Cain had known she wanted a human life, and children were a large part of that. No matter how well a vampire could pretend to be human, having children was off the table.

Would Allie tell Cain that she was now a mother? She had no idea what Allie shared with him about her, if anything. Her heart and thoughts were filled with Ben now, and Cain was a topic that Allie avoided as a general rule. She wished that somehow she could show him the incredible appreciation and gratitude she had for the difficult decision he had made six years ago.

Suddenly her eyes went wide as an idea came to her. Ben stepped back into the room with a foam coffee cup, and then noticed her expression. She looked up at him in glazed shock, torn between feeling blasphemous and completely, totally right. It was perfect, like it was meant to be. She just knew it was right. Hopefully Ben would agree. "I know his name."

Ben came eagerly closer, careful to keep the coffee safely away from the baby. "You do?"

She nodded and met Ben's eyes, hoping to convey how important this was to her, without having to try to explain it. "Christian." Although the name came out with a bit of a reverential whisper to it, it carried clearly to Ben with the force of her quiet conviction.

He became very thoughtful, mulling the name over in his mind. There was no way that he could know the name's special significance to her; that it was Cain's given name before he had become a vampire. If Ben knew, he would never agree. She felt terribly guilty over that, but in essence, it was fair tribute, wasn't it? If not for Cain, Felicity and Ben would probably not even have the life they now shared, would they? It was right, she could just feel it. She loved Ben dearly, but Christian was the only name that felt right in her heart for her firstborn son.

"I like it."

Felicity breathed an enormous sigh of relief. "You do?"

Ben pulled the gold cross necklace she'd given him for Christmas from under the collar of his shirt, just to hold the cross for a moment before putting it back. "Yes. It seems fitting."

"It does, right?" she asked him with a smile, as she gazed at him through watery tear-filled eyes.

He nodded and came to sit next to her on the bed. "It just came to you?"

She smiled as she ran a finger lightly across the baby's cheek. "Yeah."

Ben leaned over to give her a kiss and then gently took the baby from her arms to bring its little face close to his. "Sounds to me like you finally have a name. Welcome to the world, Christian Everheart."

Chapter 13 - Friends, mortal enemies... whatever

Sindy

Cain's Estate, Upstate, New York
An evening in March

Two years...it had now been two years and about six weeks since Sindy had been taken in by Cain after her injury, and invited to remain at his estate. Even if things hadn't gone entirely as planned, it had seemed very promising at the start.

She may not have arrived with the decorum she'd envisioned, but since then she had gone through a lot of trouble to refine her ways and start being more the woman she thought he would want her to be. Well, that was how she had started off, but after a while, it became clear that he wasn't truly interested, no matter what Alyson might be whispering in his ear. Sindy could act as mature and refined as she could manage, and Cain barely noticed. She could be the hot, seductive temptress, and he hardly glanced at her.

She'd stopped trying. What was the point? He didn't seem to mind her being there as a friend, but he obviously wasn't looking for anything else from her. The only time he seemed to pay her special attention, was when he felt the need to back her off an argument. Forget the new, mature, and responsible image, forget the temptress, or even the helpless injured orphan. Those personas didn't seem to be getting her anywhere. By this time, she wasn't really trying to be anyone in particular, but finally feeling safe enough to just be herself.

Funny, she didn't even really know who she was anymore. Her interaction with others was usually an act to get her whatever she needed at the moment to survive. When she wasn't playing up the sexy vamp vixen, she was usually acting the tough chick to keep anyone from thinking she might care enough about something to have it used against her. However, she had shelter and blood here, and when she wasn't consciously projecting something for a motive, she wasn't really sure how to think of herself.

When she and Cain were just taking a quiet walk outside with no alternate agenda, or having a real, honest to goodness conversation about something, in which he really wanted to hear her opinion, she would forget about trying to sway his thinking about her, and just get wrapped up in the moment. She didn't quite feel like Sindy anymore, so who was she?

Cynthia maybe; the woman she would have been, if she hadn't been forced to navigate all the dark drama in her life, always living in survival mode? Cynthia was far too luxurious a name for her. Her mother had picked it out of a romance novel. She had no business giving a name like that to a girl who would have to come home from school every day to her junkie mom passed out on the couch, and then hide from her abusive father until nightfall, when she would lie awake with her eyes scrunched closed tight, praying that he didn't come into her bedroom.

Who was she trying to kid? She had changed her name to *Sin* for good reason, because sin was all she could use to keep herself going. She was still Sindy, and she'd never be anyone else. It sure had been nice to think otherwise for a while though. To pretend that she could live in this big beautiful house, in the company of people who didn't mind having her around, and that she could fit in.

She had felt no loyalty or camaraderie with Allie when she'd first returned, but Allie seemed to have forgiven her for her past harassment, and was actually kind of fun to hang out with, a development unexpected at the very least. Mattie didn't seem to mind her really. In fact, he definitely enjoyed having her around as eye candy if nothing else. Cain...he insisted that he enjoyed her company, but their relationship seemed to be mired in some sort of platonic tar pit.

Alyson constantly assured her that Cain cared deeply for her; that being a man of old fashioned sensibilities with a wounded heart, he was just going to take a really long time before he was comfortable showing his affection. Cain had infinite patience, and Sindy needed to show some too. But could she really believe Allie's predictions, and that the girl would have her best interest at heart?

She just didn't want to face the truth. Staying here was nothing but a comforting lie. When a woman is living under a man's roof for two years and he still hasn't slept with her, that's not patience, that's rejection. She was not here to be his daughter, or his sister, and she certainly didn't come here just to be his BFF. She wanted him to accept her as his consort. She told herself that whether he cared about her truly, or sported her as a trophy, wasn't really of concern. She just wanted to be acknowledged as *his*. The rest could work itself out later. After all she had been through, she deserved to be on the arm of someone of his age and power.

She was looking for status, a station in the vampire community where she could finally feel accepted, powerful, and secure. When she'd first returned here to Cain's estate, she'd had more than one path in mind to achieve that goal, but each of those avenues seemed to have closed themselves off to her. Cain just wasn't interested enough in her. The Crimson Coven wasn't really her style, and there was no room for her to rise in that coven with Tempest there anyway. Her third option was a hidden agenda that had become more complicated than she'd expected, and was not working out well enough to be worth pursuing. None of it was working out, and it was time to go.

Cain had asked her to come out for a stroll with him this evening; something he did every now and then, when he felt guilty for ignoring her to spend all of his time working with Allie. She needed to toughen up and tell him that she was leaving. She would tell him tonight. Even Allie didn't *really* enjoy having her around, did she? She needed Sindy as a drinking coach…for now, but eventually she would manage it on her own. She tolerated Sindy as a partner to shift with, but she was still kind of territorial about her precious little coven, and the fact that Sindy didn't belong in it.

Alright, maybe that wasn't really true… To be fair, Allie had never actually rejected the idea of admitting Sindy into the coven, but that was only because Sindy had never asked. For Allie to be the only woman, the subject of complete and adoring affection from both guys, with whom she shared a blood tie… That had to be a position that no woman would want to give up to be shared with Sindy, right?

It didn't matter. Sindy could never let Allie taste her blood anyway; it would be too dangerous. The thought that Alyson could have free access to her mind, to every secret, was too great a risk. Allie was proving much more difficult to manipulate than Sindy had assumed she would be, and her plans just weren't really panning out. She was willing to scrap those plans, if Cain made it worthwhile, but she couldn't allow Allie to ever learn of them.

Having Cain's romantic attention would be worth staying, but without that, she had no real place here. She was going to have to leave; abandon Cain, turn her back on the Crimson Coven, and admit defeat in her secret mission. She would report back to Arif *without* the United One, and see if there was something else she could do for him. Maybe there was some other way to secure a place for herself at *Kana Susamiş Icin Ev.*

She wore a long-sleeved, deep-purple mini-dress, which had a very low-scooped open back. She wore nothing beneath it, not wanting to obscure the dimples of her lower back that showed at the edge of the material, just barely above her shapely ass. Her long dark hair covered much of it, but it fell to just above the edge of the material, and every time she moved, it would show a bit more bare skin. It was just the kind of thing to fan men's fantasies if she were walking down a path ahead of them. Too bad it didn't really matter at this point. She slipped on her thigh high leather boots, the ones with the lower heels for walking outside in the grass, and went out to meet Cain.

As she exited her room, she noticed Cain's bedroom door was open. He called to her as soon as he heard her come out into the hall. "Sindy? I'm in here."

She turned to stand in his doorway, feeling the thickness of unwelcome barring her entrance. She'd never actually been invited into his bedroom. She wondered if he remembered that. Even when he'd first given her a tour of the house, he'd only shown it to her from the hall. She'd always wondered if that had been intentional. She knew that Alyson and Mattie had been given invitations.

Cain was lying on his back on the bed, propped up with pillows and reading a book. He closed a bookmark in it and put it on his nightstand. She couldn't tell if he hadn't really noticed that she hadn't come into the room, or if he just expected her to stand in the hallway. He was fully clothed and lying on top of the covers, but he didn't look like he was planning to get up. "You look lovely." He gave the compliment with an easy smile, as though he expected nothing less from her.

"I thought you wanted to meet me outside for a walk?" she prompted.

He gave her an odd look, as though she was missing something obvious. Was she supposed to assume he'd rather meet with her in the bedroom? It made her pause to wonder if she'd been reading him wrong.

"Don't you hear the wind outside?" he asked. "It's like a category five hurricane out there." She sighed. No, she had not misread his motives; perfectly platonic as always. She'd been so preoccupied she hadn't even noticed the weather. "Unless you'd like to get staked by a flying tree branch, I think we're better off staying in," he added.

She nodded, leaning against the doorframe with her arms folded. "Where are Allie and Mattie?"

Cain gave her a curious look before answering, as though he wondered why she should ask. Was it too much to hope that she could have Cain to herself for an evening? She preferred privacy for the conversation she had in mind. "They're in their trailer I think…although knowing Alyson, she's probably out floating around in the storm," he added with a chuckle. "The girl takes no precaution."

Sindy had to shake her head with an envious smile. "Probably couldn't hurt her anyway. When she shifts into mist she's pretty invulnerable huh?"

"I suppose."

"Do you ever wish you could do things like that?"

He shook his head with a shrug. "Not really. It might be fun, but it doesn't really matter to me. I don't need such things. I just want to be happy."

"Are you?"

He turned thoughtful, as a warm smile stole across his face. "For the first time in a long time, I think I am."

Wrong answer. 'I would be happier if you'd come in and join me…' might have been nice to hear. But no, he was perfectly content. "That's good," she replied quietly. "Listen, I wanted to talk to you about something."

"I wanted to speak with you as well."

"Did you want to go downstairs?"

He looked puzzled. Maybe he didn't realize that she wasn't invited after all. "We don't have to, unless you want. Come in."

She just stood there for a moment as the air thinned before her, allowing her entrance. Finally, she took a few steps into the room. She ignored him as he sat up a bit, and patted the bed in invitation for her to sit. She remained standing before him, and wouldn't meet his eyes. *Too little, too late.* "I think I'm gonna go."

Cain seemed completely untroubled. He didn't even know what she was talking about. "Go where?"

"Away," she clarified shortly. "After the storm I mean. I'm taking off." If she didn't just spit the words out, she might lose the courage to say them.

As her intent sunk in, he became distressed. Now he fully sat up in alarm. "You're leaving? Why? I thought you enjoyed being here. Is something wrong?"

"Nothing's wrong, it's just…well, it's not much of anything is it? What's here for me? Don't get me wrong, I appreciate everything you've done for me. I've loved staying here in this gorgeous house, and it's nice knowing there is always fresh blood in supply, even if it's not my favorite flavor."

"Then is it Alyson, or Mattie? The Crimson Coven…did someone say something to you?" She just shook her head lightly in answer. "I don't want you to leave. Is it me?" She still couldn't look at him. He sounded almost desperate. Why did he care?

"Well, yeah." She met his eyes and was a little startled by the hurt she saw there. She softened her tone, "But it's not your fault. It's just that you guys have got stuff to do here. You've got the group coven thing going on, and you're all working on something that I'm not a part of, and that's cool, it's fine. I just don't feel like I belong here."

"You do. You can. I've told you that we might include you in the coven if you'd like, but then you never asked…"

She shook her head. He knew that Mattie and Alyson probably wouldn't be keen on it, which was why he'd never asked them. She didn't want that anyway, so she'd never pushed it. "It's not the marks."

He moved closer to sit at the end of the bed and took her hands. She didn't really want him to, but when she looked into his eyes, she couldn't just pull away. "I… I'd like you to stay," he insisted.

"Why?"

Cain gave her an odd look, as though she shouldn't have to ask. "I enjoy your company, you know I do."

"As what? A fall back? Something familiar, and comfortable, like an easy-chair, or an old shoe?" She'd never seen such immediate evidence of her words on someone's face before. It was as though he was totally vulnerable to her. "I'm sorry Cain. I'm comfortable here too, but I want more than that," she told him with quiet sincerity. "I want to be…*excited*. I need something to be excited about."

He stood, keeping one of her hands in his own, as he let the other go so that he could lightly touch her face. "I'd like to excite you."

His touch sent as much of a warm shiver down her spine as his words, but then she jerked away, turning her back on him. "Stop. You always do that," she muttered accusingly.

"Do what?"

"You try to play me. You're only saying that to get me to stay. Manipulation is a little low for you. Why do you even care if I go?"

"But I do care." She could hear in his voice that he was very chastened by her observation. "It's not that I'm being insincere. I suppose I have only been allowing you to see those feelings when it's been advantageous, and that's unfair. I'm sorry. I just do what I can to keep the peace around here, but I shouldn't use your feelings that way. I guess I just felt that I could only admit to wanting to say such things to you, when I had an excuse. Please accept my apology."

She turned towards him again, though she remained standing a pace away. She watched him for a moment, and then gave him a little smirk of a smile. "That's okay. I use sex appeal to manipulate you all the time." They both shared a laugh over the admission. She shrugged. "Doesn't change the fact that it's time for me to move on. You don't have to fake it to get me to stay. I'm gonna go anyway."

"No. It's not an act," he insisted. "I've always thought there could be something between us, I just didn't feel free to recognize it. Then I was too caught up in my own head. Now... Now I think I'm over that, but everything with Alyson has been so overwhelming it's just taken some time to work through. But that's what I wanted to tell you. It's why I wanted to see you tonight. I'm ready now."

She just stood there, trying to read his eyes with a smirk of disbelief on her face. Ready? Ready for what? He seemed very vulnerable and hopeful as the silent minutes passed. Cain didn't say a word. He just kept watching her with those clear blue eyes. Holy shit! Those eyes shone with nothing but sincerity, not manipulation or even the convenient baring of hidden emotion only to suit the moment, but honest feeling. Was he really trying to say what she thought he might be, for real?

She dropped her hand to graze the hem of her skirt, practically forcing his gaze to dart to her legs for a second, and the bit of bared thigh that showed between her tall boots and her terribly short hemline. She couldn't help but notice the little flutter of anticipation in him. That invisible, but almost palpable vibe of his sexual awareness of her. Not only did he seem completely focused on awaiting her emotional reaction to him, but she could sense his physical attraction to her as well, stronger than she'd ever felt it. It wasn't wishful thinking, she was finally seeing in him all of the little reactions she had strained so hard to find for so long, when they just hadn't been there. Sure, *now*.

"How can you not feel the change?" he asked. "Not just in me, or between us, but in yourself. Don't you see what I see in you?"

She took a step closer, but couldn't answer. What was there to see? Nothing that could be more desirable than the careful projections of image she had constructed in the past. He leaned forward, giving her plenty of time to feel the anxious tension as the heat built between them, until his lips finally brushed hers.

A soft, tender kiss, unlike what she might have expected. Where was the urgent passion? She knew it was there, she could feel it in him, but he held it back to first woo her with this simple and sentimental gesture. She had almost let herself melt into it, before breaking it off, leaving him bewildered, and wanting for more.

"You have gotta be fuckin' kiddin' me," she whispered. "*Now* you want this? I've been after you for years. We went from being friends, to trying to kill each other, to a one-night stand, to... I don't even know what we are now, but I do know that I have tried everything. Sultry, subtle seduction, brash and bold invitation, blatant force, hell I even went the frightened needy route for a while." That hadn't really been an act, but why should she let him know that? "I have been everything that you could have ever desired, and you just weren't interested. I gave up. You wanted us to just be friends, fine. I gave you what you wanted. And now that I'm done, *now* you want this? *Now* you want me...and I don't even give a shit about you anymore."

Cain smiled. "That's a lie."

"What the hell do I want with you? I'm done jumping through hoops."

"Good. Maybe it's my turn. You want to play coy, and make me work for it? I'm game. It's worth it, because now I see a woman I'd like to pursue."

Sindy laughed. "Oh, now you see what you want, huh? I think that's because you only want what you can't have. You want me when I'm walking out the door." He shook his head to dispute her, but she went on. "You are *so* fooling yourself. You've got everybody else fooled too, but not me. All that crap about being a human first, and a vampire second, it's such a joke. I know your deal now. You're just like me. If I'm the lioness," she said, trailing a finger across his chest, "you, my dear, are the drowsy old lion, laying in wait, watching for his moment. I was going about this all wrong. Lion doesn't want to be *fed*. Lion wants to *hunt*. I should have ignored you from the beginning. The lion doesn't want an offering, the lion wants *prey*."

"That's a misnomer, you know. Lions are really a lazy lot."

She stared at him for a moment, wondering what intentions really lay behind his easy smile. "Fuck you. Go back to your books," she answered with a smile and turned for the door.

He reached out for her wrist but she pulled it away before his fingers could more than brush her skin. "Sindy, you're wrong you know. Your leaving hasn't sparked this. I was never laying in wait or playing games. That's not me, honestly. I needed time. Time to grieve." She rolled her eyes at him but he carried on. "Time to *know* you. I don't want to be with you because you're beautiful, or seductive, or tempting, I want to be with you...because of you. I just...wanted to see who you were, without the act.

I needed time to leave the past behind and move on. I wanted to see you tonight, because I'm ready to do that now.

I don't want you because you're leaving. Don't you see, the real you has only just arrived? The woman who acted out for attention, hurting others to mask her own pain...she was obscuring the woman I knew was inside of you all along."

He could see that she was reluctant to believe him. He took her hands into his own and went on. "Do you remember, just a few months after we'd first met, when I was teaching you how to cloak your mark? You dropped your defenses for me, if only for a short time; you let me in. You weren't trying to be Sindy, the vampire temptress. You were Cynthia Abigail Applebaum, remember?"

The name sent a cold stab of unreasonable fear through her, fear of someone seeing through her disguise, even as his words brought tears to her eyes. She shook her head as if to deny the memory, but he cupped her chin, unwilling to let her dismiss it. "Yes, you do."

She stood very still and composed herself. *Stay in control. No reason to lose it, like an emotionally feeble little girl.* She took a deep breath, and removed his hand from her face. "I told you never to call me that, unless you wanted to lose some teeth."

He broke out laughing. "See, you do remember. Fair enough. I've been warned. But no matter what you have me call you, I know who you truly are...or at least I'm beginning to know you, and I'd like to know more. I'm ready for that now, and that is partly *because* of you.

They say that time heals all wounds, but love heals them faster. I've seen the true care in your eyes, the way that you have gently urged and pulled me out of my despair over the past, to focus on the present. Instead of letting me sulk, you make me smile. I brought you here to heal you, and instead...you've healed me. I'm ready to stop *existing*, and live again, with you.

Not that you should've been waiting for me, and if you've truly left me behind, so be it. I'm not the type for games. Subtle hints and seduction are far more your arena than mine. I just wanted you to know, I'm ready, if you're still interested. I've been truly enjoying our time together, more and more. I've been watching you over these past months, and I *very* much like what I see: you; the real you. I'd like more of you in my life."

She left his words hanging there in the air. She would have liked to watch him squirm, but his deep blue eyes never faltered from her face. His slightly hopeful smile was so genuine and sincere. She couldn't let the walls down, it was too much, but the bastard really meant it! After all of this, now he was interested? He wanted her *because* she wasn't even trying, which should be construed as a compliment, but part of her still wanted to be insulted and mad at him for not wanting her before.

He moistened his lips, drawing her attention to his face again as he spoke. "What are you thinking?" Damn those eyes! He wasn't giving her a *chance* to think. She'd never *felt* his eyes on her like this before.

He wore his usual blue jeans and a faded black t-shirt. The shirt was a little snug on him, and looking sort of thin and threadbare. Didn't the man ever shop? It looked really good on him though. She had to admit, the guy was fuckin' hot. The whole age/power issue didn't hurt either. She'd never met a man who was stronger than she was in so many ways, and yet was unwilling to use the power to try to force himself on her. It was irresistible.

Her prior plans seemed to fall apart like a house of cards in the wind blowing outside. Maybe Arif could wait. If Cain was truly serious, it might be worth staying for just a while longer and seeing how things might play out. Could he possibly see something in her that she did not even recognize in herself?

Her willful stubbornness disintegrated as he sat back down on the bed as though giving up his will to whatever she might decide. What was she going do, waste time playing games? She gave him a sultry smile as she moved closer to stand between his open knees at the edge of the bed. "I'm gonna rock your world," she promised with a sultry purr.

He gave a relieved little laugh that she wouldn't deny him, but eyed her body a bit hesitantly. "That's not really what I'm looking for...although I'm sure I'll enjoy it." She gave him a warning look, that he might be insulting her. He smiled. "I don't want what we've already had. I want to *make love* to you. Because now...I can." He reached up to slide his fingers through her hair and pull her to his lips with gentle pressure on the back of her neck. He gave her a kiss, slow burning, passionate and full of emotion she'd never felt from him before. Then he leaned back, and his eyes found hers. They seemed afire with unfathomable secrets. "I do, Sindy. I..."

She quickly raised her hand to cover his mouth before he could finish speaking. "Don't. Don't say it." He looked disappointed, but must have recognized the firm and serious countenance that had taken over her features. She softened and took her hand away. "Show me."

~~~~~~~~~~~~~~~~~~~~~~~~~~~~

Sindy lay in bed, slowly drifting to consciousness, comfortably wrapped in a tangle of sheets. It was the masculine scent of the room, which first alerted her to remember where she was. This was not the guest room she'd been using, that smelled of powder and lilac, this room smelled of the good clean scents of pine, wood polish, and the slight lingering smell of aftershave; Cain's room.

She opened her eyes to find him still lying on his stomach, asleep next to her in the bed. His arm was stretched up above him on the pillow, partially hiding his face, but from what she could make out in the dim light, it seemed that his eyes were closed. A glance towards the window told her that the sun had recently set. Even without verification from the window, something within her just knew that the dangerous orb had slipped below the horizon. The heavy drapes were drawn closed, and the seam of the curtains seemed to shine with the purple hues of dusk.

She sat up quietly, hoping not to disturb Cain as she shifted to better take in the view. The sheets barely covered him, since it seemed she had stolen them all as they slept. Her eyes played over the sensual lines of his broad back and the beginning of the nicely rounded curve of his butt, just visible above the sheet.

His skin looked so pale and smooth, it fairly glowed in the darkened room. She found herself reaching for him, amazed at the feelings his touch had brought out in her over the hours past, and wanting to somehow recapture them and prove to herself that they were real. Her fingers whispered over the bulging contours of his bicep that was stretched up on his pillow, and then her hand gently cupped the strong, rolling muscle of his shoulder. She slid her palm across it, following it down the gentle slope of his back.

How she longed to feel the tingle of a mark beneath her touch, but they hadn't shared blood. Cain was still marked against her by Mattie and Allie. That's alright, his physical attention certainly hadn't been lacking, and she would take what she could get. As her hand reached the small of his back, she turned it, to dip fingers-first beneath the sheets and continue downward, admiring the curving swell of his buttocks.

She felt him stir slightly and come to life beneath her caress. As he shifted his head and raised his eyelids, his gaze sought and found her face. She removed her hand with a bit of a guilty start, but then he smiled and she reminded herself that he had proven very appreciative of her touch over the last day and half. She hadn't really needed to remove her hand, he didn't mind. For once, she wasn't pushing limits to see what she could get away with.

He rolled to his side to prop himself up on an elbow facing her. As he did, the sheet pulled and tugged in her grasp, threatening to unveil her body as she sat holding it around her, or else uncover his, where it draped over his hip. She refused to give the sheet the slack it needed, and it slid down his thigh, exposing him as he lay on his side.

He didn't seem concerned, but did give her a smirk of a smile, conscious of her role in revealing his body. Let him smirk. He'd seen her naked body a million times, but the sight of his was something she had yet to drink in her fill of. Even partially flaccid, his manhood was an impressive sight to behold. She restrained herself from touching him again, but could easily picture her hand reaching out to bring him to full magnificence with only a few artful strokes. Damn, the man's body was a beautiful thing.

"I'm glad that you decided to stay," he told her with quiet sincerity. "I hope you are too."

Oh yeah…good decision, definitely. She allowed herself another sweeping glance down his body before answering. "Happier than I thought I'd be."

"Thanks," he said with a small huff of a laugh in amused insult. "You had pretty low expectations for my performance, did you?"

She shook her head with a chuckle. That was totally not what she had meant at all. He turned thoughtful and then continued. "Although, reflecting on what you had to compare it to, I suppose I deserve that. I've told you before, the last time I was with you was…it wasn't even about you. I was detached and trying to prove something to myself. You offered your body to me and I used you. It was reprehensible and I am deeply sorry for it."

She knitted her brow and shook her head again, wanting that night dismissed from thought. That memory didn't belong here now, showing itself with such stark contrast against the present. His actions last night were completely different in nature from that one-night stand. "Stop apologizing and forget it already. I'm used to men using me for a fast rough ride. I didn't care."

He seemed aghast at her admission. "Don't say that. You should care! And your acceptance doesn't make it right."

She gave him a look of warning to drop it. She wasn't here to be lectured. "I wasn't even talking about that anyway. I'm happier than I thought I'd be, because I figured that if I let you talk me into staying, I'd wake up kicking myself for it. I never doubted I would enjoy the night."

The night…and the entire next day after it… She had been surprised to find that not only had Cain enjoyed her company in the bed for the evening, he'd allowed her to stay after sunrise. Sharing a resting place during daylight was usually considered a serious display of trust for a vampire. Not that he should expect her to stake him in his sleep or anything, but he could have easily had her spend the day in her own room.

She had even given him opportunity to dismiss her gracefully, offering to leave and see him the next evening, but he'd told her that she was welcome to stay...unless she'd had her fill of him. It had taken a lot to keep her expression neutral and not let on to how the words had thrilled her.

He'd spent a good portion of the day 'making love' to her. The man had obviously been deprived, and was enjoying himself immensely, but he'd also seemed determined to show her that her feelings, and her pleasure were his main concern. Rather than allow her to take the lead, he instead catered to her, a recurring theme throughout the night and day.

"You, um, *exceeded* my expectations, really. But somehow, I thought I would feel differently about it." She'd expected to feel prideful and self-assured that she'd finally won him over, but she hadn't counted on feeling so emotionally safe and at ease with him. Rather than look confused by her statement, he just listened with quiet interest, making her feel that she could tell him anything. She wasn't quite ready for *full* disclosure, but it was nice to feel that thread of trust between them, nice to be able to try to put some of her newfound emotions into words. "I can appreciate good sex, but I never really thought it could change the way I feel inside."

He smiled, as she lay back down next to him. He reached over and softly brushed the hair from her face. "How do you feel?"

Important? Special? She had used sex to try to capture those feelings before, but somehow it had never really worked...until now. This time with Cain had been different. It had made her feel worth something to someone for real...finally. Voicing all of that would be going way too far though. Good enough that he should know she was happy to stay. "Happy. For the first time in a long time..." she said, echoing his statement from last night, "I think I'm pretty happy."

"Glad to hear it," he whispered. He rolled towards her, moving his leg possessively over her body, and gave her a kiss.

She sucked on his lower lip, and was rewarded to feel his erection stiffen against her. "Feels like you're pretty happy too," she teased him with a chuckle. "I know you're coming off a dry spell, but aren't you spent yet? I mean, three times would take the steam out of anybody. I'm not leaving, and I'm already impressed. You *can* slow down."

He laughed but refused to heed her advice, instead fondling her breast beneath him. "It's been four, but who's counting?" he told her, tweaking her nipple with a pinch of reprimand. She opened her mouth in surprise at the sharp pleasure/pain of it. God, she loved when he did that. He knew it, too. It sparked desire in her that melted the comfortable cozy feeling she'd been enjoying, to be replaced with renewed arousal and yearning for him. He dipped down to soothe her breast with a light, suckling kiss, and then rested his head on her chest, closing his eyes. "What can I say? It feels good to express myself after all of this time."

She stroked her hand through his hair, not quite daring to wonder if he was talking about expressing his feelings about her in particular, or just his pent up sexual energy in general. She knew better than to believe *she* inhabited all of his fantasies; a few maybe, but surely not most of them. What did it matter? She was the only one in his bed. "Express away."

He stretched up to give her another kiss, this time letting it build with passionate intensity as he moved to fully lay atop her. It was simple to dismiss uneasy contemplation when his deep kisses left her unable to think about anything but wanting more of his attention. As he began the tender, yet teasing caresses that would make her all but beg for him, she let her kisses trail down his throat.

Her shift came almost unconsciously, as demanding desire over-rode sensibility. In the heat of her growing excitement, her fangs distended, but as they touched his skin, a warning flash of pain stabbed through her temple, precursor to the migraine from hell that would surely assault her, should she try to bite him. She backed off, turning her head and retracting her fangs in sudden shock.

She closed her eyes and tucked her forehead down against his chest, trying to clear her head. She had hoped her reaction would go un-noticed, but Cain immediately froze, and rose up in concern to try to see her face. "What is it?"

She held tight to him, wanting to dismiss the interruption. "Nothing."

It only took him a second to figure it out. "It's the mark, isn't it?" he asked. He wore a coven mark shared by Alyson and Mattie, and it protected him from being bitten by any vampire outside of that coven...protected him from her.

She dismissed it with a shrug that he could feel more than see, as she held herself pressed against him. "My bad. I lost my head for a minute. My thirst is pretty strong when I first wake up, and I'm so used to blending it. Sex and blood, it's a natural combination for me."

"For any vampire," he assured her, with a small kiss on the forehead. "I understand. I'm sorry about that."

"It's fine. I just forgot for a sec. No biting allowed. You'll just have to take my mind off it," she told him teasingly, grinding her hips against him and hoping to urge him to forget the incident.

She'd been wondering if he might not feel relieved that she couldn't bite him. She knew that in some ways, blood sharing could be far more personal even than sex. It left a lasting impression, a bond to be strongly felt and clearly evident to others. No matter how 'ready' he claimed he was to be with her, that might be a bit beyond what he was willing to share.

He seemed to guess her speculations and feel badly that she was barred from his blood though. "I wish I could let you," he assured her with a kiss. "I would, you know."

"M-hmmm." Would he? He'd given her his blood while healing her, but there had also been more than one occasion in the past when she'd thought he might allow her to bite him, and then she had been denied.

He must have felt her uncertainty. "I think there's a letter opener on the desk if you want…"

She gave him a little push against his chest, to look at him with amused disbelief. "I'm not going to stab you in the neck just so I can have a drink! What kind of sadistic bitch do you think I am? …Don't answer that," she quickly added as he arched an eyebrow at her with a smile. It wasn't only about drinking his blood anyway, it was about marking him with her venom. Perhaps he would let her if he could, but it was a moot point anyway. "I'm fine," she told him again.

"It won't be long before it fades," he remarked thoughtfully. "We usually renew the marks monthly, but I could speak to Mattie and Alyson, to see about letting it go, so that you might be included next time."

She shook her head, burying her face into his chest again so she wouldn't have to meet his eyes. "No thanks. That's not what I'm looking for, really. I'm…not there yet." She wished she could consider it, but she just couldn't let Allie drink from her. It would be incredibly stupid on her part. She needed to keep her privacy protected. "I don't need to be part of your coven, I just wanted to drink from *you*.

Cain, do you remember the night you found me out there in the woods, after my injury? You brought me back here, fixed me up, and spent the whole day just holding me in bed, letting me drink from your wrist. I have to admit, even with the gaping stomach wound, I still think that was the best day of my life…before yesterday anyway."

As soon as she said it, she felt really dumb. It was totally unlike her, to just lay all her cards out on the table like that, but she felt off balance from declining the coven invitation, and had felt the need to justify her desire to drink from him if she didn't want to share marks.

The recollection of feeling so protected, safe and treasured in his arms, worth his time, blood and attention, was a cherished memory. Still, she hadn't needed to blurt out the truth like that. Hopefully it didn't sound too pathetic.

He was very quiet for a moment, and she began to fear that he felt just that, that it was pathetic for her to have no better memory than being healed from injury by him. When he spoke however, his voice held no pity, but merely sounded thoughtful and sympathetic.

"When I saw you there, lying on the snow in a pool of blood, when I saw what had been done to you, I was so stricken to think you'd had to endure that. I knew you would survive, but to see you so hurt like that, it was a terrible thing. Once I had you healed and fed, and we were simply laying together, quiet and safe, it was a wonderful feeling. To tell you the truth, I wished I could have spent every day thereafter laying just the same way, with you in my arms."

"No you didn't."

"It's true."

"Then you could have invited me into your bedroom long before last night," she pointed out. "Why didn't you?"

"I was afraid of what it implied. I didn't want it to be complicated, or to have to explore things I wasn't ready to deal with. I just wanted to hold you. I wanted to hold you safe in my arms and know that I could comfort you. I didn't know how to make that happen without other aspects of a relationship I was unready for, so I backed away."

Allie had known he'd wanted that too, she must have, having access to his thoughts and emotions. That was why she kept telling Sindy not to give up. "I'm here now," she told him in acceptance. He nodded with a smile as she continued. "I can't bite you, but you can drink from me," she reminded him.

"That hardly seems fair, now does it?"

"It's just an offer. You don't have to...if you don't want them to see." The moment he marked her, the change in their relationship would be clear to all vampires, including Alyson and Mattie.

"I'm not ashamed of you," he told her, his voice full of hurt and insult. Was he planning to let the relationship openly spill to outside of the bedroom, then? If she were going to stay, she may well need his mark. A mark not only claimed ownership, it implied a vampire would also protect that which belonged to them.

She gave him a few kisses on the chest, and then further up his neck. She could feel a shiver go through him as she placed one over his jugular. "Well, I know how much you men like to mark what's yours. You've made your feelings pretty clear, this is something real, right?" After all he'd gone through to be sure she understood that he wasn't using her, he couldn't deny it now, could he? "So go ahead, claim me. Pierce my skin and mark my blood as yours alone. You can't tell me that the idea doesn't turn you on," she whispered.

She knew it did. He was pressing against her, rock-hard and ready, and she could feel the tension in him as he tried valiantly to hold back the change. She might as well be whispering directly to his inner vampire. He had to feel the driving need to mark her just as strongly she felt the urge to bite him. Who could withstand that sort of instinct and temptation? If anyone could, it would be Cain, but he seemed to weigh the repercussions of such an act, and sway towards allowing himself to do it.

"Take me," she urged, moving to place her throat at his lips. He needed no further goading. He sank his fangs into her skin with an almost desperate moan of carnal need. His venom flooded her system as she sighed in submissive relief. He did want her, and would keep her safe. She would bear the mark to prove it.

~~~~~~~~~~~~~~~~~~~~~~~~~~~~~~

Cain drew back the covers, preparing to sit up and leave the bed, but Sindy reached up and raked her fingers across him in an attempt to seduce him to stay. As her fingers touched his skin, their newly shared mark was like a warm, enveloping current connecting them and enticing them not to part. "No, come back," she begged him. "Let's stay a little longer." She wrapped her legs around him and did her best to physically keep him from leaving the bed. "Don't stop touching me. I love being marked. It's been so long."

He relented for a moment, running his hands over her body and obviously enjoying the sensation as much as she did. But soon he gave her a slap on the ass and she reluctantly moved aside. "You know, at some point we are going to have to leave the bedroom," he told her with a chuckle.

"I don't want to," she pouted.

Cain smiled and shook his head as he stood to cross the room and find himself a pair of jeans. "Well, only one of us has had anything to drink in the last twenty-four hours. Seeing as you gave your last reserves to me, you must be thirsty."

She was. In fact, the mere mention of it drove her thirst to the forefront with neglected urgency. She'd been in need of blood even before he had drunk from her. Still, she would happily endure waves of cramping hunger if it meant he would spend the day naked in bed with her again, rather than make her go downstairs and face the others. She wanted to stay wrapped in this safe haven of sheets with him, and not have to think about the real world.

"It's late already. I should go down," Cain informed her as he pulled a tee shirt over his head.

She sighed. "Are Allie and Mattie down there?" He would be able to feel them through the coven mark if they were nearby.

He nodded as he raked his fingers through his hair. Just like that, not only presentable for company, but gorgeous. His hair fell into an un-perfect style that was casually sexy and didn't even need a brush. The scruffy shadow of beard on his cheeks and chin didn't even ruin the effect. In fact, it made him look even hotter. No wonder he didn't miss having a mirror. She shuddered to think what a mess she probably looked like. She could tell her hair was a wreck from rolling beneath the covers for twenty-four hours straight. Hopefully it was messy in a sexy sort of way, like his…but she doubted it.

"They're probably waiting for me," he told her, as he pulled on socks and boots. "I didn't speak to them last night at all, and we have sort of been working on something." He was ready to go down, but Sindy had shown no signs of even leaving his bed. "Come down with me. It'll be fine."

She had always thought that when the night came that she finally did seduce Cain into accepting her and marking her, she would be happy to show it off. She'd imagined that she would march downstairs and proudly display his mark, forcing Mattie and Allie to accept her. She thought she'd feel vindicated and glad to prove to them that she was well worth Cain's attention. She believed that they still resented her presence sometimes, no matter how Mattie might secretly admire her body, or how Alyson would claim to be supportive.

So why was it, that now that Sindy's pursuit of Cain had been justified, she felt sort of…guilty? They had all known she had been after Cain's affection. Wearing his mark wasn't odd in itself either, as Cain had said, most vampires shared blood during sex. But Cain had made it quite clear, if only through the sheer time he had waited, that he would only give his affections when warranted with love and trust. She'd finally earned that from him. Even from the time she'd first arrived, his motives had been only to love and care for her… And what were hers?

"Go ahead," she told him. "I'll be down in a few minutes. I just need to…take stock of a few things, make myself presentable."

He eyed her for a few seconds, surely trying to decide if he should wait for her. He probably thought it would be easier on her if they came down to meet the others together. She needed a few minutes alone though, to sort things out and reassess her game plan. Things were different now, weren't they?

She stood from the bed, wrapped in his sheet, and made her way towards him at the door. "I'm sure you'd rather I got dressed first," she told him with a smile. "I'll meet you down there. You don't have to wait. I'm a big girl."

"Alright then. I'll see you downstairs," he replied, leaving her with a kiss.

She took her time getting dressed, mulling over various thoughts and scenarios for the future. She chose a snug and sexy red mini-dress with a low-scooped neckline and long, blousy sleeves that were slit from the shoulder to the tight cuff at the wrist for a peek-a-boo effect.

When she was finally ready, she left her room and paused before descending the staircase. After a moment of indecision, she revealed her mark. Alyson and Mattie were sure to see it, and Cain could have a chance to tell them whatever he wanted about it before she entered the room. It just seemed less complicated that way. She would join them uncloaked and take it from there. Why was she wasting her time worrying about what they would think anyway?

Sindy went downstairs and found the others gathered around the kitchen table. Alyson and Mattie were discussing something while sitting next to each other. Allie was sitting on the end, making notes in a spiral notebook. Cain was standing, looking over their shoulders, but focusing more on the mug in his hand. He looked up with a welcoming smile as Sindy came into the room. Show time.

She held her head high and her chest out, as she confidently crossed the room to Cain. "Good evening," she said to the general room with a smile.

Allie met her eyes with a small grin. "It's about time."

Sindy turned towards Cain, giving him a kiss that was an obvious display of their new lack of personal boundaries. "Sorry I kept you waiting."

Sindy was unsure whether it was telepathy, or just a case of knowing the girl well, but she was pretty sure Allie was not talking about how long it had taken her to join them, but commenting on the fact that Sindy and Cain had now become a couple. When she glanced back at the table, she could tell by Allie's expression that she was right.

Mattie just watched her put her arm around Cain, and then turned back to the notebook on the table, with a look just short of an eye-roll. He probably thought Cain was a fool to have given in to Sindy after all of this time, but it was none of his business, was it? He had his own woman to worry about.

Cain affected not to notice any change or tension in the room, and simply gave Sindy another quick kiss, and gestured towards the table. "Join us. I'll get you something to drink."

Sindy gave him a smile of thanks, although she would rather get it herself so she had something to keep busy with. Cain wanted to be a gentleman though and serve her. She settled for standing against the counter a little closer to the table, rather than take a kitchen chair. Alyson and Mattie went on with their conversation as though she wasn't even there. "It's got to be purple," Allie insisted. "It's the only one that makes any sense."

"How do you figure?" Mattie asked in exasperation.

"Because purple is all mental. It goes with all of the manipulation and control stuff. Telepathy, thrall...power dampening fits right in," she explained.

Cain moved closer to them as he took a container of blood out of the refrigerator, and backed Mattie with an arched brow at Alyson. "That's an awful lot of power for one vampire."

"See?" Mattie replied. "It's too much, Allie. I think it's green."

"What else is green?" she asked uncertainly, scanning the page before her.

"It's the only one we don't know yet, that's why it makes sense," he insisted. Alyson slumped her shoulders, unwilling to entirely concede. Mattie pointed to lines written in the notebook as he spoke. "We already know all of ours, and we've come into contact with most of the others. Cain says that pink is definitely speed and strength, so it must be green."

Sindy was completely lost as to what they could be talking about. Cain noticed her confused expression and filled her in with a sympathetic smile as he poured her blood into a mug. "We're trying to assign all of the vampire abilities that we've discovered to their respective breed eye colors."

It was sweet of him to try to include her, but she couldn't imagine that she'd have much to add to the conversation. This was pretty new territory for her. "Oh. I know only red vamps can shift, and some vamps have other powers, but can you really sort them just by color, so cut-and-dry like that? I don't think telepathy is exclusive that way," she added, thinking of the few Crimson wolves she had seen display rudimentary aspects of the ability.

"There has been a good deal of intermingling between blood types over the years," Cain explained, "and as a result, some powers seem to have randomly bled through from one breed to another, but only to offspring. A vampire cannot gain new abilities once made, no matter whose blood they drink, they can only awaken what was within them at the time they were created. I will never gain the form of a wolf, no matter how much I might drink from you," he clarified, pausing to give Sindy a small kiss on the cheek with a tender smile at the thought of sharing her blood, confirming beyond doubt to all present, that he was unashamed to admit their new bond. "There are certain special abilities, such as your shape shifting, that seem linked only to certain eye colors."

Sindy tried not to flush too visibly with the pride and pleasure he brought out in her, with his display of acceptance through such a simple gesture. She nodded and continued the conversation, uncertainly. "Are there a lot?"

Cain chuckled. "Well, the abilities seem to be countless. Every time I think I've seen it all, we discover something new. The *breeds* we seem to have narrowed down to seven."

Allie looked up from where she'd been scribbling in her notes. "Are you sure it's not eight?"

Both Mattie and Cain answered forcefully. "Yes."

Allie dropped the pencil and threw her hands up. "Okay, sorry."

Mattie shook his head and picked up the pencil as Cain clarified. "Alyson, it can't be eight, unless you want to count white, but the United Breed is all colors combined. The separate breeds only number seven."

"There could be eight," she mumbled.

Cain was quick to correct her. "We've gone over the attack on Mattie a dozen times. There were seven. If it took eight breeds, you would not be the United One, would you?"

Sindy furrowed her brow and questioned Mattie with interest. "You were attacked?"

He looked up at her as though almost insulted by the question. Cain noticed and answered for him. "When he was originally turned," he explained, placing a hand softly on Sindy's shoulder and handing her the mug of warmed blood from the microwave.

Mattie sighed and explained it, although he affected to be lecturing to Allie and the room in general, rather than look at Sindy. She couldn't tell if he was more annoyed or embarrassed by having to repeat the details. "I was attacked by seven vampires, each with a different eye color. I staked the vampire with red eyes *before* I was turned, so only six were left to turn me.

That's why I'm *not* the United One. But when I turned Allie, she already had some blood from a red-eyed vamp in her, thanks to you." He glanced at Sindy, as though annoyed at the outcome of things.

"It's not like I fed it to her," Sindy told him defensively.

Mattie continued, focusing on Allie. "So you were turned while having the blood of *seven* vampires in you. That has to be all of them...unless you were out drinking blood from some other vampire I don't know about before you were turned." Alyson made a face at him without dignifying the accusation with an answer. "There are seven breeds, Roy G. Biv," Mattie concluded, as though that should mean something to them all.

"Who?" Allie asked in total confusion. Sindy was glad she wasn't the only one who was clueless.

Mattie wrote on the page of the notebook, and turned it so Allie could see. "Look, it's the acronym they taught us in science to remember the color spectrum of the rainbow. ROY G BIV. Red, Orange, Yellow, Green, Blue, Indigo, Violet."

"Oh, well thanks. Silly me, that explains everything," she answered snarkily. "What's indigo?"

"It's a purplish blue color. And violet is like a magenta-pink."

Cain cut in while taking a chair at the end of the table opposite Allie. "Actually, vampires with pink eyes have a lighter hue, a very bright but pale pink. It's rather disconcerting."

"Close enough," Mattie said, slumping back in his chair.

Sindy took the empty seat at Cain's side, and decided to try to be a part of the discussion. "Well, we're red, orange, and yellow. If you can't count white, the only other color I've ever seen is purple. Where are all the rest?"

"They're very rare," Cain clarified, "practically extinct really. Pink, blue and green are all but unheard of on this continent. Orange is the dominant common breed around here. Purple is hardly seen anywhere, and even yellow and red are hard to find," he said, gesturing towards himself and then her.

"How come?"

Mattie sighed, annoyed at the setback and wishing they could move on, as Cain explained. "There was a time long ago when vampires were more commonly believed in by humans, and diligently hunted. Breeds that had more obvious powers, such as shape shifting, were more easily identified and killed.

There were wars between the breeds of vampires themselves as well. Nowadays, elders who experienced the breed wars are all gone and no one seems to know details, but supposedly, vampires distrusted and killed breeds who had power over them, such as those with purple eyes. That is why their numbers are so few.

Whatever the reasons, vampires with orange eyes have had more opportunity to reproduce, and are the predominant breed in this country. They have a very subtle ability that most are unaware of, and therefore have been more discreet in their activities. They can be just as powerful as other breeds, but most know nothing of their magic."

Sindy turned to Mattie with new interest. She hadn't realized all vampires had special abilities. She'd known vampires with red eyes had the power to shift shape, and purple eyes held the power of thrall, but most other abilities seemed only luck of the draw. Some had them and some didn't. She didn't realize that eye color played such a role in other powers. Mattie had orange eyes, and she certainly hadn't been aware that he could do anything special. "What's their power?"

Mattie stared her down across the table for a moment, and she thought he might refuse to answer, but then he glanced at Cain and sighed. Cain must have given them the green light that Sindy should now be considered 'in the loop' and allowed shared information. "I can control the weather," he admitted quietly.

She raised an eyebrow, and couldn't help but wear a small smirk of disbelief. "The weather?" she asked.

"Yes. In my immediate surroundings, I can manipulate the weather."

She kept her mouth shut in a tight smile. How could anyone equate a power like that, to be on a par with her special ability to alter every molecule in her body to take the shape of an entirely new creature? Cain seemed to sense her amusement, and spoke to reassure her of his seriousness. "It can be quite impressive."

Now she had to stifle a laugh. "No doubt. I mean, who wouldn't be impressed by the weather-man?"

Allie observed Mattie's cold, hard stare, and then quickly consulted with Cain. "Can lightning come through windows?"

Cain cleared his throat for Mattie's attention. "Let's not find out."

Sindy acknowledged the dispositions of the others, and then sat up a bit straighter. Okay, maybe this actually should be taken seriously. "Lightning, really?" she asked Mattie with grudging respect.

"M-hmmm." He was still giving her that disconcerting stare. Mattie used to be fairly friendly towards her, but she'd noticed he didn't seem very tolerant of her lately. She had to wonder if he'd found out that she'd been taking Allie out drinking from humans. That would account for the attitude. It would also explain why Allie had been putting her off lately. She knew

Allie enjoyed the benefits of drinking from humans, but was afraid to do it without Sindy there for support. However, she'd backed out of their plans the last few times, probably worried to make Mattie mad at her. Maybe Mattie really wasn't someone you wanted to piss off after all.

"Ever used it?" She asked him quietly, but it still sounded slightly taunting. The Mattie that she knew, was just too boy-next-door to seem intimidating to her.

"M-hmmm." He wasn't answering to try to scare her. It was just a level, matter of fact.

Alyson leaned diagonally a bit closer to Sindy in her chair, to speak to her confidentially, although it wasn't like the others wouldn't be able to hear her. "He totally fried a guy once, into vamp dust. One strike and…poof," she said with a snap of her fingers. Sindy could tell that Allie was tickled to find this dangerous aspect within her soft-spoken man. She wasn't trying to threaten Sindy, just sharing her excitement. Dangerous could definitely be sexy. Allie knew that Sindy would understand the appeal.

Sindy raised her eyebrows, giving Mattie a smile. "Really? Wow. Watch out for the weatherman. Who knew you had it in you?" Mattie looked away with a bit of a huff, but she could see the slight smile there. He was secretly pleased to have earned her respect. "Wait a minute. Was that *you* making that ruckus last night?"

He nodded without apology, but it was Allie that Sindy turned to study under a discerning gaze. Allie smiled. "I asked him to help me work on something," she admitted with feigned innocence.

The reason Sindy and Cain had stayed inside rather than go for their walk, was because of the storm. Cain may have been planning to get closer with her anyway, but staying in for the storm was definitely a nudge that helped things progress more quickly between them. Had Allie known? Had she known that Sindy was planning to leave, or just that Cain was ready to begin a relationship with her? Either way, having their conversation in the bedroom rather than outside on the lawn had certainly put a more intimate spin on things.

"You have good timing," Sindy told her with a smirk.

Cain looked as though he was entertaining the same suspicions as Sindy. He probably didn't care for the idea of being manipulated, but he seemed more amused than annoyed. "How did that work out for you?" he asked archly.

Allie grinned. "I think it worked out pretty well."

Mattie clearly had no idea what accusations might be at play here. He looked at Allie like she was crazy. "It didn't work out at all. She tried to dampen me," he explained to Cain, "but she couldn't accomplish much of anything."

Cain's gaze bore into Allie, who fidgeted in her seat. "Is that so?" he asked.

"I did try harder towards the end..." she told them, "but it didn't make a difference. I couldn't do it."

"You must be able to do it," Cain insisted. "If dampening the powers of others is a vampiric ability, then you must have it. You're the United One."

Sindy interrupted in concern. "What do you mean, dampening power?"

Mattie answered her. "We were attacked a few months ago by a vampire who was able to keep her from using her abilities. We're trying to figure out what breed he was, and whether Allie has the power to do it too."

"She must," Cain repeated. "Weather is a tricky thing. The vampire isn't solely the source, he's manipulating natural energies. Perhaps you were affecting him, but once the storm was raging, Mattie's influence was unnecessary to keep it going," he suggested to Allie. "We need something more definitive to test it on."

"That's the problem," Allie said, gesturing towards the men. "You guys can't do anything good for me to practice on." They both looked at her with a smidge of insult. "Sorry but it's true. What are we gonna do Cain, cut you and see if I can keep you from healing?"

Cain acceded her point, and after a moment, all eyes were on Sindy. She translated their idea in disbelief. "What? You want to test stuff on me?" she asked incredulously.

Mattie was quick to agree. "You're perfect for it. The results would be immediately visible."

Cain leaned forward to pat her leg under the table. "It would help us out."

Great. When she had been wanting their acceptance into the group, the role of guinea pig wasn't exactly what she'd had in mind. "What do you want me to do?" she asked hesitantly.

Allie stood and moved behind Sindy, to pull her chair out from the table. "It's no big deal really. You'll just try to change form, and I'll try to stop you."

Sindy stood and put her hands on her hips, eying the others uncertainly. "And what if she makes something else happen to me? You don't even know everything she can do, right?"

Cain came to put an arm around her for reassurance. "It will be fine. If she was unafraid to test it on Mattie, I'm sure you haven't got any reason to worry. She won't hurt you."

"Relax," Allie told her with a smile. "I'm just going to try and keep you from shifting."

Alyson had explained to Sindy in the past, that most vampires had a natural ability to shield themselves from her power of thrall if they were on guard for it, unless they had shared blood with Allie, giving her a hold over them. So Sindy didn't need to worry about actually being under her control. Allie and Mattie shared a blood bond, and still the dampening power hadn't worked on him, so as Sindy saw it, the odds were that it probably wouldn't work on her either.

"Fine," Sindy answered, as the others moved back to give her some space. "Give it your best shot." If they wanted to put her in the spotlight, then she'd give them a good show. She reached down to skooch the skirt of her dress up to her hips with a wiggle, and then pulled it off up over her head.

When she tossed it aside, she couldn't help but grin at the expressions on their faces. Mattie especially seemed taken aback. "What are you doing?" he asked.

Sindy stood before them in her heels, red lace panties, and red satin and lace push-up bra, giving Mattie a coy smile that made him look away. "Changing. Isn't that what you asked for?"

He shook his head and kept his eyes on the ceiling. "Can't you do it with your clothes on?"

She laughed and traded looks with Cain and Alyson, assuring them that she was being perfectly cooperative. "You know I always have to strip first. Do you still want my help or not?"

Cain just gestured with his hand out, palm-up, to let her know she had the floor, but Mattie mumbled under his breath. "Allie can do it with her clothes on."

Sindy walked over to put a hand on the back of Mattie's chair and leaned closer, forcing him to look at her. "Well, I guess that's why *she's* the United One.

Us regular vampires, can't stay discorporate for that long. It's not easy trying to navigate your way out of restrictive clothing as a cloud of mist, while forming a body that doesn't fit well into a little red dress. I'm not going to get all tangled up in material and rip my clothes, just to keep you from blushing in front of your girlfriend." As she finished speaking, she unhooked the back of her bra and slid it off to let it drop to the floor.

Mattie rolled his eyes and turned away as Sindy walked back over to Cain and Alyson, towards the center of the room. She kept herself from glancing in Allie's direction, hoping she hadn't taken things too far, but they'd asked for it. "Alright," Cain said in his best mediator voice. "Let's all be adults here."

Mattie stood from his chair. It was unclear whether he was planning to leave the room or just move to a different vantage point, but Sindy spoke to stop him. "And you can stay right there and watch. This was your idea, and if she makes me explode, you're going to have to witness it."

He sat back down and met her eyes with a tight grin. "With pleasure."

Sindy returned his smile, stripped off her panties and then gave Allie the go-ahead. "Okay blondie, do your stuff." Sindy gave Allie time to focus whatever power she might have, while enjoying having everyone's full attention on her.

Her body may not be quite as voluptuous as she'd like it to be, but otherwise, she knew that it was damn near perfect. Let the men openly fault her for showing some attitude, but she knew they secretly enjoyed the voyeuristic thrill of having permission to run their eyes over her, just as much as she enjoyed showing herself off. There was something incredibly arousing about venturing into the forbidden... Mattie being otherwise attached, and Cain being far too proper to ever permit such intimacy in mixed company, under normal circumstances.

After a moment of close observation, Cain asked, "Is it working?"

Sindy grinned with thin apology for not changing yet. "I was just letting her get her bearings first. Here we go..." She was just able to see Cain shake his head at her audacity before she dematerialized into a misty cloud of particles. She thought she might be feeling some slight resistance as she began to draw herself back together, but it didn't detain her at all. She only paused for a moment before reforming herself into the shape of a large, dark wolf. Allie couldn't stop her. So much for the feared power of the United One.

She shook herself out and then shifted into her vampire wolf state, gazing at the others with her crimson red eyes. Both Cain and Mattie were impressed by the change, although they should probably be very used to seeing such things by now. She sauntered over to each of them in turn, assessing them both with her heat seeking vision, noting the blood within them and trying to discern if her display of her body had induced the effect she'd desired.

When she finally turned to look at Alyson, she was taken aback by what she saw. Not only could she tell by the shifting colors of Alyson's aura-mark, that she was straining in an attempt to use some considerable power, but she could see through her body tone of greens and blues that Allie had virtually no blood left to draw from. There was a very thin core of red enveloping her head and chest, but it seemed to be turning yellow, burning up what little blood she had left as Sindy watched. The girl was turning colder by the second.

Sindy sat down on her haunches in front of Alyson until it was clearly evident that she was spent, and nothing notable was going to happen. Sindy stood to move back to the center of the room, and then reverted into to her human form. She spread her hands with a shrug. "So much for your little experiment."

Cain seemed dissatisfied, and turned to Allie with a plea that sounded almost accusing. "Are you sure you were trying? You've got to be able to do it."

"I did try. It didn't work."

"I think she was trying," Sindy said in Allie's defense. "She just wasn't strong enough to stop me. Maybe your reserves are low," she added meaningfully to Allie. Human blood could work wonders for a vampire, and they hadn't had a girls' night out in a while.

Cain didn't seem to catch her implication, hopefully he didn't even know about their hunting expeditions, but Allie understood what she meant. Apparently, Mattie knew it too. He stood from his chair after a quick glance at Allie, and then headed for the door. As he passed by, Sindy spread her hands again in askance, standing naked before him. "Leaving so soon?" she asked Mattie, as he grimly departed the room.

Alyson gave Sindy a look of warning, not only for pushing Mattie's buttons, but for the display of her body as well. She threw a meaningful glance towards Cain and then told Sindy "Don't get greedy," as she followed after Mattie.

Once they were gone, Cain walked over and picked up Sindy's dress to hand it to her. "You shouldn't push things so far with Mattie. You're lucky Alyson tolerates you," he informed her quietly.

Sindy knew that Cain didn't understand how much Alyson truly felt she needed Sindy around right now. As long as Sindy was here, Allie felt free to explore her vampire nature without the over-bearing code of moral conduct imposed by the guys. Sindy understood her cravings, could give support and guidance, and made a nice backdrop for comparison, so that Allie could maintain her image of being 'the good one'. Without Sindy, Alyson had been feeling trapped and unable to express herself fully without condemnation. Sindy was happy to play the bad girl to Allie's good girl, if that's what the United One needed. And with Cain finally giving Sindy his mark of approval as well, the ball was back in Sindy's court to make her own decisions again. It was all working out just fine.

Sindy took the dress from Cain, but tossed it aside onto a chair with a smile. "Tolerates me? We're best buds. Don't worry, it's all good."

Cain leaned against the table and sighed, looking over Sindy, who still stood proudly naked. "Did you enjoy yourself?" he asked in amused accusation.

"Immensely," she replied with a little shimmy and a grin. "In fact, despite all the fun we've recently had, I have to admit I'm thinking I might be up for a little more. How about you?"

He chuckled. "I don't think so."

"Come on, watching him stew over looking at me must have turned you on just a little." Cain looked away as though disappointed in her for the suggestion, but she was pretty charged over the exchange and she wasn't giving up that easily. She leaned over the table towards him suggestively. "Take me right here in the kitchen. I'll bet this table's never been christened."

Cain glanced around, shocked at the brazenness of the suggestion. "I most certainly will not. They might come back."

"That's part of the thrill." He shot her a look that told her to give up. She rolled over onto her back, still half laying on the table. "They aren't coming back anyway. I'm sure Allie is very busy at the trailer, trying to erase any visions of me that might be left in Mattie's head. And anyway, you could feel them coming long before they actually got here."

He ignored her and walked over to one of the cabinets. He got himself a glass and then took out a bottle of rum. Why was this man so determined not to let himself have too good a time with her? It wasn't as though they hadn't already done plenty in the bedroom just a few hours ago.

"Cain." She waited while he poured himself a full glass and downed it, before turning to look at her. "I know that it's not just about the sex," she assured him. "But that doesn't mean the sex can't be good."

He let out a small huff of a laugh that seemed almost self-depreciating. The man was almost three and a half centuries old. It was probably stupid of her to think that he didn't understand the notion of having a loving relationship that also explored and took full advantage of exciting sex. He might come across as being reserved and proper, but she had dipped into the passion beneath the surface. She knew that he had burning desires as hot as any man's and was eager to sate them when the time was right. But right now, she was pushing him too far. She should back off and be satisfied that she'd claimed his affections, before she had him rethinking that too.

He affirmed her suspicions with two simply spoken words. "Slow down." He poured and downed himself another drink, before tossing her dress to her again and leaving the room.

~~~~~~~~~~~~~~~~~~~~~~~~~~~~~

Sindy lay on the couch with earphones on, listening to Cain's kickin' stereo play the new CD she'd bought. Her eyes were closed, and she was totally immersed in the music. She was suddenly startled to feel an intrusive burst of energy in her mind, Alyson's equivalent of a telepathic tap on the shoulder. She jerked open her eyes to see Allie watching her from a few feet away.

She took off the headphones and sat up a little more, trying not to look too shaken, as Allie gave her a verbal greeting. "Hey."

"Hey," she replied casually. She hadn't seen or spoken to Allie since their little demonstration a few nights ago. Despite what she had told Cain, she wasn't quite sure if Allie might actually be mad at her.

"What are you listening to?" Allie asked.

"P!NK. It's her new one."

Allie smiled. "I like her, she's badass."

"Yeah." So far so good. Allie seemed to be trying to give her a friendly opening at least. "So, are you pissed at me?" Sindy asked.

Allie crossed her arms and thought about it for a minute, before taking a deep breath and answering. "Nah, not really."

"Cool. Sorry if I pushed it a little far the other night." Allie visibly relaxed, pleasantly surprised to get an apology out of her. Sindy grinned. "I guess I was just feeling a little heady from...all the amazing sex," she confided with impish glee.

Allie laughed. "Probably. I told you he'd come around."

"Did he ever! Cain can be downright spectacular when he wants to be. Holy shit."

"I'm sure." Allie raised her eyebrows, giving Sindy a little nod and a smile as she perched herself on the arm of the couch. "So can Mattie. But you'll just have to take my word for it." She said the last with sudden seriousness.

"Of course," Sindy reassured her, although the warning was well deserved. "I wouldn't do that to you." Allie arched an eyebrow, questioning her loyalty. Loyal or not, she'd be pretty stupid to risk the wrath of the

United One for sex with Mattie. It wasn't worth it. "I know you'd dust me for that. I'm not an idiot."

"Good."

"I was just messing with him," Sindy assured her.

"Do me a favor, and don't give him any more reason to be ticked off. He's already making my life hell over you."

Sindy pursed her lips with a nod. He knew about their human hunting trips then... No wonder he was being extra angsty around her. "You told him, huh?"

"I had to. He's my husband, Sindy. I respect him and I love him, and I'm not going to screw that up. No more secrets from him."

Sindy shrugged. "Okay, tell him whatever you want. But he's got to know I didn't hold a gun to your head."

"He's knows that. It's on me. But he doesn't like it."

"And I'm an accessory, so now he doesn't like me."

Allie slid down off the arm onto the couch cushion next to her. "He'll get over it, just play it cool for a while, okay?"

"Sure, whatever you want." She was just happy that Cain had continued inviting her to sleep in his bedroom during the day, even after the kitchen incident. He wasn't *quite* as attentive as that first day they'd spent together, but he was receptive, which was a good start. She needed to focus on pleasing Cain and keeping him from regretting being with her. Keeping herself off Mattie's shit list was an easy request. She and Allie weren't doing anything for him to worry about lately anyway. "Shouldn't be hard. We haven't even been out since before New Year's."

"I know...it's killing me. I need a hunt."

No wonder she was being so nice. "Well, now that Mattie knows, why doesn't he take you?"

"Are you kidding? He won't stop me, but he's certainly not going to help. Besides, that's like asking a guy to take his wife to a whorehouse."

Sindy laughed at her in disbelief. "You don't even *do* them." *What a waste*, she added mentally. Drinking human blood, combined with marked sex was always a treat. She could tell by Allie's expression that she'd picked up the thought, but chose not to comment.

"Mattie's knows I don't have sex with them, but it still feels weird. Maybe to some vamps it doesn't matter, but to me, drinking feels really intimate, even without sex. It would be strange to have him there, and he's definitely not the type who'd want to watch."

"Does Cain know?"

"No. I don't know how he'd feel about it. I guess he couldn't really try to stop me, and he might even be willing to help, but...I don't know. Going out like that with *Cain* just feels like a bad idea on a couple of levels. Being caught between him and Mattie might sound like fun, but I'm already avoiding land mines left and right. There are some cans of worms I'm just better off leaving closed.

I'd rather hunt alone...but I *can't* do it alone. I need you there, Sindy. The other night, after our experiment didn't work, I went out and brought down a deer."

"So?"

"I killed it. I didn't mean to. I couldn't help it. The thirst just...got away from me. I wanted to see if live animal blood would help my abilities, and I was so damn thirsty. You know how I am when I drink. It's like I lose all sense of what's going on around me, I'm totally consumed. If I don't focus completely on what I'm doing, it just sweeps me away.

I was so busy thinking about everything, that I let myself get distracted, and before I knew it, the poor thing was dead. I can't go out drinking alone, Sindy, it's too dangerous for me. If I don't focus strictly on that heartbeat, the guy won't stand a chance, and I can't just tune out everything else without someone to cover me, it's too risky."

Sindy threw a comradely arm over Allie's shoulder. Allie was feeling even more desperate over it than she'd thought. It sounded like it was getting worse even. "It's okay, don't worry. I've got your back."

"Thanks. Can we go tonight?"

"Tonight? Need it bad, huh?"

Allie tried to shrug it off. "I just think it's important to be at my full potential. If I can block other vampires from using their power over me, that'd be huge, don't you think?"

"I guess."

"Not that I'm expecting any problems, but I think I should check it out. It's important to know if I can do it."

Sindy nodded agreeably. "What's the point of having a gun if you don't keep it loaded, right?"

The statement definitely clinched things for Allie. Sindy could just tell she'd have a regular hunting partner from now on. Allie glanced upstairs in what Sindy assumed was the vague direction of Cain's room. Allie must be able to feel him there. "Is Cain going to care if we step out?" she asked. Their hunting restriction had been lifted after the holidays, and shortly after, they had talked Cain into admitting that there was no need for them to be confined to the grounds any longer either. There had been no further incidents to cause alarm, but Cain still worried.

Sindy shook her head. "No, not a problem. We stopped at the bookstore earlier and he came home with a whole stack. He'll be busy for hours."

"I already told Mattie I was going out. He's not thrilled, but I'll make it up to him."

Sindy stood and then took Allie by the hand to pull her up from the couch. "Girl's night out it is then. Let's go."

~~~~~~~~~~~~~~~~~~~~~~~~~~~~~~~~

Sindy quickly ascended the stairs, noting the pale glow that was beginning to emanate from the border of the curtains in the entryway below. As she reached Cain's bedroom, she observed that there was also light coming from beneath the crack of his door, but rather than sunlight, this was the yellowed brightness of a light bulb, most likely the reading lamp near his bed. He was still up then.

She quietly entered the room. Just as she had suspected, he was sitting up in bed reading a book. He glanced up at her arrival, but she didn't meet his eyes, instead crossing to the chair in the corner to put down her things.

"Cutting it a bit close, aren't you?" he asked. Despite the hint of reprimand, she still loved hearing his voice. His soft British accent and tone of gentle concern were always a welcome reception after the cacophony of noise from the crowded club and the harsh howl of the wind from the journey home.

She shrugged as though unconcerned over the time. "The sun isn't up yet."

"But you were out with Alyson again, weren't you?" She nodded as she began taking off her jewelry to lay on the dresser. This was her third hunt with Allie in less than a month's time. "For Alyson, this is cutting it much too close."

"Actual sunrise isn't for at least twenty minutes. Plenty of time."

"I take it you've never been with Alyson at dawn." She shook her head, unsure why it should matter. "Alyson isn't like other vampires. Being the United One has its benefits, but it has drawbacks as well. I worry that her weaknesses may well be proportionate to her strengths, in some ways making her far more vulnerable than any of us. Everything has a balance.

I'd venture to say that even now she is on the verge of being catatonic, sluggish to the point of barely being able to move or speak. By the time the sun truly crests the horizon, she'll most likely collapse in a dead faint. It's been a gradual change, but her tolerance to sunlight and ability to function during the day has become less and less. At this point, the exhaustion overwhelms her, and she becomes completely comatose during daylight hours."

"Really? All anyone ever talks about is how the United One is supposed to be such a super-vamp. I had no idea."

He was gravely serious. "She needs to be safely behind locked doors and under Mattie's protection *well* before sunrise. Don't encourage her to push it or you'll find yourself carrying her home, and she may not even survive the trip. I suspect she'd burn far more easily than we do. Home an hour before sunrise please, no later," he sternly ordered.

Sindy mulled over the surprising, and surely valuable information, as she took off her heels and teased him for his tone. "Sorry *dad.*"

He tilted his head with a smirk for her sarcasm. "Well, someone's got to keep you ladies in line. You've been going out with Alyson a lot lately. What do you two get up to?"

She gave him a coy smile. "We go shopping and clubbing, you know, just the regular girl stuff. Nothing you'd be too interested in."

"Staying out of trouble I assume," he told her with a tone of warning.

"Of course. It's just fun to step out for some girl time now and then." He responded with a tolerant smile. He didn't suspect that they'd been hunting men. It was now common knowledge that she and Allie hunted the grounds for animals in wolf form regularly, so he didn't suspect that they would desire more. He probably never dreamed Allie would carry her over the distances that they covered to conduct their hunts far from mark range, and still return home before dawn.

He dropped his book down into his lap for a moment with a grin. "It's nice to see that you've been getting along so well. You know, there was a time when I worried to have you both here, for fear that you might kill each other," he said with a chuckle. "I guess you can never predict how relationships will change."

"Yeah," she answered quietly, thoughtful and uncertain. When she'd come back here, she'd certainly never expected Allie to accept her so easily. She'd had an entirely different agenda, but now, vulnerable as it made her feel, she was willing to abandon her plans in favor of love and friendship. The objective was too difficult anyway, and if Cain truly might care for her...then she could ignore all else. She wasn't used to making decisions that involved her heart more than her head. She hoped it wasn't a stupid mistake.

She gathered her jewelry and shoes, and went to put them into her guest bedroom, where she retrieved a negligee to wear for the day. She'd change in his room, so he could watch her over his book, as he pretended to read. She would strip slowly and seductively, even if he showed no overt interest. She was always aware to keep that all important image of desirability for his arousal. For him to be comfortable with her was fine…but *too* comfortable bred boredom.

Sindy re-entered Cain's bedroom, negligee in hand, and closed the door behind her. He glanced at her with a smile and went back to reading. She dropped her nightie and then unzipped the back of her dress slowly, the zipper making a clearly audible rasping noise in the silent room. He didn't even bother to look up. He was truly engrossed in his book.

The dress she wore was another of her very provocative snug black mini-dresses. This one had revealing cutout shapes all around the middle, showing off her thin waist. It had made her very popular with the guys at the club tonight. Too bad Cain didn't seem impressed by it. Sindy sighed and looked down at her body as she stripped off the dress, wishing she had fuller assets to draw his attention with. Sure, her body was young, slim, and firm. She had just enough curvature to be slinky, but she feared there wasn't quite enough there to really bounce and jiggle as she'd like. Cain knew what she had to offer, and enjoyed it, but it wasn't as though he couldn't take his eyes off her. It made her feel insecure in his attentions…she hated that.

She knew he wasn't usually receptive to her making direct advances lately, especially when he was reading, but maybe she could take a more direct *indirect* approach to gaining his romantic attention. "What're you reading?" she asked with a sultry tone that she hoped still sounded sincere.

He held it up a bit, so that she could see the cover, but then looked at her curiously, as he answered. "*When the Past is Present*, by David Richo."

She didn't look very closely at it, but from what she could see, there was a photo of a sunny countryside scene on the cover. She had no clue what the book might be about. "Good stuff?"

"So far." Cain looked up at her, intrigued by her sudden interest. "It's very…enlightening." He eyed her for a moment, but when she simply nodded and didn't seem to have any true interest in the book, he went back to reading.

He had not even given a second glance to her body. He just wasn't thinking that way this morning, or for the last several mornings actually. It worried her a little. "Cain," she cajoled him in a tone of pouting reprimand, "you haven't even told me what you think."

Cain looked up from his book in distraction. "Of what?"

"My new bra and panties. You like?" They were an ultra sexy little set that retailed for a small fortune. She'd convinced Allie to help her swipe them from Victoria's Secret at the mall.

He observed the erotic garments obediently and then gave her a charming little smile. "They're lovely on you."

She sighed. Lovely? Lovely was for an evening gown or a hairdo. He was supposed to say that she was sexy, hot, irresistible... "And how about what's under them?" she asked, smoothing her hands over the outer curves of her breasts and down along her body to her hips and thighs. Rather than asking in the sexy, teasing tone that she had planned, wanting it to be more of an invitation than a question, she heard it come out with a slight tremble, as a true plea for an opinion.

Cain put the book aside and looked at her more directly, trying to discern her mood. If she were to simply crawl onto the bed towards him, she knew he would make love to her, if that was what she wanted, and things would just carry on. But something froze her in place, wondering what he really truly thought.

"The way I look. What do you really think?" she asked, turning this way and that, trying to study her body without benefit of a mirror. From his vantage, did her body truly look as she remembered? She knew how to play to her strengths, and build an image to turn men's heads, but to someone who really knew her...to Cain, how did she look?

He smiled. "You're beautiful. Come to bed."

She wasn't looking to be pacified. If she had the courage to ask, he should do her the service of giving a real answer. "No, really."

Cain looked up again with a weary sigh. "Really."

She cupped her breasts for a moment, as though he hadn't given them proper consideration. "Do you think I look like a kid?"

Cain rolled his eyes with a slight smile. "Hardly." Now he ran his eyes up and down her body with a true smile. "*You* look like a budding flower forever caught in the midst of opening its petals to the world."

Damn. You had to admit, the man could spin out words as smooth as silk. It sounded beautiful...but the translation in her mind: teenager. She smirked at him and put her hands to her hips, refusing to be pacified. "I *look* like someone who just escaped teeny-bopper hell to be endlessly embroiled in adolescent angst."

Cain looked at her oddly, as he considered her uncharacteristically embellished description. "Have you been into my poetry collection?" She just stared at him in annoyance. "We both know you are *very* much a woman." It was true, but as her mind aged and her body didn't, she couldn't help but wonder and worry that others might see some discrepancy. She'd always acted as though she was an adult, from an earlier age than she probably should have, but the last thing she wanted was to look like a teenager.

"You look perfect just the way you are," he told her sincerely.

She smirked at him. "You'd say that to just about anybody."

"You're right, and it'd be true...every time." She huffed at him in disgust and he smiled. "Honestly, you've no need for concern." He sat up and looked at her levelly, trying to express that he was being straight with her. "Even at sixteen, your body looks very much that of a grown woman. You should be thankful for your form, *now* and increasingly with each year that passes. How many 27-year-old women would give anything to look like you do? And how will you feel about it when you're 47...or 67? I can tell you truly, that at 347 I am very aware and appreciative of *my* body's youth, and I would be even if I were too homely to gain your attention."

She laughed. "Well lucky for you, that's not the case."

"If you're unhappy with your appearance, perhaps you should reconsider your *wardrobe*," he added with a stage whisper and an arched brow.

"You didn't like my dress?"

"If it were a shop window I would say that it functioned just fine."

She took a moment to try to interpret that, and then shifted her weight and rolled her eyes. "You've always hated my taste in clothes. You just want an excuse to complain about them."

Cain picked his book back up with a grin. "No comment. But you'll have to admit, the image that you present is up to you. Your body shouldn't be your bone of contention. I'd advise you to make peace with it now, because you're going to be living with it until the end of your days on Earth. If you want to look more adult, you ought to start dressing more like one."

"I dress like an adult," she said indignantly.

Cain smirked at her and then turned his eyes back to his book. "Not an 'adult-film star', a *real* adult."

Sindy just pouted at him as he resumed reading. Obviously, the man had no sense of modern women's fashion. "You're no help." She removed her push-up bra, to stand only in her panties. She cupped her breasts again and considered them thoughtfully. "Do you like my tits? I'm thinkin' about gettin' them done. I don't think I was quite finished." It was something she had been considering ever since Tempest had put the idea of altering her body into her head. Sindy's attempts to manipulate her form through magic were proving to be nothing but difficult and frustrating. She sucked at it, and was ready to give up and seek other means.

Cain dropped his book again and looked up at her in exasperation. "What?" he asked in disbelief.

"You know, a boob job."

"Breast enhancement *surgery?*"

"Yeah. I'm only a 'B'. It's still more than *Allie's* got," she said with an evil little chuckle. "But come on, don't tell me you wouldn't like a nicer handful."

"Are you insane?" he asked quietly.

"I wouldn't go 'Dolly Parton' or anything. A small 'D' would be good."

"It's surgery," he said simply.

"So? It's not like it'll kill me."

Cain tilted his head to look at her incredulously. "You can't go into a hospital."

"I think they do it out-patient now."

"That's not the point! You can't see a doctor! They'll take blood, do tests."

Sindy shrugged. "You've got more money than God. I'm sure we could find someone who was willing to put them in for me without a fuss."

Cain shook his head with a laugh. "It doesn't matter anyway. It wouldn't work."

Sindy looked up at him in irritation. "Why not?"

"They use large bags of silicone gel for that, right?" Sindy shrugged. Cain stared at her for a moment solemnly. "Have you ever been shot?"

She looked at him oddly. "No."

"I have. Wasn't fun."

"And this is relevant because…?"

Cain gave her a very steady look. "It was right in the chest. Somewhere…" he looked down and brushed his hand over his heart. "Over here somewhere. Long gone now of course. Not the slightest scar. But it must have hit a rib or something, because it didn't come out my back." Sindy made a face of disgust. He smiled and continued. "Healed up just fine though. In only a day or two you could barely even see where it'd gone in."

Sindy shrugged. "See we heal fast. No problem."

Cain grinned. "That's what I thought. A day or two after it looked gone though, it started to hurt again, terribly. See the bullet was still in there. A foreign object...like your earring." Comprehension seemed to dawn on Sindy's face as she remembered her ear-piercing incident. "My body knew it didn't belong there, and was rejecting it."

Sindy blanched. "Like...pushing it back out?"

Cain nodded. "Felt like getting shot again, in reverse slow motion. Damn thing took a day and a half before it finally burst out of my chest like that bloody alien from the movies."

"Ew!"

Cain just smiled. "So, if you greatly feel the need for breast enhancement, you could certainly try it. You might enjoy them for a night or two. But I know *I* don't want to be around when they *come back out.*"

Sindy stared at him in mute horror for a moment as he went back to reading his book. Finally, she swallowed and looked down at her chest again, nodding slightly. "Yeah...actually, I think I'm good." Cain gave a little chuckle as she slipped on her nightgown and climbed into the bed.

~~~~~~~~~~~~~~~~~~~~~~~~~~~~~~~~~

Sindy patted down the dirt over the last of the bulbs she'd been planting. They were Casa Blanca Oriental Lilies, and the guy at the nursery had told her they would make a perfect addition to a night garden, being a large beautiful flower of pale white color and strong fragrance that would spread and thrive each season without taking much care on her part.

She'd waited anxiously all winter to act on her idea of a surprise garden for Cain, but she knew nothing about gardening. She had made it very clear to the guy who had helped her purchase them, that she wanted plants that could manage on their own without much care. 'Dig a hole and drop a seed' was about the speed she was looking for. Hopefully these would come up nicely by summer, along with the Four O' Clock Mirabilis she'd just finished planting seeds for.

The garden wouldn't look like much yet, except for the Dianthus Cottage Pinks she'd put in. They'd come potted, so she could just transfer them to the holes she'd dug out. They smelled nice and looked easy to manage, so she'd bought tons of them to spruce up the secluded little private corner she'd converted. They were nice bushy clumps of greenery with lots of fragrant pink speckled flowers, their pale markings showing up nicely in the moonlight.

Of course, the focus of the garden, and her favorite part, was the beautiful lattice designed wrought iron bench she had bought and placed in the corner. Next to it was a matching lantern stand with a candle box-lantern hanging from its hook. She wasn't certain of Cain's tastes, but she'd noticed that he did have some wrought iron sconces and things in the house, so she hoped he would like it. It looked like something she imagined would fit into an old-fashioned English garden.

She brushed off her hands and sat down on the bench, imagining what a nice destination this would make for her future moonlit walks with Cain. She was startled by a faint voice whispering at her ear with a slight stirring breeze. "Far out little spot you've got here."

She jumped as a misty form swam into view and then materialized into human shape a few feet in front of her. He looked like a teenage boy with a thin, triangular sort of face, and long, wispy blonde hair.

He stood before her, nude after shifting. His frame was fairly tall and thin, as though he'd been changed into a vampire after a growth spurt, and never been allowed to fill out to his potential. He'd been even younger than Sindy when he was changed, she'd bet. As her eyes took in his pale, smooth-skinned body, with its un-imposing soft blonde wisps of curls beginning below his navel, she noticed his cock seemed to fill out a bit more under her gaze. Obviously, he'd been old enough...

She quickly tore her eyes from his body to find him watching her with an amused and mischievous little smile on his face. His eyes were large and arresting, a gorgeous bright green that one rarely saw naturally in humans, although often imitated with contact lenses.

Sindy composed herself from the shock of his arrival and stood from the bench, finding her height to be about even with that of her visitor. "Who the hell are you?" she asked, annoyed at being snuck-up on.

"Chill," he said, raising his hands in surrender. "We're on the same side. Arif sent me."

She froze at his words, hoping that her feelings of misgiving didn't clearly flash across her face. Some irrational part of her had been half hoping that Arif had somehow forgotten about her, dismissing her as a long-shot not to be counted on. It was so long ago that he had given her incentive to come back to Cain's estate. She should have known better, than to believe that he wouldn't have kept tabs on the situation. He always seemed to know everything. Of course, he had spies! "You're the shade that's been hanging around?" she surmised.

The guy smiled and tilted his head while supplying a better introduction. "That's me. Kieran." She had been about to give him her name, when he put a hand out to stop her. "I know you, *very* well," he admitted.

Unsettling information, to say the least. He seemed to appreciate her though, giving a small grin to show that he liked what he knew. She found herself a bit flattered by it. He was actually very good looking and kind of sexy, in a graceful, delicate sort of way. Not at all her type normally, but disarming all the same. She shook herself out of it and glanced around worriedly. "We can't be seen together."

"We won't be, thanks to you creating this pretty little secret garden. We look like teenage lovers meeting in the moonlight for a secret tryst," he teased. After a moment, he noticed how uncomfortable she seemed to be and added, "No offense. I'm even older than you are," he informed her confidentially.

It wasn't the teenage reference that had her feeling put-off, but she accepted the apology with a grateful smile. Older than she was? She couldn't help but wonder by how much. Was he forty, fifty, a hundred and fifty year old man…forever encased in the body of a fifteen-year-old boy?

Why would he think she might be offended by being called a teenager? She glanced down at her own body, self-consciously wondering if he'd somehow eavesdropped on her conversation with Cain last night. Whether Kieran had heard her or not, she was now very happy for the years of development she'd had, however few. When she looked back up at him, he seemed to decide that he wasn't being as charming as he'd hoped, and should simply get down to business. "How's it going?"

He was inquiring about Arif's proposal to her. She wasn't sure how to answer. 'I may have changed my mind' probably wouldn't go over well. He raised his eyebrows at her hesitation. "I'm sorry, am I distracting you?" he asked. He then fogged the lower half of his body into mist, that began just below his belly button and the nicely cut lines that drew down diagonally from his sharp hips.

Sure, she thought. Go ahead and believe that's what's distracting me. "It's fine. Everything's fine."

"I've finally seen some progress," he told her, seeming pleased to have something new to report to Arif after all of this. "She drinks?"

She smiled, realizing that despite his spying and assumptions, Kieran probably couldn't follow them to the clubs to see for himself, whether or not Allie was drinking from humans. Allie travelled really fast. "Yeah. She craves it."

"Of course she does. Will she come?"

"I'm trying." Actually, she hadn't mentioned *Kana Susamiş İçin Ev* to Allie since Arif had visited and invited Allie there himself, well over a year ago. Sindy had used the opening to feel Allie out on the idea, but she'd never really followed up on it. At first she didn't want to sound suspicious, but after a while, she'd just felt no rush to go there anyway. The grass wasn't always greener… "We're not there yet. I'm working on it."

"Are you? You don't know me, but I know you. I earn my keep by observing others, and translating actions into a person's motives and desires."

"So?"

"So I have been watching you for almost three years now. That's right, since you left Arif. Did you expect anything less? I watched as you took your time sizing up the Crimson Coven and learning their ways. I saw your fling with the wolf-man. Don't be offended. How much privacy did you really expect out here in the forest? I've seen more than my share in my years, and there isn't much you could do to make me blush. I'm just following orders."

"And I'm sure you enjoy it."

"What I've enjoyed is what I've learned about you. He meant nothing to you, that wolf. What you saw in him was an opportunity. You were curious about using your other form for sex, so you acted on your curiosity and seized the moment. You experience what you want, living in the moment, knowing that any night could see you turn to dust. I like that. I live that way myself.

I'm out in the field often, and I experience what I can of the world while I have opportunity. But I will say, that when I return to the compound, I am very happy to accept a bevy of beauties in my bed and all the blood I can drink. That is an arrangement you have yet to experience, and I know you'd like to find a place where you could be so content for a while."

"Wouldn't anyone? Why do you think I entertained Arif's offer?"

"But you made him no promises. You left thinking you could play both ends. He didn't see that, but I do. I know you like the idea of keeping an adoring harem for yourself and living in luxury, but you seem to like it here just as much. Sindy is going to do whatever makes Sindy happy in the moment, whether it's playing the good girl with Cain, playing the bad girl out with Alyson, or fulfilling the master's request, which you don't seem to be in any rush to do."

"I told Arif this would take some finesse. And anyway, he never told me she was…" She trailed off, catching herself from giving information she wasn't even sure others had.

"The United One?" Kieran asked with a smile. "Yes, we know. It doesn't matter. She knows you. You said that you could convince her to come."

"I said I would try." Sindy squinted at him in annoyance. "And since I wasn't given all the information, it's a little more complicated than I thought. If you want her to come willingly, it's going to take time."

"Arif understands that. Immortality teaches patience. But you've been here for a long while already. While you may be thinking that you'd like to explore your other options for a bit longer, the master is thinking that it's time for you to deliver. Trust me, you don't want to disappoint him. I haven't shared my concerns with him, but the wait alone will soon make him think stronger measures are needed."

Jeez, her feelings over the situation were muddled enough, the last thing she needed was for Arif to send in the B team. She crossed her arms, indignantly. "It would have been a lot easier if they hadn't seen you last year," she informed him. "You put the whole place on lock down. I couldn't take her anywhere."

"It won't happen again," he assured her, moving closer, floating on his cloud of mist in lieu of legs. With the lower part of his body still discorporate, he looked like a genie somehow freed from his magic lamp. He came so close she wondered if he would dare try to kiss her. Instead, he spoke in a whisper. "You'd better decide what it is you want. Because while you're getting nice and cozy here," he glanced around with a gesture to indicate the garden, a venture that surely seemed an investment in a long-term stay, "the master waits."

With that, he shifted himself into his vampire form, giving her an eerie but entrancing little smile that revealed the tips of his fangs, as his eyes shifted to become a deep emerald green flecked with almost hypnotizing bands of a bright lime color. After a moment, he mouthed her a quick kiss and then faded completely into mist, swirling up into the sky to disappear.

~~~~~~~~~~~~~~~~~~~~~~~~~~~~~

Sindy squirted some more soap into her palms and washed her hands yet again. The gardening soil was gone, but somehow she still felt dirty, as though the visit with Kieran had exposed plans and motives within her that she had decided to pretend didn't exist.

She couldn't accept a relationship with Cain, and a friendship with Allie and Mattie, living in this beautiful house as though she had no greater fears or expectations. As gratifying as it was to have finally achieved intimacy with Cain, she'd never thought that he might actually profess love for her... She wouldn't let him say it, but it always seemed to be hovering on his lips. She didn't want to hear it, because for the first time in her life, she knew she'd be tempted to admit that she felt the same in return.

Was that genuine, hopeful, and loving woman he had claimed to see, actually inside of her? Sindy suspected that she was, but she now realized that she couldn't afford to allow herself to be that woman, not quite yet. Cynthia may be the woman that Cain wanted, but she was also a victim. *Sin* was the persona with the survival instincts, and no matter what path she decided to follow, Sindy would need to rely on those instincts to navigate this mess. Harder times had forced her to make other plans, and now she was stuck having to lie in the bed that *Sindy* had made, whether she liked it or not.

Finally convinced that her hands were as clean as they were going to get, she dried them and collected her little basket of manicure supplies to bring to the kitchen table. She sat down and began picking under her nails with a file.

Alyson entered the room, startling her, but she did her best not to jump with a guilty start. Alyson didn't seem to notice. She strode in with a huge smile and didn't even bother going for the refrigerator. She sort of twirled around the kitchen a little and then leaned against the counter. "Hey girlfriend, how's tricks?"

Sindy rolled her eyes and continued with her manicure. Alyson was undaunted by the lukewarm reception. "Wasn't last night awesome? I am pumped. You were totally right, I've been *so* limiting myself. You want to be able to break out the big guns you need the right ammo. Am I right?"

Sindy muttered a non-committal "M-hmmm". Allie had chosen a large, imposing gorilla of a guy to drink from last night. She'd wanted to be able to take as much blood as possible, and felt empowered knowing the most intimidating of men were no match for her now. Sindy understood the feeling well.

Allie had mastered her techniques of thrall on humans, and had encountered no problems luring him into her clutches. Once she'd had him all to herself in the men's bathroom, she'd drunk more than ever before, while Sindy watched the door. Sindy'd kept poking her head in, and finally interrupted Allie when she was afraid the girl was going over-board, but it had all worked out okay. They'd left the guy slumped in the corner in a stupor, but he was sure to be fine.

Meanwhile, Allie had been so exuberant over the influx of powerful blood that Sindy had needed to tempt her to leave the bar just to get her out from under mortal eyes before she did something stupid. Her powers were noticeably increased.

Over the past few weeks, a few private tests had proved that she could indeed keep Sindy from using her own abilities to shift form. She just needed to be running on human blood to do it. It was a very unsettling feeling for Sindy, being blocked from shifting like that, almost scary. It gave her new and intimidated respect for Allie's power. Not only had it made her glad that she had given up her former plans to lure Allie to Arif, but it made her nervous about Allie altogether. Perhaps it was time to let Cain in on things for support.

While working in the garden, Sindy had been thinking she should speak to Cain about Allie's drinking and discoveries, but the meeting with Kieran had thrown that notion out the window. The realization that she was being so closely watched made her unsure what she should do. She didn't want it to be obvious to Kieran that she was giving Cain aide in controlling Allie's powers, when she was supposed to be driving the girl to Arif for help. Besides, could Cain even keep Allie in check? She barely listened to him anyway. It might not be a bad thing to have Allie go join Arif's coven. No doubt, he could at least make the girl control herself.

Did Mattie know about Allie's new ability, as per the new 'no secrets from him' rule? If Mattie knew, he would probably crack and talk to Cain about it soon, along with Alyson's new drinking habits. He was too honest and indebted to Cain to keep it from him for long. Then again, she was beginning to think she might not know Mattie as well as she'd thought she did. She never would have pegged him as having the power to kill with lightning, *and* actually using it. She should have realized that Allie was a little too 'wild child' to go for a guy that had no bend in him at all. Mattie must have a certain tolerance and penchant for danger...

Sindy made sure to shield her thoughts as best as she could, and give Allie an unconcerned smile, but Allie seemed to have taken note of Sindy's solemn mood and sat down opposite her at the kitchen table, putting her feet up on the edge of Sindy's chair across the way. "Whatcha doin'?" Allie asked in a jovial singsong lilt. She still seemed to be riding a bit of a high from their hunt last night.

Sindy focused on her task, unable to meet Allie's eyes. She un-gently nudged Allie's feet off her chair. "Getting the dirt out from under my nails."

Allie looked at her oddly for a moment, and then smiled in comprehension. "From the garden? How's it going? Is it done?"

Sindy let out a huff of annoyance, looking around, as though Allie might spoil the secret. Then she realized that both of them shared a blood bond with Cain and instinctively knew he was nowhere nearby. She was still annoyed though. "It still needs some work." Having Allie act all nice and friendly to her was just making it harder for her to think clearly about her situation, and was putting her on edge.

"Did you get the bench?" Allie asked with anxious delight. Sindy just nodded, wishing she'd never even told Allie about the damn thing. Allie sat up straighter in excitement. "Ooh, I want to see it."

"No," Sindy quickly replied. The last thing she wanted was for Allie to go snooping around the garden. What if Kieran had decided it should be their secret meeting place now or something? She didn't really think he would hang around there looking for her, but after that stupid 'spot for teenage lovers' remark, she wasn't so sure. "You can't," she warned Allie.

Allie looked insulted and annoyed to be brought down from her happy mood. "Why not?"

"Because…it's private. Sorry, I just don't want to show it to anyone. Cain hasn't even seen it."

Allie nodded, trying to be understanding. "Okay, I get that. Can I see the garden *after* you show Cain?"

"*No,*" she repeated in irritation. "I'm not even sure I'm going to finish it. It was a dumb idea anyway."

"It was not dumb. It's an awesome idea. It's so thoughtful. Cain is going to love it. I thought it was uncharacteristically cool of you."

Sindy gave her an irritated glare that it should have been considered 'uncharacteristic'. "Gee thanks."

Alyson seemed to have been drawn down from her high, and was now eying Sindy discerningly. "Did you and Cain have a fight? Are you mad at him or something?"

Great. She should have just played along on the happy train until Allie left her alone. "No. I ran out of money anyway and I'm just not feeling into it." It was true that Cain had given her some shopping money earlier in the month for clothing, and although it had been a generous amount, she'd spent most of it on the garden. She still couldn't afford the rest of the flowers she wanted anyway.

Sindy chose a bottle of nail polish from the basket to show Allie, hoping to shift focus. "What do you think, good color?" It was a terribly dark shade of crimson that looked almost black. She opened it and began painting her nails.

"Yeah, it matches your mood. If you and Cain aren't fighting, then what's wrong with you? You're all disheveled and dark."

Sindy looked up in alarm, accidently painting the side of her finger rather than her nail. "Are you reading my mind?"

"No. You know I can't unless you're sending me stuff. We'd have to share blood for an involuntary connection."

Sindy took a deep breath and sighed. She'd better cool it and stop psyching herself out. She fumbled for a Q-tip from the basket, dipped it in nail polish remover, and cleaned off the paint she'd gotten on her finger while Allie continued. "I can feel you though," Allie reminded her, "and even if I couldn't, you're obviously bugged about something. What gives?"

"Cain and I aren't fighting. What's to fight about? He doesn't even care that much. He just wants someone here to comfort him so he isn't alone, right?" She forced herself to say it casually, to believe it – true or not, and she waited for Allie to confirm it. If it was true, then she could do whatever else was expected of her and leave him, not having to think twice about what could have been.

Allie slumped her shoulders and gave Sindy a reassuring smile. "It is true that you being here has helped him a lot, but he really cares about you too, and if he doesn't show it enough, just give him a chance to settle into it. He will. In the meantime, you get a cool house, a full glass, and he even buys you stuff once in a while. Pretty sweet deal."

Sindy had been thinking that herself, but she couldn't help but play devil's advocate. "It is a comfy set-up, but I don't think it'll ever be more than that. I'm not the woman he really wants, I'm just *here*, hanging on his arm like an accessory." Funny how originally, that was all she'd thought she had wanted. Suddenly it just didn't seem like enough.

She knew she meant more to him, and he would show her that, if she allowed him to, but she couldn't bring herself to truly let him in. She craved deeper love from him, but was afraid to let him give it, so she'd settled for this comfortable, indecisive limbo…and Cain seemed content with that for now. He was very happy having the United One to train, Mattie for friendship, and Sindy to join him in bed when he'd finished reading for the evening. "No… I'm more functional than an accessory," Sindy insisted. "Oh my God, I'm like a practical pair of shoes!" Allie couldn't help but laugh. "You think that's funny?" Sindy asked in outrage.

"It's kind of funny."

"It's pathetic! I am not orthopedic brown flat loafers! I am a pair of high end spike stilettos, baby."

Allie chuckled. "No, you used to be a cheap pair of red fuck-me pumps. These days, you're more like a nice pair of wedge sandals; comfortable, reliable, you can dress them up or down, they're not particularly showy, but they work for any occasion. I think it's a big improvement." Sindy thought otherwise of the description, but Allie grinned. "Just face it and be glad you're getting worn."

Sindy opened her mouth in outrage and let out a huff of disbelief. "When did you turn into such a bitch?" she asked.

"Probably around the same time I started hanging out with you."

Sindy squinted at her condescendingly. "Well it doesn't look good on you."

Allie folded her arms with a smirk. "Thought you could use a mirror."

Sindy mulled that over and then let it go. She went back to painting her nails. "Are we friends?" she finally asked.

"Sure." Allie answered her without even needing time to reflect. She wasn't thinking into it deeply. There had been a time many years ago, when they had both been human, that Sindy *had* thought they might be friends.

They'd barely met, Allie having been a few grades ahead of her in school, but Sindy knew that Allie had been Ben's best friend at the time, and Sindy had definitely wanted to be counted as important in Ben's life. Although she didn't really have any good friends of her own, it had seemed natural to her that through Ben, Allie might be someone she could connect with...

Then everything in life seemed to have gotten turned upside down, and she'd somehow found herself a rejected-ex, turned stalker-vampire, putting she and Allie on opposite sides of most fights. The result: Allie was someone that although she'd always felt an odd affinity for, Sindy'd never thought she'd have much problem screwing over if the situation called for it. And now Allie was sitting here watching her polish her nails and calling her a friend.

"That's a weird question," Allie added.

Sindy shot her a derisive look. "No, it isn't. Considering there've been very few people in my life that I could really count on as friends, without coercion or sex appeal, I think it's a very valid question. Besides, it wasn't really all that long ago that you hated my guts, Allie."

Allie was watching her thoughtfully, without answering. When it was clear she had nothing to say, Sindy kept going. "In fact, if you think about it, the two people that I am closest to in the whole world right now, have both actively tried to kill me at one time or another. Don't you think that says something about me?"

Allie was watching her with a level stare. "I never gave you a reaction you didn't earn," she finally answered quietly. "And I'm sure you would've had to push Cain pretty far before he'd snap. Read it how you want," she replied with a shrug. "But you know what they say, you only hurt the ones you love."

Sindy shook her head, dismissing the idea. "Do you think I'm a bad person? Be honest."

"Sometimes." Allie answered after a pause for thought. She contemplated a moment more, and then elaborated with a sardonic smirk. "And you used to be incredibly self-involved, manipulative and, well...basically *I* always thought you were an evil bitch." Allie smiled at Sindy's indignant frown. "But lately, not so much. Now you're almost kind of cool."

Sindy returned the smile. "For an evil bitch."

Allie grinned and nodded. "Right."

"Thanks. I knew I could count on you for honesty."

"Sure. What're friends for?" Allie traded her smile for a more serious countenance and met Sindy's eyes. "I never liked who you were, or the things you did, but I also didn't know what I know now...why you were like that."

Sindy spoke quickly, wanting to cut off Allie from saying more, and feeling annoyed and embarrassed at having to wonder how much Allie really knew about her. "I guess I just got tired of being damaged," Sindy told her. Her voice was quiet, but had a harsh edge.

"So you decided to be *damaging?*"

"If I had to choose between the two..."

Allie sighed. "Doesn't make it right, but perspective changes things," she added thoughtfully. As Sindy tried to digest that, Allie picked up a clean cotton ball from the basket and tossed it at her, attempting to shift the mood. "Friends, mortal enemies...whatever. Are we going out again tomorrow night?"

Sindy couldn't help but laugh at her enthusiasm. "Kind of soon isn't it? You're still holding a smoking gun."

Allie brushed off the comment with a wave of her hand. "Don't be dramatic. I just want to keep my levels up...you know, until I've had a chance to test out everything I can do."

Sindy gave her a dubious grin. "Uh-huh."

"Okay, I've got to admit the power trip is a rush. I feel limitless, like my mojo is off the charts! And I'm not even thirsty at all. *I* actually fed Mattie this evening, which was a nice switch."

"He was okay about it?"

"I wouldn't say he's happy, but he's stopped complaining. He doesn't want details, he just tells me to be careful a million times. We can go again tomorrow."

Sindy finished up her nails, and closed the bottle. "You know, it's kind of risky going back so soon. You start leaving lots of marks around, and somebody is bound to notice."

"So we'll go somewhere else," Allie said with an easy shrug. "Can I use this?" Allie asked of the nail polish basket. Sindy pushed it over to her and Allie began sorting through colors.

"I don't know," Sindy said warily. Kieran's visit had freaked her out a little, and she couldn't help but feel that they were safer staying home, under the protection of Cain and the Crimson Coven. "I like to get a fix now and then myself, but you've got to space them out if you don't want other vamps to know you're around. Even I supplement with animal blood. It's just smarter long term. I know you can travel really far to spread your marks around, but that's going to get old fast, don't you think? What a pain in the ass."

Sindy blew on her nails to dry them. Allie was looking at her as though she was being ridiculous. "It's worth it! Travelling isn't a big deal."

"For you. You're moving under your own power. I'm the one getting dragged all over creation like luggage. Besides, it takes half the night just flying out and back. I'd almost rather stay home. Too bad Cain doesn't have servants to drink from anymore."

"What?" Allie asked her incredulously.

"That's what he did in the old days. He told me, I swear. Back in England, he and Maribeth lived in a luxurious manor, and had a whole staff of household servants they could drink from in a pinch, when they weren't out murdering half the town."

Allie's eyes couldn't have gotten much wider. "He never told me that."

"Of course not," Sindy said with a laugh. "He's trying to be a role model for you."

"Then why did he tell you?"

"Because I've already hit lows that you've never dreamed of…being an evil bitch and all," she added with a snicker. "He wanted me to know that he understood, that he's been there. 'Murdering half the town' is probably an exaggeration, but he and Maribeth did kill people together back then."

"Maribeth…" Allie repeated the name reflectively as she chose a light lavender color of nail polish and began shaking the bottle to mix it up. "Every Christmas I expect her to show up again, with that guy Drake, like she did a few years ago. Even Cain said he thought she'd come back, that they hadn't really had much of a chance to talk. I wonder why they broke up all those years ago."

"He stopped killing people, she didn't."

"Oh. Well, I guess that would put a strain on any relationship, huh?" Allie asked, looking a bit troubled.

Sindy commented on her expression. "So does drinking, doesn't it? Mattie doesn't really approve, even if he isn't being difficult. That must be getting hard on you guys."

Allie shrugged, but it obviously worried her. "I'm not hurting anyone, that's the main thing. The whole business of violating people without consent is a little murky for him, but I figure if they were going to be willing to fuck me, they weren't against me being intimate with their bodies, and as long as I don't hurt them, it's not really so bad, is it?"

"You're asking the wrong person," Sindy reminded her with a smirk. As Allie began painting her nails, Sindy recognized an opening and decided to go for it. "That is one thing that *Kana Susamış İçin Ev* has going for it," she remarked casually. "They've got guilt free drinking down to science over there."

"Where?"

"The place Arif invited you to, in the Hamptons. I told you about it. It's a vampire community where every vamp gets their own group of human blood donors to drink from. It's all totally consensual, they know exactly what they're getting into. They like it even. You know how great a venom high can be. You must have been completely addicted to Mattie before he turned you."

Allie smiled at the memory. "I practically used to beg him for it."

"See. The vampires support the humans and the humans feed them. It's actually a pretty cool system. I'm sure it's more sophisticated than what I know about it, but from what I've heard, it's a nice set up. I was surprised you passed up the offer." Allie continued to focus on her nails, but was obviously thinking it over. Sindy went on. "If you're going to be drinking regularly, maybe you should reconsider. At least in that environment, drinking wouldn't be risky for you, and Mattie would have nothing to object to about it."

"I don't know. I just get a weird vibe from that guy. He did say I could bring Mattie, and we could stay indefinitely, having all the blood we could drink, but why such a generous offer? Why is he so worried about me?"

"Because you're the United One. It's probably like a status thing. He gets to say that he's host to the most powerful vampire there is, like he's somebody special. The guy is already rich and powerful, what else is there for him to want but image? And much like Cain, do you really think it makes any difference to him if there are a few more vampires living on his property? Having to support you is not an issue."

"He said he wanted me there so he could teach me how to control my powers, so I could learn how to shut them down and not use them too much. He said using them was going to release darkness in me and make me evil," Allie confided in her, sounding a bit shaky over it.

"Really?" Sindy asked with some trepidation. Allie shrugged, uncertainly. "That doesn't seem to have stopped you from using them," Sindy observed with a smile. "Do you think he's wrong?"

"I don't know. I think there are urges and temptations inside me that aren't completely mine, like from the vampire blood, but I don't think it's going to *take me over* or anything. I'm a pretty strong person."

"I'll bet he was just being metaphorical. Having power like yours probably could warp someone into something dark. He was just trying to warn you not to let it. I don't think he has bad intentions. He probably just wants to make sure you don't get more powerful than he is, you know? He likes to think of himself as a leader, and having you in his camp only gives him more authority, right?" Arif had certainly never spoken of motives to her, but it made sense.

"It's not like I would ever *do* anything for him though."

"You wouldn't have to. Image is everything. Just having you there makes him look better. Sounds like an all expense paid vacation to me."

Allie seemed deep in thought as she gave a small laugh. "Or a cruise."

Sindy furrowed her brow at the cryptic remark. "A cruise?"

"Do you ever think about our blood, the vampire blood inside of us that made us into what we are? I think of it as its own separate entity."

"You do?"

"I've seen some freaky stuff that definitely leads me to believe there's more to it than just blood. I think of it like a bunch of passengers on a boat in a storm."

"A boat?"

"Yes, a boat. Cain's always saying our bodies are vessels to be filled with…I don't know, the holy spirit or something."

Sindy laughed. "That's a totally different kind of vessel, like a container, not a boat."

Allie grinned, "I know, but the first time he said it, that's what I thought of, and now that's what makes sense to me. The world is a windy, wavy place, and for the most part, the blood is just happy to have a safe place to ride it out. But sometimes, when you have a strong passenger, they want to captain the ship. It's not easy to fight the storm and the tides, and sometimes the boat is just going to do what it wants, but if you have a strong enough captain, it can be steered in the general direction that the passengers want to go."

Sindy was eying her doubtfully. "Where do they want to go?"

"I don't know. I'm just the boat. But the way I see it, Arif has himself a whole fleet of sailboats, which is nice, but it's still not the same as having a luxury cruise liner in your harbor. If we're boats, I've gotta be top of the line, don't you think? I have no idea what the advantage would be to having me dock there, but…what if his passengers are thinking they'd like a nicer ride?"

"Allie this isn't making any sense to me at all."

"I just get the feeling that there is stuff going on, on levels that we don't understand. When you can't see through the storm and you haven't got a map, I guess navigating the deeper game just comes down to trusting your instincts."

"What do your instincts tell you?"

"That I want to captain my own boat, and I'm better off in open water." Allie closed up her nail polish bottle and gingerly dropped it back into the basket before looking to see Sindy's reaction.

"Well…my instincts tell me that you drank a really big guy last night, and you are still trippin'." Allie seemed disappointed that Sindy didn't seem to get what she was saying, but there was more than enough drama and intrigue going on at *this* level for Sindy's taste, and the last thing she needed was to start worrying about existential insidiousness on levels she didn't know existed. She had no idea what Arif might want with Allie either, it was just her job to try to bring her there. It seemed smarter to let it go, than to push.

Time to change the subject. "Listen, I had a question for you," she told Allie, as she cleaned up the last of the manicure supplies and dumped them back into the basket. "Have you tried any of the modification stuff that Tempest told us about, to make alterations to your forms?"

"I've played around with it a little. Nothing major. Why?"

"I'm having a hard time with it. I did that one exercise where she had us make our claws longer and sharper, but it took me forever, and I'm not very good at constructing my own designs. I was wondering, if I screw up my blueprint, is it easy to put it back to the way it was?"

"You can always revert back to your human form as a default. Then the next time you shift into the wolf, you should be able to use your original format."

"I wasn't going to change the wolf. I was thinking of altering my human body. If I do it wrong, I can still change it back, right?"

Allie seemed put-off by the idea, but answered after some thought. "That's a little scary, but I don't see why not. What were you going to do?"

Sindy spared a quick glance to make sure they were alone. She could feel that Cain wasn't around, but she didn't have that kind of connection with Mattie. "I want bigger boobs," she admitted confidentially. Allie burst out laughing. "I don't see why that's funny," she admonished sourly. "*You* of all people should be able to get where I'm coming from. You're so good at this modification stuff, I'm surprised you haven't already done it for yourself," she added snidely.

Allie narrowed her eyes. "What for? I don't really care, and if something stupid like that was important to Mattie, we would have broken up a long time ago. I hope you don't think that'd be important to *Cain*."

Sindy shook her head non-commitally. "He tells me he likes my body fine the way it is, but I don't know if I believe him, because I know he looks past that kind of thing."

Allie squinted at her in disbelief. "That barely even makes sense. Do you not see the compliment in that statement? He cares about who you are inside."

"I know, that *should* be what's important, but…let's face it, I need to prepare myself as best I can for the future, whether Cain is in it or not. We both know I'm not exactly the woman of his dreams."

Allie slumped her shoulders. It didn't matter though, even if Allie argued differently, they both knew the truth. "Don't say that," Allie admonished her. "I told you, he's not just comfortable, he cares strongly about you. If he didn't, you wouldn't still be here."

"I'm just trying to figure out modification, so I can have another skill in my arsenal, okay? Are you going to help me or not? This stuff is really hard."

"It is hard, but you can do it if you work at it. If you're going to put the time, effort, and energy into crafting a modification, do you really think you should be focusing on the size of your boobs? We should be working on amazing new defensive modifications, things we could use as weapons, and for protection."

Sindy replied with a huff of disgust. Allie just didn't understand. "Maybe you think it's trivial, but I'm not talking about something like giving myself long pretty colored finger nails. Like it or not, there is an inherent advantage in the human world to having an eye catching body, especially when you're on the prowl for a meal. Even without the vampire aspect, you of all people should recognize the self-confidence value of having larger breasts."

Allie sighed. "I'm not going to pretend that I don't get what you're saying, but *come on.* Have there been times I wished I had bigger tits…or *any tits at all,* sure. But does it really matter to me? No. Do I let it affect my self-confidence? Hell no! If anything, it's taught me to rely on things within myself that *aren't* superficial. Besides, what would I do with a bunch of extra weight making me top heavy and off balance for fighting? I think it would be annoying."

Sindy shook her head with a little laugh. "Well, I'm a lover, not a fighter. And trust me, if you were thrown out into the world, living on the street, using only your guile and your wiles to survive, you might wish you had more to work with too. Don't try to make me sound like an idiot, just because we each have different tools in our belts.

The fact is, I know what I bring to the table, and I rely on my strengths. I'm not a fighter like you, I never will be. And to be honest, being able to make some kind of clever new weapon modification might be cool and useful, but I'm a realist, and I know that I'm just not that good at this stuff. For those of us who *aren't* the United One, it's damn hard, Allie. I can't even make the bat right. How am I gonna make some entirely new thing of my own design? I need to keep it simple. I figured I'd start with a little extra padding, see if it works, and take it from there."

"I'm sorry," Allie offered quietly. "I don't think you're an idiot."

"Thank you."

"I guess I forget that things come easier to me than to other vampires. I'll be happy to help you do whatever you want. We can work on stuff together. For me, I still think it could be cool to work on something harder though."

"Like what?"

"Well, you've got me thinking…about doing my nails…"

Part 4

Crossing the Line

Chapter 14 - Auntie Allie

Allie

Felicity and Ben's new house, Long Island, New York
An evening in April

"This has got to be the cutest baby in the whole world! He's so adorable, I can barely stand it, and I don't even like babies," Allie told Felicity, while holding little almost-three-month-old Christian in her lap. "But I'll make an exception for you, little man," she told the baby, leaning down and whispering to him confidentially, "because you are very special."

"I'm glad you finally got to come out here to meet him in person."

"Well he's had so much family hovering around him I haven't had a chance! I don't think Ben would've appreciated me showing up in the middle of the night…even if I would like to finally see him, too." She gave the baby a last kiss and then handed him over so Felicity could change him for bed. "What if I was here, when he gets home tomorrow?"

Felicity shot her a look that translated as Alyson clearly being insane to think that would be a good idea. She laid Christian down on the changing table before answering. "No. You are not going to do that to me."

"Why not? What's the big deal? It could be a good time to do it. He comes back out from the city to start his new job in his new house, with his beautiful wife and new baby, and he has the support of an old friend."

"I don't think so. Have you not been paying attention? They are making him crazy at work. He couldn't even come out here with me as planned, so I had to spend our first official night living in the house, without him. When he comes out tomorrow he has one day off, and then he has to go in and start at the new office, which he is feeling really anxious about. This is not the time to dump this on him. Let us settle in first."

"I was thinking of myself as more of a pleasant surprise, than a dump…" Allie pointed out, as Felicity wrapped up the baby's dirty diaper for disposal. Felicity couldn't help but crack a smile, but still shook her head no. "But it's never a good time," Allie complained. "I don't want to wait anymore."

Now Alyson could feel Felicity growing aggravated. "Allie, I have been giving you windows of opportunity since the wedding. The whole time I was pregnant I begged you to come talk to him before the baby came. It's not my fault you were too busy out learning how to seduce guys out of their blood, and playing wolf in the woods." Allie narrowed her eyes at Felicity's description of things, but she couldn't honestly refute it.

Allie opened her mouth to speak, but Felicity wouldn't let her. "I know: time flies when you're immortal, and you've got big important things going on that I wouldn't understand. Well that's just fine, but I think you've forgotten what it's like to understand being human. I'm sorry, but our lives are going on here. We have stress and problems, and bills and concerns that you don't even have to think about. We don't spend all our time playing around like Peter Pan and the Lost Boys, we have to be grown ups and sometimes it's really hard. You think it's easy moving, and building a new life, and taking care of a newborn? We're completely sleep deprived, socially deprived, sex deprived… It's *not a good time.*"

"Okay," she said quietly, leaning down to nuzzle the baby, making him kick and wriggle as Felicity tried to get his clothes on. "Mommy and daddy are grumpy from lack of sex. I'll wait."

"Thank you," replied with a tone of thinly veiled annoyance. "I'm sorry to sound so harsh, but you have to think about the consequences. I mean, I hope things go well, and I've been trying to subtly prepare him for you as best I can, but you know he is going to be thrown for a loop. You get to leave afterwards, while I have to stay here and hold everything together, and he has not been in a good mood lately, trust me. He's spread thin right now. He uses up what little patience he has to enjoy the baby, and he's got a short fuse. That's why I wanted you to come while I was pregnant, when things were more exciting than stressful."

"You were in the middle of moving."

"Right," Felicity answered as she fit Christian's tiny legs into his feety pajamas and did up his snaps. "Did you ever think that having a friend with supernatural strength might have come in handy right about then?"

Allie laughed and rolled her eyes. "Sorry. I'll make it up to you. Want me to hold up the couch while you vacuum or something?"

"Not at the moment, but the next time I'm vacuuming before bed, I'll give you a call." Felicity lifted the baby and held him up in front of her.

"Isn't Auntie Allie silly, thinking mommy cares if there is dust under the couch?"

Allie smiled, and then became distracted by the baby for a moment. "He doesn't like those."

"Those what?"

"Those pajamas."

"Christian?" Felicity asked incredulously, realizing what Allie was talking about. The baby didn't seem to be uncomfortable though. "What do you mean?"

"They're itchy," she answered simply.

Felicity put the baby down on the changing table again, running her hand over the material to reassure herself. "No, they aren't."

"Sure they are. Inside, in the legs, there's something about the seam."

Felicity just stared at her in shock for a moment, and then ripped open the snaps to feel inside the pajamas. When she found the section Allie was talking about, she looked up at Allie, open-mouthed. "How did you know that?" Allie just shrugged. It didn't really need an explanation, just some processing. Felicity gently lifted the baby's legs out of the jammies, running her hands over his smooth skin soothingly as she thought about it. "You can hear him?"

"Kinda."

"Oh my God. What else is he thinking?" she asked anxiously.

"Not much. He's a baby, Felicity. It's not really like reading his mind, it's more the empathy."

Felicity looked ready to hyperventilate. "But this is incredible! Allie you can hear his thoughts! You know what he's thinking, when he can't even talk yet. You'll always know what he wants, how he feels, everything about him…more than I will."

"That's not true, you're his mother. Trust me, you'll know him."

"You have to tell me everything, always. It'll be amazing."

Allie folded her arms with a smile. "Felicity, I'm a vampire, not the baby whisperer."

Felicity got out a new set of pajamas and held them up for Allie's approval. Allie glanced at the baby dubiously and then shrugged. He was too busy contemplating the lamp, to notice which new jammies were coming, or have an opinion on them. Felicity began putting them on him as she asked thoughtfully, "Do you think you'll be able to hear him from far away, like you do me?"

Allie ran her hand through her hair and shifted her weight, not caring for where this was going. She could understand Felicity's interest and excitement, but she didn't particularly care for the idea of playing constant baby interpreter for the next two years until the kid could talk. "I don't know."

"You want to hold him again?" Felicity asked, holding him out to her.

"Sure." She took the baby into her arms and easily found a comfortable way to hold him. It was kind of cool that although she had never really had an affinity for babies, or felt comfortable with them before, Christian just meshed with her perfectly. She didn't feel awkward to hold him as she'd feared, because she knew just how he wanted to be held, and could anticipate his needs.

"You know I always wanted you in his life," Felicity assured her. "Not just because you can read his mind. I've always wanted you and Ben to reconcile, and for us to all be friends again. I absolutely hate keeping secrets from him. I don't want to do it anymore."

"I know what that's like," Allie muttered, thinking of her own trials over having secrets from Mattie.

"I just want to be sure the timing is as conducive as possible to a warm reception. Then we can be like a big happy...weird family." Felicity added. "Every kid needs a mysterious kooky aunt to come by once in a while and keep things interesting, even if she is a vampire."

Allie looked up at her in steadfast seriousness. "I just want you to know, that you never, *ever* have to worry about me with him. I mean, I've got everything completely under control, and I would rather die than hurt him, or you. He's safer with me than he would be with most humans."

"I know."

"Well, the fact that you have been wanting me to come see him, without even a second thought about it... I just want you to know how grateful I am for your trust. I mean, let's face it, the truth of the matter is that I *am* a blood-thirsty monster."

"No, you aren't," Felicity quietly refuted.

Allie gave her a straight stare. "Monster may be debatable, but blood-thirsty is definitely not, so I'm really honored that you have such confidence in me. Thank you for that. I will never let you down."

"I know you won't," Felicity told her with a smile. She pointed towards the bassinet in the corner of the bedroom, and Allie carried the baby over to be put down for bed. "And being that you're a telepathic empath, you must also know that no matter how powerful you are, if you were ever to hurt my son, I would find a way to dust you for it."

"I would laugh…but I know you aren't joking," Allie answered as she laid Christian down. "Don't worry mama. Between me, you, and his daddy, this boy has got to be the safest baby on earth."

"Don't forget his vampire-hunting grandpa. This kid has more protectors… Now if only I didn't have to worry about all the guardians killing each other, everything would be great."

As though right on cue, a man's voice rang out from the front of the house. "Hello?"

Both women froze in shock, although their expressions were quite different. Alyson was protectively menacing, while Felicity wore an expression of terrified worry. "That's Bernard," Felicity whispered warningly.

Allie's eyes widened. *What's he doing here?*

I don't know, and the door was locked.

"Felicity?" They could hear that he had begun moving through the house.

With a sudden shift that startled Felicity, Alyson transitioned into mist, causing all of her clothing to fall to the floor in a heap, pulling most of her down with it. She struggled to thread her way out of the clothing as quickly as possible, so that she could thin out and be less noticeable, rather than appear as a dark cloud.

Felicity watched, wide-eyed, as Alyson floated towards the ceiling. Once she was sufficiently clear Felicity glanced down and deftly kicked her clothing under the bed. Bernard knocked on the wall. It sounded like he was out in the hallway, just shy of the bedroom door, which was partially open. Felicity paused for a second of thought, and then opened the window, so Allie would have a way out, before she rushed to the bedroom doorway to intercept Bernard. "Shhh, you'll wake the baby."

"I'm sorry, but you had me worried, not answering."

"Well, what are you doing here?" she asked, coming out into the hall. "You scared me to death. And how did you get in?" she asked, while quietly closing the door until it was open barely a crack, so she could still hear the baby.

"Ben was worried about you, spending your first night in the house alone, and he asked me to stop by."

Gee, thanks honey, she thought to herself, glad that Bernard couldn't read minds. Ben was going to get an earful about this one. "I'm fine. I just talked to him on the phone a few hours ago."

"I still had the key from when I brought over the crib," he explained, taking it off his key ring to give back to her. "Ben just feels badly that he couldn't be here, but they need him in the office early tomorrow. I was going to be out this direction, so I told him I'd swing by on my way back. I'm sorry if I startled you."

"No, it's fine," she said, leading him out into the living room.

Bernard turned back towards the hallway, reluctant to go. "Can't I just peek in at the baby first? I won't wake him."

"Nope, sorry. Took me forever to get him down and he needs his sleep. You just saw him yesterday. Want a cup of coffee or something?"

Bernard read her polite expression and then smiled. "No, thank you. I'm not planning to stay and interrupt your evening any further. Just doing my duty. I've got someplace else to be and I'm sure you'll appreciate the quiet time. Just know that I'm only a phone call away if you ever need me."

Felicity walked him to the door with a grateful smile. "Thanks."

Chapter 15 - Forever in bloom

Cain

Cain's Estate, Upstate, New York
An evening in April, a few nights later

Goodbye. How was he going to say goodbye to Felicity? The simple answer was that he couldn't. He had spent a good hour sitting at his desk this evening, pen in hand, feeling pressure to write a beautiful, endearing, heartfelt letter of parting to Felicity. But although lovely, romantic phrases of star-crossed love and misled destiny found their way to the page, the letter went on and on. It would not close. He could not end it.

The letter itself didn't truly matter. She would never read it. It would be locked away in the box with all of the other letters he had written to her. He had even bought a new combination lock to put on it, so that the letters would never be found and read by another. This would be the last letter, a letter of goodbye. Then he would lock it away with the others, and not write to her anymore, out of respect for her husband, and for Sindy. He would say goodbye as he was supposed to, and move on. That was the plan.

He couldn't do it. Even if he were never to see her again, and even if after another 347 years, he still somehow roamed the earth, and she was long gone from the world, she would always be his true love, living on in his heart. He would never truly say goodbye, never.

In a strictly practical sense, their lives were separate now, and if only out of respect for those around them, each needed to move on. He would assume that after her wedding to another man, she had. Had he? Well…not entirely, although Lord knew it wasn't for a lack of trying. What more could he do? He had allowed himself a respectable mourning period, and then he had forced himself to move on.

It wasn't that Sindy wasn't a worthy woman. Others may disagree, but he saw something in her that drew him and gave him hope for the future.

She was certainly of stunning face and figure, and she was quite adept at making him feel desirable as a man, but those things didn't have much influence on his decision. They simply made it easier for others to accept, and easier for him to distract himself in difficult times. His intrigue lay more with her inner strength, clever mind, and ability to persevere through the circumstances she'd been given.

While others may dwell on her shortcomings of selfish, manipulative behavior, he knew much of that stemmed from deep-seated insecurities, which maturity and a nurturing relationship could heal. He saw potential within her. He felt love for the fragile woman beneath the façade, and honestly wanted to give her the care and confident support she needed to stop relying on her tricks and wiles; to let her feel safe to be a woman of her own choosing, not the world's. As he had told her once long ago, she had the potential to become a truly splendid creature.

But she wasn't Felicity, an undeniable fact that doomed his good intentions. Sindy could be a woman worthy of his love…but she wasn't *his* love.

Even that wasn't really true, because he did love Sindy. He knew that he did. He recognized it in himself, finally facing it, rather than hide behind denial of his feelings for her. He'd even tried to tell her so, although she wouldn't really let him voice it. Why was that? Perhaps because she sensed the truth, that while he did love her, he still loved Felicity as well. He had thought he could let Felicity go, especially once he'd fully accepted Sindy, but it was harder than he'd thought. He could never really say goodbye to Felicity, not in his heart.

He gave up writing, and put his stationary supplies away in the large box, already filled with past letters, testaments to his foolish refusal to let her go. Perhaps it was just going to take more time. He would focus on the budding new love he felt for Sindy and try not to dwell on the rest. Sindy was approaching. He could feel his mark on her growing stronger to his senses as she came nearer to him. He quickly closed and locked the wooden letterbox.

Though it contained nothing more than paper and his own musings, never to be seen by another, it felt terribly unkind and disrespectful to think that Sindy might know of them. She may suspect what was in his heart, but he would never be so cruel as to allow her confirmation. He had accepted Sindy into his home, his heart, and his bed. She deserved nothing less than his full attention. He slid the box under his bed as she entered the room. He swiftly stood and turned to face her, as she paused just within the doorway.

She wore the artfully embroidered oriental robe of red silk that he had bought for her at an auction he'd attended with Mattie not long ago. The robe was embellished with metallic threads woven into Chinese dragons of gold, jet black, royal blue and emerald green. The pattern was striking and sharp, in lovely contrast to the garment's soft flowing style.

At his request, Sindy had taken to hanging it on a hook by the back door whenever she was out shifting, then she would wear it into the house. Not only did it look exquisite on her, but it also discouraged her penchant for entering the house without clothing, a sore point that Alyson and Mattie had often complained over.

"How was your hunt?" he asked.

"Good as it could be…considering the prey. What have you been up to?"

"Nothing." Sindy raised an eyebrow, and tilted her head, eyeing the place where he had pushed his letterbox under the bed. "It's nothing," he assured her.

"Really?" she asked with a coy smile. "Then why do you look so guilty?" She moved closer, running her hands over both of his shoulders. "I don't know if I've ever seen that look on you before. Aren't you the guy who always does the right thing?"

He gave a small huff of a laugh and lowered his eyes. "Yeah, that's me."

She must have recognized the sadness that had suddenly settled over him. She smiled and gave him a gentle push away from her as she sought to catch his gaze. "Well, maybe I can tempt you with some more enjoyable guilty pleasures." As she spoke, she untied her robe and let it slip down her shoulders to the floor. She wore nothing beneath it.

He sighed with a smile. He didn't want to insult her, but he wasn't really in the mood. He was just looking up to meet her eyes and tell her as much, when something caught his attention. He couldn't place it at first. She stood there in one of her familiar poses, hand on hip and giving him a sultry smile as she modeled her body for him, as she had done many times, but something had changed.

"Have you done something…different?" It seemed a silly question. She was nude. Her hair was the same as always, hanging long, straight and dark as night down her back. She wore no make-up, it wasn't her hair or face. It was her body.

"What do you mean?" she asked with a little smirk of a smile.

His eyes widened a fraction as realization came over him. It was nicely subtle, he had to admit, but there was a definite change. Just a slightly more rounded fullness had been added to her breasts and her hips. Without looking completely different, she had somehow become just a bit more voluptuous; heightened curves replacing the slim, willowy lines he was used to seeing in her figure. "What have you done?" he asked in quiet wonder.

She turned a bit, smoothing her hand slowly down the curve of her hip and thigh. "You like?" She inhaled, enhancing the effect of her newly full bosom.

He could not stop staring and trying to figure out what he was looking at. He couldn't give her the approval she was looking for without understanding. "That depends, what am I seeing?"

She let out her breath with a laugh. "Relax. No artificial padding, or silicone. It's all me. I'm a shape-shifter," she told him with a smile and a spread of her hands. "I've just learned how to *shift* things to the way I want them."

Now he returned her smile, shaking his head at the amazement of it. He'd had no idea that such a thing was possible, although perhaps he should have guessed. The details of abilities red-eyed vampires were capable of were something he had never delved into. He assumed that their alternate forms of bat and wolf were the extent of their powers. Apparently, he was wrong. He slumped his shoulders and met her eyes. "You know, when I told you that your body was beautiful the way it was, I was telling you the truth."

"I know."

"I found your slender figure to be elegant and graceful. It pains me to think that you felt the need to go to such lengths to change it, as though it was inadequate or something."

Her smile disappeared as she furrowed her brow and studied his face. "Thank you," she finally said quietly. "That's nice to know. I just wanted to see what it was like, to try on something else for a while." She looked down at herself, seeming anxious. "Do I look okay?" She was worried by his reaction that perhaps she looked foolish.

He grinned and took her hands, spreading them and observing her new form. "You look delectable," he told her truthfully, pulling her hands a bit to shift her this way and that as she swiveled her hips. "I never thought I would use the words 'beautiful craftsmanship' or 'artistic attention to detail' in such a way, but that's what comes to mind," he admitted with a chuckle.

She cupped her breasts, lightly running her thumbs over her nipples. "If that's all that comes to mind, I may not have done this quite right."

He laughed and then reached out to cup the side of her face with his hand. "You've done perfectly. Give a man a chance to simmer before boiling over," he whispered into her ear, before giving her a soft kiss and dropping his hand from her face to caress the fullness of her curves. "You look seductively scrumptious. I *was* just as happy with your body before, though."

She shrugged. "I know. I wasn't."

"I'm glad that you didn't go to extremes."

She gazed at him through slitted eyes with a smile. "I know you too well for that, although I do plan to try it sometime, just for fun."

He chuckled, and then brought his attention back to her face, where he brushed a long lock of ebony hair to tuck back behind her ear. "Is it difficult?"

She shrugged. "It was at first. I won't even tell you how long this took me, but I've been working on it for a while and I'm getting pretty confident with it."

"I guess you won't be needing your hair dye any longer then," he observed as he brushed his fingers through her hair again.

She looked up at him in surprise. "Oh yeah. I never even thought of that. What made *you* think of that?"

"The stains in my bathroom perhaps?"

"Oh…sorry," she apologized sheepishly. "It's hard without a mirror."

"Why do you dye it?"

She seemed taken aback by the question. "I was dying it black even before I turned. I think it suits me. Now, being a vampire, it's just fitting. Don't you think?"

"It's certainly dramatic and striking, but you'd be beautiful regardless. What's your natural color?"

"Boring."

"Last time I checked, *boring* wasn't a color."

"It's brown," she clarified with a smirk. "Light, mousy, boring brown. It's totally not me."

"No? Are you certain of that?" She just stood there, looking at him in contemplation. "I'd love to see it on you sometime," he told her.

"Really?" He nodded as he watched her trying to come to a decision. "I probably could. I make my wolf's fur darker, I don't see why I couldn't make my human hair lighter. I'll see," she said, backing away from him a step.

"Right now?"

"Sure, why not? I'm no stranger to role-playing in the bedroom. Some guys want a French maid's outfit, or the bookish Librarian turned vixen, you want simple Cynthia. Let's play."

The idea startled him. She *could* change her features couldn't she? Change anything about herself… The thought was arrestingly appalling to him. He never, *ever* wanted her to get the idea into her head that he should want her to look like anyone else…ever. "No. Not like that. I never want you to change like that," he stammered.

She seemed to catch on to his thought, despite his refusal. "You sure? You like red-heads, don't you?"

"No." It carried the force of an order and shocked her to stillness. She stood there staring at him. It had been a natural enough question for her. Between knowing Felicity and his maker, Maribeth, he couldn't really blame her for asking. He forced himself to take a breath and calm his voice. "I just want you to be yourself."

She pursed her lips and nodded. "Okay."

~~~~~~~~~~~~~~~~~~~~~~~~~~~~~

Dusk…another day behind him. Nightfall approached to propel him forward further past his time with Felicity, and to try to goad him into moving on. He may not have been able to finish Felicity's goodbye letter, but he'd managed to spend another day without being miserable over her loss, a day that held its own pleasures worth smiling over, that did not involve her. That always seemed the goal: get through another night and day, and hopefully each would be better than those before.

He'd spent the day making Sindy happy, he hoped, talking, laughing, and expressing his newly blooming love for her. He had shown her appreciation and pride for the work she had done, in learning to manipulate her talent, while still encouraging her to break out of the image she felt she had to hold herself to. Hopefully, he had shown her that the aspects of herself she normally held hidden inside, were just as worthy and desirable as those she was used to being praised for.

She still slept, and he was happy to see that she had not yet shifted to change her form. As superficial a change as it was, seeing her lay there peacefully sleeping with her long straight hair spread all around her in a soft cascade of light brown, encouraged a very different perception from seeing her with locks of dark ebony black. It completely softened her, and seemed to better match the woman that Cain was always seeing glimpses of, as opposed to the image she usually tried to project. He turned on the bedside lamp as the room darkened with the nightfall, to better gaze at her. She slept soundly, without stirring.

He did love her. If he had never met Felicity at all, and then he and Sindy had reached the place they were at now, he would have been content. He would have felt that he was at a satisfactory place in his life, with a worthy goal in helping the United One deal with her situation, and a worthy woman by his side.

However, unfair to Sindy as it may be, he now had experienced a love like he had never known before, and by comparison it outshined any new ember he might try to ignite. Felicity just lit him up inside. There was no other way to explain it. They had not been together for very long, and his friends might feel he should just get over her, but how could he know love like that, and then forget it?

He wouldn't forget it, and he had his suspicions that he would never feel that way about anyone else, no matter how much time went by. But he needed to take that love and lock it away in a corner of his heart, to make room to try to nurture something new. As he had said to Sindy herself one night out in the snow, there should always be a hope for something new.

He spent some time thinking of that, wondering what hope there might be in the future, as he gently ran his fingers down the soft skin of her back, while she lay next to him in the bed. When she finally woke, she rolled over with a smile, and then he could see a moment of strange awareness flash over her features. Her body was different than she was used to, and she had forgotten. Surely, the shift of her weight felt a bit different as she rolled, and then to see her hair spread over the pillow as a lovely mess of light brown seemed very odd to her.

She noted the fact that the lamp was on, and it was fully dark outside. Normally, she was an early riser like himself. "What time is it?"

He shrugged. "It's been full dark for a bit. Your creative shifting must have tired you out."

She nodded with a smile as he moved to snuggle next to her in the bed. "And I'm famished," she admitted. "It's much harder to actively construct something, than it is to just shift to a form I'm used to."

He nodded. "Well, just so we're clear, I don't really care what form you're in. I'm more interested in getting to know who's inside." She lowered her lids and turned away with a sigh. "Why are you so adamant about trying to keep parts of yourself hidden away from me? I feel like you're always worried not to show too much. Do you think you're going to scare me away if I truly know you? Because you're not." She smiled without looking at him, as though she didn't really believe him, but then shook her head. "Are you worried I'm going to hurt you?"

Now she turned back to stare at him discerningly. What did she see? Was she gauging his love for her, words she wouldn't let him say aloud…or his love for Felicity…? Did she worry that anything she might feel for him was doomed to never be fully returned, or did she see hope in their future? He wanted to see hope…whether he really believed it could be achieved or not, so badly he wanted there to be hope for happiness, no matter how fate had twisted his life.

She smiled as she sat up in the bed. "You can't hurt me."

"Why's that?" he asked with a teasing smile. "Because you're such a tough cookie?"

She chuckled. "I'll tell you a secret. I'm no tougher than anybody else. I'm just numb."

"Don't say that." He reached out for her, but she rolled away from him to lay on the other side of the bed. She let out a groan of annoyance. It was forceful enough to startle him, and he could then see by her expression that it wasn't even for him. "What is it?"

"Allie." She grabbed a pillow to put over her head, as though she could drown out the thoughts like noise. "Get out of my head, I'm sleeping," she lied aloud for Cain to hear, with a grumble from under the pillow. Alyson had entered the house and was waiting downstairs. He could feel her.

Sindy lay still. He wasn't sure if she was having a mental conference with Alyson, or just laying there. After a moment, Cain gently took the pillow away and gazed down at her until she opened her eyes. "You're not too numb to feel this, are you?" he asked, leaning down and placing a soft kiss upon her lips.

"No," she admitted softly. "That felt pretty good…but I've got to go."

He furrowed his brow and lightly held her to the bed, as she'd been about to get up. "Where? Stay here with me. We'll see what else I can make you feel."

She laughed. "I can't. I promised Allie. She wants to go see some band."

"Mattie can take her."

"He's going to that photography thing at the college, remember? You know how Allie is. She's really jazzed about this concert. You wouldn't want the United One to take off on her own, would you?"

With a sigh of defeat, he let her go, so she could rise. "I appreciate you keeping an eye on her."

She untangled herself from the sheets and left the bed. "Sure."

Sindy left the room without really looking at him, going next door to fetch some clothing for herself. She often selected a few things and then came back into his room to dress, so he stayed in the bed, propped up on an elbow, waiting for her. She took long enough that he began to wonder if she was planning to return to him at all before going downstairs.

When she re-entered the room, he was very surprised to see that not only was her hair black once again, but she was partially dressed in tight, dark, form-fitting pants and high heeled boots. The surprise didn't end there either... She was topless, and she'd shifted the shape of her body once again, so that any of her previous bras she might attempt to wear would be completely inadequate. She held some clothing in one hand as she used the other to toss her hair back over her shoulder. "So, what do you think of going *extreme?*" she asked.

Her breasts were now quite large, accentuated even further by her tiny little trim waist and slender hips that were shown off by her low-slung pants. He had to admit, it was amazing how natural the transformation of her body looked. She must have put a decent amount of thought into it, because her breasts were beautifully formed so one would never know that she wasn't naturally so endowed. They didn't appear abnormal or artificial in the least, just...big, but she still looked odd to him. He just wasn't used to seeing her like that. "You'll never fit into your clothing," he told her after a moment of shock.

She grinned and held up the material in her hand. "I have something that'll fit." To prove her point, she slipped the spaghetti strapped top over her head without a bra. It took a bit of maneuvering to get herself properly situated in it. The top was of a form-fitting, expanding material, but was certainly stretched to its full potential, and she showed a very generous amount of cleavage in it, even once she managed to keep herself from spilling out of it.

Sometimes he looked at such garments and couldn't help but almost laugh upon thinking how they would be viewed back when he was human. He'd become used to today's more shameless styles, but back in his day, women wore layers upon layers of beautiful fabrics and lace when they wanted to be noticed. Even when their necklines were daringly low, and their corsets pulled tight to enhance their décolletage, the *full* rounded shape of their breasts were never shown, only their upper cleavage. The clothing Sindy was wearing, may as well have been body paint, and left almost nothing to the imagination. Not only was it distasteful to his sense of style, in this case, he also wasn't sure he liked the implications. "What's all this for?"

She gave him an odd look. "Are you jealous, to see me going out like this?" He just raised a questioning eyebrow. "It's not for anything in particular," she replied as she admired her chest. "I just thought it'd be fun. They're only eye candy tonight, unless you want to play with them when I get home," she added in a breathy purr.

His demeanor was serious as he sat up in the bed and asked, "Are you going hunting?"

She shook her head with a dismissive smirk for his speculation. "I'm going out with Allie."

"Yes, but does that answer my question?"

"It should." She turned her head towards the door as though being called, although Cain couldn't hear anything. It must be Alyson calling to her telepathically. "I've got to go," she confirmed.

She came towards him for a kiss. He stood, feeling almost awkward to hug her in her new shape. "Unbelievable," he muttered with a laugh at her new endowments. He supposed he could understand her wanting to play 'dress-up' with her new ability, but he couldn't shake the uneasy sense of foreboding it brought to him. Was he jealous? Not really. Perhaps he should be, but he just wasn't. He worried more for why she would want to lure men on, than for the act itself. He couldn't help but think of her newly transformed body as 'hunting attire'. "Maybe I'll come with you."

"What?" she asked in disbelief. "The last time I asked you, you said that you spend so much time in dive bars looking for vampires with messy dining habits, that the last thing you wanted to do was go to one on a night off."

"Yes, but you look like you could use a chaperone," he teased. "Besides, it's the least I can do, since you're going to the opera with me next month."

She'd rolled her eyes at the word 'chaperone', but seemed to find the word 'opera' even more annoying. "Are you really holding me to that?"

"I've already got the tickets. Don't worry, you'll enjoy it. Although we may have to find you something more suitable to wear."

She gave him a kiss and then pulled away. "Allie wants to leave right now or we'll miss the opening band." She gave him a smack on the ass, noting the fact that he wasn't dressed. "You can come to the next one."

"Aren't you going to drink something first?"

"I'll bring a flask with me."

"Where are you going to put it?" he asked archly. She just waved a hand at him as she backed out into the hall. "At least pare things down a little," he urged with a gesture towards her chest.

She shook her head. "Then I'd have to shift and get dressed again."

"Stay together, and be careful."

She was already headed for the stairs as she called back, "See you later."

Gone. Within minutes, he could feel her mark and Alyson's moving swiftly away to beyond his range. She wouldn't be out hunting men with Alyson in tow, would she? Alyson could be insubordinate at times, but drinking from humans was a major breach of their coven protocol, and he couldn't imagine Mattie standing for it. He couldn't help but notice that Sindy had never directly denied it though.

He knew Sindy drank from humans now and again. Because she knew how to handle herself without hurting them, he wasn't terribly troubled by it. She did mostly exist on animal blood these days, and a foray out for a small, carefully moderated drink from a man once in a while wasn't going to be a problem for anyone, as long as she was discreet. But she knew better than to expose Alyson to that sort of activity, didn't she? Alyson couldn't handle it, not in the least. Sindy knew that.

Cain put on some underwear, a pair of jeans and a t-shirt, and headed downstairs. He could feel that Mattie was moving about in the kitchen. Cain entered the room just as Mattie was opening the back door to leave. He paused when he saw Cain. "Hey," he said with a wave. "You just missed the girls."

"Yes, I know."

"I've got to head out too. Sorry about the mess, I'll help you straighten up when I get back."

There was a pile of glasses and mugs in the sink, and various things strewn about the counters. "That's alright." He had nothing better to do than clean up after everyone else, right? Story of his life. Mattie just gave him a wave goodbye and was out the door. It was unfortunate that they hadn't any time to discuss the girls, but Mattie didn't seem concerned with their activities in the least.

Cain looked around the kitchen with a sigh. Why did he always feel like the only adult in residence? No one ever put anything away. He poured himself a mug of blood from the refrigerator, and then began tidying up the counters while waiting for it to be done heating in the microwave.

There was a notepad out on the table. As he picked it up, a set of marks on the paper caught his attention. There were fairly deep grooves of indent in the pad, deeper than you'd expect from normal writing. The last note must have been written by someone who was pushing very firmly, probably someone who wasn't always careful to control her own supernatural strength… Alyson. He was going to put it into the drawer, but a word caught his eye. "LIE". He tilted the pad a bit for the light, to try to read the indentations. There was no mistake, it read "LIE to the end". What in the world could that mean? It didn't sound good.

He was completely alone in the house. He could feel through their marks that the others were long gone. It only took a moment before he gave in to his urge to learn more, even if it was a poor respect of privacy. He opened the drawer and found a pencil, then shaded over the indentations in the pad, to help them better stand out so he could read them clearly.

LIE to the end
24 – 27 – Town Line last left

The first line didn't make any sense at all to him. The second was odd as well, but "last left" made it sound like directions to something. Where would Allie be writing directions to? The concert maybe…but what did she need to lie about? He knew there was a place called Town Line just past the opera house in Lancaster. Was that where she was going?

It didn't really matter, but he liked having a little mystery to occupy him, and the note did seem odd. He retrieved his drink and made his way into the library. After fighting with the computer and being unsuccessful at getting it to show him one of the many maps he knew Mattie could easily access from it, he was ready to give up and get his paper map of New York from the glove box of the car. He took a deep breath and forced himself to stay sitting in his chair at the computer. As Mattie was very fond of telling him, he needed to stop fighting technology and learn how to navigate it.

He wished Felicity were here. Of course, he always wished that, but she had a way of showing him new things with the patience of a teacher. He had to smile at the thought. Now she *was* a teacher, and even the young children she worked with were surely far better at this than he was.

She had used the computer to do some searching of her own to find him, hadn't she? He could hear her voice in his mind as she told him how she had followed a lead, and it led her to find his very road…*staring right at me from the 'Google Maps' screen.* Google…that he could find.

He pulled up the Google screen and studied it for a moment, wondering what he should enter, when he realized there was a tab for 'maps' right on it. *Thank you Felicity.* He zeroed in on New York and found Town Line, but that didn't really show him anything. It was a small little hamlet, not far from them, just as he'd suspected. He had no idea what the

24 – 27 was, or what the lying business was about, but it probably just had to do with Allie's band or a little bar somewhere they were playing in. He was about to give up and find something else to occupy him, when he decided to type in "LIE to the end", just to see what came up.

To his surprise, it put a long purple line on the map. It didn't seem to be anywhere near the house though. He backed the screen away to get some perspective. It was down at the very bottom of New York, on Long Island. He looked closer at the line, and had to laugh as he realized his mistake. Allie's note didn't say the word *LIE*, as in 'untruth', it was an abbreviation…for *Long Island Expressway*. Now that he followed the line along the expressway, he saw that if he followed it to the end, it took him to a road marked *Rte. 24*, which could then be taken to *Rte. 27*, which in turn reached *Town Line Road*. Mystery solved.

Or was the mystery just beginning? What would she be doing out there? The thought worried him immensely. He didn't know very much about Long Island, except that Arif had a retreat there. Was Alyson sneaking out to see Arif? Why would she do that? Arif's offer was surely tempting to her, he could understand that, but they'd had many conversations about it. He'd like to think if she would go so far as to get directions for a visit, she would have at least consulted him about it.

Had she gone there yet? Did Mattie know? Did she have any idea the danger she could be blindly walking into? He would like to think that Arif's offer was straight-forward, but what if there was more going on than they knew of? He tried to slow down his thinking and not jump to conclusions, but the clues seemed to lead in an ominously obvious direction.

The idea of sitting home alone all evening, waiting for someone to get back so he could ask them about it, was unbearable. Mattie would be home long before the girls, who had a habit of staying out until dawn. If Alyson was meeting with Arif, and Mattie knew about it, Cain was fairly sure Mattie would have told him. If Mattie didn't know, it seemed unfair to get him upset over it without being certain. Perhaps he should wait and ask Alyson directly, but he felt time was of the essence. For all he knew, both girls could be on their way there now. No matter his current feelings for Sindy, he wouldn't put it past *her* to keep such a secret if she was in on it.

His only recourse seemed to be to visit the destination and see what it was for himself. If it was Arif's compound, he could see if the girls were there, and if they were in trouble. He would feel them through their marks if he got close enough. If they weren't there, he would come home and confront Alyson about it. Hopefully, the place was nothing more than a music venue, proving that Alyson had been hiding nothing more than traveling further than she should be. It would be a long trip for him, but he had nothing better to do, and it was worth his peace of mind.

He left a note. Alyson could surely fly there in only an hour or two, but it would take him most of the evening. He wouldn't make it back before dawn, but he could spend the day in a motel. He'd made such trips many times while investigating vampire attacks, and the others wouldn't think it odd.

Following a lead... be home by tomorrow night

— Cain

~~~~~~~~~~~~~~~~~~~~~~~~~~~~~~~~~~~~

Cain was beginning to wonder if the motorcycle had been the best choice. Not only had he been driving for the entire night and feeling in need of a break, the area he was driving through was becoming increasingly upscale. He was still out on Montauk highway, but it was only two lanes at this point, and although much of it was through farmlands and golf courses, some stretches were making him begin to feel badly for cruising along on his very loud Harley Davidson in the wee hours of the morning.

He was finally almost there, but it was already approaching the dawn. As anxious and curious as he was to find out what he was dealing with, it would be a smarter decision to sequester himself away safely in a motel, and approach the address early tomorrow evening instead. The girls would be long gone, unless they were staying the day as well, but at least he could see what was there. He pulled into The Enclave Inn and got himself a room to wait out the day. He thought about placing a call to the house, but decided against it. He couldn't speak to them and lie about what he was doing, so all it would probably accomplish at this point, was to make someone mad at him.

He was grateful that he was still too stubborn to carry a cell phone, because surely someone would have called him as soon as they'd realized he was gone. He was actually a bit surprised Alyson hadn't tried to contact him telepathically. He had not felt even a slight shiver of a mark all evening, so they must not have been anywhere close to him. That was one good thing at least. The ladies were probably just returning to the house now and going straight to bed.

Sunset came around seven thirty the next evening, still plenty early enough for people to be out and about, and for Cain to be inconspicuous as he headed out to see where this adventure was going to lead. He could only hope that he was completely wrong in his speculations, and it would somehow end well…

He was sure to drink all of the blood he'd brought with him, although it was more than he might normally require. Whatever lay ahead, he wanted to be prepared, without thirst weakening him or tempting him from making a wise decision. Once prepared, he was on his way.

He was a bit nervous when he found Town Line Rd. and saw that it led into a nice development of homes. It looked like this was not going to be a bar or place of business, unless it was a beach bar at the end of the road…which was doubtful, but he kept hoping. The road did lead right out to the beach. It dead-ended, but there were only houses here. The good news was that although they were very nice houses, they weren't particularly large and imposing, they were family homes. He had passed one or two that were surely worth a small fortune, but nothing approaching the kind of wealth he knew Arif liked to surround himself with. This was not the kind of place where he would expect to find Arif's coven.

From what he had heard, Arif's Long Island retreat *was* near the beach, but it housed many vampires and their human pets. It would have to be something of extensive size, like a gated community or condominium complex. These seemed normal homes and were not secured in any way against the public. This was not a neighborhood of vampires, and he very happily observed that there were no marked humans in the area. Alyson must not be meeting with Arif after all, not at this address. The realization brought a sigh of relief.

He took the road to the end, as instructed, and cut the motorcycle engine. The last house on the left wasn't any different from the others. It's proximity to the beach probably made it cost a bit more, but it was just a very nice, family home, with a fenced-in yard that was probably less than half an acre, but backed out onto the beach.

There were no cars in the driveway and no lights on in the house. No one seemed to be home. Was this somehow a front, a meeting place for Arif to then lead Alyson to the coven's secret compound?

Cain got off the bike and stretched, walking to the end of the road and taking a look out at the beautiful ocean view. It was a clear spring night, and the salty ocean scent was a nice change for his senses. Back home the woodland air was absolutely choked with pollen right now. He turned back to eye the house. It was lovely, but it wasn't suspicious in the least, just another human home. For once, he was glad to be wrong.

Before getting back onto the bike for the long ride home, he went to the mailbox, to see if he might read a name off some mail, to tell him anything more, but it was empty. He walked up the driveway and glanced into a few of the windows, but there was no one home. That's it then. Whatever directions Alyson was writing, if they truly led here, they meant nothing to him. If he wanted to satisfy his curiosity, he was going to have to ask her.

He was just walking back down the driveway, when a car pulled in and stopped halfway up, blocking him, and momentarily blinding him with its headlights. It seemed he was going to meet the homeowners in person. He'd explain that he was in the wrong place, and be on his way. The lights and engine turned off, and he saw that it was a woman alone in the car. He stood his ground at the top of the drive with his thumbs looped in the front pockets of his jeans, trying not to seem intimidating or suspicious, so as not to alarm her.

She just sat there for a moment. Was she afraid to leave the vehicle? He put his hands up in surrender and approached the car to reassure her that he meant no harm. He'd only taken a step or two, when he ducked his head a bit to better see through the windshield…and froze, recognition paralyzing him. He knew this car. And although it was dark, and he was only just blinking the spots from his eyes from the headlights, he knew its driver too. Could it be? *Alyson, where have you led me?*

Felicity… Her hair was pulled back into a ponytail, and her face was a bit fuller than when he had seen her last, but it was definitely her. Even accounting for the look of total shock upon her face, she looked as though she'd had a rough day. As the light came on in the car when she opened the door, he could see that she had slightly dark circles under her eyes, as though she hadn't been sleeping well. She also looked as though the very last thing in the world she had expected was to come home and find him standing at the top of her driveway.

She was going to get out of the car, when she caught sight of herself in the rearview mirror, and seemed aghast at her reflection. She quickly rubbed her hands over her face, combed her fingers through her bangs and tried to smooth back the wisps of uncooperative hair that had worked their way out of her ponytail. Finally, she gave up with a sigh and came out to meet him.

It didn't matter. He was smiling from ear to ear, even though he realized what a terrible mistake he'd made in coming, snooping around, blundering out here and disrupting things. What a fool he was. He should have known that Felicity was the one person Alyson might go out to see, without making it known to him. It had just never entered his mind. He'd assumed that she was still living in the city.

She came closer to him, returning his smile, although she looked close to tears at the sight of him, and he could tell that she almost wanted to yell at him for coming when she was so obviously unprepared. "I'm just as surprised as you are," he admitted when she reached him.

She hesitated for a moment, and then came to him for a hug. Thank God, because he wanted so badly to hold her, and was afraid that instead they would be doomed to suffer through awkward greetings and respect for personal space. He knew better than to kiss her this time, but he gratefully held her, gathering in her warmth, breathing in her scent, and not letting her go a single moment sooner than he had to.

She surrendered herself into his arms and accepted the embrace, finding the stubbled skin of his jawbone with her cheek, and snuggling in to press her face against his. It felt so good, just to feel her soft warmth pressing upon him. Her familiar scent had even his meager thirst begging for her blood, satisfied though he'd been before seeing her. The vampire within him longed to taste her again, to mark her, claim her as his own and revel in her sensuous offerings every bit as much as the man in him wanted her as well.

She pulled to back away and he had to let her, forcing back his thirst and giving her up with a defeated smile of apology. She squinted at him and then shook her head in confusion. "What are you doing here? How did you find me?"

"You sound like me the last time we met," he pointed out with a chuckle. "This was a complete accident. I found the address, and I was expecting it to belong to someone entirely different. I'd no idea you lived here, honestly, although I can't say that I'm sorry."

She let out a derisive huff of a laugh. "Of course you're not," she told him archly. "You look great, as always, and I'm a total wreck."

She smiled and it brought a spark of light to her eyes, making her seem more like her old self. Her cheeks were nicely plump again as they used to be, and when she smiled, he could see the glow of happiness within her. She wore sweatpants and a t-shirt, reminding him of the night they had spent practicing self-defense in the gym at her school so long ago.

"You're beautiful," he insisted. She was, she always would be in his eyes. She did look tired though, as though she'd been going through a rough time of late. He hoped it was nothing serious, and that things were going well for her, but part of him was ready and willing to take action at the slightest sign that it wasn't.

At this point, he wasn't sure he could turn her down, no matter what she asked of him. If for any reason things were not working out for her as she'd hoped, he *could* step in. She was 24 years old now, and still very young, but old enough to better understand what life held for her, and what he could do for her as well. If she was truly unhappy… "How are you?" he asked gently. "Is everything alright?"

She looked embarrassed that troubles might be showing through her appearance, and she brought a hand up to swipe the bangs from her face. "I'm fine. It's just been one of those days. I haven't been getting much rest lately. But everything's good," she assured him.

"Is it? Because if there's anything… I'd do anything for you," he told her with slow and deliberate sincerity.

She looked into his eyes and he could see that she knew it was true, and what it meant. "Thank you," she answered with a quiet smile. "That means a lot."

He held her gaze for a long moment. Even ignoring the predator within him, the electricity between them was palpable. No matter her worldly attachments, it felt as though he should lean close and kiss her…it just seemed one of those moments. He didn't act on it, but surely she had to feel it too, that energy, that spark of romantic tension, humming through them both, and begging to be stoked to life. Oh God, he'd missed her so much. And to have her standing here before him was almost surreal.

"I've been thinking about you lately," she said softly.

His heart swelled at the thought. "I think of you too…all the time." Why did he let those words leave his lips? He needed to stop being so transparent and let her live her life without worrying about him. "I heard the wedding was beautiful. I'm so happy for you," he said brightly, hoping that there was no trace of bitterness in the words. It seemed so long ago already, that she had given her heart to another and moved truly beyond his reach.

"Oh, yes… I got your card. Thank you so much. It was such a generous gift. You didn't have to."

"I know. I'm just glad to see you getting on alright. I want you to be happy."

She nodded. "I am, very."

"Good." He did want her to be happy, but somehow he was afraid that the word still came out sounding a bit disappointed.

"I want to show you something." She smiled with the delight of having a joyous secret. He met her gaze curiously and then followed as she led him back towards the car. She motioned for him to come around and see something within as she opened the back door.

She put her hand on his shoulder to guide him, and as the light came on and he leaned into the car at her urging, he saw that the backseat held something well worth the excited joy he'd seen in her eyes. A baby, peacefully sleeping in its snug and cushioned carrier, fitted into a base strapped to the backseat.

Total amazement froze him where he stood. He hadn't even suspected. It seemed so soon. A perfectly angelic little baby…brought into the world by this woman whom he loved so dearly. Felicity had become a mother.

The baby's eyes were closed in sleep, its cheeks and eyelids blushed pink against its light, creamy complexion. Wispy, light brown hair had lightly matted against its head from the warmth of the blankets and the car. The blankets were pale green and blue. Cain tore his tearing eyes from the baby's sweet face to meet Felicity's proud gaze.

He met her eyes and just let unspoken love, admiration and joy pass between them. He couldn't speak, only grin, and let her see how the knowledge affected him. She had her wish. She was a mother. "It's a boy?" he finally whispered. She smiled and nodded in confirmation. His smile broadened. "You have a son," he repeated in happy announcement, making it truly real for himself as he heard the words. "He's beautiful."

At the sound of his voice, soft as it was, the baby stirred, opening his eyes and then his mouth in a little yawn that Cain couldn't help but laugh and smile over. He turned to Felicity in apology though, as he realized what it meant. "I'm sorry, I've woken him."

She smiled at his repentance. "That's alright. Now you can hold him." Before he could say anything else, she guided him to back away from the car door. "Let me get him out for you."

He stood there behind her, feeling oddly separate and removed from her, inhuman, standing cold and silent in the night air as she fussed with the straps that held the baby in the seat. He felt strangely bewildered at the thought of himself holding that tiny little fragile child. "Really?"

He could hear her merry laugh from within the car. "Of course."

It wasn't something he could explain, and he would probably look like a fool if anyone was watching, but tears began falling from his eyes. He stopped breathing, as though her familiar laughter had stolen away the air. He didn't need to breathe, it was only something he normally did for speech…but there was nothing he could say. He closed his eyes, but had to open them almost immediately, because the visions that came to mind when they were closed, only made things worse.

She was lifting the baby from the car and he realized that he'd better pull himself together before she turned around. He was still wiping his eyes when she turned to him, the baby gathered to her, but she was nuzzling her nose against the child's and hadn't looked at him yet. He stood straighter and tried to smile.

It didn't work for a second. "What is it?" she asked in concern the moment she looked into his eyes.

"Nothing." She just stood there staring at him in reprimand. Did he really believe that she would accept that?

She called him on it. "I may not know you like I used to, but you're going to have to do a little better than *nothing*." His smile became more genuine at the words. She knew him. She knew him all too well. She dipped her head down to find his eyes and ask him gently, "Is it only that you're happy for me? Because it seems like something more. You can tell me anything." She said the last slowly and quietly…the way he had told her he would do anything for her.

God, how he loved this woman. She had given him an out…he could just say that he was overcome with emotion, and that would be explanation enough, but of all the people in the world, she was probably the only one he could share his feelings with, who could truly understand. He sighed, and tried to explain as simply as possible. "I haven't held a child since I was human."

He actually saw her seem to melt at his words. That was all she needed to hear. She understood. He had held only two infants in his entire life of 347 years…his daughter Amelia, and his son Daniel. His daughter had died from illness at the age of four, his premature son a few hours after birth. Felicity knew this, and looked heartbroken for him over it. She held the baby out to him immediately. "Then it's about time."

"I don't even know how."

"Yes, you do," she insisted firmly, although her voice was soft. "I'll remind you."

He took a shuddering breath, trying to steady himself as she placed the infant into his arms. She showed him how to adjust his hold and support the baby's head. He'd never believed that it would, but it did come back to him. The moment she let go and he was holding the child on his own, it was like holding Amy all over again. He'd spent so many hours with her in his arms. He could not have smiled any broader.

Felicity beamed at him. "See?" She watched him for a moment, letting him become comfortable and begin cooing at the child, who was mesmerized by him. "His name's Christian."

Such a softly spoken sentence. Just hearing the name instantly stopped him cold with a shiver down his spine…and then he realized the context of what she had actually said, and the chill turned to warmth and disbelief. He cradled the baby, who was now trying to make noises back at him, goading him to continue his dialogue of nonsense sounds, but Cain could only stare at him in silence. After a moment, he turned that gaze to Felicity.

"I told you I've been thinking about you," she whispered.

Christian…his true name. Felicity was the only living human who knew it, and she had given it to this beautiful child, her first born, as a gift of thanks to him. He couldn't even imagine how he could possibly display his gratitude. "This is, by far, the most meaningful tribute I have ever experienced in my life. Thank you."

She just smiled, reaching out to put a reassuring hand on his arm as he nestled the baby closer to his chest. "What else could I name him? I looked at him and I just knew." She watched him smile as the baby gurgled and cooed at him. After a few moments, she took a deep breath, as though steadying herself for something. "His name is Christian Everheart."

Everheart…another name that gave him a chill of recognition. But that faded; he knew that she wasn't speaking of the vampire hunter. She confirmed his suspicion of the family name. "Ben…" she said quietly. "I married Ben."

Somehow, he hadn't anticipated that. He had left Felicity six years ago, and for most young humans these days, he knew that lasting relationships could be distressingly rare. He had always assumed that Ben had probably stepped in to take a larger role in Felicity's life when he'd left, but he'd imagined that would have been short lived. "You've been with Benjamin, all this time?"

"Pretty much."

"Well, you must have a good, strong marriage then," he told her approvingly with a forced smile. "He's a fine man." He was. Cain had always grudgingly admired Ben, even if he was stubborn and combative at times. At least the man was of decent moral character. Hopefully that hadn't changed.

"Yes, he's a wonderful guy. He really loves me, and I love him."

She said it almost regretfully, afraid to hurt his feelings. Cain nodded. "Good…that's how it should be."

She turned away. She'd been smiling, but he suspected old feelings were resurfacing and she was becoming a bit overwhelmed. She busied herself by turning and taking things from the car. "Will you carry Christian into the house for me?" she asked emerging from the car with a large diaper bag, and a few other things.

His eyebrows rose in surprise at the request, before he shook his head and tried to resist. "I don't think I should."

"You're going to make me carry everything in alone? You can't just leave. Stay for a few minutes to talk at least. Ben won't be home until after nine. I want to talk to you, and I'm not keeping Christian out here in the driveway all night," she added with a nod towards the baby. "He needs to be put to bed. It's fine."

Obediently Cain followed her up to the door. She unlocked and opened it, turning to face him. "Welcome to our home. Please come inside."

Such a formal and deliberate invitation. It made him smile. He stepped over the threshold, inside to the living room to admire their house. There were a few piles of folded laundry on one of the couches and there seemed to be baby things strewn everywhere, but underneath all of that, he could see that it was nicely kept.

The house had high ceilings, and an open floor plan so that he could see through into the formal dining room, which boasted floor to ceiling windows that showed the night sky and the ocean shoreline. The large open space also had many skylights overhead. He could imagine what a beautiful and brightly lit place it was during the day. Even at night, the view of the stars gave it a feeling of airiness and a sort of grandeur that was still comfortable as a living space.

A large wedding portrait hung in the dining room. Cain resisted the urge to go and get a closer look at it. He could see it well enough from where he was. Felicity was every bit as breathtaking as she had been in the vision that Alyson had shown him. Ben stood by her side, looking more composed, competent, and handsome than Cain remembered him. The intervening years had done well for him, apparently.

Cain made himself comfortable on the couch, so that he could lay the baby on his lap. Christian lay on his back with his head reaching Cain's knees as he kicked his little feet against Cain's stomach. Cain held the child's hands and played with him while Felicity excused herself for a moment.

By the time she returned, Cain was thoroughly engaged in playing with the baby. It had been so very long since he'd had such opportunity, although he had always loved children. He had almost forgotten that special sense of private joy they could bring, when there was no one watching, and you could just make faces and noises and watch their simple delight, a shared secret. The baby seemed exceptionally small, fresh, and new to him, although he was a good sturdy child of at least twelve pounds or so, and certainly a few months old by his vocalizations and alert demeanor. He was just so perfectly beautiful, alive, and human.

Cain hushed his silly sounding dialogue with Christian, and began speaking to Felicity as he heard her re-enter the room. "You have a lovely home. How do you like living on..." he looked up and caught sight of her as he spoke...and lost the words. She'd taken her hair down out of the ponytail, brushing it out into its long, full, glossy auburn waves to fall over her shoulders. She'd also put on a little make-up. She didn't look as though she'd been made-over, she'd just lessened the darkness under her eyes, outlining them with a hint of color, and adding tint to her cheeks and lips. She looked bright, refreshed and casually gorgeous as she entered the room.

After his pause of silence, he spoke again with a smile. "You're really trying to make this difficult for me, aren't you?"

She gave him a coy grin. It was very obvious how her appearance had affected him. "Look at it from my end, Mr. ageless and amazing."

He laughed. "You're only twenty-four. How mad will you be at me if I visit you when you're sixty?"

She shook her head with a smile. "It's not the age, it's more *the amazing*... I just had a baby Cain. I haven't slept in weeks, and my body is a complete wreck. I have to wear sweats because I can't even fit into my jeans! You had to show up now? You couldn't have given me six months?"

He shook his head, refusing to give in to her objections. "It doesn't matter. You're beautiful. Look at you! You're a new mother and you're glowing with it. You are like a rose in full bloom, its petals fully open, fragrant and colorful, radiant with life." Words seemed insufficient to express what he felt for her and the beauty she exuded just by being who she was. "Honestly, I have never wanted you more." They both became motionless, frozen at his words, improper as they were. He looked down at the baby, who was now becoming drowsy in his lap, and then gathered him to give him back to Felicity. "And...that's my cue to leave."

She took back Christian, who only shifted and comfortably laid his head against her shoulder to fall asleep. "You don't have to run out the door," she told him quietly. "Maybe that wasn't something you should have actually said out loud...but it was kind of nice to hear," she admitted, "especially right now."

"Well, it's true. Forgive me for being so inappropriate. I really shouldn't be here, but I'm very glad to have had the opportunity to meet my namesake. I am truly happy for you. You've done just what you set out to do, and this is only the beginning of the wonders life has in store for you. Even clearer than before, we both know why your place is here. You should enjoy it."

He glanced up to the wedding portrait again, Felicity noting his gaze as he said, "And I'm sure you will. Ben is looking well," with a jealous little smile. "No matter what life puts you both through, if he doesn't always find you every bit as desirable as I do, he's a complete idiot."

She laughed. "He does," she admitted quietly.

"Of course he does. I never took him for a fool. And smarter than myself, he didn't let you go," he added soberly. He reached out to gently brush his finger across Christian's cheek where his head lay against Felicity. "Good thing. Look at the wonder you've brought into the world together."

Felicity blinked back tears from her eyes, snuggled the baby closer and then turned towards the hall. "Let me go and put him down. I'll be right back."

Cain sighed and went to wait by the front door. When she returned, he knew he would have to say goodbye. He tried not to dwell on it. A look back at the wedding portrait brought another question to mind. When Felicity came back, Cain questioned her with a new thought. "Does Ben know…about the baby's name?" He could see immediately by the flush of guilt that washed over her that he didn't. "I don't know if that's a good idea," he warned her gently. "I don't want to come between you."

"You won't," she assured him. "Christian wouldn't even be here if not for you. You saved my life, and then you wouldn't let me give it up. I have good reasons to name him for you, and no one else needs to know. It's a good name."

"I suppose." She came towards him, planning to hug him goodbye. He was almost alarmed at how badly he craved her touch, so badly, that he knew it could be his undoing to allow it. He put a hand on her shoulder to hold her at bay and instead leaned to place a soft kiss upon her forehead, the best way he could think of to appropriately express his love and concern, without giving in to a desire to hold her again. If he did, he wasn't sure he could let her go. "But you shouldn't keep secrets from him. Trust me."

She accepted the platonic kiss gracefully, although he could tell it caught her off guard. "I know, you're right. There are a few things I need to talk to him about, sooner rather than later." He looked at her questioningly.

"Allie, for one," she supplied quietly. He nodded. Felicity had been in contact with Allie for quite some time… She surely knew the potential that might have for disaster in her marriage, if she'd been keeping it from him. "It's been difficult. He was so hurt by her decision," she tried to explain.

"Don't turn her decision into your downfall. You have to tell him your part. Give the man a little credit. If he truly loves you, he will ultimately understand."

She wanted that hug…he could feel it. She wanted to be wrapped in his arms, held safe from the world, almost as badly as he wanted it.

He took a deep breath, renewing his memory of her subtle perfume to be treasured later alone, and then turned for the door. Felicity followed, unwilling to let him walk away from her. He opened the door and looked back, unsure what he could say that didn't sound like goodbye. She spoke before he'd the chance. "I'll walk you out."

She left the front door open a bit, as she followed him out onto the driveway. He couldn't help but notice her nervous glance down the road. He didn't know what time it was, but Ben must be expected home soon. He hated that feeling…that he should hurry and leave, as though he had something to hide, or was doing something wrong. He had nothing to be ashamed of, did he? Actually, he thought he'd handled himself rather well, considering. Still, the last thing he wanted was to make things difficult for her.

He let her catch up to him and turned to clasp her hands in his own, before she could embrace him. He gave her hands a squeeze and then brought each up to his lips for a gentle kiss. "I can't tell you how happy I am for this accidental visit." He glanced down the road as she had, showing his understanding of her concern. "But you needn't worry. I won't be back."

Rather than looking reassured, a wave of desperate anxiety washed over her and she clung more tightly to his hands. "Are you saying I'll never see you again?" she asked, her voice rising in fear of truly losing him. Her distress over the idea brought tears to his eyes.

He smiled and shook his head. "Don't be silly. You must know that even *my* self-control isn't strong enough for such a vow. We'll see each other again, I'm sure of it; but not for some time. You shouldn't expect me. You need to focus on your family."

He let his eyes wander down the road again, in the direction from which her husband was coming to claim her; lucky bastard. "Allow yourself to be happy. Keep your marriage strong and raise that sweet little boy. Some night, perhaps a few years from now, when we're both feeling a bit less vulnerable, I'll see you again. We can share a cup of tea, and talk about all that we haven't had a chance for."

She obviously loved her husband, and surely had no intention of hurting him, but this was a time in her life when stress and change had her feeling very susceptible to Cain's charms, even if he wasn't trying to woo her. And God help him but it was taking a ridiculous amount of effort on his part not to pull her in for that hug…which might inadvertently lead to a kiss…which would be completely unacceptable at this point. Just the mere thought of his lips upon her made his fangs twitch in eagerness to distend. Forget impropriety and kisses…he could easily conjure up the taste of her blood. He dropped her hands and tried to chase the thought from his mind.

Her breathing eased with the assurance that he wouldn't truly disappear from her entirely, and she gave him a little nod and a smile. As much as she hated the idea of not being able to see him sooner, she had to know how dangerous it would be for them to stay in close touch…and that was without accounting for any physical danger. Romantic temptations were too strong. The tension between them was palpable, no matter how they fought it. He could feel it like an electric current sparking between them. He backed away, not trusting himself for further physical contact, hoping she could understand without feeling rejected.

Her smile was filled with sweet remorse. "Until we meet again."

He nodded. "Yes. It's not goodbye. Until we meet again." After a moment, she turned to walk back towards the house. Perhaps she didn't want to relive the memory of seeing him ride away on his motorcycle. He could sympathize.

He called out to her before she reached the door. "Felicity, if you ever truly need me…I'll be there." The promise brought a smile to her lips as he blew her a kiss, and then left to begin his journey back out into the embrace of the night, once again leaving thoughts of human life behind as little more than a dim memory.

Chapter 16 - Secrets

Felicity

Ben and Felicity's house, Long Island, New York
Later that evening

Felicity sat on the couch in front of her fireplace, sipping a glass of red wine while remembering sitting by a similar fireplace at Cain's estate a few years ago. That was the last time she'd seen him…before tonight.

She hadn't expected to see him again, yet in a sense, somehow she always expected to see him. How many nights had she been out during some mundane task or another and suddenly thought of him? His memory would come back to her like a haunting dream just beyond her reach, and she would wonder, *why am I thinking of him now? Is he near?* She'd find herself studying every darkened street corner, every figure standing outside the mini-mart, every motorcycle that went by. It didn't happen often…but it was something she couldn't deny experiencing now and again. Somehow, his role in her life was not over, she just knew it in her heart. She had to admit to herself that most of it was probably just her own imagination, but she *knew.*

Just as she had known she would see Alyson again. Alyson was not just in her imagination. Her link with Allie had turned out to be very real. If she had such a strong connection with Alyson, how strong of a bond could she have with Cain? Cain wasn't psychic at all, by his own admission. Without wearing his mark, she couldn't really feel his presence, but sometimes she wondered if somehow she could feel when he needed her…through Allie perhaps. It just came on so suddenly and succinctly, that it felt incredibly real, hard to ignore, and it made her heart ache.

Was it Cain, hurting and missing her too during those times, or was it only her own fantasy? He had been thinking of her over the years, hadn't

457

he? He'd said so, and she knew it was sincere. He'd also said he had never wanted her more…

She was trying not to be too hard on herself for the thrill that ran through her over that statement. She was very much in love with Ben. She was a happily married woman, and planned to stay that way, but what woman wouldn't be thrilled to hear such a thing? As a matter of fact, three months after having a baby, exhausted and overweight, she'd be hard pressed to think of a time in her life when she had ever felt *less* attractive. And yet Cain was obviously smitten with her, and complimented her with such honest and unfettered openness, it was enough to make any woman melt, wasn't it?

Why did Cain affect her so strongly? It wasn't the vampire thing…although in some ways that did add to his allure, even though it kept them from being together. She couldn't help but notice as he was speaking to her out on the driveway, that he'd seemed almost afraid to touch her. She could imagine it was taking great restraint on his part not to be overly familiar with her, and he was fighting strong cravings to embrace her and to drink her blood.

Just the thought sent a shiver through her, as her body remembered the sensation and the venom, still craving it, all these years later. When she had visited him before the wedding, he had kissed her as they sat before his fireplace, and she had felt the venom in that kiss, after which he had told her *Don't ever doubt me. My love for you is eternal, no matter what the future holds.* A phrase she had treasured and thought of to comfort herself in difficult times.

It wasn't the vampire in him that affected her most though, it was his gentle, loving presence, the unshakable sense of peaceful kindness that seemed to thoroughly permeate him. She knew that he could be fiercely protective and was unafraid to fight strongly for what he believed in, but his allure lay in his moral strength and restraint. She loved the fact that he had such a desire to do right, and that using the deadly force at his disposal was a last resort.

Felicity took a large gulp of her wine, finishing off the glass. She wasn't really supposed to have more than one; she was breastfeeding. She stood and made her way to the kitchen, and after a brief pause, poured another glass anyway. She'd just have to use the bottle she'd pumped for the baby earlier. It was supposed to be for Ben to feed Christian in the morning, but she'd rather use it tonight. She'd just have to feed him herself tomorrow.

If there was ever a night when she could use a few strong glasses of wine, this was it. She wasn't quite ready to go back to facing real life and being practical just yet. Ben was late, again, and she could indulge in one more glass of wine and a few more moments thinking things over, alone on the couch.

She couldn't imagine herself sharing mundane tasks of real, everyday life with Cain, keeping to schedules and arguing over who last did the dishes, or why food shopping always seemed to cost more than it was supposed to. This was Ben's world, the good and the bad of it, and even when it was stressful and aggravating, she did love sharing it with him. He was very different from Cain, that was for sure, but he had so many wonderful qualities of his own, and he adored her just as much, if not more than her first love.

She was perfectly happy with her life, when she wasn't being given forced reminders of what could have been. She loved her husband, whom she still found very sexy, by the way. They'd only just moved in, and she'd already met at least one local woman who seemed very covetous of her gorgeous lawyer hubby, all 6'1" and 190 lbs. of him. After dinner the other night, Ben had been out in the backyard, practicing fencing moves with his sabre. God knows what their neighbors thought of him, but Felicity certainly enjoyed watching him out there at sunset practicing his parries and thrusts.

Watching actual fencing meets and tournaments wasn't nearly as romantic, with all of the equipment, face masks, and trying to remember how to keep track of scoring and whatnot, but watching him practice, alone, or with a partner from the club, was different. He'd be sparring with a friend, working up a sweat, but always so strongly in command; his precision and control were unmatched. She found his stern determination to master the sport incredibly arousing. The honeymoon might be over, but Ben still fueled her desires just as strongly as any fantasy man.

She smiled over her wine. Yes, she was a lucky woman. Her very favorite pastime of late, was watching Ben with Christian. The way he beamed with happiness and love for that boy was amazing to see. He could spend hours just tickling and whispering to him, and the baby couldn't even truly play yet! Ben wanted to be so involved in everything, even the dirty jobs... now *that* was sexy.

Her husband was not only strong, smart and sexy as hell, but he was still very in love with her, and absolutely faithful; it wasn't even a question in her mind. He deserved to feel that same assurance from her, didn't he? She shouldn't be sitting here fantasizing about anyone else, even if she hadn't done anything wrong.

She took another sip of wine and looked at the clock. It was almost ten. She hated when Ben stayed late at the office. It was always around this time that she would get a wave of worry, and terrible things would flash through her mind. Moving out from the city took away her worries over fears of muggers on the dark city streets, or in the subway, but now she had new worries. What if he's been in a car accident? And she always worried he would be attacked by a vampire, or God knows what else. What would she do without him?

The sound of his car pulling into the driveway allayed all fears; just working late. Just another night in her normal, boring life, that she was suddenly aware enough to be very thankful for. It wasn't supernaturally exciting, but she only had to take one look at the little baby sleeping in the bedroom, or take a good long look into her husband's eyes to know that her life held its own special brand of magic. Now if only she could keep thoughts of Cain out of her head…and her heart.

The front door opened, and Ben came through, bag and briefcase in hand. As soon as he noticed her on the couch, he lit up with a smile. "You're still up. Sorry, I know I said I wasn't going to be so late again. I just wanted to stay and go over everything one more time before court tomorrow." He dropped his briefcase and began taking off his jacket when he noticed her drink. "What are you having, a glass of wine? You never do that. Rough day?"

She shrugged. "I don't know. I just felt like it."

"Christian go down for you okay?"

"Yup. He's sound asleep."

Ben came closer to give her a kiss, and then assessed her appearance with a smile. "You look nice." He slumped his shoulders with a sigh. "You had something planned here didn't you? The make-up, the wine…and I screwed it up by coming home late again."

Guilt flashed through her and she hoped it didn't show in her face. She hadn't tried to initiate a romantic evening in a while, if only due to hectic schedules and exhaustion, and she almost never wore make-up since the baby had been born. She felt terrible knowing that she hadn't put the make-up on for Ben. She gave her head a little shake. "No. I just felt like having a glass of wine, and I got tired of looking like a hag."

"You couldn't look like a hag if you tried," he responded with a laugh. "But this is a nice reminder of how especially *gorgeous* you are when you try." He gave her another kiss and put his things down on the couch. "Well I hope you didn't have too rough a day, because you're starting to make me think we should stay up late tonight, even if I do have court in the morning.

She gave him a remorseful smile. "I'm not up for it. Besides, if things don't go well tomorrow, I don't want the blame. You are getting a good night's sleep."

"Fine," he replied with a smirk, "rain-check for tomorrow night, then. But I'm holding you to that."

"I look forward to it. This is a better mood than you've been in lately."

"I know. Sorry I've been so edgy."

"It's okay, I understand. Oh, and don't worry about the morning feeding, I'll do it."

"You sure? You don't have to get up that early, I can feed him."

She lifted her glass of wine. "I'll be using your bottle at 2 a.m., so the next one will have to be mine. But, since I'll be up, I can give you a good luck kiss goodbye."

"Thanks, but it's not even really my case, it's only an assist. Besides, I don't even need luck. I had a great day. I found something helpful that had been overlooked, so…good first impression for me. Tomorrow we shall be victorious, and not only that, Parker told me that I should join him on the golf course with the partners this Sunday." He dug something out of his bag. "Check it out, monogrammed golf balls. They have the firm name on them. Everybody got them, but only mine came with the invite."

"Impressive…except you don't play golf."

"Well I'm not going to turn him down! It's with the partners. I'm not even sure they know who I am. This is a prime opportunity. I can rent a set of clubs at the course. I don't have to be very good, I just have to be in the game. How hard could it be?"

She raised an eyebrow with a dubious grin. "I don't think they always show guys on T.V. sitcoms breaking and throwing their clubs for nothing, but good luck. Just remember, swinging a golf club is different from swinging a sword. Please don't kill anyone."

"I'll keep that in mind." He picked his things back up and headed into the bedroom to get undressed. Felicity finished her wine with a smile. She was pretty lucky, wasn't she? Mundane as it was, this was the life she had always wanted, and the surge of love and reassurance she felt every time Ben walked in the door, showed her that she never wanted to be without him. He was not only the father of her child and the man who knew how to make her body sing under his caresses, he was also her best friend, who had always been there for her through every trial of life, unwavering.

Cain was right, she shouldn't be keeping secrets from him, even if they were originally for his protection. Ben confided in her over everything. It was time for her to confide in him. This weekend she would plan a quiet dinner at home and they would have a long overdue talk. She would tell him about Allie…and at some point, she was going to have to say something about Bernard's vampire hunting as well. No more secrets.

She would always be grateful that Cain had selflessly helped her to make the right choice, in not giving up her life. Now she put thoughts of Cain aside and went into the kitchen to put her wine glass into the sink. She loved her life. Being human held plenty of special pleasures, and she was lucky to have Ben to share them with.

She found herself thinking back on all of the times that Ben had been there for her. Whether she was dealing with family trials, worries over work, or just generally feeling down, Ben was always there for support and a smile. They'd had some really good times too. They could have fun together no matter what they were doing, be it skiing down a mountain, hiking in the woods, rolling in the sand at the beach or just folding laundry on the bed.

Things may have been more stressful than fun lately, but she had to keep in mind that life is what you make it. Maybe she shouldn't have been so quick to shoot down Ben's invitation for a little romance before bed. Now that she thought about it, she was overdue for a reminder of how exciting human life with her sexy hubby could be.

She made her way back into the bedroom. She entered the room quietly, so as not to wake the baby. At first, she didn't see Ben, and assumed he was in the master bathroom, but then she suddenly noticed him sitting on the floor in the corner on the other side of the bed.

He was still dressed, hunched over on his knees with his hands folded in his lap and his head down low to the floor. It looked like maybe he was…praying? She'd never seen him like that before. "Ben?"

When he looked up, it almost seemed as if he didn't see her. His gaze was unfocused and he had a glazed look of disbelief on his face. His eyes were red, almost as though he'd been crying.

"Ben, what's wrong? What happened?"

He looked so terribly distraught that she was afraid at first he wasn't going to answer. She frantically turned her attention across the room to the bassinet, but Christian was still there, sound and whole, peacefully sleeping. She kept her focus on him for a moment, watching to see the rise and fall of his breathing before looking back to Ben. The baby was fine. What was going on?

"I… I dropped the golf balls. They rolled everywhere. I was picking them up, and…" he faltered to a stop, at a loss for words.

"What happened, did you get hurt or something?" It was obvious something was very wrong. He was far more upset than something like banging his head could account for, but she didn't even know what to ask him. He looked to be in complete shock.

Ben shook his head and she could see him mentally pulling himself together. He sat up straighter, still upset and confused, but now added to that was the serious contemplative look that he usually wore when analyzing a problem. He was trying to work something out. He looked up at her. "When was my dad here?"

Now she was really confused. What did Bernard have to do with anything? "The other night…um, Friday. You asked him to check in on me, remember?"

"He has a key."

"I know. He gave it back now. I told you."

"What time did you get home? Was he already here?"

"No. I called you when I got here, remember? Bernard didn't show up until later. Why? Ben, why are you so upset?"

Ben ignored her question for a moment. He looked like he was trying to work something out in his head and wasn't coming to the desired conclusions. "Was there a…problem while he was here?"

"No. What kind of problem? He was only here for a few minutes. Please tell me what's going on, you're freaking me out."

"Maybe he was here the night before, checking out the house, and it happened? But how did she find us? And how could she get in?" Even he sounded doubtful that he could make sense of his speculations.

"She who?" Even as she asked, Felicity suddenly felt a chill of comprehension. She still didn't have any idea what he was really talking about, but she was afraid she knew who the 'she' was.

"Allie." Ben said her name with a tremble that almost sounded like frightened worry. He held up his hands now to show her that when they'd been folded in his lap, he'd actually been clutching something. It was Allie's tee shirt; Felicity had kicked it under the bed when Allie had turned to mist. She'd forgotten to get rid of it later, and would now pay for her poor housekeeping.

Felicity took a small breath to speak, knowing that she needed to explain, but Ben cut her off. He thought she was in disbelief. He stretched the shirt better so that Felicity could see it. It was a concert tee, *Aerosmith's Rockin' the Joint* proudly proclaimed across the front. "It was Allie's, I know it," he insisted. "I bought it for her. We saw them years ago, drove all the way to Albany." His eyes clouded with reminiscence for a moment.

Suddenly he grew angry and threw the shirt across the room. "Why? Why'd he have to do it? He couldn't have let her be? Why were they even here?"

Felicity was startled more by his words than his anger. She glanced at the baby, who was miraculously still sleeping through Ben's raised voice, and then turned back to Ben. She couldn't make sense of his conclusions. "Exactly who do you think did what?" she asked in a forceful whisper.

Ben lowered his voice to match hers, but it was filled with resentful wrath. "My father, Bernard Everheart, our faithful protector."

Felicity froze. Did he know...about Bernard's claimed vampire hunting? It sounded like he knew. She tried to process Ben's fury as he violently pulled the rest of Allie's clothing from under the bed. Her slim jeans and tall, high heeled black leather boots; Ben ripped them from under the bed and held them up for her to see.

He was angry, but his rage fled as he looked at the articles of clothing and tears filled his eyes. "Don't you see? She must have come back and...he's too good at what he does to let that happen. She wouldn't stand a chance, not against *my* dad." The words were dripping with resentment. "He's dusted her."

Without allowing her to speak, Ben met her eyes with a level gaze. "My father, Bernard Everheart, likes to think of himself as a vampire hunter; trying to prove to himself that he really can protect his family. But he's much too late for that, and now...now Allie's really gone."

Felicity stood mute for a moment before finding her voice. "No, she isn't."

Ben shook his head in forlorn resignation, unwilling to hear her. "I don't know how, but she must have gotten in and..." he held up Allie's jeans again in emphasis, "what else could this mean?" He looked up at her with a look of profound sadness in his eyes that she hadn't seen since the night Allie had left, after revealing herself to him as a vampire.

Felicity crossed the room and knelt on the floor next to him. "It means I should have talked to you about this a long time ago." She took hold of Allie's clothing and gently took them away from him to hold them up and give them a little shake. "They're just clothes. No dust. She's fine."

Ben squinted at the clothing, daring to wonder if Felicity could be right. He picked up the tee shirt again for closer inspection. "I don't understand. How...?"

Felicity lent him her hand as they both rose to stand. "Your father's probably never even seen Allie."

"He always sees them," he told her with a quietly resigned indignation. "I don't know how, but he's got like a sixth sense about them or something. He always has. The only reason he never noticed *Sindy* back in the day, was because he was out of town during most of her shit, and honestly, I tried to keep her out of his way. If anyone was going to deal with that bitch, it was going to be me. She was my problem and I didn't want his help."

Felicity shook her head with disbelief that momentarily overshadowed her sympathy for Ben's distress. "You knew…from the beginning? All this time, I'm trying to figure out how to tell you that your dad thinks he's some kind of white *Blade*, and you already knew?"

Ben's attention was finally drawn from Allie's clothing, which he let fall from his grasp and onto the floor as he realized his wife's admission. "Me? How did *you* know?" he asked her incredulously.

"He told me," she admitted quietly.

Ben was dumbstruck. "When?" he finally asked.

Felicity averted her eyes and bit her lip, wishing she could downplay the amount of time that the secret had been kept, but knowing that Ben deserved the truth. "He told me on the day I met him."

Ben looked like she could have knocked him over with a feather. After a second, he began to laugh, which was unsettling opposite to the reaction she had expected. "Day one? You're a complete stranger, some girl his son brought home, and on the first day he meets you, he chooses to divulge the secret he hasn't seen fit to share with me for my entire life? My dad, he just keeps getting better. How much did he tell you?"

"A lot. Pretty much everything I guess." Ben let out a snort of disbelief. "He's been trying to protect you," Felicity tried to assure him.

"Yeah, I know," Ben said with a sarcastic laugh. "Sucks at it, doesn't he? Maybe he should give up the vampire hunting and try protecting me from disappointment. He just keeps letting me down, again and again." She tried to put a comforting hand on his shoulder, but he raised his own hand to stop her. "It's my own fault, because I keep coming back for more. I keep looking for his approval, like he's any kind of role-model," he added with a bitter laugh.

"When did you know?" He didn't answer. "Was it when your mom died?" she asked gently.

"I knew way before that. I didn't know *what* they were until after Allie figured out they were vampires, I think I was fourteen, but I'd known my dad was dealing with things that weren't human since I was a little kid. It's almost like I always knew.

I may not have all of the details surrounding my mother's death, but I know enough to understand my father's role in it, and why he's become the way he is today. I understand the guilt, I understand the desire for revenge, and I think both are very well deserved. That doesn't mean that I approve, but please don't insult my intelligence by assuming that over the last twenty-six years I couldn't figure it out. It's bad enough that I don't get any kind of credit from my father. I'd hope you know me better."

"I'm sorry I didn't tell you. I should have. He asked me not to and I shouldn't have listened to him. I knew that you deserved to know. I kept thinking that eventually he would tell you."

"Yeah, me too. I'm strong, I'm smart, I've even got the swordsmanship! Yet somehow, I'm still not good enough."

"Wait…good enough for what? You don't condone this, do you? Oh my God…were you planning on joining him?"

He sat there watching her outraged expression with grim seriousness. "I don't know. I don't anticipate *Everheart & Son, Vampire Slayers,*" he told her with sharply sarcastic air quotes, "but there was a time when I'd expected things to go in that direction. I guess he doesn't think I make the cut."

Felicity stared, open-mouthed at her husband, as though he was someone she didn't even know. "You cannot hunt vampires!" she ordered him in a harsh whisper.

His mouth twisted into a darkly humorous half smile. "Why, just because they give *you* the warm and fuzzies? It's not something I've been out looking to do, but I'm certainly capable and I don't like knowing that they're out there, a constant threat to my family. They're not fluffy bunnies Liss, they're demons."

She felt burning resentment rise within her. "Again with the demon thing… They're not all like that. They're people! You don't hunt people."

"You do if they're murderers."

"Who are you, Charles Bronson?"

"Liss, if our society is not willing to formally recognize this dangerous threat to the population, and designate properly skilled individuals to protect people from it, then maybe it's the moral obligation of those equipped to do the job. I'm not saying it's been a plan of mine, but it is a job that needs doing, and I have the ability to do it."

"You are a lawyer, not a superhero!"

"Are you worried about my safety, or the vampire's?"

She looked away, crossing her arms over her chest and wondering how they could be sitting here, six years later, and having the same damn argument…again. Did he really still feel threatened and resentful over the fact that she'd been in love with a vampire? She sighed as another wave of guilt over her reaction to Cain's visit flashed over her. Maybe he had a right to be.

He continued with a bitter look upon his face. "The only vampire I could never bring myself to kill is gone now anyway, so what's the difference?"

Okay, now she felt they were on more manageable ground. However unsettling his revelations about Bernard to her were, she understood now that some of his stance was fueled by his grief over Allie. He still didn't realize that Allie wasn't dusted. "Ben, she isn't gone."

"How do you know?" he asked her fiercely. "Do you have a better explanation for this?"

As much as she really didn't want Ben's anger towards Bernard to suddenly shift in her direction, she answered him quietly and truthfully. "Yes. They are Allie's, I know. I was here when she left them. She's fine."

"Wait...what?"

"Allie, she came to see me. I've seen her a few times since she left. She's wanted to see you too, but the timing has never seemed right. She misses you." Ben just took it in, in mute shock. She wished she could tell what he was thinking. Why couldn't Allie be checking in on her telepathically *now?* "Allie is kind of special...for a vampire. She has abilities... She *was* here when your dad came over, but he never saw her. There's this thing she does when she doesn't want to be seen, and she left her clothes behind. She wasn't dusted, I promise you."

"You've been seeing her?"

"It was only a couple of times, but yeah." Trying to explain the telepathy would probably make things worse, so she chose to leave that out for now. The information they were already dealing with was enough to handle.

"You invited her into our house?"

"She wanted to see the baby."

Ben glanced at the bassinet in growing outrage. "You let her see the baby?"

She gave him a look of disbelief that he would mistrust her judgment over such a thing. "Ben, take a minute," she told him, raising her hand for him to slow down and not jump into hostile hysteria. "You asked me to give you credit for understanding your dad, give me a little credit for judging Allie. I'm not a starry-eyed, naïve seventeen-year-old anymore. I probably understand vampires better than you do, and I know that Allie is trustworthy. Her body may have changed, but she hasn't, and if I think it was alright for her to see the baby, I think you should trust me. By all rights she should be Christian's godmother for heaven's sake!"

To say Ben seemed to disagree would be an understatement. He looked at the baby and then spoke in a quietly menacing voice. "If you think a vampire would make a good godmother, than I'm afraid you have a grave misunderstanding of the title."

"Ben, you said yourself that you would never dust her. I saw the look on your face and the tears in your eyes when you thought she'd been killed. I know how you feel about her, and I know that the rational, intelligent man that I married knows damn well that if I say Allie is still herself, then it's got to be true. Give me some credit.

I know that the idea of something else existing within her, and influencing her, scares the shit out of you, but I'm telling you, she has it under control. She is well made, and it hasn't changed her, not really. She isn't like one of those vampires we fought and killed years ago, she's…" Felicity shrugged with a lopsided smile. "She's Allie."

"You should have told me."

"I tried. You didn't want to hear it."

He lowered his eyes in thought. He knew that was true. It was a conversation that she had tried to start many times, and he'd always cut her off. Finally, he nodded in admission. "Still, you should not have invited her in without telling me. This is my house too, and Christian is my son just as much as yours. You can't just go and compromise our safety like that. It's not fair. It's bad enough that she knows where we live, and she saw the baby, you didn't have to invite her in!

I know you think you're right about Allie, and you know what? I hope to God you are. But you can't take a chance like that with our son's safety. There always needs to be an absolutely safe place to go, just in case. I can't believe I should have to tell you that. Do any other vampires have invitation that I should know about?" he asked her sarcastically.

Something on her face must have shown true reaction to the question, because Ben was now staring at her in wide-eyed disbelief. She hadn't planned to tell him that Cain had been there. What was the point? Cain had said himself that he wasn't coming back, and no matter what Ben believed, Felicity knew that Cain having invitation to their house was not a threat to their safety. She couldn't hide it though. She and Ben knew each other too well for that. He knew just by the split-second of reaction before she could hide the expression on her face, that there was another secret to be told, and he wasn't going to like it.

"I was just kidding," Ben said with hushed dismay. He looked at her steadily for a moment while she tried to find the right words. "He's been here?" No question in her mind who the *he* in question was, she nodded. "Please tell me that we're talking about Mattie," he asked without much hope. She sighed, lowering her eyes and confirming Ben's fears. "Cain? You've been seeing him too?" This time the word *seeing* had a different connotation to it.

"No," she asserted with forceful seriousness. "He showed up here, but it was a complete accident. He was following Allie, he didn't even know this was my house." She realized belatedly that *our house* would have been a better received phrase, showing that she thought of she and Ben as united and separate from Cain, but it was too late. It was nothing, but she knew that Ben was very adept at picking out and focusing on such minor things in an argument. That's what made him such a good lawyer.

She continued, not giving him a chance to dwell on anything. "He showed up, and we were both very surprised to see each other. I told him about you, and our life…how happy we are. He apologized for the intrusion. He said he was glad that I was doing well, and that he wouldn't be back."

"And yet somehow you still felt the need to invite him in? Why? For tea?"

Ben's questions were barked out with harsh sarcasm, but she couldn't help but smile at the tea remark. "We didn't have tea," she assured him with a quiet smile. Ben was not amused. Felicity put a hand on his arm, trying to show him that she appreciated his jealousy, but that it was unfounded.

He shrugged her off. "You don't even get it, do you? You think this is cute, a touching affectation of endearment that your husband might be jealous of some ex-lover? This isn't anything as cute as leftover rivalry, okay? This is me, feeling shaken that the entire foundation of our life might be based on something unreliable."

"What are you talking about?"

"You! You are my whole life Liss, you and Christian are the most important things in the world to me, and I am dedicated to this family one hundred percent."

"So am I!"

"Are you? Because unlike you, I'm living without a net. There is no back-up plan for me. I love you, and that's it. And I refuse to spend my life wondering if some day you're going to disappear to join the undead."

The worry in him was as palpable to her as if she possessed Allie's empathy. His words were rough and unyielding like an angry accusation, but all she saw when she looked at him was the little boy who surely felt his father had abandoned him and his mother to the supernatural, even if it was through different means. She took a step closer to him and was grateful that he didn't pull away when she took his hands. "Oh my God, Ben, no. I wouldn't. I've never thought that way. I love you too. I love our life, this is what I've always wanted, to share this with you. There is no back-up plan," she assured him.

He looked at her quietly for a moment, all emotion seeming to drain from his face. "I'm not an idiot. So don't say it isn't an option when you know damn well it is, even through Allie."

"That's not fair. We all have options. I'm sure she'd change *you* too if you asked her."

"I would never. Besides, there's nothing for me on the other side. Everything I love is here." His gaze looked into the depths of her own eyes as he said it. It didn't matter that he was a strong, smart, independent, and capable man. She truly was his world.

"I know, but being human is still your choice. It's my choice too, without a doubt."

"Is it?"

"Yes!"

"You're going to tell me that you saw Cain, and you invited him into our house…you spent time together, you talked, and it never occurred to you that you could just walk away and leave everything behind? You never even considered it?

I know how you felt about him. I know that he has an unnatural affect on you, that I can't compete with, because it's not human. But I love you, in a way that I don't think he can, and I have chosen to believe that the love we have can be strong enough to overcome anything. Please don't prove me wrong."

"Ben, I believe in us too! That is why I've made the choices that I have. No, I did not consider leaving with him! If that was what I wanted, I could have done it a long time ago. Don't start accusing me of faltering in our love just because of a visit. I've seen the man exactly twice in six years!"

She waited for a moment for the admission to register, before going on. "Yes, twice. I visited with him once before, a few years ago, before the wedding. You know what I told him? That I was in love, and planning to share my life with someone else. Until death do us part. What more do you want from me?"

He was obviously comforted by her words, but he wanted more. "Your full attention."

"You have it," she told him quietly.

Ben sighed, dropping her hands. "No, I don't. If I did, there would be no secrets."

He walked out of the room. What could she say? In some ways he was completely and utterly right...and yet, the things he worried about, she wasn't even considering, was she? How could he not feel the love she had for him and just know that she was here for him, to be his rock, unwavering, his true partner in life?

She was startled when she heard the front door slam. He was going out? Never, not once in their entire committed relationship since they'd begun living together, had he ever left without telling her where he was going. It was just an unspoken expectation. They each always knew where the other was...a result of having other people in their lives disappear.

She wanted to go after him, but she'd known the look on his face when he'd left the room. He wanted to be alone. To chase after him, would only incite argument. She hadn't thought he would leave the house, but he would come back... He had to.

Sounds of stirring, a stifled mew of an exploratory cry sounded from across the room. The door slam had woken Christian. It had been all the way out in the living room, but somehow the strength of disheartened emotion it represented had carried through the whole house like a slam to the soul, leaving Felicity feeling empty, misunderstood and regretful.

She went and soothed the baby, adjusting his covers and giving him a gentle caress or two to coax him back into slumber. Once he was drifting back to sleep, she went to her bookshelf. All of her favorites were there, worlds to delve within and escape from reality, without guilt or repercussion. Not tonight, though.

She searched the top shelf until she found the sage green spine of *The Complete Poems of John Keats*. It was Cain's copy. He'd bought it from the *DownTime* and she'd taken it from his abandoned house after he'd left. She pulled it out from the shelf and reached high up into the space behind, until rewarded with the feel of cool and delicate metal links beneath her fingers. She grasped and pulled out her hidden treasure.

The chain was attached to a tiny vial of white frosted glass held within a criss-crossing cage of tiny gold vines, its stopper topped with a little gold flower with a tiny diamond chip in the center. The necklace Cain had given her. It's vial still held a precious small amount of his blood, meant to declare his protection of her against other vampires. She remembered nights when he had first left, that she had cried herself to sleep clutching it tight in her hand under her pillow, hoping that somehow it held unrevealed magic that would call him and weave a spell to mend their fates. But it was only glass and gold, holding a few drops of Cain locked inside with all of her old unspoken dreams.

She held it now and knew in her heart, that as magical and fond as those memories were, they were dreams of the past. The man who embodied her dreams for the future had just walked out the front door.

Allie, what have I done?

Chapter 17
Welcome to the evil bitch club

Sindy

A bar, Upstate, New York
An evening in May

Allie was paying no attention to her whatsoever. The music was so loud she could barely think. Sindy could feel it pounding through her with shuddering intensity, only to be occasionally overcome by the shrill and piercing screech of electric guitar, and the obscenities shouted into the microphone by the lead singer. Listening to this ear-splitting din last night was bad enough…why did Allie have to insist that they follow the band to the next show?

However, Sindy had to admit that no matter how offensive she found the deafening music, it was definitely easy hunting ground. Earlier, Sindy had even found herself showing off a bit, by taking a nip of a drink from a guy right in the middle of the mosh pit. Allie had been suitably impressed by her stealth and control. Alyson was light years from mastering a subtle sample tasting. With Allie, it was almost all or nothing. Once she tasted the blood, she was overwhelmed and oblivious to all else, drinking a good amount before she even had the presence of mind to slow down and restrain herself at all. It was like handing a toddler a box of chocolates and telling them to take only one…

That was one of the reasons they were back. Last night's hunt had not worked out. Allie had been so busy enjoying the concert that she hadn't even staked out a victim until the show was winding down. She missed a chance to lure anyone away alone during the distraction of the concert, and then the parking lot was so full, it seemed privacy would be impossible. It was too risky to have Allie feeding in uncontrolled conditions where they might easily be seen, and it was too late to bring anyone to a hotel room.

Sindy'd had to persuade Allie to count the night as a loss. She'd had to promise that she and Allie would attend the next show to try again.

Still, Sindy didn't mind babysitting, if it was going to further her goals in the long run. The problem was deciding which of those goals was most worth pursuing. As much as she would love to just enjoy the nights as they came, reveling in the security, friendship, and romance that she had never dared to believe she could actually attain, she wasn't sure how long she was going to be able to get away with it. Until she figured out how to stay without risking Arif's wrath, or having to confess her disloyalty to Cain, and lose him, she was going to have to make it appear as though she was still following Arif's plan.

Surely, to Arif's camp she looked to be setting herself up in the perfect position to carry out her original agenda. She was fast becoming Allie's closest confidant. Sure, Mattie shared her bed and held her heart, but Sindy was the only one that truly sympathized with Allie's thirst, and that was a driving force in a vampire not to be underestimated. If Allie could count on Sindy, and only Sindy, to understand and help give her outlet to that thirst, then Sindy would have a true 'in' for manipulation.

So, now that she was gaining that trust, what should she do with it? Arif wanted Allie persuaded to voluntarily visit *Kana Susamiş İçin Ev*, and Sindy would forever be allowed a place of esteem there if she could deliver. Why he wanted Allie there was something he hadn't divulged, and Sindy had convinced herself that it didn't matter, but lately she had begun to wonder if something Arif wanted that badly, might not be best for everyone after all. It would also mean leaving Cain...

The first time that Sindy had come to see Cain, she'd had no further goal than to win his affection. Back then, she had only recently discovered her wolf-shifting ability, and had thought that she would impress him with her new independence and maturity. But when he'd spurned her advances and seemed to want nothing more than to shove her off on the Crimson Coven, she'd bolted, insulted and humiliated.

That was when she'd come across Arif's coven again. She'd heard tell of his community, *Kana Susamiş İçin Ev*, back when she had first been turned, and he had dusted her maker. It had sounded like her idea of paradise, but no matter what she'd offered in return, Arif would not allow her entrance.

Seeing his coven around again had brought back her old aspirations. The few years gone by had not erased her vision of living in vampiric luxury, so she had requested an audience with Arif, to ask once more if she might be admitted into his elite community. She had fully expected to be turned down again, but this time had been different. This time, she'd had access to something Arif wanted.

When he had told her that he knew of a young woman named Alyson who'd been recently turned, and was staying with Cain, Sindy couldn't imagine why Arif should care. His only explanation had been that Alyson had peaked his interest, and he would like to know her better. While that would seem the utmost flattery to some vampiresses, Sindy knew that Allie wouldn't go for it. But when Arif had said he would be willing to grant residence at *Kana Susamiş İçin Ev* to the vampire who could bring Allie to stay there as well, in Sindy's mind it was a done deal. 'Sure, I know her. We're great friends. No problem.'

Now that the complexity of the situation had better revealed itself, it had become a much more challenging task, but it still seemed within reach, if Sindy wanted to reach for it. It had just required slow, patient and methodical building of trust. If she was going to be practical, she knew that once she'd convinced Allie to enter the grounds of Arif's compound, it probably didn't matter what happened next, because Arif was smart enough to be prepared to handle anything Allie might do, as long as he had sound information about her abilities beforehand. And whatever Arif had planned for Allie really shouldn't be any of Sindy's concern. If the situation were reversed, Allie wouldn't waste time worrying about what happened to her…would she?

Also in line with her practical assessment, was the fact that a residence at *Kana Susamiş İçin Ev* was likely to last far longer than a friendship with Allie could survive, or a real relationship with Cain for that matter. Even now, spending each day in his bed and receiving his loving attention, she knew in her heart that his true love was Felicity; something Sindy could never surmount. The man was trying, she had to give him that, but were heart melting gazes and sweet expressions of admiration from him worth giving up her place in paradise? No matter how sublime it was to be the subject of his devotion, it was sure to be short-lived.

He was so sweet though, and he was trying to make her happy, even if she hadn't usurped Felicity's place in his heart. Earlier, as she'd been getting ready to go out, he'd found her going through her closet. He'd been thinking about their conversation over clothing the other night, and felt the need to make it up to her.

"I'm sorry if you were insulted that I don't care for most of your dresses. I just feel that you are a stunning woman who shouldn't need to put herself so blatantly on display. I'd love to go out and buy you something more classically beautiful, but I'd be hopeless to find anything that would fit, and I do respect that you have your own sense of style," he'd told her.

With that, he'd given her a credit card to go clothes shopping with. She'd never had a credit card that wasn't stolen. She'd been very surprised when he'd given it to her with a kiss on the cheek. "I know you haven't been able to fully flesh out your wardrobe with the little bits of shopping money I've given you. I shudder to think how you normally acquire such things," he'd said with a wink and a laugh. "So I'm giving you a card to use. I'll leave the shopping to you, and you should shop to your own tastes, not mine. I would just like to know that you are dressing to make *yourself* feel lovely, not to lure in a meal. Get what you need."

Sindy'd turned the card over in her hands. "Really? Whatever I want?"

At that, Cain had given her a sly smile. He was generous, but he wasn't a fool. "I didn't say get whatever you want, I said get what you need. I should think it'll be plenty to cover a basic wardrobe and a few dresses for special occasions, but there is a limit on it," he informed her with a little smile.

"What's the limit?" she asked coyly.

The smile became more of a smirk. "I guess if you need a lot, you'll find out. If you don't, it doesn't matter."

Sindy found herself smiling at the memory. He seemed happy to give her everything she could ever want, as long as she didn't make him feel taken advantage of. She could see herself staying with him indefinitely. He would get tired of her though eventually, wouldn't he? The vampire paradise offered by Arif was a much surer thing, something that would last long beyond the time that Cain grew tired of her not being the woman he really wanted...

Then again, perhaps that didn't need to hold true. Maybe she could *become* the woman he wanted, if she could allow herself to let distractions of espionage fall away, to focus on nurturing the aspects of Cynthia he saw within her. If she allowed herself to let her guard down and be the person he kept telling her she could be, maybe she could stay and it would be worth it. Perhaps what she really needed to do was re-examine her definition of paradise...

Maybe if she took Cain out to show him the secret garden she had made him, and then explained the position she was in, because of past promises she'd made in haste and selfishness, somehow he could forgive her, see that she wanted things to be different and help her find a way to defuse the whole debacle. It was a huge risk though. Once she told him, if he didn't forgive her, she would lose everything, her relationship and her chance at *Kana Susamiş İçin Ev*. Did he love her? Could she take that risk?

"Oh my God, the lead guitarist is amazing!" Even with Alyson yelling in her ear, Sindy wouldn't have been able to hear her without the assistance of telepathy. She was startled from her speculations by Allie's burst of thought in her head to accompany her voice that couldn't compete with the music. She looked to see who Allie was talking about, but could barely get a glimpse of the guy's face as his long hair swished in time with his head banging to the music. "Listen to those licks, have you ever heard anything so brutally beautiful?" Allie was unabashedly pounding her fist in the air and pointing up on stage at the guy, as he finished a particularly long and intricate solo. The guitarist noticed her as he finished his riff, and by way of appreciation, performed an almost obscene gesture towards her with his tongue.

Sindy rolled her eyes and turned to make her way through the crowd. "I'm hitting the bar. Come get me when you're ready for business."

It took four cocktails, three songs, and one more nip of a drink from the throat of a guy in the back corner of the bar, before Allie came to find her. The band's set was ending and Sindy was feeling annoyed and impatient. She'd had enough blood to satisfy, but Allie was going to miss out again unless they lured someone to follow them elsewhere. Then new music began to play, easing Sindy's worries. The bar wasn't closing yet, a D.J. would take over for a while longer, giving them a last chance for Allie to feed.

Allie took the glass from Sindy's hand and chugged down the remainder of her drink. "Let's get out of here."

"What? We're leaving?" It felt strange not to have to yell. The music from the D.J. helped the crowd noise to fill the room, but it wasn't nearly as deafening as the band had been. Her ears were ringing. Allie took her hand to start leading her outside through the crowd. "But you haven't even picked a lucky winner yet," Sindy remarked in confusion.

"He's meeting me out back. We have to find the backstage entrance," she said as they made their way outside into the cool night air. A handful of patrons spilled out into the parking lot with them to join those who were outside smoking.

Allie walked along the side of the building. Sindy realized Allie's intentions and followed, unenthusiastically. "The guy from the band? Seriously?"

Allie glanced back at her as they reached the rear of the building. "Why not?" There were only a few cars parked back here, and a long black bus that must belong to the musicians. It was almost completely dark in the back lot, with the exception of one dim light-bulb near a back door to the bar that was propped open.

"It's usually not a good idea to drink the entertainment," Sindy informed her snidely. "People notice."

The noise from the bar drifted out to them and a couple of guys emerged, accompanied by the female lead singer and the drummer from the band. They were making trips back and forth, piling speakers and things from the stage on the concrete near the back door. "Show's over," Allie told her dismissively. They watched the guys drop their stuff and go back for more. Allie turned to her with her hands on her hips. "Anyway, I'm not gonna kill him! You want me to get the drummer for you?"

"No thanks." Sindy crossed her arms and leaned against the building. "I don't get your taste in men at all."

"I'm gonna drink him, not date him," Allie reminded her with a smirk.

"Doesn't matter. In fact, a guy like that, I'd expect you to date. It's you and Mattie I don't really get. He's cute, but isn't he kind of…*simple* for your taste?"

Now Allie turned to fully stare at her. "Excuse me?"

Sindy smiled. "I didn't mean that as an insult, really. He's a smart guy, but he's simple…as in no frills, no drama, and what you see is what you get."

"Well, yeah, that's Mattie."

"So… I do remember you from back when we were human you know. He is *so* not like the kind of guys I used to see you with. Lead guitar guy I would've expected, but not Mattie. He does have a hot, jock bod under all that innocence, and it is kind of adorable how he doesn't even seem to know it. But I always thought you were more into the goth-rocker type. You're obviously drawn to the bad boys."

Allie shook her head a little, almost looking confused herself as to how to explain it. "Bad boys may be exciting, but they don't last well long term. Anyway, I've known Mattie since he was in junior high. Our relationship goes way deeper than 'types'. I love him, and there's a real foundation there. Don't forget, he's a few years younger than me. I did sample my share of bad boys before Mattie started noticing me as more than a friend. But Mattie and I always sort of clicked.

We knew each other outside of school, and when we hung out, it was like all the superficial stuff was stripped away. We're not all that different really. I'm pretty straight-forward myself, and drama is not my thing. When he started paying me some real attention, he was just so sweet and real. He was shy and inexperienced. I mean, you can see where that would be a total turn-on, right?

I knew it wouldn't be long before girls caught on to what a catch he was, so I decided not to let him get away. As soon as he started showing a little interest, I took his attention…and then I took his virginity," she admitted with a coy smile.

"And now you take him for granted. Isn't that sweet?"

Alyson's fierce glare bore into her, but Sindy refused to retract the statement. Why should she? It was true, wasn't it?

The lead singer and the roadies from the band re-emerged with more gear, and this time Allie's guitarist was with them. He was a thin, wiry guy wearing ripped jeans, a leather vest with no shirt, and had his guitar slung over his back. Dark eyeliner had streaked down his face from the strenuous performance, and he had a little tuft of a goatee on his chin. Guys who wore make-up were never Sindy's style, but she had to admit that he had great cheekbones and a very handsome face.

"Just leave the rest and we'll load it up later. We're gonna hang for a while," the singer told the men. Allie's guitarist adopted a cocky grin when he spotted the girls waiting for him. He said something to the drummer, who clapped him on the shoulder with a laugh before leaving him to head back into the bar with the others.

Allie knew he was there, but waited until he had reached them before turning around. She probably wanted to whet his appetite with a nice view of her spandex covered ass. He wasn't going to need any further tempting though. He was obviously already looking forward to spending the rest of the evening with her. He approached Allie with an almost predatory smile. "Hey sweet cheeks, wanna tour my tour bus?" He accentuated the offer by moving in closer and squeezing her ass.

Some introduction, Sindy commented mentally to Allie. *You picked a real prince.*

Allie ignored her and answered the guy with a coy smile. "Sure. You were amazing by the way."

"That was only one of my many talents…" he informed her with a subtle little flick of his tongue. "I saw you last night too. I like dedication in a fan. I've been looking forward to tasting you."

Allie just raised her eyebrows as Sindy answered him with an amused smirk. "I'm sure the feeling's mutual."

"You bringing your friend?" he asked as he seized Sindy up.

"She's going to wait out here."

"I am?" Sindy asked in surprise. Not that she wanted in on anything, but how was she going to keep Allie in check from out here?

The guy looked disappointed, but then mouthed Allie a kiss. "Lady's choice. I'll be inside getting comfortable," he told her, and then left for the bus.

"You do that," Sindy called after him facetiously. "What a tool."

"Musicians are like that."

"Known your share, have you? Why am I waiting out here?"

Allie brushed her off with a wave of her hand. "I got this."

Sindy's mouth opened as speculations began to take shape. "Oh my God, you're gonna *do* him aren't you?"

"No! I would never disrespect Mattie like that."

"Uh-huh. And I'm sure whatever else you have in mind is going to make him so proud."

"Shut up. I need you to keep an eye out for the rest of the band."

"He's all yours. Take it easy on him, though. He's kind of a light weight."

"Yeah, I'll take it slow. We'll probably talk for little first. Gimme like twenty minutes, then come check, okay?"

Sindy stifled a chuckle. "Sure, have a nice *talk.*"

Allie frowned at her. "I am not going to do anything with him."

"Whatever. I'm not here to judge. Take your time. I'll see it when you mark him and I'll come in a little after, okay?"

"Perfect, thanks." Alyson's mark was cloaked, but once she bit the guy, and her venom fully entered his system, he would become marked by her. He would be visible to all vampires nearby, unless she cloaked him too, which was something Allie had never practiced. She would only be able to cloak his mark if she stayed fairly close to him, and she never hung around after drinking anyway.

Alyson disappeared to go and claim her guitarist, leaving Sindy to stand watch in the dark parking lot. Sindy took a peek into the back door of the bar. No one was hanging around backstage. By peering down the hall, she could see at least one recognizable member of the band sitting at the bar with a bunch of people. She considered luring someone out to keep her company, but decided it was too risky.

"Hi."

Sindy spun to find Kieran standing right next to her. She was once again annoyed that he had managed to sneak up on her without her noticing. She was even more irritated when she realized that he was wearing clothing, meaning he had snuck up on her the old-fashioned way. He stood there grinning in an artfully ripped black tee shirt and a pair of leather pants that were an obnoxious shade of purple. "What are you doing here?" she asked in a harsh whisper.

He shrugged. "Hanging out, catching some tunes, admiring the ever-changing view…" He was referring to her body.

She hadn't enlarged her chest to the extreme state that she had last night, Allie was right, fun as it was, it was also a bit annoying and took some getting used to, but she had still made some very noticeable alterations. She wasn't ready to revert back to her familiar proportions just yet, and she'd opted for somewhere in between just enough, and extreme. Kieran gave her a smile to let her know that he approved.

She wouldn't let him think she cared about his opinion. "You followed us."

"No kidding. That's my job."

"Well aren't you supposed to be a little more discreet about it?"

He smirked at her and nodded his head towards the tour bus. "She's busy."

"So you decided it'd be a good time to come and bug me?" He gave her a wounded expression, but she folded her arms and refused to take pity on him. "Well you've been a *silent* observer for the past couple of years, why are you suddenly talking to me now?" Just what she needed, a stalker who'd decided she should be his new best friend.

"The silence is lifted," he revealed with a grin. "Once the master asked me to approach you for a report, you were allowed to know I was around. Now communication is at my own discretion…and the concert's over. I'm bored."

"I'm sure you could find someone else to keep you occupied," she told him with a meaningful glance towards the edge of the building. Two girls were loudly chatting as they got into their car parked out in front and to the side, just within the vampire's line of view.

His eyes never left her face. "I'm sure I could…"

"Is that all you do? Carry out *the master's* orders, follow people around like a good puppy?"

"I owe the master for my immortality." His answer was straightforward and unashamed.

"He didn't create you," she affirmed curiously.

"I was created at his command. Call me a puppy, or a lackey, or whatever you want. Doesn't bother me a bit. It's a groovy bag really. I get to be out in the field most of the time, and one week a month I get to go home to a palace, have all the blood I can drink, and…"

"And a bevy of beauties in your bed, I remember."

"Sound tempting?"

"The arrangement, or your bed in particular?"

"Answer as you like."

She shook her head and gave him a smirk to let him know that she wouldn't even consider it.

Sindy watched him for a moment, trying to figure out his true demeanor. He seemed to have a generally lighthearted disposition, but she suspected he could be much different, when the situation called for it. "Do you kill?" she asked. After all, if he was to be believed, he'd been spying on them at Cain's for a very long time now. Yet she had never seen a strange mark in the area. Of course, he knew how to cloak himself, but what about his victims? What was he feeding on? Did he travel far away to drink, or did he just kill them?

"Only when it's necessary."

"How come I've never seen your mark before? You must have been drinking nearby, all this time."

"In my job, leaving no trace is necessary," he said simply. He didn't let her dwell on it, but cracked a smile with a new thought. "That was some flight coming over here. I almost lost you two tonight. She is damn fast! I can only fly in dis-corporeal form. A couple of good cross-winds almost took me out trying to keep up. Luckily, I got close enough to hear where you were going this time."

"Luckily..." she repeated with a hint of sarcasm. She shook her head and let out a small huff in disgust at his blatant spying. They both froze for a moment in distraction as a mark flared into existence from within the tour bus about twenty feet away.

"And the United One drinks," Kieran said with a nod, seeming happy to have confirmed the information for himself. He'd probably never managed to follow them closely enough before to personally observe that Allie was drinking.

Sindy was still annoyed that she hadn't realized he was with them tonight. "You were right there with us, almost the whole time?"

He grinned. "You really enjoyed that flight, didn't you?"

She shrugged. "Sure, it's flying. Who wouldn't?"

He let his eyes travel her body for a moment. "I'll bet you're pretty light, even with the new additions," he said with a blatant nod towards her chest. "Want to go for a spin?" he came forward, to take her into his arms.

"What? No! I need to go check on Allie." She turned to walk towards the bus. Allie could drink quickly, and it was time she poked her head in.

Kieran came up behind her and locked his arms around her waist. Before she could do anything about it, he was already lifting her into the air as the lower half of his body dissolved into mist. His pants fell to the cement as she pushed against him and stifled a scream. "Put me down! What if somebody sees?"

He laughed. "They probably wouldn't even notice. This crowd's all stoned anyway. We can have some fun."

It was very disconcerting that when she kicked, there was absolutely nothing below his waist for her to connect with. He just wasn't there below his navel. She tried to grab his arms and shove at him to let her go before they got too high up. The last thing she wanted to do, was to shift form in mid-air, in order to escape his grasp, lose her clothing and fall to the ground. Such a drastic move was a last resort. "Put me down right now or I swear, you'll regret it!"

"Alright, alright." She stopped struggling as he lowered her to the ground. "Don't get your panties in a bunch. Are you wearing panties?"

"Get off me," she said as she regained her balance. She shoved him away as he reformed himself. "Go put your hideous pants back on," she told him.

"They aren't mine," he said with a chuckle. "I had to steal them when I got here."

Something changed. It only took Sindy a second to figure out what it was, and she could tell by the look on Kieran's face that he had noticed it too. The mark was gone... The mark from the guy Allie was drinking from in the tour bus, it suddenly wasn't there anymore. Sindy's eyes went wide. Was Allie cloaking him? She never did that. "Where'd he go?"

Kieran looked up from putting on his pants as directed. "Down the United One's throat would be my guess."

"Oh no. No, no, no." Sindy started backing away from him, her hands held up to her face before she turned and ran towards the tour bus. "Look what you made me do!"

"A little guilt won't hurt your cause much, will it? Tell her to come to the compound. She can drink all she wants, guilt free," Kieran called after her.

Sindy didn't even pause to answer. She leapt up the few stairs to the tour bus door and burst in. It was pretty dark inside, with only a few dim night-lights on, but Sindy could see perfectly well. The guitarist was sprawled out on the couch. He was still fully dressed, in a sitting position with his head tilted way back and a slightly messy set of puncture wounds at his throat, but Allie was nowhere near him. Sindy stepped further inside and closed the door behind her.

Alyson was sitting on the floor in the corner, seeming mesmerized by a small, lighted, decorative electricity globe on an end table next to her. "What are you doing?" Sindy asked her in disbelief.

Allie was watching the little bolts of contained purple lightning as they migrated towards her hand lightly resting on the glass. After a second, she looked up and seemed to notice Sindy. "Huh?"

"Allie! Get up." She stepped forward and took the guy's wrist into her hand to check for a pulse, but immediately dropped it when she got close enough to see that his eyes were open and glazed over. His mouth was open too, with a small bit of spittle in his goatee on his chin. He was definitely dead. She leaned back in distaste. "Jeez, look at him."

"Did you want some?" Allie's voice sounded strangely slow and slurred. "Or did you come in to hit it? 'Cause he's all yours if you want him. I told you I wasn't doing that."

"What are you talking about? This guy's already checked out of the party, Allie. What is wrong with you?"

A lazy smile spread across her face and she began to rise, but immediately lost her balance and sat on the floor again. "I don't know…but I like it."

"Wait a minute." Sindy grabbed the guitarists arm again and roughly turned it for a better view. Sure enough, the guy had dark, ugly track marks all over his forearm, and some were bruised and fresh. He'd used a needle recently. His idea of 'getting comfortable' must have been shooting up before Allie came in to join him. "Fuckin' A. Look at this shit."

"What is it?"

"Your guy was wasted. Didn't you even notice? He must have been shooting tar or something before you came in."

Allie got on her hands and knees to crawl over closer and see what Sindy was talking about, but gave up before she got close enough to see anything. She rolled over onto her back on the floor. "Is that bad?"

"It is for him. Venom is potent stuff, especially yours. When your venom mixed with the cocktail running through his veins, it must have shut him down."

"Oh… Do you know CPR?"

"Are you kidding? Just shut up for a minute, I need to think."

Allie tried to sit up to inspect the guy better, but she was very unsteady. "Who's driving the bus?"

Despite Allie's vertigo, they weren't actually moving. "Just sit down, it'll wear off in a few minutes." Sindy began inspecting their surroundings and going through the guy's stuff. She found a few crumpled up twenties in a side table drawer, which she shoved into her pocket, but that wasn't what she was looking for. After a minute of rifling through things, she found the guy's needle, tubing and spoon, along with a little baggie containing a small, grayish brown misshapen lump. She left the guy's stash out in plain sight with the works.

Allie was starting to look more steady. She also seemed to be coming down from her high and realizing there was a problem. "Is he gonna be okay?"

Sindy paused to stare at her in disbelief. "No. He's dead, Allie."

"What? No he isn't." Allie tried to stand up again.

This time Sindy lent her a hand, and she managed to stay upright. "I know a corpse when I see one," Sindy told her. "Trust me."

"But I stopped. When I was drinking, he made me feel all woozy and I stopped. I didn't take a lot. He's fine." Allie sat down next to him and began lightly slapping the guy's face as though she was going to bring him around.

Sindy tried to pull at her wrist to get her off the couch, but she wouldn't come. "He is not fine. Face it Allie, the guy is gone. Look, you need to shake off that shit so we can get out of here."

"What do you mean? You just want to leave him here?"

"Yeah. The band'll just think he OD'd. It'll be fine."

"No. No, it's not fine." Reality was beginning to set in and she could see that Allie was not going to take it well. "It won't be fine for him. He can't be dead. I didn't kill him."

"Oh relax. It was his own damn fault."

Allie stood from the couch in a panic. "No. You don't understand. He wasn't dead. Check again. I can't have killed somebody. *I* don't do that."

As though she considered herself so much better than Sindy, who had killed before? "Well, you did. Welcome to the evil bitch club."

Alyson just stared at her for a minute in mute shock. Her face seemed to melt with despair, making her look very forlorn. "But he was so good." Sindy looked at her oddly. "On the guitar," Allie clarified.

"So, he can play a harp in heaven. Come on, let's go."

Allie wiped her hands over her face as though clearing away her muddled thoughts. Just as Sindy thought she might be persuaded to leave, she could see the panic set in again. "No. I can fix this."

"What?"

"He may be kind of a jerk, but he doesn't deserve to die. And it's *not* going to be my fault."

"What do you think you're going to do?"

"I'm gonna bring him back." Now it was Sindy's turn to be silent in shock. Allie grabbed a bandana hanging out of the guy's pocket, and used it to gently wipe his face and close his eyes. "If I bring him back, it'll be okay. He'll be like us."

Sindy shook her head. "You don't know that. He's already been dead for at least five minutes. It might not even work. You don't even know how to do it."

"I do so. I know how Mattie made me. It was easy."

Sindy gave her a look of challenge for the truth. She was sure Allie'd had a much nicer introduction into death than she'd had, but she highly doubted it'd been a process anyone would call easy.

Allie amended her statement. "Okay, it wasn't *easy,* but I can do it." Allie changed as she spoke, revealing her bright white vampire eyes, and then looked down and considered where to bite her own wrist.

Thoughts raced through Sindy's mind, considering the implications of letting Allie change this guy with her powerful blood. If she were to let Allie do it, there would be a second United One...one that Sindy could easily bring to Arif, in part honoring her deal. Now that she understood that Arif knew about Allie's blood, she could guess that it was the United One he really wanted, not Allie in particular...but what would he do with such a vampire? And what would happen when Cain found out that Allie had made him?

Sindy only had a second to reach a decision before Allie acted on her own. As Allie made ready to sink her fangs into her own wrist, Sindy reached out and gave her a shove on the shoulder. "Stop it Allie. I can't let you do that."

Allie looked up at her. Even with her eyes glowing with power, her distress was clearly evident. She looked close to tears. "Why not?"

"Because...you're the United One."

"So what? I can't have killed someone, Sindy. I ended his life. It's my fault. I have to bring him back, so he can go on. Otherwise...he's just dead. It wasn't self-defense or anything, it was just my own stupid fault. I can't live with that, and...Mattie would never forgive me."

Sindy observed the heartbreak in her eyes. Sindy remembered what it was like that first time, bearing the knowledge that she had become a killer. The feeling that she had stepped off a cliff, done something that couldn't be undone. During that same moment of panicked despair, had been when

Sindy had created Ernest, her first. She didn't really know him, or like him, but it didn't matter. She couldn't just leave him for dead, a corpse to her credit.

She tried to reason with Allie, but her conviction was gone. She wasn't really trying to persuade her to stop, just to consider the implications. "How are you going to get him to drink it? He's dead. It's not so easy once they're dead. You won't know how to make it work." It wasn't all that difficult, really, but the comment served to create enough doubt in Allie to make her pause.

The light seemed to die in Allie's eyes as they shifted from white to blue, defeated. "You've done it before. You have, haven't you? How do you make it work? Please Sindy, you have to help me. We're wasting time, he'll be gone too long. Please, you have to help me...you're my friend."

She knew it was a bad idea. They should just get out of here and let the drugs on the table tell the story, but somehow, she just couldn't do that. Allie really *did* consider her a friend, someone to be trusted and counted on. Allie was counting on her to make this okay. She sat down next to the guy on the couch, opposite Allie on his other side. "It can be done, but I don't know what kind of shape he'd be in. It could be worse than leaving him."

"No. The guys you turned, most of them were okay. It'll be better than rotting in the ground. As long as...he won't be a zombie, will he?"

Sindy shook her head. "That's only when you don't give them enough blood. If he gets plenty, his body should be okay, but if too much time passes, it's his mind you have to worry about."

Allie nodded and hurriedly made ready once again to bite her wrist, but again, Sindy stopped her. "But, you can't Allie. I can't let you turn him with *your* blood." Sindy almost couldn't believe the words coming out of her mouth. "If I did...Cain would never forgive you. I'll do it."

A visible wave of relief flooded over Allie. "You will?"

Sindy nodded and quickly made ready to get down to business, before she could reflect on what an opportunity she was missing, and change her mind. Allie seemed to plan to stay and watch, but Sindy wouldn't let her. "Get outside. Don't you dare let anybody in this bus."

Allie nodded. "His name is Zach."

Sindy just shooed her to leave. After a second, worry flashed through her as she realized that Allie would be out there alone, but she dismissed the concern just as quickly. Allie was strong enough to defend herself, even if Kieran was still around. Sindy was guessing he wouldn't bother her anyway. Things were probably going just fine from his point of view. She was going to owe him a good ass kicking...

"Stay right by the bus and don't let anyone distract you," Sindy said quickly, as Allie opened the door. "Keep your guard up and your eyes white." Allie looked at her oddly, but was so relieved Sindy would help her, that she wasn't going to ask questions. "That way you can quickly brainwash anyone who approaches you," Sindy explained. "It's going to take a little while. I'll give him everything I've got, but I'll need your help when I'm done. I'm going to be pretty weak."

Allie nodded. "Anything you need." She met Sindy's gaze and held it with sincerity. "Thank you."

Sindy just gave her a quick nod and urged her to go. Once Allie had closed the door behind her, Sindy went to work. She knew the odds were slim that the guy would be just as good as new, but she'd do her damnedest to make him as well as she could. It had been quite a few years since she'd done this, but she much better understood the process now, compared to her previous attempts. Most vampires *were* created from corpses. They were then buried and left to rise on their own. Some came back strong, with their minds intact, and some didn't. But Sindy now understood that she had to be willing to drain herself to the dregs if she wanted it done well. She'd be able to give the guy a decent chance.

It was a fairly new and modern practice to give a person vampire blood before their body was even truly dead. There was no doubt that it gave better results, but as long as the body was turned within the first half-hour or so after death, and given a large amount of vampire blood for repair and change, the body should fully recover, and the mind had a good chance for full recovery as well.

The trick was to give him more blood than it seemed he needed. Apparently, the vampire blood insisted on mending the body first. Only when the body was sufficiently healed, did the blood bother to re-stimulate the mind. If she gave him blood in excess, both could be healed almost simultaneously, before memories were lost.

By the time Allie re-entered the bus, Sindy had poured every last drop that would flow from her down the guy's throat. At this point, she looked more like a corpse than he did.

Allie had been checking in with her telepathically throughout, assuring her that all was quiet, but there came a point when Sindy could barely think clearly enough to answer. She'd focused only on getting it done. Allie came in, worried by Sindy's state. "Are you okay?" She looked very concerned over Sindy's appearance, but became even more distressed when she looked at the guitarist. "Why isn't he moving? Why didn't it work?"

Sindy opened her eyes. She answered mentally, as even speech seemed more effort than she was capable of. *It's going to take a while. He was dead.*

"How long?"

You can never tell. Could be two hours, could be two days.

"Two days?" Allie asked in shock. "We can't wait two days. Look at you. I have to get you home."

No. I can't go back like this. I have to drink first. And we can't leave him here. If someone finds him before he wakes up, they'll call paramedics. We'll have to get a motel room.

Sindy wanted to stand from the couch, but the effort was too much for her. Allie quickly came to help. "Okay," Allie agreed, trying to take charge and lift the burden of responsibility from Sindy's shoulders. "We passed a motor lodge not far from here. I can get a room and then go hunt something for you, something four-legged," she added.

Sindy was ridiculously drained, but she could feel Allie trying to lend her strength. She spoke in a quiet whisper. "We have to leave without being seen, and I'm not up for travel on my own. Can you carry both of us?"

"I can do it, as long as you can hang on."

Allie led Sindy to lean against the wall, and then took a quick look around, making ready to leave. She spotted something and purposefully crossed the room. It was Zach's guitar. She gave Sindy a glance, clearly wondering if the guy would still be able to play. Sindy nodded. She wasn't entirely sure if he would come back with the capability or not, but there was no sense worrying Allie over it. Having the guitar might make things easier for him.

Allie came and slung the strap over Sindy's head and shoulder, to let the guitar rest on her back. It wasn't heavy, but the weight almost knocked her over. She had barely any strength left. Allie poked her head out the door and then came back when she saw that the coast was clear. Lifting Zach from the couch and moving to the doorway. "Can you wrap your arms around my neck?" she asked Sindy. Luckily, being much taller than Allie made it simple for her to drape her arms over Allie's shoulders from behind, despite her weakness. She grasped her arms to try to lock herself in place and hoped it wouldn't be a long flight.

It wasn't easy, but they made it. Alyson left them while she convinced the attendant of the Super 8 to give her the key to a motel room. Before long, they had Zach laid out on the bed, while Sindy sat on the floor, hunched over the last of the animals Allie had brought her. She'd already drained two medium-sized raccoons, and was now working on a large opossum. Hardly a gourmet meal, but Sindy was beyond caring, very grateful for the blood, and for the fact that the animal was a good twelve pounds or so. She would need more, but this was a good start.

Alyson observed her and said much the same. "I know it's not much, but it should be enough to get you on your feet. Then you can go take some from the motel attendant without killing him. That should be enough to get you home. I can make him give you his car keys."

Sindy looked up in shock. "What? I'm not leaving without you!"

"You have to. Someone has to be here to help Zach when he wakes up," she said with a meaningful glance towards the bed. "I know you think I was going to fool around with him, but I wasn't. We really were just talking. I wanted to practice my manipulation, that's all. I wanted to see if I could control him. I haven't ever spent any real time alone in private with a human to do that before."

"Oh." Sindy gave her a look of apology, although she didn't see why Allie felt the need to set the record straight. Did she really care that much what Sindy thought of her?

"I wanted to see how far I could push it, but I could tell right away, he was high. It was weird, way beyond being drunk. I could see right into his mind, with no resistance at all. I know he was being a jack-ass, but he's not that bad a guy."

"If you knew he was fucked up, why did you drink him?"

"I didn't think it mattered. I thought we were immune to that stuff now."

Sindy chuckled. "Not quite. It's like alcohol. It still affects you, but then the blood nullifies it. The stronger the drug, the longer it takes."

"Well, I guess I'll have to keep that in mind. In the meantime, I don't plan to be best friends with him or anything, but I've got to at least stay long enough to give him a tutorial when he wakes up."

"If I go back without you, the guys will kill me. You know they will. What am I supposed to tell them? There is nothing I could make up, that would convince Mattie and Cain that it was okay that I left the United One out here alone, and the truth wouldn't be any better."

Allie watched Zach, as though she could will him awake with her sheer desperation, but he didn't move. "Not even a flicker of consciousness yet, and it'll be dawn in like an hour. We can't just leave. He won't understand what's happening to him. That would be awful. I may have killed him, but I am *not* an evil bitch."

"I'll stay."

"But…"

"I'm sure the next few hours won't be pretty, but it's nothing I haven't handled before. I can go drink from the attendant like you said, and then I'll take care of Zach. Just go. I'll come back when I can. I'll be fine."

Allie still seemed unsure. "What do I tell the guys…Cain?"

Sindy wiped her mouth with the back of her hand and stood, resigned. "Just tell him I hooked up with some guy, and I told you not to wait."

"But Sindy, he'll think…"

Her mouth was set in a grim, determined line, although she might be losing everything. "We don't really have an alternative. You know you have to go home. I can't leave you here to handle it anyway, it's too much for you. I couldn't do that…to a friend. With any luck Cain won't even be there. He's off following some lead, and if it turns out to be a vampire, it could take a few nights. I might get home before he even misses me. If not, just tell him what I said. He knows me… It's nothing he wouldn't believe."

Chapter 18 - Time to go

Allie

Cain's Estate, Upstate, New York
Later that evening, just before the dawn

"What do you mean, she's not coming home?"

Allie shrugged and avoided Cain's eyes, knowing that even without empathy and telepathy, he was pretty good at reading her. At this point, he knew her just about as well as Mattie did; it was almost scary. "It's not a big deal, Cain. We weren't even sure you'd be back yet, so she didn't think you would mind."

After leaving Sindy and racing home before dawn approached, Alyson had been very disheartened to find that Cain had indeed returned from his own outing, and there would be no avoiding him. Apparently, whatever lead he'd been following did not require him to stay away any longer. She would have to go and tell him not to expect Sindy back this morning, so he wouldn't worry. She'd found he and Mattie sitting in the parlor.

"Exactly who was this *friend?*" Cain asked.

There was no way Allie was going to give him Sindy's 'hooked up with a stranger' story. No matter how selfless Sindy was trying to be, there was no reason to make her look like a disloyal slut...not this time anyway. What she did by herself to her image was damage past repair. Allie wasn't going to add to it, if she could help it. Besides, for some reason Cain seemed to be feeling very emotionally vulnerable tonight. "Don't worry, she wasn't into him or nothin', he was just an old friend. Someone she hadn't seen in a while, and he needed some help."

She would rather have said it was a woman, to put Cain more at ease, but she was trying to stay as close to the truth as possible, and Sindy saw most women as rivals rather than friends anyway, so it probably wouldn't have been very convincing. "He was injured, and Sindy wanted to stay with him for a night or two, just to get him some blood and help him get back on his feet."

Cain wasn't really buying it. She hadn't thought lying to him would be this difficult. "It's not as though she could feed him very well," he told her with an air of suspicion. "She's marked as mine."

Allie had forgotten that Sindy wore Cain's mark. She hadn't thought this through very well, had she? "You fed Sindy when she was injured, even though you were marked by me and Mattie," she insisted, happy to have found a precedent to cite. "She could do it like that...and I think she figured she could hunt for him."

"Why didn't she just bring him here? You both know that I would be happy to provide assistance. That's what I do! How injured was he? Surely, Sindy could have used my help."

Allie shrugged. "He wasn't *that* injured, more just blood deprived really. The guy didn't want to come back here. He's kind of a loner."

Her story didn't seem to be reassuring Cain in the least. In fact, he became more agitated as her lie progressed. After trying unsuccessfully to look into her eyes, Cain finally gave up and exchanged glances with Mattie instead. "I don't like this," he said quietly.

"Why, what's the big deal?" Allie asked, trying to sound unconcerned. "I only met the guy for a minute, but he seemed decent."

"Were you wearing your tinted glasses?" Mattie asked her. Whenever she came into contact with another vampire, that was his first concern; that she not be given away by her unique eyes; a mistake she'd made more than once in the past.

"Of course. I always wear them now."

"It may not matter," Cain said with quiet disapproval. "I never wanted to voice such worries but...any vampire that Sindy suddenly feels the need to spend private time with at this point...well, I worry that he may be working for Arif."

Both Mattie and Alyson responded sharply to the accusation. "What?!?"

Cain shook his head with a distant, troubled look in his eyes. "I'd hoped I was wrong, and perhaps I am, but I've suspected it for some time now. We all know that Arif is far more interested in you than he has any right to be, and I'm concerned that he hasn't given up trying to lure you away. What if he has decided to become more proactive about it? Sindy has had ties to Arif in the past, and I can't overlook aspects of her present demeanor that have proved suspicious."

Alyson was grateful that Mattie refuted the claim before she could think of something to say that wouldn't reveal the more simple and incriminating truth. "I don't know, Cain. Sindy's been with us for a long time now. She's not my favorite person, but if she were dealing with Arif, don't you think we would have noticed something more concrete by now?"

"Not necessarily, as much as I'd like to believe that. You underestimate the patience of an immortal. If anyone should be familiar with long-term plans, I should think it would be Arif. He may have planted her here with the specific intention of giving us time to accept her, and let our guard down. I do believe that she has sincere feelings for me, but she has also been very guarded and jumpy as of late. I've repeatedly caught her sneaking out into the woods on her own…ever since Arif's last visit as a matter of fact. What if the shade we'd been seeing was an emissary from Arif? She may have been meeting with him all along."

"She's not a spy," Alyson insisted, although she had no idea how she could convince anyone otherwise. How could Cain have harbored such suspicions without her knowing?

"I don't want to believe that either, but how can you be sure?" Cain asked her gently. "You can't truly read her, you've never shared her blood. Now she's with a strange vampire that insists on seeing her privately?"

She had to find a way to keep this from spinning out of control. Sindy was right, the 'hooked up with some guy' story probably would have been a better option. Better for Cain to think she was out having sex with a stranger, than that she was a spy! "The guy wasn't one of Arif's, okay? He was Sindy's."

Mattie seemed to accept the explanation, but Cain quickly shook his head. "He couldn't be."

"He was. She was his sire, trust me."

Cain looked unhappy and defeated. "Well then, that's no better. She's lied to me, and considering that, she could still very well be working for Arif."

"What did she lie about?" Mattie asked in confusion. "I've heard you both say that she's made lots of vampires."

Cain shook his head. "I've kept careful track. Her first was Ernest, whom I killed personally. Then came Chris and Luke, along with a handful of other young men from the college, and of course Marcus, but they've all been killed, every one of them. She's none left. She swore it to me, and she told me that she's made none since.

The making of a vampire is a serious thing, even for those who perform the act lightly and without care," he told Alyson and Mattie, who of course hadn't much experience with the act. "There is a bond between sire and protégé that cannot be severed until one of them turns to dust. Even if they go their separate ways, and end up on opposite sides of the world, a sire always knows when a vampire of their making has died. Always.

Sindy told me all of hers were dusted, there could be no mistake. So whether or not the vampire she is with now is one of her own, she has still lied about him."

Here Alyson was, trying to make things better for Sindy, and all she was doing was making her look worse and worse. This was no way to repay Sindy for her help. She was just going to have to come clean and face the music. "The vampire *is* hers, *and* she didn't lie to you," Allie told Cain forcefully. "She just made him…tonight."

"What? Why would she do that? Who is he?" Alyson's empathy confirmed the look of hurt betrayal on Cain's face, that some other man had become so important to Sindy without his knowledge. Her playing around with humans was much different than actually turning one. Even if he was harboring suspicions about her, he had still allowed himself to become hopeful that she would love and respect him above other men. "You said he was an old friend? Was he someone she knew when she was human?"

"I'm sorry, that part wasn't exactly true. I shouldn't have lied, I just didn't want you to be mad. He wasn't a friend of hers. She did it for me. I asked her to."

Although Cain was confused by this, it was the wave of trepidation that washed over Mattie, which drew her full attention. "It was someone that *you* knew?" Mattie asked, uncertainly. "Who did you ask her to change?"

Ben. Alyson plucked the name right from Mattie's mind. He was terrified that she had begged Sindy to change Ben. How could Mattie even consider that she would do that? Then again, what other human would he think she would go and change with Sindy's cooperation? "No!" she quickly refuted Mattie's speculative thoughts. "I didn't know the guy either," Allie insisted before crazy questions could arise. "He was in the band we went to see."

"Why would you want to change a complete stranger?" Cain asked.

Mattie gave her a look of jealous contempt. "You and your musicians."

"I didn't really *want* to change him, okay?" she pleaded with Mattie. She could already feel him jumping to insecure conclusions that she was looking for a more interesting vampire to spend her time with. "I didn't have a choice. I had to do something… I killed him."

Mattie's eyes grew wide with shock, but Cain was still trying to put things together. "How did you manage to kill someone?"

"Allie, you told me you were being careful!" Mattie said in distressed accusation.

"I was. It was an accident."

Cain's gaze bore through her unyieldingly. "You've been drinking from humans?" he asked. Then he turned to include Mattie in the betrayal. "And you knew? You two have been keeping this from me?"

Allie continued, ignoring Cain for now, and trying to stress her innocence to Mattie. "I *was* being careful. It wasn't my fault. I didn't over-drink him, the guy was on drugs."

Mattie snorted derisively. "Sounds like someone I'd grant eternal life, how about you?" he asked Cain sarcastically.

Cain was still staring straight through her. She finally gave in and met his eyes. "The drugs impaired your judgment," he concluded quietly.

"Kind of," she admitted. "I didn't drink too much though. Whatever he was on, it was pretty hard-core. Sindy said it probably reacted badly with my venom, and stopped his heart."

"Something I could have warned you of," Cain said, his voice slowly rising from its tone of reasonable understanding to match Mattie's betrayed contempt, "if you had bothered to come to me."

Allie refused to let him make it seem so simple. "Right, like you would have allowed it, and calmly given me lessons or something."

"Who do you think taught Mattie how to drink from *you?*"

The idea that Cain had spent time methodically giving Mattie instruction on how to drink blood from her, seemed somehow ridiculous at first, the way she would view him giving lessons on how to have sex with her…and then suddenly it made perfect sense to her that it was true.

Mattie was not the type to lead with his instinct. He would have been terrified to hurt her. As humiliating as it might have felt, surely he had gone to Cain for advice, and Cain hadn't turned him away. Cain hadn't told him not to drink, or condemned him for it, he'd given Mattie the instruction needed, just as he would have given her…if she had asked.

Somehow, she had never viewed Cain that way. She knew that he tried to help other vampires control their thirst, but his first response was always to have them drink blood purchased from the butcher, collected from animals. She knew that he was often forced to accept that some vampires refused to stop drinking from humans completely, the way he accepted such behavior from Sindy, but she never thought he would go so far as to help them with technique.

It made sense though. What better way to keep them from killing people while drinking, then to make sure they did it right? And she had opted to pretend the animal blood was enough, rather than ask for his help. She'd just assumed that with unlimited animal blood at her disposal, to drink from humans would be something he considered unacceptable, a sign of weakness in her.

"I'm sorry," she mumbled quietly.

Mattie took back her attention. "You're sorry? You killed somebody, Allie! I knew it. I knew something like this would happen."

Cain's voice was commanding and intimidating in his controlled ire. "And yet you still allowed it to go on, behind my back. I thought we were a coven? Does that mean nothing to you two? Are we equals...a family bonded by blood to honor, respect, and protect one another? Or am I nothing more than an intruder in your relationship, a necessary evil; the provider, conveniently kept out of the loop until needed? You confide in me only when things have blown up in your faces, and I'm needed to clean up the mess."

He turned his accusations to Allie, and although his voice was eerily calm, the anger she could feel within him through her empathy was more than sufficient to convey his fury. "Like you've needed me to handle the vampires you've had follow you home over the years through your own carelessness. I'm the one who's had to convince them that they should leave you be, when they show up looking for the vampire they've seen with the incredible eyes. Or how about when you went to inform Ben and Felicity of your change, against my advice, or the fact that you *continue* secret visits with Felicity, regardless of how it might affect her ability to have a normal human life? Do you care about no one but yourself?"

His mind suddenly opened to her. Thoughts and memories were unleashed as he let his guard down, and she could unexpectedly read everything from him like never before. She'd had no idea how well he could wall off his true thoughts from her. He knew all about her visits with Felicity, despite the fact that she'd tried to keep it from him. He had always suspected, and now he knew for certain, because Cain had seen her himself. That's where he had gone last night.

The knowledge that she hadn't really fooled him, and that he'd actually followed her with suspicions that she'd been doing something illicit really pissed her off, even if she was in the wrong. Maybe she shouldn't have been secretly drinking human blood, but he had no right to lump visits with

Felicity into this. "I haven't done Felicity any harm. Who are you to tell me who I can be friends with? She doesn't belong to you. That's the problem isn't it? Well, get over it. Don't think you can try to control *my* life, just because you can't seem to manage yours."

Cain's eyes smoldered with intense emotion she'd never seen or felt from him before. His words were low and menacing, and she could feel that he deeply resented her using his feelings for Felicity as fuel for an argument. "This isn't about Felicity. It's about your poor judgment. You have no idea the dangers you flirt with. You waltz into compromising positions without a thought for how you might endanger yourself and others."

Rather than argue with words, she let him know mentally that she was well aware of the fact that Ben's father hunted vampires, and that in going out alone she might encounter him, or even other vampires bent on hurting her, as she had while out with Mattie. "The only person I'm putting in danger is me, and I know how to take care of myself. I'm strong, stronger than you can even imagine. Why do you think I needed human blood? It gives me power, Cain. Mattie knows it's true, that's why he didn't try to stop me. How do you think he awakened his power over the weather?

Maybe I should have come to you about drinking from humans, but I didn't think you would understand, and I had Sindy to guide me."

"Yes, another magnificent example of your care for no one but yourself. Sneaking around with Sindy was great fun for you, and I'm sure you were very happy not to be under a truly watchful eye, but Sindy only vaguely understands the strength and severity of your thirst, and the power your venom. Surely, you don't think she understands it better than me, a man you have been drinking from monthly for the past six years.

How many times have I given you an opening to confide in me, tried to impress upon you that you could talk to me, about anything? What could possibly have made you think that Sindy would be a better mentor for such things than I? Just as you thought you would secretly have her teach you to shift shape, rather than trust that I would have the Crimson Coven teach you when you were ready."

This was news to Mattie. "What?"

Cain ignored him and carried on. "Now you've left Sindy to try and clean up your mess, making her take responsibility for your misjudgment."

"I didn't ask her to, not at first," Allie responded, doing her best to ignore Mattie's wounded expression. "I don't expect other people to take care of my shit. I was going to change him myself, but she wouldn't let me."

Mattie's sharp intake of breath drew their attention. "Well thank God! Allie, how could you even consider something like that?"

Her anger ebbed and transformed into regret, and a plea for understanding from Mattie. A tear rolled down her cheek as she hoped she hadn't crossed over the line and past his forgiveness with her actions. "I know. I know that changing him myself would have been the wrong thing to do, but I wasn't thinking clearly. The drugs still had me feeling all hazy, and all I could think of was that the poor guy was dead because of me, and how disappointed you would be in me, that I had taken someone's life.

It was so awful Mattie, when I realized that he was dead. I never meant to hurt him, and I couldn't take it back. I didn't know what to do. I was so frightened for this guy that I didn't even know, frightened that I had ended his life before it should have been over, and frightened that you would never forgive me for it. Please forgive me, Mattie. I just wanted to make things right. I thought if he could be changed, maybe it would be okay."

Mattie was silent, but hurt as he was, he gently let her know with a mental nudge that no matter his opinion on the situation, she still had his love and support. She always would. She let him know that she was ever so grateful for it.

It was Cain who spoke. "Sindy stopped you."

"Yes. She insisted that I couldn't share my blood. That's when I asked her to do it. I just didn't want him to be dead."

"You've never made another. You can't understand the severity of what you asked; the personal, unending connection she will have with this stranger forever, because you asked it of her."

"She's done it before."

"That doesn't matter! Those she created in the past were her mistakes to make. She may not have understood the consequences then, but she does now. Why do you think she has made no more since? Frankly, I'm surprised she did it."

"She wanted to leave him, to let his friends think he O.D.'d."

"I think that would have been the wiser choice. Did you use your powers to persuade her otherwise?"

"No!"

Mattie addressed Cain in disbelief. "Cain, Allie wouldn't do that."

"I wonder if you have a clear perception of just what Allie would or wouldn't do." He turned back to Allie. "I'm beginning to wonder if Arif's predictions of your powers degrading your character might not have been far off the mark."

Could he know how those words stung her? He didn't truly believe that, did he? She tried to delve into his mind and heart to see if he really felt that way, but he shut her out. Cain was much better at deflecting and manipulating her use of telepathy on him than she'd realized. She was pretty sure he didn't believe Arif though. He was just saying that for effect, to impress his disappointment on her.

"Where is she?" Cain asked.

"Sindy? She's at a motel."

"I want the address."

"What for? She said she'd come back once the guy was alright on his own. She wouldn't have agreed to change him, if she didn't think she could handle it."

Cain was unyielding and completely closed off from her now. It was very disconcerting. She had felt that she'd known him so well for so long now, and to be suddenly shut out from reading him was very unsettling. "The address please. It's bad enough that you've maneuvered her into this position, she shouldn't have to deal with it alone."

"Fine. Here it is." Allie projected the location to him telepathically. If he wanted to know where it was, let him accept her mental communication of it. After a moment of simply staring at him, he realized what she was doing, and re-opened his mind to her. Just as she had suspected, in order to receive communication from her, he needed to stop actively shutting her out. As he gathered the information, she took the opportunity to also transmit to him the emotional turmoil she felt over the whole situation, and to let him know that she was sorry to have lied to him.

He stood impassive and silent. His feelings were clear to her. He felt terribly betrayed and disappointed that she hadn't seen fit to confide in him, and that Mattie had hidden things from him as well. He was revisiting the fact that he had not allowed himself to be close to anyone, vampire or human, in decades before Felicity had pulled him back into caring for others, and now he remembered why. Others always managed to hurt him, and it wasn't worth the heartache.

"Cain, please. Don't think that way. We'll go with you to get Sindy, first thing tomorrow night. I should be the one to go back."

His thoughts and emotions went blank to her again like a television set suddenly switched off to show nothing but a black screen. "No. You've done enough. You and Mattie should stay here under the protection of the Crimson Coven. I'll go and collect her myself. This other vampire…"

"Zach," she supplied.

"If Zach seems capable, and has inherited Sindy's red eyes, perhaps he can be brought to the Crimson Coven for a time of adjustment to his new situation. That's unlikely though. Sindy's blood isn't pure of breed, and so far, none of her making have inherited her gifts. If he isn't of crimson stock, I'll assess his situation and take care of things as I see fit. I don't think that *you* seeing him again will be good for anyone."

Alyson took offense at the idea that seeing her would upset him…even if she was his murderer. Oh my God, she *was* a murderer, wasn't she? But Zach wouldn't see her that way, would he? Would he understand that she had admired his talent, and been drawn to him for it? She'd simply wanted some kind of connection with him through his blood. She'd never meant to hurt him.

Cain must have deciphered her hurt expression. "Your desire to believe in people's capacity for forgiveness is very sweet. It's also a bit naïve. You'd be better served if you didn't need to ask for it quite so often."

Cain turned away, to head for the door. Mattie reached out to stop him, but only got him to pause for a moment. "Cain, you can't go now. It'll be dawn soon."

It was true. Alyson could already feel the fatigue creeping over her, making her thoughts become muddled, and her limbs feel heavy as though weighted down. Damn the sun.

Cain opened the door anyway, making Allie cringe. The sky was only a lesser dark than before, not even showing true signs of sunrise, but Alyson was more sensitive to it, and found herself looking away. "I'm not leaving Sindy alone to deal with him all day," Cain told them. "I'll take the car. I can get there before full light if I hurry."

He was about to walk out the door, when Mattie stopped him for one more exchange. "Cain, I'm sorry. I shouldn't have kept the drinking from you. I just…"

Allie was almost surprised to feel Mattie's emotions and incentives for keeping the secret. It was simple jealousy. She'd never recognized it as much of a problem for him before, but he *was* a bit jealous of Cain, and the intimate relationship that she shared with him, even if it wasn't romantic. Not only did they share blood, but she and Cain confided in each other over so many things. For Mattie, it had been reassuring to know that Allie had secrets with him, that Cain didn't share.

Cain turned and met Mattie's eyes, seeming to instinctively understand, as perhaps only another man would. "What you two share is special. You don't need to keep secrets from me to highlight it." He gave Allie a last glance of disapproval. "She's all yours."

Mattie stood frozen with self-reproach, as Cain turned and walked out the door. After a moment of watching him leave, Mattie glanced at the sky and held the door open for Alyson. "We'd better get you to bed."

She turned away from the coming dawn, feeling its approach quickly leeching strength from her body, and reason from her thoughts. She lightly shook her head, feeling repelled by the sky beyond the doorway. Unreasonable as it was, she'd rather sleep here on the floor, than have to go outside now. Mattie took only a second to assess her state, before scooping her up into his arms. Alyson hunched herself tightly against him, burying her face in his chest as he carried her out across the lawn. It didn't burn yet, the sun wasn't up, only threatening, but she could feel it insisting that she flee, panic-stricken to some safe dark place. She let Mattie feel her fright, and he clenched her tighter to him. "Hon, it's not even light at all yet."

"Yes, it is," she mumbled. "I feel it. Please hurry."

"We're almost there." She could feel him trying to unlock and open the door to their trailer without putting her down. She felt so physically weak, but the panic that always began to rise within her at dawn if she wasn't safely indoors, lent strength to her powers. With her eyes scrunched shut she pictured the locking mechanism within their doorknob, and exerted psychic force on it, impatient with Mattie's fumbling with the key.

There was an audible click, and then the door burst open before them. Mattie only paused in a moment of surprise before rushing inside. He took her directly into the back bedroom to ensconce Allie safely in their bed beneath the covers, far from the burning rays of the sun.

"Did you do that…open the door?" he asked, as he tucked her in.

She snuggled under the blankets, answering only in thought. *You were taking too long. The sun was coming.*

Mattie was still talking, trying to make her understand that her actions were significant somehow, but the words were lost, as her mind shut down to prepare for the death-slumber of day.

~~~~~~~~~~~~~~~~~~~~~~~~~~~~~~~

"Allie? Come on, sunset was an hour ago, how can you not be up yet?"

Mattie's words floated to her on a hazy wave of awareness, slowly washing her back to the beach of reality. She'd been dreaming of heavy metal music, and having fun drinking beer and dancing with friends at a bar. There was no blood, or regrets over acts of moral ineptitude. She scrunched her eyes tighter, not wanting to wake up. You'd think she'd be having nightmares over taking someone's life. Was her conscience really untroubled? The thought startled her to open her eyes.

Mattie was sitting on the edge of the bed, watching over her. "Finally."

She closed her eyes again, unwilling to fully awaken yet. Who could tell why people dreamt the things they did? She felt awful about Zach, and the fact that she hadn't had nightmares didn't mean anything, did it? Ever since awakening her full powers, she was in a dead, vampire-trance state without living thought during the day anyway. It was only during the twilight time after sunset that her mind became alive enough to give her dreams. Perhaps if she'd stayed asleep long enough, her dream would have become a nightmare. That was a thought that made her abandon the idea of going back to sleep. "I can't help it that I don't rise as early as you do," she mumbled. "You know I'm more sensitive to the sun."

"Well, I'm glad you're up. I've been waiting for news." He pulled the covers back down off her head. "Can you reach Cain?"

"I'm getting tired of playing switchboard operator," she remarked in annoyance. "Maybe you guys should invest in a cell phone plan." Mattie just rolled his eyes, and waited for her to contact Cain telepathically. "I can't reach him."

Mattie sighed, but didn't seem very surprised. "Well, he is awfully far away."

"That's not it. I can reach him anywhere, just like I can with you. He's shutting me out."

She could tell that Mattie was a little taken aback to realize that her connection with Cain should be as strong as the one they shared, but just as Cain had said, she'd been sharing blood with the man monthly for almost six years now. Mattie would always be her sire, and their romantic relationship gave them a stronger bond, but her connection with Cain was as close to that as anyone else could get. "He shut me out last night too. He's just pissed at me."

Mattie seemed confused. "Last night, while he was here? How could he? I can't do that."

"Sure you can. You shut me out that night you were mad at me, when you went out to that coffee shop alone."

"Yeah, a coffee shop two hours away. The only reason I could shut you out, was because I traveled so far. That was kind of the point. Otherwise, I couldn't keep you out of my head if I tried. Why do you think we're always telling you not to pry? We can't stop you!"

"Cain can. He always knows when I'm in his head, he can just tell. I hadn't realized he was shielding stuff from me, but last night when he opened up, I saw all kinds of things I didn't know about, and when he cut me off, I got nothing. If I can't reach him now, it's because he doesn't want to talk to me."

"What about Sindy? Can you talk to her and find out what's going on?"

She shook her head. "She really is too far away. I can't use telepathy on a vampire I've never shared blood with, unless they're close by and willing. I guess we'll just have to wait until they get back."

"I don't think we should."

"What do you mean?"

Mattie shifted on the bed and glanced at the night sky out the window. It was full night now, with barely even any moonlight to ease the darkness. "I don't think we should be here when they get back."

Allie squinted at him curiously. "Where else would we be?"

"Anywhere. I say we take the trailer and go."

She sat up in the bed. "Seriously? Why would we do that? I know Cain was mad, but he doesn't want us to leave. Trust me, we'll all get over this."

"Remember when Cain said maybe your powers were having a bad effect on your moral character?"

"You don't really believe that, do you?" she asked him pleadingly. He'd assured her of his support last night, but she knew he just hadn't wanted her to feel like both guys were ganging up on her. "I know I've made some bad decisions. I should never have kept things from you...or Cain, and I feel absolutely terrible about what I did to Zach, I really do. I guess I haven't been a very good person lately, have I? But I didn't mean to hurt the guy, you know I didn't. It's not the blood, or the powers, it's just selfish carelessness and stupidity, which I guess is worse in a way, but I am sorry, and I'm not evil. I'm not a lost cause, Mattie, I swear. Please don't give up on me."

He reached forward and gently moved the hair aside off her forehead to tuck behind her ear. "Never. But do me a favor, and stop making it so hard to back you up, okay? I know it's not evil blood, and so does Cain. He just said that to show you the severity of your actions, and how they look from our point of view."

She flinched at the word 'our'. He hadn't ganged up on her when Cain was there, but he wasn't happy. By all rights, she knew she was lucky that both of them hadn't left her already. Mattie went on. "Cain just thinks you've been immature; reckless, and irresponsible. I can't say I disagree, but I don't think the blood is having as much of a negative effect on you, as *Sindy* is."

Allie shook her head. "No, you can't put all of this on her. I know you don't like her much, but it's not her fault. I have to take responsibility for my own actions."

"Allie, you never would have even considered drinking human blood if she hadn't been here, sneaking out, and doing it herself, making it seem like it was no big deal, tempting you to join her. You can't deny that."

"You're right, but ultimately it was my decision." She took a deep breath and sighed. "If I hadn't done it, you never would've discovered your power over the weather, and I wouldn't be nearly as strong as I could be. So, no matter how badly I feel about Zach, and wish I could take back *that* drink, I can't say I'm sorry for drinking human blood, or that I won't keep doing it. I just need to be more careful."

She waited for an argument, but none came. At this point, it seemed Mattie agreed that they needed to have all the strength for protection that they could get. He was staring back out the window. She noticed it was getting awfully windy outside. She hoped it wasn't an expression of his pent up anger with her.

"How did you learn to shift shape?" he asked quietly. "You told me that Tempest taught you, but that's not true, is it? Sindy showed you how."

Allie pulled the covers back up around her legs where she sat, making a little nest for herself, wishing she could just crawl under them and go back to sleep, nightmares or not. She gave in and answered. "I saw Sindy as the wolf, and I wanted to know what it was about, so I made her show me."

"Behind my back, like you do everything these days. Why didn't you just tell me?"

Allie sighed, wishing she could make him understand. She tried to use empathy to back her words a little as she spoke, and help him feel her side of it, even if it wasn't entirely a fair thing to do. She needed all the help she could get, to allow him to understand that she wasn't just being disloyal. "Shifting is such an inhuman thing, and I can't share it with you. It really intrigued me, but I was afraid that it was going to drive us apart."

"The only thing driving us apart is all the lies; the lies and Sindy. You know she wants it that way, don't you? I'm too strong a foundation for you, and she wishes you'd drive me away." She opened her mouth to comment on that, but he wouldn't let her. *"When* did you see her as the wolf? It was that first night, wasn't it? You didn't just find her injured, you saw her as the wolf first." She couldn't deny it. "That's a long time to keep a secret from me, Allie. That is a lot of nights of sneaking around to get wolf time with her, instead of talking to me."

"It helped me with my thirst," she pleaded insistently. "I know that you don't really have thirst like I do, and you can't understand, but it was making me nuts. I didn't want you to think I couldn't handle it, but it was really rough there for a while, Mattie. The wolf let me drink my fill of live blood and keep me in control. You're right, I should've told you right away, but it wasn't some plot on Sindy's part to split us up. You don't really think she could be working for Arif, do you?"

He took in her explanation of thirst and rolled it around in his mind before answering her question. He knew she was telling the truth. He was still hurt that she'd hidden it, but he understood why, and grudgingly accepted it. Sindy, he wasn't so sure about. "You spend more time with her than I do, you tell me. Has she ever tried to sway you in Arif's direction?"

She felt the need to defend Sindy, but knew she was just feeling grateful because of Sindy's willingness to help with the Zach situation. She tried to think back over past conversations with Sindy with an objective eye. "Yes, a couple of times, but it wouldn't exactly be out of character for her. She's pretty impressed with the idea of his compound, but that doesn't mean she's playing secret agent."

"How come she won't share blood with us?" Mattie asked with direct seriousness. "We've talked about it before. You and I have been sharing blood with Cain monthly since long before Sindy came back. Cain drinks from her all the time now, so you know he wouldn't object. We keep waiting for her to ask to be included in the coven, but she hasn't. So why doesn't she want to share blood with us?"

"Maybe she doesn't like you," Allie offered with a smirk.

Mattie chuckled. "Yeah, right. We both know she would *love* an excuse to drink from me, even if only so she could rub your face in it. Yet she passes up the opportunity, month after month. The only explanation I can think of, is that she doesn't want you in her head. So then the question is, what's she got to hide?"

Allie had always known that Sindy didn't like the idea of anyone being able to read her mind. She'd even assumed that it *was* the reason Sindy didn't include herself in the coven, but she'd never thought of it as anything more than Sindy wanting to hide her own insecurities. Maybe it was something more… "You're right. We should probably talk to Cain about this."

"What for? We don't know anything he hasn't already figured out. It sounds like he's had suspicions for a while now. Even if you had something incriminating to add, what do you think he'd do about it? I've been going over things in my head ever since I woke up. Think about how long it's taken him to allow himself to move on from Felicity. He's finally opened up, and accepted someone else into his heart, and his bed...do you really think he's going to just kick her out? As long as she isn't actively hurting you, he'll give Sindy a chance to redeem herself. He'll give her the benefit of the doubt, and try to help her become a better person. That's what he does. But *I'll* never trust her again, now that the doubt is in my mind."

"I see your point. But we can't just leave."

Mattie took hold of her shoulders, radiating a stern determination she hadn't felt from him since the time she'd been afraid that he might really leave her, back when they'd battled it out over her drinking human blood. Last night he may have tried to hold back and remain supportive of her in spite of his hurt feelings, but now he was done letting her take the lead. She could feel the force of his conviction building with the howling wind outside.

When he spoke, she was almost surprised that the words were grimly calm and moderated. Mattie was always soft-spoken, but judging by the emotion she felt in him, she'd almost expected him to growl the words at her. "I know you've been having a good time with Sindy, hitting the clubs and running the woods, so you're not in a rush to leave, but don't be stupid. I've told you before, I'll never give up on you. I'll always love you if you let me, but I'm not going to stand by and watch you self-destruct. You have to start giving me a stronger say in things. I can't be a silent partner, Allie, I won't. You think you've got things in hand, but you don't, and no matter what her motives are, Sindy is not helping the situation. I don't think this place is safe for you anymore, and I want to get you out of here for a while. You have to let me."

He was completely committed and not willing to budge, she could feel it. He softened his tone though, sensing her hesitation. "Allie, do you really think you're going to uncover any more powers that we can't handle alone? I know Cain's been very helpful, and he feels responsible to guide you, but at this point, I think we're better off on our own, despite his good intentions. He doesn't need us here, not the way he needs Sindy right now, and with her around, I don't think this is the safest place for us to be anymore. We should leave before they get back into range, so Cain won't feel our marks to follow. If we let everyone see where we're going, what's the point?"

Allie sighed, feeling that he was right, but not wanting to admit that there was another reason she wanted to see Cain and Sindy before leaving. "I need to know how things went for Zach," she admitted quietly. "I didn't make him, but I'm still responsible for him."

Mattie looked very disheartened by her sentiment, but she realized in a moment that it wasn't for selfish jealousy. "Allie, I doubt they'll have anything to tell you that you'd want to hear." She knitted her brows and tried to understand what he could mean. Even though Zach had been dead for ten minutes or so, Sindy had still assured her that he had every chance for a successful change. "Why do you think Cain went out there?" Mattie asked.

"To help Sindy."

"Help her with what? The guy's already been changed, all there is for him to do is wake up and get an explanation. Allie, for the past few years, Cain's top priority has been working with you, but what do you think he did before that?"

"Help other vampires," she answered simply.

"Help them how?"

"He teaches them to drink animal blood instead of drinking from humans."

"And if they don't want animal blood?"

"He teaches them to drink from humans without hurting them, doesn't he? That's why he was mad at me for not coming to him about it. I just didn't realize."

"Right. But what about vampires that just can't handle it? You forget that we have the advantage of being very carefully made under the best of circumstances." He cringed a bit, thinking of his own transformation. It had been traumatic and terrifying, but at least the vampires who had done it had been sure to do it well. "A lot of vampires just aren't that well made. They don't have the conscience, the discipline, or the self-control to stop killing. And some of them are just sadistic creeps who kill for fun. What do you think Cain does with them?"

"Tries to persuade them…" she answered, uncertainly.

"He gives them every chance, but if they can't change their ways, or they won't, he kills them. If it's a choice between dusting a vampire, or letting humans die, he'll dust the vamp without regret. It's a hard thing to do, to decide someone has to die by your hand, but that's the job he's set for himself, because he feels it's for the greater good."

"But he won't kill Zach, will he? Sindy gave him all the blood that she could. He must be decently made. Cain's got no reason to dust him!"

"I'm sure he didn't go out there just to kill him, but if Zach was left with nothing but Sindy's instruction, what do you think he'd do?"

"He's not a bad guy!" Allie insisted. "He's not just going to go out and start killing people!"

"You don't know that. All you know about him, is that you like the way he plays guitar," Mattie told her bitterly. "He might not be a vicious killer, but what about when the thirst hits? What about the first night that he has a hard time buying butcher blood, but there are people all around him? Even if he does manage to keep himself under control, then what do you think he'll do?"

"What do you mean? He could still continue his life. A goth-rocker's lifestyle isn't much different from being a vampire anyway, is it? Look at MCR," she joked with a smile. "He could still tour with his band."

"Right, and how long before he *tells* his band, and then maybe changes them too, if he can figure out how? Allie, you might have effectively signed the death warrants of every groupie that stays after every show, in every town for years to come. Do you really want all that blood on your hands?"

The scope of what she may have done began to come clearer, and heavier than simple guilt over one death could ever weigh on her. "I didn't think…"

"I know. Look, the loss of Zach's life is your guilt to bear, but Cain went to make sure that it ends there. Whether or not he thinks Zach can handle an existence without hurting humans, will be Cain's decision. Trust him to make it, and let it go. Cain has been judging these kinds of situations since long before either of us was born, and that's on his conscience, not yours. I think you should make peace with it, and let me get you out of here."

The decision was made; they were heading out on their own. It was amazing how quickly they could just pick up and leave. Just about everything they owned (which wasn't much) was already in the trailer. They took a last look around in the house before leaving. "I feel so bad," Allie said as she downed a last helping of blood from Cain's refrigerator, "about just skipping out like this."

"I know, but it doesn't have to be forever, it's just for a little while. Give Cain some time to sort out which side of the fence Sindy's on. I keep hoping that as more time goes by, Arif will get bored and find something else to think about, besides you. I don't like that he knows just where to find us, even if we are well protected."

"You're right. Being off Arif's radar for a while can't be a bad thing. I just feel so bad to leave Cain."

Mattie gently took the empty glass from her hand and put it into the sink. "Cain will be okay. I know he'll be hurt, but he'll understand. We were here for him, to help him through the worst of his heartache. He has Sindy to lean on now. He'll be fine. If you really can reach him telepathically from a distance, at some point, once we're far away and hard to find, you can get in touch and talk. We'll just have to make sure you do it before your mark wears off of him."

Allie reached into the sink, and washed the few mugs they'd left there, feeling bad to leave Cain more of a mess to clean up than she already had. "It's going to be weird isn't it, when his mark wears off us? I'm so used to us being a threesome," she said, drying her hands on a towel with a sly smirk. She could imagine Mattie wasn't going to miss their monthly coven marking sessions nearly as much as she would.

His expression confirmed the fact as he met her eyes with a steady stare, although he did sport a hint of a smile. "Well, I'm just going to have to be man enough for you."

She licked her lips with a grin and then pulled him closer to her by the belt loops of his jeans. "Don't worry babe, you're all I need."

She gave him a kiss heated enough to prove her point, but he ended it to bring them back to the task at hand. "Time to go. I can prove that I'm all you can handle later." She had to laugh. That was the kind of boast she usually made to him, not the other way around, but Mattie was proving to have more quiet strength and smoldering desire than she knew others would give him credit for. She was definitely in good hands.

"Leave a note," he told her. "I'll grab your CD's out of the media room."

"Don't forget the Playstation," she added. Mattie headed downstairs to collect the video game and discs, while Allie sat at the kitchen table to write a letter of parting explanation to Cain and Sindy.

She was still sitting there a few minutes later, when she heard Mattie making his way back up the stairs. She was having a hard time figuring out how she could put their concerns into a note that Sindy might possibly find and read before Cain. If Sindy was involved in any sort of betrayal, Allie didn't want to tip her off that they knew, and if she wasn't, Allie didn't want to hurt her with accusations. "Let's go," Mattie urged her.

Short and simple. That would be best. They were pressed for time anyway, not knowing when the others would be back. She would just have to trust that she could give a better explanation later. For now, she would just tell them that she and Mattie needed some space, and were leaving for some private time alone. 'Nuff said.

They were outside hooking up Allie's Charger to be towed on the hitch behind the trailer, when she felt with uneasy certainty that they were being watched.

Who would be watching them? The Crimson Coven was the first obvious conclusion, but she didn't think it was one of them. They rarely cloaked their marks, using them to communicate their locations to each other during hunts. They never came this close to the house unless they were here to speak to Cain, and they would consider it rude not to unveil their presence psychically first.

As Mattie finished the job, Alyson tried to observe their surroundings without showing that she was alerted to the fact that they weren't alone. She was just beginning to doubt her suspicions, when she saw it. The shade was hovering in the trees off to their left.

At first, it was impossible to distinguish from the dark shadows of the trees, especially since there was only a bare sliver of a moon. Then she saw it drift forward as a cloud, in a direction opposite the breeze, almost as though it was fighting the wind to stay in place; a dark nebulous shape, about the size of herself, separate from the shadows cast by branches.

She took her eyes from it, and pretended she hadn't noticed anything out of the ordinary, waiting until she and Mattie were safely closed inside the trailer before sharing her discovery telepathically, still afraid of being overheard even with the windows closed. *The shade's back,* she told him. *It's been watching us.*

Mattie was instantly tense and alert. *How do I kill it?*

Allie smiled at his protective ferocity. *I don't think you can while it's dematerialized. Besides, I don't think it's here to hurt us, or it would have done something by now. It must be here to watch us, and report back to someone else.*

Mattie nodded and glanced out the window, although its tint made it impossible to see much outside in the dark. *And I think we can assume it's reporting back to Arif. Who else would care what we do?*

Allie agreed. *We know it can't carry a cell phone in that state, and unlike me, I doubt it's telepathic. Telepathy is a trait of purple-eyed vampires. Cain said it can sometimes show up in others, but it's rare. So we can assume it can't report anything until Arif decides to check in.*

Mattie began securing things for the ride, trying to keep busy and look natural in case they could be seen through the windows. *We have to be pretty boring to watch lately, and Arif is a busy guy. He probably doesn't bother to check in more than once or twice a night. We should have a few hours before anything gets back to him. We can't let the shade follow us. If I can't kill it, maybe I can use the wind to blow it to pieces. I'll bet that would take some recovering from. Then we could take off before it knew where we went.*

Allie became thoughtful. *True, but it would still report us before morning. That's not much of a head start, and in this giant camper, we aren't all that hard to find for someone who's looking.*

Do you have a better idea? Mattie asked.

As a matter of fact, I do. She couldn't help but smile as a plan began to take shape. *There's something I've sort of been working on…*

Mattie groaned. The sound seemed pronounced after their silent conversation. *Another secret?*

She sent him a wave of reassurance. *This time you are the first to know, I swear.* She took him by the arm into the bedroom, where she closed the tinted windows, and then shut the curtains for extra privacy. *I've been working on something, but I'm not sure if I've perfected it yet. I'd need the shade to materialize to use it, but I'd sure love to try it out.*

Mattie was understandably confused. *Try what out?*

What is my most formidable weapon?

He grinned. *Your stunning good looks and deceivingly cute size?*

What else? she prompted with a smile.

Well, as much as I know you could beat the heck out of anyone who tried to hurt you, that's not what I find most formidable about you. I'd say your eyes. One look from those babies and your enemy is helplessly in thrall.

She sighed. *I wish it was that easy. It only works like that on humans. A vampire isn't as susceptible, unless I've infected them with my venom first.*

Your venom…now there's an interesting weapon.

My thoughts exactly! Not only can I immobilize someone, but I can even control them. I haven't practiced it, but Sindy can call victims to her, and if I use it in conjunction with my eyes, she thinks I could even give a victim orders for the future, like subliminal directions to follow. She says I could tell humans to come back and meet me somewhere to let me drink from them again… Mattie gave her a disapproving look. *I'm just sayin'…but I'm sure I could use it for other things too, even on vampires. It could be useful, don't you think? Not to mention fun.*

You could tell him not to report on us, Mattie suggested.

I'm sure we could come up with something even more creative than that. But I have to get my venom into him first.

Mattie's growing interest suddenly deflated. *You'd have to bite him.*

Not necessarily. That's where my new project comes in. I have to admit, biting someone isn't always the best course of action for me.

Mattie laughed. *Finally, something we can agree on.*

Once there's blood involved, I tend to get caught up in it and lose my focus. Not a plus if I'm trying to defend myself. So I wanted to find a way to inject someone with my venom, without biting them. Then I got this idea while Sindy and I were doing our nails... Watch.

Alyson stripped down her jeans, and then turned to mist without bothering to unfasten the rest of her clothing. As long as it wasn't too restrictive, it was easy enough to navigate. She dematerialized and floated up out of her clothing as it fell to the floor. She hovered as a cloud for more than five minutes as she constructed the alterations to her form that she'd been working on in her mind, and hoped that they translated properly.

Mattie was beginning to grow impatient, when she finally took shape once again. At first, she looked just the same. Pretty and petite, nude Allie just standing there before Mattie as he tried to imagine what she could have changed. Then she held up her hands to show him her considerably lengthened nails. They didn't look inhuman, but they were close to it. She'd seen in a magazine that there was a new manicure trend out in L.A. called *talons:* nails that were pointed and just long enough to look almost dangerous. She'd modeled her nails after that.

Mattie was unimpressed. "Pretty," he muttered sarcastically.

She turned her hands palm up for him to inspect. *That's just for show, all the real artistry is underneath and inside.* She showed Mattie the thin hollow tube she had constructed up the middle of the underside of each long nail. Each tube ended just at the edge of her fingernail. *And when I flex my hand like this...* She arched her fingers and tensed her hand into a claw-like pose, as though she were going to scratch someone, and it made an even thinner pointed tube unsheathe from each shaft, natural needles to poke out further than her nails.

"Wait...you can actually..." Mattie began to speak aloud before she shushed him, worried their spy might overhear. *Can you actually inject your venom with those?* he asked, continuing the question in thought.

She smiled. *That's right. I'm hypodermic, baby!*

Allie, that is amazing! How did you do that?

It wasn't easy, and I still don't know if it really works. We have venom in all of our bodily fluids, but I couldn't just make a direct needle, because I don't want to give the victim any of my blood. The easiest source of pure venom I could figure out how to tap into was my saliva. I had to construct little venom lines that run from each nail, through my hands and up my arms into my saliva glands, which are now basically venom sacs in my throat...if I did it right.

Mattie was staring at her, completely bewildered by her work. "Now I'm beginning to understand the anatomy and physiology books on your side of the bed. When you said Tempest gave you homework, I never dreamed you'd take it so seriously and actually read them."

Allie laughed. Academics were never her strong suit. *I could barely follow most of the passages, they use the Latin names for everything, but the diagrams were really helpful. As long as I can picture something clearly enough, I can build it. And I have an advantage over Tempest, because I can take all the time I want preparing my blueprint before I reform. Crimson vampires can't spend much time as mist, they have less than a minute before their particles pull back together, ready or not.*

Mattie shook his head, still in disbelief over the implications. *How long have you been working on this?*

Couple of months.

When?

While you were busy playing Modern Warfare, she answered with a smirk.

He laughed and took hold of her wrist to better examine her nails. *No, this is modern warfare. Let's see if they work.* She glanced up at him and he realized her thought. He dropped her hand and backed away. *Uh-uh, not on me,* he said with a grin. *I need to be able to drive.*

That's okay, I don't need to actually inject anybody. Allie laughed and then moved to flex the new muscles in the fingers of her left hand over the dresser top. She was rewarded to see a small droplet of clear liquid form at the tip of each nail. After a moment, they began dripping steadily, but then they actually produced thin streams before Allie straightened her fingers and made it stop. "Shit, that's not right," she mumbled, observing the puddle of venom she'd left on the dresser.

"What are you talking about? That's awesome!"

It's too much, Allie explained. *I made little muscle valves at the tip of each finger. They are supposed to moderate the flow, but it seems like all I can manage is open or closed.*

Mattie seemed almost giddy over her creation. To him, anything that kept her from having to bite some other guy, seemed like a successful invention. *Who cares? It works! Better too much than not enough.*

Although Allie was proud to see her idea come to fruition, the thought of actually using it on someone made her pause, especially if she couldn't control it well. *Vampires can't be killed by a venom overdose, can they?*

Now *you're worried about killing someone?* She gave him a sharp glance of reprimand for his hurtful sarcasm. *Sorry, but still...he's the enemy, hon.*

No he isn't. He's just some guy who's working for the enemy. If there even is an enemy. I mean, we don't know anything for sure. Why should anybody be out to hurt us? We didn't do anything. It's not my fault, what kind of blood I've got in me, any more than I can control the color of my eyes.

Mattie came to put a hand on her shoulder. *I hate to break it to you, but people have been hating other people over things as stupid as the color of their skin since…forever. Small-minded people are afraid of anyone who is different. And your case goes a bit deeper than differences. There is an incredible amount of power packed into the beautiful little body of the woman I love. People are afraid of that.*

But I'm not trying to do anything with it! Allie insisted.

I know, but people who desperately want power, can't believe that you would have it and not wield it. That's why I'm afraid that Arif will never stop trying to sway you over to him. That leaves us three choices. We could join his coven, but I think we can both agree that we've got bad feelings about that. So either you stand up and claim your power, using it against him, or we disappear, in the hopes that he'll see you're not a threat and leave us be. As long as we're around other vampires, I think Arif will always feel taunted by it. He may even worry that we're planning to act against him, just because we're well-protected here and have others willing to back us up.

Allie shook her head, sitting down on the edge of the bed. *I know I've said some arrogant things about having divine power or whatever, but I don't want to lead a revolution or anything. His system works for him and I don't care about his coven, as long as they leave us alone. I'm not trying to make enemies. I just want to be left alone, you and me. I don't want to kill anyone, not even the shade. He's never tried to hurt us. It doesn't feel much like self-defense if he's just standing there. I just want my venom to keep him from ratting us out, not kill him.*

Mattie came and sat next to her on the bed with an odd smirk on his face. "Don't worry," he whispered to her confidentially. *You won't kill him, you'll just make him cum in his pants.*

Allie couldn't help but let out a surprised laugh before covering her mouth, her eyes wide at the ridiculousness of knowing that with her aphrodisial venom it was probably true. After a moment, she shook her head while still not quite being able to hide her grin. *He's a shade. He isn't wearing pants.*

Mattie raised an eyebrow and gave her a look of amused disgust. *Then I guess you'd better stand back.*

She shoved him back onto the bed as she stood up. "Wise ass…" *I've still got to figure out how to get him to materialize so I can use it.*

Mattie sat back up, still chuckling. *If I were a spy, I'd stay mist all night. Why risk being seen?*

He can't stay mist forever, Allie told him. *He's got to take form to sleep…and to drink. I'll bet he's burning up energy like crazy staying scattered like that. He'll need to drink plenty. He must take breaks to hunt.*

Mattie shook his head. *We've never seen strange marks in the area, and if he was killing nightly, wouldn't we have noticed bodies?*

Allie smiled thoughtfully. *You're right. But being a spy I'll bet he's learned to be pretty resourceful, and make do with whatever is easiest to find without much risk. I'll bet we've been feeding him.*

The garage! Mattie realized. *The Crimson Coven is always bringing containers of blood in tribute for use of the land. Cain's got that sign up, 'All who come in peace are welcome within'.*

Right, Allie agreed. *As long as he isn't trying to hurt us, he can enter the garage and drink his fill. Still, we can't hang around and wait for him to get thirsty. We don't know when the others will be back.* She took Mattie's hand to have him stand from the bed. *Go ahead and get us moving. I've got an idea.*

The shade will follow us, Mattie reminded her, unsure of her intent.

I'm counting on it.

After twenty minutes on the road, Alyson had Mattie pull into a gas station. "This is the perfect spot," she told him. It not only had pumps and a mini-mart, but there were picnic tables off to the side, next to the bathroom. There was also a small, enclosed gazebo-type structure out on the grass labeled 'Visitors Center', where people could get maps and brochures of fishing spots and local interests.

Allie went into the back and prepared two large Styrofoam travel cups of blood to take outside. "I'll be out at a picnic table."

The gas station wasn't very busy, seeing as it was approaching 10 p.m., but Allie was still sure to have Mattie park the trailer to block the view of the tables from anyone at the pumps or inside the station. She sat down at one of the tables alone, put down Mattie's cup, and took a sip from her own. After a moment, Mattie came out with two gas cans in his hands.

He spotted Allie and came over to the table. "What are you doing?"

"Sit down, I fixed you a drink."

"I have to go fill these." He held up the gas cans for emphasis.

"Come on Mattie, we're already on our way. What's the rush? You haven't even had a drink yet tonight, have you? Come on, while it's still warm."

Mattie just shook his head and turned to start walking away towards the pumps. "Allie, I will not relax until we are far out of mark range. I'd just feel safer knowing that no one knew where we were." He stopped for a moment, as though just considering something. "Go and get us some maps," he told her, gesturing towards the visitor center. "As many as you can find. See if they have anything for Canada, too."

Alyson called after him just before he disappeared around the side of the trailer. "What about your drink?"

"Leave it."

Alyson let him go, and took another quick sip from her cup before putting it down beside Mattie's untouched one on the table. Then she headed for the visitor center as directed. Once inside she began rifling through maps as she tried to inspect her psychic view of the area, and discover any discrepancy that might give away the shade's shielded mark.

Sure enough, it was only a few seconds before she was able to pick out a darkened, empty seeming space in the life energy near the table. The grass, being a living thing, gave off its own weak life force to her psychic view, although it was something vampires learned to tune out automatically. But Cain had taught her to observe it for inconsistency. The space where a vampire shielded their own mark also shielded that which was immediately around them, including plant life. If she was close enough, she could pick out the blank spot, and also know the location of the vampire, no matter how well they were disguised.

She transformed herself into mist, silently floating out of the structure, leaving her clothing behind. Just as she had suspected, the shade was not above pilfering a quick drink where it could. It had been afraid to lose them as they'd traveled, and had followed diligently behind without a chance to hunt. Now it was powerfully thirsty and thought to drink Mattie's cup of blood without being noticed.

She slowly let herself take shape, to better observe him through her eyes, while carefully crafting her adapted fingernails and their workings. The shade in his human form was a slight young man, with wispy blonde hair. Allie didn't recognize him at first from the back, but he turned to face her with a start as she reached out to lay a hand on his shoulder.

Something odd happened. She felt him try to turn to mist. She knew that his first instinct would be to dematerialize when he sensed her approach, and she had meant to inject him before he could do that, but she was too late. He began to shift before she could inject him, but it didn't quite work. It was as though every bit of his body loosened and tried to separate, but then couldn't. He froze like that for a moment, with her hand engulfed in the particles where his shoulder used to be, but then he reformed again, somehow thwarted.

She didn't bother to waste time questioning it, although she could see by the surprise on his face, that he didn't understand what had happened either. Then she firmly drove her new needle-nails into his skin, taking him under her control. She felt him tense and stiffen as she pierced him. Her empathy assured her that his anxious instinct to fight or flee was quickly dissipating under her narcotic onslaught. She felt her venom flow into him, washing over his body in waves of tranquility, followed by euphoric ecstasy.

She took Mattie's advice and turned him to face away from her, as she led him to the gazebo.

He could hardly walk at first, his muscles seeming disobedient as her venom stole away their strength. He didn't bother trying to resist her. By the time she had them enclosed within the semi-private space, his legs were trembling and he would need to sit on the bench-ledge before he collapsed. She finally withdrew her needles. She had probably injected him with a ridiculous amount of venom, but she had been afraid to let go before she was absolutely certain that she had him under control.

He passed out almost the moment he reached the bench, and she was afraid that too much wasted time would pass before she could awaken him, but with some mental nudging, she was finally able to bring him back around before too long.

He looked up to meet her white vampire eyes, as she stood before him. Now there was truly no doubt. He was hers. "Your name is Kieran, isn't it?" she asked. "I remember you. You were at the meeting with Arif, in Atlantic City."

He nodded, but there was really no need to respond. His thoughts were completely open to her. She wished she had more time to sift through them. Surely, they held all sorts of interesting tidbits. She needed to keep to their schedule though. She knew that Cain had a pretty far-reaching psychic range, and she didn't want him to pick up their marks on his way home.

Kieran's immediate surface thoughts were filled only with how good her venom had made him feel, and that he would offer up anything she could possibly desire, if only she would touch him once more and not let the ecstasy fade. She hoped her venom would allow him to coherently answer her questions. "Why are you following us?"

"Master's orders," Kieran answered in a lazy sounding slur. He was staring into her eyes, mesmerized and unable to look away.

She had to admit, even just standing before this stranger, exposed in her nudity, she'd never felt so powerful. He wouldn't even bat an eyelash if she disapproved. She could see where some could find such a feeling addictive and alluring. "What does Arif want with us?"

Kieran answered without thought or hesitation. "He wants your blood. He hopes you hold the key to creating more of your kind, under his strict supervision," Kieran's speech was still slightly slurred, but he was seeming to become more aware of his words by the second. "He's been trying to create one such as yourself for decades without success. It seems your lover had a magic touch," Kieran noted with a smile, a bit of his own personality coming back to him as his body fought the venom. He was still tightly under her control, but thinking independently as well now. "So do you, apparently."

She broke their gaze as she tried to comprehend the fact that Arif did not want to destroy her as they had thought, but had actually been *trying* to create one like her for years. "Well, Mattie made me, not Arif," she mumbled indignantly, "This is *my* blood. I'll decide who to share it with, and Arif is definitely *not* on the list. He's not getting hold of blood from the United One, not if I can help it."

When she looked back to Kieran, she caught him sweeping his gaze over her body. She squinted at him in annoyance and sent him a slight mental reprimand not to tick her off with juvenile thoughts. "You're mine now. You know that, don't you?" she asked, as she collected her clothes from the floor and put them back on. "I am your only *true* master."

He smiled at her sweetly, as if there was never a doubt of it. "I knew it the moment you revealed yourself to us at that meeting table. You *are* the United One, and it's as though I've only been waiting for you to collect me. I'd expected to be under your control much sooner, my queen," he told her in a sincere voice barely above a whisper. It was a bit un-nerving, but he seemed to believe it utterly. He had always been faithful to Arif, but it was like the blood in him had known she was its true superior, to be obeyed without question.

She could feel his unguarded reactions to her clearly. To be under her control now was a welcomed state, no matter what his prior intentions had been. Past orders from a vampire beneath the United One were over-ridden and forgotten. "And what sweet control it is," he added, savoring the fading sensations her venom had brought, and wishing once again that she would touch him, so he could feel her marked connection on his skin.

Allie ignored his wishes, sitting down opposite him, trying to decide her best course of action without wasting too much time. "You've got my signature on your mark now, don't you?" she asked, regretfully. He nodded, confirming it, although his aura remained hidden from view. "Are you expected to meet with Arif soon?"

"No, I can keep it from him if you want. I usually return to the compound to report monthly, but it's very irregular, based on the movements of those I observe. I mostly return for the comforts of drinking from my harem. I won't be missed if I can't return until the mark is gone."

She nodded, almost amazed by his willingness to help her. He was coerced by her venom and mind control, but she thought she'd need to work harder to pull information out of him. He was being pretty helpful. She realized that this was because although he obeyed Arif and felt indebted to him, he didn't really have any personal interest in helping the coven master with his plans. He followed his instructions, giving Arif no more or less. He was also enjoying *her* mastery of him more than any pleasures Arif could grudgingly give.

She quickly ran down her mental list of directions, so she wouldn't forget anything. "You are never to speak to anyone of this conversation, or the fact that I have any control of your actions. Outwardly, you are to act normally and continue following your orders from Arif. However, you are never to act directly against me or Mattie...or Cain either," she added belatedly after some thought. He may not be with them, but she certainly didn't want any harm to ever come to him. "If you know we are going to be harmed in any way, you have to find a way to stop it, without giving away your betrayal. Is that understood?"

He nodded, with a smirk on his face. She could read that while he must obey her orders without fail, he still had enough free thought to observe the exchange almost as a third party. "Yes, Ma'am." He seemed interested to see just how clever her directions would prove to be.

She tried not to let him distract her. "When will you be expected to report to someone?"

"Arif will contact me telepathically at some point. He's kind of busy with recent new developments, and probably won't check in with me until tomorrow, seeing as I only just saw him last night."

Good, they had even more time than she'd thought. "Whenever he does check in, you are to tell him that we're on Cain's property as usual, doing nothing interesting to report. He doesn't need to know we're gone until it can't be hidden any longer.

If Arif is going to find out we're missing, then you can pretend that you only just lost us, okay? If at any point, Arif does figure out where we are, mislead him if possible, but you must be discreet. You are never to betray us, or the fact that you are helping us, got it?"

"Yes, I understand perfectly. I am your loyal subject. I shall protect you and yours to the best of my ability. I will obey the Coven Master Arif only so long as his interests do not conflict with yours, and no one is ever to know that the United One directs me. Your welfare and desires are now my foremost concerns."

She nodded. "I might try to contact you in the future, but don't count on it. Once my venom is gone from you, I don't think telepathy will be an option, so you'll be on your own."

"You have my complete devotion, my queen," he assured her, bowing his head in acquiescence.

"You don't have to call me that."

He looked back up at her with a lopsided smile. "You must feel the truth. Your blood gives you the divine right to lead us all. It's your destiny. The title fits."

She shook her head, dismissing it and trying to be sure she remembered everything. "You are to carry out these directives, even after my venom has faded from you. You can never tell anyone about this, even after my mark is gone."

He nodded. She probably hadn't needed to add that. The effect her eyes had on him was aided by the venom, but once she had him in thrall, her eyes held their own power that should allow her directives to remain in place even without venom control. She just wanted to be sure.

She knew that she should let him go, they'd spent too long here already, but she couldn't resist a last question, although she was almost afraid to just come out and ask it directly. "Do you know Sindy?"

"I do."

"Does she know you?"

Kieran smiled, which didn't seem a good sign. "She does."

Allie gave up skirting the question and asked it with a sigh. "Is she working for Arif?"

Kieran met her eyes and answered gently, "She's been made an offer, but she has not acted against you."

The answer was a relief, but she knew that it also implied an unspoken 'yet'. Apparently, Mattie had been right. They had chosen a good time to leave, before Sindy lost the will to resist Arif's temptations. "I guess that's it. You should go back to Cain's estate and hang out there. Don't bother them or anything, just stay inconspicuous and wait for my mark to wear off. If Arif calls you in too soon, you find a way to stall until my mark is gone. He can't see it on you."

"You can count on me. But before you leave, would you grant your lowly subject one last rapturous reminder of your mastery?"

She arched an eyebrow at him. She wasn't giving him any more venom. She'd given him so much, it would take a long time for her mark to wear off as it was. Instead, she reached forward and took his hand from the bench. As she held it in her own, the electric shiver of their shared mark arced and tingled between them. It was so odd to feel it from someone other than Mattie or Cain.

Kieran closed his eyes for a moment, reveling in the sensation, and then lifted her hand to his lips for a kiss of thanks. "You are a gracious, indulgent ruler," he told her in adoration.

She pulled her hand away with a smirk, aware that although he sincerely meant every word, he was also sporting a teasing grin. He knew that she was torn between feeling uncomfortable with his devotion, and eating it up. "Mattie and I plan to disappear for a while. Do not find us," she told him sternly.

"If there is one thing I have become good at in my time as a vampire," he assured her, "it's following orders."

Allie could feel Mattie's mark growing stronger on her as he approached the little visitor-center structure. She stood as he appeared in the doorway. He eyed Kieran for a moment, sitting naked on the bench. Kieran watched him as well, and then lowered his eyes and gave Mattie a respectful nod of his head. Mattie looked to Allie curiously. "Everything okay here?"

She smiled. "We're fine. Everything is under control."

"Good. We'd better get going."

Allie nodded. "Kieran?" He stood and waited for her orders. "You can go on now. And remember everything we talked about."

"You can rest assured that I will, my queen," Kieran replied with a deep bow. Allie looked away with some humility as she saw Mattie raise his eyebrows at the title.

Kieran made ready to walk past Mattie, out the small doorway, but Mattie blocked his path. "Kieran, you'd better obey everything she's said, and don't let me catch you spying on us again, ever."

Kieran grinned. "She knows she has my consummate devotion. As consort to my true master, I pledge *you* my allegiance as well."

Mattie just stared at him for a moment, at a loss for words, before finally mumbling, "Thanks," and moving out of Kieran's way.

"She's amazing," Kieran added confidentially to Mattie on his way out. "I'm deeply jealous of you." He said it with a smile and a wink, that Allie could tell made Mattie unsure whether to agree, or slug him. "You won't see me again unless it's at your request," Kieran told them, and then dissipated into a cloud of mist that took off towards Cain's estate.

Mattie stood, open-mouthed, staring in the direction Kieran had taken. Allie came over and took his hand before he could say anything. "Mattie? I just wanted to say…thank you, for keeping me safe, and for taking care of me, even when I'm too stubborn to want to let you. I'm sorry for all of the shit I put you through. I know I don't make it easy for you to love me sometimes.

Things are gonna be good now, though. It's going to be just you and me for a while, safe and hidden from the world, and just enjoying being together. I know that's all you've ever wanted. It's about time I gave it to you. Just because we aren't human, doesn't mean we can't have a 'happily ever after'."

The words brought a deeply grateful smile from him. She felt bad to know he hadn't really thought his patience with her would be rewarded with the time alone together that he craved. He'd assumed he'd always be chasing after her, and private, peaceful, happiness, without much hope of tying down either. "I just want to make sure you know, you mean everything to me. You're not just my consort," she told him, repeating Kieran's nickname for him with a grin, "you're my king."

Mattie looked down into her eyes, a smile warming his lips. "I'm glad to hear it, because United One or not, you will always be my queen."

Chapter 19 - Alone

Cain

Cain's Estate, Upstate, New York
About 16 hours earlier (sunrise the morning before)

Where is she? Cain was pulling into the motel that Alyson had directed him to, and by this time, he was getting very worried. *Something's wrong.* Alyson couldn't hear him of course. The sun was ready to peek over the horizon, and Alyson was surely tucked away in bed and unconscious by now.

As he had approached the motel, he had been reassured to see that two humans nearby clearly sported Sindy's mark. She had drunk from them within the past few hours. He was in the right place, but as he got closer, he still could not feel Sindy herself. She was marked by him as his personal victim, not to be drunk from by any other. Even if she cloaked her mark, he should be able to *feel* her proximity. She could not effectively hide from him if she was within a thousand feet or so. So why couldn't he feel her?

There were only two practical reasons that he would not be able to feel Sindy. Either she had been killed, heaven forbid, or she just wasn't there. So close to dawn, where would she go, that was far enough from here that he would be unable to feel her? He couldn't imagine why she would risk travel, rather than stay in the perfectly safe motel room. There were no strange vampire marks in the area either, so the man she and Allie had changed was not there, nor any other vampire.

He parked the car, and noting the lightness in the sky, grabbed his leather jacket from the backseat and put on his sunglasses before leaving the vehicle. He entered the front office just as the first rays of sunlight pierced brightly over the horizon, making him flinch and squint as he moved further into the room, which was distressingly full of eastern facing windows.

There was a young man sitting at the front desk, reading a graphic novel; a skinny little guy with glasses and poor fashion sense, probably just over eighteen. He seemed in good spirits though, which was understandable, because he wore Sindy's mark, and knowing her, she had surely made the marking very pleasurable for him. Cain was not jealous, but relieved to observe Sindy's visit had probably been of a friendly nature. It meant that she hadn't been dusted by him.

As the kid looked up from the book, Cain saw her bite on his neck, within some slight bruising consistent with a hickey. She'd definitely drunk from him. His complexion was rather pale, although that could be normal for him, but however much she had taken, at least she'd left him enough to bruise. He seemed healthy and happy enough. Still, sloppy of her not to heal it before leaving him. The fool would probably be showing it off to his friends later. "You want a room?" the guy asked.

"No. I'm looking for a young woman who was here, Sindy. She's just under 5' 9", long black hair. You know who I'm talking about. Room 111."

The kid looked past Cain, through the window to the door of Sindy's room, and then back at him. "Did you try knocking on the door?" The guy would have clearly seen Cain pull into the parking lot, and he had come straight into the office. He hadn't been anywhere near room 111.

Cain didn't feel like wasting time, standing here uncomfortably exposed to the ever-brightening sunlight, playing games with this kid. "She's not there," he assured the boy. "Did you see her leave? Was she alone?"

The guy squinted at Cain curiously, and then shrugged. "It was another girl who bought the room, a blonde, but I didn't see her again. I saw the one you're looking for…but that was a while ago. I don't know where she went."

Cain sighed and tried to check his impatience. This kid didn't know anything useful. "Thanks." He turned and went out the door, quickly jogging across the parking lot into the shadow of the building. Even from just the brief exposure to the sun, the side of his face felt burning hot. It wasn't enough to have actually burned him yet, especially considering his heightened resistance and healing rate, as compared to most vampires, but if he was forced to run across the parking lot a few more times, he was going to have a hell of a sunburn.

Going to the room Sindy had occupied was useless, but he could see that someone wearing Sindy's bright mark was in the room next door. He headed to room 112 and knocked there instead. It took them some time to come to the door. This was most likely because it was now just a bit past

6:00 in the morning. Well, they had obviously been awake enough to let Sindy in just over an hour ago, so they could very well open the door for him too.

An older man answered, probably in his late fifties, a bit on the heavy side, with a scraggly, unkempt beard. He wore Sindy's mark, but no bite marks were visible near the neckline of the soiled undershirt he wore. Cain found that he had no desire to learn where the man *was* bitten. "What do you want?" he asked.

"I'm looking for Sindy. Long dark hair…she was here earlier."

"What for?"

"Do you know where she went?"

"You her husband?" the man asked warily.

Cain smiled. If the man thought Sindy might have a disgruntled husband, odds were that he also thought she was human. That meant she was not a pile of ash on this guy's motel room floor. "No, I'm just looking for her."

The guy scratched his butt, and began to close the door. "She's not here."

Cain stuck his boot in the doorway to keep it from closing. "Look, I'm not here to give you grief. I know she's not inside, and I don't care why she was here. I just need to find her. Did you see anything that might help me?"

The man looked down at Cain's boot and then eyed him suspiciously before deciding that the best way to get rid of him was to tell him something. "She just left a little while ago. Big black car came and got her."

It was a moment before Cain could dislodge his shock to ask for more details. "Did she get in alone?"

"Na, there were a couple a guys in the car, but I couldn't really describe none of 'em. She brought someone with her, too. Tall punk, in leather. That's all I know." He spared another pointed glance at Cain's boot.

Cain backed up for the man to close the door. "Thanks a lot."

Arif…it had to have been men sent by Arif. What the hell was wrong with that woman? Why did she have to keep disappointing him? He'd really believed that she was different this time. She had changed, grown; she'd finally seemed to have realized the value of allowing herself to have a true connection with someone…with him. Or so he'd thought.

How could she be working for Arif? She truly cared for him, he'd felt it. He knew her faults and illicit tendencies, he wasn't completely shocked; disappointed was more accurate. Because for all her faults, she did display traits to be genuinely admired as well, and he had really believed that she was finally beginning to see for herself, those things that he admired in her; and that she didn't need to lower herself to be appreciated. Yet she'd gone off with Arif, rather than stay with him.

He was unsure what to do, but the sun made the decision for him. The shadow he stood in was growing smaller by the minute. Unless he wanted to hunch down in his car until he figured out what to do, he was going to have to return to the office and get a room.

Sindy had never returned her key to the office, and the room had been paid up for two nights according to the clerk. Of course, Cain found it doubtful that any money had actually changed hands. Allie had probably just made the clerk *believe* that she had paid, but that was effective enough. It was still officially occupied until check out, at noon tomorrow. Cain was able to take room 110 on the other side of hers, so that he would feel her if she returned.

He knew it was unlikely that she would, but in his heart, he still wanted to believe that she'd come back. He could not help but hold onto the slim hope that she would return, see him, and confess that she had made a terrible mistake. Perhaps she would admit to having true feelings for him, tell him of her indiscretions, and somehow they could untangle the mess together.

Even if she had impure motives through and through, there was a chance she'd only gone to meet briefly with Arif, planning to return and carry on her charade. If Arif ordered her to lure Allie out alone, it would be easy for Sindy to call her back to the motel, stating she needed assistance with the new vampire, Zach.

But why had Sindy turned Zach? If she truly wanted to further Arif's cause, wouldn't she have let Alyson turn the guy herself, and get into as much trouble as possible? It would lend credence to Arif's case, that Alyson was not to be trusted to keep her powerful blood secure from misuse. Instead, Sindy had kept Allie from making such a mistake. For that, Cain had to believe she was not beyond reprieve.

Cain lay on the bed, and finally allowed himself to submit to emotional exhaustion. What a night he'd had. It had begun with suspecting Alyson of deceit. Then he'd unwittingly stumbled into a reunion with Felicity. Not only was he assured that she was happy and fulfilling her potential, but he'd learned she still carried love for him in her heart. Given that he could not share her life, their visit this evening was more than he could have hoped for. He was so happy to see her firmly ensconced in the family life she had always desired. Then, to hold her baby, named for him... The happiness that memory brought, could last him a lifetime.

He ached for the loss of his own children, and for the fact that he was not human any longer, to share in a new incarnation of life with Felicity. But it was a sweet sorrow, because the joy he had in knowing she would have the life she deserved, comforted him. Isn't that little baby what life is all about? That made everything else worthwhile. It was *slight* comfort, as he lay here alone, but she had what he had wanted for her, and it satisfied him. It was good to know that at least the sacrifice of his happiness was not in vain.

He had truly believed that although Felicity was lost to him, he could still find some sort of happiness with Sindy. He hadn't expected it to be the same as the sweet, pure love that Felicity had given him, but Sindy had her own breed of love to offer. She had led a difficult life, and been forced to make trying choices. Sindy had allowed herself to be led down a dark path, but it wasn't very different from dark paths in *his* past. He'd thought he could take her hand, and they could find their way together. Was it fruitless to believe that could still happen? Only time would tell.

Although normally an early riser, ensconced in the dark silence of the motel room, recovering from his mental fatigue, he didn't open his eyes again until a few hours after sunset the next evening. He had to wonder if perhaps subconsciously he was trying to protect himself from further heartbreak, by tuning out the world and remaining unconscious for as long as possible.

When he awoke, the humans that Sindy had marked were both gone, off to resume their lives and leaving him no trace of her. He wouldn't bother to try to look for her. He could probably manage to contact Arif, but to what end? Arif would never admit to any wrong-doing on his part, and if Sindy had chosen to go to him, then her choice was clear. If she came back on her own, he might be able to talk to her, and turn things around, but the ball was in her court.

Cain ignored his thirst for blood and instead wandered over to the office for a complimentary cup of coffee. He knew he might as well go back to the house and let Mattie and Alyson know of Sindy's absence, but he was taking his time, hoping that she still might come back. The coffee was truly terrible.

The ride home wasn't long, but Cain drove slowly, attempting to pick up the slight sensations of Sindy's whereabouts through his mark on her. It was an uneventful and lonely trip, made worse when he pulled up his driveway. As the car's headlights flashed across the house and yard as he topped the hill, something looked strangely out of place. He pulled around slowly towards the garage, but nothing seemed truly amiss, just a nagging awareness of something being different.

He parked the car inside, and closed the large garage door from the outside, opting to walk around the front rather than enter the house from within. What was wrong? As he began to follow the path, the house was lit before him, rising up out of the darkness of the surrounding wood. Now he realized what he was seeing.

The house was surrounded by trees, but they were back a bit, leaving a fair clearing for landscaping and paths around it. There was also a nicely sized lawn in the front and off to the left. That large, open expanse had always been left clear, and used to be the place where he would normally go out to lure those few deer who wore his mark and would donate their blood for him. Except for the fact that for the past few years, Mattie had kept his trailer parked over there. Now it was gone.

The large, hulking luxury motor coach had become a fixture on his property. When coming up to the top of the drive, along with the magnificence of the house with its little solar landscape lights all around it and brightly lit porch, the trailer could always be seen off to the side and a bit behind it, with its own lights shining dimly from within its tinted windows. Now there was only a vast open space of darkness, seeming all the more empty in contrast with its recent occupancy.

Cain took a deep breath and let it out slowly, wondering what it could mean. His first instinct was to reach out for Alyson psychically, but he didn't carry the gift of telepathy. The most he could ever do was open his mind and hope that she would attempt to contact him. Usually, just opening his mind to her was enough, but at the moment, it seemed she was focused on other things.

He entered the house, the foyer dark, and silent. There was a light left on in the kitchen though, he could see it dimly from where he stood in the entryway. Funny, the first thing he noticed as he entered the room, was that the kitchen looked cleaner than it had in a while. There wasn't even a mug in the sink. Somehow, that told him that they weren't planning on coming back any time soon.

There was a note, the only thing on the kitchen table. He picked it up and scanned it with some trepidation. It was Allie's handwriting and said next to nothing. They were taking off for a while. He was not to worry, they would be in touch when they could. What in the world would provoke them to leave?

...Him, perhaps? Less than twenty-four hours ago, he'd stood here accusing them of disrespecting their coven bond with him, and treating him like an intruder in their relationship. He'd called Alyson selfish, and questioned whether her powers were degrading her character. Everything he'd said, had been provoked and well founded, even if a bit over-blown, but it was no wonder that she might want some space from him for a while. If she wanted a break from being here, Mattie would naturally join her, rather than side here with Cain. Who could blame him?

They were his coven though, his family. He knew that they loved him, as he loved them, even if they needed a break for themselves at this point. Alyson had said she would contact him, and he would apologize when she did, smoothing things over, and inviting them to come back before their mark of the coven faded. Knowing them as he did, he expected that Mattie would begin worrying about him and want to check in, or Alyson would begin to read things from him and decide that he needed company again. They would be back before long. Until then, it was going to be very quiet around here, though…

They couldn't know that Sindy would not be here to distract him from their absence. He'd even suggested to them that Sindy might be a threat, and apparently, he'd been right. Maybe that had been a deciding factor for them as well. In a way, it might be best, and he was relieved not to have to deal with sorting out loyalties and keeping the peace between them all. Arguing a case for Sindy to remain may not have been easy. Still, it might have been better than being alone…

Alone again. He'd spent so much of his life alone, he should be used to it. But it was amazing how quickly he'd grown to appreciate and expect the camaraderie of his coven and his lover. No more talks around the kitchen table, or before the fire. His bed would be empty come daybreak, until he climbed beneath the cold sheets himself.

One never knew what to expect from the future, though. Look at all of the unexpected twists and turns he had found himself navigating over just this past decade! *Each day, we must make every effort to do what is right, and pray that we have the strength to do it again tomorrow.* He had done what he could to set things right, and each night he would continue to do so, trusting his destiny to unwind as it should.

He poured himself a cup of blood, and prepared to face the future, wondering what unforeseen turns lay in the road ahead...

Chapter 20 - Leverage

Elric

Kana Susamiş Icin Ev
Montauk, Long Island, New York
An evening in late May

Latisha's blood tasted sweet, thick and hot as it poured down Elric's throat. She moaned and writhed beneath him, reminding him that her body craved his attentions just as much as he craved her blood. He paused in his feast to part her thighs with his knee. Her blood was intoxicating, but he was hard and eager to enter her moist warm flesh as well.

Her long, supple dancer's limbs wrapped around him, holding on for dear life as he deftly thrust his body into hers, striving for climax. Her voice was husky and deep, as her sexy purr became a growl in his ear. "Yes…harder…I'm so close."

A summons from the master, Arif, cut through Elric like a sudden shiver of ice down his back. Elric froze in his movements and muttered a curse.

"Don't stop," Latisha pleaded, unaware of the call. She clung to him tightly, her fingers digging into his buttocks, desperate for him to continue.

He couldn't go on, not with the master's attention on him. "I have to go," he muttered regretfully, rolling off her to lie on his back.

Latisha tried to keep her hold on him as she pleaded for him not to ignore her need. "What? No, you can't leave now!" She turned on him like a frenzied wild thing. She climbed atop him and took his face into her hands as she straddled him. "What is it, what's wrong?"

He met her eyes, and as soon as she allowed herself to calm down for a moment, she instantly realized the situation. Now she was pissed. "Damn it, he does that on purpose, doesn't he? He's let me stay only so he can remind you that it's by *his* grace. He takes pleasure in undermining my relationship with you."

Elric replied, aware that Arif was likely listening in on their conversation. "It's just bad timing. I'll come back to you as soon as I can. I have to go."

She still lay astride him, straddling him with her hips, very near to causing him to enter her again and complete what they had begun. She leaned down to his lips for a seductive kiss, and whispered with teasing authority, "No. I won't let you leave until I'm finished with you. He can wait."

Elric's chuckle was cut short, as she sat up and her hand found its way behind her, down between his legs where he lay beneath her. She cupped the full firmness of his balls, drawn up tightly in tensed anticipation, waiting for release, and gave them a gentle squeeze. "You need me just as badly. I'd be a poor head concubine to send you out there so full of frustration and need."

As she let her hand move to close around the thick length of his shaft, his erection stiffened further at her touch, despite his better judgment. He made a token attempt to sit up and move her off him, but she refused to let him, unless he was prepared to use true force. Technically, he owned her. She belonged to him utterly, yet he knew that at this moment, it was she who mastered him, and she was always the master of his heart.

He was loathe to displease her, and she made it very difficult for him to ignore her wishes. She guided and then released him with her hand, but slid herself down upon him, holding him captive instead within the shuddering, clenched muscles between her thighs, a satisfied hiss escaping from her lips.

He couldn't speak, he could only focus on the building, boiling sensation of ecstasy that was quickly growing to engulf him. She wasted no time but immediately regained the rhythm of passion interrupted. She rode him mercilessly, pounding herself down onto him with a ferocious drive to match the carnal sounds rumbling from deep within her throat.

Elric opened his eyes to see her beautiful breasts bob and dance to the cadence of her motions. He reached up and pulled her face down closer to him, to kiss her luscious lips. Then he nuzzled the crook of her shoulder and throat so that he could pierce her sweet, salty skin with his fangs once more. She let out a cry of pain mixed with pleasure, as climax washed over her in spasms of delight with his bite. Once again, her blood filled his mouth and he allowed himself to revel in the taste, until his body was overcome by the rapture of sensation building in his groin. Orgasm roared through him, overwhelming and most welcome.

She is still delectable isn't she? Arif's thoughts intruded in his head. *And quite the hellion in bed too. I can see why you would be reluctant to give her up. Thanks for sharing.*

Elric steeled himself to control his thoughts, shielding his true emotions over the invasive trespass, and refrained from answering. Rather than hold Latisha in his arms, he immediately rose from the bed to get dressed, robbed of his awaited moment of satisfied bliss. Latisha reached up from the bed and caught his attention, pulling him closer with just the slight whisper of her fingers on his hip.

Surely, she understood; knew that the master lurked within his mind. He prayed she wouldn't say anything incriminating, to prompt Arif to send her away.

"Don't let him vex you," she told him quietly. "I'm grateful that he allows us this time. As always, I am your indebted and humble ward, here only to obey. I hope you aren't angry that I overstepped, but I needed to show you my fierce appreciation for what I haven't lost."

She knew the master was listening. Before rising from the bed, Elric had not kissed her and told her how he loved her, as he normally would. It had alerted her that they were not alone. She must have realized how mutinous her words and actions had seemed against Arif, and now was trying to soften them, so he would not be offended. Luckily, the master appreciated her spunk, and the voyeuristic thrill she had unwittingly supplied.

Someday things would be different; he could love whom he wanted without care for rules. Until then, he had to play the game. He gave her a smile and a slight nod of his head. It didn't matter if Arif required that he treat her as a slave. She knew the truth. "Such disobedience should not be tolerated," he informed her. "But because I value what you bring to my house and harem, I'll overlook it."

Elric stood above her where she still perched on the bed, and reached down to cup the side of her face. He tilted her chin upwards, as though inspecting and appraising her beauty. It wasn't ungentle, but neither was it the loving sort of gesture he usually graced her with. It was more detached, as though he was inspecting his property to assure himself that it was worthy of him. Arif would surely approve. "You please me," he told her. In his heart, he hoped she knew enough to replace the words with 'I love you'.

When Elric reported to the master's office as requested, Arif sat behind his desk with a taunting grin. Elric was sorely tempted to say something truly mutinous. Luckily, he was startled from his thoughts, to find they were not alone.

The vampiress Sindy, whom he knew from her past involvements with the coven, was sitting in one of the large leather chairs before Arif's desk. Next to her, in a smaller chair to the side of the desk was another vampire, a young man whom he did not know. He was cloaked, but hardly seemed of interest. He sat tapping out a tune quietly on his leg with his fingertips, and looked as though he couldn't care less what was going on around him.

"Come in Elric, sit." Elric took the second leather chair before Arif's large mahogany desk next to the vampiress, who was looking even lovelier than he remembered, but very unhappy to be there. "I hope this impromptu meeting isn't too great an interruption. I know you're a busy man." It sounded a perfectly polite comment. Elric refused to allow himself to be goaded into replying with the words that leapt to his lips in response, but instead bit his tongue and forced a smile.

After a brief pause, Arif continued when it was plain Elric would not speak. "You remember Sindy. This is her new youngling, Zach. Kieran suggested that I have them brought in for a conference regarding our painfully slow progress with the United One."

"And is Kieran joining us?" Elric asked. Kieran could be annoying at times, but Elric still counted him as a dear friend, and was always happy to have him around as a buffer between him and the master.

"I'm afraid not. After arranging Sindy's transport, he went back to check on the United One with the intention of joining us after, but he now feels that it would be more prudent for him to remain in surveillance. I would have Lorelei here, but she is currently still settling that business in Albany, so it's just us."

At least he would be spared Lorelei's presence. As Elric sat, Arif promptly ignored them. Sindy met Elric's eyes with a look of confused impatience, but Elric knew Arif was probably having a mental conference with one not present. After a brief silence, someone else entered the room from a door in the back corner, which opened on a hallway that led to Arif's private suite of bedrooms.

A beautiful woman entered, a marked human of Arif's personal harem. She had thick, luscious, dark curls, and wore a sari of truly exquisite design and material. It was gold, grey and green, embroidered with flowers of deep violet, and draped to best display her full curves and thin waist. She looked exotic and lovely.

Her eyes were lowered respectfully to the floor, as she entered and then waited for a directive from her master. When he spoke to her, Elric paid closer attention, recognizing her name. "Marguerite, I have a guest in need of hospitality for a short while as I meet with these," he said, with a gesture towards Elric and Sindy. "Zach, you may go with Marguerite, and I will send Sindy to collect you later." He turned back to his concubine, who stood as the perfect embodiment of beauty and obedience. "Give him a tour of the grounds and then perhaps he would enjoy some refreshment from the bar."

She nodded humbly. Zach looked like he thought he had just won the lottery. Elric hoped he wasn't stupid enough not to realize that if he so much as laid a finger on the master's property, he could be killed for it, or at the very least spend a few nights in the reform cellar.

Sindy looked almost panicked that Zach was being sent off on his own. She must have had the same worries. "Behave yourself," she muttered to him as he stood. "No fangs, and if you touch her you're dust."

As Zach moved out from the chairs, Elric caught Marguerite stealing a glance at him through her lowered lashes. She worked up the courage to ask her master for a favor. "Master, if it pleases you, may I speak?"

Arif smiled at her fondly. She definitely seemed to have assimilated well to her situation. Something Elric was grateful to see, because it was the main reason Latisha had been allowed to stay. Arif would never have trusted a human to wander the grounds alone with a strange vampire unless he trusted her explicitly to obey his every order. "What troubles you my dear?" Arif asked. "I can assure you that you have nothing to fear from our guest."

She gave him a sweet smile of adoration. "Oh, I would never worry for my safety as long as I am yours, Master. I wondered only if I might have permission to speak with Elric."

Elric was shocked, not only by her question, but at how she had picked up the affectations of speech that he knew Arif preferred from his women. She must be paying close attention in her classes for social grace and harem etiquette. Arif seemed curious and amused by her request. "If you wish, you may speak."

Marguerite moved before Elric's chair, and executed a deep, graceful curtsy. "I never properly thanked you, sir." She looked at him with her large dark eyes and seemed quite sincere. "For your kindness and care, and for your role in bringing me to my master. I am eternally grateful."

Whether it was entirely truthful, or an act meant to gain favor with Arif, it was quite an artful and effective display. It was certainly a far cry from the kicking and screaming she had done when he had been forced to drag her to the car for the ride here. Did she really care for the role she had been given? She was treated as nothing but a pretty piece of property, but she was also well cared for. Was she happy to accept her fate, or was she simply biding her time? He may never know.

"It was my pleasure to present such a fair gift to my master. I am glad to see you have adjusted so well. Harem life suits you."

She nodded in thanks and then, after an even deeper curtsy to her master, she led Zach from the room. Arif seemed pleased with the exchange. But as soon as they closed the door, his mood became more serious and he got down to business. "It seems that Sindy has been having a difficult time convincing the United One that joining us would be in her best interest."

Sindy shocked Elric by not only speaking out of turn, but actually arguing with the master. "I'm not having a difficult time. She's coming around. I just need a little longer to clinch the deal. You didn't have to swoop in and abduct me for an update. Kieran could have told you. Everything is coming along fine."

Arif's cold stare was surely accompanied by a brief telepathic reminder that she was not to speak unless spoken to. Sindy slumped back in her chair in a huff, seeming more like the teenager that her body showed her to be, than the twenty-something woman she actually was.

Arif continued as though uninterrupted. "It has been over a year since my sire graced us with his presence, remarking on the fact that my many endeavors have our coven widespread and unfocused. He is right that I have perhaps been too patient, too trusting that my plans would come to fruition if I waited," he said with a pointed look at Sindy. "I think the time for waiting is done.

The situation is becoming more pressing for our dear Alyson, I'm afraid. She is losing control of her thirst, as I am sure our new friend Zach could attest. It would surely be best for all, if she was under my supervision."

Why did he have to make it sound like he was going to do everyone a big favor? Why not just say he wanted her for selfish reasons? Did he care what they thought? And what did Arif mean by saying Zach had felt the United One's thirst? The master had said he was of Sindy's making.

If Arif felt the time for waiting was over, what did he plan to do? "You don't believe that you will acquire the United One by force, do you?" Elric asked.

"No," Arif assured him. "It seems that inexperienced as she is, her powers of defense have come to her rather naturally. She has somehow thwarted every team I have sent against her. The small group I sent after she and her lover at Mardi Gras in New Orleans a few years back, were weak minded, easily manipulated by her, and unable to properly carry out their directives. The pair that followed her to that wedding she attended were killed. Lorelei and her team were similarly ineffective. Direct measures do not seem the proper course. She is far too strong. She must be convinced to come to us of her own free will. If Sindy cannot accomplish this, perhaps there is someone else who can."

Sindy became annoyed. "If you would've just left me there, I told you I can do it. Let me go back." Apparently, she had learned nothing from Arif's reaction to her last outburst. Perhaps she was trying to stress the fact that she had not been accepted as a member of the coven, and so was not technically subject to Arif's rule. She expected to be treated as an equal. *Good luck with that,* Elric thought with a smile.

Sindy must have interpreted the expression on his face over her demeanor. She softened her tone and tried to speak to Arif more reasonably. "Allie's not an idiot. If she's going to be manipulated, it has to be slow and subtle. There are very few people that she trusts."

"And I don't think you are one of them," Arif said, uninterested in her excuses. "The young Mattie and the vampire Cain are her coven, and those are the only advisors she will listen to. Sindy, you wear Cain's mark. Apparently you have become important to him during your stay. Perhaps you could persuade *him* that Alyson is safer with us. She clearly respects his wishes."

Sindy answered quickly. "Sure, I can do that." It seemed to Elric that she would swiftly agree to anything just to get the hell out of here.

Arif assessed her for a moment, and then remarked, "Forgive me, but I find you unconvincing of late." Arif sat back in his chair, his fingers steepled before him, tapping his chin as he considered something they weren't yet privy to. "Direct force will start a war that we will not win. Guile seems not to be working either. Perhaps what she needs at this point, is simple incentive. The problem is that we are not in a position to strike a deal. If we want samples of her blood, we must sit her down and plainly draw up terms for a trade."

Sindy was obviously uncertain what he could mean, but afraid to ask, so Elric expressed the obvious. "We do not have anything that she wants."

"Precisely," Arif replied. "So tell me how we are going to rectify that." Elric was mute. What could he say? He had no idea what he could offer. "Nothing?" Arif asked. "You are my senior guardsman and you have nothing to say? You cannot find me the piece for this puzzle?"

"Time, my lord. Let me consider it a while."

Arif was disgusted with the request. "We've wasted enough time. I already know the answer. Kieran supplied it to me over his last few reports. Sometimes it seems he is the only member of my coven of any true use to me.

There is something valued not only by the United One, but by Cain as well. Something she should be happy to trade for, and if she is not, Cain would surely convince her. Such a thing would be very useful to us, don't you think?"

Elric traded a glance with Sindy, who displayed a wary sense of foreboding. "Very useful, sir," Elric agreed.

Elric knew that the master was beginning to lose faith in him after his disobedient arguing for Latisha's sake. He needed to put himself back into the master's good graces, before Arif began to consider demoting him and giving his position back to Lorelei. He needed to keep his status, if he ever expected to enact the plans he had brewing. "I will fetch it for you without fail."

Arif smiled at his obedient, unhesitant answer. "Good. I'm sure you will."

This quest seemed just the thing to prove his devotion. He would fetch this thing of value, his loyalty unquestioned, so he might plan his true rebellion. Elric prompted Arif eagerly. "Tell me where to find this object, Master."

"Her name is Felicity."

~~~~~~~~~~~~~~~~~~~~~~~~~~~~~~~~~~~

TO BE CONTINUED

IN

ALMOST HUMAN

∽ THE SECOND TRILOGY ∽

VOLUME 3

DESTINED FOR DIVINITY

~~~~~~~~~~~~~~~~~~~~~~~~~~~~~~~~~~~

If you enjoyed this book, please take a moment to leave a review online, on your favorite book review website!

You can join author/reader discussions about the series, and get updates on upcoming book releases for this series on the author's web site at:
www.MelanieNowak.com